ALSO BY GARTH RISK HALLBERG

A Field Guide to the North American Family

City on Fire

The Second Coming

The Second Coming

A NOVEL

Garth Risk Hallberg

 Alfred A. Knopf * New York * 2024

THIS IS A BORZOI BOOK
PUBLISHED BY ALFRED A. KNOPF

www.aaknopf.com

Knopf, Borzoi Books, and the colophon
are registered trademarks of Penguin Random House LLC.

A portion of this book appeared, in different form,
in *Granta* 139: *Best of Young American Novelists*.

Library of Congress Cataloging-in-Publication Data
Names: Hallberg, Garth Risk, author.
Title: The second coming : a novel / Garth Risk Hallberg.
Description: First edition. | New York : Alfred A. Knopf, 2024.
Identifiers: LCCN 2023027159 (print) | LCCN 2023027160 (ebook) |
ISBN 9780593536926 (hardcover) | ISBN 9780593536933 (ebook) |
ISBN 9780593802380 (open market)
Subjects: LCSH: Fathers and daughters—Fiction. | LCGFT: Domestic fiction. | Novels.
Classification: LCC PS3608.A54827 S43 2024 (print) | LCC PS3608.A54827 (ebook) |
DDC 813/.6—dc23/eng/20230615
LC record available at https://lccn.loc.gov/2023027159
LC ebook record available at https://lccn.loc.gov/2023027160

Jacket photograph by Cyndi Monaghan / Getty Images
Jacket design by Oliver Munday

Manufactured in the United States of America
First Edition

For Amos,
Walter,
Nora,
and Soren:
resurrections all.

Against the dark wall a figure appears slowly . . . a changeling, kidnapped.

—JAMES JOYCE
Ulysses

I am that name you give me, but I am also something else that cannot quite be named. The relation to the unname-able is perhaps a way of maintaining a relation to the other that exceeds any and all capture.

—JUDITH BUTLER
"Reply from Judith Butler"

Contents

The Second Coming

2 Whom It May Concern...

They were just kids then, despite everything, and full of hope, so at first the window's size must have seemed a selling point. Only after the move-in would they discover how badly the glass had been compromised—by which point it was already too late. The putty of the sash having long since failed, moisture had knifed its way in so that a residue of atmospheric solids (bus fumes and boiler fumes and exhaust from the Chinese place downstairs) scumbled both the upper and lower panes; this was a window for looking at, not out of. Yet sometimes with daylight and southern exposure, that could feel like enough. Even the November of his second collapse, his first of the new millennium, there could come an hour when the sun found some deep grain in the waterstains and the whole window became like a wall of pale wedding-band gold . . . or a waterfall, he now thinks, with a hollowed-out place to stand behind. He could sit in his life as the Romans did in their baths and feel in his heart like it wasn't just some fuckup brought him here.

Then he reminds himself that he's not here; not really. As far as his wife knows, he's still working a lunch shift downtown to cover preschool tuition, or trying to revive his abandoned poems at the big library on Forty-Second Street. She'll come in past sunset, somehow laden even after the stroller is stowed and the bags set down, and having hidden any trace of his real day, he'll affect in the most minimal of ways to have arrived home only minutes ahead: keys dropped on the counter near the door and a lamp or two switched off that by day he's had on.

But oh: the night. The night in this city is like a magician's coat, full of false linings and pockets you can't reach the bottoms of, and no sooner has it dropped than he can feel this apartment, their refuge, being altered right down to the smell. Which becomes, for instance, the slightly seaweedy smell of a beachhouse her family rented half a decade back, the slightly seedy cushion of an old porch glider on a night when he'd had one too many.

Though of course that was another trick, wasn't it? Two different locations, two slightly different times. Only at the first had she offered to take off her clothes. She had been, even then, a girl of good sense, brilliant and self-contained and lancingly pretty—a survivor, which was part of why she'd stood for him in the silvery light she did. They'd lain together in one place while in the window of the other, glass rippled: bees bumbling around hydrangeas, a dry-docked catamaran, two heavy-limbed old evergreens beyond which the day-bright day was never going to end . . . Now there's his breath, with everything it might give away. The moaning thing he does unless he sleeps on his stomach. Did I never moan before? he wants to ask. Did my breathing never stop? But no, what is between them started with the fact now weighing on her: this other life. Their little girl.

It is true that the crying, that first year after her arrival, came almost on the hour, attended by surges in the adrenaline spectrum—panic and desperation, the emotions least congenial to sleep. But of course quiet too can induce a sort of panic, at those hours of the night when dads count hazards instead of sheep. Radon. Toys purpose-built for choking. Is there a more terrible phrase, or excellent name for a thrash-metal band, than Sudden Infant Death?

Before he is even aware of it he is up and crossing the dark to check on her. Brushing back the door, he reminds himself that she is four now, and himself twenty-four, a grown man. From the gray plane of the bed, shapes swim into relief: a cataract of sheets, the night's buncha books. But where is the body, the life burning furiously inside? There—buried down at the center, away from the cold. He thinks of doing another tuck-in. Then of the messenger bag where he's stashed a last pill and one of his few remaining liquor bottles, easily enough recovered to be plausibly not hidden at all.

What can't quite resolve itself, as he steals back out to bed, is the window. If it could just stay its daytime self, extend its shelter made of light . . . but in the night you have to open it a crack against steam heat or street heat; and in the night the steep ascender of the fire escape gets printed on the translucence, green then yellow then red with the traffic signal down at the corner; and in the night these days, it's the shadows that demand attention. When he was his daughter's age this one might have looked like a monster. Now it is a ladder leading to a spacecraft hovering just out of view. The lack of exterior weeping or screams would seem to confirm it: his is the last life left unvaporized in New York, and even now the craft has begun to scan with those probes, red for heart, green for mind. It can see in advance what he is about to do—though probably not why he is about to do it, since that's something he was hoping the booze might tell him . . . He is just considering waking Sarah up and risking the truth—what he's been holding inside for these last months (years), and how far he's ready to go to avoid repeating it—but before he can finish the thought, something out there beyond the window stirs.

It hasn't occurred to him till now that no signal has been discussed; the old one seemed to work just fine. But here comes this new thing again— the green going a paler green, then dark again, then paler again, twice: a visitor from a far planet or just the person closest to his own true self. He hasn't heard an engine running. He hopes the car isn't stolen this time.

Perhaps his mind's already made up, though, because there on the knob of the bathroom door hangs the denim jacket of his youth. Three hours twenty each way, this time of night. If he isn't back before they wake, he tells himself, or if he is but his absence gets noted, he can claim to have just slipped out for a long walk. He undoes the several locks, deft as any Houdini. Goes down.

The car is parked this side of the street but aimed away, like there's no worry he won't come. It gives him a feeling of wanting to call this trip off, frankly, just to prove that he's still free. But maybe through some conjunction of panes and mirrors he's being watched after all, since a dome light blinks on under the oblong strapped to the roof.

He stops to catch his breath. The sidewalk glimmers; gutters.

And at this point, from the psych ward where I now sit, writing all this, I want to mix in sound, warn him of what he's forgetting in his jacket pocket, but every time I try it, calling to him across the years, I can feel a whole ocean rushing in to fill my mouth, my throat . . . I'm being dragged back under.

And now my voice is trapped somewhere inside, the voice of a parent withheld from a child. The voice of Charlie Brown's mom, forever overheard.

Still: does something make it through? Because for a second, he does what every story says not to: looks back. Imagines he sees on the window the glassy outline of the person or persons he's decided he's destined to lose. But likely their sleep even now is that of angels, he thinks, and those human-sized figures are just the same old weathermarks, only seen from outside. And right before he steps off the curb and into the rest of his life—this shadow I can still feel hanging over me; my father—he will catch himself wondering if it has ever been possible, or even desirable, to have the one without the other. The hugeness without the compromise. All that exposure, without any flaws.

I

UNDERLAND

Winter–Spring 2011

Turning and turning in the widening gyre
The falcon cannot hear the falconer

—W. B. YEATS
"The Second Coming"

1

ALL LIFE IS SUFFERING. *Well, duh,* Jolie would remember thinking, the one time Roshi Steve ever stooped to bullet-point the noble truths of Buddhism. Her phone, secure in its cubby, was more or less a snuff film of the world's entangled miseries: bread lines, forever wars, the beehives gone silent, the coral reefs bleached white. Yet there at the zendo to which she'd been sneaking off each Thursday the spring of her seventh-grade year, wisdom wasn't supposed to come in such pithy little nuggets. So it was only later, toward the end of April, that she would realize this First Noble Truth had been the through-line all along.

I don't mean to suggest that it had shown up in quizzes or drills. Only a few other times had she even encountered it as a verbal formulation: once among some pamphlets on a wire rack by the door, once in a piece of supplemental reading. *The Dhammapada,* maybe. Or Wikipedia. But at a certain point that afternoon between her escape from sixth period and her stop in a nearby garden to bolt a little liquor, a thing or two had been (shall we say) brought home. And now here she was, late to what would turn out to be her final meditation.

Also possibly—let's just get this out in the open—slightly tipsy. Possibly obviously slightly tipsy. Vodka was undetectable on the breath, people said, but it's not like Jolie Aspern, at that point barely even a teenager, could smell her own breath to check, any more than she could catch the back of her head in a dressing-room mirror, or hear her own voice absent the walls of her skull. She succeeded in getting her violin case stowed and squatting to remove shoes, but would recall her backpack only when she stood again, whamming it into the little end table behind her—the one with the porcelain alms bowl on top. And as she whipped around to keep the bowl from falling, there it was, suddenly: her own sadness, flashing back at her like neon from every surface.

Take the mats, for example, reed mats so thin their only conceivable purpose was to emphasize the cushioning they refused to provide. Or take the roshi, nearly as thin in his masochistic sweater. Her mental imagery going into this had been inflected, admittedly, by the statues in Chinese restaurants—smiling and slightly louche Buddhas in '70s vests and love beads, their plump bellies begging to be rubbed—but Roshi Steve on his best day could muster at most a glower. And then suffusing everything was the light from the picture window that ran the basement's far wall. It was like something had been done to the glass back there or to the courtyard outside to lend each object within this terrible clarity. The brutal linoleum. Her idiot fingers. The kamikaze bowl.

Which shattered on the floor just as people were starting to look around for the source of the commotion. The usual crowd here was office workers in their twenties, a few fixie dudes with man-buns and frockish shirts mixed in, but the light brought out lines in their faces. (Rivers, she used to call them, running a thumb from the corners of her mother's eyes. *Mommy, another river.*) Mindfulness on such faces could look like anything from fatigue to a sort of pinched constipation, but never like actual enlightenment. Still, it was the roshi's gaunt face she would return to later. Could he tell she'd been drinking? (Could everyone?) In any case, what she saw there when he finally sighed and used his bamboo thingy to indicate a mat wasn't anger, but its opposite. Like: those shards at your feet are an illusion, Jolie, and can wait. Your soul cannot. And the suffering you might spend a whole lifetime trying to writhe away from?

Well, that's just what life is, cupcake. The way a fire is its burning.

BUT HOLD ON A SEC, wait, I can already hear you saying: What were you—sorry, "she"—doing at the Kips Bay Zendo in the first place? And why, if the life-to-suffering equivalency was hardly a secret (if most people growing up managed to figure it out for themselves, thank you very much), why did she keep going there weekly to shove a few more dollars of her bat mitzvah money into the now-defunct bowl?

Even all these years later, I can't be sure. One hypothesis involved the many different ways there are of knowing things. Or rather, the different *kinds* of things, corresponding to different kinds of knowledge. Knowing, say, that Juneau is the capital of Alaska isn't the same as living there. So maybe for Jolie Aspern in Manhattan in the precarious springtime of 2011, learning to kneel in place for an hour at a stretch and ride out her kneecaps' distress signals was an attempt to nudge certain facts from one category to another.

Then again, it's possible she was just hard-wired for this. Her paternal grandfather, she knew, had been a chaplain in the navy, and then rector of an Episcopal boys' school on Maryland's Eastern Shore. And though Mom's own people had been among the nonobservant elite of prewar Vienna, it would be foolish to rule out the possibility of a rabbi in there somewhere. Genetic explanations had a way of begging the question, obviously, but on the other hand if Jolie, at thirteen, had a superpower at all, it was the tug she used to feel toward anything even remotely metaphysical: the smudged foreheads flooding the streets at Ash Wednesday; the Sufis she'd once heard belting out their version of "Happy Birthday" at a vegetarian restaurant downtown; that filament of Shabbos string she'd wasted a whole Sunday in fifth grade trailing around the Upper East Side, not quite trusting Mom's assurances that it was a closed loop. For her, the things of the spirit had a taste, almost, the way the air in a Catholic church had a taste even though you weren't eating it, some stone-cool and incensed unreason at the heart of the late-capitalist world. (She loved, too, this faintly churchy phrase, *late capitalism*, which she'd come across on one of Mom's syllabi and repeated any chance she got.)

So maybe the deeper mystery was why she hadn't chosen a more proximate place to stage her rebellion, the nearest synagogue or cathedral or mosque. But here, too, there were strings. And they would seem, when she followed them, to recede into the dreariness of the previous fall and winter.

SEE, THAT WAS ALSO THE YEAR she'd been transferred to a new middle school. Not one of the out-of-zone catchments to which the rest of her elementary's white population had fled a year earlier, but an honest-to-God prep school way down at the foot of Third Avenue. Her mother's political commitments should have put them squarely on the side of public education, but Mom had lately seemed more and more resigned to slippages between theory and practice. Or anyway, a glance at Jolie one morning near the end of sixth grade had spooked her into submission. "What's that on your face?" she'd said. "Is that Vaseline?"

"It's protective," Jolie heard herself say. "Some girls have nails."

"Honey, what are you telling me? Are you saying people have been fighting at school?"

"What do you want me to do, Mom? The minute they tag you as a brain, you're done for."

The burst of candor had an unintended effect: Mom would spend a good chunk of the following summer at the kitchen table, her sun-streaked head bent over financial aid packages and average test scores, and when school started up again in September, Jolie wasn't walking the few blocks to P.S. 166 anymore, but heading to the subway for the half-hour trek to Broad Horizons Academy. Progressive education. Rah.

She would carefully slick a sticker that first day onto the pebbled skin of her instrument case: *This Machine Kills Fascists*. A conversation starter, from the Bluestockings Bookstore on Allen Street. But the school's cliques had formed long ago, and worse than being singled out, she drifted through the halls between periods like just another ghost. Back home, she drew her room's blinds and lay prone on the bed in her underwear, smelling the brick dust kicked out by the secondhand window unit. Not that she had any right to feel sorry for herself; she wasn't a civilian in Mosul (she knew) or one of those Mediterranean boat people just starting to haunt her newsfeed. She was young, white, reasonably privileged, with a whole afternoon—a whole life, really—ahead of her. But maybe this was the problem: all those years already in the rearview, all those hours weeks months spent in empire's soft prison, had in the end boiled down to nothing.

At some point, she opened her iTunes. The Bach and Shosta-kovich pieces that had lit her up at seven or eight now seemed distant, historical, as if produced on toy instruments under a bell jar. But beneath her bed was a box of old CDs she'd long been avoiding. Now she dragged it out, plucked free a burned disc that had caught her eye once before. Other People: A Requiem, said the label, but when she put it in, the music for some reason wouldn't play. So she reached for another jewelcase: Prince. The cover, though, featured not the purple lothario of legend, but a cropped blur loitering by a pile of junk in a turtleneck and big glasses, looking like nothing so much as that "Coffee Talk" lady from *Saturday Night Live*. The music was at first equally off-kilter, a looped drum and a cheeseball synth locked in combat with what could have been either a heart monitor or a dial-up modem. But if you hung around for a minute (and again, Jolie had nothing better to do), it was like you got sucked through a veil, into a rich velvet space of guitar and organ plus whatever was the opposite of falsetto, a tenor beamed back from the far side of apocalypse, recounting the addictions and afflictions and other hells you had to struggle through to get there. Halfway through the song, she pressed repeat.

She would wake to find the light murky and a note on the nightstand:

You seemed exhausted last night, sweetie, so I decided to let you sleep straight through. Had to go meet students but laid out some breakfast. Don't forget to floss.

And indeed in the kitchen two packets of instant oatmeal had been left on the counter, along with an ugly banana and Mom's frenemy *The New York Times*. What would seem telling in hind-sight was the weird moment when, waiting for her gums to stop bleeding in the bathroom mirror, Jolie imagined the shower-curtain being tugged back to reveal her own slumped corpse in the tub. But at the time, it was only a moment. After eating what she could and squirreling away the rest at the bottom of the trash, she shouldered her pack and headed to the train alone.

And this would become her routine in the weeks that followed: shuffle through the stations of her classes; avoid all common areas; spend the better part of the afternoon laboring through the bleary underworld of swim practice and then do the commute in reverse, a caustic chlorine scent in her nose. Showering seemed beside the point when you could go the whole day speaking only a few dozen words to actual human beings. The latchkey time in her room, working her way through the music collection of a grandmother she'd never got to meet, was the one thing she now looked forward to—the one thing authentically hers—but there are certain kinds of balm that only worsen the underlying injury. And as the leaves continued to scab from the trees outside and the little upload wheel to spin, she could feel a black spot blooming at the center of her head's darkness, like a stain across a microscope slide. Or like someone out there had trained the sun on her through a series of lenses. Like some black/white queer/straight imp of the perverse had "produced, arranged, composed and performed" this *Sign o' the Times* for her alone.

THEN IT WAS FEBRUARY, the last day before midterm break, and her school was holding another dance. The fall mixer, three months prior, must not have been a total wash, because this time some of the girls in her class did get asked by boys. Yet if you'd happened to peer at eight that night through the square windows of the gymtorium doors, you'd have seen the sexes stuck to discrete walls as if parted by a comb. You might even, if you were a feminist, have felt a certain vindication. On the Sojourner Truth–to–Paris Hilton continuum of feminism, Jolie graded herself somewhere around a Beyoncé: alert to the workings of patriarchy yet unable to get fully outside them. Which was practically the only Bey-like thing about her, what with the acne. The eyebrows. Still, she wanted to believe it was a sign of progress rather than of surrender that she'd agreed to meet up beforehand with a girl named Precious Ezeobi.

Precious was a year further along in school and a head taller, not to mention preternaturally poised, with one of those voices that made you realize acting was eighty percent voice. In the fall production of *Into the Woods*, while Jolie dutifully sawed away in the orchestra, Precious had played the baker's clever wife. It had been hard to tell from the pit whether her high-waisted apron had done more to hide her curves or call attention to them—but probably hide them, it seemed, for Precious had now swept back in from off campus in a tight black-and-white wrap dress and her hair done up in a dozen mini Afro puffs. And the one thing Jolie could do to prevent a sense of gawking was to push into the gym.

Which is to say, the auditorium with no show running. The stage lights at the far end bore colored gels, she noticed, and in place of the fluorescents overhead, Christmas lights snaked through the winched-up basketball goals. Seeing Precious take a sodacup from a table and go lean against the lip of the stage, Jolie did the same. Between speakers opposite, a laptop had been loaded with the kids' requests, Rihanna, Diplo, Weezy . . . or possibly it was just Pandora, working subtle variations on the theme of mononymous pop.

Five or six songs drifted past like this. Then, as if at some invisible signal, a cluster of girls from the wall crossed to a cleared space near the jump circle. They started shifting back and forth without looking at the boys, yet with a listlessness that seemed directed at them, somehow. Was this what Jolie was supposed to do, too? She couldn't unsee the image of chickens from a certain movie from her childhood: stop-motion hens, scratching and stupidly pecking. Yet saying so out loud wasn't going to make her feel any happier—only meaner. And when Precious, after a few minutes' thoughtful watching, got up and moved toward an exit, Jolie hoped they'd fulfilled the minimum required attendance and could bounce out of here altogether.

The plan was for Precious to spend the night at the apartment where Jolie lived with her mom, uptown. (There was track work in perpetuity on the C train, and cabs to Brooklyn could be a pain in the ass, even to the gentrified parts where families like the Ezeobis had gut-renovated brownstones.) It was this sleepover element, in fact, that had sold Jolie on the dance. But Precious was now tacking around the corner to a seldom-used faculty bathroom. She scanned the hall, put her ear to the door. Then, with a regal jerk of her head, she beckoned Jolie inside.

Far from the little Versailles you might imagine, it was a glorified student john, the same smell of bleach and brown paper towel. The only perk was a deadbolt set high in the door. "Tell me if that still works," Precious said, meaning the transom window above the lone stall.

"Okay, but dude, what are you doing?"

What Precious was doing was shooting the bolt, dumping her Coke into the sink, then running the faucet to rinse the cup. Her overnight bag thumped to the counter. From its depths came a squarish bottle Jolie failed to register much of, save for some woodland creature in full affront on the label. Perhaps she was distracted by all that liquid inside, throbbing faintly with the bass through the foot-thick wall. "My sister left a stash in her room when she took off for Barcelona," Precious explained. "The middle one I was telling you about. Grace."

As always, the mention of Precious's sister brought a tiny, jealous pang. "You stole it?"

" 'Stole' is such an ugly word. Anyway, I had a hunch we might need to liven things up." As the tempo shifted, Precious measured out a practiced draught and knocked it back without visibly flinching. Then she refilled the chalice and held it out.

Jolie sniffed. She'd never had anything stronger than Manischewitz, unless you counted the gin her Nana had let her dip a finger in that one time. She'd been warned since of various hereditary risk factors, but again, wasn't that just a copout? It's not like one measly drink could ever change anything . . . or at any rate, a close-quarters hang with the most interesting girl in eighth grade hardly seemed the place for scruples. She took a demo sip, trying not to breathe through her nose, and swallowed as quickly as if it were her own spit. The result was controlled fire. Survivable burn. The second time the cup came to her, though, Jolie miscalculated, so that a whole hot finger of whatever it was was now making the slow transit of her throat. She thought of a PET scan she'd had to undergo once to check kidney function—contrast dye lighting up her gag reflex. Then the booze touched some deeper opening, the rupture she'd been doing her best to rise above. And Oh, she realized.

Oh.

As a city girl, born and raised, Jolie liked to fancy herself sophisticated, but her cheek, when next she touched it, had a gauzy quality. The air held either more or less oxygen than normal. Precious said something funny, and she heard herself do this horsey sputtering thing. A Pez-hued pack of American Spirits appeared on the counter, and for once she had to give props to the fell power of DNA; were even a bag of angel dust to be produced, she saw, she would immediately have tried to snort it, or smoke it, because what did nasal passages matter, what did kidneys or lungs (or for that matter heart), when the disease was life itself?

But now the bolt rattled near her ear, followed by a knock. A voice came from outside, male, teacherly. "Hello?"

Shit, Jolie would remember thinking, just as Precious said, "Shit." And louder, in the same register she'd used to tell off her baker husband: "*¡Es ocupado, señor!*"

Then she slipped down off her wedges, climbed nimbly atop the commode, shoved the bottle with its fiery remnant through the transom. Jolie braced for the sound of breaking, but Precious must have pre-positioned a receptacle on the street below—or anyway, you wouldn't have put it past her. "If somebody asks," she hissed, "you got your period and the dispenser in the girls' room was out."

"But what are you doing here, in this scenario?"

"I'm your moral support—duh." And before Jolie could wonder why it had to be *her* period: "Is he gone yet?"

Jolie put an ear to the door, unsure how a person was supposed to detect signs of life over all this echoey percussion. But when she slotted the bolt back and peeked out into the hall, there was just an old couch and some half-spooled volleyball nets and a red stripe spanning the cinderblock wall, its stenciled exhortation: *EAGLES!*

What came next she would experience less as a seamless tracking shot than as a series of stills stuttering forward at the brush of some cosmic thumb. Yet the overall impression was of the darkness starting, finally, to wane. Like, here was the sheen of sweat at Precious's neck where the hair had pulled it tight . . . and here they were, dancing. Here was a chubby girl whose prettiness she'd never noticed before gliding closer and pumping a fist to Jay-Z. Here, at the start of a tribute spin of "Billie Jean," were dud clouds of dry ice courtesy of the Physics Club—and here was an Asian boy effecting an uncanny moonwalk. Another boy whipped out a phone to memorialize the memorial while the fat girl whooped with a knowingness that couldn't quite hide her genuine delight.

The deejay-slash-algorithm must have decided to bypass any slowdance, though, because at ten sharp, amid the audible chock of levers being thrown, a blue light kindled in the overhead cages, and teachers too clueless to avoid chaperone duty were shouting idle threats about getting locked in over the break. Cool air gusted from doors that led to the street, where the faces of the older parents, glowing, gathered. A few bigass cans of Arizona iced tea lolled on the floor.

Jolie's own mom's omniscience no longer seemed to extend to public transit, or really to anything below about 110th Street, so she and Precious would set out for the subway unobserved. They didn't actually *stagger*, she didn't think, but she would later retain an inordinate amount of sidewalk in the B-roll, a fatal dazzle of mica under the streetlights—unless this was just the glitter in the moonwalking boy's hair. "I think he's into you," Precious said.

Jolie wondered if her brain had gone audible. "What? Who?"

"Peter Yang, with that whole *Thriller* routine." She was just unpacking the finer points of the crotch-grab when a hand touched Jolie's arm.

"Hey, you two want to slow down for a minute?"

Jolie felt Precious trying to pull ahead, but her own reflex in the face of beseechment was still a shameful obedience. She turned to see a leather jacket, then a head of floppy blueblack hair a few inches below where she expected it to be. It was Mr. Koussoglou, who taught Exploring Cultural Richness and had recently taken over the literary magazine.

"You ladies looked like you were having a good time back there," he said, eyeing Precious through his architectural glasses.

"Oh, you know," sputtered Jolie. "I don't know. It was fine."

Mr. Koussoglou was one of the younger members of the faculty, and they'd thus far been on good terms. In the fall, he'd let her linger in his classroom well into the lunch hour, perusing the ethnologic bric-a-brac, the long shelves of academic paperbacks that recalled Mom's study at home. The rumor was that he'd dropped out of grad school during a bad breakup before coming to teach; hence the faint hipsterish air, like his necktie was a prop he couldn't quite get behind—though now he was really inhabiting the role. "I saw you out on the dance floor. It looked like a lot more than 'I don't know.'"

"What's your point, Mr. K.?" Precious had a way of making nonchalance seem almost flirtatious, but her face tightened as he went on.

"I know that was the two of you in the faculty restroom. I assume you have an explanation?"

"It's kind of a personal question, no? And for you to be dogging me this late in the game—"

He wasn't dogging anyone, he said. "In fact, I've been trying to stay out of your way, Precious, but when I go to take the recycling out and find *this* on the dumpster lid beneath the window . . ." He pulled something from his jacket. A light rain was falling, adding to the general mistiness, the mingled clouds of their breath, but Jolie didn't have to look too closely to see the defiant stag logo, dragging everything behind it into clarity.

And naturally a merchant across the street would choose exactly that moment to start cranking the security grate down over his storefront: half a minute of graveyard rattle. More excruciating still was the silence that followed—or what, on the northern fringes of Manhattan's East Village on a Friday night in winter, passed for silence: ambulances screaming their heads off, housing-insecure pigeons winging darkly overhead.

"It's mine," Jolie blurted. "Precious has nothing to do with it."

She waited for her new friend to jump in with some matching feat of nobility, but Precious just said, "Everybody knows you have it in for me, Mr. K., but I'm not in your class anymore, we're not on campus. So unless you're ready to bring a proper accusation"—her top-notes of litigiousness were pretty much unmissable—"my date and I will be going. Let's book, Jolie."

The clomp of Precious's wedges on the sidewalk had a bracing authority, but Jolie couldn't get her own feet to budge. She seemed to catch a flicker inside Mr. Koussoglou as he turned the bottle in his hands, a disappointment out of all proportion to the offense. Like he'd glimpsed whatever she had, the hole at the back of the universe, and still couldn't get past it.

"This is yours?" he said. And when she didn't answer: "I'm surprised at you, frankly, Jolie. Drinking on school property's a serious violation of the honor code—though right now it's your safety I'm more concerned about. How were you proposing to get home?"

"It was just a couple of swallows, Mr. Koussoglou. To see how it felt. And I told you, Precious is sober, you saw her. The train's right there."

"You know I'm going to have to contact your parents none-theless," he said.

"My mom lets unknown numbers go to voicemail."

"So we use your phone to call her."

"It died." Which was true, actually. She held it up.

"An email, then, and let's see what comes back."

The lit face of his phone lit his own fine face as she watched him thumb-type the letters of an address she felt helpless to with-hold. Then he stopped and frowned. "Jolie, this isn't going to end up in some dead account, is it? Like a fake number someone gives out at a bar?"

She was used to people in official positions wondering why her last name failed to match her mom's. Even on her birth certificate, she was the only Aspern. "You got me, Mr. K. I'm a total criminal mastermind, and this is all just a really long con."

"Because it's easy enough to go back to the office and pull your mother's contact card. And let's cut the sarcasm, shall we, given the circumstances?"

"The university email's the one synced to her phone . . . It's Kupferberg because she never took my dad's name, okay? I was four the first time he got arrested. And then like ten when they made him go to rehab."

His eyes seemed to swim slightly behind their lenses, unless it was the booze making her see things. "Sorry," he said. "I didn't realize."

"Why would you?"

"I could try him instead, if that's who you'd prefer picking you up."

The assumption that her father would now be anywhere reach-able was telling, she thought. Maybe even a resource to exploit.

Not that Mom was one for traditional discipline, but the breach of privacy that had opened up this intriguing closeness with her teacher was going to be unbearable from the woman with whom she already shared meals, a hair color, an apartment, and a habit of biting the ring finger of her right hand when nervous. Then again, the goal seemed to be someone capable of coming down here and retrieving her, as in corporeally. Plus trying to escape your mother was like trying to escape your own body. Or so, in as many words, she was about to tell Mr. Koussoglou—she was a big girl, and would face the music—when that glimmer, closer to pain than to power, stole again across his face.

"Look, Mr. K., Precious is waiting for me right there at the subway. It's half a block, and then like six stops on the express. Let me go now, and you get the entire break to draft your email."

"Which accomplishes what, exactly?"

"Well, it gives me some time to own up to my mom myself first. Isn't that the real punishment?"

"Not per the student handbook, I'm guessing."

"Yeah, but the people who wrote the student handbook never had to admit human fallibility to Sarah Kupferberg," she said, trying to find the right distance to pooch out her lower lip.

In the end, he would insist on putting her into a cab, handing the driver a twenty while she rattled off her cross-streets. But at the first red light after turning the corner, Jolie would ask to be let out and then double back to the subway. She must have sensed already there'd be no one on the platform save herself and the homeless. But apparently she wasn't yet ready to abandon that other reality—the one where a girl like Precious Ezeobi would be the type to stick around.

WITH MR. KOUSSOGLOU, TOO, she'd been dumb to get her hopes up. He wasn't going to let her off the hook for the drinking just because they both had a week off school. Some adults were like psychological Mormons this way: admit them as far as the vestibule and the next thing you knew they were in your innermost sanctum, testing the couch cushions and straightening the pictures on the wall. Then again, Jolie knew that if he'd passed by her door without so much as a knock, she'd have felt pained by the rejection. And so that first Monday back, leading her mother past a scrum of staring eighth-graders and into a first-floor classroom, she found herself in the position she'd come to think of as her default: wanting things so many different ways as to pretty much ensure her disappointment.

The room was unoccupied, but up near the whiteboard three student desks had been dragged into powwow formation. Mom folded her long legs under the writing surface and fiddled with her pledge-drive go-cup. To sit down beside her to wait would have been to encourage more of the conversation Jolie had spent the last forty-eight hours ducking ("How am I supposed to know what he wants, Mom? Didn't he mention anything in the email?"), so she lingered by the bookshelves, taking another inventory of Mr. Koussoglou's library—its umlauted authors and promises of disenchantment. And here came the man himself, bustling in with an armload of papers, so chipper it made his earlier attunement seem like a front. "Sorry to keep you waiting, folks. We've got only the one copier serving all of Humanities, and it tends to get a little jammy this time of day. Anybody need coffee before we start?"

"I brought my own." Mom indicated the go-cup. Then she pushed up her glasses like a crown and put out a ringless hand . . . and as always, it stung a little to be reminded of how young she still was. She might have been out there living her own life— might even have wanted that—had it not been for the accident of Jolie. "It's Sarah, by the way."

"Right, forgive me—Brandon. Ahem. Koussoglou. I keep forgetting email isn't actually a form of introduction. Jolie, you fixed for caffeine there?"

Jolie had in fact been experimenting with the idea of herself as a coffee drinker, but the question seemed rhetorical. He had already launched into his prologue with Mom: how good of her to come on such short notice, how good to sit down and finally get to know each other . . . It occurred to Jolie that the cheerfulness was itself the front. Something was making him nervous—which explained why he kept delaying any specific charges. "So I gather Jolie's told you why I called you both in to meet?" The question hung in the air.

And maybe it was just the Inuit transformation mask on the wall behind him, but she found herself thinking of the fire in Precious's eyes. Of rituals where people symbolically consumed their gods in order to become them. "To be honest, you're going to have to spell it out, Mr. K.," she heard herself say. "Because neither of us has the faintest clue."

"Interesting. No clue why you're here, Jolie, really?" He steepled his fingers, as if inviting her to reconsider.

But her habitual obligingness had vanished, leaving her strangely reckless. Strangely free.

He cleared his throat again. "Well in that case, I guess let's all just take a step back and try to start with the bigger picture. I took the liberty of glancing at the permanent record, and I was surprised to discover a certain Jolie Aspern on the honor roll going back to . . . ah, basically back to whenever the public schools start the honor roll. You understand why I say 'discover.'"

"This year's report cards have been less than stellar, I know," said Mom. "But Jolie's still pulling what, a B in here?"

"She'll be lucky to salvage a C minus, now that the midterms are graded."

He had a marked copy of her exam at the ready. Jolie felt some unease as her mother flipped through pages.

"Brandon, if this is just about grades, I teach, too—"

"Right. Urban Studies, I think she mentioned, at Columbia. Geographic displacement and, ah, 'economies of desire'?"

"Barnard, but same difference. Anyway, I don't want to get hung up on a few stray data points, or try to shield her from adversity. I've seen how destructive this whole rise of the helicopter parents has been."

"Again, though, the academic record's just for background," he said, before sidestepping the obvious segue. "Look, here's a copy of her final paper from the fall. Choose your own theme: a comparative study of the genocides in Cambodia and Rwanda. Or really just an essay on the brutality of human nature—very loose with the citations, I might add, hence the low grade." This too he slid toward Mom. "The nihilism by itself would be one thing. But looking back, I'm also seeing the various recesses Jolie's been sitting out. The lunches eaten alone, if at all. The weltschmerz, the 'Rude Boy' pin, the cloak of inky black—"

"It's a fucking—!" said Jolie, who'd been caught off guard. "I mean, pardon my French, but it's a tuxedo jacket, from a thrift store. Itzhak Perlman, hello?"

"Black jeans, black fedora, black tee-shirts on Casual Friday, now shading into various other forms of acting out." The hand gesture felt gratuitous. "Jolie, I'm offering a choice here. Can I just cut to the chase of what this has all started to look like from where I'm sitting? Or do we really need to go back over the most recent warning signs?"

It wasn't his place to offer a diagnosis, but the effect was the same: of a bandage being ripped away. Of a wound, exposed.

"I'm saying, is there something going on with you I should know about?"

Asshole, she thought. With your puppydog eyes. You could never imagine what it's like in here.

Yet Mom was looking at her as if for the first time. "Well, I can't identify anything specific. But now that you mention it, I do seem to have noticed some moping around lately."

And suddenly Jolie's fear surged in a new direction, and had to be throttled back. "Uh, maybe I'm bored? Anybody thought of that?"

"Honey, how can you be bored? There was the musical, you've got swimming—not to mention, you're growing up in one of the least boring places on earth."

"Everything is context, though, isn't that what you're always saying? Maybe in the context of what it ought to be, American life is, like, really, really boring."

"Jolie, it's more or less an objective fact that we're among the most lavishly entertained people in the history of the world. If you're bored, it does seem to say something about you."

"That you've raised a boring person, I guess. But that doesn't mean I need some *intervention* from the social studies teacher." She was almost daring him to bring this back to the gravamen, the drinking: about any larger crisis, she was prepared to concede exactly nothing. "Or are you just going to write off my take on things because I've started to think for myself?"

"Jolie, I hate to point to your financial aid package." This was Mr. Koussoglou. "But there are baseline expectations you're starting to bump up against. And what I'm trying to suggest is, maybe the solution could involve us actually getting to the root of whatever's eating you?"

"Well, wait a minute, though." It would be unclear for a long time afterward just what had caused Mom to return so swiftly to first principles. "Before we get ahead of ourselves, these are survey classes you're teaching, right? No offense, but is it possible school really has been a little underwhelming? I mean, Jolie *is* the one having the experience."

"I have reason to think it's bigger than that," said Mr. K., blushing. "I'm not trying to prosecute any particular case here, but I think you'd agree I have a duty not to pull punches when I see behaviors that concern me. As an educator, or just as a human being."

And from somewhere in memory a tactic for dealing with men returned to Jolie: Don't resist. Steer into the skid. "Okay, Mr. Koussoglou, yes. But what you're trying to read as warning signs are just noise, is what I'm saying. What do I have to do to prove to you that this has all been a big overreaction? Or aberration, or whatever—that I'm already back on track?"

He studied her face for another long count. Then her mother's. Then, perhaps seeing the legacies of self-protectiveness to which the Kupferberg women were heir, he rose to reconnoiter his bookshelves. When he returned, it was with a battered paperback, black cutouts on a purple ground. The cover he tipped toward Mom. "This one you're familiar with, I bet?"

"Geertz, sure," she said. "We had to read him for comps."

"Jolie, your contention is that you're just bored. What I hear your mom saying is that everything is interesting if you look at it closely enough. Which happens to be the argument of this book . . . mutatis mutandis. At any rate, the suggestion on the table is that we could be doing more to challenge you here at school, and this other 'noise,' as you call it, would clear up. So what if I proposed a kind of test?"

"This is my punishment. More homework."

"But remember, it can hardly be a punishment—right?—so long as no one's pointing to any specific rule you've broken."

And only now, too late, did she see how neatly their little secret could be turned to his advantage, rather than her own.

"Call it an independent study instead." Her mission, he told her, would be to visit a site of Cultural Richness, however she construed the phrase, and to produce five to seven pages of thick description, on the model of Geertz's "Notes on the Balinese Cockfight."

"—which I'm guessing you would have to read," added Mom, clearly relieved to be back in harness with the forces of self-improvement.

"Along with the rest of *The Interpretation of Cultures*, plus let's say three more secondary sources of your choosing," Mr. Kous-soglou said. "You and I could meet weekly through the spring to track your progress. I'm sure we could enlist your mom as a resource, too. But the real commitment would have to come from you. If you got a credible paper in by the last day of the semester, we'd have evidence you were right all along: this year was strictly an adjustment period. Your final grade would get a bump—we might even think about your piece for *The Gyre*—and I could consider my larger concerns addressed. Meantime, I'd try to hold them to one side . . ."

It was like a dare of his own; was the idea that he'd keep piling on the work until she just threw up her hands and confessed? She was still trying to figure out the shortest path to liberation when Mom said, "Sounds like we have a deal."

"Hey. I'm right here." But it was as if at some point Jolie had been put on mute, as if even her own mother could no longer hear her.

"You know, you have this fear, with middle school, that you're packing them off on some three-year voyage. So even if this is all just typical teenage stuff, Brandon, I'm grateful to have someone looking out for her."

Jolie entered a message into the phone in her lap.

> I'm. Right. Here.

But Mr. Koussoglou was saying, "You know how it is, I'm sure. Sometimes you don't know where the kids are coming from until you get everybody in and get a dialogue going. Still, I'm willing to try taking Jolie at her word." And turned once more to zap her with his vaporous soulfulness. "There's nothing I'd like more than to have misunderstood."

"FIELDWORK," was how Mom kept trying to dignify the assignment, but Jolie's first instinct was to just refuse to do it. The way Mr. K. had set this up, though, the alternative was to cop to the drinking, which she couldn't quite bring herself to do either. And so, after an interval of token resistance, she began scouting around her neighborhood for whatever would be the least boring subject. Maybe the drum circle that met on those project benches near the park? Or that Dominican social club by the cathedral? She used to love on warm days to watch the old men in Ban-Lon sling dominoes across a folding table. But since she'd last looked, a sheet of glass seemed to have arisen between her and the Cultural Riches of Morningside Heights.

It was already mid-March when one of her dilatory walks from train to school took her past a wisteria'd townhouse on East Twenty-Fifth Street with an oblong of wood bolted to the basement level. The word carved there was one she'd never seen before, yet after school ended, she would find herself delaying the eighty-block schlep uptown to pass it again. Sometime between, the sign had broken into syllables. Punctuated itself. ZEN: DO.

The floor above looked residential—half a lampshade visible in a second-story window, a sill of leaning DVDs. But the basement blinds hadn't budged, as if a secret were being harbored there. The idea that anything could still be secret in this city—in this century—seemed indisputably non-boring. Even a little daunting. For ten minutes or more, she hung on the nearest corner, pacing a guano'd stretch of flagstone, ghosting her finger across hours and Yelp reviews on her phone. To anyone watching, she'd be just another passerby. Yet at two minutes to four, seeing no obvious place to ring, she seized the knob at the center of the plain wooden door.

Immediately, a buzzer somewhere began to buzz. She pictured a whole audience turning to clock her faux pas, but inside was just a bare room, aqueously lit; what she'd read as pulled shades were in fact sheets of rice paper. Her eyes adjusted to take in the alms bowl with its crumpled bills, and then, past the doorframe, a larger room, nearly shadowless, a rigid grid of mats on the floor. The people already in there looked normal enough from the ankle up, yet the way they were padding around in stocking feet was almost weirder than if they'd been nude. The odor was weird, too, toasty but also loamy, like fishfood.

It was when she turned to flee that the buzzer buzzed again and two finance types jostled in behind her. She had to weigh her need to escape against their bro-ish vibe of possessing the space—but in complete silence, for the strangest thing about the basement (so strange she'd only just noticed it) was that nobody was talking. In true Jolie fashion, she ended up doing this pantomime-yield thing, almost a bow. And once the guys were past, she saw them making for a shoe rack no more exotic than you might see in the front hall of a family apartment. It occurred to her to get through this the way she'd gotten through her first time being panhandled on the subway: study other people and do as they did . . . though it was too late to do much about the socks hiding under her black Chuck Taylors, besides wait till these guys cleared out and hope no one noticed the individual sheaths at the toe-caps, the Christmas bulbs stitched at the end of each. It seemed a neophyte's dead giveaway, somehow, toe socks at the zendo.

TWO HOURS LATER, when she let herself into the apartment, her head would still be an exquisite blank. It was the sight of the second keyring on the mail table that sent her hurtling back to meatspace. Her mother must have canceled office hours and come home early. "How was practice?"

"It's not practice, Mom, it's voluntary free swim." Technically, Coach Duff wasn't allowed to require pool time in the offseason, but it was understood that any girl who didn't turn out weekly for the quote-unquote free swim was forfeiting her spot on the team in the fall.

"How was voluntary free swim, then?"

Her hair was dry, her eyes lacking that raccoon look they got after eighty minutes in goggles; she hadn't been planning to keep the afternoon's discovery to herself, necessarily. But if there was a moment to speak up, the tableau that greeted her as she entered the living room foreclosed it. "I thought that thing was in storage."

Atop the black arthropod of her futuristic exercycle, Mom's legs were churning at roughly twice the speed of anyone riding an actual bike. It did something to the handlebars, swept them backward and forward in quarter time, an effect obscurely reminiscent of folk dance.

"I had Vikas bring it up."

"Yeah, but why?"

"Look at you, Jolie. You're in the pool four hours a week. Me—" She was short of breath. "Yesterday a kid your age offered me his seat on the subway." A pause. "I don't know, is thirty-four actually old?"

"Maybe he thought you were pregnant," she said, though Mom could still pass for a model (if now for hornrims rather than for X-Girl).

"That's not funny."

"Some people join a gym."

"I've got a membership through school. But I never go, so."

"Well, don't let me screw up your rhythm." Jolie turned to leave.

"Oh, honey, before I forget, though. Your laptop was doing its blurbling thing. That's Skype, right?"

Instantly, Jolie's guard was back up; there was only one person in the world she ever Skyped with, and whole seasons of her life could pass between attempts. But it would be just like her mom to engineer one. "This wouldn't by any chance have anything to do with that stupid meeting at school, would it?" Because for all her due deference toward deconstruction, Mom still clung to the idea of history as it had once been lived. She seemed to think that if you weren't happy, it must be down to some intentional decision by human agents—a late-night smuggling run, say; a narcotics charge—rather than the fathomless fucking gyre of existence itself.

"Jolie, it's not my habit to go running after your father about things like that, even if I could reliably get ahold of him. But don't you think if you're going to have a relationship, you should fill him in on what you're up to? I know you've started to claw your way back academically, for instance. Or anyway, that's what your teacher says, Mr. . . . ." She snapped her fingers.

"What, Koussoglou's briefing you behind my back now? Oh, forget it."

That she'd managed to make the pedaling stop brought no real satisfaction. In the hall, she waited for the flywheel whir to mean it had resumed. Then she turned toward the kitchen. In the cabinet above the range hood were a few old bottles, greasy and streaked with lint. She wasn't quite sure where they'd come from, since as far as she knew Mom had never taken a drink in her life; they saw the light of day only on those rare occasions when Nana and Albert visited here, rather than having them up to Riverdale. But now she took one. Or liberated it, as those agitators at Blue-stockings might have said—promoted it to the recesses of her bulgy backpack, stopping only to press her nose to the neck for the flutter brought back just by the smell.

AND SO, BY APRIL (long story short), it had become part of Jolie's ritual to seal off her weekly meditation with a drink or two. If there was no one around, she liked to do it right after in the lit-tle community garden down the street from the zendo: squeeze through the warped gate, duck behind a bush, ride home with her head like a slope cleared by brushfire. Nothing could hurt her then. And the secrecy was important, as the ritual was important. The secrecy was how she knew she hadn't totally knuckled under. It was a positive pleasure, for instance, to sit debating the prem-ises of humanism with Mr. K. while in the rosin compartment of her violin case not three feet away hid a grenade-sized Poland Spring bottle full of vodka. Even when she submitted the required draft in a few weeks and revealed that there was something in the world actually worth her interest, she'd be holding back more in the margins. For the time being, she stalled, saying she'd identi-fied several potential subjects and needed time for further inves-tigation. And it was true, in its way: whether kneeling seiza-style in Midtown or getting blotto in her room to *Dirty Mind*, she was investigating the body's capacity to detach itself from the shift-ing pageant all around and burrow down to the ground zero of consciousness—to either the something or the nothing she now could sense lurking there. In the spirit of scientific inquiry, she'd even resorted to drinking *before* school let out for the day. Which perhaps was why, floating north into Kips Bay after the last bell that afternoon (the one where what she'd later learn to call her "depression" caught up with her), she would be slow to spot Precious Ezeobi on a street corner ahead, waiting for the light to change.

In the two and a half months since the dance, Precious had become just another figure to avoid during lunchtimes and passing periods; they did the chin nod if they had to, but never acknowledged they'd been in the trenches together. Nor was either of them about to surrender this corner to the other, even as the pedestrians massed around them, even as the trees shimmied in their boxes and the year's first blossoms clung like fliers to the wet windshields of cars. Jolie wondered if something had gone wrong with the signal. Then she said, "You didn't have to sell me out like that, you know." The words had just arrived in her mouth, as if the intervening months had been erased (though without them she'd have never found the courage to speak).

"Sell you out like what?"

And now Jolie thought she understood the reason married couples were told not to go to bed mad. It was a third presence on the sidewalk between them, restless, motile, prickly. "The night of the dance, Precious. You abandoned me, basically."

"What I did was try to drag you away," Precious said. "You were the one who stayed behind jawing with Mr. Kissyface. No one asked you to like *volunteer* you'd been drinking."

"I'm a terrible liar! And I was trying to take a bullet for you."

"Oh, I get it. I make a mistake, that makes me a bad person, but when someone like you makes a mistake it's like, 'Typical Jolie,' right? Too honest for her own good?" Then, just as Precious had her pinned, she relented. "But notice, I'm admitting it was a mistake." Amazing: that she should even still smell like herself. And here like some soothing chaser came the old solicitude. "I see now we should've stuck together. Plus it's my fault he stopped us in the first place. That asshole's been after me since last year."

"He's just doing his job," Jolie said quietly.

"See? There you go shoring up the system again. You sound

like that heiress, with the Stockholm syndrome. 'Oh, my Tiko's such a sweetheart.'" Ever since they'd met, she'd assumed Precious to be the one with the power and herself the one with the need, but perhaps they'd both had something at stake, and if she could just have accepted the terms of the armistice, taken Precious's tone here as teasing, whatever future they'd had together might have been restored. But the Jolie of that winter had been a different person, apparently. This one was already a block past her destination—and either found a quick way to square things with Precious or failed to score a mat before the bell that tolled the hour. She could have just told the truth about where she was going, of course. But the last time she'd opened herself up to Precious Ezeobi, it had landed her on a cold bench alone, with a twenty-minute wait for the train.

"You know what?" she heard herself say. "Maybe my mistake was ever trusting you to begin with." And turned to double back toward the zendo, but not before she got a look at the sucker-punched contours of Precious's perfect face.

Which almost instantly she would wish she hadn't, for they'd stay with her in the garden where she paused to numb her heart with another swig of the fake Poland Spring. And in the shoe room soon after, above the dissipated alms and the million shards of bowl. And even deep into Open Meditation, invading the fragile white space she'd been counting on to render immaterial the vast mess she'd made of this year. She tried for the umpteenth time to recenter. To attune herself to the ant wobbling its mindless way across the reeds of her mat. To the bead of sweat reposed between her shoulderblades. Repression was the one thing she'd always been good at. But repression took effort, and effort was the opposite of mindfulness—not to struggle was such a struggle! Even the booze had lost its hold. Then a car alarm erupted outside, cycling through its insistent jingles and springing loose the treacherous moisture that was somehow in her eyes, and she knew she'd blown her one chance to escape this meat suit—oh, how had she imagined there might be a way to get free?

The roshi betrayed no evident surprise as Jolie rose from her mat and blundered past the kneeling bodies, the faces too vacant to flinch. "Sorry," she told them. "Sorry," and put a hand on her middle as if the problem were with her stomach. Which did in fact feel a bit rocky all of a sudden. In the shoe room, in the grip of compulsion, she plucked up a few jags of what had been broken, deposited them in the trash. And the last she would see of the Kips Bay Zendo, framed by the outer doorway and the inner, was the roshi's expression, which she now seemed to have misread after all: the opposite of anger wasn't commiseration, so much as a cosmic indifference.

Then it was rush hour on the street and the universal was in full flight behind the particular, the truth of what the world was receding again behind the manifest fucked-upness of the world not being some superior and palpably adjacent way. Someone's medicine-ball handbag came slamming into her arm, and she narrowly avoided the shit some dogowner must have thought too tiny to pick up, and men in helmets had the sidewalk cleared for the erection of yet another oligarch's redoubt, and people were pouring up the down side of the subway stairs. Strange, how the object world conspired against you. Strange, how the beauty withdrew. Down below, she found a pillar mid-platform to lean against and put her subway face on and her earbuds in and sucked a bead of blood from her pricked thumb and was just about to pull up the Albums menu and lose herself in a Prince bootleg called **The Second Coming** when she felt the phone slip from her grasp. There was a slight, distinct tug at the end of the knotted white cord—a fish striking the end of a line. Then the jack gave way and the phone continued its downward arc, clipping the yellow braille of the platform edge, spinning off and clattering to the tracks below.

"Mother*fuck*er," she said, and checked to see if anyone had noticed, but this was New York; the lone flutter was of a bird that had gotten stuck up under the girders. Nearer the mouth of the tunnel was a risible little gate with a notice too small to read, a swimming-pool ladder leading down to the tracks. It was one of those stations from which, when the tunnel was empty, you could see clear through to the lights of the next. She had more than enough time, in other words, to get down the ladder and back to the middle of the station and then do the whole bit in reverse. And the thing no one ever tells you about being fully and unjudgmentally in the present is that your choices don't always feel like choices, especially not when your four-hundred-dollar phone is at stake and your mom's unlikely to spring for a new one.

She wouldn't even be convinced these were the actions she took, really; threading through the crowd, clambering down the semi-ladder, picking her way along the sooty ties toward the subway station's center, keeping a nice wide margin from the third rail. Yet there at eye level, inescapably, were the shoes of commuters. Their heads should have been a million miles away, lost in news or in novels, in dramas public or private, but after a couple of folks cried out from beyond the far track, her own side began to stir. *Hey . . . Hey!* She pretended not to hear, because fuck you. And when she got up onto the platform again, she would walk right back to her spot like butter wouldn't melt. Her fingers closed around the phone, whose glass, amazingly, was not cracked. A major deviation from her recent run of luck. Then, in what order was hard to say, a puff of sour air lifted the hair from her forehead and the ties began to quake, and a small white light to tremble in the tunnel's mouth. *Huh*, she just had time to think. *I did not see that coming.* At which point whatever string she'd been groping her way along these last months seemed abruptly to have run out . . .

Or maybe I should say: to have split. Because there must still be some world in which she breaks panicking toward the ladder behind her. Shouts gusting from the platform above, a horn cleaving the air—and no way was a train already coming, she protested in her head. Not unless she was a whole lot drunker than she thought.

But in the story I now find myself again at the outer limits of my ability to tell, her body felt oddly calm, as if a hole had been wiped in a foggy window by some obliging sleeve. She turned to run mainly because she could see how anything less might have appeared to Mom. To Mr. K. To Dad, even. But then a snatch of that Sufi birthday song came back. What they sang, instead of "Happy Birthday, dear Blah-Blah" was "May you rea-lize in this life-time . . ." To a child's ears, it had sounded so mysterious: Realize what? But of course some verbs need no object, can simply exist on their own. Her whole pointless life had been a failure to realize, she realized, yet all she had to do to change that was to stay here with the calm, to close her eyes and still the grasshopper mind and see her research through to what now seemed its logical conclusion: that even a nothing was preferable to this something.

There would be the one voice rising above the others as the headlight swelled and she wheeled back to kneel before the train, a swarthy-looking guy with a shaved head and a boxer's squashed face dropping to his knees at the edge of the platform as if in sympathy or anticipation. His outstretched arms were as thick as small trees, but the tattoos made them seem somehow fragile. *Don't,* she wanted to say, waving him off. *I'll only drag you down.* But then, what did her intentions even matter in the end—what do they even now—if at the moment that would feel the heaviest in her thirteen years on earth, it was this other part of her, the thing beyond naming, stepping forward to call the shots?

2

THE WAY ETHAN HAD ALWAYS HEARD IT, Alan T. was a programming honcho who'd developed, alongside one of the big reality franchises of the late '90s—*Outraged!* or *Naked Terror* or some such—a powerful taste for crystal meth. And then, as the housing bubble metastasized, had been talked into buying a ten-acre retreat on Santa Catalina Island by an unscrupulous mortgage broker (redundancy *sic*). The pitch was multipronged: he could borrow at two percent and hold bonds at four, the island was a short hop from the mainland, and Alan T. already had his pilot's license plus a little six-seater Cessna gathering dust at the Long Beach Airport. Not that Alan T. needed much persuading; by that point, he was going days at a clip without sleep, and you could probably have sold him beachfront property on Mars—which he'd have visited about as often, come to think of it. But one fogbound morning, stumbling home after thirty straight hours in strip clubs, he'd decided, in a fit of expiation, to fly his wife and kid across the channel for the weekend. Only now the sleeplessness caught up with him. The Cessna overshot the island's runway by about a mile and dropped into the drink. The lone survivor the Coast Guard managed to fish from the debris was Alan T., suffering from minor contusions.

He'd subsequently become a kind of cautionary legend in L.A.–area recovery circles. Also a lurker at meetings, it was assumed, though no one could quite establish what he looked like. Some said fat, some stringy; certain Latinos believed him to be half Latino. Most described his eyes as haunted, while the small but vocal minority who claimed to have heard his story first-hand had him as unflappably—even alarmingly—cheerful. The one thing everyone in AA could agree on was that Alan T. had emerged from great loss determined to pay the gift of his sobriety forward. Every so often, some especially touch-and-go noob would receive via his or her sponsor a second chance: a sealed envelope. Inside, neatly typed, would be a note in the first-person plural offering a three-month retreat on Santa Catalina, away from the temptations of Babylon. Away from the interminable meetings, too, Ethan would figure when his own offer came. It was part of why he'd said yes. But the program was relentless like that; you could have been hiking the Yukon and made camp for the night and within a mile there'd be at least one other tent where four or five people sat under a lantern chanting the serenity prayer. Or at any rate, this island, with its year-round population of five thousand and its handful of liquor licenses, turned out to be rife with ex-addicts—a couple of them alums of Alan T.'s halfway–halfway house, now rechristened the Casa del Sol.

Like the island itself, the property was impressive in its way, built out in stages from its humble origins until it hovered undecideably between janky ranch and modernist masterpiece. The largest structure was an angular strut suspended out over the hillside like the house at the end of *North by Northwest*. Or maybe Ethan was thinking of *Zabriskie Point*; either way, from the soaring plateglass of the great room, you could see clear to the Pacific. And save for the maids who came through once a week, you had the whole space to yourself—"alone with your thoughts," as the invitation put it.

After a couple days lingering in bed, sweating out the last of the dope, Ethan would find himself ransacking the *Casa del Sol Guidebook* in the butler's pantry for some chore-sheet or list of instructions he might have overlooked. Wasn't that how these places were supposed to work? But aside from a laminated sheaf of business cards, a few loose takeout menus, and a schedule of local meetings, there was only a long list of prohibitions: No guests, no feminine hygiene products down the toilet, no alcohol or drugs, no using the pool (liability), and so on.

Laying aside the binder, he slid open a door to a set of stairs leading down to a terrace. The salt smell stung his nose, though you couldn't really hear the surf over the crunch of the south lawn like a cheap plastic mat underfoot. It was a desert island, basically, in the midst of another drought, and maybe because the Casa itself was so devoid of life, Alan T. had let the landscaping go. In the gardens where Ethan now wandered, even the bromeliads, ostensible air plants, seemed to be hanging by a thread. The weeds pushing up through the white gravel beds were, by contrast, like alien opportunists who'd hitched a ride on a meteor and would thrive even in the absence of sunlight. Then he thought of his auteur mother kneeling in a mid-Atlantic garden, trying to disentangle bindweed from her hostas—that inch of fiery hair grown back only thinner; her shaky hands and neuropathy gloves . . . and soon he was kneeling, too, inveigling free a weed, then another, pinching low on the stem as she had ended up having to teach him to wrest out the always surprisingly long taproot. Each pulled weed seemed to disclose two more. By the time he remembered to look up, his lower back ached, the winter-small sun had dropped, and the shadow of the house reached halfway across the piebald lawn.

Over the next week, Ethan's bubble of involvement would likewise expand. He sketched a rotation of beds to be cleared. Found a few bags of compost in a disused stable and troweled them around the bases of the worst-looking plants. He moved moss from treelimbs to gravel until he found one that might work as a weed guard, or at least made pleasingly organic patterns against the white. And at nightfall, when the water would get the most time to soak to the roots, he used a hose to send hoops of silver out over the grass. There was no indication at that point of anyone else on the estate, nor a single soul at the church-basement meetings he attended who could have fit a plausible description of Alan T. (unless Alan T. was a leathery blond woman in her early fifties), yet somehow word must have gotten back, because as Ethan's three months neared their end, he received an email asking would he like to stay on as caretaker. In addition to a small stipend, he could have the little gardener's hut at the back of the compound rent-free. And given the charnel-house of his résumé, his present unlikelihood of clearing a background check for any other job—plus the fact that he hadn't taken a drink or injected

so much as an aspirin since he'd been out here—it was an offer
he'd have been crazy to refuse. Even crazier than he sometimes
feared he already was.

Since then, in the same way the sun had sunk that first day in
the garden, three years had slipped by. Such social links as he
maintained were with the little town of Avalon a mile away, the
site of his tenuous fellowshipping and endpoint of his daily con-
stitutional. A half-dozen other tenants cycled through the house
up the hill, but he experienced them only as lights coming on
at odd hours in the pitch of night, or at most as a bright-toned
sweater on a balcony of a morning, an unreturned wave, a plan-
gency he pretended not to notice as he continued on his rounds.

The daily highlight—the part that, despite his hopelessness
at marshmallow tests, he tried to save for last—was the forbidden pool. Having fertilized dead spots, edge-trimmed walks,
raked limes from under the trees, he might even squeeze in a run
along the ridgeline and attempt a ghazal or two before retrieving the needfuls from the poolhouse. The next twenty minutes
he'd spend emptying each filter in turn. With a litmus kit and an
almost Hippocratic attentiveness, he'd test and retest the water,
add chemicals as indicated. Only then, as the golden hour crept
in, would he untelescope the net and begin his skim.

The big stuff, the palm fronds and feathers and the occasional
bag blown over from Dump Road, you could clear in five minutes,
but there was this whole universe of flotsam you missed if you
went too fast: insects borne along on the surface tension, para-
chutes from silkwoods, other fuzzy variants of pollen. Depending
on the light, you had to keep squatting to avoid glare, and the
finer the pollutant, the more work required to wrangle it into
the net. He evolved a technique that had something of tai chi in
it, something of the golfer sizing up his putt, something of the
rhythmic poling of the gondolier. Maybe there was a larger metaphor in here, but the point was not to think too much. The sky
burned down to pink. A bat or two might start tumbling around
up there, like socks in a dryer. Then, when the surface of the
pool was immaculate, or anyway as immaculate as he could get it,
he'd allow himself this one concession to the whole AA gestalt: to
pause on the concrete lip with his eyes closed and try to frame an

emission of gratitude to the Higher Power of whose nonexistence he now felt like living proof.

But Ethan was nothing if not distractible, and one day at the start of the third spring he heard a crashing on the deck behind him. He turned to discover a barelegged girl with dark hair and an upturned nose, clambering into a metal lounger. From the killing fields of long-term memory rose an email: a new tenant was due to check in, Magnolia yclept—Magnolia Doyle. He'd assumed that like her half-dozen predecessors (like himself when he first arrived) she'd be in some early-middle stage of recovery. For a few months she would rattle around the big house, grieving the loss of her substance; then, like the others, she'd be gone. Yet here she was, a blur of neon beneath a thin weave of tee. He decided not to be rushed; she'd eventually figure out how all this worked. It was when he turned away to fumble in his head's darkness that she announced he was missing something.

"Beg pardon?"

Without putting down her magazine, she curved a propped foot and swung it toward a spot on the water. Her expression was lost behind sunglasses. Then again, his might have been, too. "I'm saying, you missed a spot."

And damned if she wasn't right; there, plain as day, was a tawny flaw, a fur-clump beating boatlike against the breeze. "Thanks," he said, without conviction.

She let her leg linger a moment in the air between them, then marked her place with her gum. "No worries. I reckon I owed you anyway."

"For what?"

"For the soft landing, obviously. For me and Rerun."

He shrugged. "It's not my place. I just unlock the doors."

"Oh, come off it. You know I brought a pet." It was true; apart from lights, the one sign of habitation up at the big house of late had been a dog patrolling the terrace near dusk. "It's Ethan, right? Call me crazy, but I had this idea that maybe you were the one who got the powers that be to lay off."

"If you mean Alan T., my access is strictly email, and even then the guy keeps his own counsel." He felt obscurely accused; how to hide behind Alan T. without sounding childish? "Maybe he's taken a shine to you from afar—"

"In which case I'd owe you for *not* telling him about the dog, right? I hear he's still got suction with some of the casting directors in L.A."

Ethan moved to change the subject. So she was an actor, too; how was that going?

How did he think it was going, she said, if she was stuck out here at some goddamn sanatorium? "My last audition was for prestige cable. I'd just crawled out of a k-hole, and I guess I came off kind of strident about my dignity, like no sober person ever stooped to showing tit. And now every time the phone rings up at the house, I'm like, Oh, there's my agent. Instead, it's someone wanting to sell me a time-share, or shaking a cup for the Sierra Club . . . But here I go cozying up to strangers again, when you must have tons to do, probably."

"Nope, that's pretty much it," he said, and began to collapse the skimmer. "Good luck with your stay, though, Magnolia. It works if you work it."

The length of the pole magnified the tremor in his hands, but as he returned the gear to the poolhouse, he tried not to let it show, or to notice her shucking her tee-shirt or hooking her fingers into the bottom of her swimsuit, wriggling it into place before executing a splashy cannonball. She'd return a few times that month to rap about the weather and the dog, but he was careful to switch up his rituals—took the excuse to break off his desultory attendance at meetings lest their paths cross there; even shaved his shaggy blond beard, in case it was the whiskers she was into—and gradually she seemed to grasp (or maybe he got better at conveying) that as people seemed fond of saying, in those days of every man his own island, he hadn't come out here to make friends.

THEN A MONTH INTO SPRING there'd come a knock at his door. It was Tuesday, the maids' day, and he was following the usual protocol: lie low in the bungalow, keep the blinds drawn and the volume on the TV down. Not that he had anything against maids—he himself was a glorified maid—but he struggled with the Spanish, and liked to preserve the illusion of solitude. The knock, obviously in error, would go away if ignored. Except here it came again, the pneumatic wheeze of the screen door and a series of sharp reports on the wood underneath.

It was Magnolia, shoeless, her dog nosing around loose-leashed on the path behind her. "You want to tell me just exactly what the fuck this is?" A crumpled piece of paper was being clutched inches from his face. Chipped nails in shades of industrial decay. He had to steady her hand to read the printout.

Dear [Visitor's Name Here]: As per House Rules noted on your invitation and reproduced in the Guidebook, pets are strictly "non grata." We offer you the freedom to make separate arrangements for your animal or tender a deposit of $200 against any maintenance charges to be incurred, cash or check to the caretaker.

"I can't believe you'd narc me out," she said. "I thought we were cool."

He told her she had it wrong, they were still cool (though how *had* those urine-bleached patches he'd hosed off the grass been detected, unless Alan T. was pulling a Boo Radley here and had been watching them all along?). He groped for a new angle. "Look, I've suspected ever since he hired me instead of a professional that he must be overextended on the mortgage. Maybe he needs to feel like if a potential buyer walked in off the street today, or stepped off a yacht, or what have you, a realtor could show it at its best."

But Alan T.'s selling the place ran pretty much directly counter to her interests as its current occupant, she pointed out. "Its supposedly fragile current occupant?"

"Magnolia, I'm an occupant, too. One who'd be out of a job if Alan T. was serious about selling. Do I look worried?" The question might have been asked of the air, though; she'd already crashed past him into the bungalow's dim interior. And when he reached for the leash end to secure it to a planter, the dog gave a monitory growl. *Fine*, thought Ethan. *Have it your way.* Inside, Magnolia was curled in the papasan chair, vaguely sculptural, hands to head. "Hey," he said. "At the end of the day, it's a couple hundred bucks."

"It's just . . . right now I can barely feed myself, you know?"

"Something will turn up. You said you have an agent—"

"Yeah, who's scheming to drop me."

"I'm sure that's not true."

Down came the hands. "It's a hundred percent true. You remember that audition I told you about? They called to offer me the sister."

"Really?" Conversation with Magnolia was like a flurry of punches it was impossible to track any one of. "That's fantastic, Magnolia. Hats off."

"Ethan, I read for the heroine. The sister's supposed to be thirty. And divorced."

"You say that like it's a bad thing."

"Do you understand what happens to ingénue types who get cast as the thirty-year-old divorcée?"

He hung fire. "They go celebrate?"

"Wake up, Ethan. It's a one-way ticket to ballbreaking lawyer, with a terminal stop at dried-up old nun." And now her tears were no longer the big, open-eyed, discreetly spilly ones, but the ones that blotched and crumpled and uglied up the face. He had that warping sensation that precedes an earthquake, the brief shimmer just before your possessions go dancing across the room. But what was he thinking? The obvious move was to send in some twenties from his own meager stash and try to cover it with a bluff. "Look, if a few hundred dollars is really all that's standing between you and career hara-kiri, why don't you let me compose an email to Alan T.? He seems to feel kindly toward me. Or anyway, to feel something. People used to say I had a way with words . . ."

She bit her lip (he feared more tears) but then appeared to come to a decision. "For me, you'd do that?" And all at once she was on her feet, grabbing his hands. He pulled away as from a hot stove, reminding himself that if she could cry like that on command, she'd have landed any role she wanted. "Now I really do owe you," she said.

"It's no big deal."

"No, I hate being in anyone's debt." She came closer. "You've got to let me at least make you dinner or something."

"Um. Wouldn't that set you back further, financially speaking?"

"Peasant food, if it makes you feel better. Tex-Mex or whatnot. Saturday?"

"Magnolia . . ."

"Just say you'll come. This Saturday, up at the house. It's got two kitchens, for fuck's sake, both of which are currently going to waste." For a second, he thought he heard a snatch of melody from one of his mom's old soundtrack candidates: *Gigolos get lonely, too.* But when he consented, he would tell himself it was purely to get her out of his hair.

NOW BEFORE I REVEAL why Ethan's policy of irresponsibility to anyone but himself was doomed—how his story is my story, too—I should stipulate that there were reasonable people who might have agreed it was for the best. For among those he'd left back east was a sister who'd already underwritten an earlier attempt at rehab, not to mention a probation officer from a prior case. And after his second bust, in '08, there had been a feeling on both sides that some local day program wouldn't be enough to cure him. Inpatient waitlists were backed up all across the opioid belt, but his P.O. had pulled strings at a facility outside San Pedro whose director was an old friend, or Facebook friend, or Friendster—close enough at any rate to land Ethan a bed. The plan was for him to dry out and detox, hit enough meetings to get his sixty-day chip, and then return to his obligations a new man . . . but within weeks of his release, he'd found himself on a late-night phone jag, slurring to his replacement sponsor about how New York itself seemed to have become the obstacle to his sobriety: not only his personal rock bottom but also a whole fucking museum of triggers. And it's not like anyone back there wanted him home like this.

Thus the persistence of most of his worldly belongings in a storage space in Queens for which thirty dollars a month got autodeducted from his bank account. For Saturday's dinner, it would be either the board shorts he unseriously ran in, his Clorox-splashed jeans, or the funeral suit he'd worn on the plane.

He ended up going with the shorts, not wanting to give Magnolia the wrong idea, yet even before he reached the big house, a Bach piece seeping from inside gave a sense of ceremony. He had to knock several times at the delivery entrance to the butler's pantry. And when she did answer, a blast of garlicky humidity rolled out. "Ethan! I was starting to think you'd flaked."

"I had some stuff I had to take care of—"

"I'll bet." She rose on tiptoe to offer him a cheek he didn't know what to do with besides kiss. But something about her greeting felt performative, like he'd come from the far side of the earth, rather than of the lawn, and indeed, when she let him past, there was a third person in the vaulted kitchen, a buzz-cut millennial in a pink polo shirt thumbing around on an iPhone, shades still on—not necessarily a drug dealer, Ethan thought in alarm, yet not necessarily not one, either. "My brother Patrick," she explained. "On shore leave at Point Loma for the week. Don't worry, he's got a room booked at the Hyatt," she added, for if the purported brother were actually staying here, it would be a further flouting of house rules. This was not to speak of the fish-shaped wine-bottle sitting open atop the table.

"And Rerun?"

"I set him up with food and water in the solarium."

"Never was a big Rerun fan," Patrick allowed, glancing up from his device, and now Ethan could see the resemblance: sharp chin and green eyes, faint twang.

Well, me neither, he thought, but I didn't know we could just come out and say it. On the other hand, Magnolia was for the time being no longer his personal mitzvah. He took one of the empty seats at the table. When Patrick tried to fill the glass waiting there, Ethan put a hand over the rim.

"Christ, you too?" the guy said. "It really is some kind of a cult out here."

"Oh, leave him be," said Magnolia. Ethan couldn't fail to recognize the guilt-trippy look her brother shot toward the counter where she stood abusing a salad with some tongs; it was like something from his previous life, the one he was doing his damnedest to put behind him.

But as plates and then food appeared on the table, these winces and nods and related gestures continued to pass between the Doyles. They amounted to a kind of subfrequency, carrying bewildering little signals about vector and position, facilitated perhaps by the glass of wine now in Magnolia's hands. Ethan wanted to say something—bringing booze to the Casa really should have been the last straw—but if her personal vice was ketamine, and Chablis her way of avoiding it, who was he to stand on orthodoxy?

All through dinner the talk would stay strained, an engine struggling to turn over. Patrick, a Navy SEAL, was coming off his third stint in Iraq, and seemed not overly inclined to let anyone forget it. Though perhaps Ethan was the one fixating, feeling like either a pacifist or a pussy. He asked questions with the same sheepishness he might have adopted to say Thank you for your service, and got answers so clipped he started to wonder if the guy had killed people over there. Or no—lost buddies, he thought, kicking himself. But when the conversation turned at last and he dared to take out his phone to check the time, it drew a whistle from Magnolia. "Whoa, look at you, Hollywood."

"What is that, a Jitterbug? I didn't know those still existed," said Patrick.

Ethan affected what he hoped was an air of high-mindedness and set his flip phone down by his plate. "I save like a grand a year in charges and fees. Plus I'd sooner drill a hole in my own skull than have internet in my pocket—assuming there's a difference."

They couldn't let it drop. "You should get one of those holsters for your belt," Magnolia said.

"An external battery with a strap," Patrick suggested.

"Go ahead, you two, yuk it up." He knew his weaknesses were no one else's fault, but blamed Magnolia for having involved him in this occult sibling dynamic, whose silent contentions would now be leavened with jokes at his expense. By dessert—slices of Viennetta plopped on the same plates they'd eaten from—he decided just to focus on the Bach partitas, their eerie fidelity. Which as if on cue went silent, for it was only during the last course, when appetites could no longer be ruined, that one learned the true purpose of a meal. Patrick turned to him. "My sister says the landlord here's a piece of work."

"They're in a standoff about the no-pets policy," Ethan replied carefully, looking at Magnolia. "But it sounds like you can understand his thing about dogs."

"He has a thing about a lot of things. She showed me the binder."

"Overkill, I know."

"Yet you stayed here even after your tour was up."

He had to remind himself not to be ashamed, or annoyed—

whichever feeling covered for the other—that Alan T. had gauged his neediness so acutely. "What can I say? I thrive on order."

"You don't find the whole setup a little odd?"

"It's not my place to judge," he said, retreating to AA-voice. "I keep the grounds, that's all."

"I'm just saying, I don't see how holing up on an island is preparing anyone for real life."

Ethan brazened it out. "And is that what you think we're after here? Real life?" You almost had to laugh. Far from a special operator, the brother might have been a concerned parent swooping in to deprogram a Moonie bride. "Look, with respect to Alan T., I've already agreed to try to talk him into being a little less implacable; it's kind of a specialty of mine. But I need your sister to promise she'll stop dragging me into the middle of things. Maintaining detachment is pretty much an island's whole point."

She beamed as if he were a pony she'd just put through its paces. "Didn't I tell you, Patch?" she said. "When he gets that little hitch in his voice, you just want to put him in your pocket and take him home."

"Now can we move on, please? I'll go see if I can find some more tunes."

He rose and headed for the conservatory wing he'd always given a wide berth. Unlike the books and TV series he'd depended upon to pass the time, music was still a desolation—what of his own he hadn't pawned was in a box back in New York—but maybe he could scroll the library of whichever device she'd hooked up and in this way obtain a little space to breathe. Not having been in the house for a while, though, he managed to get lost. Eventually he reached a room he didn't recognize, the piano at its center so gleaming black he could see himself suspended in the side. It smelled resinous, as though unplayed (had he somehow missed a delivery?), but before he could touch it, ghostly fingers began to work the keys. And only now did he spot the module affixed beneath like an ankle monitor or a suicide belt, spewing shards of spectral jazz. Beyond the glass wall, night had fallen, ebony ocean and the woozy lights of a sailboat. He should have been out there sloping homeward, he thought, another blackness in the blackness; if he spared a look back toward this prism of sound and light, it would be as an astronaut looks back toward the forsaken earth. But when he returned through the entrance hall, it was the brother in his windbreaker being shown the door. "Be seeing you, bro," Patrick leaned back in to shout, or threaten. Gave Magnolia an inscrutable squeeze of the arm and was gone. And before Ethan could think, *I am not your bro,* he and she were alone, unless you counted the dog, who'd been let out to Roomba the kitchen, leaving a sponge-painting of saliva on the floor. "Don't even start," Magnolia said, when Ethan made a feint toward the dishes. "I'll deal with those in the morning."

He pretended to yawn; yawned. "I should get going, then. But thanks for the invite. The tacos were superb." And kissed his fingers in emphasis and farewell. He didn't think he'd left room for further surprises, but she told him to wait.

"Rerun needs to go out—don't you, Re? Let us walk you to your cabin or whatever, make sure you get in all right."

"You mean because of the muggers."

"What muggers?"

"The ones I keep flushing from the bushes."

She smirked. "I'm just saying, it's hella dark out there, with no one to hear you when you fall. If you think about it, it's a damn good thing I brought the dog."

He went down to the terrace while she closed the door behind her. A metallic ping quickened—Rerun's untrimmed nails on the steps—but then stopped to let leg address bush. The air felt moveless, heavy . . . as if recovering from some disturbance.

At the door to the bungalow, he turned to say goodnight, only to find her reaching past him to flick on a light. "You know, it was awful gloomy in here that other time," she said. "I didn't really get a sense of— Oop!" And since Rerun, leash dropped, was already inside, thumping up the carpeted stairs, there wasn't much to do but let Magnolia follow.

The little bungalow, like so much of the island, had last been updated during the Reagan era, and downstairs was nothing to write home about. Kitchenette, formica peninsula, white wall-to-wall in the living room, a balsawood door behind which lay a room just big enough for a bed. But she was quick to spot the exception. "Oh my God, tell me that's not what I think it is," she said, hurling herself athwart the mattress that had come with the rest of the furniture. "Waterbed!" The other, less dubious extra was the empty room upstairs, under the eaves, or, more specifically, the balcony attached to it, which offered a view to the west through a screening mass of jacaranda. Granted, you had to climb through the window to reach it, but then your privacy was complete. An island off an island. Noticing Rerun sniffing the two-by-four used to prop the sash, Ethan removed it and eased the window down. He found that by pretending to throw the wood, he could conduct the dog generally doorward.

Back downstairs, Magnolia was still on his bed. She smoothed a spot on the comforter. "Come on, Ethan. Make some waves."

He sat beside her, wordless. The motion took a while to subside.

"Hey." She cleared her throat. "You're not mad at me, are you?"

"Don't be ridiculous."

Then she said, softly, "Good. Because I can't get up."

"That's waterbeds for you."

"No, I mean I never should have mixed pinot grigio with tequila."

And though you'd think by this point he'd have found other people's intoxications tedious, the feeling that shot through him was indeed closer to rage. Sometimes it seemed he didn't want to be sober any more than he'd wanted, in the end, to be fucked up.

"You know my brother liked you," she said. "It's why I had him at dinner in the first place."

"I'm at least eighty percent heterosexual, Magnolia."

"I never said you weren't. His job was to argue you're all wrong for me."

"And did he?" He expected her to have something prepared, but now she was the one biting her tongue. He tried to summon what was left of his vaunted persuasions. "Because I am all wrong for you, for about a million reasons. You hardly know me, for one, or you'd know I was wrong for anyone."

"Hubba hubba."

"Plus I'm old enough to be your father."

"I'm twenty-four and you're what, thirty-two? Thirty-three?"

He backpedaled. "You know what I'm saying. We grew up in different worlds. 'Old school' for you is, like, *Wu-Tang*

Forever. Plus the web, et cetera. What you're feeling is a species of transference we all go through—thirteenth stepping, they call it. Besides which, you're hammered."

"So what if I am. Can't I just sleep here, Ethan?"

And in case it was consent that still hung him up, she moved a hand to his thigh. He closed his eyes, tried to slow his breathing. To observe rather than judge the fact that he wasn't immediately pulling away, because he couldn't yet tell which direction it was tugging, this force intruding on his oblivion—whether she meant to blast apart his little fortress of solitude or draw him deeper in. Finally, somewhat painfully, he stood, trying to think what a better person might have said. "You're welcome to pass out here, Magnolia, so long as you keep the dog off the mattress. But in case it changes your calculus any, I'll be crashing in the spare room tonight."

HIS DREAMS must have been of his mother again, though, because when he woke the next morning, his face was wet, guilt draped across his chest like a dentist's lead apron. Usually it was daylight that came crashing in to save him before Mom could lower the boom, confront him with his crimes, but now the world outside was dark. Or at the very least, deep gray. And in place of a bed beneath him was hard floor. Carpet chafing his jawline. A canted ceiling above, submarine light through a lone window. He had passed the night in the room upstairs, but couldn't remember why, and for a second feared he'd been wasted again. Then it came back to him: Ah, right. Jesus, right. The girl.

Sure enough, when he got himself together to venture downstairs, her pit bull was by the closed door to the bedroom, the blunt artillery of its head resting on crossed paws. The dog seemed in the dimness to slit an eye, to track him to the kitchenette, but without raising its head, so maybe their relationship had evolved. Or more likely, having established dominance over the first floor of the bungalow, the dog saw further aggression as a waste; they both knew Ethan Aspern wasn't going near that door.

He had already gotten down the coffee beans when it hit him that the grinder noise might wake her. Nor could he dash over to the Tradewinds for coffee, even had it been open—his wallet was still in the bedroom. The best he could manage was a half-can of Coke from the back of the fridge. He eased open the front door on its querulous hinge, willing the dog not to bark, the rooster on the next estate to hold its peace. Then, still in boxers, he stepped out to the south lawn, that revived plenitude of desert grass, and stood for a minute swilling flat cola, trying not to wish it beer.

At six a.m., the sky out here was mother-of-pearl, uncharacteristically overcast for the dry season. A wildfire had been raging for weeks now on the mainland, but no amount of smoke blown across the channel could have accounted for this gray. It was a fog denser than any in years, of which patches remained closer in, shrouding the heads of the pathway's squat lights, beading on the pergola, clinging to the surface of the pool. The grass was dark, the lime bark the same glossy black as the paling around the poolhouse. Yet the hand he held out for inspection seemed steady enough to get the key to the lock. The lights inside he could do without (not to speak of the mirrors). Somewhere among the nets and poles was a used shortboard he'd scored on Craigslist a few months ago in a moment of weakness, thinking he might take up surfing again. Plus in the waterproof pocket of the wetsuit, bundled with its lighter, unless he was mistaken—nope, here it was—a little clingwrapped twist of grass he'd been too cowardly to touch, much less to throw away. Tossed in as a freebie by the hippie who'd sold him the board, it was the one affirmation he'd had in his whole time out here of the kind of creature he really was.

Of course, if the recovery clichés were to be believed, the more important question was what he chose to do about it. But then he recalled how, on the last day of detox, a fellow drinker, perhaps sensing some frailty in his resolve, had reminded him of the David Crosby method for avoiding drinking and what inevitably followed (so called because every time the thirst came upon you, you rolled a Crosby instead, until you pretty much forgot what drinking was). Ethan had dismissed this at the time as simply swapping a better crutch for a worse one, but hadn't that summed up AA, too? And say this was all just the disease talking and a couple of innocent tokes would put him right back in the hole—

wouldn't it at least show Magnolia she should have done as he said and left him the fuck alone? In any case, he'd already shut himself in the changing stall to tug on the seal suit and cough down half of the joint (the first substance he'd put in his body in some twenty-seven months, for those keeping score at home). And within minutes, as if to affirm the rightness of his decision, he was padding along the highway shoulder with the board under his arm, already feeling less pain. Local custom dictated that when you showed up somewhere and found a *Back Soon* sign, a vanished merchant or coworker, you figured there was a swell on, and so, when he ran into Magnolia again, this morning's vanishing act could be one of those matters not spoken about between friends and neighbors, or whatever third thing they were now.

And how subtle were the gradations on the dimmerswitch sun! By the time he hit the beach, it was bright enough to see that the surf wasn't up to much, that he'd have the water to himself. Neoprene kept the temperature shock to just a faint pressure. With three minutes of hard paddling and a few hundred yards of open water, all markers of human enclosure—the resort down the beach, the pier, plush houses hiding in the hills—had faded to a delirium of green.

It would be tempting to infer from the session that followed some lingering irresolution; over the next several hours, he managed to coax from the slop only five or six bunny-slope rides. But the truth was, he'd been on this board fewer than a half-dozen times since buying it, and though the knowledge did loiter in your bones, there was also that conditioning element possessed only by the maniacally committed and the dumbshit young. Besides, even if he mostly just sat here correcting for drift, wasn't that a kind of practice, too?

And at some point he must have taken the joint back out for a second go-round—the one that makes the meaning. The sky, he was pleased to rediscover, grew higher as he did. Clearer. Tiny vacationers stepped down from their shuttles. Watching them unpack toy chairs, inches of newspaper, Ethan pictured himself as some kind of voyeur angel, like in that German movie Mom had made him watch back when he was still her little sidekick: the one with the *Columbo* guy and the telepathic voiceovers she had later adapted for her swan song. He made a game now of composing them in his head. These folks would of course be consumed with normal-person things, rather than the tortured consciences of post-wall Berliners. Or rather—had life taught him nothing?—torment and normalcy would be all jumbled up. *Is it turpentine or witch hazel that gets beach tar off the feet?* he had a woman in a floppy hat think. *And either way, could it soak through the skin, be bad for the baby? Maybe it's time we talked about the baby* . . . But suddenly, as if spooked by Ethan's thoughts, the man next to her leapt up from his towel. A dervish of powdered sand was streaking across the tightrope of coast, and even at this range, Ethan could make out Magnolia's pit bull, sixty pounds of solid muscle churning up fragments of light. The dog pulled up short at water's edge to muzzle the onshores. And as sure as a thunderclap follows lightning, here came his mistress in all her actuality.

At proper scale, she was cuter than he'd been letting himself see. Compact, deeply tan, whatever was the midpoint between gamine and zaftig . . . were this in fact a film, they might have been spooning in his waterbed right now. Reality being only itself, though, he bent low to the board. When she turned and began talking to the man, Ethan thought he'd escaped unseen. But then she turned back and began to gesture animatedly, directly at him. The fact that she was wearing his bathrobe suggested some urgency in coming down here. But as long as whatever she was shouting stayed lost to the wind, Ethan could dismiss it as mere disappointment, or sour grapes. She made a phone out of her hand and held it to an ear. Ethan patted his sides, trying to semaphore the complex idea that bringing a cellphone surfing would be like smuggling porn into morning chapel. But now that she'd given up and fell to simply pointing, people around her stared past Ethan as if at someone more important standing behind him (so maybe they were native Angelenos, not European at all). He turned in time to see an eight-foot wall of water pushing in from his blind spot, a rogue wave or the bleeding edge of a set, he was too far inside to tell, with at most a few seconds left to escape impact. Yet his instinct remained—he was surprised to discover—that he wasn't totally a lost cause, that redemption might even now be possible. Instead of duck-diving under, he went flat, thrashed, let himself be lifted, popped up . . .

And for fifty yards or so, he could feel the sound and the image, the past and the present, bending and touching and clicking back together. It might have been the summer of '91 at the fading point-break off Henlopen Acres, when the God who hadn't yet left the building would sometimes still bestow the kind of ride Ethan was too green then to realize he didn't deserve—the long barrel forming nothing out of nothing and translating him across the shallows. Was it the drugs that had done it? Loosened the arms, softened the pose, placed him right on the magic axis between casual and careless? At any rate, it was like being back onstage, like the onset of a poem, he could feel the utter legitimacy of his performance erasing all cowardice; he was out here chasing something, rather than simply running away. It was when he put out a hand to test the wave face that some inner doubt, vectored and amplified, inverted earth and sky. He felt his body break the surface, the tired Velcro rip from his ankle like a Band-Aid. Then, in rapid sequence, he was slammed shoulder-first against the bottom, scraped across the face, rolled like a drunk by a gang of delinquents. Held under and robbed of breath.

He came up sputtering and blinking in what was now a broad and sunny daylight, in whitish spume that barely reached the knee. No use pretending not to see Magnolia dancing back from where the wave had died a few dozen yards down the shore. She cupped her hands and shouted again.

"Still can't hear you," he shouted in turn.

She stepped closer, looking baleful. "I said, you've got a phone call."

"No, really, Magnolia, all my bones seem intact, thanks for asking." He dragged himself toward dry land, trying not to look high. "Plus what are you doing answering my phone?"

"The cradle's on your nightstand, fuckhead. It woke me up."

"What, the landline?" A banana-yellow thumbnail shot onto the beach past her shoulder: his board. Later, unable to find it, he would remember thinking he'd go down there once the daytrippers stopped gawking. He turned back to her. "Well, who is it?"

She shrugged. "Some chick."

"And you came all the way out here just to tell me?"

"It seemed like something you might want to know." Another shrug, a downward glance, a bit lip, and now, in the split second before she spun and marched off up the beach, he would feel a foreshock pushing the board and everything else from his head. "I mean, seeing as how it involves you having an ex-wife. And a daughter I guess you didn't see fit to mention."

AFTER AN AWKWARD TRIP BACK, essentially chasing the terrycloth form of Magnolia along the highway, he entered the bungalow and found the cordless unit face-up on the coffeetable, its red light beady as any eye. The call must have been active for like half an hour at this point. Yet when he picked it up, Sarah was right there; even her silences had that recriminating vibe. "How did you get this number?" he burst out, an octave above target.

"The probation people had it as a backup," she said. "I was trying you on your cell all last night . . ."

His cell, right. Probably still somewhere up among the dishes at the big house, but how to explain this without inviting a charge of dereliction? He reminded himself again of the dangers of seeming high. "Okay, but voicemail is a popular option. People send texts. And is that even legal, them giving out my info like that?"

He could almost hear her stockpiles of restraint dwindling. "Ethan, please. You know I've tried to respect whatever curtain you've felt you needed to draw around your life . . ." The reference was pretty clearly to the dismayed young woman who had answered his phone and now stared accusingly from the doorway. *It's not like that*, he wanted to say. *Sarah—I don't love her.* But she pressed on: "I wouldn't be calling if there was a better way to do this." Then, "Hello? Are you even there?"

Magnolia having ignored his attempts to shoo her from the room, Ethan was turning back upstairs. This time of morning, the temperature under the eaves had risen, and the center-line where the roof peaked was the one place he could walk without hitting his head, yet all this buttressed his concept of himself as a person situated amongst fixed, oppressive forces, doing everything in his power to stand up. He wedged the phone between jaw and shoulder, used the two-by-four to re-prop the window. "Listen, if this is about Jolie's orchestra camp, I'm still scraping together the cash—"

"Would you let me speak? There's been an, ah . . . accident, I guess you'd call it—"

"Fuck—what?"

"In the subway, Ethan. She dropped her phone on the tracks, and somehow got the notion she had to go down after it."

A violent numbness seized his hands, his chest, as if an ice-pick were being jabbed through his solar plexus. "Oh my God. I'm going to be sick."

"No, wait: she's okay. I should have started there. She's okay now—"

"Jesus *fuck*, Sarah."

"There was this delivery guy who somehow managed to pull her back onto the platform before the train could come—"

"—are you trying to give me a heart attack?"

"I mean, she's got a big goose-egg on her temple, and they had to relocate her shoulder after she came through triage at Bellevue, she'll be in a sling for a while . . . But all things considered, we got amazingly lucky. I just thought, since it's in all the papers, it was better you hear it from me. It was only on account of her being a minor that they didn't run her name." Then she added, "Sorry. I've never had to do this before, obviously."

Was that a note of solidarity? But even as he closed his eyes and tried to summon an image of their daughter on a hospital gurney, the two of them reunited above, his darker mind was slipping back to when he'd been all of twenty, wheeling a year-old Jolie around Harlem at odd hours of the night to buy Sarah a bit of sleep before the day's first classes . . . and thinking he would wake to find this had all been some crazy dream. Certainly, he'd gone for long stretches more recently acting as if that were the case. All the same, if Jolie were in mortal peril, shouldn't some paternal ESP have kicked in to warn him? He squeezed through the window to the balcony, picking up a splinter from planks warmed by the coins and puzzle-pieces of California sun. "Where is she? Let me talk to her."

"I'm out getting more sushi to take back to her room, Ethan. She's got another day left in the hospital."

"I thought you said she was fine!"

"Well, that's the other thing. I tried to bring her home Thursday night, but they wanted to hold her for observation—and then Friday we got snarled in red tape, a liability thing. Somebody handing her off at intake got the wrong idea off the police report, and since it's a public hospital, they apparently can't discharge her until someone from the city comes to verify that she's not, what's the phrase . . . 'a danger to herself and others.'"

"That's crazy," he said. For though it couldn't be outwardly acknowledged, they both knew Sarah had done a tremendous job with her. Yet he could feel the cracks forming in his project of sounding not-high. "Jolie's the most level-headed human being I've ever met."

"As I would have explained to whoever screwed up the file, Ethan, but I guess nobody works weekends. It's not like there weren't witnesses, you know? It was rush hour. The whole reason Jolie froze down there is she had no idea the train was so close."

He struggled to take it on board. *(Froze? Close?)* "But wait, did you say this all went down *three days ago*?"

"You know I'd have called earlier if she'd been seriously hurt. And if it were up to Jolie, we wouldn't be talking even now. She's really embarrassed, I think, at having run an idiotic risk like that. And concerned about freaking you out. Her phrase, not mine."

"I feel like I'm losing my mind here, though. What happened to my right to know this stuff in real time?"

"But what possible difference could it have made if I'd tried you first thing Friday? And if now . . . God. See? This is why I held off. *My* rights. *My* mind. You can't get over yourself for like three seconds, Ethan, is why nobody ever wants to tell you things."

"What things? Are there more things?"

"You should ask *her*, but when was the last time you even tried?"

And now, like a cold front, their estrangement descended. "I guess it's been a couple months." Though really, it had been just before Christmas.

"But since you asked about orchestra camp, you're off the hook. Her arm being what it is, a mid-May audition's not in the cards."

"And then school's out before you know it," he heard himself say.

"So?"

"So?" His hands fumbled with the wetsuit's zipper, but his

voice held oddly steady. "Why not send her out here to recu-
perate? Give me more than a few hours with her, for once? Even
just a long weekend."

"Ethan, the custody agreement was pellucid on this point . . .
and for good reason, if you recall. You couldn't take her across
Houston Street, much less to California. And that was before you
gave up visits altogether."

"But don't act like that was without your approval, Sarah," he
said, feeling something shake loose. "When I told you I had to
come here and why, you gave your blessing."

"Is that what you thought it was?" For a second, she seemed
ready to go further—to talk about it, even. But no: she could no
longer acknowledge the feeling still between them, or whatever
you called the scar tissue left behind. "I'm not alluding to anything specific, Ethan. Anyway, she's already missing half a week
of school, and now there's P.T., most likely, and this independent
study . . . she's got enough on her plate without being whisked all
the way across the country—"

"You want me feeling guilty, though. Admit it. You want me
feeling like the fact that our daughter could have been lying in a
coma for three days now is in some way my fault. Or in the fucking morgue."

"*Listen*, please. What I'm telling you is, it's nobody's fault but
Jolie's, going down there like it wasn't the very *first* rule of the
subway . . . Or if you want to blame someone, blame me, I guess,
for banging on about the cost of the goddamn phone."

"So why even scare me half to death with this, Sarah, days after
the fact? What's the ask?"

"The *ask*?" More silence. "The ask was for you to show up
for her for once. Be her father. But maybe that was too much to
expect of you, I don't know anymore. You know what? Forget it.
Just forget it."

And down like an axe came the dialtone. He was seized with a
sudden desire to chuck this handset as hard as he could, hear its
cheap plastic innards smash on the path below. Instead, he tried
to recover his balance. Sat with the timbers burning beneath him
and a leafblower droning somewhere beyond the dusty verdure,
the stuccoed wall of Alan T.'s property. With each passing year

they were out earlier, the feral leafblowers of Southern California, though the leaves seemed to be dying faster also, the whole earth on fire. And only now, when it could do him no good, did the fatherhood instinct punch through his haze: it wasn't the seeming high that had been the problem, it was the *being* high to begin with . . . and the most level-headed human could only be Sarah herself, since half of Jolie's wiring came from his side, too. He tried to console himself with the memory of their last Skype session, watching her unpack the stocking he'd sent, but found he could recall substantially nothing of what had been said, for along with hoverboards and virtual reality and most of Ethan's adult life so far, video-chat had fallen far short of its promise. You got distracted by things offscreen, talked over the ends of each other's sentences, were prevented by the very structure of the technology from ever looking each other in the eye (connectivity being to real connection what airline food was to food). No, what haunted him now was her face, blue in the gloom, a certain withholding in her voice, and a fear of what he might have seen himself three days ago, had he been there at the intake desk—a sixth sense that something was wrong here, that he had somehow left his daughter to get caught inside, in that impact zone he knew better than anyone. And besides, grant him even the most perfect record of Jolie's state of mind at the moment she'd gone down onto the tracks . . . wouldn't it still be missing the point? For if his little girl could have held her life such a worthless thing, even for so much as an instant, then the last few years of Ethan's own life had been not an act of self-preservation, as he'd wanted to believe— much less one of bravery—but just another in an unbroken line of unforgivable mistakes.

II
A NEW MAN

I'm sitting here thinking of something one of the rehab counselors said once, Jolie, shortly before they let me go. Not a regular, I should say, but an older guy I didn't recognize, with salt-and-pepper stubble and a Hawaiian shirt buttoned so low I'm tempted to call him a ringer. At any rate, he was doodling on his notepad, letting me flail around with questions of culpability and regret (as I was doing even then, honey—I promise), when suddenly, out of all patience, he looked up:

The way I see it, Ethan, the problem seems pretty straightforward. Sure, there may be a well-intentioned dude in there somewhere trying to put his life back on track. But how's he supposed to hang on to the wheel when he's also got a raging ego riding shotgun and a terrified kid in back and a four-hundred-pound gorilla who wants them all dead—

The beast, I must have said.

Along with how many others he refuses to acknowledge? Point is, you keep acting like you're one specific thing when that's exactly what you're not.

The thrust, I'll be the first to admit, was lost on me at the time. To be honest, I'd almost forgotten it until the document you emailed last month brought all this back: the hot-lunch smell on the air, the glass door to the smoking terrace, the junkies puffing away out there, seeming to smolder at the edges in the sun . . . and how a guy who'd been your father could have ended up among them. Maybe that's all you meant, reaching out to me in writing after nearly a decade of silence—a reminder not to get too comfortable with the adult I seem to have become here at forty-three, and the miracle that either did or didn't save me.

Particularly if, as it seems from your prologue, you've ended up in the hospital again. I know of course that what went down with us after that phone call back in 2011 wasn't actual magic, that the depression doesn't just go away; surely this is part of what the rehab counselor was trying to warn me about. And I remember this idea of storytelling as therapeutic from AA . . . But I suppose the last thing you want to hear, this late in the day, is how I see myself reflected in your struggles. Or no, maybe the last thing you want is me repeating how very sorry I am.

Still, I expect you wouldn't have sent along the first sixty pages of this experimental memoir, your novel without fiction or whatever, if you weren't looking for a response from somewhere out beyond what you've called your "outer limits." So for what it's worth, when I think back now to the year you seem to be trying to excavate (the one that recalled me to life, the one that nearly got you killed), what I'm seeing aren't so much figures of wholeness and consistency, facing well-defined choices, as mystifying fields of enmeshment and contradiction: people in the loosest but maybe also fullest sense of the word, hazily delineated, at odds even with themselves.

Which means what, in practical terms? Well, first, that you may actually have gone a little easy on me as your co-protagonist. Take the dope, for example, and the drinking, and the glancing allusions to my mom. You leave open the possibility that I was a victim, "self-medicating" after the loss of a parent—as would obviously bring our stories into closer alignment. Yet the fact is, I was out of my mind well before she got sick, and on whatever I could find: cough syrup, bagged glue, in a pinch the pep pills sold over the counter at Ducky's Sinclair next door . . . This would have been, I don't know, the year of Nirvana, when Mom was logging long afternoons by herself out in the artroom at St. Anselm's, cutting together her magnum opus. Even the great god Jehovah was still in the sky. Let's not gild the lily, then: I started using for the sheer pleasure of it. Or at least, something in me was swept up enough in being high that when her diagnosis came, it felt less like a cause of addiction than like a conspiracy to get me better drugs.

This isn't to deny the notion of context; in a way, I guess I'm trying to widen yours. The one physical elevation there in town, maybe you remember, was called Keel Hill. It was rumored to contain a continuity-of-government bunker from the 1950s, but as far as I could tell was just covered-over landfill. And if I concentrate, I can still summon the vibe of almost scary freedom up there above the countryside—can still see the alterna-kids from the middling but unisex public high school who used to retreat to the hilltop to smoke and play music at sunset, when rougher trade took over Ducky's parking lot.

It was early in the winter of my third-form year that we would make that climb, too, me and some classmates I can't even say were friends. There was Eczema Jeff; Eli Sernovitz, the bee-charmer boy who stuck pushpins in his arms and claimed immunity from pain; Judd McGrath, my surfing buddy from back before his mom, our extremely part-time guidance counselor, divorced his dad . . . plus that first day, a bracingly assertive Immaculate Heart girl you may have heard me call Natasha. By no means a girlfriend, really, but the person who would show me another facet of Mom's illness. We'd been sharing a cigarette on a loading dock after rehearsals for the interfaith Christmas play when she'd asked me point-blank why no one came to pick me up anymore. And then, when I confided in her about the chemo, assumed a look of compassion and said she knew something that would help. And before I could suggest we just keep talking, she'd shoved my Joseph robes up around my ears and (not to put too fine a point on this, Jolie, but you need to hear it if you're to understand what comes later) was initiating me into mysteries more enduring than mainline Protestantism. Now, careful to avoid jostling the Reddi-wip cans I'd shoplifted from the Sinclair, we slumped back against the storm fence in our uniform jackets and catalog flannels, not far enough from the regular group to be singled out yet not close enough to blend in. And I can recall the blackness descending as I sucked down my first hit of nitrous . . . the flash of fear on Judd's face as I went under, and how, when I returned to the colder light of consciousness, I sat up and motioned for a second straight away. That's the rector's kid, I imagined the high schoolers saying—no one to fuck with. Obviously any figure I cut, sliding farther down the fence amid the strange wail of brain cells dying, was less intimidating than pathetic; nor was I so far gone as to miss how quickly Natasha's interest (or whatever) had moved on to Judd. As some part of me must have known, neither of them was willing to follow where I wanted to go. Maybe that was why I was so eager to go there. And by a week or two later, when I'd discovered how easy it was to steal prescription Vicodin from the room where my mom lay weakened by tumor pain, I'd be too strung out on what felt like true love to care . . .

Only here's the rub, right? Every time I get to this part, the deep heart of my shame, I can hear the narcissism, the self-pity, the guile—that whole manipulative side an addict is warned against, and will frankly be the first to cop to, if it gets him closer to the thing he wants. And all this when the thing I really want, the context I know I have to offer you, has nothing to do with myself or -selves, per se. Rather, it involves the one person in your story thus far who might deserve more of the understanding you've extended to me. I'm talking about the person I did love, Jolie: your mother. That she couldn't reach in to make your own pain stop, wouldn't even see it until it was too late . . . believe me, I know how much that hurts. But anger, in my experience, can be no less a prison than numbness, and cold comfort though it might seem, I think what you deserve now is the truth. People are complicated; there is no other story out there where some winged figure swoops down from on high to change what isn't yet ready to be changed. And your mother, Sarah Kupferberg, was only ever doing the best she could.

But see, here come the paradoxes again: How to explain to you the multitudes she must still carry inside her without first showing you more of the wilderness she was trying to lead me out of when I met her, years ago? And how to justify the choice she'd make later to leave me without helping you to see all the times and ways I'd already abandoned you both? And then, how to do any of this—to convey what I'm frightened got lost in the mix of that last night I saw you—without raising questions of some ulterior motive? How to be sure that my dubious-sounding lifeline isn't just another ploy to secure what I <u>really</u> really want, way down on the lower frequencies: your acceptance, some lessening of the gulf between us?

For a long time, I'm saying, your email felt irresolvable. And replying impossible. Now, though, after weeks on another coast, on motel wifi, saving and deleting and fretting this won't reach you in time, I think I'm finding much as you are that certain stories need certain people to tell them. And that to become the person who can follow a story to the finish, across its gaps and over its walls—to relive it all the way through in hopes of leaving it behind—you just have to start telling it, any way you can. So if you're still out there, Jolie, still willing, despite the high, hard border we both know lies ahead, then follow me back to . . . how did you put it in your opening chapter? To the "wound, exposed." To a blazing bright Monday in June, 1995, and the forest where our story begins.

I guess the first thing I should say about that summer is that it had started two days earlier, after senior convocation, when my father, your grandfather, took off on a six-week sailing trip up to Newfoundland. It was something he'd talked about doing ever since our move to the Eastern Shore: trading in the cat boat for one that slept four, spending the long school break as a family, chasing the sun. There were now only three of us, but Mom had arranged her life insurance to cover not just college funds and medical bills but also the twenty-nine-foot yawl she'd picked out for him and decided would be called the Molly A. Odds are she'd sworn him to follow through on the trip, too. She could be stubborn like that—even perverse. Come to think of it, the fact that Dad's plans now included the new woman he'd started dating might have seemed almost a tribute to his late wife's sensibility, Fitzcarraldo meets The Breakfast Club. But I kicked and screamed against it. Or no, that's not quite right, for with my father, the rector, one didn't throw tantrums; one exchanged views. His view was that it had been almost eight months, and Mom had wanted above all else for us to live . . . not to mention the trouble I was going to face getting around without him, given what he still believed to be my reckless-driving bust that spring. My view was, recklessness was in the eye of the beholder—Corinne had been her hospice nurse, goddammit. And fine, there were only so many ways to meet people out here in the boonies, but at seventeen I should be doing something I could put on a college application, and everyone knew I couldn't sail if my fucking life depended on it.

Let me just add for the record that by this point I hadn't the slightest intention of applying to college. I'd scored high in all senses on the SAT verbal, was besotted with Shakespeare as with Mobb Deep, but my ambitions no longer ran much beyond Ocean City, one town over, where, at least in the offseason, my survivor benefits would cover a bay-side one-bedroom with enough left over for music, poetry, and the weed I'd come to rely on to help me live without morphine. As if practicing for emancipation, I spent the weekend after Dad left hotboxing my room. But Sunday night, finding my fat half-ounce down to seeds and stems, I felt the fever of relapse seeping in. My dealer hadn't returned a page in weeks, and if I couldn't even ration pot like a normal person, what was to stop me from slipping back to that underworld I'd only barely escaped? I chain-smoked. I paced. I turned the Wu-Tang up till the bass blew. I may even have had some kind of flashback or breakdown, since when I woke in the morning, my voice sounded shaky and "Shimmy Shimmy Ya" distinctly Satanic. In the old days, I'd have grabbed my board, seen if I could hitch to the beach and disappear; instead, I pounded a backwashy Gatorade, bagged my bong, scraped the last germs of dope from my desk into the Altoids tin where I stashed my contraband, and removed the fan from the window to escape the private way: out to the tarpaper roof of the sunroom, down the wisteria, past beds of riven hostas, and into the woods.

Yet even "woods" seemed delusional all of a sudden. The multi-acre preserve back of our house, once a selling point, had in the last forty-eight hours shrunk like the rest of Cheshire County to just pine and thorns and poison ivy. Still, I slipped past Ducky's above-ground tanks, hopped a catenary of chain marked AUTHORIZED VEHICLES ONLY, tracked a hip-high Mohawk of nameless beachy grasses north along the railroad cut. To the west, where the treeline swelled to accommodate the back slope of the hill, I would sometimes run across spent fires, old forties; once a waterlogged cache of Playboys. East of the tracks, though—in the quarter-mile seethe of green I thought of as my own—I had only ever found a clearing with a rusty glider someone must've dragged out there to sleep on, shielded from view by the fields flanking the bypass but close enough to take in the car lots and the hospital, the chain restaurants that were the lone salient to date of the Clinton-era boom.

This was the blind spot where I'd once gone to feed my habit. And later, where I'd put the scraggly pot plants my dealer, a certain Eddie Sixkiller, had asked me to see if I could revive for him. They hadn't responded to my efforts, and would ordinarily need curing, but maybe by mixing them together with the crumbs I'd brought, some loose tobacco from my tin, I could get a leaf to spark. Though possibly I was just looking for an excuse to dump the smokes, get at the escape-hatch I still kept hidden underneath? Such were my thoughts, anyway, when a crashing sound came from the corn. An animal, like as not. Yet I scrambled to hide my gear, in case it was a cop. (Or maybe it was Eddie, riding to the rescue?) It was in some ways worse: my sister. She continued plumbline-straight across the clearing and plunked down on the glider, as if by prearrangement. And was instantly back up, swatting at the seat of her work-issued khakis.

What the fuck is it with you, Ethan? That thing's wet.

Codswallop, I remember telling her; the cushion was waterproof.
I'd bought it myself with my SSA check, bungeed it to my back like a
shortboard, and pedaled over from the Home Depot, tacking against
the wind. Plus she had chaff in her hair, I added, or words to that effect,
indicating something in her boy-short mop that immediately took wing
and flittered away.

But maybe just start with what you're doing here?

What's it look like I'm doing? she said. I can't let you spend the whole
summer sitting around getting wasted.

What I'd meant, really, was how she'd known where to find me, but I
shammed perplexity as to why my summer was any of her business. Plus
who said I was wasted? I was reading. I held up my scribbled-in <u>Masnavi of
Rumi</u> or whatever as if to say, Look. Perfectly innocent over here. Her gaze
narrowed.

Dad left me in charge. And I feel like I'm watching you rot.

But see, now I'm struggling with "watching," I said. You're back all of two
weeks, Moira. And then you're either out—

Yeah, working for a living.

—or holed up in your room with the phone like you never left thirteen.

You're familiar with the concept of projection, Ethan? The whole
argument for not getting on the boat was we were both going to do
something constructive. Instead, you spend this entire period post-exams
in literal hiding, to the point that you really can't say <u>where</u> anyone is or
<u>what</u> they're doing.

Touché, I thought. But the concepts of projection and denial (as I've
since come to understand them) have certain properties of recursion, and
her attack felt unfair largely because I'd learned the dark arts of withdrawal
from Moira herself. As witness the fall of '92, when, through the heating
grate, I'd heard our parents in urgent colloquy downstairs and crossed the
landing to alert her to what I figured must be the inevitable split. Her room
had the kind of emptiness that's adjacent to occupancy, as cleanliness is
said to be to godliness, so when I spotted the phone cord, I followed it to
her closet. Sure enough, there she was: huddled over a physics textbook
with the phone's Kermit-shaped cradle in her lap and the receiver to an
ear. Yet before I could speak, she'd covered the mouthpiece and told me
to fuck off. And a couple of years later, undeterred by anything in between,
she'd been raptured from her perch as salutatorian of Cheshire High to the
groves of MIT.

You're the one who's never around, I insisted, more feebly.

But when I got out my tin and lit a menthol from the carton I'd nicked off Corinne, she took it, took a drag.

Ethan, we can talk about my shit some other time. I thought you wanted to get out of here for good. Live la vie bohème and so forth.

Now who was projecting? I said. After a bit, though, I allowed her to hand the cigarette back and followed her toward the corn tiger-striped by darkness. She'd come by the fields and not the tracks, though I wouldn't see why till we debouched at the highway fifty yards on to find the Subaru glaring from the shoulder. Then she offered the keys, and I realized Dad had been either too embarrassed or too preoccupied to mention the suspension of my license . . . unless she was testing to see if I'd level with her about that, too. As I might even have done, had someone in a passing truck not just then chucked a water bottle at my head, shaking me back to adult experience.

Our destination was in Ocean City, the Howard Johnson's at the bottom of the boardwalk, which depending on your angle was either a midcentury icon or a poor man's Bucky Fuller—its polygonal fantasia collapsing somewhere between the airy front dining room and the windowless bolthole behind the kitchen where I was delivered to the assistant manager. This was a muttonchopped twenty-one-year-old I'd been told to call Squatch. What I wasn't prepared for was the psychedelic dressing gown he wore over his turquoise polo, the lush frizz of curls in his chopsticked topknot. As he tilted back to appraise me from the office's one chair, I must have looked equally unprepossessing, because after a searching look at Moira, he explained that the dress code here "back of the house" was loose; if hired, I too could wear mufti. He paused to pick his teeth with the chewed end of a pen.

But don't let that stop you showering, you know?

What he did care about (he went on, when I didn't react) was the work; it may not have looked it, but by one o'clock, this place was jumping. Tradition held that dishwashers got tipped out ten percent by waitstaff—my lovely and talented sister, for example—so if I busted my ass, I could walk out of here with a decent roll. He'd probably been about my age when he'd started bussing tables . . .

And look at you now, said Moira behind me. He's not running for president, Squatch. Either cough up the paperwork or admit you're welshing.

His eyes filled with injured dignity. The incisor his pen cap traced was oddly small and snaggly, like a baby tooth. Finally, he began to spelunk a desk drawer for an application sheet and a badly xeroxed W-9. With no clipboard to write on, I had to sort of stoop over the metal desk to steady myself as I printed my full name and checked the little box indicating I was a U.S. person.

You left off your driver's license number, he observed. (There were no flies on Squatch—at least not yet.)

And maybe now's as good a moment as any, Jolie, to address this business about my "way with words": it turns out to mean mostly that I was a practiced dissembler, as well as a drug addict and sometime thief. In any case, not wanting to raise in his mind or Moira's the issue of how I'd get to work, I said my license was in my other pants. Could I get it to him later?

I can't ask HoJo corporate just to take it on faith you are who you say you are, he replied. If you want to start today, I'll need some form of photo ID.

Jesus, I heard Moira say. But I dug in a pocket, unvelcro'd the wallet where I kept a laminated charge card for the St. Anselm's cafeteria. Refectory, rather.

And can fingertips be described as chubby? Then let Squatch's be chubby, even if it was only the tightness of his grip making the grooves.

But so hey, man . . . what's it like being his son, anyway? he asked.

Whose? I said, glancing back down at the page. You know my dad?

The whole clan, he said. No one told you this? I was at St. Anselm's too, back in the day. Coach was my coach. Your mom, God rest her, helped me learn how to use a darkroom. Even Moira here managed the regatta equipment. Senior year, we were this close to nationals.

The season he held pinched between thumb and forefinger, it occurred to me, was the fall of 1993, the last before Mom's chemo had stopped working. For a moment, I stood there feeling like the Visible Man—like somewhere beneath my thin plastic shell I was still wrecked on her pain pills, be-drooled in my clearing in the woods. But with a striking alacrity, he was now up and patting my shoulder.

Why don't I introduce you to your shift partner, Aspern, and you two can get cozy while I run this sucker off?

Through zones of noise and humidity, we trailed Squatch to the chlorinated hell of a dishroom where, in the weeks to come, I would spend upwards of a hundred hours. There was a conveyance of silver rollers like a hot dog machine; a stainless steel box with a cartoon lever; a sinewy kid in all black racking glasses into the box's maw. I noticed the straps of his plastic apron cutting a cross in the back of his tee-shirt, and the hairnet he wore, as I'd probably be forced to do, too. Then through bleach and old milk came the distinctive whiff of Drakkar Noir cologne . . . and he turned to me with his arms out, a smile just lighting the eyes.

My man.

Surprise, said my sister without inflection.

It was Squatch's turn to sound confused, or even double-crossed. Wait—I didn't realize you all had met.

Come on, Anthony, keep up, said Eddie Sixkiller. Who do you think convinced Moira to haul this wastrel in off his sorry ass in the first place?

Yep, that was him: Eddie Six-K. He'd first crossed my radar some eighteen months prior, when Moira had fallen in briefly with the techno-clique that, along with goth-curious farmboys, punks who'd missed the memo, and girls who followed Phish, hung out at the Sinclair after school. There wasn't enough of any one group to form a coherent subculture, but they were all drawn to Ducky's pool table and video games, his militant free-traderism vis-à-vis teens and tobacco, and—crucially, though I didn't know it yet—his joker poker machine with its illegal payout. Besides which, on the Eastern Shore, you kept your freak flag trimmed to a ringer tee and maybe a hemp choker or a wallet-chain regardless. Eddie alone really stood out: black cargo shorts in all weathers, brown brogan shoes, tube socks worn to mid-calf, spotless black shirt, and, when he felt like emphasizing his supposed bisexuality, eyeliner. With the leaves down, my room had a clear view of the parking lot, and one afternoon, Nine Inch Nails pounding outside my window, I'd looked up from the Vikes I was crushing to see him and your aunt, my sister, going at it in the bucket seat of a T-top Trans Am—or rather, him in the seat and her atop him, hands in each other's cropped hair. As I watched, a biker-looking dude coming out of the store called them faggots, only to have Eddie, despite being a full head shorter, leap out and ram him against the side of the building with a grip on his throat and an arm cocked back like: What?

If I had to guess, Moira meant on some level to draw our parents' worries to herself. But a year's worth of being pulled away for doctors' visits had left Dad more immersed than ever in the running of the school, and Mom, at that point still in remission, started asking all kinds of questions, such as would Eddie be willing to sit for an interview on-camera, so Moira lost interest. Not me. I already knew him to be a transplant like us, arrived at twelve to join the half-dozen other foster kids being raised by the town comptroller and his evangelical wife. I knew as well that he didn't belong among them. Maybe it was the Cherokee side he'd talk up if given the chance: cheekbones, eyes so horsey black there was no real distinction between pupil and iris, the surname I'd assumed was de plume or de guerre; but maybe it was just Eddie's apostasy against every law of God and man. Even with Moira back in her closet, I continued to take note when I saw him next door in one or another of his foster dad's numerous cars or at Wendy's at off-campus lunch. Though hyperglycemic from birth, he could hold a booth for hours, making sugarless lemonade by crunching fistfuls of lemon wedges and multiple NutraSweet packets into his empty cup with ice. The staff not only didn't object, but would come out to join the stream of well-wishers proffering elaborate hand-grips and then skulking after Eddie into the bathroom. And I might plead innocence in all this, say I didn't quite grasp what I was seeing (I often didn't quite grasp what I was seeing), except that the following fall, when I could no longer pretend that my bottomless supply of opiates was going to last, I knew just whom to seek out.

It was the first time we'd spoken, and his response was Nothing doing; didn't I know that pill shit would be the death of me? That was if the cancer sticks I was smoking didn't get me first. (A pause here of almost fraternal concern.) But he could probably see his way, he said, to furnishing a decent-sized bag of weed at an ex-family discount. I gave him the money, and he excused himself and went across the tarmac to the store. Here at Ducky's, I reckoned, where the cops too came daily, he kept his stash separate from his person. Then the panic I'd been trying to keep ahead of caught me: maybe he couldn't help after all and was ripping me off . . . but one thing you can say for Eddie, as opposed to yours truly: he never out-and-out lied. Five minutes later, in a wood-paneled minivan under an aging English oak, on the jewelcase of what I'd like to remember as Illmatic but knowing him was probably just Pretty Hate Machine, he walked me through the rolling of a blunt. And fine: hospital-grade morphine obviously wasn't what he happened to have. But wasn't I being transactional myself, assuming he'd heard that my mom had only weeks left to live, and trading on his pity?

He was, moreover, the one person who knew about my spot in the woods. There in the last days of analog, the cellphone was still a brick, and generally confined to cars, but Eddie had his pager, and whenever I couldn't outwit the increasingly suspicious hospice folks and was facing withdrawal, like the ground rushing up to meet a jumper, I'd punch in 158, our agreed-upon code for Come find me at my clearing. His fleet now included a foster sister's bike several sizes too small, the seat too wide, brake levers girlishly high. But he'd Kryloned the frame black and wrapped the bars in electrical tape to oddly badass effect, somehow only reinforced by his decision to leave colored beads on the spokes. If you knew how to listen, you could hear him coming from a long way off: tick, tick . . .

Now, just to finish tracing the historical ground: on the wall by the walk-in fridge at the restaurant was an honest-to-God time clock and a pocketboard of manila cards. To mark your hours, you found the card with your name, inserted it into the clock's slot, and waited for a jolt like the world's tiniest handgun to leave a new stamp: precise to the second, if slightly misaligned with the pre-printed grid. Moira's card was doubly jumbled, since for reasons known only to herself she'd been working five lunches and six dinners a week. I'd been given the less glamorous shift post-breakfast, as had Eddie, who'd proved unaccountably indifferent to showing up on time. Or maybe what I'm flagging here is that Squatch proved unaccountably cool with Eddie's indifference, or else didn't notice I was punching us both in each day, eager as I could manage after biking the seven miles past drainage ditches and fields and then across the Assawoman Bay.

Don't get me wrong. The job was awful: hauling last night's grease out to a dumpster ripe with heat; polishing splotched flatware as the opening "sidework"—then, for hours, slamming plates into the machine, hosing the stubbornest of orts into a fine, almost dental mist, pulling the lever for ninety seconds of quantum pandemonium. Nor could we even talk, really, given the din. The best I could manage was a kind of speculative, listwise kibitzing I would strike up on smoke break to forestall Eddie's lectures on the evils of tobacco and then continue in the privacy of my own head. All-time optimal Orioles lineups . . . unrealizable mixtapes . . . theories as to why the Monahan brothers, our two carrot-topped line cooks, were already at work no matter how early I arrived. For a while, I mulled a vampire hypothesis, but when I finally unveiled it—they were hiding from the sun, I suggested, using the walk-in as a crypt—Eddie seemed nettled by my creativity.

Nah, Prep. Those guys moonlight as carnies. Get ripped, pass out under the arcade, slope in early to avenge themselves on tourists.

Avenge themselves?

You don't know about the clam chowder? he said, and did the universal sign language for whacking off. It's that extra jigger of protein puts it over the top, Ethan.

No way, I said, after a second. Someone would notice.

Would they, though? And shook his head: Humiliating, the life of a carnie.

But mostly we killed the hours with music from the ghetto blaster (Eddie's term) perched on a shelf above the slop sink. We'd at first tried the radio, but two-thirds of the signals were Top 40 or country, and the dining room's compulsory oldies soon wore thin, so one night at the end of June, after stripping off my work clothes and showering, replenishing electrolytes with a piss-warm Mello Yello, I did what I hadn't dared to since the previous December: opened the French doors to the sunroom downstairs.

The scene inside reminded me of the artroom at school once all my mom's film stuff had been packed off to God knows where. The TV monitor had been returned to the living room; the cot folded away by Corinne or the other guy from hospice; Mom's afghans and space heater restored to the cedar closet, yet a few things still persisted from those months when she could no longer make it up to a warm bed, much less out to St. Anselm's to work on her film—including the vast archive of music she'd wanted me to pick through for a soundtrack. I grabbed the milkcrate of CDs nearest the door, in such a hurry to get out of there that I didn't worry about leaving tracks in the dusty carpet.

Her filing system, I'd be reminded by daylight, had been idiosyncratic, so that it was hard to say what was holding together the items in this particular crate—Who's Next, The Lion and the Cobra, Dylan in his surprisingly funky born-again phase. I would pass them off to Eddie Sixkiller as just my monthly selections from the BMG Music Club, and mostly he abided them. But when I tried him on her dub reggae or skronking free jazz or even the wonderful, terrible techno-sex album that was the last thing Prince put out before the name change, he made the same face he did for hip-hop and said, What is this shit? Notwithstanding which, when the black guys from Delaware, Ernest and Dre, showed up to take the second shift, he'd vanish with them into the bowels of the restaurant to talk, sticking me with the closing sidework.

By then it would be close to five. There were no lights on my Schwinn, only reflectors, so I'd have no more than an hour on the boardwalk unless

I wanted to bike back to the mainland under a perilous gloaming. But this was the hour when Ocean City suited me best anyway. The sky behind the high-rises was bloodied, the air thick with fry oil, amusement bulbs making a travesty of the dying sun, spreading the hot butter of flattery over the mob. Eddie used to point out girls he'd seen at the restaurant during the day, claiming to have chatted them up while I was off smoking. (For a bisexual, I might have noticed, he was a real poon-hound. Also: Where did he keep disappearing to after sundown? Why was I never offered a ride?) But by that point my brain was empty. It was as if physical labor had become its own narcotic, a numbness of body blanking out the mind, even as days and ultimately weeks slipped by with Eddie alluding vaguely to some static with his supplier, and thus without so much as a nickelbag through which I might treat my condition.

Then, that first Wednesday in July, Squatch rematerialized in the doorless doorway to the cube where I toiled. It was early, so the dishes hadn't yet begun to require meaningful triage, but a Squatch sighting was now rare enough this far back of the house that I muted the volume on the blaster. Even Eddie, having just rolled in from the parking lot, seemed chastened. Not that Squatch wasn't also a figure of fun—not that he didn't probably know himself to be one—but the balance of power depended on a whole complex kabuki of deference and authority that could be read several ways, a very '90s kind of ironic regress. When he wondered aloud if he could bend an ear, for example, it meant simultaneously that an ear was about to be bent, so shut up for a minute and listen.

I've got to admit, he began, three weeks ago I didn't have much in the way of hopes for either of you. To be honest, you seemed like a pair of zombies.

I looked at him, blinking, determined to give away nothing, and could feel Eddie doing the same. He edged on.

But you've both pulled your weight. I want to say: the work has been seen.

And here, for a second, I felt my father's influence . . . could almost summon some shipboard interaction where Coach James Aspern, the infallible rector of St. Anselm's, would have favored Anthony "Squatch" Pessoa with this same tone of hard-won approval.

As a token of his gratitude, he ventured, he'd arranged for a lunch opening front-of-the-house. And when even his most game-showish pause got no response, he added a caveat: there was only the one spot available. A hand shot from the folds of his kimono, holding a server's rolled half-apron.

Eddie, congrats, fella.

Fucking ridiculous, I thought . . . compounded by the ridiculousness of how badly I'd wanted that apron for myself. Here I'd been, sweating out my dry spell like some actual goddamn straight arrow—

Then Eddie said, Nah, I'm cool. Give it to Ethan.

I tried to catch his eyes, but they were busy fielding a downright pleading look from Squatch, disturbing what I'd taken to be the settled order of things.

You sure? Squatch asked. It's like double the money, even after everyone gets tipped out.

Yeah, but who says I'm still hurting for money? If nominated, I won't run. If elected, I won't serve. Ethan can act as my eyes and ears up there. And your music's for shit anyway. Fucking Boomers.

Now, it never was wise to think you'd gotten the best of Eddie Sixkiller— a rule that was soon to have repercussions. But otherwise, Squatch had been right: the front room really was a step up. There was the rest of the summer waitstaff he'd assembled, for one thing, coltish college girls with Aquafresh smiles and impossibly short shorts, tans deepened on the decks of sunboats moored out at Assateague Island. Except for one girl from Towson (and even she was named Becky) they were exclusively white, with competence levels ranging from ninja to inept, but it wasn't the service as such that brought you back to the Ocean City HoJo in 1995. It was more the hot dogs and the Beach Boys, the nostalgia for some endless nonexistent summer where no one ever died. And if this made my presence there and Moira's that much more anomalous, hailing as we did from the lunar side of sublimation and rage, the work at least came naturally. I learned never to let a plate sit empty on a table, and to atone for the culinary sins of the Monahans with baskets of hot rolls comped behind Squatch's back.

The money, as promised, was considerable. By the day of my first paycheck, I'd amassed a pile of extra cash that, even after tithing to the back of the house, seemed a threat to my sobriety. Exemption from sidework was another of the waiter's prerogatives. Still, out of solidarity with Eddie, who'd been left solo with the dishes (or maybe just prodded by the burning in my pocket), I joined him around 3:50 that afternoon in the unused banquet room where he sat folding napkins into bishop's mitres, sorting flatware into pill-minderish trays. With no machine roaring between us, we should have had plenty to talk about, but the moment I took a seat, he was up picking fries from a bussed platter, and glancing through the door's porthole glass. Nor would he act any less distant once I'd confessed the true scale of my windfall. Didn't he see? I said. Now I could pay him full retail for whatever drugs he could lay hands on, pot, Valium, ecstasy, or whatever, and at least stay fucked up Tuesdays and Thursdays, our days off. My pulse was already twitching as he punched me on the arm and bid me come check something out, so my first impulse was to ignore him.

No, seriously, E, he said, sounding almost angry. This is the stuff I'm trusting you to keep an eye on, and instead where's your head at?

I figured he was just jealous of my promotion, but rose nonetheless to peer into the great rhombus of the dining room. All seemed peaceful out there . . . smoke haunting ashtrays, TV tuned to golf; behind the bar where Moira stood working a double, the iced tea machine burped amber liquid into a vitrine. Then I saw what he meant, sitting on one of the bar's white pleather stools, elbows spreading a book under her coffee, hair like sun-tea falling over the fine plane of exposed skin where her tee-shirt's collar had been razored away. Were it not for her blinding detachment—her apparent unawareness of being watched—the black x's on her hands might have seemed for show. But I knew solitude when I saw it: that feeling of all other life having been snuffed out around you. And even so, it was the wetsuit, worn as pants and dripping on the rug, that brought her presence home. I'd occasionally seen girls out at Frank Loves Emma, the word-of-mouth break up in Delaware we used to make Judd's dad take us to back when he had a car, but still, it wasn't something you encountered every day, circa 1995. A surfeuse.

I recall the girl glancing up as her soup came and then just as quickly going back to the book. It was only after she tore open a packet of oyster crackers that it dawned on me what she'd ordered. And before Eddie could make his move, I was across the dining room, banging into her elbow.

Yo! she said, sweeping her clunky reading glasses into a fist. Can I help you?

The voice had layers—like velvet, I thought, only tougher. Also: it should have been my line.

Word to the wise, I managed. Don't eat the chowder.

Though her eyes, grayish, had locked onto mine, it was Moira the voice now addressed: Your colleague says something's off with the chowder.

My brother's a waste product, said Moira. Ethan, this is my check.

Yeah, well, let me cover it, I said. And to the girl: The chowder really is no bueno. Here, I can comp you some rolls while you wait.

She looked from my face to my sister's as if at two squabbling children.

You know what? All this smoke in here was killing my appetite anyway.

A pair of damp singles from her wetsuit's pocket appeared under the coffee. As she recovered a shortboard from the coat area and made for the door, I just had time to register how tall she was. Then, without the least compunction for Moira or Eddie—without even consciously realizing how badly I wanted to change—I did it: plunged after her into the parking lot's white heat.

I was still weighing how to phrase the increasingly far-fetched notion that a Monahan had jizzed in her chowder when I must have touched her again, for she spun from the side of a tawny Volvo wagon, the board clipping me right under an eye. I tried to catch myself as I went down, only to find the adjacent car on fire, and I landed on the shaded pavement in between, cradling my hand.

Ow, Jesus, I said.

Well, what do you expect, she said, flushing. People will think you're out to get them. You all right?

I guess so. I'll just . . . I'll just sit here on the ground, thanks.

For as hot as she burned, she was quick to cool down:

Don't be a hero, she said. Knowing my mom, she'll have a first-aid kit in the car.

No, I don't want to keep you, I said, absurdly, for unless I moved, she'd have to drive over me to get out. And the next thing I knew she was propping her board against the Volvo, her upper half disappearing inside. The Tupperware that emerged unleashed a wet-wipe smell; an astringent pad seared my forehead before becoming a cat's rough tongue, licking. Then it was vanishing pinkly back into its wrapper as she warned me she'd have to check me out. Gently but firmly, she held my chin, tilted my head thirty degrees sunward for inspection, gave me her name—Sarah—and asked for mine again.

Which was not, I should say, how this was supposed to go. By spring of my freshman year, every high-school girl in the county had known who I was, the guy with the dying mother . . . and that I was an ardent if somewhat inconstant lover, since in those months before the drugs killed my interest, I'd gotten hooked on this, too, making mixes for specific girls, peeling them off from the pack on the hill, taking them on long walks where I'd reveal just enough for them to feel the specialness of our connection. Maybe it was their pity I wanted. Maybe it was the control. Or somehow the disgust with myself, afterward. But with my mom gone, using what had happened to us (or even talking about it) was one of the things I'd made a hard rule against; it had been a long time since I'd let a girl touch me like this. Or like anything at all.

Now I felt Sarah's warmth, smelled the coffee on her breath, but could see her only as a goldish haze in my periphery. The view beyond was of more asphalt, then arcade stalls, seagulls dotting bollards. Finally, she sighed and got out a Band-Aid:

I don't think stitches are called for, she said. But what's your deal, anyway, sneaking up on me like that, with no warning?

I wanted to apologize, I began—but then started spinning a story (my refuge, my curse). There'd been this red tide thing, a couple of other folks had gotten bad clams . . .

Listen, Ethan: I'm eighteen, okay? I can handle myself. And apologies are all well and good, but it's a little hard to hear yours over the roar of your explanation.

Sorry, I said. I'm sorry.

Out there on the boardwalk now, noon crowds were on the prowl, scarfing popcorn from the Fisher's stand, rolling past on skates, on Earth Cruisers. For a second, they felt like some lost and inscrutable civilization. But closer in were nostrils flaming with sun; the subtler tranches of color in her hair you'd need a jumbo box of pastels to do justice to. And those gray eyes, still doubting:

You'd have warned any of your customers, you're saying.

Just the ones who dig Lorca. The rest can fuck off and die.

What, this? she said, seeming to remember the bio she'd set on the roof of the car. This was just the most interesting-looking thing on the shelf at the rental.

I thought those were all, like, <u>Reader's Digest</u> and John P. Marquand.

She shrugged. In Ocean City, maybe. It's a little tonier up at Rehoboth Beach. Tony and calm. I came down here chasing a wave.

I thought about seeing and raising her posture of objectivity, claiming summer-person status myself, but already part of her power was to make me feel weird about even the one lie.

Yeah, what would I know? I admitted. I commute from the next dorp over. You probably blinked and missed it on your way out 50 from the Bridge.

Except we took the ferry, yesterday. Drove down from New York.

Right, I should have known, given, ah . . .

I had started to say something taking in her whole person, that armor of self-possession I recognized from TV, but wussed out and noted how she spoke, her accent.

My accent? she drawled, sliding her board into the trunk. You heard of "chutzpah," Ethan? (But was that a smile?) Look, I'd ask for more book recs next time, but since you've just put me off HoJos for life, and I'm not really one to change plans, this is vaya con dios, I guess.

And honestly, that might have been the end of things between me and Sarah Kupferberg, Jolie, just as it might have been had I never come out to the parking lot to begin with, or shaken Eddie's hand off my shoulder. You might have remained inconceivable, literally; I might have ended up the one on the stretcher, being borne up out of the dark.

No, wait, I blurted. You want a killer break, there's actually one near where you're staying. Like twenty minutes from here, if you can drive.

Just between you and me: it was closer to forty. But I suppose I was remembering how fast the time went at double the speed, all the arc-lights blinking out as I whooshed underneath on the night I'd lost my license, and the radio offering up the only possible song at the last possible moment— the one right before the sirens had come on to drag me back to the land of the living. It was just a matter of knowing where to look, I heard myself say, thrashing my way up toward the daylight world again. Or of having someone with you who does.

Inside the Volvo, the first thing I'd notice was a two-disc set of West Side Story I had to move off the blazing seat. Before I could further embarrass myself with a reprise of "Somewhere" from the second-form talent show, though, she explained that it was her mother's. Not that she herself didn't like musicals as much as the next guy, Sarah said, but her tastes these days ran more modern. Anyway, moot point, since the stereo was on the fritz. She cranked back the moonroof; hotels white as sepulchers loomed in the heat. But soon these and the condos thinned and we were cruising the rough landward side of Ocean City: busted bus shelters, corroded water tower, the lone government building where Dad had taken me to collect my first Social Security check. To an outsider, it must have seemed even bleaker. She didn't comment, though, or if she did we were already on the highway, some combo of her hair and the wind making it hard for me to hear.

Still, I had to admire her focus behind the wheel. Once a choice had been made—even a drastic one—there could be no looking back. Steering with her right hand, signaling with her left, she somehow found the wherewithal to downshift and pass a semi while yelling how she hardly knew the area; her family usually did summers on the east end of Long Island. I tried to explain that we too were city mice at heart, that I'd lived in DC till I was eight. Was DC really a city, though? she said. Then: Kidding, kidding . . . There'd been a school trip the year the wall came down, the Reagan-Bush cheerleading had just left her a little cold, was all. But that meant I knew Dischord Records, right? The band Minor Threat? Not personally, I said, but it had already occurred to me that the x's marking her hands might not have been leftovers from some all-ages show. When I asked, she confirmed they stood for "straight edge," no drinking, no drugs. And you'd think that by now I'd have known better than to mistake wishes for signs, but I remember a feeling of quickening as I warned her about Delaware troopers, the inverse correlation between sales taxes and speed traps. Then quietly, as if she'd felt me feeling it, she said:

This is probably the place to mention I already have a boyfriend.

What?

Just so we don't get our wires crossed.

No, wait, I yelled—here!

The sandy turnoff to the state park threatened for a moment to skid beneath us, but if you recall that Volvo, it was a tank. Its treads held. Then we were bumping along a paved drive in search of the graffitied boulder marking an otherwise indiscernible tunnel through the scrub pine. Given the cultish nature of mid-Atlantic surfing, the beach at the end was halfway secret, and now that the tide was out, the wind dying under the needles, there were no other cars, just Rosa rugosa, orange and purple flowers that retained, in the privacy of my mind, a sacramental aspect. Still: whatever transformation I'd been imagining for myself seemed to be dying, too. The surf bug had abandoned me around the same time as my religious sense, and no sooner had I talked Sarah through the takeoff specs than I'd be turned back to face Squatch and Moira and the long pedal home: the emptiness that was adjacent only to emptiness. I was just pointing out the spot where a culvert hit the water when she said,

But aren't we going in? You said you were going to show me.

I don't have a suit, I reminded her. Or my board.

It's no problem. We can take turns on mine. And the wetsuit . . . that's just me getting the temperature wrong. I've been in once already. It's bathwater, Ethan.

Right there in the car, she started tugging off her funky tee-shirt— a flash of bikini I thought for a second might become something else—and then hopped out to zip her black rubber top and fetch her board from the back. As she ran down the beach, her long, dark form launching a volley of blond and silver, I was left to my confusions, among which was how I might look myself. The tallest boy in my class, I'd never regained the weight I'd dropped my bombed-out sophomore year. But then, reminding myself this might be the one chance I got, I stripped to my skivvies and went charging in after her.

Of course with no wind, the surf was so distinctly un-killer as to make me seem even more of a liar. Treading the bright water, trying to distract her from its slackness, I asked how a city kid like her got to surfing. And to the best of my memory, Jolie, that's what got us digging into her past as a skateboarder. It had been pretty much the standard progression, she began—

Though in my case maybe not the cleanest, you know? What I mean is, my parents were already big on independence, and when they split up a few years ago it gave me even more time to explore the city.

She then explained that she'd fallen in with a middle-school crew that ran every library porch and project courtyard from West Sixty-Third Street to the Village. It was how she'd gotten sucked into the fashion thing, too, she said: a photographer had spotted them one afternoon in the dry fountain at Washington Square.

Shit, don't tell me, I groaned, watching her climb down off the board and motion for me to take over. You're a model.

Only for a year, she protested. At fifteen. And then just street clothes: Sassy, Spin, a couple smaller labels.

And she went on to tell me, as if pushing past defensiveness, that the checks had mostly gone to pay for stuff for her skate buddies:

One of them was like full feral latchkey, Ethan, so for a while we had access to this apartment in the Amsterdam Houses that I swear was almost like a commune. Picture a bunch of kids hanging out on winter afternoons, truants and strays plus some slumming kids from the private schools, watching videos, tagging walls. And there's me rolling in after a shoot flush with beer money—

So you did drink, at least, I said, before catching myself: Not that there's anything wrong with that.

I didn't, though. I was still only fifteen, for one thing, and probably a goody two-shoes at heart. And I don't know . . . my dad's moving out had me thinking about certain lines he'd crossed back at academic conferences where the wine was flowing and he could be away from my mom. I guess it was easier to blame alcohol than who he was. But anyway, this thing now . . . it was other people's lives I was being offered a peek into, and I felt like it would be wrong to judge.

A set of waves seeming to mass out there, I insisted we switch places again, though by the time we did, it had failed to amount to much. And when she started talking again, it was about how no utopia ever lasts.

See, by the next spring (she said), the attention I was getting, the money, the extra autonomy or whatever it was, had started to tear little rifts between the Ethical Culture kids and the ones from the Houses. And then my agent starts trying to sell my dad on orthodonture, like ten grand for a new-model Sarah's supposed to be some kind of apology, and—

Fuck that, I said. You had yourself straightened out already. I mean, you are who you are.

Right, my sentiments exactly, Ethan! What's so wrong with my teeth?

Her smile, beautiful, faded. She trailed a hand in the water.

And then I come home one day and find my dad just sitting there on the couch like he never left, with no apology even needed. Which truly: fuck that.

Another pause here, as it became clear that I didn't know what to say. (Besides, why was she even telling me this?) Something roughened in her voice:

My mom had obviously decided to forgive him. But she also made it clear that she now expected us to be home more, acting like a family again. And it was my mom, you know? I didn't know what to do but try to be the person she wanted. So I cut myself off from my so-called dropout friends, however much they'd meant to me. The worst part, though, was how she sort of had their number after all.

And out of nowhere, before I could backstroke away or dive under, she was telling me about the day she'd gotten the call one of them was dead and not a thing she could do about it—an overdose on heroin.

Christ, I heard myself say, feeling my face go numb, as if she somehow knew my secrets already. And there's you, left behind to deal with the guilt. No, hey, listen, that shit's not easy.

You asked how I got to surfing, Ethan, she said; here's how. Two years ago this September. You want to guess how many surf shops there are in the New York City phone book? One.

And then she was walking me through how she'd put down the phone and taken the train out to where the track ends, Rockaway Beach in Queens, where she'd blown her last check on a board. The waves had been trash (not unlike what we saw here, in fact), but after a while, just being in them had made her feel steadier.

This is the first time I've ever told that story, by the way, she said a minute later. You're a weirdly easy person to talk to, anyone ever tell you that? There's a look you get, not exactly in your eyes, but . . .

For a second, it seemed she was going to reach across to where I still clung to her board and touch the place she meant. And though she stopped, it wasn't before I got the feeling that she'd been trying for a while now to show me something. How a person might start to be honest, maybe. How to open up while still keeping control. At any rate, as my muscles found some equilibrium between the fatigue of the lunch shift and the fatigue of swimming, I realized I too had stabilized. The sun was a hot disc of metaphysics; the water no longer stung my cut cheek. And when I went back to talking, as the lull seemed to invite, it was about a thing my mom had told me once. Who always was a sucker for a pretty phrase, I heard myself start. And then, catching myself:

Still is. Joanna's her name. An artist, but also an insatiable reader. And then in the early part of the '70s she was doing street photography, too. This was back when she was finishing up at the Corcoran and there were still protests all over DC, the war seeming right on the verge of ending. And I remember coming across her old contact sheets later when I was a kid, being fascinated. These longhairs with their bongos over here, those people over there with the National Guard, and for all I knew, my dad inside one of the buildings under protest, about to step out front and lay some rap on the girl with the camera. You'd think she'd have had more resistance to it, since she basically was one of the hippies herself. Her big thing at the time was going to see the Dead, you know? Hendrix, the Who . . . But when I asked her one day why she hadn't just stayed on her own side, photographing her own people, she told me—this is going to be in Latin, sorry—"Humani nil a me alienum puto."

No, that's sort of a famous line, right? Sarah said. What is it, "Nothing human is alien to me"?

Right. Terence, I think. Which is funny, actually, since by the time she taught it to me she was in full flight to these abstractions she could have done just as easily on an uninhabited planet, paintings, sculptures . . . even the coffeemugs she sculpted for Christmas one year came out sort of vaguely cubist. My folks had by that point gotten hitched and moved to a rowhouse behind the National Zoo, but for a while in the middle there, the war had dragged on. And I guess between that and having kids, depicting the reality of what humans actually are got to be too much. It was only in the '80s, after she got invited to shoot a friend's wedding out here on the Eastern Shore, that she finally remembered what she was supposed to be doing with a camera. Or anyway, that's the story she liked to tell.

And now I heard myself recounting the part about the camcorder Mom had special-ordered to take along with her that first time, and certain days the following fall when she'd let me skip school so I could ride back out to the Shore with her, get bribed with Mickey D's (our secret, she'd said). How she used to drag me all around the countryside to scout locations, or record me plonking along on the piano back home to the little bits of footage we'd made. And the flattery of her wanting me with her like that, but also the confusion of it.

Honestly, Sarah, there were times when I almost wondered if she was training me to take over where she left off, I said. Like if I turned out to be an artist too it would somehow vindicate everything she'd had to give up. The hell of it was, though, I never got what I was supposed to be seeing. Because I didn't really inherit any of her visual gifts, you know? Only the magpie thing, an ear for what sounded good—words words words.

No, there it is, Sarah said, in her alert way. Keep going.

But I wasn't used to being taken so seriously, hadn't intended to go even this far, so I decided to leave my poetic ambitions where I'd left the fact that I knew every last song from West Side Story: passed over in silence.

I mean, I talked you out here, didn't I?

A decent set was finally starting to come in, and I proceeded to catch a not-terrible pair of rides. And in case you're wondering: your mother took her share even less badly. I wouldn't call her a natural, exactly; you could tell she was thinking about something up there on the board. But it was like watching a wire-walker think about a bowling ball, rubber chicken, and chainsaw being juggled at high speed, which is to say there was a countervailing sense of not thinking at all. Unless what I'm trying to get at is those times when they feel like the same thing.

Only now for some reason she began to talk about this boyfriend again; let's call him M——. M—— taught me that, she might say. Or, I've got to remember to tell M—— you said that. As if M—— would care, as if M—— were someone I knew. In addition to his being, by her account, a Dalton School grad, a family friend since childhood, a committed socialist, a punker shredding faces with his upside-down guitar—the Finn MacFuckingCool of the Upper East Side and basically everything yours truly was not—they were both bound for Columbia come the thirty-first of August, neither having wanted to leave New York—

I can't take much more of this, I broke in at last. It came out opaque, but also sharper than I intended. And when she looked at me: Let's call this a wrap, I'm saying.

The evening had begun to pale. Or rather, to darken. To thicken and thin somehow simultaneously. That's all you've got in you? she said.

At which point I could feel the beast roil inside, urge me to stick the knife in before she did:

Yeah, socialism's all well and good for folks who can afford an Ivy League education, but the rest of us have to get up and work in the morning.

I dragged myself up the beach, no longer worrying how I might appear in my soaked briefs, though I did duck behind some bushes to swap them out for the still-dry HoJo khakis. I don't know if I expected her to come in after me.

What else do I remember? The warmth of hot sand through thinning cotton. A feeling of wanting to flee my petty jealousies, my own head. Watching the X-acto blade of a plane, on fire with reflected light, draw silently north, expose the batting of the sky.

Hey, it's cool your mom's an artist, though, she said after a while, as if she'd never meant to shut me down. Does she have like a studio or a gallery where I could check out her stuff while I'm down here?

I'm not really allowed to talk about her work, I said tightly. Which at least had a germ of truth: it was one of the few rules I'd set for myself and actually observed.

But you were talking earlier about something she had to give up . . .

No, just . . . I was thinking about how hard it must have been for her to keep all those fires inside her alive while still trying to be a mom. Be a wife. Especially when my dad was part Vulcan.

No accounting for taste, I guess.

And here I relaxed a little, since the Dad part of the story seemed so much simpler to understand.

Yeah, Naval Academy, Yale Divinity, a summer sailing for William F. Buckley of all people. And then right back to Annapolis for a chaplain gig.

But she'd grown alert again, in this way I think I already loved: Man, that's got to be a lot for you and your sister to juggle, though, right? Navy brat and preacher's kid?

I shouldn't have made it sound like that, I said, where normally I might have run with it: I mean, it's not like he was out firing torpedoes or anything; he wasn't that gung ho. Even going back to the service after grad school I think was more a kind of penance for taking a deferment than because he'd believed in the war. But he had this natural ease with logistics and chain of command, so eventually he got promoted to an admin job in the Office of the Secretary. My mom put up with the work through the tail end of Vietnam, but by the time we invaded Grenada, she was like—

"Check please!" Sarah said.

Or anyway, I told her, such had been my impression.

See, Sarah, I already knew there was stuff Mom wasn't saying out loud, even before those road trips of ours. And then gradually she starts slipping away to the beach some days without me, not being home when we get back from school, leaving Dad to heat dinner. And if anyone asks, it's like, "Let it go, son, your mother's on a project." So when his former thesis adviser calls one day to say he's stepping down from his role at an Episcopal boys' school out here, where my dad can run the place and coach sailing and her trade travel time for teaching and collect a salary to boot, and me free tuition . . . well, no one was really in a place to ask what's the catch, you know? As for preaching, that was just a thing Dad used to drag me and Moira to go hear twice a month from a pew in Ocean City. If anything, Mom was the seeker between the two of them, with her Rumi and her Enneagrams and all the music she used to subject us to—wait, don't look disappointed.

Sorry, she said. It's just, there it is again, all over your face. Something else you're thinking about . . . And this time she actually did touch me, Jolie, fingers to my temple, just a brush of thumb above where the Band-Aid sat, but long enough.

Yeah, no, she's dead now, I said. She got cancer. She died.

There was an inhalation of breath.

Then: I think I knew that.

But she'd definitely have liked you, Sarah, I added after a minute, not having meant to make her uncomfortable (unless I had). For whatever that's worth. I'm saying, you've got those x's on your hands, you're into DC hardcore . . . Nothing human is alien, right?

Ethan, I wish I was half as hard core as you make her sound. To be honest, I still get mad at myself sometimes for being such a dilettante. I'll spend a month listening to Tribe, or Madonna, or Sonic Youth, anything with that sense of plugging into some secret little scene, but then it's on to the next.

But that was her, too, by the CD era, I said, this huge pile of dub and rock and funk she'd spent her whole life burning through . . .

And as the words left my mouth, it struck me how even the fragments of her late obsessions, early Sinéad and mid-period King Tubby and that Prince album Come, had been more of a piece than I'd thought.

It's just, she would have said the goal was less about plugging into whatever was handed to you than looking for a way to transcend it, Sarah. Granted, she kept a carve-out for the Grateful Dead, who were pretty much her definition of immanence. "Like a bunch of carpenters banging away at a house," is the phrase I remember turning me off the tapes. But when I think about all those other phases she passed through . . . what she was chasing was always a mystery, you know? The Van Morrison thing. The Joshua Tree thing. This kind of call you heard burning behind the everyday. Like, for jazz it was Coltrane over Miles, every day of the week. Or when I played hip-hop for her once, she wanted all my Nas but no Biggie. She either heard that call or she didn't—it was the one distinction that mattered. How much of it was there, and how loudly. And films and theater used to be like that for her, too (I heard myself go on), when she could step outside her professional box, get things in their proper perspective. I think her basic idea of a work of art was that it should put you in touch with all the stuff you can't connect with on your own . . .

I know connection feels safer when it's like that, Sarah said, gently. I've done that: connection in the abstract, and then you move on. But don't you think it's what we're supposed to be finding with other people?

And when she saw me frown:

Like that thing where someone just opens their mouth and all of a sudden you're inside each other's heads?

It was us she was talking about, I knew that much; it was the last half-hour. What she didn't seem to realize, though, was that even this connection remained a little abstract. I'd told her about my mom, which was indeed a mystery. But beyond that, she didn't know the first thing about me. And I guess I must really have wanted to see if I could trust what was developing between us, or to prove to myself that I wasn't running game again (a reliable sign that I was somewhere mid-slip), because as I stood, I began to fish from my khakis the smokes I'd thus far managed to keep hidden. An ugly habit—and in light of what had gone down with my mom, arguably even a desecration—but if it was concreteness Sarah Kupferberg wanted, here it was.

Then again, maybe I was just fiending, because my hold on the tin proved shaky, and when at last the little notch released and the lid popped open, a half-dozen menthols and some pot seeds scattered across the beach, dangerously close to exposing what I'd forgotten underneath: a dimestore razor and the last stolen pill I'd been toting around with me everywhere for half a year now.

To her credit, she didn't seem particularly shocked to learn I was a smoker; in fact, she started picking up the cigarettes, brushing the sand off as if for closer inspection. It took me a second to realize she was handing them back.

I thought you'd be appalled, I admitted. I mean, you being straight-edge and all, and me with the, uh, sob story . . .

No, it's your life. Plus I could smell them on your breath.

Having broken my rule, though, I had to press on:

Don't let my little-lost-boy act fool you, Sarah. As long as we're uncrossing wires, I should probably go ahead and warn you what a world-class fuckup I really am.

Are we back on the clam chowder?

—and this trip about being in other people's heads . . . that was always going to just be a fantasy, you know? Like if we could really know each other, we probably wouldn't even like each other.

Whoa. Did I do something to piss you off?

Because there she was, I continued, talking like cities were the only place where anyone ever OD'd—

That wasn't what I said, she said.

—when on the Shore you could get even more of that shit per capita. And sitting right in front of her was just the scuzziest kind of wastoid, headed out to score just as soon as he got home tonight . . .

Something seemed to catch in my throat.

I'm trying to say, Sarah: smoking's the least of my problems. I've got a drug habit, okay? Tranquilizers, lithium, paint thinner, speed . . . that's always been me, more or less. Like I'm afraid of life or something.

I could see her having another of those moments of intense concentration.

Then before I own up to worse she said, Okay, I hear you.

It was what came next, though, that caught me completely wide-open:

But nothing says you have to keep going with any of that, right?

And after the second it took me to recover, I would find myself struggling to explain why it was never going to be that easy: Keel Hill, eighth grade, Ducky's after dark, things I seldom even let myself remember. The pool shark, now dead, who in exchange for some secondhand Ritalin had once taught me how to chop them up and snort them—I know I made it that far. And the weatherman from Channel 5 who'd come to recount his coke addiction at chapel one week and a particular line of his that kept coming back to me later, under the pines: Cocaine . . . she was my lady.

And this from the guy they called in to dissuade us! But that's just Boomers, like my friend Eddie says . . . we might as well have been raised by wolves.

Remember, though, Ethan, I've pretty much had the run of Manhattan since I was thirteen. And I get it: freedom can be scary, at least in the early going. But isn't the real issue what you're planning to do with it now that you're not a kid anymore?

The thing I knew I still had to tell her, of course, was the place where I'd ended up: the Vicodin and then the morphine pills and whose nightstand they had come from, and the thing in me that had been so hungry to lay hands on them, day in and day out; what it had felt like to be in that room, and in those woods, and in the end, on this very beach. It was right there, Jolie—at my goddamn fingertips. But no matter how honest I'd set out to be, the best I could do was explain that I was trying to give her an out.

And I hope you'll take it, Sarah. Because if you let me trick you into thinking I can be like you, I'm only going to let you down.

And to this day, I believe she did weigh her options, in the silence that followed. But again what she came out with surprised me.

You're still selling yourself short, though, Ethan. Look: it sounds like it's been a rough few years for us both, she said. But like . . . say what I really want is to be the kind of person who doesn't run and hide anymore—who might actually help someone this side of a toe-tag. And say you want to stop letting people down. Well, okay then . . . does either of us want those things badly enough to try to make them real?

At which moment a thing happened that I must have revisited a thousand times without ever quite understanding it: I decided to let myself imagine that what was clearly some type of oversight or category error on her part was instead a kind of pact. Reached out to dig a literal hole in the sand. Dropped in what I hadn't let her realize was my stash-box and began to smooth it over.

I wasn't saying to take up littering instead! she said, but she must have glimpsed something in my face when I could no longer pinpoint the exact site of the burial. Sorry, kidding again, bad joke.

No, you're right, I said, forcing myself to look up from the sand. About cigarettes, the pot, drugs, everything. If it means we could keep hanging out like this, I could just . . . not.

It was one of the only times I would ever find her tongue-tied.

But you have to really believe me when I say that, Sarah, I said, or the trick won't work.

What—does it seem like I don't? It will. I mean, I do. But look, she said, before I could change my mind (and turned toward the now-fat contrail, pale pink in the bruised sky. It's getting late, no? I should probably run you home.

I thought about mentioning my bike, still chained to a dumpster behind the HoJo, but had already resolved that this was the ride I'd be taking; I could worry tomorrow about how to get back to work. And so in full dusk, after a half-hour of awkward small talk in the Volvo, we were pulling onto my street. There was a big old Victorian right on the corner, and I directed her to the curb out front. I suppose I didn't want her to see where I actually lived, redolent as it was of the vacant horizons I'd just sworn off. But as with my pledge to try to go straight-edge, she seemed uncertain at first.

What, here?

The car had rolled to a stop. The trees and wires were inky above the moonroof. Down in the parking lot at Ducky's life ran on; everything green, everything belated, the air roiled by choppers, by cicadas. Then I thought, Oh who the fuck had I been kidding anyway, since my confession had stopped short of the full truth of myself—and since we'd obviously never see each other again?

No, sorry, I said. There. Half a block up.

She crept the car forward to where the moon hit the oystershell drive, the tin-roofed garage still resisting my dad's attempts to buttress it plumb. And then the pink-tipped hostas run riot along the walk; the sunroom where no one went anymore, windows all dark.

So that's you, huh, Ethan?

There was that odd husk to her voice again, but I couldn't make out her face to know was I even meant to answer. So I thanked her courteously for the ride and the pep talk, said maybe I'd catch her in the lineup sometime. I was about to unbuckle my seatbelt when I heard a second click, and all at once she was in my lap, lifting my face to hers, a long, stale, sand-grained kiss. Then, just as I braced for her to touch the Band-Aid, the tender place beneath, she pushed me back and returned to her seat like it had never happened. In this context, her promise to call would seem hollow. But she did call, the very next day; she'd driven all the way back to Delaware before realizing she had my wet briefs in her glovebox.

And I swear that became the summer of no rain, Jolie. Clouds would sometimes boil up like dirty mountains over the fields of an afternoon, but it was as if, through sheer force of will, your mother could hold them at bay. The real magic, though (and for me the sting), was her insistence that we remained just cool or casual acquaintances—even as I'd promised her what felt like my life; even as, during the four weeks left on the Kupferbergs' rental, we saw one another almost daily, and twice on my days off. If I was working, she would wait for me on the boardwalk, where I'd invariably pretend to pitch her on coming back the next summer after I graduated. Hamptons Schmamptons, was my angle. Like, did the Hamptons have stand-mounted binoculars that offered up only darkness unless you paid a quarter? Or the game with the giant mallets and the flying rubber frogs? Did the Hamptons have that? How about not one but two amusement parks called the Jolly Roger, each with a Tilt-a-Whirl so ultra-sketch you had to sign a waiver? And I remember the feeling in my chest when the floor would drop away and I'd look over at her distorted face looking back at mine, each of us almost dying with laughter at something the other could never quite see. No longer saving my money for some annihilating bender, I was flush with tips, and would slip a twenty to the non-Monahan carnie so we could cut right back to the head of the line. Or if I'd blazed through Eddie's sidework and slipped off when he wasn't looking, she and I might squeeze in an hour at Frank Loves Emma before the sun went down, since my swim trunks and board were now fixtures in her Volvo.

I told myself Eddie would be cool with this further dwindling of our time together, having been the one to turn me toward the dining room to begin with. Instead, as July wore on, he assumed in my presence a wearied air, as if remounting the platform he'd long ago descended to become my friend. Increasingly, he even insisted on closing out his shift himself, not wanting to queer the pitch with Whatsherface (as he rarely neglected to call her). And I'd like to report that I told him to stop being a dick—as I'd like to report that I'd challenged him on his habitual use of the n-word—but if I'm being honest, I think I counted on my demurral reading as embarrassment. Embarrassment that I was indeed getting some.

Still, put yourself in my position: How could I have explained what was actually going on, those times when she and I were alone up at our secret beach? I now saw why no one went there anymore: the tides having resculpted the sandbar left by the Corps of Engineers, the destruction of the '91 hurricane was nearly over. The break, smaller than in the past, was tapering away to nothing. We'd sit at the takeoff spot mostly to see who'd be the first to admit boredom or defeat and then hurry back up the burning shore, lean back on elbows to put as much sand as possible in contact with our bodies. If our arms touched, she never let on that it was anything but accidental, or warranted pulling away. The angel of sobriety, Sarah Kupferberg didn't lie, didn't cheat, didn't break her troth to M—— (except what had that been in the car? Oh, torture! It was torture!). One lesson learned from the months alone with my dad, though, was that it was easier to talk facing something in common, a TV, a windshield—and the bigger that exogenous thing, the better. And now, clear-headed, facing the Atlantic, I was having some of the best conversations of my life.

What were they about? Politics, for starters. For your mom back then, everything was politics, and she claimed to see, in the still-fresh ruins of the Cold War, not an end, but a beginning: a field razed for what people might build, free of everything that oppressed them. I told her about Moira's Cabaret fixation in high school, and how she'd then taught herself German out of Mom's West-östlicher Divan, hoping to get over there and see Europe for herself. But had I read Joan Didion's thing about El Salvador? Sarah said. Or how about Gustavo Gutiérrez? The city of Lima, Peru, had seven million people—just try to wrap your head around that. In an ideal world, where her Spanish was good enough, this would be her fieldwork toward an anthro major. Go down to Peru or Managua or Santiago de Chile, look for new life springing up from the ruins: magical urbanism.

The position I adopted, mostly for the sake of being argued out of it, was that maybe stuff didn't really change that way. Sure, you could take the Olympian view, but what happened once people turned back toward their own backyards was that they grew compromised again. Fearful. I was thinking specifically of the racial situation out here, which I hated. My mom had been a humanist, in her esoteric way, and even my dad, from sheer righteousness or whatever, had gone to Alabama as a grad student to register voters; in DC, I'd walked to public elementary school alongside countless Salvadorans and Guatemalans and black Washingtonians. But if you looked at us leaving, how was that not white flight? St. Anselm's Academy had been founded, when, 1954? There were like two black kids in the entire upper school, and as far as I knew Sernovitz the only Jew. Not that the graduates of Cheshire High seemed a whole lot more cosmopolitan.

I mean, Eddie Sixkiller's half Cherokee, I said, and he's like the most racist person I know.

No sooner had she frowned than I saw I'd miscalculated, unless my goal was for some reason to worsen rather than amend the dislike she'd contrived for Eddie. That guy's nobody's friend, she'd told me after the one time I'd tried to introduce them at the shift change; he was using me, she hoped I could see that. Which was ass-backward, I thought—using me for what? Now, out loud, I declared that there was a lot of good in him, too.

Whereupon the clouds parted: But see, there you go, Ethan . . . the essential goodness of human nature. We'll make a socialist of you yet!

The world with all its problems, then—and as if for contrast, her helpless and unanalytic love for the particular corner of it that had shaped her: bucket drums, rent control, Howard Stern, egg sandwiches, New York, New York.

I remember telling her about my single, brief trip up there, when Mom had made me her chauffeur and we'd just barely made the curtain for The Who's Tommy on Broadway. The show was a mess, probably, had narrative holes you could drive a truck through, and even so, it had blown me away: light and sound and color all bleeding out across their own borders, like in the poems I'd imagined myself writing. And I recalled how on our late-night ramble back through Times Square to an overpriced garage (all ten minutes of it, me walking, Mom in the wheelchair I for some reason dropped from the telling, along with the half-dose of Percocet I'd crushed and chased with coffee for the drive home)—I'd had a sense of the show continuing to swell outward; maybe what I'd inherited from her, really, was just a weakness for total art.

So roll up, then, she said, after a moment. Next year. The city has a ton of colleges, some with writing programs, and you've got all fall to decide, right?

Anxious at this mention of my future (which I'd shaded even more carefully than my past), I said, Or maybe we wait till you have your degree in hand and do a roommate thing . . . rent an apartment above a storefront somewhere with a big neon sign, like that diner on Seinfeld. The only living surf bums in New York.

I braced myself for a prophylactic mention of M——, but none ever came; instead she said, That's right by Columbia. Same diner as the Suzanne Vega song. You could put your writing desk by the window, watch for me to come home. Though in this fantasy I suppose I'd be writing, too. Typing up my field notes. Going for the dissertation.

But that's really what you fantasize about? I said. Becoming a professor?

She didn't answer directly, instead telling me:

I remember when I was little, that was my word for what my dad was doing in the spare room every day he wasn't teaching: professing. He was in the home stretch of the book on Lady Gregory, I think, so it was dead silent in there. My mom said not even to knock. And then one day the door opens; he's got galley proofs and needs a second set of eyes. Holding out a stubby blue pencil, like this professing business is the most important thing in the world. Total solipsism, I know, but from then on, he used to always let me help him edit. The magus in his temple.

And this was the other subject we kept returning to, I noticed—her parents—though only now, in August, would she spell out the other thing she hadn't told anyone: the real reason the Kupferbergs weren't in Amagansett this year.

It was the looks we got the summer after he returned home, she said. The way that even out there, people seemed to have known what he'd been up to behind my mom's back. So he'd ruined it . . . I refused to go out there and just play pretend.

That's men for you, was all I could tell her. Chasing their appetites. Unable to see past themselves. But hey, are you okay?

Already, she seemed to be shrugging it off:

I just don't see why a person ever gets married, Ethan.

Well there's kids, I pointed out. But I'm guessing you wouldn't want to risk passing it on to them, huh? The solipsism gene, I mean.

She wasn't so sure the solipsism wasn't something environmental, she said, after sending me a funny look. But maybe it was time for me to see first-hand what she was dealing with: Why didn't I come to dinner and meet her mom and dad?

If I'd thought harder, I might have seen this as an irrelevancy rather than a sign, since the Kupferbergs were due to leave Rehoboth the morning of the tenth—too soon for any one dinner to stop it. But when I consulted the wall calendar at home, that was also the day starred for Dad's return, which perhaps accounts for the frenzied quality of my optimism. In any case, I pushed for a date two nights prior. With no shift at the HoJo, I wouldn't have to show up in my smoke-smelling uniform. And since Moira happened to be working only the dinner rush, I could talk her into dropping me beforehand, a whole hour out of her way.

It would be just shy of five, I remember, when I shooed my sister from a gutterless street on the highway's ocean side. The houses here were stilted, freestanding, and had carports of latticed cement and placards with cutesy names. Look for one called "Paradise Found," Sarah had told me, levelly. Seeing no sign of the yellow Volvo there, I went through the carport and climbed some back stairs to a deck, but aside from a giant umbrella and a table set with flatware, I was alone. Then a door rolled back, and out stepped the magus himself, Albert Kupferberg.

You must be Sarah's friend; no, please, take a seat.

Far from the moody Don Juan I'd been imagining, your grandfather was short, paunchy, rumpled in his beachy linen, but with a handsome Easter Island head beneath his Yankees cap and a certain self-satisfied charm. In one hand were two martini glasses, and he set down the shaker with the other to shake mine. So vivid was the impression of a breeze caressing the unkempt tips of his hair—of his whistling without having to whistle—that I almost didn't notice your Nana, Eleanor, slight but impeccable, coming from behind to take the glasses from his grip. Gradually, however, I saw how closely she attended to the questions he seemed merely to cross off and flip to the bottom of some mental stack.

—good Old Testament handle, he was saying. But this "Aspern" of yours is what, German?

Some kind of Scandinavian, I think? An Antrim on my mother's side, though.

Unionists?

You'd know better than I, I said, doing my best to twinkle. I hear you're the maestro on all things Irish.

I sound Irish to you, though: Kupferberg? Sort of twinkling back.

Enough! we heard, and turned to find Sarah (whom I'd never known to wear anything more formal than jeans) in a white sundress, her hair pinned up in two loosely Leia-like swirls. From her hands hung plastic delivery sacks, and as I jumped to take them, I could have sworn I saw her blush.

The food they'd ordered was Italian, too much of it, from a red-sauce joint down the beach, and though we could have eaten straight from the takeout containers, Eleanor would insist on using real plates. Martinis dispatched, she poured wine for the adults and seltzer from a glass bottle for Sarah and me, the white blaze in her hair slightly atremble as she struggled with the cap. She seemed most interested in finding out where I'd come from, exactly, but when I mentioned my dad and his time at Yale, Albert slipped deftly into a monologue about his own postdoc year in Dublin in the early '70s. Cycling out into the countryside at the time had been like riding back into the nineteenth century, he said, only with bits of the twenty-first shooting through, dairy farms and council blocks and the tricolour in every window, a ferment like you wouldn't believe. The car-bombings had been a boon to his work on Joyce, actually, as they got him thinking about Ulysses again in the context of Zionism . . . and then that led naturally enough to Yeats's Orientalism, and the secular myths out of which a nation had to summon itself:

"The same people living in the same place," as the poet said, Ethan. But I gather you've played Orpheus a little yourself?

I admitted, as I now had to Sarah, that it had been some time since I'd managed to complete a poem to my satisfaction—that I no longer seemed able to get from the winning address to the meaningful turn; that whatever knack I'd maintained was just for reading them.

Ah, well, my daughter tends to collect bookworms, he said. I suppose she told you she'll be starting at Columbia at the end of this month, along with her young man M——. I've got colleagues clamoring for them to come over from Anthro to the English department, but I tell them, Save your breath. Too hungry to see the world, those two! Now if only I could get them over to Ireland . . .

He seemed to have missed the pain crossing my face, just as I'd barely registered Eleanor's attempt to catch Sarah's eye.

But Ethan, she said, tacking away, I notice you said your parents "were" in education; what is it they do now?

Well, my dad still runs the high school where I'll be graduating next spring, I said.

Which led to a gig for his mom there too, Sarah added, touching my leg beneath the table as if to reassure me that no more needed to be said: An artist-in-residence.

But then I heard a person, apparently myself, say that that was before they'd diagnosed her with breast cancer.

She died last year.

It slipped out so easily I might have rehearsed it. And Sarah seemed to know better than to leave her hand on my thigh—which, so long as she didn't, left me fine. Or beyond fine: fit to be here. Meanwhile, a flustered Albert quoted some lines about a "gathering into eternity." And then raised his glass in memoriam and found it empty as, for the second or maybe just first time, Sarah blushed.

Once the food was done (she'd only picked at hers) Albert would propose that he and Eleanor walk down to the pier to fetch gelato, give us kids some time to say our goodbyes before he ran me home.

You know my dad's big fear going into tonight was that I might be using you to get back at him, Sarah translated, once they were gone.

She'd brought me indoors ostensibly to let me copy out her new address and phone number at the college, but after I'd done so, she'd led me further, downstairs, to a concrete rec room air-conditioned to raise goosebumps. Past a thin sheet of storm glass, hydrangeas shaded the still-brightness outside. I figured we might watch TV. Instead, she sank to the couch, not even turning on a lamp.

What are you talking about? I said. Your dad loved me. He thought I was a poet!

That was just condescension, Ethan. He didn't feel threatened by you, is all. Or not at first.

It's your mom who can come off a little dismissive.

Less streaky radars than yours have misread my mom. But at least she didn't treat you like some dreamy yokel with nowhere better to go. Anyway, mission accomplished, I guess. Now we don't have a lot of time, will you get this?

Having turned her back to me, she pushed up stray wisps of hair to expose her dress's clasp, so delicate I could barely make it out. It sat just below the top bump in her vertebrae, inches above the pallor of her swimsuit line. And when I didn't move, she reached back expertly with her other hand to unfasten it. Then she tucked her shoulders, letting the dress fall forward, pale everywhere the sun hadn't touched. Unable to look, I couldn't look away:

But hang on—what are you doing?

This is what you've been waiting for, Ethan, right? For me to take your maidenhead or whatever?

On some level, that was obviously true, so it must have been simply the frankness that set me off. Either she didn't really want us to sleep together, because I'd revealed the kind of person I actually was, or worse, she did— meaning she still couldn't see me. And whichever was the case, it seemed to reduce my performance back there at the table, and even on the beach a month ago, to one more version of the con I'd been running ever since Natasha showed me its power: slipping back toward my using, all the while I'd thought I was in control.

I'm flattered you think I'm a virgin, I managed to say. But don't do that, Sarah, okay? Don't pity me.

Ethan, this isn't pity; this is me knowing who you are, underneath. And choosing.

What about your boyfriend, though?

I'm sure my mom's filling my dad in right now; M—— and I agreed to end it on the phone this morning. I told you before, transparency's the only way I know how to do things.

But what about that first kiss, Sarah—you already cheating on him, with me—did that not happen? I said, rising from the couch; for I was furious, suddenly, at what she claimed to be able to know, and to decide. Or could you just not see how it would blow up my whole summer?

I thought blowing up your summer was the whole project.

Is that what I am to you now, a project?

Will you stop, please? You're making me have second thoughts.

Turning to the window, I pressed my forehead to it. Looked past at what were indeed two trees. They seemed to move with my breathing, imprinting themselves on my mind's eye: someday, maybe even soon, they would be gone. And of course that was why Sarah had decided to give in to me—two days from now she would be gone, too, and our story over. What the trees were doing was waving goodbye.

Listen, I'm sorry, Sarah, but I'm not the person I've apparently let you believe. You act like people can just snap their fingers and change—

That's not true, Ethan. And that's not how I'm seeing you at all. But look: the glass . . .

Had something started to give? All I could feel now was the pressure in my head.

—except what do you think happens when you leave me here with all this shit everywhere, I said, and a whole depressed countryside set up to funnel me toward it? Do you think letting me sleep with you for consolation is going to make it any easier, being in here? And then how do I know you're not leaving for good?

Ethan, don't do that, please—I don't want you to get hurt.

There had been a sound this time, almost a crack. I backed off. And in the quiet behind me she paused to think things over again, as if among the millions of paths leading out of this moment, there was only one that could end with our friendship intact.

I hear what you're saying, okay? she said. I hear the pain. But to me it seems crazy to regret the choices you've made so badly you'd just . . . wish it away the next time someone offers one. Sometimes you've got to take the leap, you know?

I feel like you're not understanding me, I said.

So help me understand, goddammit!

And here I turned to face her:

Sarah, who would someone like me even be on the other side?

Then, when I kept on, turning toward the door, she gave me that look again as if she were puzzling something out . . . and began to tug up her dress and said okay, change was hard, maybe this was all happening too fast, and if I still needed time to get my head around the fact that it was obviously too late to go back, then no need to storm farther than the front yard—she would call me a cab.

I had never been late to work before, but there was no Squatch around to chide me the next day at noontime, and when one of the girls complained about covering my tables, a lie slid off my tongue like silver: I'd been up all night celebrating my birthday, go easy on me. In truth, I'd just been too shaken by my outburst to sleep, and caught sunrise from the roof outside my room, where it was at most a degree cooler.

Was it any surprise, then, that my last day at the HoJo should also be my worst-ever day of tips? At one point, a trio of beefy guys in knit shirts, reddened as if they'd made an enemy of the sun, left a little pile of cash under an ice-cream dish, precise to the penny, along with a note scrawled on the check, TIP: TRY ACTING LIKE A WAITER. I slipped back to the banquet room at shift's end hoping to laugh it off with Eddie; instead I found Ernest (or was that Dre?), his hands counting receipts, his <u>Fresh Air</u> on the radio, his hairnet a blurred memory.

Surprise inspection this morning, he said, glancing up. The owner caught Squatch drowning his grief in blow. Your man Eddie's gone, too—it's a total housecleaning.

And after a minute, when I hadn't left:

I'm only spitballing here. But my feeling is, you can't be bothered to be on time, you might as well not show up at all. Why don't you go figure out what you want to do tomorrow.

It remained at least theoretically possible that I could now reach Sarah from a payphone, tell her I was sorry, see if she still wanted to meet on the boardwalk for one last night on the Eastern Shore. Yet I stepped back into the daylight feeling like Schrödinger's cat . . . or no, sorry, that's weak, let me rephrase. Unable to stand knowing if my chances with your mother were alive or if I'd managed to kill them—or which I even feared more— I chickened out. Pedaled the half-hour home.

Even before I reached our corner, though, I could hear a tangled spaghetti of music coming from Ducky's, or more precisely from the cars out back. There must have been three times as many loiterers as usual— the high-school no-goodniks, yes, but also some motorcycle guys and even jocks in cherry tie-dye, all drinking in the broad daylight. My thought as I ditched the Schwinn (still not having caught the import of a fully functioning slot machine in a state where gambling was illegal) was that it was a wonder the cops didn't come. But what at first seemed a bacchanal turned out to be a wake. Watery-eyed Phish girls chewed their hempen necklaces; even the bikers looked ruminative. Then a hand drew me into a circle spaced as if for hacky-sack. It was Squatch, sans robe but compensatorily solemn.

You haven't heard about this morning? he said, placing a joint in my hand.

The firings? I was about to ask, when he said:

Jerry died.

Jerry?

Yeah, Jerry, man. Garcia.

Now, as I say, I'd never really gotten into your grandmother's Dead tapes, having internalized her rap about immanence versus transcendence. Yet I could recall her nonetheless citing them as the one band of her era who'd managed to construct inside this conflicted world an alternative vision of itself. And if the last remnant of that vision had passed away, I thought—Jerry Garcia, the patron saint of acid and grass, now a suicide by heroin at age fifty-three—wouldn't it be wrong not to allow myself a hit or two in commemoration?

Of course for me there could be no such thing as one or two, and in no time I was sliding from circle to circle, sucking down blunts, and cadging the beers that continued to roll out of Ducky's by the case. You'll have noticed I still wasn't much of a drinker, but that's only because, sliding backward down the ladder of downers, I hadn't yet reached the lowest rung.

It would be six, maybe seven beers later that I found myself in the backseat of a car full of folks I didn't know, swept away on blue highways into the dark as, through the speakers, the band played on. A girl with a shadowy face sat on my lap pressing another luke-cold can of Natty Boh into my hand.

Then another parking lot, skirted by weeds, and a more percussive music trembling puddles of water giving back arc-lights staked on poles down into the dark heart of everything. My upward stumble sent a nautical mural on cinderblock smearing past; we'd reached the Dockhouse, an all-black nightclub said to exist out toward the county line. Maybe someone had thought it would be funny to actually go there, but I knew there were certain lines you couldn't cross; it's just that I was having trouble getting the words out. Well-dressed clubgoers trickled past us on the gravel, mildly curious. Then, under a bulb like a bug zapper's, a bouncer in a muscle-tee gave me just enough of a smirk to confirm that, between him and me, we knew who the joke was on.

Inside, though, the club was so standard-issue that people soon splintered off my party, some to try to get a drink, some to hit the dance floor, where the waywardness of white kids would be tolerated, if not indulged. I lingered near the entrance with the girl from the car. Did I remember who she was? she kept asking over the music. Her attempt at a kiss bordered on violence; I had to reach for the top of a payphone to stay upright. People laughed, but there were also women my mother's age beginning to look on with concern. I patted my pockets, couldn't recall where I'd left my Altoids. Then one of our party came back to report that someone was selling crack in the men's room, where the guy who'd driven us had disappeared five minutes ago. Someone else said don't worry; he probably just had to piss. My thought process, to the extent I still had one, was like, Crack, sweet, and I slurred something about a rescue mission as I shoved through a door to the bathroom only to stumble out into the parking lot again, but whatever; by this point, passing out in the backseat of the car I'd arrived in sounded like a plausible alternative. I found a rear door unlocked and had just finished emptying my guts into the footwell when I heard a woman's loud voice behind me.

Hey, what's that whiteboy doing in your car?

I crawled back out to find the lot already swollen with grown men and women, a weird inversion of earlier at Ducky's. What the hell is this? the bouncer asked, his arms bulging under the lights like Easter hams.

Somebody died, I wanted to explain, but a woman's voice, younger, said I bet you money this is the motherfucker's been stealing from motherfuckers.

What's that smell, though? the bouncer said. Because I know that's not vomit. Not when I just cleaned my car.

The crowd now numbered a couple dozen, and there was a moment when it seemed anything at all might have jumped off. Then a slight figure in a black workshirt and black khakis moved into the light, saying let him handle this. I must have been just brightening with recognition when he cold-cocked me in the face, one-two, and dropped me to the gravel with a jab to the gut.

What comes next, in memory, is just the weird bright taste of my own blood. A sense of sucked-in breath around me . . . of people turned away in a kind of secondhand pain. And of Eddie Sixkiller, squatting nearby to wipe the wetness off his fist with his shirttail, ignoring my moans. As soon as we were something like alone, he began to drag me back across the gravel.

And I want to say I remember "Shook Ones Pt. II" on the stereo, just as I want to locate my head in Eddie's lap, but of course that's impossible, when the forensics all have me lying in the backseat of a cavernous SUV now whipping along country roads. Let's just go with the smells, then, black-leather new-car smell, autoerotic exhalations from the cornfields, and over top of that, a Christmas-tree air freshener. The clock in the center console might as well have been Proust in the original French, could have said eleven at night or three in the morning. When I tried to beg Eddie not to make me go home, his answer was, Don't you dare fuck up the leather, Ducky'd kill me for letting anyone in here. He must have heard my request as literal, though, since sometime later (I know not how) he was plopping me onto my secret glider in the woods—which was indeed damp, but only because of my tears.

Jesus, what the fuck is wrong with you, he said. You have everything, Ethan. Everything. Now stay here.

Something minty hit my chest: a soft-pack of menthols, already torn open. Then he was in the wind, and the stars aswim; I had nothing.

The fuck you do, Prep, I heard him answer in my head (the one place I could still make myself intelligible). Because I've seen how things happen for you. How doors open at a word. And those plants you brought back to life for your mom; how you can make things grow.

But you tried to use me for it, I imagined myself protesting. And then up and left me. And just got done beating the shit out of me.

Ethan, what the hell do you think love is sometimes?

Or okay, perhaps my thoughts weren't that linear. But they would end, I know, with his spraypainted bike: the bright beads blurring into whatever was the neon equivalent of brown from the speed with which he'd crashed in on my clearing that first time . . . And now I felt as sure as I'd been of anything in my life that he'd known the way because it had been his clearing first: that the one sleeping here in the woods behind Ducky's on nights when he'd found himself locked out at home was Eddie Sixkiller. And that, in exchange for a guarantee of safety, Eddie must have consented at some point to let Ducky hold his stash and bribe the cops, and then take over as his supplier, and ultimately back Eddie into whatever he'd started dealing out of the HoJo this summer, the rock cocaine my friend and protector had done his level best to keep me from—oh, how was it possible for one person to miss so much?

And maybe I passed out again for a while, because suddenly there came a voice whose cloth-wrapped susurrations I'd have known anywhere, crossed by the cries of the insomniac birds. The person on whose behalf I set out to write all this however many pages ago, Jolie: your mother. We still haven't gotten you into the world, it seems . . . and here in 2021, I'm increasingly worried you might take some drastic step before we do. But I guess if there's a thought I want to leave you with before I head home from the Costa Brava, it's about how certain kinds of hopelessness are almost a precondition for a second act. Just watch.

Make sure you keep his head up in case he boots, Eddie said, after throwing a blanket over me. I don't want him choking to death.

Then he was gone again and it was just the two of us. Your mom thumbing my black eye by moonlight, climbing onto the wet glider beside me. She shushed me after a bit and at some point fell asleep, but drunk though I was—stoned though I was—I couldn't find my way back to unconsciousness, nor work up the courage to move. Nor can I even point to any particular moment when the sky would have gotten brighter, but once the birdsong went continuous and I could see the top of her hair, I rose, jabbed by a headache.

Hey, wake up, I told her. Hey, Sarah: it's the next day. Fuck—damn it. I'm late for work. And your folks are going to kill you. We spent the night together.

She blinked, sat up groggily . . . and then said, Grow up, Ethan. Who do you think let me take the car? My mom knows she can trust me. But you're right. I should go. Vacation's over.

And already she was out of my arms, folding up the blanket, moving across the clearing for a canvas tote she'd set on the ground.

No, wait, I said, too slow to see what was happening and desperate for some line that might stop her leaving. But when I started to explain once more what I'd been trying to for a month now—the problem we'd been ignoring, the nature of the beast—she cut me off. There's nothing else I need to know about you, Ethan. We're hardly even friends anymore . . . and definitely not more than that, remember? We're just people who hung out one summer.

So why'd you come back for me, then?

Your pal Eddie tracked down the rental through Moira and showed up at our door—said he had to get back to work. And if it's a choice between a person staying alive and that person dying, she said, of course I'd rather them not die. But you ought to be able to take care of yourself from here on out, Ethan. I mean, that's pretty much the choice you've made, isn't it?

Then she bent to touch her lips to my forehead, just barely, before jerking upright, as if it burned.

Watching her fade back into the corn, some part of me was trying to see how it could possibly be the case that I'd chosen anything at all. But away on another channel, a different part of me kept turning over that kiss: how she had winced away in pain at the very moment she should have been letting me go. Any old person could offer you their body, I thought, or cast aside another, but only someone who loved you a great deal would let you in deep enough to hurt like that. Which maybe meant that we weren't so different after all, your mother and I—selves irreconcilably at war—but also that I'd lost her before I'd even realized I had her.

And perhaps she might even understand what I did next, I thought. Or perhaps you will now, wherever you are. For the obvious move was to get the twigs out of my hair and make for the highway, hitch a ride to the HoJo with all due speed, plead for my job back so I could live up to my sister's expectations, hold my head up before my dad. Instead, having fixed myself up with a cigarette (my absolute last, I swore), I turned back toward the brush that edged the clearing—my failed early-warning system, those shoals of birds now calling and responding in the green—and watched myself drift deeper into the woods.

III

BRAN'S CAULDRON

Spring->Summer->Fall 2011

Nobody sings anymore.
And then last night, I tiptoed up
To my daughter's room and heard her
Talking to someone, and when I opened
The door, there was no one there . . .

—AMIRI BARAKA
"Preface to a Twenty Volume Suicide Note"

3

THAT WHOLE FIRST HOUR of what was to become her second life, Jolie kept expecting someone to tag her with the obvious question: Had she been *trying* to kill herself back there or what? No matter how she braced for it, though, the fact would remain that no one she encountered in the turmoil of ambulance and emergency room and radiology lab seemed overanxious to hear the truth. Not the cop who'd squatted by her on the subway tile to take down the basic timeline; not the huge-handed medics who would lift her onto their board, stirring a brief throb of submissive lust; not the TV reporter already blurring past at the gate up to the street, holding forth about these millennials and their devices to what might have been thin air. It was the phone, apparently, that made the story. You had it right there on the tracks, an iPhone 3G, followed by a thirteen-year-old girl, and finally the train, and if life was short and time indeed money, who needed all the murky bits in between?

To be fair, there had been the one EMT who seemed to have missed the memo, making gentle noises about confiscating shoelaces as he readied the gurney for exit. And then hung around at the triage desk to try to find out why the Aspern kid was marked for ortho and not psych. But not even the nurses saw it as their job to go overturning rocks. (And was it the woman stonewalling him there at intake, or some other one, who'd finally let him submit the form that would prevent Jolie's release? Funny, how the nurses of Bellevue kept turning into one another when you weren't looking, like a single, seraphic creature with a range of possible faces but a multitude of busy wings.)

Still, Jolie was under no illusion that the truth could stay hidden for long. For as soon as a rush-hour cab could make it from the Upper West Side, her mother would arrive, and they would both be in tears, and Jolie wouldn't even have to speak, her mom would just know, from the look on her face, what had gone through her mind back there on the tracks . . .

For the record, though, Mom must have fabricated out of Jolie's assurances the same cautionary tale as the newsbreak on the cab's talk radio, because the first thing she said after "Honey, are you sure you're okay?" was, "But God, what were you thinking? Don't you know these phones are replaceable?" Her voice was eloquent with frustration. Her eyes slid to the bruise on Jolie's temple, the slinged arm, the vertical blinds covering the window—everywhere but her daughter's own eyes. And when she did finally cross to the bed and press Jolie to her, it seemed almost a way not to have to see her as a person with her own thoughts and feelings. So no, maybe now wasn't quite the moment to start dissecting the finer shades of intent.

Mom would spend much of the following morning trying to find someone in one of the relevant bureaucracies who might discuss with her the clerical screw-up that was delaying their going home. In the same bedside chair she'd slept in, she sat through endless hold music, which she punctuated with irate hand gestures. By midafternoon, however, it was starting to seem as if they might be stuck here till Monday, which meant a different set of calls, to what Mom referred to as "concerned parties." And at this, Jolie, who'd spent hours flipping through the suckiest possible menu of channels on the wall-mounted TV, turned it off. "Do you really have to go spreading around the gory details, though?" She let the remote swing on its rubber umbilicus. "I mean, the whole thing makes me look so dumb . . ."

"It's in the news already, Jolie."

"But no one knows it's me, you said, and unless someone blows the whistle, no one has to."

"Your school will need to know you're in the hospital, at least. Mine too; I may have to reschedule Monday classes. And if we ever get out of here, it's hardly going to escape notice that your shoulder's in a sling."

"Yeah, but isn't there some other way to explain it than the phone?" said Jolie (who'd already tried applying concealer to the bump on her forehead).

She was just sketching the kind of fig leaf she had in mind when Nana called, threatening to rush down here in the Volvo. From four feet away, Jolie could hear the consternation she'd caused. *Please?* she mouthed to Mom. Then repeated aloud, quietly, "Please?" And all at once, with a look that was pained, not to say grudging, Mom let transparency go. No need to panic, she told Nana, everything was okay, Jolie had simply been walking under a scaffold, listening to her music, when she'd been knocked to the ground by falling debris. All of which she then repeated minutes later to the attendance secretary at Broad Horizons.

AND IT WAS AN INTERESTING FEATURE of little white lies, how much you could build upon them. Mom continued to sleep in the chair, but by Saturday was using the daylight hours to venture back out on errands as if there really were no need for alarm—laundry, for God's sakes! Sushi!—leaving Jolie with long stretches of time in which to try to work out the underlying truth.

The underlying truth was this: she couldn't see how she'd been suicidal, really, or at any rate was anymore. In the ambulance, that medic had kept harping on "plans" as opposed to "thoughts," and when she'd told him, No, she had no immediate plans to hurt herself, wasn't she just being honest?

Of course, she was pretty sure there had been no plan when she'd left the zendo, either. She spent a decent part of that Saturday considering the possibility that this cleaving of decision from action signaled an even greater disorder than the one she obviously had. But by this point, "thinking" and "planning" seemed the wrong words altogether, when her fear of the train and her turning to embrace it were more layered on top of each other, like different cross-sections of the same planet, or different Jolies splayed across the M-space of the universe.

THEN SUDDENLY it was Sunday noon and she was alone again, the ward charged with the emptiness of all Sundays everywhere, and she was just wishing she hadn't in the confusion lost track of her violin case and its incriminating booze when knuckles rapped on the doorframe. Mom might have been back with lunch already, but instead it was the hunky paramedic, now in off-duty jeans, his dubious look having vanished along with his coveralls. He seemed to be counting on the patient to know why he'd come; when Jolie reached for her navy surplus backpack, he told her, "You can leave all that stuff behind."

Which, strangely enough, Jolie did: rose to tug on sneakers and then, without the guy so much as touching her arm except to occasionally flash her bracelet to a nurse, let herself be led through endless corridors, skyways whose glass seemed to run with mascara—everywhere the sad late light of winter trying to claw back spring.

The coffee-odored dayroom where they ended up was if anything even sadder. Tube lighting, hyperactive radiators, a glum-looking klatsch of teeshirted teens seated at maybe half a dozen folding tables, absorbed in the kind of work that might have seemed artistic but for the total absence of scissors, glitter, paint . . . At the center of each table was just a parsimony of printer paper. Pencils somehow pre-blunted. Also: Who was even in charge here, now that the medic had evaporated again? The only other person who even seemed to see Jolie was a tall boy slouched in a corner armchair, pointedly refusing to participate, his flannel sleeves buttoned to the wrist.

It was mostly to get him to stop staring that she found herself drifting to an empty table. From above, the oblong of paper stacked there had the aspect of a pool viewed from a high dive, a sense of vertigo only slightly lessened by her sitting down. But from the next table over, she could hear now a phatic purr she recognized from the artrooms of her youth. A wraithlike girl in a hijab and another boy, sibilant, were murmuring almost tenderly about being pumped full of charcoal—which must also have been what their hands were busy writing about. She kept expecting her mother to appear in the doorway, calling her back to where she belonged; and still there was this brief, sharp longing to stay here among the tribe. But though it was easy enough to say, Follow that feeling, Jolie—just start telling what's wrong with you—where would she have even begun? It was like trying to play music when someone had ripped up the score.

After a while, though, she found herself thinking for some reason of her other grandmother, her dad's dead mom, the one who'd made art. Of somebody—Dad?—talking about a film project whose original had at some point been lost, and a soundtrack some part of which was now stuck in a box under her bed. And then with a whoosh she was both watching a movie and in it, deposited back on East 112th Street in an apartment she hadn't seen for years—standing behind glass at what seemed to be the edge of the world. Because of course what you had to begin with was the beginning.

Picking up a pencil, she wrote down the words, *In the beginning*, then heard Bible and crossed it out for something that sounded more like herself, *At first . . .* and then crossed that out, too. *The window was full of flaws, but they did not know it then*, she tried—but who was this "they"? She went on to make more attempts after that; it was like she couldn't get each one down fast enough before crossing it out. But eventually Jolie found herself back at the old apartment, the window, the concreteness of where she'd begun, and things just started coming out of her about her father in the years when she was little. His own afflictions. His own sadness, and stuck-ness. His inability to tell Mom the truth, and how much worse that made it. The sentences came fast. Her hand seemed to be melting. Yet as long as she stood here trying to look through this flawed glass rather than down at the marks on the page, she was no longer quite so stuck in herself.

Time passed. Possibly a lot of time. She was still eighty blocks plus however many years away, but somehow her story was all here, too, or at least a lot of it, in a code she couldn't have concocted through any more purposeful effort. But now the neighboring girl started laughing and she felt eyes on her again, which made her realize: Who was she kidding? She'd written down part of the story, okay, but where was the person with whom she could have shared it? And without that, nothing had changed, nothing even ceased. Then the wave broke, and she found herself tumbling back out into the world again, just as scared and as lonely and perhaps somehow even more hopeless than before.

From the armchair, the tall boy was still watching. She stood, embarrassed, and retreated outside to where she recalled seeing vending machines and some garbage cans. Before dropping her crumpled pages in the nearest of these, she checked left and right and saw the boy rounding the corner; she was just trying to seem engrossed in her choice of candy bar when he caught up to her. He looked high-school aged, she thought, skinny jeans, hair mussed either carefully or not carefully at all—the wry expression of the welcoming committee. And as he held something up between them, she would catch herself trying to read the name off the plastic bracelet around his cuff, so that it took a full second to realize that the something was an instrument case, and that it was hers.

"Nurse Ratched suggested I bring this along with me today, see that it gets to its rightful owner," the boy said, with an English accent she at first took for fake. "Nice sticker, by the way."

But which one? The Amnesty dove? The motorcycle glyph from *Purple Rain*? He seemed to mean the Woody Guthrie. "That doesn't make sense," she said. "My violin went missing Thursday, during triage. How did it end up on a psych ward?"

He released his hold on it without seeming to cede any ground. "I literally just told you." Lich-rilly. "But things do tend to get lost in the shuffle 'round these parts; you should pay better attention."

"There's been a mix-up. I'm not even supposed to be here!"

The look he gave her was somehow off as he said he knew the feeling, but she persisted.

"No, really, I'm not one of you." It came out harsher than she'd expected, yet carried with it the same thing she'd felt when writing, only now brought under her control. "As soon as my paperwork's straight, I'm on my way home. In fact, I should be getting back to my own ward now."

She had already spotted an exit sign farther down the hall, but strangely, there were still no adults in view to stop her. Around the corner, it was true, she would then come to a sealed set of doors where a nurse or whoever glanced up from a computer ten yards back, but she was surprised to find that when she held up her own bracelet and sort of jangled it as the EMT had done to get her in, it was enough for them to mash the button that let her out. Well, that or the violin, which conceivably made her look like a visitor. At some point, feeling the narrowness of her escape, she ducked into a bathroom to dump the vodka from her rosin compartment. And finally, some twenty minutes later, she reached somewhere she recognized: her mother with a takeout bag, looking pensive by a door. At Jolie's appearance she brightened. "Oh, great, you found your violin."

"Yeah, turns out some jerk tried to make off with it."

"I was wondering where you'd gotten to. But listen, I think I did it."

"Did what?"

"I had to walk all the way over to adolescent medicine, but I found the person I think can get us cleared for release. She's just pulling your chart, let me go grab her. And then you tell her everything you told me about how you came to be here." She was already steering Jolie by the good arm, not to her room, but to a tiled cell in the other direction, where a table sheathed in coarse paper sat under the vaguely dysfunctional lighting of a pre-glasnost *Waiting for Godot*.

Godot turned out to be a white woman with flat Midwestern vowels, a Child Services credential clipped to her lab coat, and a no-nonsense face that could have been anywhere from forty-five to sixty. As she took Jolie's measurements, medical history, and vital signs, struck both knees with a mallet, and gauged her injured arm for range of motion, Jolie could feel herself relax: she'd jumped through these same hoops three times already. But then the woman looked at her clipboard and frowned. "It says here you're down a couple pounds since Thursday, Josie . . ."

Jolie, she wanted to assert, but the tone brought her up short. "I'm always a bit lighter this time of the month."

"Your cycle's been normal, then?"

"Honestly? It's not that big of a sample size . . ."

"Okay, menses variable, I'll put. Now are there any other physical irregularities you've been noticing, before we move on to the mental-health portion of the screen?"

Who said anything about my mental health? Jolie thought. And then remembered the boy slumped in his chair, his loneliness and pallor. "You mean irregular like nearly getting flattened by a subway train while I go to get my phone off the tracks? I know it was an idiotic thing to do, but it wasn't crazy. I should have been out of here Friday."

The woman flipped ahead a page, paused. "Wait, that was you, in the subway last week? With the iPhone? On the cover of the *Post*?"

"Did my mom not explain the mix-up?"

Another reconnoiter of the chart. "You know what? Why don't we get her in here to iron out a few discrepancies, if you don't mind."

As the woman stepped into the hallway, Jolie let her gaze go back around the room, taking in an abdominal cross-section straight out of *Our Bodies, Ourselves*, the mean-looking mouth of a metal box marked Sharps . . . Then the doorknob turned, and she realized she was holding her breath. What if the woman had been walking Mom through the holes in Jolie's story? (Except wasn't that on some level just the opening she'd been waiting for?) *Look at me, Mom*, she thought. *Please look at me.*

But Mom's whole focus was on getting her home, as it must have been out in the hall, for now the woman was saying she'd heard enough to sign off on discharge—"with my apologies, Josie, for the initial confusion."

"It's Jolie," she and Mom said in unison.

"One thing, though," the woman continued. "Since 9/11, we do try to be vigilant about post-traumatic stress, so I'm going to leave you with a card for a specialist . . ."

"A shrink, you mean?" The word still attached in Jolie's mind to Dr. Sam, the boyish family therapist she'd been sent to once or twice the year of the divorce: his condescending magic tricks, his easily stymied patter.

"The approach is called 'shared subjectivity,'" said the woman, with a glance at Mom that was either significant or meaningless. "You may find that the ordeal you've just come through isn't something you want to try to handle on your own."

Yeah, but it's not my first rodeo, Jolie got as far as thinking, when the full scope of what she'd been inching up to took the words away. And before she could think further, much less have time to make a final decision, she said, "Okay, sure."

"Sure what?"

She scooched from the table, stooped to one-hand the recovered violin. "If it means getting out of here," she said, "then we'll take the name. Please." The backpack she would leave to her mother, who could be straightened out on the shrink later, when they were alone. For the present, Jolie had done it—had secured her release after a three-day hospitalization and one near-death experience with no further reference to depression, or ideation, or addiction, or whatever had led her onto those tracks. And why bring any of that stuff up, after all? She hadn't swallowed poison, had she? Or taken a razor to her wrists, as that boy in the flannel obviously had. You didn't plan on a train, or calibrate your near-miss with one as a cry for help. So no: she didn't belong among those kids back there, she thought—the depressives, the suicides—and the bigger lie would have been to pretend that she did.

WHAT JOLIE HADN'T COUNTED ON, though, was that even the smaller lie required care and feeding . . . was hungry like any living thing to grow. And how it would begin as soon as she got home to interpose itself between her and others. To begin with, there was Vikas, the doorman. He'd seemed older of late, silver threading into the black above his ears, but beneath his Yankees cap and beetled brow, he had one of the great all-time pairs of eyes, slices of pale gold at once soft and sharp, somehow. And remarkably, in this city that turned everyone inward, the eyes' searching quality had only deepened. Now he stopped her. "A sling I knew to expect, kid, with the dislocation, but don't tell me the debris clipped your head, too?"

Her fedora must have slipped in the cab, further experiments with concealer having left her right temple looking like an incipient horn. "No worries, Vikas. Swelling's going down already. It's only a scratch."

Even with the door to the street propped open, the lobby was so quiet she could hear keys hitting tin when Mom went for the mail. And the slight whistle of Vikas's nostrils, like a jazz show she and Mom used to listen to on Sunday nights in winter.

"I could ask around for an attorney," he offered at last. "An old neighbor of mine fell down a manhole once, got enough out of court to retire."

Brighter, Jolie told herself. Lighter. "I'd settle for a newspaper, honestly, if you're done with today's."

"What, the *Times*? The *Journal*?"

"You get the *Post* back there? I hear there's a column says we might take the whole division this year."

"You and your Mets." Vikas shook his head as he rifled through the four or five newspapers he read daily, but seemed secretly relieved. The offending tabloid came to her folded in two. And in the same mild tone that might have crackled through the intercom system to announce she had a package, he told her to take it, with best wishes for a speedy recovery.

SHE COULD OF COURSE just have found the *Post* online, but its website in those days was a labyrinth, actively de-optimized for mobile. The quickest shunt to the urban unconscious remained the old four-color pages—which loved little so much as a subway caper. She'd already known about Friday's front page (**APP-ETITE FOR DESTRUCTION!**), and now she braced for a sequel, with enough identifying information for someone nosy at school, Mr. K., say, to connect it to her own absence and injuries. Instead the lone follow-up turned out to be a human-interest thing about the guy who'd pulled her free, his grinding Guatemalan childhood and ambitions to open his own gym. It should have spelled relief: New York, briefly burdened by Jolie's existence, had caught the next wave and moved on. Some do-gooders had even set the guy up a GoFundMe. But in fact, trying to connect his potted biography with the tattooed figure being grilled by an interpreter on the far side of the MetroCard machine only raised new questions about what Jolie had been thinking down there. Her savior could have ended up deported, or killed—and for what?

No, the truth was, each cleared hurdle in the steeplechase of her cover-up led not only out to freedom, but also deeper into guilt. She now had to take two separate buses to school to avoid the subway, and on the dot of three o'clock, as if sliding all the way back to the year's beginning, she would take these same buses straight home. There could be no more zendo, the way she'd left things (nor, given the shoulder, any speedy return to the pool), but neither was there further talk of P.T., or PTSD, now that Mom had seen the out-of-network deductibles. Nor drinking, which couldn't be trusted not to make her try to do it again . . . drinking, somehow the hardest thing for her to let go. All she had left to fill the time was that box of her grandmother's CDs. And Prince had lost her long about 1993, become the dour and transactional ♀. She found solace in the Who, those songs that seemed to speak directly to her condition: "Behind Blue Eyes," "The Real Me," "I Don't Even Know Myself." But even after her sling came off, she would sometimes still find herself delaying the listening session, lingering by the mailboxes on her way in, feigning absorption in grocery circulars until Vikas got called away for a cigarette or a delivery and she could raid the newspaper pile on his desk. Each time, she wondered: Was there something she'd missed? For her darker self remained skeptical that you could come as close as she had to your own extinction—even just scare the shit out of the conductor and make a bunch of people late getting home—and then wave it away with a few pale flourishes of your hand.

Small wonder then that in late May, when the mail brought an official-looking envelope with her mom's name in lawyerly copperplate, she would have a premonition of the other shoe, dropping. She thought about steaming it open, even as she worked a finger under the seal. Yet instead of a bill from the MTA, or a duplicate of her police report with the half-truths marked in red, what fluttered to the floor was an onionskin insert. The card she was left holding, on cream-colored stock almost too thick to bend, announced that on the last day of school, the faculty of Broad Horizons would be hosting its fifth annual Academic Achievement Awards. And la-di-dah, right? At public school, they'd have just showed movies. But Vikas was already flashing a thumbs-up from his smoking spot under the awning, like he could read the insert's tiny font from there:

GYRE PRIZE (BEST UPPER-SCHOOL ESSAY): JOLIE ASPERN, FINALIST

NOW, JUST SO WE'RE CLEAR, there was never any chance of her taking home this uncoveted award. Even the nomination—for two thousand words banged out in a Red Bull–fueled spree and submitted a week after deadline—felt unlikely. Yet here was her grandmother, the living one, phoning down from Riverdale to reserve tickets to the ceremony. And here was Mom insisting, as the big day neared, that Jolie wear something nicer than just her Casual Friday jeans.

Mom herself would waste almost an hour that morning trying on tops in the mirror, and though they still reached school ahead of time, seemed oddly anxious about snagging a seat. Nana and Albert had been told to save one, she explained, scrolling her phone, but were caught in some kind of traffic apocalypse on the Major Deegan and might have to meet up with them at the lunch after. Then she said good luck and vanished inside, leaving Jolie to languish in her tux jacket and least skirty skirt among the four hundred other kids bunched around the entrance, along with entourages of family and friends chattering and mugging for selfies.

At length, order formed from the chaos, teachers with batons of rolled program herding the mob into homerooms. Jolie drifted toward her line, attached herself to the back, shuffled when it shuffled, stopped when it stopped. From the gymtorium doors came a great orchestral yawn. But right as she was about to surrender, fingers reached from behind to cover her eyes as in a game of Guess Who?

"Hey! Hands off the merchandise!"

Twisting away, she felt a ripple of what might have been déjà vu, were it not completely sui generis: instead of some pimple-faced creep, the person she found herself facing—impossibly tall, impossibly young, and basically just fucking impossible—was her father. The hairshirty beard he'd worn as recently as their last Skype session had been shaved down to stubble. Otherwise, it was like the image had been frozen back in the middle of the '08 crash. Or if anything, the tanned jawline made him look younger, unless that was a blush she now saw rising there, the recovery of some capacity for shame. He held up his hands in defense. Cleared his throat. "I hear you're up for an award, Jolie. Nice school, by the way," he added. "I can see why your mom chose it."

And now her own shame burst free, like softness from a bruised pear. "Oh my God, Dad . . . did she put you up to this? Because she swore she wasn't going to tell—"

"Tell me what? That my daughter's twice the writer I ever was? Give me a little credit, honey. The school mailed invites to all the parents. Mine's taped to the fridge in California, right by that photo you sent at Thanksgiving."

"But please say she knows that you're here!"

What she meant was, *Please say she doesn't*, but his failure to catch the nuance seemed to confirm his obliviousness: "I wasn't sure about the timing, coming from JFK at morning rush, and I knew if I said I would show and then didn't, it was going to be held against me."

"So what . . . so you decide on a whim to come back after three years and let me be the first to know?"

"I don't need your mother's permission to visit New York, do I? I mean, what if I said I had some business to take care of?"

What business?

"But look at you: getting so tall." The hands had come to rest on her shoulders, a posture she knew would ease into a hug at the slightest hint of permission. And in fact there was little to prevent her giving it; aside from teachers releasing the kickstands that held open doors, they were the only ones left in the hall. Later, looking back, she would picture herself as standing on an event horizon, being sucked toward the inevitable reunion. But however oblivious Dad might have been, he had that way of peering into her, too, when he could be bothered to see . . . as, if they stood here much longer, he doubtless would—though really, it was as much the vision of an unsuspecting Mom sweeping around the corner to spot his messenger bag and marked-up Vans that sent her scrabbling for a pen.

"Sorry your timing sucks, Dad, but I've got to go catch up with my group. If it's really so important that we see each other, why don't you write down where you're staying, so I have some firm way to reach you?"

"We can handle logistics later, Jo. For now, let me find a seat."

"Oh, but please don't do that. Please. Nobody calls me 'Jo' anymore. And these things are a drag. You truly don't need to stay."

"Sweetheart. I took a redeye specifically to be here."

The direct appeal was excruciating, and her time short; amplified voices had begun to carom around inside. "Then make sure you take a seat near the back, okay? I don't want Mom seeing you." She grabbed a program from his hands, starred a margin on the last page but one. "My bit should be done right around here. There's a nut cart on the corner of Third Avenue. You slip out where I marked and meet me there, and we'll figure out some way forward." And before he could attempt a one-sided embrace, she broke for the gym (or auditorium—whatever) suddenly grateful for its lowered lights. Otherwise, pale as she was, you might have thought she'd just seen a ghost.

THE ACADEMIC AWARDS CEREMONY was like a low-rent Oscars—you were expected to sit through scores of presentations that didn't concern you just to catch the few that did—and would have been trying under even ordinary circumstances. As it was, Jolie felt her need to turn and scan the dark rows behind her as a kind of burning, impervious to anything she might have learned sitting zazen.

By hour two, kids around her had their programs folded into fans. She tried to distract herself from the mystery of Dad's reappearance by seeking patterns in the oscillations, but they were pure randomness, like the syllables tripping out of the PA. Up in the second row floated the elaborately braided head of Precious Ezeobi, bound in the fall for the high school from *Fame*. Precious, whose own refusal to look back was starting to seem deliberate. Might a narrow enough beam of pure thought make itself felt on those glowing zags of scalp, the fiery mind beneath? *I'm sorry!* Jolie thought. And *Take me with you!* But dammit— the name now garbling from the speaker must have been hers, because a boy down the row was motioning wearily for her to rise. And here she was, as in a dream of disquiet, shuffling toward the rostrum where her certificate and complimentary pencil awaited, under the penetrating gaze of her nominating teacher.

Which meant she then had to stand up onstage for a minute or more with this hot male hand on her lower back and who knows how many eyes boring in on her from beyond. And as she waited for some sign of release, the gaze that felt the most discomfiting out there in the blackness was Dad's. Wasn't it possible, or even likely, that Mom had at least relayed that his daughter had been hurt, and had had to spend a couple nights at the hospital? For why come back like this if not in some misguided attempt to comfort, and to help? And if Mom had told him that much, then why not the rest of what she'd taken to be the full story? How close was Jolie here to real exposure?

You were supposed to exit stage left and recirculate to your seat, but Jolie found herself shoving through a door to an outer corridor. *EAGLES!* the wall screamed. Otherwise, the school was like a body emptied of breath; even the front office was inert, blinds drawn. And when she reached the avenue outside, Hamid the nut guy had been raptured away. Dad would have no idea which corner to meet on, assuming he'd remembered they were supposed to meet in the first place . . . or that, out of some unconfessable need (she thought, scanning the bright clots of pedestrians that kept failing to contain him), she hadn't hallucinated him altogether?

For ten minutes, she traipsed from one end of the block to the other. Texted the last number she had for him, not even sure it still worked. Watched her award-winning syntax decay:

But by this point the ceremony was over, the other audience members starting to spill from the school. And the one catching her on the steps, on the verge of plunging back in, was Mom. The certificate shot from her hands. "Oh, Jolie, don't look like that.

This award is a good thing, right? Brandon says you're a born ethnographer."

"It's not that," she said, and was struggling to frame another fib when a two-tone whistle rang out behind her.

"Perfect," came Dad's voice. "Both of you in one place."

The flight of Mom's hand to her heart seemed to douse any remaining whiff of conspiracy. "Ethan! What the hell . . . ?"

"Sorry, I wasn't trying to spring anything on you, as I told Jolie. But what with all the packing, the mad dash to the airport—"

"Hang on . . . you knew about this, Jolie?"

"Yeah, as of about a minute before the ceremony."

"Breathe, Sarah," he suggested. "I'm only back for ten days."

But now that gorgeous fat girl was passing a few yards away. "Have a great summer!" And though it wasn't clear amid the throng whom she meant, the three of them must have looked like a travesty of a family, the parents scarcely more than teenagers, their spacing slightly off. Jolie could see only one way to smash the picture. "Uh, Mom? Wasn't there supposed to be a lunch or something?"

"No, you're right." Mom reached out to tuck a stray hair behind her daughter's ear, a gesture that at first seemed grateful but was maybe just proprietary, because out of nowhere she was turning to tell Dad he might as well come along and account for himself over a meal like civilized people. "Unless of course you have somewhere better to be . . . ?"

The ensuing stare-off would find Jolie trying to melt into the sidewalk; the sidewalk actively resisting; and these unimaginable lovers, her parents, grappling silently past the moment when Mom might have backed out or Dad backed down. Then came that curious flush again beneath his tan. "This is all the baggage I brought with me, Sarah. So unless there's something else you need to go back for, I reckon go ahead and lead on."

THE RESERVATION was at one of those Szechuan caverns on Lexington, though booking ahead had hardly been necessary: this deep into lunchtime, they could have taken any two tables in the dining room and shuttled Jolie back and forth in between. Still, the fiction that everyone had outgrown bitterness entailed Mom upgrading the reservation to a single party of five . . . that is, herself and Jolie and Dad, plus Nana and Albert, already waiting at the larger table with foreboding looks, as if their opinion of Ethan Aspern had sunk even lower than Mom's.

Or interesting question, actually: Does the absence of any love to begin with lessen the eventual hatred? Seated there under a canopy of upside-down umbrellas, Jolie would have plenty of time to consider. Albert, to her right, seemed determined to proceed as if Dad, to her left, wasn't there, while Nana's insistence on a round of dumplings to start seemed equally punitive, insofar as it would prolong the meal. It fell to Mom to keep the shuttlecock of small talk aloft. At intervals, some remark about Jolie's essay or the upcoming pennant race would sail forth into the ether. But even a noisier space couldn't have drowned out the lack of reply. And that was before Dad excused himself, ostensibly to visit the men's room, and came back with his sunglasses still on. Nana reached for the duck sauce, sending a brisk little jiggle through the Lazy Susan's tchotchkes. The central air, cycling to life, clacked the umbrellas softly together. In the end, Jolie would have to nudge him, touch fingers to temples. He mimicked the gesture and in so doing discovered the sunglasses and removed them. "Sorry, honey," he said, sotto voce. "Must be a bit jetlagged still."

At which point, as if to curtail further embarrassment, Albert hoisted onto the table a yellow shopping bag he'd had at his feet. "We felt sorry about missing your big moment, Jolie, so we ducked into the Strand for a birthday present."

"Geez, guys. What did I say about this? Besides, my birthday's not for another week."

Far from dragging him down from Olympus, retirement had wafted her grandfather higher into those realms of tweedy abstraction where even the rattle of ice cubes in his glass could count as raw emotion. "Go ahead, Jolie, open it."

"Go on, dear," Nana said.

The book inside was a slim brown hardcover, sans jacket. Mircea Eliade. *The Myth of the Eternal Return.*

"Your mom said you've been interested in this sort of thing," Albert said.

Yet how to explain the last ember of Jolie's interest being snuffed at precisely that moment, except to say that the number of people poking around in her inner life had grown insupportable? "Really, you guys didn't have to get me anything. But it's great, thanks."

"Well, we didn't want you to think we'd forgotten," Nana said.

"Amid all this other mishegoss," Albert added.

She was just starting to worry again what Mom might have let slip, and to whom, when Dad leapt in defensively. "Don't think for a second I forgot, either, honey. In fact, that's the other reason I came here."

"Oh, not you, too," said Jolie, since the indiscriminacy of his gifts—violin, socks, the box of his mother's old music—had a way of drowning out the recipient. "Can't you just donate to something in my name?"

"No, listen, the great anti-materialism campaign of 2010, I remember that, I respect it. But my thinking was . . . your birthday's the third, right? I've got a hotel room in Brooklyn till the fifth, and in between is the holiday. So why don't you come spend one of those nights with me? We could see some music, hit that place Roberta's for pizza, or however you wanted to celebrate."

There was a fifty percent chance he was ad-libbing and a fifty percent chance a full-blown sleepover had been his goal all along and he'd just confabulated the rest of his comeback tour. At any rate, half of what he was peddling here was bogus, but Jolie's main concern was to slip through in one piece. Maybe, she said. We'll see.

At which point Mom tried to change the subject. "Hey look, fortune cookies, who wants one?"

But her father remained that rare personality type, impulsive-compulsive, meaning no matter how lightly he'd gotten onto a thing, he couldn't let it go. "Sorry, did I miss the part where we finished our entrées? Jolie's barely touched her pork."

Mom seemed unmoved. "I'm just trying to be polite, Ethan. You and I can debate the wisdom of a formal custody visit later, but you know this isn't the time or place."

"Hang on, though. Isn't your whole line that Jolie is old enough now to make her own choices?"

"She's thirteen, Ethan."

In the pause that followed, Nana could be heard rubbing a pair of chopsticks together beneath her napkin, as if to start a diversionary fire. Then Albert, who'd been brooding over his fortune, slid back his chair and rose to the full majesty of his five feet eight inches. "An army of waiters, and where are they when you need them? I'll just go and rustle up the check. Or was someone else going to pay for all this . . . No? Didn't think so."

After a few seconds, Nana's napkin dropped to her plate. "Let me just go see if Al needs help."

But then she didn't move. Jolie could feel the knot of her earbuds in her skort's pocket, like a tether to an Earth One just out of reach. "Yep, this sure is fun," she said. "Let's be sure to all do this again sometime in the near future."

"It isn't something to be flip about," Mom said. Meaning *Go easy on your grandparents*, but now Dad had his wish: everything had become about him.

"My point exactly," he said. "It's a serious proposal I'm making."

"Ethan, I might have believed that if you could live up to even the most minimal expectations of a serious person—like calling ahead before you come flying across the country."

"Can't you see I'm trying here, Sarah? The flight's not something I undertake lightly; you know the kind of budget I'm on . . ."

Having lost the thread, Mom tried to recover with a flourish of open-mindedness. "Jolie, is a sleepover with your dad something you feel strongly about?"

"You're right," she answered quietly, "we can discuss it another time."

"Why not now, with us all in one place?" Dad said.

"Because I feel a little ambushed, Dad, is why. Is there even a spare bed where you're staying?"

For the third time, he reddened (though perhaps an hour of open hostility from his old in-laws had at last sunk in). "We can fix it in the mix, as they say. Come for the Fourth, we'll go walk the bridge, catch the fireworks from up there . . ."

Nana was giving Mom the tiny headshake of the third-base coach—which, when Dad noticed it, became less subtle. "We'd talked about that trip to Montreal this year, Sarah, remember?"

"Canada? For Fourth of July? Eleanor, honestly, does Jolie even have a passport?"

Jolie loved her grandmother (and in fact did have a passport) but it was oddly gratifying to see her wrongfooted like this. "Well, we *did* talk about it," Nana huffed.

"Listen," Mom said, with finality. "I should have mentioned this earlier, but I've arranged for us to spend Jolie's birthday out at Montauk. It was supposed to be a surprise. A girls' weekend, just the two of us."

What the phrase "girls' weekend" conjured for Jolie was the furthest thing from excitement—turbans made of towels, coins of cucumber over the eyes—and this was the first she'd heard of it. Yet the effrontery paled next to Dad's, so when Mom said she was glad, really, to see him taking an interest but he should have given advance notice, Jolie kept her trap shut.

As she would five minutes later under the awning outside, when he buttonholed her to ask if he could at least walk her home. She looked around for backup, but Albert had withdrawn to the Volvo, and Mom, debating with Nana the relative merits of the Henry Hudson and the Transverse, seemed not to hear. "Dad, seriously. That's like four miles, at least."

"Just to Union Square, then, and I can be your chaperone on the train."

She could physically feel the air leaving her body. "Who said anything about needing a chaperone to go on the train? You're the one arguing how mature I am."

"Cicerone, sorry. I only meant the ride would give us a chance to catch up."

"I'm sure Mom has thoughts . . . ," she said.

But Mom was just turning to say it sounded like a reasonable request. "You have your key, sweetheart? I'll meet you back at the apartment." Then, as if this were secretly her daughter's wish, she slid into the car's backseat and was whisked away by a light, leaving Jolie the very thing she was suddenly keenest to avoid: alone with her dad.

It was that post-lunch hour in warmweather Manhattan when office workers struggle to stay awake and even the traffic dies a little. As she walked, she could hear the scuff of her own sneakers on the pavement; it had never occurred to her that their name might be onomatopoetic: *Chuck*. Then he tried to loop an arm through hers, and she flinched.

"Sorry. Forgot about your shoulder."

It was the slip she'd been waiting for. "So she did call to talk about the shoulder, huh? And the bump on the head, too, I'm guessing . . ."

A minute passed. "Honey, listen. You can't really have expected your mother to keep something that serious from me, right?"

"As serious as getting dinged by loose debris?"

"As serious as being on the wrong side of an oncoming train."

And oh, how she hated the way he called her mother "your mother." The way he made the whole thing sound like a crisis rather than a lapse. "And that's the real reason you came back? Mom telling you?"

She waited for a denial, but he just said, "Don't hold it against her, Jolie. It was a hundred percent true about her not knowing my plans. We're just trying to figure out how to give you what you need."

She turtled deeper into her jacket. What she needed was for everyone to stop acting like the return of Ethan Aspern could mean anything but further misery. There were six other kids with divorced parents in her homeroom this year, and you didn't see any of *them* having meals together, except Enzo's, and Enzo's dad was gay. But to say that aloud would have been to abandon a principle. *Chuck. Chuck.*

"You had to have been terrified down there," he continued. "I know I was when I heard. And regardless of the party line, I was thinking you and I could figure out a way to steal some time to get together, like you said, before I have to go back to Avalon. Even if it's just going for walks like this."

"What, so you can make sure I don't chase a ball in front of a truck or something?"

"Is that such a terrible thing for a father to want?" He seemed to brood on it for a moment. "But look, there's something I need to make sure of first," and the gap that followed was just long enough for her to think: Anything else. Let it be literally anything else besides this. "It *was* an accident, right?"

"Jesus Christ, Dad. How can you even ask a thing like that?"

"Well, okay, then. It's not an accusation. Just . . . I have my reasons."

"You're a poetry person, you ever hear of this guy Larkin?" she heard herself say. "We read him in English last semester. He has this one poem, it starts, like, 'Parents, they fuck you up.'"

Intending to alleviate a pressure, she had somehow only made it worse. "Honey, I practically *wrote* that poem," he was saying. "The thing is, in certain key familial respects, maybe you and I aren't so different . . ."

"It's been three years since you took off without me, Dad. I don't know why you'd expect me to know the first thing about the way we are or aren't alike, much less where it comes from."

"I guess you never got around to watching that video of my mom's, then? The big quote-unquote requiem? *Other People?*"

Great, just her luck: not a mixtape, but a whole fucking DVD's worth of origin-story, yet scratched beyond playability.

"Anyway, what do you want me to say here, Jo? Sooner or later, you're going to have to try a little understanding."

"And let me guess, you thought you could just show up and it would magically happen?" They'd reached Park now, where from a couple blocks down, a bus was approaching. She was amazed to realize again that there was no decisive moment—only a before and an after. And still, crazily, she almost yielded to her earlier longing to let him pull her back in, press her face against his chest and smell his smell. "Look, you've obviously come a long way and spent a ton of money to be here, but if my needs are the issue for once, then what you can give me is my fucking space, okay?" She could feel a busload of reinforcements arriving behind her. "Which doesn't cost you anything, which is free. Maybe I'll feel differently when you're back out in La-La Land or whatever, and we can talk. But meantime, best of luck with your other business."

"What other business?" he said, as she mounted toward the stone-faced driver. She didn't look back, though, since nowadays the knife she'd sought to twist seemed double-bladed—meaning there was no way to jam it any deeper into her dad without bringing more pain upon herself.

IN THEORY, AT LEAST, the big draw of a weekend getaway on Long Island's East End was proximity to the city; you weren't completely cut off from your air supply, noxious though it may have been. But what Jolie would come to discover, that weekend she turned fourteen, was that you also weren't getting far enough away for meaningful escape. Here she was in hour four of a three-hour drive, for example, and it was like, lane closure for road work: check. Absence of verifiable roadworkers: check. Fender-bender as result of said lane closure, banksters in white BMWs standing red-faced and bluetoothed on the shoulder of the L.I.E.: check, check, check. And here came the Tea Party on the radio again, trying to blow up the government, because socialism. Albert's diesel-powered Volvo was a dinosaur, comparatively, but as she manually cranked her seat back down to watch the dirty clouds scroll by, she couldn't shake the sense of her own malady stretching all the way to Montauk—of everyone both fleeing the nightmare of history and crammed with it to bursting.

Though was this maybe the teensiest bit dramatic? The town, once they reached it, would seem placid enough. Ornamental roses and a grassy commons with a gazebo and a duck pond and folks reading salmon-colored broadsheets on porches with gay-pride windsocks and oaken No Vacancy signs. Mom had booked on short notice, apparently, because they ended up at a poured-concrete motor lodge right across the main drag from the public beach.

Apart from a miasma of Lemon Pledge, their room might have been untouched since the fifties. The bedsteads were brassy, the comforters synthetic, the carpet the deep crimson of an anchorman's jacket. And back near the bathroom was a high counter with barstools that looked superfluous until she spied the little hobbit-door of a minifridge underneath. She waited for Mom to go shower before taking a chance. Inside was a moldy hamburger still in its wrapper. But then, farther back . . . paydirt: a crumpled McDonald's bag full of airplane bottles, two brown and one clear plus some vile, apple-green elixir. Water rushed on behind the pasteboard wall; her mom wouldn't be out for several minutes. But just as she was about to expropriate the bottles to her bag, her phone's buzz on the nightstand startled her. She shut the fridge, took the phone out to the breezeway, slung herself down in an

Adirondack chair. Even this far east, it was still so bright out at eight p.m. that she had to strain to make out the backlit number—doubtless Dad, whose messages had grown increasingly plaintive as his time in New York wound down.

> Hey—was just thinking maybe we could start over, tabula rasa.

Three more days of no response, she reminded herself, and he's out of your life for good. Which was when she noticed that the sender was a string of digits with an unfamiliar area code. She stared at it as though, with enough concentration, it might resolve into language, a name. Her personal rule was, if you had to text *Who is this?* to someone, that was a person you shouldn't be texting. The phone bestirred itself.

> I never meant to steal yr violin or anything

> Was just playing the good samaritan.

Oh, God. Not Dad, but . . . that boy from the hospital? She'd done her best to blot this out: his eyes with their glimmery intensity, the blinks that seemed to arrive at premeditated intervals. He'd been the first person to whom she'd out-and-out lied about her mental state. But then, he hadn't totally leveled with her either; he'd said nothing, for instance, about having finagled her number.

> Anyhow, just wanted to say, my bad back there. Hope yr feeling a bit more yrself.

"Jolie? What are you doing?" said her mom, who'd been standing in the doorway for some unspecified period, watching.

Jolie dropped the phone in her lap—and again had that sense of being mugged by reality. "Gah! Would you put something on?"

"It's not like you haven't seen me in a two-piece before."

"It's not me I worry about," she said. "There are other guests."

But how had she missed this? Those hours on the exercycle had left Mom, never far from beauty, looking positively glamorous. "I thought we could hit the pool," she was saying.

"Who showers *before* swimming?"

"And then walk to get seafood or something. I know the expressway was a grind, though, so I won't be offended if you didn't feel like going out."

Even more unnerving than the swimsuit was the care being taken with Jolie's feelings here. "Or we could just raid the fridge," she snapped. "There's like half a Big Mac the last guests left." For a second, she almost wanted the booze to be found and confiscated, her decisions all made for her . . . but then, that wasn't her mom's M.O., was it.

"No one cleaned it out? Geez, honey, let me call and complain. The place had decent enough reviews online."

She was instantly ashamed. "I'm just messing, Mother. No pool for me tonight, but I guess I'd be willing to go to dinner . . . Of course that's assuming you brought any actual clothes to wear."

THEY HAD TO ROAM only a few blocks to find Mom's favorite, shrimp scampi, which she would insist on ordering for them both. And maybe it was the salt air, or maybe just the low expectations, but after months of diminished appetite, Jolie was shocked by the animal pleasures of the meal. Possibly they weren't even anything special out here; possibly in olden times, back when Mom was still riding waves, the whole Hamptons economy had rested on these high-lipid fruits of the sea—large families of Catholic fishermen roistering in taverns on Fridays as furtively Jewish mothers and daughters hunkered by candlelight. Mom disappeared briefly, and soon after, the kitchen staff came out bearing a wedge of sweaty cheesecake impaled on a candle. Having momentarily forgotten she'd be fourteen at midnight, Jolie didn't even totally hate it when the whole restaurant began to sing.

Back at the motel, she would use her birthday's imminence or immanence to push for a half-hour of MTV. And though a series of Frankfurt School sighs issued from Mom's side of the room, you couldn't go to the shore and not watch *Jersey Shore*, Jolie pointed out. It was like trying escargot in Paris. It was a when-in-Rome thing.

Then the tube was off and the climate unit filling the dark with its metallic smell yet somehow failing to dent the humidity. Her preferred sleeping position was a cocoon, but she ended up atop the comforter (so called), which stuck to her arms and legs each time she pivoted toward a cool patch. What the AC did provide was some auditory cover when at last she rose. Going for air should have been no biggie, but in Mom's mind the protective forcefield of New York extended only as far as the Hudson and East Rivers . . . and so those aspects of the room that had seemed the most outmoded now revealed themselves to have merely been awaiting this moment: the noise-absorbing shag; the analog lock that, when Jolie pulled it tight, gave a tiny, intimate click.

Outside, a guy with a military haircut and a neck tattoo and a bleached-blond lady ten years his senior were drinking beer in the turquoise lozenge of the pool. Jolie followed the breezeway around to the building's dark side and took some stairs down to the grass. She would hardly notice the burrs accumulating in her laces; she was surging out ahead of herself, the deathless riff to "Won't Get Fooled Again" pummeling her brain. The blacktop wasn't even black, actually, but brown shading to yellow under a line of sodium lights. In one direction, where the shoreline dog-legged east, lay the grand estates. In the other, lights dwindled to an emptiness of woods. Or not quite emptiness; a motorbike revved behind the trees. She focused on the concrete barrier that edged the beach, its stenciled warnings and jayvee graffiti and the gap sliding through. A quick hypotenuse, and the couple sucking face in the pool would never notice her, much less the airplane bottle jouncing in the pocket of her Umbros.

And then the beach at night, like an Etch A Sketch lately erased. All the caprices of the tourist season, the little civilization pitching itself daily against the tides, had been shaken down to dark water and a shelf of slate-gray sand. Farther along she passed an exposed pipe carrying God knew what out to sea. She'd been earnest enough in pleading with her father for space, yet now that she had it, she got out her phone. There were no new messages, but pulling up the last took her back to the moment of receiving it, the butterflies she was now determined to power through . . . because the time to text *Who is this?* was of course when you already knew who it was. She thumbed it in.

> Who is this?

It was 11:23, according to the little clock at the corner. The boy would be asleep—not that it mattered. But before she could decide that this was all another mistake, the phone made a double pulse.

> Who's this? Its Grayson.

> From Bellevue.

Grayson, right. She now got what had happened: tapped by that one intake nurse to schlep her violin along to his writing-therapy group, he'd started to worry she wouldn't show and copied her number off the "If Lost . . ." tag inside. For some reason, she no longer felt this as a violation. Nor could she account for her impulse to fudge her coordinates, except that, given his apparent affinity for Woody Guthrie, she didn't want to come off as part of the whole Hamptons haute-bourgeoisie.

> Hey, Grayson from Bellevue.

> Greetings from the Jersey Shore.

His reply arrived almost instantly.

> The Dirty Jerz!

> What u doing down the shore?

Asking myself the same question, she thought. But apparently she'd been overtaken by someone to whom answers came more easily.

> Practicing non-attachment.
> Watching TV with my mom.
> Plus GTL, obvs.

A package tour in other words.

She scrambled for some authenticating piece of Jerseyana.

> Exactly. "See the Beautiful Carnage Light."
> *Barnaget Light.
> Damn you, AutoCorrect.

Google Maps is showing me "Barnegat" tho

he wrote.

With the e in the middle

Then, gratifyingly:

But what do those assholes know.

Plans for the 4th?

> Honestly? Probably more of the same.

She had already hit send when she realized it had been an invitation. He wrote:

Not in the city, got it.

Hardly time to sort anything on my end anyway.

Just home from Putney. (Boarding school.)

> They let you back out, huh?

A disconcerting lag here. Had she said something wrong?

> After we met that day in the dayroom, I mean.

Oh. That was just my spring break.

But speaking of which . . . how's yr head?

> Good as new.

> Must be all that journaling.

> You?

Nothing the drugs won't fix. 😉

There followed a longer pause, during which whose turn it was to text became gradually unclear. She was reminded of how she must look, the breeze bleeding through her shirt, a lit slice of screen: a girl on the beach with her phone.

> Someone should make a Top 10 List:
> Most overrated NYC holidays.

For shizzle.

New Year's, San Gennaro, Brooklyn-Queens Day. (Actual thing, btw.)

What am I missing?

> Um.
> St. Patrick's Day? Earth Day?

She had almost added *my birthday* when she realized that a logical follow-up might involve him asking her age. Then again, why was she worrying how she came off to a stranger? She swept through a matrix of icons to find one of a sleepy cat.

I'm boring you.

No! Just tired, is all.

Long drive to get out here today.
Crazy traffic on the expressway.

*Parkway.

Still, it's minutes to midnight,
I should let you turn in.

Yeah, let me let you go,
as my Nana likes to say.

Heh.

His descents to the vulgate felt strained—an old, trying to meet her on her level—but later she would have to admit to herself that she'd chosen to ignore this.

Good to hear from you, though,
Grayson from Bellevue.

Likewise. Keep it crunk, homie.

*Jolie.

Which was another thing he must have gone to some lengths to procure, she realized, as her energy saver preferences dimmed and then killed the phone, leaving her once again alone and defenseless and fourteen on the beach. She didn't recall ever having given him her name.

SHE HADN'T FORGOTTEN, of course, that the Montauk trip was a kind of bribe, meant to distract from her subway disaster and Dad's return. Apprised of his ongoing campaign for a visit, Mom had seemed as eager to facilitate Jolie's nonresponse as she'd been careful not to endorse it. But the thing about bribery and distraction is: they work. By day, she and Mom drowsed and read and ate, hit the cineplex and the lemonade hut and the one ice cream parlor with the coconut chip; swam in the ocean and the pool and then bathed until she felt like a photo being cycled through solutions, growing more and more solid with each. Yet it was this time after Lights Out that she found herself looking forward to—this pocketing of another bottle for courage, this catlike slipping out to the breezeway where the hot damp salt-smelling air pressed itself upon you in waves. And then the beach, a blackness you never got in the city, that sense of exposure in its full range of meanings, as if she were no deeper than the surface of her own skin, the tips of her own fingers reaching out to coax light from the dark.

Grayson had suggested they move their conversation onto Facebook, claiming it would be more private. And his idiom, which had seemed a bit blunt in person, turned out to be made for this, basically, because there was so little nuance to be lost in translation. Mostly he just wanted to hear what she'd done that day, or gathered from her dips into *The Myth of the Eternal Return*—her general state of mind, she figured, which by Sunday night he'd condensed into an all-purpose opener:

How's life in the Garden State?

To which she replied, trying to wax philosophical without sounding naïve,

Same as it ever was.

And because Grayson, being male, would expect some reciprocity, she went on from there:

And how are things in the glittering heart of it all?

Grayson Aplanalp
Eh. You know. Mustn't grumble.

She could almost hear his intonation, hanging at the exact midpoint between earnestness and parody. Somehow, without seeming to actually choose anything, he'd made her the one in charge of generating a current. Which she learned to do by simple alternation. Half the time, she played glib, coy, sardonic—a natural gift of girls her age, but one she now polished to a high shine. If he tried to message her before dinner, she might pretend to be too busy to reply, and even later, in the dark, she would occasionally let the screen blink off, let her mind fill with the ocean hurling itself forward before pulling back into the void. At such times, she could almost convince herself that she was someone she wasn't, clever and distant and not really giving a fuck about the nexus of technology and capitalism and death. But then the phone would blink with another message, pinging the night to see if she was still in it. And having managed to knock Grayson off balance, she would go the other way, flood him with intimacies he never really sought. Just now, for example, she was explaining that her dad, from his self-imposed exile in California, had surprised her last week by showing up at her school, angling for a visit. And how she'd been blowing him off ever since.

Jolie Aspern
You asked me what I'm doing down here. I guess I'm running out the clock on his return. Freezing him out or whatever. Maybe for good.

Grayson Aplanalp
You sound pissed.

Jolie Aspern
Well, he's been somewhat of a flake, historically.

Grayson Aplanalp
Flake? Or dick?

The Venn diagram was a bit of a mess, she allowed after a minute, fighting a sense of disloyalty.

Grayson Aplanalp
But it's yr Mum yr with now, yeah?
She cool, at least?

She found herself risking more, yet pleased with it, almost.

Jolie Aspern
Once upon a time I think she was. Honestly?
I think she needs to get laid.

Grayson Aplanalp
As who among us doesn't?

And, three minutes later:

Grayson Aplanalp
Still there?

Even at their edgiest, though, these exchanges had a Nerf quality that chafed as much as it reassured. She sometimes noticed herself thinking of Magic 8 Ball and Ouija, and of ELIZA, the chat-bot she'd spent hours talking to at the library in sixth grade: Grayson on his island, her on hers, and how to bridge the distance between them when, for one thing, she had no way to verify he wasn't shading certain facts, too, and when, for another, the incoming messages felt more like ideas bubbling up from inside the terminal of her own being? The thing that made it real, the thing that seemed both the safest and the least guarded, was when he would use her name. She'd never liked to see it written out, this French word for "pretty," which would have been a perfectly normal name in Lagos (she was given to understand), but not in the good old U.S. of A. But Grayson, with his matter-of-factness, made "Jolie" feel new and strange, a referent encompassing both the girl who not so long ago had had thoughts of packing it in and the fiercer figure she might yet become.

AND WAS SHE? Pretty, that is? On the evening of their last night in
Montauk, while Mom took a valedictory lap in the pool, Jolie stood
in the bathroom, considering. Her hair, which she'd always felt
to be mousy, had lightened a shade in the sun. She pulled it into a
streaky knot atop her head and made, in the mirror, a face just shy
of fishlips. Then actual fishlips. Then dropped the towel, trying to
catch herself before the filters snapped into place, to see herself as
she might appear to someone out beyond her own head—to a boy.

And if the thought here was calming, it was because for a while
now she'd been worried she might be gay. Even at the store where
she'd found her new swimsuit—with the porno-chic posters and
the electroclash soundtrack Nana registered in a series of deco-
rous winces—Jolie had wondered at the flutter inside her ribs.
She'd had to remind herself that she didn't want to fuck these
models, so much as to *be* them. Yet when she'd pulled the clasp-
less white two-piece from the bag back home, it had carried all
the erotic charge of a spent balloon. Her sudden sense of the ten
thousand other baffled girls who were the fools in this particular
marketplace, the ten thousand other moments of deflation, was
softened only by a nagging awareness of the further ten thousand
girls in Bangalore or wherever whose tiny fingers had probably
done the stitching. And so she hadn't revealed to Mom even now
that she'd brought a bikini of her own. Had continued to wear
the menstrual racing Speedo, right up to this moment of double-
checking the lock and looking back over her shoulder at the mirror. The hips she'd used her thrift-store jacket to hide were not,
in this context, displeasing, but otherwise all the soreness of the
last year had left her with like a junior B cup at best. She was just
balling some Kleenex from the vanity when Mom knocked on the
door. "Honey, it's getting dark out. Show's going to start soon."

Another thing about Montauk: it claimed to have the best fireworks east of NYC. Grayson's reply, when she'd mentioned earlier her love of a grand finale, had been succinct:

Send pics?

And though it seemed likely he was referring only to fireworks,
still: that left a nonzero chance he wanted to see more.

"Just a minute," she yelled now through the door, trying to keep cool but maybe overshooting and landing somewhere near annoyed. This much did seem certain: there was nothing cute about how the bikini top had to be rolled off like a wad of panty-hose. Somehow it fixed the trouble with her chest, though. She was just small enough to crook an arm around. Or crook and sort of cup, simultaneously; she knew it would be the flourish of modesty that read as sexy. She downed the last of the green airplane bottle and held the phone out at arm's length, lens turned toward her and slightly elevated for the best angle, and then pouted just slightly before pressing the button.

No, damn. Finger over lens. She snapped another picture, and another to give herself options . . . and then one last one with the bottom half-off like the Coppertone girl. Then she tugged it back on and reversed the camera to check the results. A second knock.

"Jolie? I'd really rather not watch from the breezeway here."

None of the images looked like her, was the thing. But maybe that was good? Or maybe she simply didn't know how she looked. Maybe all along she'd been a different Jolie than she'd thought. One who could swipe and click send and not feel the least bit creepy or weird.

Still, here on Earth Two, the place where you'd already come within seconds of killing yourself, shame was ubiquitous as oxygen. The permission structure as she'd understood it was Mutually Assured Destruction: you gave the boy something over you, but he was supposed to give you something over him, too. And though there were certain mysteries of sexting she'd been eager to get to the bottom of (Was the convention, e.g., for him to have his junk covered, or al fresco? And then rampant, or couchant?), his reply kept not coming—so what if her body and its urges, rather than luring Grayson in, had driven him away in disgust?

A thud sounded through the wall: the first municipal shell out over the ocean or just some freelancer closer in. The knob jiggled. "Honey?"

"I said give me a minute, goddammit!"

But the clairvoyance of old hotel rooms could cut both ways, it seemed, for the lock knew just when to give out, and as the door swung open, here was Jolie, shielding her scanty bosom. Another thud as the door hit a wall, troubling the mirror, but at least she'd managed to put the contraband back in her bag—no, wait. Damn.

"What is in that bottle, Jolie?"

"It's nothing." Jolie tried not to breathe as she set it down.

"Excuse me?"

"I'm stating a fact. It's empty." She was just making a bid for open space when Mom grabbed her arm, hard enough to leave marks. Jolie had a sudden sense of talons, feathers, some mythical thing that could lie dormant for years but when awakened was pure fire.

"After all we've said about this? You're in here getting loaded?"

The facts looked sufficiently bad that the impulse was to meet Mom's fire with her own, fight back until only one of them was left to soldier on. Yet there remained in the background the whole problem of April. Of the train that seemed to have split her life in two—and exactly how much she'd meant to end it. And who knew what would happen now if her public self and her private one, just millimeters apart, were to cross. No, the drinking had to result from rather than precede the trauma, Jolie decided. For post-traumatic stress could say nothing about her, personally; post-traumatic stress, in America, in 2011, was the new normal. She gestured toward the minifridge. "Have it your way. This thimble-ful was in there with the burger. I thought it might take the edge off, like a Xanax. I've had an awful lot to deal with lately, as you might remember."

And you could almost see it happening, the wings refolding, Mom forcing herself to accept what, for complex reasons, she obviously couldn't bear to probe too deeply. She took the bottle. Scrutinized the label. "Oh, honey, shit, though. Is *this* why you've been slipping out at night? I'm not saying it hasn't been a hard year, but this . . . ? This is exactly what you *can't* do. You with your family history. At thirteen."

"Fourteen."

Into the pocket of Mom's jeans went the bottle. "You know what? I think when we get back to the city it's time to call that number."

"What number?" Jolie said. But of course she already knew: the referral from the hospital had been her hole card for a while now. And honestly, maybe the idea of sharing her subjectivity with a professional wasn't as awful as it had once seemed. At least not compared to the alternative, which was to continue to watch it get stripped away like this, piece by piece.

4

THE ORIGINAL CONCEPT—Magnolia's, anyway—had been for Ethan to drive. Before coming to the Casa, she'd left a jeep in a friend's carport in Van Nuys, she said, and though it could probably use a jump-start (and to be honest, with a couple hundred k on the odometer, was at this point held together with baling wire and wishful thinking), she was hereby putting the keys at his disposal. Or *their* disposal, rather. "We can take turns at the wheel while the other one sleeps it off in the backseat."

Ethan didn't know how to respond; he'd expected her to still be steaming at all his artful indirection around the past; the one benefit of his ex-wife's call, from a certain angle, should have been to spare him the hassle of disillusioning her. But he'd seen this in meetings: a true story had a transfixing power that, once you began to unfold it, got hard to control. It seemed a particular mistake to have mentioned his suspicions about his daughter's alleged "accident" in the subway. He wouldn't repeat it by going into chapter and verse about his missing license. The blood was still up in Magnolia's cheeks, her nostrils slightly flared. Somewhat distressingly, she refused to change out of his bathrobe.

"If we can get the engine started now, we're in Times Square by noon Wednesday," she told him, "like Han and Chewie making one last run at the Death Star."

"Magnolia, my problems don't have to be your problems."

"The hell they don't. What's that thing people say in the program? 'Be of Maximum Service'?"

"I appreciate the sentiment, really. You'll never know how heartening it is at a moment like this to feel that someone's in your corner . . . But doesn't air travel seem more reliable? Probably cheaper, too, when you get down to it—"

"And what were you planning to do once you got there? Have you given it the slightest thought?"

She had a point: in the hour since Sarah had hung up on him, his mind had been consumed with an almost molecular drive to eliminate the three-thousand-mile gap between himself and his little girl . . . the rest he could tackle one day at a time. But Magnolia was getting at something else entirely.

"I saw you twitching along with my music last night, and that was just *The Well-Tempered Clavier.* So what are you going to do when you're walking home after a dinner or something with your daughter and all of a sudden you hear a jukebox wafting 'Under Pressure' from a bar? You like to play the bodhisattva, Ethan, two steps farther along than everybody else, but when was the last time you even attended a meeting?"

"I never could find one that didn't make me feel uncomfortable," he protested. "All that so-called fellowshipping, on and off for years, but every time I get up to speak all I hear is me me me. I'm self-obsessed enough already, you know? Which may have been the issue to begin with."

"It's like you're playing the record backward, though. My brother was right: you think you're staying sober under your own power, but really you've just stumbled into this walled garden where you don't have to confront the decision of whether to go get high."

" 'If it works, work it.' "

"I'm saying, how long do you reckon on lasting back there by yourself, with the added stress of fatherhood and an ex it sounds like hates you?"

"I promise you she has her reasons."

"If you come to in a gutter somewhere, do you even have a sponsor you could call?"

"Magnolia—"

"See? I didn't think so. Besides, we can write it off as a professional junket. I've never been to New York. Ethan, let go and let God."

And if there was one place she had him dead to rights, it was his helplessness in the face of a compulsion; he was going to take whatever steps would lead him back to Jolie most efficiently. To wit: though he couldn't afford both airfare and lodging even with the money he'd been saving for her camp—and though he'd sworn to himself never again to lead a woman on—American Express (in pretty much the definition of irrational exuberance) had bumped Magnolia's credit limit up to twelve thousand dollars, enough breathing room to cover her own ticket, she said, plus half of a ten-day stay together at a chain hotel in deepest Brooklyn.

"You can see all that on your phone?"

"Priceline, kemosabe."

"And you realize the credit-card company isn't giving you the money out of the goodness of its heart, right?"

The touchscreen already to an ear, she put a hand where the mic must have been. "I'm calling the agency to see if Showtime left an offer on the table. In a pinch, I can always take the begging bowl around to my brothers and sisters. I mean, what the hell else is family even for?"

IN FACT, it would be the Navy SEAL, Patrick, who ended up watching Rerun and house-sitting the Casa del Sol, either sweetening or wasting his furlough as, unbeknownst to their mutual patron, Ethan and Magnolia streaked through the night at thirty thousand feet. But that sense of everything hurtling toward absolution would last only till the next day, when Jolie announced that she didn't want to see him anymore—as Ethan would doubtless have known already, had he bothered to consult with her ahead of time.

From where she left him near the end of the Shake Shack line after their Szechuan lunch catastrophe, he took a long, digressive walk through the canyons, trying to figure out where he'd gone wrong, and how to break it to Magnolia that she may as well have set her credit rating on fire. Yet when he reached the hotel room at dusk and roused himself to a kind of honesty, she took it remarkably well. Or perhaps, in the *Star Wars* remake she was casting in her head, she'd had herself as the wisecracking rogue all along, and him as the inarticulate Wookiee shaking a hairy fist at the sky.

In any case, as he waited for Jolie to cool down, Magnolia would stay glued to his side, brandishing a visitor's guide disguised as a hipster notebook. She dragged him to what was left of Little Italy, and to St. Mark's Place . . . to feed gulls from the back of a ferry on a futile quest for Staten Island's best pizza . . . but whatever she'd achieved in the way of distraction she would nearly demolish by taking him to the Egyptian wing of the Met, for what people seemed to want most in their tombs, he couldn't help but notice, were a million little effigies of their spouses and children.

She then attempted to cheer him with an overpriced tea in the courtyard of the Plaza, "paid for with points, don't worry. And later we can skimp on dinner." A piano man played torch songs behind a line of palms. A pigeon had somehow gotten in. She kept repositioning the ziggurat of petits-fours so they could see each other whole, but he kept nudging it back, finding it easier to deal with Magnolia in tranches. The whole week was tranches, really, the connections snipped away everywhere he'd drifted into worry or anxiety or dream over the messages Jolie continued not to return. Oddly, the overall effect would resemble nothing so much as the courtship montage from a romantic comedy, right down to these foam-rubber soundstages Magnolia kept managing to unearth from her *Not for Tourists* guide, the generic old fake real New York.

On the last night before he turned tail in defeat, they squeezed at her behest onto the packed Brooklyn Heights promenade to watch the triplicate burst of the fireworks show: in the air, in the obsidian towers of the Financial District, in the still-blacker water below. He felt a story about Sarah and the Brooklyn Bridge and the mid-'90s swelling in his chest, but couldn't find the voice to share it. Car radios blasted Copland and reggaeton from down on the packed BQE, the whole gemütlich waveform of New York syncing itself to the colors. And when at last they returned to the hotel via subway, he undressed with virginal shyness, his back turned, but then would lie awake waiting for her to press her luck one more time.

Or press his luck, maybe—for if she hadn't, he might actually have gotten some sleep that night and displayed better judgment. Might not have ended up in the cramped cubicle of the hotel's purported business center at three a.m., in a final swivet of email-checking to distract from his shame over having given in and fucked her. Or at least might have been able to come clean with her sooner about what he'd found there at the top of his inbox. Instead, he was left to fret over the implications of an email from Sarah in the same bed where Magnolia now snored in a puddle of sex. And by the time a rag of sky started to pale between the blackout curtains, Ethan was surprised to find that his own path had become clear. He felt in his bag for his running shoes, his board shorts and bleachy *Ill Communication* tee, and slipped back out to drop his bag at the front desk; there was a good chance he didn't make it back before checkout. Then he went racing up Eastern Parkway toward downtown's insta-skyline at too fast a clip (he could already tell), but fleeing a sunrise as pretty as the mouth of hell.

FROM THE AMPLE HILLS around Prospect Park, the descent to the waterfront was as much ontological as topographic—like the problem of how to get from Sesame Street to Mordor. After blocks of stately brownstone, you hit the skeleton of the elevated Smith/Ninth station, the peeling hulk of the expressway, a sulfurous canal that may as well have been a moat . . . and abruptly the beergardens and cafés of Strollerville gave way to scrap-heaps and salt yards and vacant lots fuzzed with ailanthus. Now that the sun was up, only a blue dome of heat seemed to connect the two Brooklyns. Well, that and the stitch in Ethan's side, the failed metronome of his Nikes on the pavement. Chunks of windshield glass surfaced underfoot, along with spent fireworks from last night and the occasional tampon of tobacco cleft from its blunt. Outside a poultry plant, Cambodian men in piratical high boots reclined on flattened cardboard, seeming not to notice the chickenshit smell or the frantic gabbling within.

Then came sleepy Van Brunt Street and a corner Ethan seemed to remember. On a tenement stoop with a propped-open door, two boys of indeterminate complexion were divvying a bag of fragrant egg sandwiches. He'd already found the illegible buzzers when a bus whooshing past drew his eye to the stoop. The taller of the boys, nearly a man, wore a face that might have been sympathetic were it not so busy trying to seem hard. "You looking for somebody?"

"Yeah," Ethan admitted, counting his breaths. "You know a neighbor here, last name Morales? A tenant?"

"Depends who's asking," the guy said. The stare that followed was too long to be a once-over, but Ethan knew better than to reply. And sure enough, as his cut-rate running costume sank in and made clear he wasn't a cop, a faint amusement seemed to twitch the corners of the kid's mouth, under an equally faint moustache. He scrounged for a key to the inner door. "Six F. There's no elevator, so you know."

Which: of course there wasn't. Nor the mildest zephyr from the vestibule falling away as Ethan mounted toward a square of sooty light. The stairwell was a blast furnace, essentially, its color that charred brown specific to the prewar buildings of New York and certain Detroit-made sedans of the late '70s. On the sixth landing, though, came a retrofitted door, an anomalous little window with three wire-reinforced panes curtained off at eye level. He knocked. Put an ear to the glass; heard quiet within. Touched the painted-over mezuzah for luck, if that was indeed what a mezuzah had to offer, then knocked again, harder. Still, a buzz of fluorescence was the lone response. Probably at work already. It was only as he was reminding himself that he had no plan B—no other way forward—that tumblers began to tumble and the doorway to part to a length of chain, a handsome woman in hospital scrubs blinking through the gap. It took him a second to hold out a hand. "Mrs. Morales? I'm Ethan Aspern."

There was another blink behind her glasses and then, from deeper inside, a ventriloquized groan:

"Oh, cripes, Mami, no. Whatever he's selling, tell him we don't want any. Tell him I gave at the office."

The interior was too dim for the speaker to be seen—meaning, conversely, that Ethan would be lit up for her in all his dishevelment. And even before the door slammed shut, it was feeling like a misstep not to have called ahead. Gingham resettled over the window, immuring him in heat. Another bus rumbled distantly past, or maybe just the same one, dead-ended, turned back toward whence it came.

Then a miracle: along the curtain's left edge, he spotted a tongue of light. Leaning in, he could just make out a sofa, legs, the scrub-clad woman to whom he'd been speaking. With the back of his hand (as if this were somehow more polite), he knocked a third time. A moment distended. Something started to rattle around in there, a coin inside a meter. And when the chain came off, the metamorphosis was complete. Before him stood a petite goddess with wet hair and soy-milk skin, a towel around her neck: Erica Morales, his erstwhile probation officer. "Fucking A," she said, like it was his name, and then frowned. "You need to have your head examined."

"Nice to see you, too," he replied, as somewhere in the dimness the mother sucked teeth.

"It's barely even day out. Did you not hear me say to get lost?"

"Yeah, but people say a lot of things. I remember you saying, for example, that if I ever found myself on the verge of throwing my life away again, to reach out to a sister first."

Her gold eyes flared. Only a single time before had he seen her in street clothes, it occurred to him, and not even then had her hair been down. Always the ponytail. Always the androgynous slacks. Now her ribbed tee seemed not even to conceal a bra—not that he was noticing. "I sure as hell wasn't *inviting you to the crib*," she said. "Just once was a disaster."

"Look, about that: I know I fucked up. And was fucked up, obviously . . . I meant to apologize, or I'd never have sent you those poems. But since you then went ahead and closed my case, no more conflict of interest, right?" With each additional second she kept the door open, the odds seemed to tick in his favor; neighbors would at some point start leaving for the Tuesday commute, and Erica Morales wasn't the type to enjoy her private life laid bare. "A glass of water's all I'm asking," he said. "Five minutes, tops. Then you want me gone? Poof. You never saw me."

As in one of those Impressionist paintings where an apparent purple turns out to be an effect of green and orange, her look moved through shades of impatience and irritation with no real physiognomic shift. The problem remained the body, still barring the way. "How do I know you're not fucked up again this minute? You smell like a circus animal."

"The sweat's just from the run. Humidity outside is pushing eighty percent, and I had to hoof it all the way from East New York. Would you believe Atlantic Avenue now has its own Best Western?"

"You're supposed to be in L.A., though, was our deal. If they knew, Probation could have my balls—"

"So to speak."

"—and Lord only knows how your judge on the custody case would react. You couldn't find some legal clinic to take you on out there?"

With what felt like a mighty effort not to just confess the whole truth, he reminded her, "I can't defend myself if you won't let me in."

A last flicker of scruple, and something seemed to change. "One glass of water, capisce? Ma, Ethan here's an apparition—poof." The mother had moved to the couch-end farthest from the door. He declared it a pleasure and offered his hand again, but Erica forbade her to rise, or him to sit. "He's just passing through."

And indeed, as he trailed her into a darkened hall, he was able to summon surprisingly little of his one other incursion here, the night Obama was elected—the night his sister had wanted him home to attend his father's wake. It was as if all his mnemonic horsepower at the time had been busy not letting on how wasted he'd let himself get instead. A scent of unseen cats, that much matched up, as did the doorway through which he could just glimpse a wedge of damp tile, a showercurtain beaded with droplets, a canted mirror. A memory of a freestanding sink, cool to the touch—or more precisely, of plunging his head into it, his own face dripping in the glass—threatened to recur when a shout sounded ahead. "Keep it moving."

The kitchen was a ship's, not meant for two. A bulb like a hemorrhoid pillow lit a medal at her neck as she set a glass on the wood-grain formica and gestured at the tap like, *Knock yourself out.* A gift from another admirer? A splurge on bling? In any case, it suited her, this softer look. Fatigue, frustration: these suited her.

Yet before the glass could be filled, she was pushing through a screen door in the narrow rear wall. He caught up with her on a fire escape stocked with mismatched flower pots and a lone folding chair. The bricks back here had a baked and jagged look, as if exploded by the heat. On a deep sill beneath the window, a textbook bristled with Post-its. "Geez, this yours?" he said, hefting it.

She pulled the door shut, presumably so the mom wouldn't hear, then cupped hands around her elbows and leaned back, sort of holding herself. "I should warn you up front, I quit the department about a month after I bailed your ass out in South Jersey. So until I pass my actuarial exam, I'm living on unsubsidized loans and whatever of my mother's paycheck she can kick toward rent. In short, there's nothing for you here, Ethan."

"Insurance, though—that's not a career change, it's a midlife crisis."

"What can I say? Adjust a claim, it stays adjusted. But can we please stop pretending to have some ongoing interest in each other's lives?" she said, taking the book back. "Because that would be some wishful-ass shit, even for you."

The vision that had carried him through the dawn—that sense of having seized the wheel and made for open seas—now seemed to dim. "Yet still you felt empowered to give out my work number." He'd planned to keep this in reserve, but when she turned away to fiddle with a loose brick, he kept going. "I mean, that had to be you giving it to Sarah, right? No one else had the landline. But I don't suppose she let on why she wanted to reach me?"

Evidently not, for Erica only stiffened further, pulling a cigarette and some matches from a squashed pack of Kools.

"A courtesy call, Kupferberg edition: she wanted to let me know our thirteen-year-old had nearly been run over by an IRT train. Maybe you heard about it on the evening news? A near-miss, but still."

And now from somewhere in the urban environs came the whizz and pop of a last rocket launched skyward, tearing open new textures in the silence: bugsong in the ragged grass of the courtyard below.

"Try seeing that from my perspective, Morales. There's my daughter on the tracks, people probably screaming and shit. And here's me, three thousand miles away, in the absolute dark, no clue it's even happening. Now, why would a person call and tell all this to her ex-husband, if she didn't expect him to come running? But for some reason my being back has Jolie so pissed she won't so much as answer my texts. Ten days should have been more than enough to fall back into a rhythm, make some amends . . ."

"No, you're right," she said at last, exhaling a long plume of smoke as she held out the open end of her pack.

He hesitated before waving it off. "I am?"

"I'm saying, I should have hung up the second I heard whose ex it was. But what is it you want from me now?"

His appeal to compassion having been to uncertain effect, he switched to that old war-horse, flattery. "You always were the queen of wraparound services, Erica . . ." And when she refused to fill in the blanks: "I'm throwing myself on your mercy here. Seeing as how you came through for me once before, I thought maybe you could help me find a place to stay till I get myself right with my daughter."

No sooner was it out of his mouth than he heard how ridiculous it sounded. Perhaps at three this morning he'd been recalling that Erica had a second bedroom in her apartment, but the presence of her mother (not to mention an interpersonal dynamic he'd pretty clearly misjudged) had more or less put paid to that. And if a short-term rental was what he was after, as she now pointed out, he could always look online.

But for this at least he had an answer. "No browser on my phone, remember?"

"The library has computers, Ethan."

"Which require a library card, tied to a stable address, and as of"—he glanced at where a watch would have been—"as of like an hour from now, when my room key self-destructs, I'm functionally homeless."

There was a pause. "Spend a night in an actual shelter somewhere, maybe we'll talk," she said. "But for now your plan is to what, just eat the cost of the return ticket and stay on?"

" 'Plan' is maybe a little grandiose, but I sure as hell can't leave things the way they are." He swallowed. "Jolie needs me. I can feel it."

"This despite the not-talking."

"You'd understand if you had a kid. Hey, let me see your phone."

Wincing only slightly, she handed it over. He groped his way through to Hotmail, was briefly annoyed to find a solicitation from saintanselms.edu at the top of his inbox (what was Moira thinking, subscribing him to the fundraising list?) . . . but here it was in last night's messages:

> Just so you can't claim to be blindsided, Ethan: I've decided to send Jolie to a therapist after all. Not P.T., but a proper psychologist, or anyway, some group modality that came recommended to me—which we can almost afford. Full disclosure: I caught her sneaking liquor here at the beach. Teen angst, most likely, but given the larger context, you'll understand my need to rule out anything more serious. The deductible's 2k a year, your share is half (reminding you of the address below) or else I can go through the lawyers. Meantime: please stop trying to contact her—or me. Please. Whatever it is you think you can still make better, hanging on like this, you've only been making worse.

His first impression had been of anger, a sign that she still cared. But as he read it again now, that last line seemed as impersonal as an AA bromide. He handed back the phone. "See?"

" 'Teen angst,' she says."

" 'The larger context,' though—"

"What, that you've driven your daughter to drink?"

He'd moved around from the shade of the fire escape to try to see the message from her angle, but now it was Erica's posture that seemed to have changed, like he'd trod on a loose floorboard. Then a throat was cleared—her mother's, inside the screen door—and he hurried back to his former spot. The mother asked something in Spanish, like a grown-up keeping secrets from a child (and it was true that the lone word he recognized was *borracho*). "Yeah," Erica answered, "but can you give us some privacy, Ma? Go get your work shoes on or something. Our five minutes are basically up."

"So this is the way the world ends, huh?" he asked as the mother receded, gloom spreading to fill the screen around her. "All this history between us, and you're not even going to try to help?"

Her gaze intensified, and he had an unwelcome vision of how he must look to her, leaning in his dingy running gear against the low iron rail of the fire escape, where a hand to his chest would be all it took to topple him. Instead, she reverted to small talk, said if the backup number had worked, he must still be employed . . .

If you could call it that, he admitted.

"Food service again, right?"

"Manual labor. Landscaping, mostly. At least till my boss figures out I'm AWOL."

She absorbed this. Looked him up and down. Then: "I can think of exactly one place that might do for a case like yours. Even if it's a long shot. I'm up at Medgar Evers all day, cramming, but let me put in a call and try your cell around dinner."

He drew back out his dumbphone to check the time. "I'm realizing I've got some loose ends I should probably tie up; is there any way you could make it lunch?"

She sighed again in what he took for assent, but was maybe just her way of saying, *Jesus, Ethan* . . .

"Really, though, you don't know how grateful I am."

"It's purely to get you out of my apartment, I swear," she said, flicking her smoke out toward the grass. "And for good this time. You try to contact me again, I put the dogs on you. You understand? No calls, nada."

"Like I said," he said. "I'm getting an awful lot of that lately." And felt almost like a gentleman as he held the door to let Officer Morales precede him into the smallness of her own kitchen.

AND STILL, if he'd had it all to do over, he probably wouldn't have slept with Magnolia. Not that it made any difference—not directly—but apparently he'd been in California long enough to weaken a little on the numinous, the vibrational, and he couldn't help but think that the sex was somehow related to his feeling of having upset the power balance between them. Guilt, was the word. Guilt was back. Guilt-wise, for Ethan Aspern, this whole week was a real shit sandwich.

She was one of those people who'd sleep until noon if she could, so as he entered the room, the blackout curtains admitted only the faintest intimation of day. Heeling his shoes off for stealth, he set down the bag he'd reclaimed from the front desk. Then he padded to the bathroom and unvelcro'd the pocket of his shorts, began laying out the contents by feel on the vanity—ATM card, depleted MetroCard, clutch of wizened bills. The idea was to shower off the stink of almost having ghosted her, but before he could get the door shut, a voice came from out in the sleeping area: "How did it go?"

He peeked back around the jamb. Gradients were now emerging from the blackness, but only after an LED bulb snapped on did he realize she'd been sitting up in bed this whole time, doing something on her phone. The shirts pants bras that had erupted across the room upon check-in must have vanished into the knockoff luggage she'd bought as a souvenir. "How did what go?"

"Your run, dummy. It's supposed to hit ninety-seven today."

"Yeah, but I was down by the harbor. With the breeze, windchill . . ."

"Heat index."

"It wasn't so bad. Been up long?"

"You were noisy going out, and I couldn't fall back asleep. There's no TV to speak of at that hour."

"Right, well. I just figured I'd make one last loop. For old times' sake."

"I thought your old place was in Manhattan."

"Same water, though," he said. And quickly reverted to the packing. "You didn't have to do all this cleanup by yourself."

"That's funny, I was starting to think you were trying to avoid any opportunity to help."

She was propped on her elbows, the sheet stretched across her chest as demurely as a debutante's gown. Yet the bags under her eyes spoke of hungers they'd fed in the night. It was mostly to stop himself from unleashing them again that he blurted, "No, that's a lie, about where I was. The truth is, I can't go back west with you."

"What?"

"While you were sleeping, I got an email from Sarah. A request for money, ostensibly, but really just to tell me she's calling a shrink."

"And that's why you're saying you have to stay? Lots of kids have shrinks, Ethan, and for lots of things. Lord knows Patrick had like six of them after our folks split up."

"That's reassuring, Magnolia, but you're not letting me finish. The reason is, Sarah caught Jolie drinking."

Her look wasn't the alarmed one he expected, more a mingling of concern and disappointment and confirmation: "Like father, like daughter, is the fear."

"If that's how you want to put it . . ."

"Damn. In that case I guess you were right to be worried. But doesn't a therapist put a safety net in place going forward?"

He went to the window, pulled back the curtain, only to be blinded by the sun. How to begin to explain what you couldn't even see? "I'm not sure Sarah gets the scale of the danger, Magnolia. Or is capable of that. You have to understand, she's not . . . like us."

"Ouch."

"Sorry. Like me, I'm saying. But like Jolie too, if this is something I passed on to her. Or if it dragged her down to my level somehow, me having to go away to get sober . . ."

When he turned back, Magnolia was ashen, as if something had knocked the wind out of her.

"Sorry, no, you're probably right," he said. "I'm overreacting. Solipsism again."

"You didn't tell me you were still in love with her, though."

"Jolie? She's my daughter."

"The mom, I mean. Sarah."

He thought about this. "Honestly, I can't be in love with anyone, Magnolia. Love is dangerous for me."

She hardly seemed to hear him. "And still you let me gift you your plane-fare. Among other things." Gesturing to the bed. "I mean, here I was thinking I was a user, but you are the worst. The absolute worst."

I tried to warn you, he wanted to say . . . but was that even true? Or had he just confined himself to vague noises of self-pity?

"Can't you see? This must be a signal we were right to come here after all. A kid that age needs a father."

"Maybe the signal is that a father like you is exactly what she doesn't need. Maybe you're supposed to be setting each other free, you know?"

"Come on, Magnolia. You heard how Sarah sounded when she called that day. And what did you do? What you saw needed doing: came and got me." She looked miserable still, in that way that couldn't be faked. "Here, let me show you something." In a flash of inspiration, he'd knelt to his bag to retrieve one of his two purchases from an hour they'd killed among the waning dollar stalls of Booksellers' Row. The first, weighing down his clothes, was a Mailer omnibus justifiable mainly for its soporific qualities, the way it dissolved upon reading into the Esperanto of dreams. Digging past it, though, he found an elusive little anthology of poems by the Brownings. Maybe so soon after the lunch with Sarah, he'd been looking for the one about the damaged lovers who ended up wanting to strangle each other, but then he'd come upon a sonnet from the Portuguese that had seemed to illuminate something about himself to himself, and in so doing, to physically hurt. Now, in the hideous energy-saving light, he found it again. "Read this one for me."

"Out loud?" She seemed skeptical. "'O Beloved—' . . . What is this, *The Jungle Book*?"

"'Belovèd.'" He wanted her to feel what he had. "Like it really counts."

"'O Belovèd, it is plain / I am not of thy worth nor for thy place! / And yet, because I love thee, I obtain . . . ' This is a little much, Ethan."

"I know, but keep going."

"'. . . I obtain / From that same love this vindicating grace, / To live on still in love, and yet in vain, — / To bless thee, yet renounce thee to thy . . . face'?"

"You see what I mean?"

"Not really."

And suddenly the *saudade* of those last lines struck even Ethan as somewhat ambiguous. Was he the Belovèd, as he'd thought, renounced by Jolie—by Sarah—but secretly being asked to stay?

Or was he the speaker, the unworthy one, which made Jolie the . . . wait, was the poem inviting him to look at this from *Magnolia's* angle? "I'm saying, I've got to hang on here until Jolie at least talks to me. Now come on, I'll ride with you out to the airport. I'd hate for you to miss your plane."

THE SUBWAY would prove even hotter than the street above, and as she stood on the platform peering into darkness, Magnolia seemed to armor herself in silence, girding for further renunciation. As why wouldn't she? Among the old batteries and chicken bones, the Santería leavings strewn along the tracks, there was still plenty of time for Ethan to change his mind, to try to mend what he had broken. Yet as if under some kind of spell, he stayed silent himself until, ten minutes later, they were seated in a cool, bracing cylinder, launching out toward the place where the city ended.

Indeed, his fear that he'd somehow permanently scarred Magnolia may only have been anxiety over his own soul, since once they were in motion, she began to speculate idly about the odds of making the last ferry to Santa Catalina and finally sleeping in her own bed tonight. Or rather, Alan T.'s. And now Ethan was the one who hardly heard, focused as he was on the urban structures winnowing in the heat above him—and the question of what the actual fuck he thought might be accomplished by staying here. He was thirty-three years old, same as Jesus when he died . . . Jesus who, whatever else you wanted to accuse him of, had founded a billion-person religion while setting generally accepted benchmarks for meekness and humility. Well, fatherhood, okay: Jesus hadn't managed that. But had Ethan, really? He felt himself to be a child trapped in some kind of costume, the big suit from *Stop Making Sense*, except instead of the businesswear of his father's generation, he persisted in kitting himself out like an adolescent, leaving his surface self doubly false. And now here they were, rising toward birds wheeling over some graves. A subway poem in a scratchy frame. The text he was waiting for was never going to come, he had just started to think, when the phone, reestablishing contact with the grid, jiggled.

At Howard Beach, almost the entire train departed, lugging duffels and wheelie bags. Magnolia would insist on carrying her own things this time. He braced a hand against the doorframe to let her pass, not expecting the door to close on him. Black streaks bloomed on the sleeves of his shirt. The platform, when he squeezed through, was aflame. He looked up to see her trundling toward the escalators.

A couple of levels above was a Jetsons-style atrium from which you could watch the train you'd just left glide onto a causeway across Jamaica Bay, and ultimately (he shuddered a little) to Sarah's old break over at Beach 116th. The connection to the airport wasn't direct; you still had to board a monorail that would take you to your terminal. Between here and there, a line of gates demanded another swipe of the MetroCard, and he had only a single transfer left. "Magnolia," he heard himself say as she passed through. But with all the travelers rushing around them, she seemed not to hear. He managed to grab the strap of her bag before she moved out of range. "Mags. Wait."

They were blocking the flow of pedestrians through one of the half-dozen inbound lanes, and out of the corner of his eye he could see a neon-vested station agent swelling with institutional importance, preparing to swoop in. "I know I haven't been the ideal partner here, but I just wanted you to know, if I'd had to sit for ten days by myself waiting for Jolie to let me in, I'd probably be in a gutter somewhere as we speak."

"Who's to say you don't still end up in a gutter, though?" she asked. And before he could answer—there was no answer—she said, "Besides, you should know that as far as gardening goes, my thumb is absurdly brown. It's like the thumb of death."

"Wait . . . are you offering to cover for me?"

"I draw the line at straight-up dishonesty, Ethan. If Alan T. asks where you are, I lay the whole mess out for him, to the degree I even understand it." She moved closer to the gate, put her hands to the sides of his face, and studied it long and hard. "But you should know this already: I'll do what I can, for as long as I can."

She could have been the mother in a Folgers commercial, packing her son off to war. And suddenly he could see how much it was costing her, this fortitude in the face of rejection. (In the wake of acceptance.) On an impulse, he took the strap, pulled her to him, kissed her as he hadn't been able to last night—trying for once to give all of himself. Or better: none of himself. "Magnolia, I don't deserve you."

"Oh, Ethan, fuck you, though. That was never for you to decide." Then she put on her shades and shouldered her Llewys-Vultrons and flapped in her sandals toward the tunnel through which he could hear the peculiar non-sound of a monorail, arriving.

THE TEXT HE'D RECEIVED from Erica Morales consisted solely of a name, a time, and an address, the last of which was in the teens, on a residential block that jerry-rigged the slice joints of Sixth Avenue to the designer flagships of Fifth. As he blundered east from the train, he had a feeling like when he used to emerge in his twenties from back-to-back matinees at the AMC Union Square. (Double-header. Trifecta. Superfecta.) It was bright, strangely quieter here than in the tunnels. Building numbers stuttered and jumped alongside him like digits under a roulette ball, and though the address on his phone doubtless corresponded to another half-way house, he couldn't help hoping it occupied one of the older brick three-flats, rather than this quasi-Soviet infill. The right slot failing to eventuate, though, he checked his messages again and saw that he needed to backtrack a hundred feet.

Across the way, where 40 should have fallen ineluctably between 38 and 42, stood a grime-blackened, four-story church. And out front was either the street life he'd been missing or the cause for its disappearance: from an entry gate trailed two queues maybe forty or fifty deep, sorted by gender but jumbled by ethnicity, with every other person seeming overdressed for the heat. He could think of at least one thing that might have drawn this sort of crowd to a church at off hours, and the downtroddenness was about what you'd expect with twelve-steppers, but nowhere did he detect the beatific look of the reformed addict—what he privately called "the white light." At any rate, had there been some mistake? Surely Erica Morales wasn't expecting him to wait in line for another of those infernal meetings.

He edged around to climb the shadowed front steps and breached a door like a bank vault's. The architecture inside might have been Gothic, except that the church (which probably predated the rest of the block by fifty years) had, as the city grew up around it, been starved of sunlight, cast back toward gloomy Romanesque. The rose window was a faint purple above the portico; it was the dark itself that seemed to draw the eye deeper, to gain height and volume the longer he looked. And all of it, pews altar side chapels . . . all of it empty. Had he been allowed to cut the line only because no one else was coming up here?

His spidey-sense tingling even more forcibly—AA invariably met belowdecks—he found a switchback stairway off to the side and pursued a familiar clamor along a subterranean corridor, trying not to knock into asbestos-wrapped pipes. At the end, though, was a large, low room where in addition to the usual chairs, long tables had been set, every place occupied. A smell of ham pervaded. Through a rectangular expediter's window, a half-dozen people zoomed back and forth, attending to what soon became steaming pots and foil containers. He marked a couple of high-school-looking kids; a pair of elderly black ladies with island-tinged vowels; a sourish woman in a stained apron sitting heavily on high stool, carving a joint with one of those electric knives from ads on cable. The only gaze that seemed to spot his presence in the passthrough belonged to the one person not moving: a middle-aged guy leaning against the fridge in denim cutoffs, cowboy boots, and a stretch-necked gray vee-neck. With his salt-and-cayenne beard, he looked like one of the homeless (for that's obviously what they were) who'd wandered in off the line out there. A toothpick flitted sideways. Then he sighed and made his way over. "'Fraid you'll have to take a number like everybody else, brother."

"Oh—I'm not here to eat. I was told to look for Leslie? She's the, uh . . . coordinator here, I think?"

"I guess you found her. But nobody calls me Leslie." The guy's voice seemed to issue through layers of charcoal. The gray of his shirt was white plus dog hair. Still: that Leslie was a man seemed almost a relief.

"Erica sent me," Ethan said, as if that excused his mistake, and adjusted his bag nervously at his side. "Officer Morales, rather."

"Hm. So you're Erica's golden boy, is that about the size of it?" And now a couple of people did glance over. But the guy's grin never wavered. "From her description I was expecting a little more meat on the bones."

"Sorry, I'm just . . . I'm confused. You two spoke by phone? What did she say to you?"

"Said you'd probably be good for a few hours of work. We're short-handed here."

"And I'm chopped liver, McGonagall?" said the carving lady.

The toothpick stabbed toward a closet. "Grab some gloves for the health code," he told Ethan. "Then you can help with the ticket line up front. A face like that, you've got greeter written all over you."

The contours of the P.O.'s trick began to resolve; he should never have likened himself to the involuntary poor, and she was damn well going to teach him the difference. On the other hand, his return flight had long since departed, and he had nothing better to do before bedtime. Or pavement-time, as the case may be. Which made Erica right, if not quite in the way she thought: since he'd probably be sleeping on the street anyway, he might as well get a feel for the milieu.

It was helpful, actually, to be reminded of his own free will as he headed into the heat again. The cheerful Canadian who was taking tickets at the street-level door handed him a stack and told him his job was to go down the line distributing them. The point of this ticketing ouroboros would remain somewhat murky, but Ethan did as he was told, trying to copy the Canadian's hail-fellow tone—to meet gazes, to go out in spirit. And all things considered, this part of his penance would pass with surprising quickness. A couple of times he almost had to bite his tongue not to say, "Keep coming back."

By five, though, the shadows were longer and the lines gone, and he found himself holding a surplus of tickets he had to return inside to dispose of. The dining area was now like a theater after the day's last show. The tables were folded; he could see a few guests exiting to another street out back. But the scullery crew and the Canadian had joined in some kind of postgame huddle that unmistakably meant prayer, so he slid past to the kitchen. The only meaningful God he could conceive of was one with the power to grant wishes—and who could have wished for any of this? The indigents slipping out the door with their damaged shoes . . . the damaged lives retold in the rooms: house fires set with crack pipes, all those incinerated pets. He felt now as he had at the start of his first attempt at rehab: like he'd developed an allergy to higher powers tout court, some autoimmune thing. (In the end, though, weren't these volunteers just as self-interested as he was, priding themselves on their service, savoring the little philanthropic treat of their own lives made to seem righteous by contrast?)

The coordinator, head unbowed, had trailed Ethan to the kitchen. "Well, Erica was right about one thing," he said. "You've got a certain hustle about you."

"Extra tickets," Ethan said, thrusting out the roll. "I guess I'll be off, then. Wait . . . crap. Did you see a shoulder bag full of clothes?"

"Not to worry," said Les McGonagall. "I carried your stuff outside hours ago. Now look alive, brother. We've still got deliveries left to make."

THE VAN THAT WAITED at the curb was white and windowless, but as McGonagall slid foiled trays into the rubberized cargo area, Ethan wondered how he'd missed the spring-mounted faux-terrier tail protruding like a cockamamie antenna above the butt-crack of the rear doors. Even in the cab, into which he was told to go ahead and climb ("Don't be shy; lock's busted"), the smell of air freshener didn't lessen but only compounded the scent of dog. Then three crisp twenties were being pressed into Ethan's hand. "An advance, understand. We were slow off the mark today, missed the start of rush hour, so this might take some time."

McGonagall had already turned on a Spanish-language radio station and was working the van around its own massive blind spots, into the one-way traffic. Soon they were double-parked by a concrete island near the Lincoln Tunnel on-ramp where the now inevitable-seeming dozens queued. "How about you take the wheel while I pass around leftovers?" he said.

"What, like drive?"

"More like sit in neutral and try to sweet-talk any heat that comes along. That's your bailiwick, isn't it? Talking yourself out of trouble? Slip them something from your roll if need be, and I'll reimburse. There's no legal parking to be had."

Without mentioning his rap sheet or the years since he'd last driven, Ethan clambered across to the driver's side, there to ride out the urge to change the station or look away once more from the dispossessed. Who knows? Some of them might even have been the very people he'd greeted earlier, returned for seconds. Then McGonagall was climbing back in, ordering him over to the passenger seat, and they were headed downtown again. The sun was falling further, the light softening; presumably they would come to a corner where McGonagall would turf him out with his sixty bucks like some eleemosynary rent boy. But he could feel the tension dropping out of him, leaving only a weariness of everyplace he'd touched down today: East New York, Red Hook, Howard Beach, Chelsea, the traffic now stalled on Canal—a weariness of himself, too, that left him willing to accept the ride as far as it led.

Where it led, after a jog onto a fingerbone sidestreet, was down toward the East River. At a four-way stop at each block's end, pedestrians parted around the van like water around a rock, making him glad he couldn't drive. And maybe here amid the chopped-up tenements a night's lodging really could be had on the cheap, and he could view his problems afresh in the morning. Maybe that was the point of this otherwise shambolic journey. This otherwise interminable day.

But after a couple more blocks, McGonagall swung straight up onto the sidewalk and threw the van into park. He hopped out to unlock some storm fencing. The pedestrians seemed to see this as no big deal, even when the van jerked into a vacant lot, scattering feral cats from puddles where they'd gathered to drink. Ethan didn't realize the headlights were on until flakes of old whitewash and yellow mortar showed on a wall, along with a sinewy vine trying to snake its way skyward. Then the lights died, and he could see the hulks of other parked vans and trucks between him and the street, and the city rising unvanquishable in the dusk beyond. "Convenient, right?" said McGonagall—the first words he'd spoken since Astor Place.

"Convenient to what? You haven't said where you're taking me."

"Oh, you weren't worried I'd put you out on the street tonight, were you? No, you're too rare a find for that. I'm taking you home."

Biting his tongue, Ethan followed him out of the lot, onto the sidewalk. Old men stood in doorways under fire escapes wired with kanji boards, while farther off, people loitered at fruit stands or swirled into crosswalks, shopping bags adangle. And these kids in their ballooning tees dashing out to rap with stopped cars, the fireworks hawkers: how could Ethan have forgotten them? Now that the holiday was over, it must have been a buyers' market.

After a few blocks' walk, they came to a cluster of high-rises set back from the street and out of scale with the rest of the neighborhood. They looked like any of the city's housing projects, but the lobby inside was newly mopped, its bulletin boards kempt and orthogonal, and the blazered security guard was careful to log Ethan's ID: the passport he'd learned to carry in lieu of a license. One of the elevators was out of order. It was while waiting for the other that McGonagall volunteered that he was a Bronx native, Parkchester and Co-op City—that this place with its stabilized rent and second bedroom had come to him only after he returned to the city and his aunt had entered assisted living a few years ago.

Upstairs, Ethan followed him down a cheerless hall to a door McGonagall unlocked without looking. Behind it lay the apartment in question, large but spare. Bachelorish, you might have said, were it not for a whiff of monasticism, along with a small clumsy painting of what appeared to be Friar Tuck in a remake of *The Birds*. "Empty room's down the hall," McGonagall said, dropping the great keyring onto the kitchen counter as if casting off a discipline. "You can stow your bag there, and towels are in the closet if you need a shower. Which, take it from me, you do." Then incongruously, given the lack of AC and the smattering of empty winebottles: "I'll put on some tea."

Ethan would return after a bit to find a barnacled hotpot sluicing its contents into mugs on the living room's coffeetable. When he raised the nearest one to blow on it, he got a whiff of seaweed. Toasted rice. McGonagall, now shirtless and red-faced but either surprisingly buff or younger than he looked, had swept several rollerblades off a couch cushion by the window, beyond which the nightfall over Manhattan made the lamplight seem almost homey. He sat, closed his eyes, appeared to nod. In Ethan's hand the hot mug soothed as it burned. Yet he was suddenly at the limit of his capacity to take things as they come. "Can I ask you something? Why are you doing this?"

"The tea? A thing I picked up in Damietta. I used to go around outside the walls of our compound in the afternoon, you'd have a hundred-, hundred-ten-degree day and these Egyptian guys would be squatting in the doorways of shops with their thousand-degree tea. I ask one, he says it cools you down. I'm like, Who am I to say better?"

"No, I mean, doing this *for me*. Giving me a bed for the night. What is all this?"

"Well, for starters, it's not for the night, the bed's here as long as you want it. But I'm not giving—you're leasing. Sweat equity, pal. You have your advance already; at eight sharp tomorrow, the real work begins."

"What . . . the soup kitchen serves breakfast too?"

"That's just volunteerism, Ethan. No, my real life is that van out there. Any fool can do it, dogwalking, though the grooming takes some skill. As for why I'm making you this generous offer," he continued (while Ethan thought, *You've got to be kidding*), "the short answer is, my last assistant walked on me in June."

"And the longer version?"

"Let's just say your Officer Morales and I have been through some things together." And boom, there it was, the white light; *so how exactly do you know Erica?* he'd been wanting to ask, yet now he had the alarming sense that McGonagall might just go ahead and let him in on the secret . . . or all the secrets. Ex-junkies? Scientology? Amway? Or were *they* fucking? Suddenly he felt too exhausted, too weak, too unhoused to care. He clunked his mug down on the coffeetable. "You know what? I've been up since like eight a.m. yesterday. I'm really, really tired."

When McGonagall made no move to stop him, he retreated back down the hall to the vacant bedroom, scarcely big enough for the sheetless mattress on the floor. Stood at the door on aching feet, listening. Maybe his ingratitude had given sufficient offense that he'd be kicked out in the morning, but for now there was no stir in the apartment except the slurping of tea, faint or possibly imaginary. Across the room the open window had faded to a patch of navy, and as the sounds swelled from the street ten stories down he felt himself long for a tumbler of gin, a bag of dope, a time-release tab of sweet MS Contin, his ruined youth back again.

Instead, he reached for the dresser where he'd set the dumb-phone to charge before showering. Earlier, on his way back from JFK, he'd dashed off a quick text to Jolie explaining that his business in New York turned out to be more complicated than he'd thought—that he'd be sticking around indefinitely. The nominal goal here was transparency, but he must also have been hoping for some sarcastic retort by now, or any other chink in her wall. Yet six hours later, still nothing.

It was obvious he was being tested. Well, fine, he thought, and stretched out fully clothed with the phone on his chest, his hands folded over it like the Nosferatu of the 2G grid. If at some point she did respond, there would be no gap between message and receiver. He'd be shaken awake in the dark by that vibration like death, all the more surprising when you were already expecting it. Meanwhile, he would send his thoughts out over the Lower East Side and the luminous constructions to the north, those immensities even the FM waves had trouble finding their way around. He imagined his dreams as giant hands, trying to grope their way past the Pan Am Building, the Empire State, to reach out and touch and gently turn his daughter toward him. It was the fifth of July, the year of somebody's Lord 2011, the longest day of his entire adult life (such as it was), yet his little girl remained out there somewhere in the city thinking she'd been left all on her own. Alone in the radio silence.

5

IT WASN'T LIKE Jolie hadn't known spells of confinement before, but they'd always been hers to initiate, and to control. Since Montauk, however, her mother had been overcompensating, monitoring sleep, whereabouts, appetite . . . even standing too close in the kitchen, as if to sniff her. And no sooner had Summer Session II put Mom back in the classroom than Jolie began to suspect Vikas of logging her own departures and returns from her part-time gig digitizing records at her pediatrician's office, so that for a while there, evening became just a dull blur of *Quadrophenia* and occasional self-touching; of lying facedown in a version of the dead man's float, waiting for her text-addled father to give up the ghost and be gone.

Still, his refusal to leave New York turned out to furnish a useful alibi. By the time her therapy group broke for vacation, in August, she'd let Mom assume from various hints and implications that she'd caved and decided to see him, and though Mom herself kept up a punitive embargo, she seemed unwilling for some reason to block the relationship altogether. If Jolie said she was going out to grab coffee, a timer would be set: "See you back here in twenty minutes." But she could say *Dad* wanted to meet for coffee, and all at once time was an open sea, no questions asked. Jolie was careful to attempt the trick only sparingly—there was always the possibility that Mom would commute his sentence, reach out to compare notes—but once school started, she found herself more and more using the excuse to hang around the Bluestockings Bookstore after class.

And it was there, trying to make contact with the self she'd

been before her life went off the rails, that she would first hear
of the protestors camping down on Wall Street—or, to be precise, in a park a few blocks away. She dismissed it initially as just
another pseudoevent in a world shorn of significance. There
might be an item on NPR, another groaner on the cover of the
Post, but after a few spins of the news cycle, the regression to
the mean would begin. On her next visit, though, she heard a
guy over in 'Zines discussing a protestor who'd been maced by
the NYPD. "The video's brutal," he said appreciatively. Jolie
wasn't going to take out her phone and start googling on the
spot, but when she did get a moment to check, "brutal" seemed
the mot juste. The cop might have been a ringer from the '68
Democratic convention; the girl he was blinding, a college under-
graduate, looked no older than Jolie, her shoulders crumpling
like wings. And most startling, perhaps, was how clichéd power
appeared once you stripped away its evasions and disguises.
She clicked refresh and scanned for any artifacts of fakery even
while wishing she could trade places with the girl onscreen, feel
that burning in her eyes. Then, back in her room, she fished
her laptop from under the bed and wrote her impressions
down.

See, this was her other innovation of that fall: to wait up wired
on endorphins and caffeine for Mom's bedtime noises to subside.
It could hardly count as a violation of Lights Out Means Lights
Out (could it?) this screen just big enough to hold the missive
to Grayson Aplanalp she'd spent all day composing in her head.
Should he ask about the sexting fiasco, she'd told herself, she
would try to make him jealous, insist that her selfie had been
meant for someone else, had just slipped in by mistake. He never
did ask, though; simply popped up again to message without reply
or apology several weeks later. Now her fingers flashed like quick-
silver over the keys. What was left when they stopped would be
not staccato blips of imposture, but a coherent version of herself
as she'd been that day—what she'd seen, read, thought . . . and
by morning, she'd have Grayson's long reply, followed sometimes
by two or three postscripts; whereupon the whole process could
begin again.

Tonight, for example, she sent him a rumor reposted off some
anarchist listserv: the band Radiohead was supposed to be playing

a surprise set at Zuccotti Park on Saturday, in solidarity with the occupation. The reply waiting for her at sunup seemed painfully curt until she read it through:

I'm back down from school for Columbus Day.
What say we go check it out.

And she found, to her surprise, that she'd planned for this already. She had therapy Saturday morning, springing her from her cage. And now she could tell her mom how Dad had bought tickets to a musical on Broadway—that troubled *Spider-Man* thing, say, whose run time they couldn't seem to unbloat. Plus then of course dinner to follow.

THAT SAME FRIDAY, she was on her way to the elevator, earbuds in, when Vikas stopped her in the lobby. "Don't forget your package, kid."

"I got a package?"

On the narrow little parapet that delineated Vikas's work area from the rest of the building, he set a padded envelope someone had rolled into a cylinder and girded at each end with a rubber band. There was no return address. Her first thought was of the liberties Dad used to take with giftwrap: circulars from Macy's or P.C. Richard repurposed into paper by a man who didn't seem to understand the physics of Scotch tape. The scrawl with her name wasn't his, though, which perhaps was why she dodged Vikas's gaze.

"Okay, Vikas, thanks. Check you later."

When the elevator doors closed, she ripped open the mailer. Inside, in a further tube of bubble wrap, a note had been affixed to a paper towel, itself wrapped around a fistful of off-brand crayons.

4 The Rainbows With In Rainbows....

the note said, in its entirety. She almost didn't bother with the little tatter of whatever had fallen off. Then she realized it was two tiny stamps, albeit on sturdier paper, joined by a perforation and printed with cartoony black stars that seemed to wink at her as they grinned. She'd never seen tabs of LSD before, yet somehow she knew them on sight.

The elevator doors had opened again. Mercifully, no one was around. But as she neared the apartment, Mom was just heading out. "I can't face cooking, I'm going to pick up Lebanese . . . hey, what's with the crayons?"

Jolie looked down: envelope, note. Though she'd managed to palm the acid, her hands seemed sweaty, and there was that one urban legend where the hippie, pursued by cops, tripped in a puddle so that however many hundred of the doses he was carrying osmosed instantly through his skin; to this day, he was said to be in a padded cell somewhere, talking to God. She willed her hands not to sweat. "You remember my friend who was supposed to spend the night in February?" she asked, knowing Mom would be at pains not to think ill of Precious. "She sent these."

"I don't get it—we have crayons already."

The crayons were probably to throw off the drug-sniffing dogs or whatever, but the true genius of them was the non sequitur. "An in-joke. You remember she's off at art school now. Such kidders, those Ezeobis."

Safe in her room, Jolie repacked the package and cranked the AC to its most polar setting. The headboard of her bed had a secret panel of the kind that seemed whimsical when furnished to a child yet increasingly shortsighted as that child approached adulthood. In the spring, she'd used it to stow her pilfered fifth of vodka, and then subsequent ones bought from an enterprising member of the Broad Horizons senior class. It was almost like Grayson had known about this, too. But instead of hiding the drugs in her hiding place, she wrapped them back up and shoved them in the bottom of her bag, since he obviously meant for her to bring them along tomorrow, and hadn't wanted to risk a bust coming through Penn Station from Putney.

IT WOULD BE a quarter to eleven the next morning when she finally hoisted herself up from bed. Finding no further updates online, she grabbed the backpack she'd packed full of needfuls the night before: trail mix, a notebook for documentation . . . and, somewhat less rigorously, an old *New Yorker* in case her bus got stuck in traffic.

Her mother, a creature of the daylight, should have been up for hours by now in her sun-splashed grading alcove, but when Jolie passed the door to the bedroom, there she was at the mirror, doing something to her eyes. Undoubtedly she felt Jolie behind her, and could have turned at any moment to ask why she needed so much gear just to go to a Broadway show. But of course Jolie could have turned it back on her, asked why the eyeliner, so perhaps on both sides there was this appeal to the unsaid: the way it preserved a zone of autonomy. Keeping to the edge of the hall so as not to squeak the floorboards, Jolie made it to the front door. Laced up her new Doc Martens, undid the bolt, yelled, "Okay, Mom!"

"Okay what?"

"Okay I'm headed out. Remember? Group with Dr. Loesser, then I meet Dad for *Spider-Man*."

"Wait, sorry, did I miss something?" A tremor went through Jolie. "I thought you said showtime was at three o'clock. That leaves a whole hour for lunch in between."

"Yeah—with Dad. Lunch plus show plus dinner equals more free time for you. Don't look a gift horse in the mouth." And before a directive could be issued to have fun, she was gone.

FOR THERAPY, she had to catch the M7 to the Hotel Valhalla, a onetime palace right down Twenty-Third Street from the school for the blind. Probably the second floor's high-ceilinged banquet room was just the cheapest space Dr. Loesser could rent by the hour, but passing through the dropclothed lobby, Jolie would find herself fantasizing that no one had signed off on her presence there—that she was some postapocalyptic runaway, and New York its own future ruin.

The conceit seemed to extend even to the meetings themselves, an intergenerational mishmash of show-and-tell and *Lord of the*

Flies. In theory, everyone went clockwise speaking in turn until their eighty minutes was up and they all headed off for another week's worth of neurosis. In practice, the conch tended to make it less than halfway around the circle before getting hijacked by Bitter Stuart, out of work since the crash, or Wilting Mary, containing whom was like trying to contain water. Dr. Loesser, a thin-wristed woman hunched over a yellow pad, seemed to lack the personal mojo to stand up to either of them, but two months into her treatment, Jolie had learned to welcome their filibusters. However close the kinship of rage and melancholy, Stuart and Mary seemed genuinely to loathe each other, showing up early to grab seats at opposite poles of the circle, and by coming early, too, and grabbing the chair immediately to Stuart's left, Jolie, the group's youngest member, had coasted through seven sessions with little opportunity to talk.

Now she arrived upstairs to find Bitter Stuart spooning Folgers from a giant can into an equally giant filter basket. Of course the thing about him was, he was actually kind of a sweetheart if you managed to get him alone. When she went to help him unstack the chairs, he was like, Please, forget about it. But she couldn't choose a seat until he finished, so she drifted to a window behind the long folding table. Over the street hung a marquee thing that in better times must have sheltered limos. At present, it just lay there like a pigeonshit Pollock, shadowing the working stiffs passing below . . . among whom, for some reason, she kept picturing her dad.

Then the elevator out in the hall made its analog ding. This would be Wilting Mary—just in time to avoid any obligation to set up—but Jolie stuck by her window, trying to trade out the image of Dad for one of Grayson. Which was silly, obviously; she wasn't supposed to meet him for another couple of hours, and then only way downtown. Nor had she told him about having started outpatient therapy. Yet she hesitated long enough that when she went to go sit, she was out of position, somewhere to Bitter Stuart's right and only three slots down from the doctor herself . . . whose lulling passivity had perhaps been more strategic than had been appreciated, for now, almost casually, she said, "Jolie, it's been a while since we heard from you. Maybe you could start us off, tell us what's on your mind these days?"

Jolie trawled around inside herself like a mechanical arm in an arcade game. But the thing she kept thunking against, beneath the plumage and the guile, at least had the virtue of taking the focus off her attempt to self-destruct last spring. It was her dad.

What she would end up offering the group—what seemed safest to offer—was her earliest memory of him: winter afternoon in a city park glazed with rain, playground brightness under a birdbath sky, and Dad warning her repeatedly, and slightly too loud, to watch for slick spots. She recalled his hands as damp and ungloved, her own as frozen from the wet rails of the slide. Wet seat of pants, wet underpants, numb butt . . . In the fogged window of a coffeeshop across the way, her mom sat over a slab of interview transcriptions, making a point of not watching through the hole she'd cleared on the glass, as in better weather she'd have been stationed on the playground's far bench. There was no way the three of them had spent the whole day like this, Jolie said, but that's how it felt at the time. And of course she and Dad had only ventured outside in the first place because at that point what other neutral meeting ground was left?

"Supervised visitation was all they'd give him after Mom moved out," she said. "And then only every couple weeks."

Really, she'd meant to break things off there: a historical thumbnail from which the relevant arcs could be inferred. Not wanting to mislead a room of possibly volatile head-cases, though, she found herself hastening to clarify that the dynamic had shifted somewhat—the element of surveillance abated—once she'd reached grade school and the divorce went through.

At the time, Dad had still been living in the old studio apartment on the edge of Spanish Harlem, the one that had been her home when she'd been a baby, and now on Thursdays she headed over there to watch whatever Netflix he'd forgotten to mail back while he transformed a brown pound of bodega ground beef into one of his three *plats du jour*: burgers, spaghetti, tacos. His spaghetti always had this faintly smoky taste he couldn't get off the pan. Always and only the spaghetti, for some reason. The waiter bit was because that was what an out-of-work actor who'd copped to felony drug-running charges did for money, waiting tables.

Afterward, washing up, he would send Jolie downstairs with a couple bucks for Baby Ruths, and then they would shoot the breeze about school and work until it was time for the crosstown pas de deux of subway and bus that would carry her back home . . . unless it was summer, and she could be out later. Then, depending on that week's tips, he might take her bowling at the bus station or to hit shag balls at Chelsea Piers, or, if Mom agreed, out to Coney Island with its Whac-a-Mole and batting cages and Single-A baseball team.

Had some court order cleared the way for these longer visits? Not as far as Jolie could tell. Everything beyond the original, narrower covenant seemed to be Mom's call alone. She was tenure-track at Barnard by this point, so her teaching load probably figured in there somewhere. Mostly, though, she seemed to be relying on her own sense of what worked for Jolie and/or exactly how far Dad could now be trusted—assessed with the same rigor she'd brought to her field research on the sex trade in Jackson Heights, as if there were no longer any personal stake to seal off.

And maybe that was the model Jolie had internalized, because with respect to whatever had gone down between her folks in the time before consciousness, she'd come to think of herself as basically Switzerland. Not that she knew all that much about Switzerland—chocolates, watches, banks . . . a general sense of cuteness and boringness and precision—but she was aware that, oddly for the birthplace of the Swiss Army knife, Switzerland either didn't have or didn't use an army. This wasn't to say it never felt a tug toward one side or the other when tensions flared between neighboring principalities; in fact, you could sort of picture Switzerland glancing up from its workbench with its little loupe thing in its eye and seeing even *more* clearly which party was to blame. Still, war was a waste. And Switzerland, with its tiny drills and hammers, had better things to do than get sucked in.

No, the real trouble had come a few years ago, when Dad stopped being around so much to get sucked *into*. Jolie had just turned eleven, and had finally been granted her own phone, when these messages started cropping up Wednesday nights. E.g.:

> Sorry, Jo—rentt due, had to pick up a shfit tomorrow.

> Make it upp to you next wek?

And then a frowny face cobbled together from a colon and a parenthesis, like it was still 1999.

Mom's whole argument against the iPhone had been caveat emptor—blah blah Adorno blah. She'd bought herself the worst possible Huawei to drive home the point, as if her refusal to learn how it worked was an act of resistance. But you had to distinguish, Jolie felt, between a technology and its user. Honestly, her dad was one of those people for whom texting should have been forbidden, in that he had no internal governor telling him *This at least deserves a phone call*. And as the one now tasked with going down the hall and informing Mom of the change in plans, Jolie could see the appeal: if her own conscience had let her, she'd have broken the news via emoji.

It would take a dozen more of Dad's skipped visits for her to start to wonder if there had been something beyond mere flakiness at work. A new girlfriend was a possibility, for unlike Mom, he'd been known to date—or at any rate, to plunge into gray areas with coworkers. Although the girls themselves remained invisible, she could infer the mayfly arcs of relationships from certain gaps in his stories about restaurant life. (Well, that and the strip of condoms she'd found under his futon the previous fall, accordioned like tickets to the fair.)

But then at the final meet of her first season swimming, he'd shown up unannounced—and with a full beard. He hadn't come to any of her other meets, so when she degoggled after her leg of the 200-meter, it had taken a few seconds to grasp who that even was, whooping for her up there on the top bleacher. He looked like a member of the Taliban. Or like a CIA agent preparing to infiltrate the Taliban. A Method actor preparing to play that CIA agent. As he stood there making his joyful noise amid the rafters, it struck her that the secret-girlfriend hypothesis was now moot. The man before her was not one who knew the steadying influence of a woman. And by the time she exited the showers, he was gone.

She would have to wait a couple more days for an explanation to come. Email this time (so he did have *some* sense of decorum). He should have let her know before the meet, he wrote, but he'd just been told his own father had passed away—kidney disease. A short, sharp decline. He'd thought that he could keep it together until they could grab dinner and he could break the news to her in person. Wrongly, as it turned out. "Anyway, even if you only met him the one time, I thought you deserved to know."

And was Jolie supposed to feel guilty here for having resented his erratic behavior? Well, mission accomplished. But she felt an unexpected anger, too—he could at least have mentioned her Grandpa Aspern was sick—and then, like, guilt about the anger. Even when a parent was practically a stranger, as his had been (even when a parent was practically a stranger as hers had been), you had to assume losing one was a big deal.

She made plans to address this with him. There were certain things they could talk about with each other that they couldn't with people they knew better. (Or less well.) Like the previous year, when a girl in her class had been diagnosed with a malignant neuroblastoma: Mom had been all grit and high-mindedness—as had the whole earnest host of grief counselors and oncologist uncles who'd descended on the lunchroom for a school-wide "community meeting." They'd broken into small groups and talked about five-year survival curves and death as a part of life; whereas Dad, when she mentioned it after dinner one night, dropped the scrub-brush into the dishwater. "Jesus, that fucking sucks."

Well, they were saying her friend had a fifty percent chance, Jolie had said, a little shaken by his anger. But of course there was nothing to be sorry about: it did fucking suck, and on East 112th Street, it was okay to cry.

Then came the night when he'd shown up in the lobby of her building with a box in his arms. Some things from the Eastern Shore he wanted her to have. "Um, okay," Jolie said. *But couldn't you have taken me with you when you went back for the funeral?* She noticed him shifting from foot to foot the way he had at the swim meet. "Dad? Is everything all right?" He had no umbrella despite the rain, nor anything warmer than a windbreaker. His dirty-blond hair was dark at the nape where his Mets cap failed to cover it. But he smiled: yeah, everything was fine. She almost invited him upstairs to dry off, but of course Switzerland's integrity depended on its punctiliousness about borders—and Vikas was already eyeing Dad doubtfully from behind his desk. Only when she lugged the box upstairs would she find that it was full of her dead grandmother's compact discs and mixtapes. (Plus at least one video, apparently.)

Which she would still be puzzling over when his second email arrived. There was something he'd meant to tell her about back there, he said, before he lost his nerve: a chance he'd been given to dig out of the hole he'd fallen into. *(What hole?)* The bad news was, it meant he had to go to California; he'd miss a few visits. But on the plus side, he'd be returned to her in a couple of months, good as new. Or better, even . . .

"And that was almost three years ago," she found herself admitting. "Since then I basically haven't seen him, except for one time this summer." Her stare stayed affixed to the faux-Persian carpet whose designs she'd been tracking through much of her monologue. For what felt like a further month but was probably just a few seconds, the group around her stayed silent. Then the blind person's traffic signal outside began to beep, the automated voice to deliver its robotic assurance that it was now safe to cross.

"Okay, Jolie—thank you." Some kind of bangle slid down Dr. Loesser's forearm as she turned to a woman in a tracksuit. "Now, what about you, Deb? You've got the parent's perspective on joint custody, does any of that resonate at all?"

And had Jolie's real fear been that they might start murmuring their disapproval? Or conversely, gather 'round for a laying on of hands? Or had it been precisely this: that her thrown stone would provoke no ripple, but go under the water as noiselessly as any other?

The rest of her session would be spent absorbed in her cuticles, but no one seemed to notice. Afterward, not wishing to be caught in an elevator with any of them, she retreated to the window again. A little kidney of overspill had pooled on the plastic tablecloth below the coffee urn's spout. She was just looking around for napkins when Bitter Stuart materialized next to her, holding a roll of paper towels. "Hey. Just wanted to say, that story you were telling really got me right here." Prodding his thorax. "And don't sweat running long—it happens."

Whatever "shared subjectivity" was, he was clearly trying to perform it with his face. But Jolie had cooled once more to the idea of Group as anything other than a means to keep Mom off her back. She blotted at the coffee and then, to distract him, asked about his shirt.

"What, you like?" He touched the front again until a Grey Poupon–colored handprint appeared amid the brown. "Hypercolor. From back in the day. Ten bucks on Canal Street, I could probably get you one."

"That's all right," she said, the way you might to a toddler offering a bite of his cookie. "But I'll see you next weekend, Stu, okay?" She swung through the circle for her bag, and then, coast clear, made for the door.

It was still Indian summer down on the street—the kind of weather for which you endured the hurricane months of August, September—and she tried to will her way back toward her earlier hopefulness. Scanned the street for cabs, grabbed the pole of the hotel awning, angled her body out over the gutter and let herself feel vaguely nautical as one of those crimped hot-dog trays gusted past. But splurging on a cab was obviously a tone-deaf way to arrive at a demonstration, so she retreated to the green globe of the subway entrance.

It had been months since she'd been in a station by herself, and the platform here was flush under the street, with voices and traffic noise and bits of reflected light filtering down: that whole sense of life unfolding just above your head. She toed a pock of gum with her Docs and tried not to dwell on a thing she'd heard recently, about the brown stuff on the tracks being not just soot but particles of rust, and capable, should fate decree, of carrying voltage from the third rail.

But at some point her mind seemed to have slipped from her control. Once on board, half watching for the sign for Wall Street, she found herself remembering the last time she'd been down here, years ago, to march against the Iraq War. Or rather, to roll against it; the route had stretched all the way to the tip of Broadway, so Mom had to dig their old umbrella stroller out of a closet. From its threadbare seat, she recalled, Albert had seemed to float above like a parade balloon, a great tweed bear. And Nana in her smart little boots, the ankles so thin you feared they might snap every time she had to negotiate a curb. They'd slowed to point out to her the Stock Exchange as if it would someday be essential that Jolie know exactly where the meridians of global finance converged. But what would stay with her, actually, was Wall Street's smallness: a checkpoint like a telephone booth, a line of gleaming new security bollards, a flutter of pigeons resettling themselves under a raggedy flag . . . it had felt like the least occupied street in all of New York.

If her plan now had a hole, it was how to find Grayson Aplanalp upon surfacing, but when she rose, there he was on the far side of a thoroughfare drained of cars, sitting cross-legged on the sill of a boarded-up menswear joint. His chin propped on his hands, his sleeves still buttoned protectively, he was bent over a book . . . and she was touched, too, by his flimsy imposture of not having seen her—as if he'd just happened to choose this spot to read.

She approached slowly, and when he didn't look up, she said, "Hey," trying to keep the warmth from her voice. He snapped the book shut, shielded the cover so that all she could make out was the ATM slip he'd used to mark his place. But the hand doing the hiding was elegant, and the effort at concealment pleasing: it was the first time in their friendship or whatever that he'd seemed remotely nervous. "Reading something juicy?" she asked him.

"Just some religious tripe I picked up somewhere, for a book report. One would have thought they'd let us have the long weekend sans homework, but no."

"Yeah, people don't seem too keen on celebrating genocide these days."

"Was Columbus genocidal? I find I'm hazy on the details," he said, with that distance from all things American he sometimes seemed to affect. "But here, hold this for me, yeah? I didn't bring a bag." Having unfolded himself from his perch, he put the book out facedown, like a dare. She declined to flip it over, instead shoving it into her bag, and saw his shoulders relax: "You're a mensch, Jolie." And as she followed him toward the blue saw-horses now looming in the distance, she wondered, not for the first time, how he'd known just exactly what she wanted to hear.

Zuccotti Park turned out to be not a park at all, so much as a bland little corporate plaza done up in pinkish quartz, a few trees spiked here and there like toothpicks through a sandwich, plus a dozen news vans . . . and maybe a hundred fifty protestors, total. Their sparseness elicited the kind of pity she might have felt for a wayward animal. Yet Grayson seemed not to register it, turning to her instead with his cracked grin. "This must be where the magic happens."

"So I gather," she said, resisting an urge to break out her phone and see where all the people had gone. "You mind if we take a lap?"

And though she didn't let on, the scene felt as disappointing demographically as it did numerically, skewing notably white and male: a frathouse vibe of sodacans and shoeprinted placards, posterboard snagged in the struggling branches above. Tucked in every available cranny were wadded sleeping bags and little goiters of laundry. Yet by the time they finished their loop, Jolie had started to intuit, if not a logic, exactly, then at least some kind of organization. That folding table over there with all the books served as a library; this one with the sterno tins and pizza boxes was the cafeteria.

What was missing was any sense of an impending performance. The closest thing to a stage was a cleared place at the center of the park where a balding man like a street preacher fulminated about election funding. His cadences seemed odd, even halting, yet she noticed the echoes bouncing back from the younger people gathered around. "You've seen clips of this?" Grayson said. "The People's Mic." He had reached the group's outer edge, but since organized chanting made Jolie self-conscious, she touched his shoulder.

"It's twenty past two. Is Radiohead planning to play via People's Mic, you think?"

"I wouldn't overanalyze it, Jolie This hardly feels like the most tightly run ship."

"Still: any objection if we sit down to wait?" Her feet, accustomed to their buttery Chucks, were already contracting blisters from the Docs' stiff leather.

Grayson seemed as game as ever. Complicating the search for a seat, though, was a kind of shadowboxing that had emerged around the use of space—i.e., how, exactly, it was supposed to be occupied. The homeless-proof benches were already full, and through most of the bald man's speech, every time they found a spot on a plinth or planter, a uniformed rent-a-cop would approach to shoo them away. At last a bench came free on the far side of the listening circle. The plaque's worth of rules bolted to an adjacent wall went from *NO LOITERING* to *NO OVER-NIGHT CAMPING*. She ran a finger over the type. "This last one's awfully on the nose, don't you think?"

"What? Oh." Grayson, who'd been using his phone to film the speech, now gently moved her finger to the margin of pale granite that fringed the plaque's perimeter like the edge of a summer haircut. "They probably subbed in new rules last week; the mayor's a Wall Street guy, right? I think the general plan of attack is to harass us into leaving of our own volition, since no one's quite sure how to kick anybody out legally. These bureaucratic gray areas being the downside of public-private space . . ."

"Or upside, depending on where you stand."

Somehow he must have been continuing to track the campaign-finance lecture, for now he raised his cupped hands to echo back a phrase: "They give us social policy based on individual greed!" But then a more professional cameraman came trundling past, and as his lens swept across them, Jolie reflexively hunched her shoulders, flipped up her sweatshirt's hood.

"Crikey," Grayson said. "See, this is what I do. I embarrass people."

"It's not that; just . . . NY1 is like my mom's guilty pleasure. I can't have her turning on the TV and seeing me down here."

"She should be proud! 'A woman of the left,' you called her . . ."

"Yeah, but I still had to come up with an excuse for if we were planning to be out past curfew."

"Ah. And is that what we're doing?"

"She thinks I'm with my dad at a play." She felt herself blush; in much the same way she hadn't brought up the topless pictures of herself, she hadn't mentioned Dad since their exchanges of that summer.

But his look now was curious. "The gaffer's still around, huh?" he asked. And when she didn't answer, undertook a piss-poor British Brando: "You want I should go jump this mook for his footage?"

"I'd rather just hang back."

"Joking. It's all in the cloud anyway. You know, if I ever have a punk band, that's what I'll call it."

"In the Cloud?"

"Public-Private."

Punk is dead, she wanted to tell him, but applause had begun to build, and also, from around the corner, a sound so ubiquitous she wouldn't ordinarily have noticed it: heavy traffic, rumbling down Broadway. As they watched, a series of charter buses drew to the curb and began to disgorge a throng that could have been a tour group save for the placards being handed out and the way the dispersed listeners had already formed a kind of phalanx. A whistle shrilled; a new and louder chant came forth. What did they want? *No foreclosures.* When did they want it? *Now.*

And all at once, something clicked. What if the modest numbers crashing here overnight had only been a beachhead? A sort of vanguard, awaiting backup against the many-armed armies of austerity? She floated this theory to Grayson as if it were mere guesswork, but he said, "See? This is why I like you, Jolie. So effing precocious."

"But someone should tell whoever's in charge that it's pointless to be marching downtown," she added, secretly invigorated. "Battery Park's a morgue on Saturdays. You head that way, the only people who see you are going to be the cops enforcing your free-speech zone and the tourists snapping pictures."

"Maybe that's the point."

"Yeah, fuck NYPD, I guess." Though compared to the park's officious security guards, the city police with their bad haircuts and beleaguered expressions seemed less hateable than the dark powers she'd watched on YouTube—as much the potential beneficiaries of democratic socialism as obstacles to its enactment.

"I meant the tourists, Jolie. The cameras. Think about it . . . what's the one way you know for certain something's worth your attention these days? Someone puts video of it online. 'No pictures, it didn't happen.' This occupation's been in the paper for over a month, but it took streamable footage, a narrative, to draw us both down here."

He looked to her as if for a response, and when he didn't get one, pushed on.

"And still the very nature of narrative is to falsify, right? Smooth away the tensions, or whatever . . . make them photogenic, jack them into fantasy. So imagine the kind of change we could provoke—or at least the nervous breakdown—if we could somehow trick all the screens into showing, even for just a min-

BRAN'S CAULDRON   191

ute, how people are actually feeling down here." Suddenly, he
was on his feet, his hoarse shouts trebling in the empty afternoon.
And already the assembled crowd was raising itself on its thousand legs and filing along Broadway toward the narrower spill of
streets running down to the harbor, the counting houses and custom houses that were the first, rough draft of New York.

They soon fell in step with an attractive Spanish couple, the
man carrying a baby in one of those slings. Conversation was
inaudible (amid the carnival atmosphere it seemed a miracle the
baby could even sleep), but for now it felt like enough simply to
be walking at Grayson's side. From time to time the march would
slow to harangue the headquarters of Corporation X or the Royal
Bank of Thus-and-Such. The chants, Jolie thought, remained
weirdly indifferent to their targets—were in fact the old standbys
she recalled from sad little street actions sprung up at the Columbia gates whenever a Bush cabinet official or an Israeli head of
state came to talk. Yet every minute or two, when they fell out of
sync, a tambourine would shake as if for quarters—*Da da-da da-
da-da-da da-da*—and a woman up ahead would again demand that
they show her what democracy looked like.

These banalities at first seemed not to trouble Grayson, but by
the time the marchers paused outside a retail branch of Citibank,
he'd started to veer off-script. "Hey hey! Ho ho! Convenience
fees have got to go!" The Spaniards laughed as other folks took up
the refrain. *Hey hey! Ho ho . . . !* And attention, of whatever kind,
seemed to galvanize him. He sent a new one climbing up the walls:
"Now heed our . . . incitements . . . we want to see indictments!"

Jolie had picked up enough browsing Bluestockings to be wary
of her tendency to aestheticize. Still, she couldn't help feeling that
Grayson's gag was a failure somehow: too specific, too beholden
to the existing order, no glimpse of the change he'd just been
talking about, even if that other world felt mostly out of reach.
But now two uniformed cops from the next corner had awakened
to the growing disorder and come striding this way. She steeled
herself for pepper spray or worse—for the image of her own face,
flashing out to all points of the grid. But they were only here to
harass a news crew about blocking the sidewalk and then order
the marchers to keep marching. "That's unless you want to see
somebody get hurt," she heard one warn the Spaniards, as if all

this—the protest, the spectacle, the recession itself—were their fault.

It was at this point that Grayson looked around and noticed Jolie straggling behind with her hood up. He turned to resettle it around her face—the third time he'd touched her, counting the handoff of the violin. "Of course: how careless of me to yell. I couldn't do more to blow your cover if I tried."

"No, it's just . . . I don't think these boots were made for actual walking, you know?"

"But look how far you've come!" He pointed west, to a gap between buildings. By some commodious recirculation, they'd been brought back to within rock-chucking distance of Zuccotti. "I know a pizza spot near here, if you feel like chilling for a bit over a slice. Or my father's place is like a ten-minute walk."

"What if we miss Radiohead?"

"Right. Well, let's see . . ." He bent over his phone. She was amazed at the dexterity of his thumbs, almost a blur. But now he seemed puzzled. "Hmph. Look at this."

He held out the phone. A message-board posting, scaled up to fill the screen, lurched outward as he rotated it sideways. Someone whose avatar was a photo of Slavoj Žižek was flaming someone else for calling out the Radiohead hoax; if it got bodies into the street, was it not ipso facto good for the cause? She looked to where Grayson's finger was tapping; the post was two weeks out of date. And this would be hard to explain to anyone later, but as the implications hit, she felt herself relax the way she always had in the presence of a force she couldn't outrun. She appreciated especially that he didn't try to make her feel the three-year gap in their ages. "You know what? Your dad's place sounds great."

Not looking back, they peeled off from the march, and were soon crossing the invisible boundary that marked off Tribeca: black cars on standby, the deeper stillness of weekend streets, topiary bushes out front of the old factories with their cast iron faces, their façades of the real. It was to one of these that he led her. The doorman in his Trekkie headset must have been new, since Grayson didn't attempt small talk, just strode past to insert a key in a panel by the elevator. The doors rolled back on a shimmering mesh interior, gold to auburn to bronze. "I should have mentioned," he said, as she caught herself gawking. "You talk about the one percent, you're basically talking about my father."

"No, I had kind of figured you weren't a charity case," she said. And when he cocked an eyebrow: "Putney, Grayson? Please."

But if New York had anything left to teach, it was that there was money and then there was money, and when the doors parted again she found herself stepping straight into the kind of loft space that only great gobs of the latter could secure, a remove further deepened by glass walls on all sides. He did something with his phone she didn't even know you could do, and then as if by magic lights came on, hurling into relief club chairs and rugs and other articles of power-decoration. A wall behind a couch connected to nothing, for example—existed purely to support a comic-strip panel she was pretty sure was an actual Roy Lichtenstein. She felt a compensatory urge to try to impress him. *My grandma was an artist,* she wanted to say . . . *I don't suppose you've ever heard of Joanna Aspern?* Yet Grayson moved around the space as if it were just another place to live. She could make herself comfortable while he got drinks, he said, but the thought of being alone in this vastness unnerved her, so she followed him to the marginally less vast kitchen. The dog dish looked vintage. The fridge might have been another art piece or a space probe crashed through the wall. "What's your pleasure? Water? Coffee? Beer?"

She was attuned now to the briskness of his invitations, that open-endedness in case she turned him down. "Sure, beer's fine," she said, not wanting to discourage him, though the last time she'd checked, she hadn't loved the taste.

Then they were facing each other across a marble island the size of an actual island, sipping on Amstels Light, and she could feel the old relief, the compensation, seeping into her bones. One of them was going to have to say something, though. He looked down at his shoes. She wanted to ask how he was doing with his depression, which they never seemed to talk about. Instead she blurted, "Which one's your room?"

"Lord, where are my manners? I was about three swigs from asking if you wanted to see it. But here, probably you'd prefer something stronger?" He opened a cupboard. All those gleaming bottles.

"The vodka, maybe?" she said, as if she couldn't feel her cells quickening.

He poured her a few fingers, and she followed him down a hall you didn't notice from the elevator, past pantry and bathroom and laundry and at least one more bathroom to a door tucked away like something the rest of the apartment was ashamed of. A padlock hung open on a hasp, and in the second when she might have paused to contemplate this, it occurred to her where she'd last seen the blue x spraypainted on the door: clips of Hurricane Katrina. Inside, though, his room had the same expensively neutral look as everything else, built-in bookcases, stodgy rug. The only real signs of habitation were a battered electric guitar and a desk with three contiguous monitors like a Japanese screen, towers of light whirring softly nearby. When she dropped her bag on the desk, the mouse must have moved, for a document got startled out of the rightmost screen's far corner. A page of line-broken lines, most of them crossed out. Poetry? Song lyrics? He was across the room instantly, hitting a button to douse the screen. "Sorry, don't know what that's doing there."

"Some rig you've got, though."

"Same setup as a trading floor. The master's house with the master's tools, that sort of thing."

To cover her embarrassment at having invaded his privacy, she moved toward the window. A storm front was edging in over Jersey. Twelve floors down, the river was a runner of dark baize, the tandems of headlights on the West Side Highway already starting to come on. For someone used to facing neighbors across an airshaft, the altitude was dizzying, but there was a deep ledge with a grate the radiator breathed through, and here, with no more than an inch of glass to shield her from the city, she took a seat. She was still trying to decide how much of his vodka would actually be safe to drink when he asked about the package he'd sent: "Did you bring it?"

She looked over to find him sprawled in his ergonomic desk chair. The acid tabs were right there in her backpack, a door waiting to be stepped through, on whose other side lay who knew? Especially since they said you never really knew how much of a dose was on there. Still, she owed him something, didn't she? "Sorry," she heard herself say. "Was I supposed to get a package?"

He looked momentarily pinched, but then recovered. "The web led me to believe it would arrive by last night—so much for priority mail. But just to alert you, Jolie, I posted something from Vermont, which I reckon you can now look forward to. Meantime, I can probably scare up some other stuff here . . ." He recovered from under his desk a baggie he must have taped there and proceeded to empty it on the desk blotter. His posture was a jeweler's, hunched forward.

She thought again of her dad returning to the lunch table in his sunglasses. Had he been high that day? No, of course not: rehab had been the whole point of California. He had done that for her (well, right up to the point when he hadn't). "If that's pot, I should warn you, I've never really smoked."

"Ah, you'll love it, Jolie. It's made for people like us."

As he began to sort through the little pile, she reached for the guitar and picked out a few unresonant chords. The intervals weren't what she was used to, each fret a half-step where she'd wanted a whole (nor was she prepared for the frailty of her calluses against the coiled steel), but she landed quickly enough on the opening arpeggio from "Baba O'Riley."

"You didn't tell me you played guitar as well!" he said, not looking up.

"Oh, I don't, really. Just messing around by ear."

"But messing around by ear is pretty much the Public-Private enterprise in a nutshell, Jolie. And a chick guitarist might lend the whole project a certain allure."

She tilted closer to punch his arm. "Don't be a pig, please."

"Hey, I'm not the one into the Who."

"What's wrong with the Who?"

"Some of those songs are pretty misogynistic, don't you think? And what about your hero Prince?"

"Prince is no more a misogynist than I am! I mean, he's practically half girl." But even as she said it, she was flashing on certain vignettes from *Purple Rain*. Was it possible Wendy and Lisa had been included in the Revolution not as a feminist gesture meant for Jolie personally, but as eye candy? And how did Grayson know she was into Prince in the first place? Oh, right. The sticker.

"Come now, Jolie . . . 'I sincerely want to fuck the taste out of your mouth'?"

The line had never troubled her, oddly. "It's satire, I think."
(Though of what?) "Anyway, always a mistake to confuse the writer's point of view with the character's."

"Irony: last refuge of the bourgeoisie. I'll tell you my favorite
Prince story, though." He'd been tonguing a lighter flame over a
rolled joint, drying the saliva.

"Is this the Dave Chapelle one? The pancakes?"

"No, no, different. People are mad for him in the U.K., this
is from around the time he got huge there. The story concerns
The Black Album; you know *The Black Album*, Jolie?" She nodded, but already he'd gone on. "The most famous bootleg in the
world, supposedly. It was made available at some point, but now
has vanished from circulation. Anyway, Prince had intended it as
the follow-up to his triple-decker, what's-it-called . . ."

"*Sign o' the Times.*"

"That's the one. I guess his nose was out of joint because
radio didn't play it, or black folks were into hip-hop instead, or
something."

"Are you kidding? It's an acclaimed masterpiece."

"Yeah, people loved it, but they didn't love it the way he *wanted*
them to love it. Anyone who insists on playing all the instruments himself obviously has some control issues. Anyway, Prince
decides he's going to do a one-eighty, make this album of uncompromising black dance music. Or whatever that sounds like in the
imagination of a light-skinned polymath from Minnesota. Original title: *The Funk Bible*. And it's like, rapping, disses of rappers,
murder fantasies, stalking, whatever, I've never actually heard any
of it, but that's beside the point. The point is, dark, cynical, angry
music, sort of the opposite of his purple love vibe thing. And then
a jet-black cover with no name, no human language on it at all."
He took a couple of experimental puffs, the joint smoldering like
debris caught under a stove burner. "Only something holds him
back, Jolie. You sure you haven't heard this story?"

She shook her head. She hadn't known to ask.

"The record company is on the phone by this point and is like,
Prince, babe, what's the holdup? And Prince is prevaricating, pick
your excuse—maybe because he knows he's about to blow up his
career. So one night, he goes out to a club, which is where he likes
to spend his time, but in a kind of non-nightclub-goer's fantasy

of a nightclub. The guy doesn't even do drugs, reportedly. I think his favorite drink was Madeira. No, the beauty of the nightclub, from Prince's perspective, is that he can arrange to have his own music played and watch how people are reacting, like does it get them moving. He has the DJ put on a test pressing of *The Black Album*. Now at this point the story turns a little fuzzy. Maybe nobody likes to dance to uncompromising black dance music about, like, bondage and squirrel meat. Or maybe everybody does. But Prince, watching, gets this distinct feeling that what he's done here is wrong. Is against the God he's always claimed to believe in but maybe hasn't thought about for a while. Does God exist, in this story? You tell me: a girl suddenly appears out of the darkness—radiant. They start talking, she ends up feeding him ecstasy, the first time he's ever done psychedelics or whatever, and they stay up the whole night, talking, talking. No one knows what is said. But come sunrise, he calls the record company and orders all copies of *The Black Album* destroyed, which they are, except for one. And in the course of the next three weeks, he records a whole new album from scratch, which is *Lovesexy*, the one with him on the cover cuddled naked in an orchid and no breaks in between the tracks: the single continuous story of how he almost spiritually died but then received a vision *which the album doesn't even fucking tell you what it is*! The single in the U.K. is 'Alphabet Street,' which is huge, as I said, but in the U.S., *Lovesexy* tanks his career, and Prince is never really the same again. Now get over here."

Having taken her hand, considerately, he led her down off the ledge.

"Breathe in when I say."

He reversed the joint so that the burning end was in his mouth and leaned forward as if to kiss her, a centimeter of wet end smoking faintly between his lips. Then he blew, and she understood she was supposed to inhale at the same time, the very thing she'd planned not to do. Into her boozy mouth came a hot dense fog. How was it, you ask? Confusing. Slightly painful. It was mostly to get him to stop that she put a hand on his chest. And just like that, the joint was on the edge of the desk and his eyes were closed and his hands were on her breasts and they were kissing.

She found herself thinking of a brace-faced boy from orchestra camp two summers ago, Zack, or Zach, whose tongue had been a sweet little blip of plausible deniability. Grayson's, by contrast, was beer-cold, all business. Through his shirt, his stomach muscles felt tense; she had somehow been expecting more give. Away on another track, she said, "Wait." *Your door's still open, your dad could come in. You're going to burn a hole in your carpet.* But as their mouths clunked back together, he took her hand and moved it to the front of his jeans, as if to confirm that this wasn't his first time. She tried to keep it flat, but when her fingers flexed autonomically, he seemed to take it as a signal to pull her toward his bed—though maybe the signal he was responding to had been the selfie she'd sent back in July, which she just had time to decide he must have received after all.

Then the choreography grew more involved. More consequential. His skinny jeans were down by his gymsocks, revealing engorged tighty-whiteys. He fumbled a bit with her buttonfly before resigning himself to copying, along the inseam, the same pressure she was giving him. Not a patch on the shower's massage-head at home, yet connected to another human being. Still, she thought, as his hips began to move, did she even like him like this? Did she like *anyone* like this? She heard herself years in the future trying to tell someone, *Grayson. Grayson was the boy I lost my virginity to. With.*

It was only upon opening her eyes that she realized she had closed them. She was on her back now and he was sucking her earlobe, making noises that sounded like he was really into it and seeking out her nipples with his thumbs. Dead center on the ceiling hung an incongruously cheap fixture, a glass dome like a candy dish, and for a second, she was up there with it, an oversight, floating. Then into her ear, in a voice that at first seemed a stranger's, he murmured, "I should get some protection, yeah?"

To buy time, she slid out from under him and put her head on his now-bare chest, planning to ask could they maybe just hold each other until her buzz faded a little, but this, too, he seemed to misread, because now his hand was on her recovered shoulder, nudging her down toward what she still wasn't ready to see. So maybe she could use her fingers to sort of confuse him? Some saliva would be required too, probably, if he was to mistake her hand for her mouth. She closed her eyes again, felt for his jock, was briefly turned on by her own power, and ducked to apply just the slightest bit of tongue, since what could it hurt? Maybe she'd like it. Then he lurched his hips and a hand was on her head, forcing it down, and for a whole minute she was choking on potted ham and couldn't breathe. He winced—"Ow, teeth!"—and eased off temporarily. And as she opened her eyes again to the gleaming pale bareness of him, the torso, the arms, something cold went through her: *I'm not here. This isn't happening.*

"Wait . . ." She coughed. "Where are the scars?"

"What?"

"Your wrists, Grayson. Shouldn't there be scars?"

"Scars from . . . ? Oh, Christ, you didn't still think—ah, of course, right." He'd wriggled free and was sitting up now against the headboardless wall with his knees drawn, suddenly chaste. "Look . . . if you're going to go all the way with me I should probably just clear things up once and for all: you realize I wasn't part of that group, the day we met."

"I wasn't part of that group either! But what are you even talking about? I thought you were a cutter."

"I don't know why you'd assume anything of the sort." The stiffness seemed to have passed into his whole body. "As I said at the time, the nurses told me that's where to find you. I wasn't trying to give the impression I was a patient myself . . . I mean, I did tell you."

"Not a patient? But then why would you even be at the hospital?"

"Well, I had to get you your violin, didn't I? It was those stickers on the case that had caught my eye from across the tracks, you see . . ."

"Oh my God—"

"And when I saw you put it down and walk off to the end of the platform, the first thing I thought was that some stranger might try to take it—"

"You were at the *station? Watching?*"

"Before you get angry," he said (though it seemed awfully late innings for that), "I thought what I was watching was someone die, okay? But then the train pulls away and there you are, Jolie, a perfect miracle. By the time I get over to your side to see what I can see, there are so many EMTs and cops and whatnot that I can't get through, but then I spot the case getting left behind and

I just . . . grab it. And since someone mentioned the ambulance was bound for Bellevue, I knew where to go."

"Jesus Christ. And you weren't going to tell me *any of this*—"

"I thought on some level you already knew! Besides: When was I going to bring it up? Hey, don't act like you've always been a model of forthrightness."

"You must be out of your mind."

" 'The Jersey Shore,' though, Jolie? Not Montauk? You know people can see your location when you message on Facebook, right? Do you even know how privacy settings work?" He gestured vaguely—infuriatingly—toward his screens.

"So you caught me fibbing about what beach I was at!" She'd stood now to tug on her clothes. "How is that anywhere near the same thing?"

"And if you truly weren't meant to be in the dayroom that day, or on the train tracks, then what is this?" From under his desk blotter, he pulled some smoothed pages, their creases like those of a weathered face. The piece she'd written. He must have dug it out of the trash at the hospital, maybe looking for her name. She felt herself go numb.

"That's not mine. I don't want that."

"Maybe you shouldn't be so quick to disown it, though. But listen, I'm sorry! Think how embarrassed I must be!"

"On behalf of the suicidal fourteen-year-old whose throat you just left a pube in? Or was my age not the kind of thing you snoop around for online?"

"Shit," he said, and banged his head against the wall behind. "Shit, shit, shit." But already she was running back down the hall, fumbling at the top button of her jeans. The blueprint had been knocked from her head, and she ended up passing a laundry room and a third bathroom before reversing back toward the kitchen. He was calling after her to stop, but by the time he came sliding into the entry hall, shielding his crotch with a pillow, she was at the elevator. Never before had a "Door Close" button responded to her touch, but maybe this, too, was a prerogative of the one percent, because a moment later she was in a sealed metal box, plunging down through the bluing throb of Manhattan.

And again briefly choking—this time on tears.

Off-duty lights drifted like windblown seeds through the dusk beyond the lobby. For once, her luck would hold: at the corner, a cab was letting out a fare. She grabbed the door and threw herself in back and gave the henna-bearded driver her address. As he glanced at the rearview, she willed herself not to turn and check for a pantsless psycho skidding out into the street.

Then they were passing along the highway, and after that the surface streets: papaya spot, synagogue, some film shoot taking up a whole section of Broadway as Jolie shielded her eyes from the cabbie, fought to stifle her crying . . . and finally, the long, dark residential frontage of her block. When the dome light revealed that there wasn't enough cash in her wallet for a decent tip, she shoved the entire wad plus some coins through the cab's partition window and then fled before it could be counted. She'd almost reached the stairs inside when Vikas touched her elbow.

"I can't talk now, Vikas," was all she could say, pulling away; for another memory had just assailed her. It was their first day in the building, and she was on a stoop nearby, struggling her numb-fingered way through a bag of pistachios while a couple of Mom's grad-school colleagues milled behind the U-Haul. All at once, Vikas had swooped from the lobby, seeing past their bright chatter to the manual incompetence underneath. He found the catch, rumbled the iron ramp out, fetched the dolly from its hiding place as she looked on—in secrecy, she believed. But then he'd reappeared before her, flapping his long coat to shake off the brownish-beige detritus of her life to date. She hadn't been sure how to respond except with a different problem, a particularly obdurate nut. His manicured nails had the shell halved instantly. Still, the moment she reached for the green flesh bare on his palm, he'd popped it into his own mouth. And watched for a reaction with those all-seeing eyes, like a tailor's inspecting a fabric for holes.

Now, just as she was realizing that the whole sordid truth was going to have to come out, to her mother at least, he gently suggested she buzz up first.

"Buzz up to my own apartment? I don't . . . Is everything okay?"

"Here." He retreated to his desk to hoist a telephone onto the parapet. With its chunky buttons, it seemed to hail from the time of the flintlock, the victrola. The line beeped four times before her mother answered, her voice strangely muzzy. "Hello?"

Which is when Jolie caught another voice, a man's, in the background. Eyeliner . . . swimsuit . . . exercycle. "Mom?"

And suddenly all was alertness. "Jolie, what's going on? Are you downstairs?"

"Of course I'm downstairs, I'm using the intercom, aren't I? I'm at Vikas's desk. Why don't *you* tell *me* what's going on?"

"I thought Dad was supposed to keep you till ten."

"So? We ate a big lunch, I wasn't hungry after the show."

"God. This is really awkward, but . . . honey, I'm not exactly alone." A long pause. "Do you think you could go walk around the block for a few minutes?"

"What the hell, Mom?" she said. "What kind of parent sends her eighth-grader out to wander the streets of Manhattan at this time of night?" She hung up, grateful to Vikas for having retreated outside to smoke but unable to return his gaze when he swept the door open for her—unsure, in fact, that she'd ever be able to again.

At one end of the block, the low trees of Riverside Drive clawed at a violet sky. At the other: the TV kliegs of Broadway, and the train tunnels running into the distance. The track on the near side led back downtown, but to what? To Grayson, and his lies. To Precious, at a stretch. And over there was the track that ended somewhere in the farthest reaches of the Bronx. But did only two tracks even constitute a choice, really? Did anything? Neither politics nor psychology nor even her own apartment had offered any respite from the pain that seemed to surround her. And drinking, the one thing that had, had betrayed her no less than had Grayson. Or worse: she had betrayed herself. And so all this would be swirling around inside her—her mom and escape and *The Black Album* and the question of any way she might make the betrayal stop—when she looked over from her spot behind a girder on the far side to lock eyes with the man in his leather jacket bouncing down onto the platform headed the other way: Mr. Koussoglou, from last year's Cultural Richness class. Here she'd been, that is, nursing her griefs and little grievances, dithering over whether to push ahead or turn back, and all the while, her motherfucking teacher had been fucking her mother.

6

AND NOW SOMEWHERE in Brookhattan a jingle of keys could be heard, and a merry little string of dogs came tripping out into a crosswalk, the tall and increasingly fragile young man at the cynosure of their leashes seeming more in pursuit than in control. It was a Monday or it was a Friday or it was anything in between, and was also, to judge by the half-mile of ripe garbage-can behind them, well after lunchtime—itself now falling mere hours before dusk. And even so, wasn't the vibe out here a bit dark? A cool wind off the river, Hudson or East, ripped through the nylon track-bottoms he'd grabbed off a discount rack months ago. Beyond that, he wore only his Beastie Boys tee and a fast-fashion corduroy jacket, since no other job, up to and including exotic dancer, boasted sumptuary codes as loose as those of dog-walker. You could have stayed in pajamas if you wanted. You could probably have gone topless. The client cared mainly about your smell, "client" in this case meaning "canine," because the creative destruction of New York seemed immune to recession—or even stimulated by it—and the work-hours of its humans commensurately long. In the utilitarian terms on which the system was constructed, no one here should have wanted a dog in the first place, yet loneliness was the system's great byproduct, so these dogowners were now counting on Ethan Aspern, at nine fifty an hour, to supply what they couldn't.

Depending on how many walks he'd booked at once, the accrued lucre could be substantial, not to say filthy. Then again, his own personal liquidity crunch hadn't so much subsided as given way to a graver problem, one of how a person like himself might ever attain solidity. You could subtract right off the top the cost of food, for example: the freezer-case Tex-Mex, the takeout Chinese. And then the thirty percent commission owed back to Les McGonagall on every walk, plus another grand in rent due the first of each month, once you factored in the price of the storage space. And then subtract too the cash for Jolie's therapy he'd shrouded in notebook paper and mailed off mid-July and had to assume Sarah had received, never having heard back; subtract, in theory, another return ticket to L.A.—though each milestone that passed without word from his daughter (Labor Day, equinox, Halloween) seemed to argue against his leaving as much as for it. And oh, right, he thought, bounding for the shelter of the High Line as the first raindrops prismed the glass above his negative bank balance: subtract the hundred dollars he was now shelling out monthly for a smartphone.

This had turned out to be one of the gig's few fixed demands. The other—that in a pinch, he be able to drive the van—remained more of a working assumption (one he'd thought it best not to undermine with talk of suspended licenses). But at the end of Ethan's second day as a trainee, his last before being dispatched to far-flung ZIP codes, McGonagall had shown him how to send each client's owner a high-res photo documenting the day's walk. "Then at Christmastime, I email everyone a personalized album, see? And don't be afraid of a little creativity. If Monday was a shot of Princess tucking into a bowl of kibble, maybe Tuesday's you rubbing her belly. No need to be skittish, though, she won't bite. And like this: only the hand. In my experience, people will trust a stranger with their keys and valuables right up to the point where they're forced to actually see him as a whole human being." He was tweaking the iPhone's "crop" feature when his glance fell on Ethan's lumpen Samsung, its two-pixel lens. "Aw, you're joking."

Ethan must have been holding his breath. "I don't suppose Erica mentioned I'm, ah . . . coming out of a substance-treatment program?"

"'Course she did. Why do you think she paired us up?"

Et tu, McGonagall, he thought, *after all that?* but then felt sheepish for having judged another man's sobriety based on a few Chianti bottles pressed into service as candlesticks. "So you'll understand if I say wifi's a huge trigger for me—"

"Have you looked around lately? It's a huge trigger for every-one. But so is the fact of other people more generally. I'm notic-ing a lot of these 'for me' statements, by the way."

"I'm trying to use my 'I' voice."

The vigor with which McGonagall stroked his beard made Ethan wonder about fleas. "Just feels like you might be going about it wrong."

"The internet's an anxiety machine, I'm saying."

"Life's an anxiety machine, brother. And I'm sorry, this is 2011. Time to come down off the mountaintop and get yourself a real phone. It's a what-do-you-call. Condition of employment."

Later, reviewing his service contract at a sleek tech outpost on Delancey Street, Ethan would regret not having pushed for a raise. Then again, dogwalking only filled fifty hours a week, with another five at most for the soup-kitchen shifts McGonagall insisted were "good for the soul," and he could always moon-light washing dishes. No, if he balked at signing, it was less an artifact of cost, or of the skeins of fine print set to bind him for all eternity to the T-Mobile corporation, than because the phone broke the personal rules that had so far thwarted Magnolia's worst prophecies. *No chasing. Don't feed the beast. Never let them see you bleed.*

Yet this slip turned out not to be fatal—or anyway, not at first. As late as the end of August, mushing his charges across mol-ten sidewalks, the Android a nylon whisper against his thigh, he would find himself admiring the churn of neighborhoods—the reinvention of whole boroughs—from within a sturdier sort of pocket, one insulated against the occasional nostalgic wisp of Madonna or blast of barroom air. It seemed almost shameful at times: How much might have turned out differently between him and Jolie, him and Sarah, had someone suggested three years ago when his father was dying that his mom's whole *Wings of Desire* trip could be prophylactic? That all he'd ever had to do to fight relapse was to hover at an angelic remove from his feelings and wait for them to pass? And say McGonagall had a point, and it was less his own feelings than other people's that had tended to make him crazy—or rather, the incommensurability between the two; then, with this wedge of flatulent canines bounding ahead, pedestrians abandoning the curbs like fielders ceding basepaths, he was spared any real confrontation, short of an argument about whose cans he'd chosen for the deposit of his baggies.

The insulation persisted when the workday was done. On the subway, women no longer checked him out as they used to. In otherwise packed cars, empty seats persisted to his left and right; at some point he'd look down to find himself like Shakespeare's Bottom, half-covered in fur. A discreet sniff of the tee yielded only fading Speed Stick, but there was another, deeper musk, he knew, a funk of cutaneous oils and dried ammonia it would take twenty minutes in the shower to wash off. McGonagall's preferred soap, a mail-order jade bar hanging on a rope beside a scrub-brush about which the less said the better, dwindled to a rusk fortnightly, as a curling decal on the shaving mirror commanded, "Don't Worry, Be Happy," above a face as teasingly familiar as a crossword clue.

It was over tea one night in September, when Ethan finally gave in and asked what the story was with this sticker, that McGonagall saw fit to mention the time he'd spent at the state correctional facility at Wallkill. He did so in the same blithe way he'd mentioned having been in the touring company of the '80s roller-musical *Starlight Express*—a biographical oversight, an odd job he'd held once—and for a second, Ethan pictured him in law-enforcement regalia, rubbing elbows with Erica Morales at some upstate convention. At the phrase "B felony," though, the lobster buffet turned to gruel, and Erica was whisked away on creaking tracks, replaced by McGonagall and Eddie Sixkiller in matching pinstripes. But no: it wasn't Wallkill but Moriah where Eddie had been sent after the bust in '01, Moriah that Ethan himself had barely skirted and then failed to visit, and instead of the jailhouse nitty-gritty that might have salted old wounds, McGonagall was now recalling the various sects that used to dump their tracts on the prison library. He couldn't always make heads or tails of the donations, he said, but in the particular one that had turned his life around, heads and tails were revealed to be a vanity anyway . . .

He paused, waiting for some encouragement to keep going. At this late date, though, talk of changed lives had the same effect on Ethan as the shibboleths of AA, or his late father's Episcopalianism, which was a kind of gag reflex of solitude, like he was the last person on earth shut out of these simple doctrines of subjection and oneness and love. And how could he ever have imagined himself relieved that McGonagall was a man? Men were the creatures he feared the most . . . they jammed him up, somehow.

So here was another thing that kept Ethan on the narrow path, those first few months of waiting: if he high-tailed it back to Chinatown after work, he might reach the apartment ahead of McGonagall and not have to hear any more about clouds of unknowing or the motions of the soul. It could be tricky at first to know if he'd succeeded, as McGonagall tended to take his evening tea with no lights on. More than once since the start of Daylight Wastings, Ethan had lit the living room lamp only to find McGonagall sitting there already, head bowed, spectral in his jean shorts. But he'd since learned to keep his own keys distinct from the three-pound hoop of others in his messenger bag; to work the lock with all due stealth and push the door swiftly past its squeaking point; to stand there motionless in the paint-smelling entryway, feeling for the subtle dislocations that would signify he wasn't alone . . . and, in their absence, to whisk from the fridge whatever he'd ordered over the weekend as takeout and spirit it off to his refuge.

By Columbus Day weekend, however, his refuge was back to feeling more like just a crash pad. After covering what he owed Sarah, one of his first moves had been to buy, at one of the last surviving miscellany shops on lower Broadway, a little *Murphy Brown*–era countertop TV. The government had auctioned off the rabbit-ears spectrum in favor of squarish new digital antennas that came at six price points: Excellent, Exceptional, Supreme, Best, Ultimate, and Supreme Plus. After some hesitation, Ethan had plumped for Exceptional, but now only two channels came in, fewer if the weather was bad, and eventually he'd ceased to futz with them. He had YouTube, after all, and a running text thread with Magnolia if it was friction he wanted, or friction cut with salaciousness. But let's be honest, what he really wanted after a season of toeing the line was more like the deliciousness of free-fall: Wikipedia rabbitholes, celebrity misbehavior, a whole warren of seeming emergencies that wouldn't matter tomorrow, provided he even remembered them. He liked to keep several tabs open simultaneously, one atop the next, the collapse of perspective being in some way essential . . . for the phone also offered new channels through which to try Jolie (friend requests, chat apps, e-vites), and increasingly, after a wallow in the shallows, he'd feel reckless enough to test these lower depths.

Hey, this you?

Jolie?

Ethan Aspern wants to be friends with you on Facebook.

The silence he met there felt even louder than in the summer, amplified by everything since, but at least this way he got a sense of escalation—as if instead of merely an unanswered call or text, it was now the whole edifice of cyberspace reverberating with her absence. With the fall wearing on, he would even catch himself bending his route home after work to let him pass by her school. Night now came at like five p.m. His breath was a fog machine, his shoulders hunched conspicuously in the ever-more-unseasonal corduroy, but there were hardly any lights on inside, or faculty or staff to look out and spot this stunted ape-man typing frantically with his thumbs.

Hey, sweetie—can we talk?

And still, a normal person might have been able to stop there, without the whole chain of sequelae that was to upend both their lives. A normal person was allowed to want things, wasn't he? And even, here and there, to slip? October had become November, though, Ethan's bad moon rising, and he was finding it harder to abide the other injunction he was under: not to misuse the access he'd been granted to the lives of perfect strangers.

It started like this. He was on his knees one afternoon, dumping a can of food into a bowl for the day's last client, a French bulldog named Bruiser, when a random snatch of erotic magnetic poetry—*hips my glistening suck* or some such—had caught his eye from amid the welter of menus and coupons and collection notices on the fridge door. But to whom could the line possibly have been directed, when everything else about this drab two-bedroom apartment said the owner was celibate and lived alone? And suddenly, out of nowhere, he found himself recalling again the VHS cassette he'd discovered among his mother's archives a year or so after her death and digitized with his own two hands and built a whole elaborate con around and then (possibly out of guilt) misplaced the only full copy of. It had been her last film project, and, like the fridge door now facing him, a kind of collage—one from which the human form had been sheared away, as if an H-bomb had gone off or the day of Judgment come at last. And yet the soundtrack, to the first half at least, was this procession of voices, internal monologues of people he thought he knew from around town, whom she'd somehow ensorcelled into sharing their secrets.

Before he could think what he was doing, he'd raised his phone's camera at one of the oblique angles Joanna Aspern had favored, opened the owner's fridge and scooted back, tried to conjure this person's private pain or the technique that would coax it out into the open . . . but the lit rectangle remained mute, might have been anyone's: single-shot yogurt, clamshell of spinach. So too with the kitchen drawers he pulled open (one for flatware, one for mail, one jammed tight with deli bags) and with the hall closet that felt like a novelty, scaled to match. But past these lay the larger back bedroom, and there, on the dresser, he spotted a rosewood lockbox. It was above all the lock that drew him in, and by the time he confirmed it was undone and peeked inside and saw a glass pipe and what looked to be about an eighth of an ounce of high-resin hashish, he'd forgotten again that the inner life he'd been seeking was anyone's but his own.

THE QUANTITIES he then began to nick of the drugs he found were hardly big enough to be missed . . . and anyway, legal exigencies would have prevented their owners from reporting them stolen. But the weird part was, he didn't ingest the drugs or even end up stealing them this time—not for good. Not the benzos he took from the nightstand at Mr. Pickles's in brownstone Brooklyn, nor the poppers from Princess's in Chelsea a few days later, nor even the stash of coke discovered, mirabile dictu, in a leather gimp suit in the downtown loft of doleful Wantohantoweh. He hadn't known this at first—or maybe he had, and that was why he'd been careful to avoid medicine cabinets—but the point seemed to be more to carry some talisman back with him to his lonely cell at McGonagall's, and to know for as long as he kept it there that he could have chosen to consume it, but didn't: to prove to himself that he still had some measure of control over the object world.

Or no, the point was the residue of excitement left behind, even after he'd contrived some subsequent dogwalking itinerary to facilitate the return of the drugs. For given the historic ugliness of the visible part of his life, it was Ethan's proclivity to believe that the real you is the one that other people *can't* see. That secrets make personality, or (putting it another way) that to have a personality, you had to have secrets . . . as now, even after checking the returned contraband against the clip he'd shot to make sure nothing was out of place, he manifestly did.

And that it all lived on as reference video on his phone . . . was this even creepier, somehow? Or at least not what the geniuses out in Mountain View quite had in mind? Well, to the extent that it generated monetizable data, human behavior was probably fungible anyway. And if some other Power out there wanted him to stop, he told himself, then it could damn well have his daughter give him a call.

IT WOULD ACTUALLY be Bruiser's owner's hash he'd have the hardest time letting go of, and most seriously contemplate using. Pot had helped him through a rough patch once before, after all, and he'd smoked that joint back in California without major repercussions (unless you chose to credit his sometime fancy that he'd been trapped in a bad hallucination ever since). But now, entering Bruiser's apartment three weeks later, he steeled himself to let even this temptation go. Draped his damp *My So-Called Life* jacket over the back of a kitchen chair, paused at the sink to wash hands as the dog collapsed dripping on the floor . . . and then, as if destroying evidence, tossed the paper towel. The squirming live weight in his gut as he crossed the hall to the bedroom was strangely familiar; for a moment, he almost hoped to find the wooden lockbox locked, but it wasn't, and in the weeks since he'd last touched the lump inside, it looked basically unchanged from the video version on his phone. It was only as an afterthought, then, that he went to inspect the medicine chest in the second, ensuite bathroom. Or maybe this was a little gift he was giving himself; looking down at his ringless finger, he'd just remembered that today would have been his thirteenth wedding anniversary.

And of course inside the medicine chest was where he found what he'd been seeking, between an alloy tube of jock-itch cream and a pump of steroidal nasal spray . . . no longer a longshot, but in the America of 2011, something like an inevitability: an amber cylinder of Purdue Pharma's OxyContin CR. Obtained for legitimate reasons, he figured, juddering a finger across the label, since the prescription was some three months out of date, and the bottle more than half full. If the owner *were* a junkie, of course, Ethan could almost have justified filching a few pills, in the golden-rule sense that a junkie would have done the same to him. He decided, however, to have this person be in terminal pain but avoiding the meds so as to remain clear-headed—meaning that to remove a few, however temporarily, would be to go beyond reciprocity to outright gift. The logic came out somewhat garbled, though, given the half-dozen pills already threatening to melt in his palm as his free hand readjusted the shelf's contents and reached for the mirrored door.

Which was when the thing that happened, happened: in the glass clicking shut appeared a face not his own. Nor am I speaking metaphorically; when he looked down to check the mirror captured in his phone, this other face was there, too. Not a stranger's face, but one he would have known anywhere: a face he had loved and hated, had fought against and failed, and above all, a face he'd been assured as of three years ago he would never see again. It didn't say a thing; just stared at him, impassive. A psychological symptom, perhaps, but an unnerving one, since even in the depths of withdrawal his delusions had never quite hit the level of a visual disturbance:

"Dad?"

It was to appease this face, as much as anything, that he opened the door, put the pills back inside. Before he could check their position on the shelf, though, he heard the scrabble of the dying owner's return, bearing in on him how this all was going to look from the outside. The least dignified job in the world, yet still one far above him. He would be caught—fired, ejected from the McGonagall ménage—and at this point it was unclear that the earnings pressed between the Brownings and Mailer's *Orgones & Ethers* would suffice to get him back to Avalon . . . or that there was even an Avalon to go back to. He used a square of toilet paper to wipe a print from the mirror and then, to account for his presence there, flushed. Again, though: Who would ever buy that he couldn't just have used the front john?

As fate would have it, the sound was only Bruiser, wrangling last night's sushi from the trash. And once Ethan had the rice and the black mercury of the soy sauce cleaned from the kitchen floor—and had located the cord with which he'd apparently failed to re-lash the can—he noticed that the sky had gone ombré beyond the Norman arch of the window. Even the wall-clock had jounced forward. The dog kept his head on his paws, but the eyes showed pleading crescents of white as his tail half-heartedly thwacked the linoleum. "Sorry, bud. Just walked you, if you'll recall." Ethan squatted to disburse a few pats, worried that it might be his own memory misfiring, as in one of those nightmares where his mom returned to earth to save him (but too late—he was already high).

Down on the street, the raindrops now seemed to precipitate directly out of the air, along with the ramifying impressions of rush hour: heavy smell of receding halal carts, cabs grousing along the thoroughfare, great chunks of Hell's Kitchen gone dark like an instrument panel someone had smashed with a fire extinguisher. The lights of the far buildings seemed remote enough to be Hoboken, but in the other direction was Eighth Avenue, a cauldron of actual New Yorkers swirling past at the herky-jerky speeds of a silent movie. And again he had the feeling that had defined so much of his youth: of a secret disaster just barely averted. But then why, when he caught sight of his own ghost in the scratched convexity at the subway steps' first switchback, did it look so furtive, so ashamed?

He would surface on Broadway a quarter of an hour later to find the rain had stopped. He couldn't even really say where he was going—which of the near-identical monoliths on Sarah's block was hers. She'd been so careful since moving to keep them off each other's turf, and his one other time here, in the fall of '08, he'd been fresh from a South Jersey drunk tank, by way of Erica Morales and her city-issued car. True, he now had the building number scribbled on a Post-it back in his other life, but fat lot of good that did him, unless he was ready to call Magnolia for it, hat in hand. Then he remembered the email from July where Sarah had broken the news of Jolie's drinking. Scrolling back through the migraine of his inbox, he passed that solicitation from his high school: homecoming moved to Thanksgiving, help honor the late rector and rechristen the sailing team's newest vessel, all donations tax-deductible . . . His sister, listed here as a member of the Committee for Saint Anselm's, had clearly ignored the long and mostly sincere apology he'd sent her after he'd blown his last detox, and was now trying to punish him. But ah: here we go, Sarah's address, third awning from the end.

To his surprise, he recognized the doorman reading behind the desk there, which meant potentially vice versa. So he retreated to count up a dozen stories. Then re-counted to make sure he hadn't skipped one. The L in 12L meant Left, but his left or the building's? Either way, their apartment must have been one of those two lines of windows above the lower cornice. He was starting to wonder again just what he was doing when a choir of pigeons exploded from the rooftop into the mist. And then a shadow seemed to step up onto a parapet . . . because what else were parapets for, or shadows? But don't be an asshole, Ethan: there was of course no one up there, no casement or parapet, conceivably even no birds. More likely, it seemed, he had somehow *needed* Jolie to be in danger all along. Had his idea in returning, then, been that if she fell he'd be here to catch her, even at the cost of his own survival? Because the only myth that mapped onto real life, it seemed (sorry, Eurydice; Abraham), involved not the efficacy of sacrifice but its long, barbed tail . . .

He was just emerging from these reveries when a woman in a too-large parka and a plastic hairdresser's kerchief plowed into him: "Watch where you're going!" The city hadn't yet spun him so thoroughly as to prevent a mumbled *Sorry*. Before he could even get it out, though, she had the kerchief down around her neck. "Oh, for God's sakes—Ethan? Don't tell me you're coming from upstairs."

It was Eleanor Kupferberg. Back in June, he'd noticed the white blaze at her temple starting to range Warholically through her slate-colored hair, but now she'd pulled it back to a tight demi-Sontag. And her thinness, unchanged, read as impatience, as though Ethan's own alibi were a test he was flunking. She went on:

"Though I suppose I'd be the last person Sarah told if the two of you were . . . reconnecting."

The inference was too close to his own secret longings for him to correct it; inasmuch as it offered a reason for his still being in New York, it may even have vindicated him a little. But as she continued on toward the canopy, he imagined her relaying this encounter to her daughter—or to his. "No, wait, Eleanor, stop. The truth is, neither of them know I'm here, okay? I was in the neighborhood, and I just wanted a clean look at where they were living. It's our anniversary, you know. Just a little moment or two of feeling close before I moved on."

"Close to Sarah?"

"To Jolie," he said quickly. "I know it sounds stalkerish, but I'm trying to be more honest with myself and others these days." And in case that wasn't plain enough: "Please don't rat on me."

He could have no concept of the look on his face—was too busy locking down the inner fallout shelter to which he fled in moments of greatest shame. Maybe she thought he'd fallen off the wagon, or didn't realize he'd been on it in the first place. But when she raised a hand, it wasn't to strike him, but to take him by the elbow and march him toward the nearest brownstone, where she unzipped her parka and spread it on the still-damp stoop, commanding him to sit.

Which, what else was there to do? With the fat iron banister to his right slicing the awning into frames, he felt as he had in various courtrooms of the early aughts, awaiting a sentence so painfully deferred.

"Ethan, let me ask you something," she said. "How long has it been since the air got cleared between us?"

He gave it some thought. "I don't know," he said. "Did it ever?"

"All the more reason for us not to mince words: I don't know what you think has been going on this last month, but whoever said your daughter's up there misled you. She's out in Riverdale right now, with Albert."

"Christ—did something happen?"

"You tell me," she said, with a hard stare. "She's been with us since Columbus Day weekend. She and Al are probably just settling down to their four hours nightly of television. Part of what I've come to talk to Sarah about, in fact."

He wasn't sure which felt more crucial to hide: his relief, or his despair. "You're worried Albert's wasting his brainpower on *Real Housewives*?"

"For once, my husband's not the problem." And now she took a seat on the step beside him, albeit far enough away that the coat did her no good. "Sarah really didn't call you about this? Jolie hasn't uttered a single word to us since her arrival in October— but what am I saying, why would you need filling in on what you already know?"

"I know nothing," he said, in all truth.

"Nothing about that afternoon you took her to see *Spider-Man* on Broadway, Ethan? Because at ten fifteen that night we get a knock on the door, and there's your daughter with her lip buttoned and a look on her face like somebody died. And though I'm sure Albert would have happily run her home in the car, nothing could have been plainer than that she needed a place to stay the night. To be frank, I assumed it was you she was trying to get away from."

All this was news to him (not least that he'd taken Jolie to see a show), but he didn't want to interrupt the telling. "Seems like I probably am what she's running from, one way or another," he said, to placate her. "I mean, whatever she's been giving you and Albert in the way of a silent treatment, she pioneered on me back in July."

"But it's not just us; she won't talk to Sarah, either. Who, when I reached her, said there'd been some kind of a blow-up between them. Even in school now, Jolie's gone silent. The way you do when you're stewing on something."

"She's still talking to that therapist, though, right?"

"They're group sessions, Ethan, and I don't think I'm violating a trust if I say she shows up, sits there mutely, glowers at her phone. In fact, it was the therapist who suggested letting her stay with us for a month while things cooled off at home."

Precisely the offer he'd tried to make Sarah in May, he thought—the one whose rejection had led to this moment. But now a cab sluiced past, dissolving any sense of having told anyone so, and touching the edge of Eleanor's kerchief with a brief glow. She hunched forward, elbows on her trim black pants, as if exhausted by the sheer ongoingness of life.

"And a few days not speaking, Ethan, a week of it, and then she opens up: okay. But we've passed the one-month mark now, she's supposed to be back with her mother starting a week from Wednesday last, and the only change I've seen is for the worse. Schooldays she slips out of the house at six a.m., comes back in the early dark without so much as a hello. Then she and Al sit there in the dark with the tube on, him musing about God knows what and her not talking. And that's not to mention her appearance. I tried taking her to dinner last week, and five minutes ahead of our leaving she blows in from the bus stop—reeking of tobacco, I might add—with a fourth earring in her ear and one through the nose. And when I ask her, *That's* how you want people to see you?, I get nothing in return. Ethan, the piercings aren't so bad, the holes will heal, but how can I fix what I can't even talk to? The therapist was wrong. This let-the-grandparents-handle-it strategy hasn't worked."

"I guess that puts us in the same boat," he said, struggling not to see how it might feel to his daughter that even Eleanor was ready to cut her losses. "I mean, it's not like I have any pull with her either."

She looked up. "But quite obviously you do. Whether or not you're the proximate cause, we all seemed to be getting along just fine until this great comeback of yours. And I fail to see how it's doing Jolie any good for you to be hanging around like this against everyone's wishes—stalking, to use your word. Don't think I haven't seen those messages you keep sending her, by the way, before her phone locks up again. From watching her wince, I had an idea that maybe she'd asked you to stop."

"Maybe I'm just not a good person, though. Remember?"

"Even at your lowest, Ethan, I could never quite believe that about you." He was reminded of how she'd softened in those first few visits after they'd brought Jolie home from the birthing center. Beguilement at his transformation, he'd thought, when of course she'd seen through him from the very start. And were she now to touch his face, do something even minimally maternal, it might be the death of him—as she seemed to sense. "But what if I were to try calling on your better angels? What would I have to offer them, Ethan, to drag you back to California, restore things to what they were?"

He stood and faced the street, ready to tell her what he'd learned: nothing restores anything . . . and he'd been on the brink of leaving regardless. But already something in him must have been realizing how Jolie's silence could be put to work. "Honestly, Eleanor? I'm already not seeing any of you, Jolie's headed back to her mom's, and you can't stop me being her father, so beyond the aesthetic pleasure of knowing I'm faroff and suffering, what's it to you if I stay or if I go?" She seemed to have no answer to this, so he pushed on. "All I wanted, as I told Sarah six months ago—all I came here for in the first place—was to spend some time talking with my daughter. Which you'll recall I was legally entitled to—"

"Under direct supervision."

"A day, maybe a night. And things being what they are, you and I both know it might have done her some good if I'd gotten my way. Or at least couldn't have hurt."

He suppressed the paltry satisfaction of having won the point; what mattered was whether she rose to the bait. Which she seemed to, at first: "Am I to understand that if I could somehow bring about a custody visit—'a day, maybe a night'—you'd be prepared go back west and leave the four of us alone?"

He was surprised to catch something calculating in her look.

"Because it's almost Thanksgiving break, Ethan. I know Sarah's finalizing her own plans. I could talk to her for you, I suppose, provided Jolie doesn't put up a fight."

"And if you could arrange for my visit to fall over the holiday, I guess that would be a bonus, or anyway, a fellow can dream. But now I'm confused: What's in this for you?"

She stood to face him. Raised the kerchief like a cowl over her hair and slinked her frail frame, always tougher than it seemed, into her coat. Leaned forward but did not touch. For a second, he wondered if she was the one who'd been drinking, but the smell was of course just chemicals from the salon. "It remains the case that you're her father, Ethan, whether I like it or not. But I think if you're being truly fearless with your moral inventory, or what's the other one—"

"'Searching.'"

"—you'll find that it does entail having some power over her. Which is the exact thing I'm asking you to give up in return." Then she reached out to help him to his feet, the same brusque woman he'd met sixteen years ago on the Eastern Shore.

"But how will I know if Sarah has agreed to any of this? I've got a new phone, don't you want the number?"

"You think I haven't already gone and copied it off Jolie's texts? Let's not kid ourselves, Ethan: you've been campaigning months for this, so I'm confident you can wait a few more days for my call." In all the ways that counted, he would remain in the dark, she was saying. Yet as she walked off, he found himself for the first time in a long while full of hope. For if his daughter didn't want his messages, why hadn't she just taken whatever steps were needed to delete them?

"YOU SURE you're good to do the holiday alone?" asked McGonagall early the next week.

Ethan stayed crouched before the refrigerator, hunting for Sunday night's Chinese. There had been little of this solicitude lately—no more "soul" talk or auditions for some kind of guru position—and he wondered briefly if McGonagall was trying to distract him from the fact that he'd eaten all of Ethan's General Tso's. But no, there it was, behind the mayo, and what had seemed a sort of schtick was just ordinary fellow feeling. Out of gratitude, he almost confessed then and there about Jolie's proposed visit. Instead, he ventured that Thanksgiving was revisionist history anyway and it had been years since he'd spent it other than by himself, which in some respects seemed easier. "As witness . . ."

He gestured toward McGonagall, who, though clad only in boxer shorts and a dingy Pilgrim hat, was alternately holding up before the mirror a striped necktie and a shinier, more abstract one, perhaps waiting for Friar Tuck to weigh in from the painting he'd prematurely garlanded with tinsel (and clearly done himself).

"My vote is for stripes, by the way," he continued. "And again, don't worry about me picking up your shifts, McGonagall. At this point, I'm an old pro."

Actually, if Ethan was an old pro at anything, it was pretending his ability to abide in this world wasn't hopelessly fucked. But it was true that his host's departure in the a.m. for a long weekend with an ex-cellmate's family in Cleveland would solve certain logistical problems. Not only would Ethan be spared the expense of last-minute lodgings for two; after consolidating his and McGonagall's dogwalking itineraries, minus holiday cancellations, he might even end up running a surplus . . . one he'd already blown mentally on hot chocolates, ice skating at Rockefeller Center, and a climactic feast bound to fix whatever was wrong with Jolie. The important thing here was that someone in a position of responsibility just hurry up and confirm. No, scratch that—the important thing here was that he not call Sarah directly and ask what the hell was taking her so long; for were he to tumble once more from the brink of self-control, he could pretty much count on these fantasies of reconciliation having come to nothing.

After quarantining the smartphone between books in a dresser drawer, he would spend the rest of that Tuesday with an itchy feeling, like a limb had been amputated. The weather remained a mess, moils of rain seeming to time their arrivals against his dashes between awnings with clients in tow. He had finally accepted his lot, invested in calf-high wellies and a water-resistant shell, but Gore-Tex and India rubber had clearly been designed for some less apocalyptic age. And a wet dog shook, he discovered, for the same reason you boiled tea before sweetening it: to allow supersaturation. On his way home, drenched, he made a stop at the Whole Foods Union Square, that unlikely synthesis of Soviet commissary and neoliberal free-for-all, and elbowed aside a lanyarded techie to snatch from the case the last organic, humanely slaughtered bird, "fresh frozen," whatever that meant. It cost eighty-seven dollars and weighed twice as much as he needed, but perhaps the train of ethical dispensations would buy a little indulgence from his daughter. And when he reached his room and dared get out the phone to check, there was a voicemail from Magnolia about some water-main issue in California . . . but also one from Eleanor with the time and location of the Broad Horizons fall recital, where, she informed him, he could come to collect Jolie tomorrow.

It should have been thrilling, whole vistas of fatherhood reopening before him, but when he turned to inspect the apartment through his daughter's eyes, what he felt instead was an obscure sense of failure. The living room looked grotty. Ill-used. Yellowing tabloids, waterstains, boluses of loose tea slumped in saucers like sleepers on the subway. From the arms of the lampshade luffed filaments of cobweb he'd never noticed before, borne aloft by the heat of the bulb. He thought of that Camus book Moira had sent him the spring of his senior year of high school, apropos of ostensibly nothing—Camus with his blackfoot conscience, Camus who insisted on certain doors that, once opened, could not be closed. Yet neither (it seemed) could Sisyphus get on with his life, begin reimposing order. He tested the turkey's rubberized membrane for leakages, but the moisture he'd noticed was just precipitation, so he wrapped the corpse in a towel, set it at the bottom of his closet to thaw. He would move it to the sink tomorrow, once he had the place to himself and didn't have to worry about explaining what he was up to. Well, bathtub, maybe, given the size.

THEN MORNING WAS UPON HIM, like a jaguar from a tree. A low-angled sun, making an uncredited cameo, drove shafts of brightness through the miniblinds. And in the kitchen, McGonagall stood over a wheelie bag and several boxes heaped on the parquet, waiting for the coffee to brew. The oddity of his white oxford shirt was only heightened by the fact that he'd tied his tie a good three inches too short. He'd had the wisdom to go with the stripes, at least. But now, for the first time since Ethan had known him, he looked impatient, seizing the carafe even as the burner spit acrid billows across the room. Then he turned, mug in hand, and coolly took a sip. "Didn't realize you were up."

Chop wood, carry water, Ethan wanted to say, but knew it would come out as sarcasm, or self-pity. "Does it make a difference?"

"I've got more luggage than I thought," McGonagall said, "what with Christmas coming early for my little godsons. I suppose I could always ship it FedEx, take the bus out to LaGuardia, but I thought maybe you'd like to give me a lift instead. You'll be needing the van anyway, you're planning to hit all your marks." He nodded toward a printed spreadsheet on the counter, names of clients plotted against hours of the day. And if only there had been some hint of pressure, Ethan might have tried to talk his way out of helping, ended up on foot. But McGonagall's artlessness was somewhere between kid asquirm in his Easter clothes and lead guitarist for AC/DC. Worse, he was right: if there was to be any hope at all of getting forty dogs walked in the next five hours, it was going to involve driving between appointments.

Or so Ethan kept telling himself a half-hour later, gingerly piloting the van—to which McGonagall had now clipped a pair of festive reindeer antlers—along the congested FDR. Driving was among the many things in life said to be like riding a bike (along with sobriety, come to think of it), but as he dropped his employer near the skycap at Terminal C, Ethan felt there was much he'd forgotten. In the end, the van didn't even yield any real gain in efficiency. You'd think meters and alternate-side parking might have been suspended in view of the holiday, but no. And where the traffic should have quickened as the matutinal throng got digested, the cross-streets in fact grew more sluggish. At some point the radio reminded him, mockingly, that the Wednesday before Thanksgiving was the busiest travel day of the year. Then it was lunchtime, then two thirty, and suddenly he'd missed his window to dash back to Chinatown and tidy up, or change clothes, or even just be rid of the van.

And so, reaching Third Avenue, he grabbed the first meter he saw, sat in the driver's seat brushing bristles off his jacket, and used the corner of a loose subscription card to clean his teeth, trying not to guess how much he'd devolved since last seeing Sarah.

There were a few minutes still left before the recital, which he could use to pick something up for her, a little token of gratitude for going along with all this, but what? Flowers were probably too naked in their appeal to auld lang syne. But didn't there used to be a bakery a few blocks down—one of those old-timey places with a twine dispenser strung up from the ceiling? It was Thanksgiving, for God's sakes, and they could be adults about this: he would get her a pie.

The storefront, guarded by a fiberglass pig in a toque and apron, was more or less where he remembered it, but the mob he'd feared was nowhere to be seen. Even as he entered, high banks of fluorescents were shutting down preparatory to an early close, and though the smells carried him back to the time when all was promise, smells could be deceptive; the glass case was bereft of all but a tropical cake spectacularly inapposite to the holiday. Then again, Sarah always had liked coconut. When asked about coffee, the clerk, an apronless middle-aged man, seemed to scowl.

"It's not fresh."

"Just so long as it's hot."

"It's not really hot, either."

"Then you'd be willing to give me half-price on a small if I took that coconut cream off your hands?"

"Hell, you take that cake, I'll throw the coffee in for free. Just don't expect it to be any good, is what I'm saying." When the guy was done tying up the box, he slid it across the counter with a blue deli cup on top:

WE ARE HAPPY TO SERVE YOU

Per Eleanor's message, the recital was to take place in Stuyvesant Square, a little park that, like the train platform in the Harry Potter movies, seemed to exist only if you were looking for it. The route, though, took him right past Jolie's school, both the main building he'd spied on earlier that fall and the annex farther along the sidestreet, former rectory to a now-condoed church. As he passed, he experienced another twinge of regret (especially since nothing had come of those stakeouts), leaving him wide

open for the next of his visions: in one of the windows, the love of
his life perched on a desk with her hands braced behind her, head
thrown back in laughter. But already the angle had cut her off; the
street was a blank again, and obviously Sarah was still fifty yards
ahead with their little girl, at the concert whose strains he couldn't
hear.

He hustled on to where the street T'd into a somnolent lane.
On the far side were fenceposts and psoriatic sycamores and a
glint of Second Avenue, the first lights coming on. A wintry wind
whipped little gyres of drying leaves from the gutter, but the park
itself remained a wave of green, culminating in the verdigrised
likeness of the dead white male who'd lent it his name. Ethan's
fuzziness on the respective C.V.s of Peters Stuyvesant and Minuit
was of course beside the point; what mattered about the statue
was its lordly mien. *Without me, no this*, it seemed to say—the
hook on which fathers the world over hung their claims. Then,
about to pass through the gate, he spotted a mottle of drying coffee on his left hand, like a phone number written there against
forgetting. He licked at it, rubbed it against the grooves of his
corduroy, and, when he couldn't get all of it off, chucked the cup
with its faulty lid into a can; the clerk had been right anyway—
everything was terrible.

And now it was possible to make out a rabble of folding chairs,
heads chockablock above: families, hatted and scarved. But so
many onlookers were packed into the standing room along the
margins that at least some of them had to be tourists, he thought,
sucked north from walking tours of the old CBGB and Heaven
and Hell Club to hear his daughter play. Or not hear, since there
was still no sound, just a folding table barring his way. Behind a
plastic dropcloth motley with school crests and anchored by a
donation jar sat two girls roughly Jolie's age. They seemed both
over- and underdressed, somehow—ample accessories, not much
to keep off the cold—and when he tried to sweep past, one of
them shot him a look of appraisal so frank it took him a second
to recover. "Sorry, is this ticket-holders only? My daughter plays
first violin, maybe you know her . . . Jolie Aspern?"

"It's a bunch of schools playing," the other girl said.

As a finger rose to the first one's lips, he marked a leather cuff battened to her slim brown wrist; the wheel of fashion had turned back to the grunge years, apparently, everything old new again. But what really startled was her nail, painted a blue that was nearly incorporeal, as if to match the washed-out segment of moon floating overhead.

Then she slid back, plucked from under the jar a sheet of copy-paper he now saw was a program. Broad Horizons was the third school listed. Before he could read further, the girl was guiding him through the congestion behind the table, so that presently he found himself in a narrow space between the last folding chairs and the wrought-iron ankle-breaker bordering the beds. He was searching for Sarah—wanting her to see how he'd made it here with time to spare—when an ambient noise drew his eye toward the front. An Asian American girl seated at an electric keyboard, presumably the soloist, was mutely closing a binder and pushing back her bench to stand. And there in profile among the music stands behind her: his own daughter in a tux jacket, bow raised above her violin as though the performance had just ended. In which case, had it started ahead of schedule? Again he checked the program. "Fall" from *The Four Seasons*, something from *A Charlie Brown Christmas*, something called "Let's See Action" . . . and finally, ha ha, very funny, "4'33"." Not J. Aspern, but J. Cage. And when he looked back up, the hands lowering the instrument seemed paler than the cold could account for, and the face beneath the hatbrim thin to the point of severity. At this age, five months was long enough for the last of the childhood softness to have burned away, so that now the true action beneath stood revealed: youth ending at the very moment the beauty comes in.

The other adults, having glanced around to confirm that the show really was over, were rising from their chairs in an ovation as absurd as the minutes of silence. The chief effect on Ethan was to rob him of Jolie again. Still no sign of Sarah, either, but there in one of the front rows were Albert and Eleanor Kupferberg, visibly overcompensating with their applause. All he could manage to do was drum his own on the lid of the cake box. Then a curious reorganization began, whereby the seated claque dispersed and the one on the margins swooped in. A path opened to Jolie, who was squatting to return violin and bow to their velveteen housings. The little trapdoored rosin compartment seemed to bulge, as if holding something back. Her navy surplus bag looked likewise overstuffed (so at least she was planning to stay the night). And here was his chance to bypass the Kupferbergs altogether; by the time he remembered her touchiness around being touched, he had closed the distance between them and was already reaching for the fedora.

What he was unprepared for was the artificial pink tingeing her light brown hair. He saw, too, the silver hoop through her nose, the surrounding skin still a little inflamed . . . and that was before he realized she was chewing something and heard a clanking that recalled a girl he'd dated briefly in rehab, the tiny barbell through her tongue. "Hey, your Nana didn't mention another piercing." It was a provocation (probably the business with the hat had been, too), but her poker face was total; even the chill in her gray eyes might have been something he put there. "Or wait, sorry," he said, more softly, "are we not communicating in meatspace, either?"

She continued to favor him with an absence of expression—or rather, to unfavor a point somewhere around his right shoulder. But now her grandparents came whooshing in, Eleanor saying, That was wonderful, honey. Just wonderful.

Albert, for his part, took no notice of Ethan's attempted handshake; only of Jolie's manifest unhappiness. "You know it's not too late to change course, Jojo, come back with us to the Bronx for Thanksgiving."

But the rescue attempt probably came too late, since Jolie had already begun to re-shoulder her gear; and anyway, it had been years, Ethan knew, since Albert was in any position to oppose his wife's wishes.

Only when he asked after Sarah—"I brought a peace offering"— did the man deign to acknowledge him.

"You should have been on time."

"I was on time. Four o'clock, Eleanor said."

"Then you should have double-checked the website, where it said three thirty. But you wouldn't have seen Sarah anyway."

"You did tell her I'd be here?" For it wasn't like her to miss a chance to make him suffer, he thought.

"Sarah's taken the opportunity to go up to Connecticut for the holiday, Ethan," Eleanor said.

"With a friend," Albert added, and here, at least, the import was crystalline; Ethan had once been such a "friend" himself.

He waited until Albert went and congratulated the Asian girl to tug Eleanor aside. "So Sarah's overnighting with some boyfriend now? I guess that explains a lot . . . including why you're so eager to usher me offstage. But I didn't come here to have your husband rub my nose in it. Even Jolie's giving me dirty looks. Did you not have time to get everyone on board with our agreement?"

"Candidly, Ethan, I spent much of last week doubting the wisdom of it myself. But then this morning I go in to make sure Jolie's all packed, and the only things out on the bed are her phone and that passport we got her back at the end of fifth grade . . . which I hadn't looked at in years. I mean really looked. I can still remember taking her to sit for the photo, how excited she was. That smile. And now here she was snatching it from my hands, a different person. A wounded child I know is still in there. Which you may have some power to reach the rest of us don't." *Being one yourself*, she perhaps thought but did not say.

"And Sarah?" he said. But Eleanor seemed for a minute not to understand.

"If you can succeed with Jolie where we failed, and Sarah can get a night away from all this, maybe she'll forgive us a little last-minute rejiggering of plans. At any rate, I'll be there at the hand-off tomorrow to smooth out any rough edges and drop off the rest of her clothes. We'll look for you at nine o'clock, in the lobby of their building . . . which of course you know how to find."

"Nine meaning nine," said Albert, having just rejoined them. "Not nine thirty. Not eleven."

Ethan wanted to protest again that this wasn't about winning their daughter's forgiveness, or their respective successes or failures, but since Jolie had now slipped into the crowd massing toward the avenue, there was no time. Instead, he lifted the cake box and foisted it onto Albert, who only barely missed dropping it. "Well, bon appétit to you both, anyway."

Ahead of him, Jolie had pushed on toward the corner at an automaton's pace, too slow to quite count as fleeing and too fast to be seeking to be chased (particularly as it wasn't clear she knew he'd spotted her). But then the signal changed and crosstown traffic became a wall, damming her up with every other mortal. The tallest of the westerly buildings now blocked the sun. Headlights multiplied, holes punched through tin. *You could have told me your mom was seeing someone*, he thought . . . but then how would she have done that, if she really was going to insist on this silence? Out loud, he said, "Wrong way, honey. I'm parked over on Third."

And had that been a little glimmer of resistance just before she locked back down? He chose to construe it as surprise (not to say encouragement).

"As to why I'm driving, that's a bit of a saga. I thought I could fill you in over dinner—your pick—and then we'd loop up to Central Park to watch balloons get blown up for the parade. But here, let me at least carry some of your stuff." Her knuckles visibly whitened when he reached for the handle of her violin, but after a brief skirmish he was allowed to take the backpack, making him think of that game Operation, the tiny tools used to extricate a bone or organ without setting off the electrified rim.

Rather than cutting across the park again and risking further unpleasantness with his in-laws, he led her along its lower bound and around the corner, past the school. In the quiet of the side-street, he could hear the weird clank of her tongue-ring behind him. Was she really not going to say anything? The rectory was by now a mouthful of dead teeth, every last light gone save for an emergency-lit stairwell . . . assuming things hadn't been like that before. Then, as they rounded onto Third Avenue, he noticed a uniformed woman half a block north eyeballing the parked van with its horns and tail.

"Hey," he called, breaking into a trot, "how about cutting me some slack?" To have someone to unload on was almost a relief. "I've already had to re-park like a dozen times today; it's Thanksgiving, you know?"

"Thanksgiving's tomorrow," the meter maid corrected him. "And the law's the law, you need fifteen feet to the hydrant."

"Look, I've got my kid here and everything . . ." He had turned to point out Jolie, but she was nowhere to be seen. Fear came flooding back in (he'd been a dad again for all of ten minutes, had he screwed up already?) when he spotted a smear of stickers, a flash of chrome: Jolie's violin case disappearing into the chain drugstore some thirty yards back. "See? You scared her off. Now what say we give each other something to be thankful for . . ."

He was just unvelcroing his wallet for a gratuity when the meter maid said, "Sir? System's automated. Once your plate gets scanned, it's out of my control." With the push of a button, the machine ground out a citation in the style of a register receipt. "You two have a nice holiday, though," she added before walking away.

The drugstore's interior was one of those weightless postmillennial spaces, newly renovated but also already festooned with kitsch. And why does so much of my life seem to depend upon a Duane Reade? he wondered, as the pabulum of yuletide filtered down from ceiling-mounted woofers too discreet to even see. Half the cashiers had been cashiered in favor of self-service machines, but Jolie, clutching the organic-cotton pads she must have come for, was holding out for an actual human. He joined her on the foreshortened line: "Christ, is this Shania Twain doing 'Hallelujah'? Someone should tell her this song's about adultery," he said. And again, in the second before she recovered, it seemed possible that Jolie had lost control of her face, though not in the longed-for smile. What she was conveying, he realized, was that he'd been supposed to spare her the affront of his existence and wait the fuck outside.

At which point the clerk motioned them forward. Jolie set the pads on the counter, added a giant torpedo of Fiji water from an adjacent display; an entire carton of green granola bars; and then, so blankly he almost missed it, a turquoise pack of American Spirits. At which point she wrenched the backpack off his shoulder and began to stuff the scanned items in. The cashier, a kangaroo-smocked young woman with elaborate fingernails, had paused over the cigarettes, skeptical, but Ethan was not above weighing the benefits of placing his daughter in his debt, which . . . no, sorry, fuck that, absolutely not. With a croupier's deftness, he returned the smokes to their rack and stooped to replace them with a Hershey bar and Jolie's old favorite, Baby Ruth, as if she'd grabbed the wrong thing by mistake. Then he raked up her crumpled bills, reached for his wallet. Perhaps the cashier's relief was really his, too. At any rate, it was short-lived; Jolie had used the confusion to make a run for the door, bag in tow, leaving him holding only her cash.

He would manage to grab on to the trailing violin case as she lit out the wrong way outside, back toward Fourteenth Street, and the subway, and though he could feel the tension radiating through the nubbed black plastic, he knew better than to let her go short of the van. And of course outright mutiny would have broken her silence. The way he swept aside the passenger's-side door and got her bundled in and the heat going might have been gallant, were it not for the incongruous smell of drying fur and the same air fresheners used once by Eddie Six-K. He reached past her again to stash the parking ticket in the glovebox and snag the backpack, just in case. Then he was out on the curb, the city looming above him, feeling somehow more desolate than even before.

It was when he went around to his own side that he would discover she'd locked the door. He knocked on the window, signaled her to open it, but she wouldn't respond. Some part of him he hated wanted to bang on it with his palm, not stop till she acknowledged him as her father. But he knew the passenger's-side door wasn't locked—was not in fact lockable—so he went around, tugged it open, and clambered in across Jolie, trying not to jostle or even touch, but wedging the backpack in on the driver's side so that if she wanted it she was going to have to ask. When he got his seatbelt buckled and looked over, she was arrow-straight, facing forward. The dome light had died, leaving the cab too dark to read her profile, but then again, what was there to read? The radio was silent; the instrument panel the merest blur of light. He felt himself hit a boil. "For the record," he said, "if you ever decide to try running off on your own like that again, you come talk to me first, okay? I'm not saying it even has to be verbal, exactly, but you're in my care now, Jolie, and my job is to make sure you're safe."

Had it worked?—was that another quiver of disbelief on her side? Or even hatred? No, probably just the rattle of the engine. And when she took out her phone to check something, it was only

in his fantasies (or whatever they were) that she went to type out
a message:

> Please Dad, don't make me do this . . .

Besides—do what? His own phone remained a dumb slab in his
lap, nothing to check, no voicemail or messages from the beyond.
And people like to gush over benchmarks—first step, first word—
but no one ever wants to talk about the first time the child who
used to run to you for Band-Aids manages to draw your own
blood. He watched himself thumb in a missive from his side, one
she wouldn't be able to ignore.

> I get it, honey: life sucks, dads are the
> worst, you don't want to join in the whole
> holiday spectacular thing—fine. But as
> long as we're stuck together for the
> next twenty-odd hours, why not figure
> out something you actually feel like
> doing?

He could hear her phone buzz, see it jump in her hand, but still
she failed to react. He was losing her, he thought . . . or in truth,
had already lost her, at the moment three years back when he'd
blown off his fourth or fifth meeting post-rehab and instead sidled
off to score heroin. And if there could be said to exist some point
of no return, a single moment where he decided to take both their
fates in his hands (he would realize later)—this was it.

"I mean, I'm just thinking out loud," he said, "but I remember
you saying you don't know the first thing about where we come
from, you and I. And there's this memorial thing for your grandfather I seem to be expected at tomorrow: a boat dedication down
on the Eastern Shore . . . more of that business I mentioned last
summer. I wasn't planning on going, but from here it's only two
hours and change to Cape May, and if we leave now we could
probably make the last ferry. I could show you around the old
haunts of the Asperns and have you back before anyone was the
wiser."

And when she still refused to respond:

"Or how's this, Jolie: you know of some easier path to forgiveness, say the word."

He would justify this to himself as an attempt to give her a voice, not to rob her of one. But Jolie's voice was her silence, and she clung to it for all she was worth. And anyway, as with so much about him, he thought, the idea had been cockamamie, had been bullshit; he had no valid driver's license, no one's permission to take her across state lines; for that matter, it was increasingly clear that her mother, his ex-wife, hadn't signed off on them going even this far. And there were of course laws in place to protect Sarah's rights as a mom—he wasn't an idiot. Nor was it like he had a ferry schedule at his fingertips, any more than he could have pushed a button and whisked them all back to a life where his little girl would know she was loved. It wasn't 1997 any longer. It wasn't, God knew, 2001. Except, creature of impulse that he was, he was recalling now that in the year of our Lord 2011 there was a button for everything, and that maybe all he had to do was find the right one here and push it. And take her. And in a flash the icon of a shopping cart with ferry tickets was rising before him. And directions to the tunnel, and New Jersey. And a memory of Norman Mailer, late of Long Branch—those ridiculous third-person essays where he called himself Aquarius, as if he weren't in fact the one in control—and two poets, male and female, clashing violently in his head . . . And what was that thing Sarah was always saying about choices?

It was in this way, Belovèd, that I'm afraid my dad, Ethan Aspern, would make his.

IV

THE VINDICATIONS

But again, Jolie, there I was: on the Eastern Shore more than a quarter-century back, slinking south with a hangover along the railroad cut, in approximately the same stunned state you've just left us both in. Or sorry, no, your point is well-taken: I was the one in control there, in 2011 . . . and maybe as early as seventeen, the confusions afflicting me were my responsibility alone. Still, your line about "choices that don't feel like choices" pretty neatly captures what was ringing in my head, that morning of reckoning it feels ever more crucial to get right. What do I mean? I mean that though the Sinclair's awning, looming up between tanks a quarter-mile on, wore its innocent daylight aspect, I was already scanning the shade below for anyone who might be in possession of prescription painkillers they'd be willing to part with. What brought me up short was the sight of my own house as I exited the woods, along with the one other person I'd spent all summer letting slide from my view.

That is, I'd been counting on several more hours of not having to deal with my dad, but Corinne's hatchback was already parked trunk-first in the driveway, and there he was behind it, squatting to inspect some cardboard boxes. Before I could step back into the woods and retreat, he looked up. So I continued across the grass, hoping he hadn't noticed my shift in tack. Or possibly hoping he had.

I see you came through the summer all right, he said, when I'd drawn close enough that he wouldn't have to call out to me. You look good, Ethan. Tanned. Sturdy.

Resisting the urge to reach up and check my hair, I shrugged: Yeah, well, I've been working.

So says your sister.

You talked to her already?

You know there's a phone in every port, he said, in that measured way of his. But here—why don't you go grab a pair of coveralls and help me get these into the garage?

No mention of the hour, no wondering where I'd been, just: here, don't soil your clothes, son. And all this, I thought, when if he'd taken the slightest interest in the person beneath, he couldn't possibly have missed the puke flecking the cuffs of my khakis. But he was right, something had changed in his absence. Previously, I'd have felt compelled either to do his bidding or to stalk off in protest, but it was as if the presumption of industry, duty, tensile strength—of having a son who was anything like him—could no longer touch me. Instead, I went and sat on the top step with my heart snuffed in my chest and watched him take boxes from the staging area and reconstruct them in neat stacks in the garage. And after a while, maybe just to see what he would do, I shouted idly that I'd been giving some thought to this whole college thing we'd been talking about in June.

Oh?

Specifically Columbia. It's in New York. Maybe you've heard of it.

And now, at last, I'd managed to provoke him. He pushed back his O's cap and scratched his forehead and peered up at me, the rims of his glasses flaring gold in the sun.

That's an Ivy League school, Ethan. But is this about a girl? Moira mentioned a girl . . . she must be smart.

Yeah, but she's gone now, I said. Left this morning. Then: I did tell her about Mom, though.

There was a long pause.

Well, that's good, he said. (It could have been a line from a script.) And I'm glad to hear you bring that up, actually, because I've had time to do some thinking too . . . or maybe what I mean is had space. I was starting to worry we were somehow letting you get stuck—

Was this some angle Corinne had been working? I wondered. Had Mom's vials of missing pills come up, out there on the boat? But whatever Corinne knew, or guessed, she must have preferred to keep to herself (blackmailing me into compliance, I felt) since he'd rolled right on into his leader-of-men routine:

—in any event, senior year's a big one, Ethan, and what comes next is going to be the better part of your life—

And before he could get to the line about hard rights and easy wrongs, something in my fogged-over brain made a click:

Wait—are those her boxes, from the sunroom?

Just the music, he said. And the video stuff from that editing suite she used to keep out at school. I stopped by on my way back from the dock. I was thinking it should all end up in one place.

And Corinne put you up to moving them out of the house?

Corinne has nothing to do with this, he said, I'm just borrowing her car.

And glanced back over his shoulder as if to double-check, but the only other traces of Corinne were a dreamcatcher hanging from her rearview and a welter of bumper stickers: the Darwin fish, the hospital parking pass, the imperative to "coexist."

Ethan, you might not like to hear this, he said, but it isn't doing anyone any good to let these things sit around eighteen different places collecting dust. We've got to make room to move forward. I thought maybe we could set you up a greenhouse in the sunroom, let you start your seeds there this winter . . .

But for Pete's sake, don't just stick it all in the garage, I said. Or let me do it, okay? This needs way more time than you're giving it.

He raised his hands as though in self-defense, but then seemed to catch himself, saying that would be great; in fact, provided I didn't have to be at work now, why didn't I go ahead and finish up in the sunroom, and he could use the time to fix me some lunch.

I had little choice but to obey, I thought, lest he decide to stow the boxes somewhere harder for me to reach, or for all I knew send them to Goodwill. Yet nor did I feel inclined to accept so much as an inch of extra space under my father's roof. So while the material he'd already moved sat untouched in the sun, I'd spend the rest of that morning and several thereafter trying to busy myself on the periphery: pushing things around in the garage, sweeping, vacuuming, clearing a five-by-five corner of bare concrete I then kitted out with an extension cord and a utility lantern. I shrugged off Dad's periodic offers to help, since lurking on the obverse, I knew, like the fine print on a credit card mailer, would be his ideas for how to do everything different. And when it could no longer be avoided, I hauled back those boxes he'd been so eager to get rid of and there in the coolness began to re-sort them by format and then alphabetize each in turn. The holiest of the holies, Mom's LPs and camcorder cassettes, I then smuggled out to the sunroom, where her stereo and tape decks still lived. I never did turn up so much as a reel of the last thing she'd been working on. But the CDs I'd keep with me, nine cartons I then stacked into a wall, flapped sideways for ease of access—or rather ten, after Moira retrieved the missing crate from the HoJo on her last day before heading back to Boston. I didn't tell her why I'd set up where I had, or kid myself she'd have cared (she was still too pissed about me and Eddie squandering the strings she'd pulled two months ago with Squatch) but when she was gone, I took her old Discman out to the garage and buckled down, belatedly, to listen.

Of course, with no real sense of what I was listening for—what was in the missing footage Mom's soundtrack candidates had been meant to score—my efforts proved futile . . . Or anyway, that was my excuse for how quickly I gave up. But the preliminaries alone had kept me occupied just long enough to quell the pain I'd been carrying around for weeks now, or at least to prevent me from running back out to get high.

Then again, enraging as I found Dad's refusal to look back, how was it any different than what I'd been trying to pull here with the loss of Sarah Kupferberg? It was out of a resolve to become my own man, I think—the one I'd once tricked her into thinking I could be—that I sat down in early September to write her a long and seemingly earnest letter apologizing for last month's freakout. And then, on the last day of the month, another. Knowing me, I was probably on the verge of sending a third when, out of the blue, a response came with the afternoon mail; I didn't recognize the handwriting, but whose else could it be?

I can still recall hunkering on the tarpaper outside my room, scrutinizing the address with an intensity I'd previously reserved for poems. And then the letter inside, begun without so much as a greeting. Perhaps I'd been too drunk and/or high to remember much about that night in the woods (it said):

. . . but your justifications at the time were pretty copious, Ethan. Either way, no need to rehash old apologies here, since you know I've never done anything but accept them. To me, though, the problem with any kind of relationship going forward comes down to that thing about choice I was always trying to get you to see—from that day on the beach to the beachhouse. In hindsight, you may not have understood what I meant by having to "take the leap," but I took mine, Ethan—I believed in you. And as you'll see if you stop to think it over, it's the kind of trick that can only be worked once . . .

End of letter. Well, that and the closing: Love, Sarah.

Skipping dinner, my heart in my throat, I banged out a reply on Dad's hand-me-down Mac with its Post-it-sized screen. Yet when I read back over my own pleas and protests, all I could see were the ego-trips I'd honestly thought she might cure me of, projection, manipulation, hiding . . . right down to the postdating I'd done at the top to make me seem less desperate for forgiveness. So I trashed the file, fetched the Kermit phone from my sister's room, allowed myself to dial the number I'd been given. It was a communal line in Sarah's dorm, just down the hall from what I imagined as a kitchen full of microwaves and a TV room where debs in black turtlenecks would watch the kinds of movies my mom had called "films." The girl who answered, Indian-accented, identified herself as Rita. Was it Sarah K. I was looking for? she said. Because Sarah K. was out, did I care to leave a message?

I apologized, claiming nonsensically to have had the wrong number.

But the next night, I would try again. The extralong phone cord that had served Moira so well just barely stretched to my roof, provided I left the cradle back inside and lay out in the dark with my head against the siding. This is what it feels like to choose, I reminded myself, as the ringer repeated its leaden circles and the dry leaves clashed overhead: maybe the noise I was hearing underneath was Christ himself, come back to earth to make her answer. But nope, there was only old Rita on the line, asking two or three times, who was this? And listening to Ducky or one of his emissaries lock up next door, I caught myself picturing the rows of malt-liquor bottles lined up inside, the pot and raw cocaine I now figured to be in the safe, along with some pills, maybe some morphine, maybe even some smack, a burglar alarm he'd have bought on the cheap. Then the pump lights were doused, and all those stars that had been trying to hide burst into visibility . . . like stigmata, I thought, still trying to wrest order from the nothing. Or no: stigmata were the echoes down the years, signs of favor to the true believer, when what I meant was something more like the original wounds. And that's when I thought back to the test I'd set my dad on the day of his return, and his inability, too, to believe me capable of change.

But then why expect otherwise, from anybody? Didn't I know this already? The solution to any one person's shattered faith couldn't be to ask another leap of it. It could only be a tangible miracle: something as vast and improbable as a resurrection.

And so it was that I'd land a week later in the shared office of my ex-best-friend's mom, the guidance counselor, announcing my intent to gain admission to Columbia University's class of 2000. How hard could it be? I said. There were three whole months before the deadline, more than enough time to pull together an application: straight A's for senior year, obviously, a smattering of volunteer work, and then a personal essay about, like, the lessons to be taken from adversity? Maybe I'd even get extra credit for having come from the middle of nowhere . . .

She wheeled in her office chair and removed from the file cabinet a tabbed yellow folder.

You recognize this, Ethan? Your permanent record.

It was a term I hadn't heard since lower school, where teachers had used it to enforce discipline. Yet somehow it had gotten entangled in my mind with the idea of divine invigilation absorbed from my father's chapel lectures and lunchtime prayers and from twice-monthly services at St. Paul's by-the-Sea. The file now before me wasn't as extensive as I might have feared: no mirror and blade recovered from behind the radiator of my room, no huffed bags of glue, no Kleenexes (Kleenices?) stiffened with my DNA. But academically, it held enough material from the last couple of years—or rather, little enough material—to bar my way forward. Not only were my grades wildly out of step with my board scores, she said, leaning in to take back the folder; any sense of the extracurricular person seemed to have vanished. I'd been prefect of my first-form class—had sat with her son Judd on their deck out back, scheming about surf trophies we'd bring home; what had happened since?

Well, there was that freshman-year Side by Side by Sondheim, I pointed out. (I gave her a couple of bars of the tenor part from "Barcelona," trying to distract from my own spreading blush.) And the year I'd run cross-country; the cycle of ghazals I'd been working on. Oh, and I'd just started covering regatta as a stringer for the county paper, that intern spot they hired for each fall; I'd been thinking of maybe trying a writing concentration.

Her fingernail scratched redly at the folder.

It's your fifty dollars, you want to waste it applying, she said. And before you say it, NYU's not likely to be any easier.

How about City College? I said. I'll go anywhere—just so long as it's New York.

This is a volunteer position, Ethan, she said, not unkindly, but I'm pretty sure City College is for city kids. Even Rutgers is feeling like a stretch.

Wasn't Rutgers in New Jersey, though?

Her eyes went down the page, not reading, but stalling, like the finger. The thaw I expected to find there when they swung back up—the flicker of intimacy my waywardness so often seemed to inspire—turned out to be embarrassment on my behalf.

Look, I'm sorry if this comes as a shock, she said. We all assumed, from who your father is . . . well, that you'd had ample warning, and were flaming out by choice. Clearly for Moira to achieve what she did was thrilling. But whether it was youthful excess or just a different way to grieve, Ethan, your SATs plus some newspaper cuttings are an awfully thin reed to hang an application on.

And it's funny, even six months ago I'd have blown out of there disappointed, or at least enraged, but on the rarefied plane where I was now living, I could hear only a suggestion to look elsewhere. I spent several hours with the phone to my ear, copying out recorded NJ Transit timetables from New Brunswick into New York–Penn, scanning for rides shorter than an hour. I thought, too, of the competing chains of for-profit technical colleges that advertised on cable, DeVry and ITT, though it was hard to imagine stomaching the look on Albert Kupferberg's face when I told him I was studying to be a computer technician.

Anyway, aside from drafting love letters, my sole interest in computers to date had been their usefulness in backing up the visual portion of Mom's archive in case Dad tried to bury it again: all those videotapes she'd made in the '80s before perfecting her crazy Bolex contraption and moving her editing rig out to school. This was no job for the Macs of that era, but our local paper, the Press-Times, had a fancy new Compaq hooked up to exotically blinking towers and recording equipment, and now, as a roving high-school sports correspondent, I'd been given my own key. Amid a larger effort to steer clear of Eddie and other forces that could derail me, I'd been spending a lot of time in the empty newsroom at night, even when not on deadline. And there, messing around, I'd taught myself how to rip each tape to a .mov file and then burn it onto a recordable CD.

Which was how, not long before Halloween, still brooding over a way forward, I finally stumbled upon the project I see you're struggling to incorporate in your telling. My mother's last opus, it was also, I knew, her first film on film, so she must have mixed it down to cassette from Super 16-millimeter to store among the earlier work shot to VHS. The quickening I felt was partly at the subtitle on the label, partly at the run time underneath: If I'd known it was so much longer than those three-minute haiku I'd helped her shoot back before we moved, I might have looked harder for it in the first place. But it was the damnedest thing: what the monitor showed when I started the VCR was stuff I thought I knew already—a long and apparently unbroken shot of the picnic tables at the Sinclair early of a summer morning, a cat doing slow yoga and then vanishing into the high grass—yet from such an oblique angle that I'd still be trying to figure out whether that was my window she was filming from when the camera somehow broke the plane and a steely monologue kicked in from offscreen . . .

At one o'clock that morning, when I finally locked up the building and slipped out to the stadium-lit parking lot, I had only just hit the halfway point where the various voiceovers started to run out and the passages of silence to grow obtrusive. I stood dumbly by my bike but didn't unchain it. Instead, I sat down on one of those concrete barriers meant to keep you from rolling through a space, watching weeds crack the asphalt into unnamable patterns and wishing I could run everything back together in my head—as if, given it all to do over again, I could stand to see her vision cut short like that even a single time.

But an odd thing seems to have happened that night, for by morning I had realized, with only a twinge of misgiving, that since no one else had ever seen the tape, I could pass off its finished half as complete . . . and as my own. Some research into the film school at NYU revealed it to be part of the larger college, and consequently (if Judd's mom was to be believed) too good for the likes of me. Juilliard, closer to Columbia, promised in an otherwise insufferable recruitment brochure to put special emphasis on applicants' "thespian endeavors" (and had the appeal of a pedigree that might impress the Kupferbergs), but for all my gifts at deception, I couldn't figure out how to leverage a dubbed tape of plagiarized documentary into a plausible body of work onstage. I noticed from the map, though, that Fordham University, which I'd thought of as a parochial school in the otherwise unknowable Bronx, also kept a campus right there at the south end of Lincoln Center. More to the point, its "Drama and Theatre" program seemed to presuppose not only a scope beyond the footlights, but also an agnosticism about directing versus acting, movies versus stage. Or at any rate, if it was good enough for Denzel Washington, it was good enough for me.

I would spend the rest of that fall covering boat races, cramming to raise my G.P.A., reading the novels I suddenly found myself preferring to poetry (the ones where stuff actually happened), and frantically bending the trajectory of my life toward that of Sarah Kupferberg, writing and rewriting a personal statement in response to the prompt I'd selected from a whole vague menu of them. "What do the dramatic arts still have to offer us, here at the dawn of a new millennium?" My answer was nearly as diffuse as the question, but I enclosed a burned disc of Other People: A Requiem as a "creative portfolio" to back up my basic premise: that although the wider world these days was only a mouse-click away, real art had to feed three hungers simultaneously—the hunger to get the facts, yes, but also the hunger to transcend them, and to change. And even before an acceptance letter came, with its note of double-edged praise from the review committee for the "thrilling arrogance of [my] ambition," I felt that the liberties I'd taken with my dead mother's work were in service to a larger truth: the truth of your own mother, Jolie, and the past I was going to have to outrun if I was to win her.

I don't think you'll be shocked if I say that, in my whirl of activity, the question of whether Sarah would actually want to be won had somehow receded. But maybe that was part of the design. At eighteen, I was only myself, after all, and absent any finer feel for how she might be seeing me, surprise seemed my best shot at getting her to let me back in. Surprise plus the crazy scale of my longing. Or anyway, it had worked for me once before.

Still, by the following August, doubt had returned. There she was four hours to the north, unaware of the plot I'd set in motion and under no obligation to receive me even if I followed it through. And here I was on oystershells on the Eastern Shore, facing a Subaru packed for departure with pretty much everything I owned: a trailing moonplant, extralong linens fresh from the store, a Macintosh like a nuclear football, and box upon box of my mom's CDs—the rearward tilt of the chassis suggesting less a man boldly striking out from home than one a little afraid to leave it behind.

And that was before Corinne crossed the lawn and climbed into the corner of the backseat not crammed with junk. For among the things she had told my dad was that we'd need someone to watch the car while we unloaded—she'd lived in New York in her youth, and could attest personally to the dodginess of parking, not to mention thieves. Moira, the more obvious copilot, had taken off that June for a year of study in Berlin . . . and now Dad was turning to ask did I want to drive. An oblique apology? Sobriety test? Reward for how I'd triumphed at last? But of course any of these would have required acknowledging there was something to apologize for, or triumph over, which, for reasons still obscure to me, he couldn't do. I pointed out that my license hadn't yet been reinstated.

Can't hurt to practice while you wait, he said. The state didn't revoke your learner's permit, did it?

And because some tests are also dares, I gestured for the keys.

Perhaps even more frustrating than his customary dryness was my dad's comfort with long silences. Or, less charitably, an obliviousness to the kind of tension he could have relieved by just popping in a cassette. Even the pedagogical little grunts from our stick-shift sessions were gone, though I suppose with no drugs to dull the friction, I'd become harder to talk to as well. This left Corinne to fill the gap the way she had at so many mealtimes this past year—as if suborning my silence weren't enough, as if she still felt the need to earn my approval. Making us stop for lunch at a health-food place near Philly, she regaled us with memories of all the many times she'd done this drive, and of her old apartment directly above the Holland Tunnel . . . calling it "the City" like there was only one, dropping in "Barbizon" and "cold-water flat" while Dad nodded along like this was her true reason for coming. What followed, though, when the Turnpike began to widen and planes to dive-bomb the traffic and exit signs to arrive bunched together and to bear the names of poets, was a kind of vindication. The skyline jabbed up briefly past an inlet, and even allowing for my doubts and the heat, New York resembled less a city than a ship glimpsed at the far end of a desert, the two pale promontories at its tip blurring into a single mast, with a second farther off at midtown.

And now came the Hudson steaming silver under the GW Bridge; the ironwork, the Palisades, the whole West Side exploding at midday in a green surprise of trees. Craning my neck, I could feel my hopes starting to revive up there behind the sawtooth roofs . . . but damn if Corinne hadn't been right about the parking. The only space to be had was at a hydrant a

full avenue from the dorm. Jolted back to real life, I suggested to Dad that
we alternate: I'd grab a load, and he could be ready with a second by the
time I came around to get the third. Then I hefted my messenger bag, one-
armed a box, unbungeed the longboard, and hurled myself past the police
barrier blocking Sixtieth Street.

The board barely fit in the elevator, and seemed in this context a plea for
attention, but I was trusting my edginess to read as cool. Up in a lottery-
assigned fifth-floor double, one Henry White, Jr., of Marblehead, Mass.
(hereinafter White Henry), stood with his parents amid the shipwreck of
his own possessions, not least an expensive stereo system that would
have played LPs, had I thought to bring any. He was almost my height, but
thicker set, with dirty-blond curls and lips you might call cherubic if cherubs
could pout. His stonewashed jeans and plain white tee were tempered in
like fashion by the gossamer-scarfed mother fussing as though over a four-
year-old, and by Henry Sr., who looked ready to break into a golf swing at
the slightest encouragement. I shook hands, suppressed a drawl, imagined
the short work Eddie Sixkiller would have made of these people, but when
White Henry offered to help me unload, I said no worries, my dad and I
had things under control (though the grander spaces I'd been conjuring
from the size of the student loans now embarrassed me, and the boxes I'd
brought would remain largely unopened beneath the jacked mattress of
the ectomorph bed).

Some dozen trips later, all that remained outside was a trashbag full
of shoes and Corinne in the car with the windows rolled to conserve AC,
plaiting her dark hair and mouthing along to her smoking-cessation tape or
one of Mom's epic mixes. Knowing she couldn't see me, I allowed myself a
flipped bird. I'd planned to ditch Dad there, too, but reached the dormitory
to find him still standing around with the Whites, laughing over something.
The doorframe gave the same illusion of life peeking into life I'd later
get from Vermeers at the Frick . . . but what was his life? I found myself
wondering again, or still. There was the wry charmer of parents' nights, the
Ahab of Chesapeake regatta, the meek suitor I'd just spent the day with—
but otherwise my personal experience had long since dwindled to the cold
dinners and strained Jeopardy! battles of home, the widower baffled by my
existence.

Sorry, he told them, breaking off. If you'll excuse us . . .

The hallway was even less private than the room, but maybe what I'd
really feared was a formal leave-taking slash settling of accounts, and now

we could at least skip that: I was free. Then, by a window, he put a hand on my face as if to tug it forward. A hot wind gusted up.

Come on, Dad. You know we're not the kind of guys who do this stuff.

You're going to fill me in on your adventures come Thanksgiving, then?

I was thinking more like Christmas, I said.

Is that right? he said, and studied me for a minute before making the adjustment. Okay, Christmas, at the outside.

Depending on how things go, I added. Barring disaster.

And with this as the last word, I turned to the room to rejoin the Whites. But they, too, were parting, a scene whose mawkishness swept me back to the hall. From the window, I scanned the blocked-off street below. I had only just spotted Dad walking down the center line when, suddenly, I had the feeling of watching Mom's film again: first the leveled-out car; then his view from the doorway into my room at home with its stained mattress and greebles of Blu Tack, stars I hadn't bothered to pick off the ceiling now faintly aglow—and beyond, the darkling town the four of us had rolled into like conquerors a decade ago. But so long, Ducky's, I thought, with your peeling dinosaurs, your petty enticements; catch you later, two-bit forest and railroad tracks that wouldn't melt a penny; goodbye, bypass, fast food, farmland. Good luck.

Back inside, White Henry was alone, his teariness gone like a stage trick.

So I guess this is paradise, he said.

He rifled the clutter for a wheelie suitcase and flipped back the top to reveal what nestled there: a pint of Scotch glinting evilly among his boxers. Maybe he'd anticipated us clinking glasses, sharing a rueful laugh . . . and I know I thought about setting aside my new rule, Jolie, just this once. But after shoving a few boxes to my side of the room and mastering the urge to turn away as I changed shirts, I told him I already had plans, and not to wait up.

It would be one hour and two train fuckups later that I recovered Broadway three miles from where I'd lost it (though what I actually recall from my first few subway rides was this curious sense of the outer world dissolving and reforming while I stayed in one place). There was even less sign of a campus here than back at my own, but if you could get yourself aimed north, you saw stone walls and black-gated checkpoints stitching up the blocks to your right. At a gaunt residential building on a sidestreet, the guard seemed hesitant to let me through without an all-clear from somebody inside. I could have made a run for it, I thought. Could have leaned across the desk and socked him one right in the moustache. I could have done almost anything, save for the obvious thing, calling up.

Is Rita here? I asked, in a flash of ingenuity. Try Rita.

The guard lugged out a ring-bound directory, but then something in my look made him drop the whole Cerberus act and wave me on to the stairs. At whose top I'll freely admit might have waited any manner of comeuppance: a wrong address, a deadbolt clicking shut, a love affair that would split my life in two. And yet somehow I had let myself believe that it wouldn't be anything other than what I'd been promised a million years ago last summer. I ran my lines again: I was ready. I'd had a little breakdown, one teensy little lapse, but was finally ready to become the person she'd known I could be. There could be more, too, depending on her reaction; if need be, I was ready to go to my knees. Instead, all she said when the door opened was,

Jesus Christ . . . Ethan. Followed by: Where have you been all my life?

And right there in the hallway where anyone could have seen us, she slipped into my arms and, for only the second time in our personal history, kissed me.

Which is not to say that all our problems vanished in a single moment. There was, for one thing, the note of probation that set in as soon as I saw her and wouldn't stop that whole first night in New York. Not at the diner where we caught up so hungrily our food got cold; not at the party later where she introduced me to one of her professors as though we'd been together for years . . . not on the rooftop where, still later, we tried to tune out the ramblings of a photographer who shot portraits of feet. Nor even back in her dormroom, in bed, watching the window go blue with the dawn. By which point it was probably too late anyway for me to confess the scheme that had brought me here; I'd been up for twenty-four hours without chemical assistance save the caffeine, and hadn't felt this close to another human being since the morning she'd left me in the woods. Instead I heard myself ask, in the half-light, how she'd known I would come for her. And only now did she bring out certain facts she'd thought already in my possession: that Moira, learning of my acceptance to Fordham in the spring, had tossed my room looking for a 212 number and called ahead to warn her that I wouldn't be giving up.

Moira, I said. Damn. But that was way back in March. Weren't you seeing anybody else by that point?

Do you really want to know, Ethan?

And still for six months you didn't call me. Or even write.

But your sister's expectations were clear: I was supposed to be letting you down easy. I don't think anyone in our respective corners is really seeing this as a long-term bet, you know?

And with a yawn, she tilted up to kiss me.

I returned the kiss; tried to stop thinking about anything beyond. (But what if Moira got wind of the "portfolio" I'd submitted of our mom's work? Would she rat on me to the administration? To Sarah?) Sorry, I said. Is that what's going on here, you letting me down easy? Or were you just not going to listen to any of them?

I sent that letter, didn't I? And you read in it what you read—we'd talked about you coming to the city.

Yeah, a year ago. Before you were in touch with my sister.

But I wasn't knuckling under, Ethan. I was always going to wait and see.

Then, when I continued to hold back:

Look, idiot: she loves you. She wants to protect you. But whatever can still happen now between us, it's not going to be quite that simple anymore, is it?

Proving otherwise seemed to demand I keep my duplicity a secret . . . which, as you learned in your own narrow escape from Bellevue, involved a kind of doubling-down. So the days that fall, or the late-morning parts of them into which I managed to shoehorn my classes, I spent playing at student life, assuring myself that this was what any real actor would do. The core curriculum was rigid, the foldable desk-things in the classrooms likewise, and I felt some relief in my daily descent to the basement's black box theater, even if, in another sense, it entailed further fraud. I mean, my colleagues there had all been onstage since nursery school, been choristers at muni operas or acted in commercials on TV. And each time they warmly wished each other broken legs before a table-read, it felt like a club from which I'd been excluded. Still, I had two things going for me. One was that success couldn't mean for them what it now meant for me (since any failure to sustain disbelief would get me kicked out of school in a trice, remanded back to the woods of Cheshire County). The other was Hank Gregory, the tall black Wooster Group alum who'd signed the note on my admission letter and ran our freshman workshop.

But maybe I should just linger here a minute over this whole question of protection versus care. Despite his initial encouragement (by which I guess I mean mostly his obvious favoritism), Hank was blunt whenever I took on a leading role, insisting that I would never venture much beyond the limits of my own character unless I could find some way to tune in to the reality of the other actors around me . . .

Like the way you were trying to see those other people in your portfolio, Ethan, he said.

And this alone might have been enough to trip me up—in the excerpt I'd sent, there <u>were</u> no other people. Yet his bigger problem had to do with still others, even harder to see:

All this facility of yours, I remember him saying to me once . . . with realism, with fantasy, but at a certain point, man, if you can't break through that fourth wall and touch some person other than yourself, then what's it all for? Why tell a story, ultimately, if there's not someone out there as important as you are to hear it?

Which is, I might add, the question that increasingly haunts me about these slabs of memoir you keep sending, Jolie . . . But then, with all you've had to go through (are going through again, I fear, in whatever sad room you may be writing from), it's not my job to ask you for further exposure is it? No, the choice of which parts of your story to share and which to hold back would seem to be exclusively your own, and maybe my job here, with respect to that story—no matter whom it concerns—is just to make sure you have the facts you need from mine. Such as that the more I stopped trying to dazzle your mother with my performance of sobriety and instead just invited her in, the lighter my burdens felt. That my afternoons, nights, weekends were all set aside for her. And that, far from freakish, this soon revealed itself as just the nature of courtship under coeducation: in September, I hardly saw my roommate; by October, hardly anybody else was seeing theirs.

Here, then, is a typical weekday. I'd reach the Columbia gates around three or three thirty and would immediately lay claim to one of the wide benches in the median strip of Broadway, sometimes with a pizza slice as big as my head, sometimes with a paperback at odd angles to my studies—<u>Song of Solomon</u>, Stephen King—but always with one of the blue cups of deli coffee we liked to call "sugar bombs." The sun was strong, the rain absent again, the breeze warm from traffic, napkins rustling like cheap feathers between the wheels and the trucks of the skateboard she'd found for me second-hand. She'd come ambling up 114th after swapping out textbooks for her own skateboard, and then we'd cut over to the Hungarian Pastry Shop by the cathedral for more coffee, light and sweet, before launching on one of our epic trips downtown. The city around us—Sarah's city— seemed even more chimerical now than from afar: no longer what it had been in the stories she'd told me back on the Eastern Shore, but not yet settled into what it was to become. From street to street, or within a single block (within Sarah herself, recalling whatever this or that place had been five years ago), the boundary lines between order and entropy, reason and unreason, all seemed in mid-'90s New York to be up for grabs.

In a way, it was the specifics of this tension that transfixed me: elders chumming to watch a playoff series through the window of a discount store while uniformed schoolkids jockeyed for rider toys out front; the park entrance across from the old Coliseum where breakdancers congregated opposite Lost Tribes of Israel, and again, miraculously, these same dudes in their Aladdin drag shouting into a megaphone ten blocks south while Lubavitchers with dangling loupes watched without comment . . . and deeper into the transformation zone, inflatable rats shaming non-union construction workers, actual rats skirmishing over a bagel, Chuck Close at the MoMA, Chuck E. Cheese in Times Square, hookers ducking cops with Peep-o-Rama to one side and The Lion King or whatever on the other, army recruiters recruiting, men in cutoff shorts holding hands and openly Frenching . . . and us rolling south, hopping off onto the sidewalk and then on again to cruise the widened bus lane on Broadway below Fourteenth, where cabbies dragged cardboard from their trunks to pray; and at dusk drifting off of Broadway into the Village: shops where I bought hip-hop, fences of gutted brownstones hung with perfectly good clothes (a designer hoodie, the denim jacket I wore all that fall); and restaurants where we refueled, cheap sushi under a Springsteen poster, rare burgers on a paper plate, the best Brazilian, the best pastrami, egg creams whose egglessness she vouched for chased by more coffee in an anarchist café or that one tavern on West Fourth Street where fifty years ago, I informed her, a young Allen Ginsberg and a young William Burroughs either played pool or helped conceal a murder, I couldn't remember—all those non-carding bars holding nothing for me to fear anymore, since she'd now x'd both our hands and we grew more and more sober on refills as the people around us grew more and more drunk. Yet in a different sense, any moment could have been anywhere, our conversations installments in a single, thousand-hour conversation we carried around the island of Manhattan as a snail carries its home.

Our Rubicon was Houston Street, where even the most jagged path would lead eventually. Its dozen lanes were darker back then, and seemed wider, its cabs in more of a hurry to be elsewhere. After six, seven miles walked or skated in as many hours, we would have to decide whether to catch a train back uptown to her room or continue all the way to the harbor. There was a complex calculus involving time of night and week and month, but here's how I had changed already: I was often just as happy to keep going, since there seemed to be so much more she had to show me.

So say we do roll onward. Maybe it's a Tuesday and Sarah's heard about a gallery opening in SoHo, or it's a Friday and someone is having a loft party somewhere, or there's an all-ages slam at the Nuyorican, or a scholar of the Spanish Civil War has, for his fiftieth birthday, rented out the back room of a dim sum joint that doubles as a massage parlor. You can't just pick up these things from your phone yet, but it's her job as a person to know as much as she can of the world around her, she says, even if all you can ever know is a fraction. And how easily, how hungrily those black x's slide her from one world to the next, in the flow but not of it, meeting people, on the qui vive, and then picking right back up where we left off, talking Eduardo Galeano, talking Joe Brainard. Me? I remember the first time a tourist ever asked me for directions. I remember training myself to say "on line." I remember dissecting the inaccuracies of the TV show <u>ER</u> with some nurses headed home one night on the F train. I remember the actress Parker Posey calling me a suave motherfucker on line for Two Boots pizza. I remember jointly karaoke-ing Iggy Pop's "Candy" with your mom in a bar of tolerant gays. I remember a schizophrenic homeless woman named Debra Little who insisted Delancey Street was no place for children to be messing around at night and then guided us across it with her shopping cart of thunder, telling each of us in turn, You my favorite. No, <u>you</u> my favorite. And Sarah's mental map of every last public toilet in Manhattan, having to pee constantly from all those sugar bombs we kept stopping to buy, a condition she called East Coast Bladder.

At times, my sense of imposture still flared. The night the Yankees won the pennant, for instance, we went to a party literally inside the Brooklyn

Bridge. Crossing the river was a big deal then, and there was little about the great anchorage on the far side to suggest hollowness, but past an unremarkable door and some bushes where we stowed our skateboards, we found a space like a cathedral or fortress, different vaults reaching three and four stories high, all walled with refrigerator-sized sandstone. In one, we danced for an hour, not well, to a music accurately enough called drum 'n' bass. In another, a frontman who'd once been on MTV's Buzz Bin was soloing on what sounded like a power drill. There were breasts, bare. There was body paint. Ecstasy being slung behind the port-a-johns, I could hear it call. The closest I'd ever come to a rave on the Eastern Shore was a <u>Newsweek</u> cover in the upper-school library at St. Anselm's, and now I recovered enough to ask her: Was this one of them? But for better or worse, that moment was over, she said, and pointed to the corporate logos flying above the open bars, the dim grottoes of sponsored beer; these days nobody used the word "rave" except with quotation marks. Then she recognized one of the bartenders and they embraced like long-lost sisters.

I felt sweaty and slightly chastised, and neither of us could even pretend to dance to industrial, so we went out onto the bridge to get some air. It was late, the pedestrian walkway empty. The harbor below us stretched darkly, a wild air of desolation after the catacombs. Above the traffic, no music could be heard. Turn the other way, though, and there was the city racked upon itself, lights doubling and quadrupling, staining the violet sky and recasting the darkness as just shadow. Atop the nearer pier, a flag stirred against some clouds. Huge cables looped lazily upward. And without much warning—even to myself—I began to pick my way up the nearest one, holding on to two guy wires for support.

Hey, what are you doing? she yelled.

And to this day, it remains a fair question, Jolie: Why did I climb the Brooklyn Bridge? Likely I felt I still owed her restitution, had to swap in for my fugazi some proof of how far I'd go to secure her love. I mean, sure, I was no longer acting like a junkie—rave or no rave, I'd hung in there stone sober—but I'd lied my way into college, pawned off my mother's film as my own, bad juju, all of it, and bound, I think I knew even then, to blow up in my face. Or maybe I just wanted what I always wanted: for someone to see the risks I was running and to say "stop." But I shouted back, Hey, were we not surfers? Stay balanced, keep hold of the wires, and don't look down. And true story, I swear: she followed.

About a third of the way up the slope was a barred security gate you had to clamber out and around, so that for a few moments there was nothing between you and the lanes of traffic now however many stories below. Even more terrifying was the second gate, another hundred yards up, where you could feel even the big cables sway. Then, incredibly, I was pulling myself up a short ladder onto a platform as broad and solid as the top of Keel Hill. I knelt to kiss the sod, pretending I was joking but for some reason near tears. Her own look, to the degree I could even make it out by the light of the lit-up flag, split the difference between shaken and transformed; she had trusted me again—the one thing about which she seemed incapable of resolve—and for her troubles, had been given an experience few people ever had.

The other crazy thing was how invisible we'd become, New Yorkers so rarely thinking to look up. And what does a person do with a gift like that? Forgive me for saying so, but sex would have been impure, done for bragging rights. (Also, I was afraid she might notice I'd wet myself a little at the first gate, though for all I knew or cared, she had, too.) Yet how could we return to earth so soon when we might never again get so high up—and when the descent was probably that much scarier? Instead we keyed our names into the flagpole's base as proof and then resumed the old political debate with legs dangling over the side, having broken through to some whole other level. We went a few teasing rounds about socialism. Then, as if out of nowhere, she said,

There's something I'm still struggling with, though.

And already I was thinking: oh fuck.

Remember how I kept talking this week about that essay "The Magical State"? Well . . . the part I was trying to get myself to say was this thing I just found out, Ethan. The author's supposed to take a bunch of us to Caracas to study, starting in January.

Uh . . . okay, I said, and waited for my stomach to catch up to the fact that I was being dumped. Again. At the top of the Brooklyn Bridge.

Just for a semester. I applied last year, before I'd heard from your sister . . . and even if I could figure out a way now to cut myself loose—

No, I mean you should go if you want to, I managed. You've done so much for me already, Sarah. Really.

Have I? Because I couldn't go if I thought it meant having to give up . . . whatever this is turning into. You know I'm in love with you, right?

Then I take it back, stay, I said, and laughed to cover my gasping for air; for a minute, I'd felt myself going back under. I bumped my heels against the stones. Felt their solidity. No, seriously, that's months from now, Sarah, and if I waited a year for you, I can do another semester standing on my head. Besides, this'll give me the excuse I need to stick around for Christmas break.

But . . . how can I put this? I know it hasn't always been easy for you, Ethan, coming like this to New York. She studied the palm she'd grabbed in the darkness. And sometimes I worry about what you might . . . you know. Do. Left on your own, in the city.

What's the alternative, though? That you don't go? We can write letters. And in between I'll be busy with my poems . . . my play. It's your future. Really, I'm fine. The drug stuff is in the rearview, I told you.

But I notice you never talk about home anymore.

So what? Who needs home, when I've got all this? I said, leaning all the way forward—meaning I'd still have the city while she was away. Or maybe that, at the moment she'd followed me up here, they'd become the same thing . . .

But let's say this is a different night, and back on Houston Street we've instead boarded an uptown train. With her spare key and my student ID, my whiteness and my maleness, no one questions my presence in Sarah's building anymore. The floors are staggered by sex, so her neighbors are all girls—women, I should say—but I'm far from the only boyfriend, and if I'm spotted in the kitchen or on my way to use the men's room two stories down, I never hear complaints.

Her room is just big enough to fit a narrow mattress and a desk and the old parlor chair I've dragged in from the trash one day; the game is to get from one piece of furniture to another without touching the ground, like primates moving around an understory or kids playing fort. We end up in the safety of her bed, of course, but my own favorite may just be those mornings when I wake to find the chair angled so that she can read by the light of this sidestreet the sun can't quite reach, the window cracked to the cool rush of uptown traffic. Another gift I've brought her: an old typewriter with a snap-together case and some ribbons from a dusty shop down in the printers' district. She persists in treating it like an art object, without practical purpose, and on writing her papers in the computer lab in the dorm's basement, but when the hour gets late enough that my typing won't disturb the neighbors, I pull the case onto my lap and start pecking away at the one-act Hank Gregory has assigned to our class as a yearlong project. And finally, I think, I am starting to discover the voice I need. To work alongside each other in peace, breaking only for oatmeal from the hot pot or, if we're feeling bourgie, brunch—to look up from the page where I've just begun to lose myself, as if taken by a wave, and to rediscover Sarah Kupferberg, the friend, the fresh-air fiend, tapping her imperfect teeth with a pencil or letting it ripple over the fingers of her right hand the way a swan runs across the water as it lands—that's my favorite.

Or no, this is my actual favorite, probably: the moment when I'm the one in the chair and she's just left for class and I can start to miss her all over again . . . with enough distance from the life I'm now living to be both in it and not in it, to see and not see what a kingdom it, or was. For depending on how you count, Jolie, this happily-ever-after of ours will last all of sixty-eight days.

There was a presidential election that year, and we were both newly eligible to vote. I'd registered as a proud citizen of New York, and had warned her already that I'd be late reaching 114th from my notoriously understaffed precinct. In fact, the queue was no worse than any other in this city of queues, though once in the booth, unable to find the Workers' Equality candidate we'd agreed on, I wussed out and pulled the lever for the Democrat. Still, I came up out of the subway feeling I'd done my part for the cause of organized labor.

At that point, you see, it had been just over a week since Hank Gregory had pulled me aside after workshop to mention a friend of his from the Performing Garage who now ran background cast for Law & Order—it's never too soon to start working on that union card, he'd told me. Ignoring the implied judgment on my efforts as a playwright, I cut class the next day and went down to a theater-district office where they sized me up against my photo and, without asking me to read, gave me a call time for the following Tuesday: not a speaking part, but a step toward the SAG membership needed in order to land one. And sure enough, Jolie, that's me, season 7, episode 13, Panicked Drug Gang Member Number Three in a basketball game Detective Briscoe rolls up on in Little Italy. What I remember most is the length of the shoot just to get this one blip, and worrying I'd done something wrong each time the director yelled, "Cut!" Well, that and the size of Jerry Orbach's head (and the implausibility of the drug gang having worked up a full-court game in the dwarfish environs of Mott Street). But on film, you bought it, and for half a day's work, a check for eighty dollars was cut right there on set, which I cashed before going to vote. It would cover not only cabfare, but also the dinner where I planned to surprise Sarah with my news, and despite the slight distance I'd had to put between us that week to keep my activities secret, I couldn't help feeling that I was finally unraveling my curse, covering the bet I'd made on myself—becoming worthy of her.

Or I suppose, given your point of view, that I was going to get away with everything.

In any case, I reached her room an hour later to find the door standing open and a tall and blue-jawed young man sitting up in her bed, shooting me a stern look from under his dreadlocks. Then the floor creaked behind me, and I turned to find Sarah carrying a Solo cup of what smelled like booze. The light outside was as bleak as a trashcan fire, and her face as pale as a ghost's. I was afraid to look back down at the sheets.

Ethan, she said. Shit. This isn't how I wanted you to meet, but I guess . . . let me introduce you to M——. M——, Ethan.

And people talk about seeing red, I get it, red the color of eyes closed against the sun, red the color of your blood on the walls from a vein she slashes as easily as flicking out a light. It seems to me now, though, that what I was seeing was closer to gray: all the color of a minute earlier, park-bench green, taxicab yellow, sucked right back out of the world. A severe localization of pewter, of lead. I came unstuck just long enough to spit on the floor and then turned back the way I'd come, giving thanks for the emptiness of stairwells, the thickness of fire-stairs doors.

The subway felt even less survivable than making the long trek downtown by my lonesome, so I steamed east toward the park, where at least there'd be trees to hide in. Two blocks later, though, my East Coast Bladder rebelled. I ducked into a Mexican restaurant. The restroom was past a smoke-filled but otherwise empty front area where a bartender stooped to stock beer, and with the door closed I could hear the muffled arrhythmia of music from the kitchen and then the clank of dishes, as if the barrier between me and my primeval self had never been any thicker than plywood. On my way out, I asked the bartender if he had anything Irish. Since he wouldn't, I could be on my way.

Cervezas? he said instead. I've got Harp. Five to the bucket.

I stammered that just one would do. It seemed urgent, suddenly, that I be able to drink just one beer like a normal human. Then, with three sips to go on my second, I asked the guy if he had a cigarette to spare, and he

said why didn't I just go do like everybody else and buy a loosie. At which
point I threw down a spiteful <u>Law & Order</u> twenty and ran to take the train
after all, riding in the frontmost car, my forehead pressed to the window,
imagining myself flying through.

Though White Henry seemed pleased to find me no longer playing the
ascetic, he directed me to the blinking light on his answering machine.

Your lady friend called, he said. Joan of Arc, or whatever. I offered to take
her message, but she said she wanted it to go to tape.

And all at once I saw Sarah in her dorm, in a blue-carpeted alcove heady
with dry-erase while she murmured into the phone how sorry she was for
having betrayed me.

The actual message, so loud I had to hold the phone away from my ear,
was to get the fuck over myself. I had until midnight to call her back.

I sent White Henry out to get coffee while I waited for Rita (good,
dependable Rita) to come to the phone. But it was Sarah who picked up:

That was fast, she said.

Must be the implied ultimatum, I said, scraping up every last ounce
of my obnoxiousness. Those are catnip for people with an abandonment
complex.

You're the one who spat on my rug, though, remember?

I guess I was hoping to hurt you back. But of course, that would assume
you ever cared enough to get hurt, wouldn't it.

Have you lost your mind? Why would I say I loved you if it wasn't so?

Why does the sun rise in the east, Sarah? Why does the caged bird sing?
People lie, you know? Or fine, maybe not you—maybe out of all the world
you've never broken anyone's trust, that kiss in the Volvo notwithstanding,
and all along you meant to tell me M—— was back in your life. Kind of like
you meant to tell me about Caracas. But be honest with me: He's going
with you, isn't he? What is it he has that I don't? Aside from the hair, and
the body—

I almost can't talk about this, is how much I could kill you right now.

He was in your bed, goddammit!

And me in the chair. Where else was he going to sit? Look, if it made
you jealous, I apologize, but M—— has known me since we were little, you
were nowhere to be found for two days, and I had to talk to someone. What
the hell else did you want me to do?

It's funny, though, I can't hear your apology over . . . wait. Talk about
what?

Ethan, I'm late.

White Henry, having returned with a coffee in each hand, saw my face and backed out into the hall.

Late as in . . .

And now a new sound: your mother at a loss. Right. As in late.

She didn't want to go to the university clinic to confirm the three separate home tests she'd flunked, so the next day, on a silent noontime train, barely touching, we went down to St. Vincent's in the Village, where there'd be no one either of us knew. They put us in a dim room where she was handed a pink gown and told to remove her pants. Then a doctor came in, Japanese-seeming but with the incongruous name of Franz. Though possibly the accent, too, was German? And possibly the regular ultrasound tech had the day off? I would later learn that Franz was somewhat famous in his field, and also that this floor, the seventh, had been an AIDS ward at ground zero of the plague. My hatred of hospitals being honestly come by, I looked at the coarse sheet covering Sarah's legs and could see only sheets covering stretchers, the silent lights of first responders crimsoning the snow. But on the other hand, these piecemeal recollections of my mother's dying offered something like a form of steadiness, which, mixed with the last day's apologies, I tried to stream into Sarah via handclasp even as I winced along with an experience whose inside I literally couldn't imagine. Please, I kept thinking, as she submitted to the wanding. Please, I'm sorry, I didn't mean . . . Please you have to understand . . . Relax, said Franz. The lunar image of her insides shifted with each tremor of his moderately famous hand. His words, meanwhile, seemed more a soothing auditory element than a vessel for meaning, so it took me a minute, squinting at the blobs of darkness, the grayscale seas, to realize that what he was murmuring now was, That's stool. And that, too: stool. And when at last he found his quarry, he didn't pause for effect or sigh. Just loosened his grip, fixed onscreen a blob that for all I knew looked like any other: "And that's baby."

Verbatim quote, by the way, if you want to use it. This was a Catholic hospital, post–Evangelium Vitae, so I guess he must have thought we'd be stoked.

My memory of the week that followed is of Sarah calling in sick to class and then spending whole days in the green parlor chair, half turned toward the street, arms wrapped around her knees to shield her belly while I lay on the bed not sleeping. I hadn't been sleeping much before the ultrasound, either (nor, to be honest, that whole fall), but now, strung out as I was by daylight, going over and over it, how we could have fucked up so badly, and whose fault that was anyway, and what would come of it—my real dread was of the coming of night. The one thing that seemed to calm us both down was physical contact, working closer in the extra-narrow bed. But then, just when we'd finally gone quiet and begun to drift off, I'd taste metal in my mouth, get this feeling dropping through my core like the elevator I'd been riding in had had its cables cut—this claustrophobic freefall I remembered from withdrawal. The attack would be that much worse because nudging her awake to confide it would be weak where she needed me to be strong; I already knew that if she saw how this had reduced me to just another burden, helpless, needing her care, then I would lose her. And besides, if I didn't shut up about all this, how was either of us supposed to get any rest at all?

It was a Thursday when Sarah returned to class, and I led her to believe I'd do the same, but instead I would find myself back in my own neglected dormroom, the safest place I could think of, standing in the window by the deep ledge where White Henry had left the phone. With a calling card I'd picked up along the way, I tried reaching Moira, figuring it was probably dinnertime where she was. No answer, though; just a recording in a language I couldn't understand. At home, meanwhile, I got Corinne: Ethan? Your father's out, but I know he'd love to hear your voice . . .

It wasn't quite a hang-up, what I did then, but nor did I leave a message. And now, reversing my angle on the silent room, I saw what I hadn't been able to before. A moonplant in need of watering; a bodega geranium. And the tail end of my old longboard, balanced on unopened boxes, sticking out from the end of the bed.

It took me less than an hour to reach the last stop on the A train. I don't know what I was hoping to find there, any more than I can tell you what I'd been looking for on the phone, but walking down the desolate frontage of whatever street ran past the train shed, I felt almost like I'd been here before. This was two weeks into November, the sky gone a flat gray, but the water at the shoreline was still bearable enough that I left my wetsuit in a pile on the sand with my shoes and jeans. I could see only one other surfer, far down the beach where there must have been a break, but I didn't want to be that close to anyone anymore, even at the cost of rideable waves.

Though I should clarify that there were a few of those even here, Jolie, long muddy lefts, so I should have been in my element, the way your mom was on stable ground; the problem wasn't the surf. It was more like I'd lost the urge to get caught up in something bigger, to walk on water, and instead of that sense of dissolving into motion, I was just sinking deeper into my fears.

Somehow in all our agonizing we'd managed to skirt direct talk of when to schedule an abortion, yet I could feel its inevitability right below the surface, pushing any question of what to do next toward the rhetorical. We were way too young to have a kid, after all—that was part of it. But beyond or behind this, for me at least, was the awareness that once you did, there could be no unhaving it, not even if it cost you an education or a career, not even if you had to move three thousand miles away and forget to call . . . not even if you found yourself sucked back into addiction or illness or depression or whatever it was had almost killed you at seventeen. That, and the terror that you'd be passing this on to your child, who hadn't asked for any of it. Becoming a parent, I thought, would be like running toward a locked door with your hands tied behind your back—at some point would come a pain from which there could be no protection. So why hadn't I just gently opened the conversation about making the appointment? Why hadn't she? I don't know. On my part, I guess I kept thinking of Dr. Franz, that word "baby" on the one hand and the small clump of cells on the other, and my dad's little tabbed collar from before he left the service.

I know first-hand, I'm trying to say here, Jolie, what it is to be haunted by a God you don't believe in. Not to believe in something, I'm saying, and also not to be able to bear the thought of its never coming back to save you.

And as I sat there watching the light go, that other surfer drift into eclipse behind the waves, I was put in mind of a not-very-good play we'd read in Hank's class, and the line my mother must have cribbed for the title of her movie, about hell being other people. Because with the way I seemed to keep failing to show up for them, wasn't hell no worse than I deserved? I mean, there was your mother, whom I'd knocked up and accused of cheating, now left on dry land, returning after classes to find no one there. And if she hadn't come out yet and said to me, Let's take care of this, it was obviously because she was waiting for me to get my shit together, mentally, and say I'd help her salvage her future the way she'd once helped to salvage mine.

When I burst through the door of her dormroom, an hour after dark, I hadn't even bothered to shower the salt from my hair.

Listen, I said. I know we haven't talked specifics, but I want you to hear this. I just made some extra money, all right? So I'll one hundred percent be behind you if you want to take care of it, Sarah.

And even as I heard the clumsiness, I felt relief flood through me as I hadn't there on the beach—as though it were the evasions themselves that had been trying to push me back out past the edge.

I mean, you should know I'll stick with you in whatever way I can, I said, go with you to the place, sit with you, be around during the recovery to care for you as much or as little as you want . . . if that's what you want.

She paused for what felt like a long time, looking out the window, chewing a nail.

But you still haven't said what it is you want, Ethan.

And for a second I almost wondered again.

Come on, Sarah. I'm the guy, what I want doesn't matter. My job is just to support you.

I went to take her hand, the one with the nail she'd chewed ragged.

And if ending it is going to be the decision, then you should always look back and know that was the right one, because it was what you needed to do.

There was another pause here, even longer; but then she said okay, if it was on her alone to decide what to do, then I was right, the question answered itself, didn't it.

The clinic we found was in a beige office building in Turtle Bay, not far from Tudor City Place. This was one of those periods in America when doctors were being murdered left and right just for doing their job, and though the protestors I knew from TV were nowhere to be seen, it may have been due mostly to the heavy barrier of planters out front and the two armed guards. Upstairs were banks of attached seats like the boarding area in an airport, but they were all aimed the same way, and it took me a second to realize that the point was to keep you from having to look anyone in the face. Which naturally, being the asshole I was, I did. What did I see then? I saw what seemed to be a mother and a daughter. Two nervous-looking women in opposite corners, filling in forms. And one other man, he could only have been Eastern European, with a gold chain and track pants, legs crossed, jiggling a trainer. It was this, the jiggle, that I couldn't tear my eyes off of. I'd spent the predawn hours trying to soothe myself with images of a waiting room, and myself in it, standing supportively by the woman I loved (still just a girl, I see now); but what would come next had until that moment been a black box. It somehow hadn't occurred to me that this room was as far as I'd be allowed to go, and that everything after they called her back she would have to face alone. Nor that beneath her resolve, Sarah would still seem so conflicted.

And maybe she felt me starting to spin out, the panic setting in again, because she suggested I run down to the drugstore while she finished up the paperwork; she would need pads. I didn't want to go, yet had promised to support her in every possible way, so what choice did I have? Guards again, a burst of gilt November, and then I was in another drugstore, facing a wall of feminine hygiene products. As recently as that summer, I might have been embarrassed to be seen among them, but now it was as if the connections linking inside and out had come undone; here beyond the clinic walls, no one looking in could have imagined the moment I'd just come out of, or how unintelligible, how profoundly unlike a TV commercial, it felt.

And then for some reason my mom in her last days came back to me. All that music, with no one left to hear it. And frail men my own age in saffron-colored gowns, arms hickeyed in lesions, on the seventh floor of St. Vincent's, waiting for the end to come. And the women in the waiting room, the nervous guy: each in their own situation, Jolie, every bit as unimaginable as yours or mine. From somewhere in the ceiling of the Duane Reade (believe it or not), a Prince song had just begun to play, and the spoken intro, always so tossed-off-seeming, now revealed itself as specifically about this feeling: the moment when even Sarah Kupferberg had started to become a stranger to me. And as I stood there, I felt increasingly sure that, whatever she experienced in that room, or was experiencing right now (a something, a nothing, or scarier still, some confusing thing in between), the fact that we could never be facing exactly the same set of choices marked some kind of boundary or outer limit. And so by July, the month of the birth that never came—maybe even before she left the country—we would be driven as far back inside ourselves as we'd been before we met. Whatever was between us would end, and I would be exactly as I was now: trapped inside what I'd thought would protect me, which was somehow the very thing I'd been trying to escape . . . And still I couldn't get away from the echo of what she'd said in the dormroom— what I'd felt there on the beach. For what if I'd had everything backward again? What if some secret part of her had wanted to have a kid? What if what she'd really needed me to admit in order to even know what she wanted was that some part of me, just as secretly, had wanted to go through with this, too, be the father of her child? What if the choices she faced somehow depended on who we both stood ready to be? It was as if, by my inability to acknowledge that we might be in this thing called life together, I'd as much as made her choices for her.

Three minutes later, winded from running, I was standing before her.

Listen, I had everything backward, I said, loud enough that the tracksuited man and the nearest woman looked over. I know this probably isn't time, but there's something I should have said to you back at the very start.

Which is what?

I lowered my voice, not wanting to make anything harder for anyone than it already was:

Which is just that if you decided you wanted something different, I'd be with you in that, too.

It's okay, Ethan. I've thought a lot about this. You made it clear that wasn't your decision.

I had to force myself to stand there and own it, not turn away.

All I want, Sarah, is for you to feel as free as you possibly can. So you have to hear this. No, listen: if going through with the pregnancy turned out to be what you wanted, then whatever it cost us, I would take responsibility for it. Be a dad, you know? It could be my child, if need be.

I couldn't ask you to do that, she said, still quiet. All the work you did just to get here, Ethan. And the union card—

—would take a backseat, I'm saying. Or shouldn't be the deciding factor. Anything that makes your decision easier. I'm not saying any of this is wrong. But if having it was what you wanted, then that would be right, too, do you see?

She thought for a minute, in that way she had. But you're still not telling me if it's the decision you'd make, if it was you.

I can't tell you that because it's <u>not</u> me. Or because who I am depends on who you need me to be. It has to be both of us acting together, maybe.

Me choosing to show up for you, no matter what—for real this time—and you only having to worry about what matters . . . which is whether or not you want to become a mother right now.

The breath she took then was audible. Like it hurt. Okay, she said. And after another, more silent breath, this one with some tears: But what if I told you I did want to have it, and for us to stay together?

Then I'm here with you in that, is what I'm saying. For as long as you want me.

I don't recall us ever telling the nurses we were canceling, but there must have been some bureaucratic hurdles left to clear, because by the time we walked out, a few protestors had indeed appeared across the street, unless I'd missed them on the way in. I tried to stay inside the seam of whatever had been filling me up, making every move so clear. Yet if I'm honest, it may have been closing me out already, since I couldn't quite forgive those protestors, Jolie—still can't. And all this editorializing bullshit aside, what am I trying to say? I'm no longer sure your mother and I were even talking about the same thing when we used words like "decision" or "choice" but I do know this: if we hadn't both felt like we had one, I wouldn't be writing you this letter.

Per the countless '70s-era childbirth books we found in the public library, we weren't supposed to tell people about the pregnancy for three months, but we'd decided given the various givens to wait only until semester's end to read her parents in—just long enough, she said, to present it as a fait accompli. So the morning after finals found us headed down to West Seventy-Third Street for brunch and crucifixion. Sarah had dressed as if for an Interview shoot, but the lobby of the Kupferbergs' building was dowdier than I'd have guessed. A plastic fir tree abutted a non-working fireplace, on whose mantel stood a plug-in menorah with weird blue flames. And I was struck by an asymmetry: though she already knew most of my secret places, I'd never in all our countless treks downtown seen the apartment where our child's mother-to-be had grown up.

I remember it seeming significant that Sarah, who must have had a key, would choose once upstairs to knock. And how cold her hand felt in mine, and wondering what was even the point of fingerless gloves. Then Eleanor was standing in the doorway with a cheek-kiss for her daughter, and another, much brisker, for me.

Come in, you two. You're like icicles. Al's just wrapping up some work, don't mind the disarray. Ethan, can I get you coffee?

Decaf, ideally, I said. Then, recalling the stationery set I'd had White Henry help me pick out at Bloomingdale's, I asked for my coat back, pulled the box from a pocket. Here, I said. A Hanukkah gift.

How thoughtful, she said, making no move to open it.

Sarah had assumed an exasperated look, as if to signal, This isn't about you, Ethan, but I shrugged; I was only ever trying to make a good impression.

At any rate, Eleanor was already gone down the hall to the kitchen, taking the stationery with her. And as Sarah Vaughan began to warble "Let's Do It (Let's Fall in Love)" from somewhere back there, the cavernous front rooms came into relief. The parlor, walled with Albert's books, boasted not only a library ladder but also two separate seating areas, the lesser a constellation of loveseat and chairs by the window onto Central Park West. After pushing up the sash, Sarah took the loveseat and indicated that I should follow. It was as if the architects had chosen to apportion all of the building's natural light to this one apartment, the sun homing in low over the park like an interrogator's lamp. And that was even before her mother had taken up position across from us.

I hear congratulations are in order, she began, and must have set the coffees on a side table (for, had mine been in my hand, I would surely have already spilled it). But don't be embarrassed, Ethan, Sarah's been telling anyone who'll listen about your star turn on <u>Law & Order</u>.

Thanks, I said, trying to regain my composure. It's just . . . there's some other news we were hoping to share.

Having reached for my hand at "congratulations," Sarah now squeezed it to remind me: she'd be the one to lay out our plan. But perhaps we'd both underestimated Eleanor, who seemed troubled by something and now glanced up to catch the look passing between me and her daughter.

Oh, she said. Oh no, oh God. Don't say it.

Then Sarah had my hand in her lap, and the two of them were talking over each other in low voices.

We didn't mean for it to happen, obviously—

But please, it's still early? Please tell me it's still early—

About three months, said Sarah.

But you can't be sure . . .

We can be pretty sure. Like, obstetrically.

There would be no time to correct her math, go back to the script we'd prepared, because now Albert was upon us in herringbone slacks and an open-collared shirt, his neck and cheeks pinkened by shaving. A more sensitive man might have pulled up short at some point since the room's threshold, alert to the shift in pressure, but still he had that look like cartoon bluebirds might alight on his shoulders. And suddenly I saw how close it was to charisma: this ability, against all the evidence, to place yourself right at the center of the world. Then briefly, as Sarah told him she was going to have a baby, I imagined I saw the pain this wall of mirrors had been thrown up to protect.

I don't understand, honey . . . how could this happen?

I would think you'd know better than anyone, his daughter said sharply.

But it seemed to glance off him: Okay, Sarah, birds do it, bees do it and so on, but we assumed you were being careful!

It was my first chance to observe Eleanor in a crisis. She held up a hand like a crossing guard to keep him from going further; their daughter would be the one to chart our path forward, during which time there was to be no panic, no gnashing of teeth, no fury directed my way. In fact, I seemed to have slid into a side-pocket no one could even see.

We could move in here for a year or two, Sarah was explaining, halfway between her college and mine, and with a careful enmeshment of our schedules one of us could always be with the baby . . .

What about spring semester, though? he objected. What about Professor Coronil, and Venezuela? You're planning to get that doctorate, Sarah, you need to have native-level fluency in Spanish.

She told him she'd change fields if she had to. Anthropology had started to seem a little conceptually problematic anyway. And if it was his colleagues' good opinion he was worried about, no one at Columbia would have to know, or not yet. Not that we were ashamed—we weren't—but her courses ran only till early May, and everyone gained some weight on the meal plan.

Which was where I leapt in to note that my mom's survivor benefits ought to be enough to cover some expenses. And I could get a part-time job, juggle it with school; I had some experience in restaurants, I heard myself say—

And anyway, you should know, if one of us had to take a hiatus, Sarah's studies would one hundred percent come first. I would be the one responsible for the baby.

Oh God, Eleanor said again.

Not what I was looking for, of course, but I pushed on:

I'm saying, school doesn't have to be such a priority for me. Name an actor who needed a degree to succeed.

Peter O'Toole, Albert replied without thinking. The <u>Schindler's List</u> guy. Sir John fucking Gielgud.

But Ethan's already getting parts, Sarah told him; didn't Mom say anything about <u>Law & Order</u>?

And in a couple of years, when I've got a play or two under my belt and we've built up some savings, we could get our own place, I said, ignoring them both. Move in together—it isn't the nineteenth century. Or if it helps we could tie the knot, make it official.

After a silence Sarah Vaughan could have sung a symphony in, Eleanor said, Well, you've certainly looked at all the angles. But just so I know: you did think about . . . the alternatives?

Mom, I already told you: I'm not going to try to justify it, but the alternative isn't what either of us wants to do.

I hadn't ruled out Albert trying to assault me physically, but he'd been watching Eleanor's face, and when she turned to him, some wordless thing seemed to cinch tight between them. Fix this, she seemed to be saying. Meet her halfway.

No, I don't suppose it would be like you, Sarah, to have told us if there were still doubts, he said, and sighed. I remember worrying in my twenties that having a kid too young was going to upend everything . . . but when you get to my age and look back, it ends up being the least of your regrets. I'm saying, we can find room to pack you all in here, he continued (as if oblivious to how it sounded), just as long as you hold off for the time being on deciding what comes next.

Telling my family should have been easier, at least on paper. Dad still being a man of the cloth, I thought, choice qua choice wouldn't enter into the equation, leaving pregnancy as one of those things you were supposed to just accept. (Another of his favorite lines: It's not ours to ask why.) And yet did I relish returning home a scant four months after leaving, with my glittering palace of September all in ruins? Jolie, I did not.

The bus I chose out of Port Authority was the opposite of an express. After lurching to a stop at seemingly every backwater along the mid-

Atlantic, it arrived under cover of darkness on the eve of Christmas Eve. Moira had opted to stay abroad for the holiday (a greeting card in performatively rusty English had reached me in New York, along with a photo of her with her hair grown out, drinking some kind of flaming wine) so I feared disembarking to an unchecked Corinne, but Dad, too, seemed inclined to avoid conflict, and Corinne wouldn't be seen until dinnertime the next evening, followed by midnight mass at St. Paul's by-the-Sea.

I suppose what I was really dreading was Christmas Day itself, recalling as it would the threadbare gift exchange of '92, when Mom had first been laid out on chemo, and myself struggling not to nod out on the couch. Dad's presents this year were only marginally less perfunctory—a waterproof watch and a laptop weighing roughly twelve pounds—but we did somehow manage to go the entire morning without TV. Then the Navy game was on and Corinne off to Hagerstown to see relatives; I'd double-checked her timing before finalizing Sarah's visit. She would arrive for lunch on the twenty-sixth in Albert's Volvo—ostensibly to meet Dad, but really to be by my side as I broke the news—and then late afternoon we'd start back.

Naturally, the rains came that next morning, though with a softness that seemed almost tentative. I lay in bed trying to reread Mom's old <u>Masnavi</u> but not quite remembering what I'd seen in it. I assumed the plink-plink distracting me was the gutter until I heard a mallet come down like a librarian's stamp and realized it was crabshell going into a bowl, a sound I hadn't heard since the last time Dad had wanted to impress someone. I took my book over to the window with some inchoate idea of running to catch Sarah before she could ring the doorbell. Somehow I missed the Volvo, though, which she'd parked in the side lot at Ducky's, and by the time she turned up our walk, it was too late to stop her. She was wearing one of Albert's blazers over her <u>Blond Ambition</u> tee, sleeves jeujed up, but underneath I could see the glow. I hurried out the window just as if these were the bad old days, and rather than shinny down the wisteria, leapt straight from the roofline to the lawn. My jeans were damp, my feet smarting. The rain had stopped, but around us everything was still drowning, water gurgling audibly in the storm drain, the trees like slashes of a wet brush. And the love I felt then, too, a kind of drowning. I imagined myself guiding her back around the hydrangeas to where no one could see and sliding my hand inside her belt to feel the softness of her belly. Instead, I asked her had she been okay, was everything okay?

It was just three days, Ethan, she said.

And kissed my face and gave a little pat of my chest, like, everything's fine, you have nothing to worry about.

Then we were in the small living room and Dad in the doorway to the kitchen, toweling off his hands for shaking, sizing her up with the same scrutiny he'd used to gauge the length of hair and tucked-in-ness of shirts between periods out at school. But Sarah gave as good as she got, and seeing him through her eyes, I almost began to wonder if there was less to the rector of St. Anselm's than I'd feared—if his demands, his disapproval were just things I'd put there in my imagination. When he offered to take her jacket, as I'd forgotten to do, she turned with a perfect admixture of surprise and bashfulness to shake it off:

Whatever you've got cooking smells amazing.

Ethan says you're studying anthropology, he said. We wanted to give you the full local experience. But I'm sorry, Sarah—I'm realizing I forgot to ask him if you ate crab.

The implication couldn't possibly have been ethnic, since I hadn't mentioned her being Jewish, but by the time I remembered the shellfish allergy Corinne had purportedly developed, Sarah was on his arm, giving rise to what on anyone else I'd have recognized as a blush.

Was he kidding? she said. Crabcakes were all she'd eat, given the chance; they were one of the first things she'd fallen in love with on the Eastern Shore.

He cleared his throat—Hang on to this one, Ethan—and excused himself to the kitchen to finish up. This wasn't rudeness, I knew, nor again exactly shyness; rather, my dad's notion of hospitality was that the most remote person in a room should always be the one put at ease, even if it was you yourself who'd made them uneasy. Not that we'd been left to just chill on the couch, either; so as not to seem disinterested, he'd propped open the kitchen door and was talking to us through it. Meanwhile, blocked from view, Sarah had taken out a creased photo strip from an appointment with the midwives two days earlier. Still a blob, but our blob, she pointed out: my Christmas gift, along with a silent kiss. So by the time she started arguing, through gesture and look, that we should go in and try to help, I had softened.

In short order, she was in an apron, working at Dad's side. I could see that she hadn't given up on the idea of mending the breach between father and son; if anything, it had acquired force. And maybe she was right to want that, I decided. Where I'd long taken Dad's habit of busying himself while talking as a strategy to deflect any real exchange, it now occurred to me that maybe he too felt congenitally embattled, and distraction was just what he needed to be able to relax. Anyway, she seemed genuinely interested as he brought out his good knives, the ones with the fading old zip case, and showed how to whet one on the heavy stone, the preparatory cuts that would let you dice your celery or what-have-you in casual staccato. And before I knew it, he was telling her about the flexibility forced on you by a destroyer's galley, some crossing to Singapore he'd made in the early '70s—a place I didn't even know he'd been.

As she practiced her knifework, he emptied the block of crabmeat into a sieve from an upcycled tub of I Can't Believe It's Not Butter! and shocked it back to life in the shell stock he'd set to simmer, loosing a fragrant layer of steam. Then into the colander it went, to be checked for missed fragments before it joined the celery and scallions in a bowl, along with some mayo whipped from scratch and a good punch of Old Bay.

Back when Mom was still alive, we'd typically eaten around the little table there in the kitchen, but now he'd set what he called the "formal dining room"—really just an alcove between the china hutch and the wall of the front room. He'd worked hard on this, too: the good napkins in holders, an arrangement from the florist, salad forks for whatever fell from buns he'd baked himself and buttered and warmed. And without waiting for us to adjust, he bowed his head and in his mild baritone offered one of his pre-lunch prayers from school—not the one I'd dreaded (the hard right, the easy wrong, the help we need choosing), but some anodyne thing about the blessings of family and the workings of grace. We were three bites into the actual meal when he excused himself, disappeared into the basement, and resurfaced with three dusty cans of National Bohemian lager.

Almost forgot, Sarah. But I promised you a complete immersion in the native culture.

Oh, I'm fine with water, she said, with uncharacteristic diffidence—normally she'd have turned the offer of a beer back on you, made you start questioning whichever assumptions you'd made. Then: I have to drive.

But it wasn't the feint to spare his feelings that set me off; it was that I honestly thought he knew better than to put alcohol in front of me. I mean: Didn't he have to know at least that much?

Sarah doesn't drink, Dad, I said. Me neither, since we've been together.

I see, he said, slightly nonplussed. Well, good for you both.

Which for some reason got further up my nose.

Anyway, I continued, there's something you should be aware of.

Burning to be seen now, I took the ultrasound strip from my pocket and shoved it toward him across the tablecloth between us.

The best way I can describe the look on his face then is, "puzzled." As if a blade had been driven in, but the blood hadn't yet begun to flow.

Ethan, this is . . . ? Why are you . . . ?

You're going to be a grandpa.

Jesus. What? I can't believe this . . . But you should have said something, to Moira if not to me. Are you okay? You're both okay?

It occurred to me that the Kupferbergs hadn't thought to ask. And also that his sudden show of concern was making me look like the real bully here, bullies being the one thing Sarah hated most. As if trying to close up the wound, amend the slip, I began to rehearse for him the deal we'd struck with Eleanor and Albert—how they'd agreed to us moving in. And if there was a plea for him to endorse all this, resume his old spiel about learning to cope with life's responsibilities, I kept it where only he could hear it. He just let me run on. Then he repeated, as if insensible to the foregoing,

The most important thing to start with, though, is just that you're okay.

We're okay, Dad, really. We've had time to get used to the idea. People have been through worse.

He looked at the picture again: And the due date is . . . I'm sorry, Sarah, when did you say it was?

We didn't, she said, still circumspect.

July, I said.

He took it in.

More than six months away. That's good. So you still have a little time in which to weigh your options.

Options?

Because the next thing you need to hear, both of you, is that you're going to be supported no matter what.

Still slightly stunned by how quickly he had gotten to the right things to say, I said, What, by you and Corinne? Who the fuck are you right now, Dad—options? And what have you done with my real father?

Ethan, you just turned nineteen. I'm only saying, you're under no obligation to carry this through to term. Neither of you are.

What happened to "God's will," though? I said. What happened to "accepting the mystery"?

This last, from the funeral, was just cruel, but I couldn't help myself.

A human life is not a mystery, Ethan, he said. Or not only.

I should have fucking guessed, I groaned. You talk such a big game about, like, duty and sacrifice and all that, but what did you do after Mom died? Moved right on.

I waited half a year to start seeing Corinne. You know that.

You waited four months! It was nothing!

He needed a moment to recover.

But people have a duty to themselves, too, Ethan, is what I thought we discussed. We're not honoring anyone by just condemning ourselves to more suffering. Which is why I'm asking you to think long and hard about the real work of parenthood.

I didn't realize it's been that miserable for you.

That's not what I meant, Ethan. The opposite, obviously. But it's so much more difficult than either of you seems to realize. And just because a person makes one mistake—

For fuck's sake, nobody's saying this was a mistake! I said.

But when I looked to Sarah for backup, she seemed to be searching his face for something.

You think I'm not ready, is that it? I said. Or no: you're scared of being called in to clean up my mess?

Well, it's probably not the wisest thing to try to live on the good graces of your girlfriend's parents. But what I'm trying to say is what I'd say to anyone who came to me for counsel, Ethan. We're talking about the next twenty years of your lives. Sometimes more than that.

And now he took off his glasses, folded them, rubbed the little divots they'd left on the sides of his nose.

One misstep, or whatever it was, son, shouldn't require the sacrifice of your entire youth. I'm telling you: you owe it to yourselves to think the next part over very carefully.

We have thought it over carefully, Sarah said at last, her gaze still fixed on him. If you'd been with us, you would see that.

Then she reached out to put her hand in mine, but I didn't want someone translating for me anymore.

We didn't come to you for counsel, I heard myself say, steadier. What we came for is the boat.

What?

I wanted to take her out one last time before we left, I said. The Molly

A's not dry-docked yet, right? Sarah's never seen her. Don't worry, I won't try to actually sail, just use the motor.

For a second his eyes stayed closed. If he was praying for me, I thought, I was out of here. And conversely, if he objected on the grounds of the pregnancy he'd just tried to talk us into ending—out of here. In fact, so long as he continued to dismiss the reaction to him and his whole way of being he could at least no longer deny I had, maybe I was out of here anyway.

You know I'm not saying you can't do it, he said, finally.

But whatever he meant, it was too late in coming. Your mom pushed some food around on her plate, but my own appetite was gone; the crabcake had turned to cardboard in my mouth. I wouldn't give him the satisfaction of anything so dramatic as a door-slam, but I pointedly didn't offer to clear dishes, and made sure he saw me take my messenger bag as we walked out to the lawn. I already had his old computer, so the new one could just be something to remember me by.

You really want to take her out? the marina guy said, peering from the open wall of the warehouse-like structure, then back at the one license I did possess, a little fill-in-the-blanks card from the state of Maryland certifying me fit to sail. Off-season, we close at six, so if you can't be back—

We'll be back, I said, trying to sound like I did this all the time. In fact, I hadn't been shipboard in two years, nor meaningfully engaged with the business of sailing since the summer's worth of lessons I'd bluffed my way through at thirteen. The guy motioned us into the dinghy, and, once I'd helped your mother step down, ferried us through the rows of listing powerboats waiting to be wrapped for the winter like gifts.

And soon we were puttering out alone on the bigger boat, the docks and trees and the lit-up boathouse sliding past. The idea, to the degree that there was one, was to venture only a short ways into the channel proper. The air was moist but still balmy. Your mom stood next to me and slightly behind, in the life-vest I'd grabbed for her from a locker. Channel markers listed and clanged with no other traffic to read them. A trace scent of Clorox was probably just recent cleaning, but I told myself instead it was that deeper sterility that had doomed my dad—this refusal to dirty his hands with the disorder that was life on earth.

And even so, it was a kind of relief to have Sarah be the outsider once more, and me the one gesturing cryptically toward what I could only hope to show her. I pointed out the line of sunset spreading under the overcast, and the low mound of Keel Hill. Then Ocean City wheeled whitely through ten o'clock, its stunted skyline of condos and hotels now empty for the season. Sarah edged closer to the bow, keeping one hand on the rail, but however she was seeing what had happened back there, she didn't say, and anyway, her whipped-up hair was hiding her face.

It wasn't until open water that I cut the motor and let our little wake slosh past us. The summer we'd first met, our excursions had brought us north, toward the mainland; now we were facing the barrier island called Assateague. Like Chincoteague to the south, I told her, it was still undeveloped, not that different from four hundred years ago. Once a year, in summer, wild ponies got swum at low tide from one to the other, and then auctioned off to thin the herd. But sometimes you'd get a stray or even a little family of them this far north.

And that's where your mom's buried? she said. Where her ashes were put to rest, I mean?

You're not supposed to drop anchor there, I said, but that was what she wanted. Moira and Dad scattered their part by the water, but I went off and did mine right where you see that rise. I had this little wooden paperweight I'd made for her in Scouts. They give you such a shitty knife . . .

Hey, she said, after a while. Look at me. What your father thinks ultimately doesn't matter, you know that, right?

It matters what you think.

I still think maybe you don't understand him, she said. But now I can see why.

This isn't about reasons, Sarah, it's about choices. As long as he chooses a life with that woman, I don't know how I can face coming back here.

You don't have to argue it to me, I'm on your side, she said, and laced her hand through mine. But there is one thing he was making some sense about, which is how much we should be relying on parents at all. I mean, we're the parents now.

Point being . . .

Don't you think we should probably get our own place sooner rather than later?

And God almighty, did I ever love her then.

Hell yes, I do, I said. But didn't you say the brokers want like three months of rent up front? Plus assurances we're not just some flash in the pan?

Well, on top of your SSA, I have my holiday checks, and that little mutual fund thing from when my aunt died. You're going to be getting more TV work. And I'm pretty sure my parents would cosign a lease, if only to get us out of the house . . .

But wouldn't it look better on an application if we said we're engaged? I asked. Then I saw it: Hey—marry me a little, Sarah.

What?

Let's get married, I said, my knee wet again (or still). No big fuss, just City Hall. People don't even have to know.

She moved my hair back out of my eyes; smiled down on me. If that's really how you feel, Ethan, then I should tell you I've already been looking at apartments.

You have?

How do you think I spent my Christmas? I may even have managed to find one.

A drive, a night's sleep, a joint shower, and a bus transfer would leave us standing in an unfinished loft above a Chinese carryout over toward the east side of El Barrio. She'd charmed keys out of the broker, saying she wanted to show the place to her fiancé before the holiday ended, and now, on the poker-chip chain she tossed in her hand, they made a surprisingly large noise. As did her voice:

It's great, right? You could keep your plants over here . . .

I reconnoitered the small apartment, listening to her echo. No closets, so we'd have to hang everything on doorknobs, living right out in the open. My takeaway from our visit to the Kupferbergs, though, had been that the real making of a New York apartment was the light. The tiny lavatory and bathtubbed kitchen each had a transom to the east, but the main exposure was to the south, out a huge industrial window whose panes had patches of what looked like freezer burn, diffusing the day outside. Through the clearer parts I could make out a fire escape, and beyond that the street, the corner. And after the never-brightness of her dormroom, all that glass had the effect of a white light burning off the lingering haze of my trip home. She pointed out the top of the carryout's sign:

Not neon, she said, but otherwise awful close to what you dreamed up that time on the beach.

No, it's perfect, I said, not mentioning how long it would take me to get across town, down to school.

We signed a lease that very afternoon, and though we couldn't technically move in till the first of the month, it's not like I owned any furniture to speak of—just the longboard that for all she knew had never made it out to Queens and the too-many boxes I'd carried with me to Manhattan (which maybe it really was time to start letting go of). The broker agreed to look the other way if we brought a chair over early, and so we rang in the start of 1997 using its cushions as pillows, sleeping or not sleeping on the floor as car-horns and fireworks and cheers from the neighborhood filtered through the uncurtained window, altered slightly by the snow. And aside from that and the lovely slight rounding of her hips, there was hardly any physical reminder we weren't back in October, on the last night of the World Series, in a kingdom now big enough for three.

What came next in that apartment, Jolie, was just joyful immersion. The schedule she'd fashioned out of the jetsam of Venezuela now included the maximum number of credit-hours the university allowed—as if by taking her studies far enough, fast enough, she could outrun the distractions of motherhood. It was still mostly underpaid TAs handling Columbia's sophomores, but by the first week of May, she was donning bulky sweaters to go meet with professors from the three different programs now urging her, on the strength of her term papers, to switch majors. When she declared for Urban Studies, I insisted on a celebratory dinner out—the one, you'll recall, I still owed her from November. And in general, I relished my vocation as her caretaker, stocking the fridge with seltzer and limes and all the brined foods she couldn't stop eating—kimchi, olives, capers, the warty little French dill pickles she could absently down a whole jar of while studying—plus ridiculously expensive vitamin supplements and the whole-milk, whole-everything yogurt the books recommended, which I had to get on the subway to even find.

We could afford to splurge in part because I was indeed getting more TV work. Another friend of Hank's had decided the camera liked me, whatever that meant, and because I needed only a few additional background roles to earn my SAG card, he'd referred me to an agent—or junior agent, I should say. She wasn't the best about returning phone calls, but the door, once opened, led to others. My secret, aside from having lied my way into college? I'd say yes to anything. There I was, transferring a call on Sprint's "Flatiron Press" campaign . . . trying to seem tense in the waiting room of a short-lived <u>Doogie Howser</u> spinoff . . . and, if you look closely, delivering cappuccinos to the friends of <u>Friends</u> in a pair of episodes now ascended to the Valhalla of syndication. At no point would you have seen me, nineteen playing twenty-one, or sixteen, and imagined I was about to become a father. And out there in the world, too, I kept my secret, feeling it somehow gave me mystery, gave me substance.

Amid all of which, did my schoolwork suffer? Very well, then: my schoolwork suffered. I'd bought a beater of a ten-speed out of the back of <u>The Village Voice</u>, and from our apartment I could whip downtown via the ring road in Central Park, arriving chill with sweat for the day's first class. But I muddled my way through midterms, played chicken with deadlines I then discharged with halfass reams of bop prosody hammered out on Sarah's Underwood while still safe in her bed, and when the comments came back, "See me," I never did. Even my one-act, which I fitfully continued to revise and extend, kept collapsing into monologue, drowned out by Hank's elegant scrawl: You're still stuck in your own head, man, you need to push harder, let's talk . . . I started blowing off his rehearsals, blaming each absence, in my mind, on the new long commute, and telling myself I needed no instruction in how to build a character. For what could even the most well-meaning other person teach me that Sarah, that New York, couldn't? Out of gold and out of junk—out of sobriety, lust, fat beats, and a dream of my mom's bohemia—I had fabricated for myself a new life to replace the one I'd been born with, and had finally crawled from one to the other, zipping shut the passage behind me.

So far had I come in the course of nine months, it appeared, that when I found myself standing by an eleventh-floor window at St. Luke's–Roosevelt early the next July, nearly visionary with exhaustion after twenty hours of Bradley-Method labor coaching, and saw a white tower two blocks north turning seashell pink with the day, I at first didn't recognize it as an elevated view of my own dorm. Behind sun-blind windows, the kids were of course all gone for the summer. But even if one had stayed behind, White Henry, say, and had thought to look out at the delivery ward where I stood, he'd never in a million years have imagined that the man in the window was me.

But now the midwife was calling me back to bedside where the crowning had commenced. Sarah, even more exhausted than I was, had gone someplace deeper inside while the surface calmed like the sea after a storm, but as the labor grew heavy again, I took her hand and tried to give her anything I had for the final push. And then the sheet was thrown off and everyone was yelling, and for all the waiting, it was so quick, that last step through the veil—so quick, I swear, and the light so real, and the sounds so beyond coachability, that I almost couldn't grasp what had changed. Nor was I allowed to go straight toward it; I was the only male figure in the room, and these women had plans for me. Shears with a funny kink in them were being shoved into my hand, but at the last minute I recalled Sarah saying something from the books about delaying the cut. I could feel the cord pulsing, the life still sloshing back and forth between, neither two nor quite yet one. As if dealing with an idiot, they guided my hands to where they were supposed to be and said, All you have to do is cut. But fear seized me. What if I fucked this up too, somehow, right from the start? And suddenly someone was at my elbow with a clipboard.

What's the name, Daddy?

The name? I said. I don't know, is it a boy or a girl?

I heard Sarah laugh . . . somehow, miraculously, herself again. You didn't think to look? It's a girl, Ethan. You have a daughter.

My mind was a blank. I honestly couldn't remember what we'd decided, in that case; then the fear lifted off me like a wave.

We'll call her Jolie, I said. Jo for short.

And there you were.

V

OTHER PEOPLE:
A REQUIEM

November 23–25, 2011

these are dangerous days
to say what you feel is to dig your own grave
—SINÉAD O'CONNOR
"Black Boys on Mopeds"

7

ONLY NOW SHE WAS . . . well, where was she? Not "safe in her bed," to judge by the tamped-down mattress beneath her, but someplace bright despite sealed eyes, and with this ominous whirring back of the quiet, a sort of mechanized death rattle. And though her New York childhood had comprised whole syllabaries of urban noise, still the acoustics here felt off, somehow: rustle of vegetation, faint crake of crows. Or were those gulls? Then came a cascade of glass into iron, heedless of anyone's sleep, and within the frail compass of her eyelids, she had it: recycling truck. Even unto the blasted heath of Maryland's Eastern Shore, nothing, however broken or empty, could go to waste anymore. If life on earth was to survive, everything redeemable was going to have to be redeemed.

Jaysus, though, but it sounded like a motherlode out there, a couple thousand bottles sluicing from dumpster to truckbed, thence to be ground down to something just short of sand and packed on container ships belching carbon all the way to China. Having spent the last few weeks trying to stifle thoughts of pointlessness, of self-annihilation, Jolie might have done better to ignore all this, go back under. Instead, recalling the shards her plans now lay in, she forced herself awake and groped alongside her to find the floor less far down than she'd imagined. Then jeans. Then phone. And when her eyes opened, it was on the little glyph that meant no new messages (no one back home having noticed she'd gone missing), and beyond, projections of treeshadow and gold on a scrim of wall . . . so maybe it was the brightness and not the truck that had roused her after all: the dappled emergency of

late November here at 6:23 a.m.—when the train she'd be needing stopped through Philly at noon, and for the life of her she
couldn't remember what she'd done with her passport.

Of sleep she had no memory either, though her ass, itself
underpadded, seemed mostly recovered from those hours spent
captive in a doggy Econoline. Yet the instant she sat upright, her
head banged against the ceiling, sending such a jolt through the
tender place where metal pierced tongue that it took her whole
self not to cry out. Slowly, more carefully this time, she rose on
her elbows. Had she grown giant in the night? No, this wall next
to her was just knee-high, the ceiling swooping down as if to greet
it. And the bed was a futon, and the quilt a SpongeBob sleeping
bag she couldn't recall unzipping or spreading over her. And of
course her father would have gone ahead and claimed whatever
in the way of a proper mattress did exist, this being the room he'd
grown up in. Allegedly.

It was when she got up to unmoil the jeans that she realized he
must have crashed elsewhere. In fact, this looked to be no longer a bedroom at all, but the new owner's study, with built-ins
near the door and a hutch for the A/V sprawl. In the air a smell
of fresh paint hung whitely, vented by the one window, partway
open. A peek through the blinds yielded a brief tar roof, a truck
marked **FLAHERTY HAULING,** and the gas station that had flickered in and out of Dad's monologue speeding south last night on
the parkway. And then off to the left, at the curb: the horned van
where of course her passport must have been all along, stuffed
into the rosin box of her violin case along with an emergency supply of booze and the dual-language packet of legal advice she'd
printed off the internet. She could go right now out the window,
she thought; but when she tested the sash, a little safety bracket
blocked it. Shoulders might fit, but the head would be a near
thing. And anyway, this whole notion of captivity was just the
sort of childish bullshit she would have to leave behind if a future
was to be salvaged; when she crossed to the doorknob, it turned.
And still: time was tight. Wherever Dad was sleeping, he wouldn't
be for long—not with those birds to croak up the sun. Not with
the airbrake of the truck bursting like one last bottle, the engine
grumbling off down the street.

In a hurry now, she jammed her feet into legholes, unscrunched legs, and squatted to gather such supplies as had tumbled to the faux-Turkish rug: cash; Midol; a jerry-rigged cigarette lighter whose outsized flame leapt obediently at her touch. That there were no actual cigarettes remained galling, possibly because in trying to smoke away the urge to drink she'd acquired another addiction, but also possibly because the not-talking was harder than you'd think and a cigarette plugged the hole at the center of your face. Still, the gas station's claim to fame, per Dad, was its dealings with minors, and if she could ride out a two-hundred-mile detour without a single word of protest, she could surely finesse the negotiation of a couple domestic cartons on her way back north, or northeast . . . or however one got from here to JFK. She swilled a capful of antiseptic from the piercing place, spat it into the trash. Donned her black jacket and hat. Cinched her leaden Docs. Was just slinging the backpack over a shoulder, messenger-style, when something snagged in her gut like a hook. Say she made it out undetected—would this then be the closest she'd ever come to her lost grandparents? In which case, was there not some memento she could maybe take with her? But a quick snoop of shelves and closet did nothing to substantiate what little she'd been told: church art school sea. The person who'd redone this room had wanted no part of the past (unless you counted the VHS player under the flatscreen).

The door too was new, or at least noiseless on its hinges. And out on the landing, it might have been midnight still. Three open doorways framed the gloom, one leading to a bathroom, one to more steps, but through a crack in the last shone a nightlight. She squatted to work her boots off again so no one would hear them clomp. Held them by the leather toggles and toesocked down the stairs. Only on the first floor came more signs of the renovation she'd failed to notice six hours ago, when the woman with the shorty bathrobe and the eyes slitted to unreadability (an old flame who'd bought the house, she'd surmised through her exhaustion) had more or less ordered Jolie upstairs to the futon while trapping Dad on the porch to talk, arms crossed in the flicker of fall's last moths. Down here were wood floors darker where carpets had lain; an open kitchen with those stone countertops everyone seemed to want nowadays; a stand-mounted mixer still in its box . . . all of it a far cry from the Dickensian workhouse of Dad's imaginings. Only the French doors below the flat little roof seemed unaltered, and for a second she paused with her hand on the knob, fearing him drowsing behind them with one eye open, like the watchman in a fairy tale. Though maybe with his keys not on his person? Instead what she found, pushing through, was a wheeled cot, a mildewed rug, and a line of musty cartons tagged with handwritten Post-its. And inside those, neat stacks of audio- and videocassettes and scores of her grandmother's old record albums. There would have been CDs, too, she knew, were they not already in a box back under her bed at home, jumbled with Dad's own boom-bap—plus at least one malfunctioning video disc that had gotten mixed in. Still, was it possible some prior version of Joanna's lost opus might have washed up here? Movement beyond the glass drew her gaze. A twitch of the van's tail, breath wisping from a palsied muffler. Somehow amid the din of recycling she hadn't noticed the engine had been left on all night, the keys waiting in the ignition. And here it was after all, like a charm, under *O:* the missing link, holy grail of Aspern studies. Into the bag it went. Maybe she could even sneak back upstairs to see if it worked, snag the VCR needed to play it . . . ? But no, best not to give Dad another reason to come chasing after.

So now courage, Jolie: the front door, replete with deadbolts and chains, the breeze lancing through her sweater and the cold porch chivvying her boots back on. Across the lawn lay a glitter of hoarfrost, the strong southern light through two exfoliated trees. And as soon as she'd retrieved the violin, it would be on to the nearest bus station. How did she know there'd be one? The whole place just had that vibe. Also Google. Oh point four miles.

There was a moment here when the van's passenger's-side door might not have come open, but then she was reminded of its busted lock . . . and how he'd insisted on moving her instrument to the back last night before hauling her out for hot chocolate and candy bars on the ferry, that king-sized Baby Ruth she'd refused to even touch. The rear doors too were unlocked, but when she swept them apart, the grooming table had been shoved to one side, toward a pegboard of clippers and shears, and there in the cleared space—not a foot from the violin—stretched the supine form of her father. Under a dusty afghan, he could have been a cathedral, his great feet the towers, long legs the nave, arms the transept, crossing at the heart . . . and above that, a head unfinished as St. John the Divine. A fucking wonder her gaze hadn't wakened him, but maybe this is the closest we come to predestination: even spewing pollutants all night, even with worsening apnea, even with the door unlocked so that anyone with the requisite will could have just bashed in his face with the instrument case and then taken the entire van, there was the heaviness with which we sleep when back in our hometowns.

Gingerly, she re-closed the doors. Twisted the stud in her mouth; a dull pang of memory. A boy's hand on her head, forcing her down. And no one there to help her after, or even just to hear her cry. She almost sat on the bumper but was afraid to rock it. How could something you felt so sure of one minute just give out on you the next? She could neither reach the goddamn passport without waking Dad nor escape this burning without it.

But again: that caw.

Trying to reduce her mind to a camera, to master the pain, she backpedaled up the oystershell drive. Past a yawing outbuilding (was there a pole inside that might help her fish out the case? a bike to make up for lost time?), the yard ran to a line of evergreens, and as she scanned for the sound's source, a redness came streaking from behind the siding, bright against branches before vanishing again. A swingset, and on it a black boy of five or six, pumping away at what must from his perspective have seemed an overwhelming velocity. She tried to duck out of sight, but too late. In conjunction with his red jumper, the hand he raised at the top of the next backward sweep had an oddly adult effect, like one of those baby Jesi in the Renaissance wing of the Met. Then he came down stiffly in a swale of sand.

"You leaving already? Because I t-told them last night you wouldn't b-b-be with us for long. I just duh . . . I d-d-d-duh . . . I c-couldn't say which way you'd g-go."

Struggling to parse the stutter, Jolie tracked his eyes to a person not quite herself, the navy surplus strap further flattening her chest under the cardigan, the tee. For a second, she couldn't recall if kids got an exemption from her vow of silence. But no, rules were rules. If she ever spoke again, it was going to have to be on her own terms—because she'd finally gotten free. What followed was a queasy spell, like the temptation to falter had been planted in her from the outside.

"Maybe first you g-give me push, though? So you can see how I g-g-get over the bar?"

It would be hard to say why she didn't turn on the spot and flee; there was curiosity, sure, but also the implied threat: if she did, the boy might start shouting loud enough to wake the dead. And communication being ninety percent nonverbal, Jolie couldn't put a finger to her lips, much less gesture toward the front of the house without betraying herself anew; even a nonresponse was a response. Perhaps simplest just to keep him quiet while she figured out her next move. She set her bag in the frostless sand and stationed herself behind, trying to minimize contact with his warm little back. The resulting push was weak, he said . . . try harder. (His *h*'s seemed to come more naturally.) And as his hushpuppies went horizontal, that avian creak started up again. Impossible to tell, really, whether the swingset dated to her dad's era or whether things out here just aged faster; the air felt saltier than it would have deeper inland (though maybe this was just Jolie, still clinging to the notion that her forebears had commanded an ocean view). At the margins of the house's shade, the grass grew beautiful and wet and soft and dead. The shot, it occurred to her, was the reverse of what her grandmother might have framed from the kitchen window, the dead artist grandmother she'd lately come to picture as a cross between Sally Mann and Laurie Anderson and the Lady of the Lake. And what she'd taken to be leaves, curled in upon themselves, were in this wider angle pecans, littering the ground like pieces of an abandoned puzzle. *Oh please don't leave me here though*, she caught herself thinking. *You can't just lead me out like this and then strand me . . .*

But now the door to the back steps had opened, and at the top stood a woman she hadn't seen before, albeit in the same robe as last night. "No, Jesus, Izz—too high!" Or had Jolie failed to notice Dad's ex was Cambodian, or Thai? Slash American, she amended. And perhaps some pain had slipped her defenses . . .

for the woman had halted halfway down the stairs. "Sorry, but it's about time everyone slowed down and gave some actual thought to what they're doing. For instance, did you even say hello to your Cousin Jolie, honey?"

"Hello to your Cousin Jolie!" he sang out, with pleasure at his own joke.

"I'm Teresa. This is Izzy." A tone firm and clear. "I know we didn't exactly roll out the red carpet for you last night, everything's a bit . . ."

"It's okay, Mama," he broke in. "Jolie doesn't feel like t-t- . . . like t-t-t . . . But she was j-j-j—" The stammer overtaking him again, he braked the swing and traced along his forearm a curious, vein-opening pattern: "Just being on her way."

The woman seemed barely to notice. "Guess your dad must have gotten the message, then."

"What message, T.?" said a voice. "I thought we'd agreed not to decide anything before this morning."

A short-haired woman, the one from last night, had appeared higher up the steps. She began to explain how she'd gone out to fetch the afghan from the van just now only to find Ethan still adoze there, but the import was unclear until she said:

"Look. I know my brother can be . . . well, actually, I don't know what he can be anymore. But I've waited a long time to meet my niece, and it seems a waste to run the two of them off this way."

Teresa eyed the bag, the sheer bulk of it, a toothbrush and a trailing bit of shoelace come loose from the top. "I don't know, though, Moira. Feels like the idea was maybe for the running to commence without him."

"Well, he does have that effect on people," said Moira, taking it in. "But what were you going to do, Jolie, hop a bus back to your mom in New York? The routes all got consolidated through Ocean City two years ago, some austerity thing."

Clank, clank. Even with all her practice, despair was probably the hardest feeling to hide.

"How about this," Moira said finally, a little softer. "Let me at least fix you coffee and some cereal . . . then, you still feel like heading home before the festivities get started, I'll personally drive you over to the station. It's not like we've got anywhere to be this side of one thirty. And if your dad should happen to wake before your mind's made up, Teresa's already lobbying to ban him from the house. Mi casa, su casa. Not Ethan's anymore."

"The answer is yes!" Izzy announced from the swing where he'd resumed his labors (whose squeaking seemed almost the point).

"What's the rule, Izz?" Moira said.

"Not before s-seven? And weekends only . . . Moms need rest."

"It's six fifty. On a Thursday."

"But it's Turkey Day! And I c-can't tell time!"

For all his clamor, Jolie made no move to shush him, and back in the kitchen she would do her best to conceal her glimpses at the clock as this woman, her aunt, prepped the shredded wheat and the coffee while her partner lingered at the island, in a sulk. Still, the lack of walls meant that when Dad entered (as inevitably he would) he'd have a vision of her sitting down to breakfast as if under anything but duress. Without a word of thanks, then, or even the eloquence of hesitation, she accepted mug and bowl and looped back upstairs to the empty cell she'd believed as recently as twenty minutes ago she'd left for good. Locked the door behind her, rolled SpongeBob into a tube and jammed it into a closet and wrestled the futon to its upright position so that at least something would have changed. But of course something had already: her silently nurtured dream of flight had been revealed as hollow—not just the train from Philly she now seemed doomed to miss, the plane she'd have no shot at making, but the whole notion that overseas, in some country far away, there might be some chance to avoid her own eclipse . . . impossible, all of it. Whose impossibility had maybe even been intentional; maybe that was why, despite weeks of preparation, she hadn't yet pushed "buy" on the ticket from New York to Barcelona. Maybe what she'd been angling for, ever since another package from Grayson had showed up (this time in her grandparents' mail dish in Riverdale), was not the moment of takeoff, but the one where Mom came rushing up the concourse before she could be lost completely and said Wait, Jolie, I wasn't there for you, I'm so sorry—and stopped her.

But now through the floor came a trickle of conversation—

what you got for exposing the rafters—which soon, she knew, was going to ripen into an argument about the discord she was causing. Unwilling to feel again that eavesdropper's sense of nowhere belonging, she recrossed the room, fired up the flatscreen, turned up the volume, fed the tape she'd stolen into the VCR, and pushed play. But of course the sound she'd been looking for to cover the others was missing. And the images that arrived were the very ones she'd seen with her own eyes this morning, give or take a couple decades and some frost: grass, trees, convenience store. Her grandma's parting shot had been no requiem, it turned out, not a Mass for those left behind, but just a note of solitude held endlessly, a fermata from which there could be no escape.

She reached for her phone. Then her thoughts went back to Precious, from whom she'd gotten the idea to run in the first place—Precious whose sister Grace had taken that gap year in Spain before disappearing into an anarchist squat along the Rambla. Had Grace Ezeobi needed shifting rationales, or constant self-doubt, or reams of research into visas and legal emancipation? No, she'd just done it—made the leap. So why not risk everything here, try for this redeye that left out of BWI? The cost would be higher, it seemed. But here in her savings account sat the rest of the bat mitzvah money she'd been holding aside to rent a flat, and a nine p.m. flight would give her all the way till nightfall to make her escape, a whole day full of moments to choose from. And even as she thought, Jolie began to unpack her please-notice-me backpack and place the bulkiest items in the closet: the extra sweaters, the hair dryer, the jug of antiseptic . . . and finally, after a pause, even her beloved old Chucks. Reduced to bare essentials, the bag would fit under a back-row seat, should it come to that. And by this time tomorrow, if she could be brave enough to surrender every last hope of being caught—the hope she now saw had doomed her—Dad would be forced to confront this same closet full of juvenilia and accept how the story had changed. Whereas she would be on foreign soil, with at least one door where she knew she could knock and ask to be taken in.

Which is really where she might have ended up, too, reader, I swear—Barcelona—had a belated voice not just then started up from offscreen in the room behind her. It wasn't the words themselves that would strike the chord, make her turn to see what she'd missed on the TV behind her, but the steely tone beneath, what I only know how to describe as a harmonic—how the whole project could suddenly have been singing Jolie's own song back at her, her own emptiness, her desolation. So the piece entitled *Other People* was a requiem after all, it turned out . . . but not necessarily the sound of all hope lost, was it? For even now, as every pathway out seemed to her to thrum with danger, these human voices persisted . . .

8

INTERIOR, DAY: Moira Aspern at a farmhouse sink runs mentally back over an email she only half-remembers sending four months ago. Given that its subject—the twenty-nine-foot yawl being donated to the school for the tax deduction—already limited the audience to St. Anselm's alums (of which she wasn't one), there were bound to be names in the bcc field that aroused no goodwill . . . Frank Gutfreund, for example, whom she'd let fuck her back when she was still managing equipment for the sailing team and who now ran his dad's Chevy dealership. Or Anthony Pessoa, last seen leaving a basket of condolence fruit on the front porch around Christmastime of '08, along with a pamphlet averring 𝕬𝖑𝖑 𝖄𝖔𝖚𝖗 𝖘𝖎𝖓𝖘 𝖂𝖎𝖑𝖑 𝕭𝖊 𝖋𝖔𝖗𝖌𝖎𝖛𝖊𝖓. Remarkable, then, that her own junkie brother should be the very last person she'd wish to find sleeping in a van out front of her house at a quarter to seven on Thanksgiving Day. He hasn't shown his face here in fifteen years—not even to bury their father—yet had allowed her to max out three different credit cards to cover his court costs and legal fees and most recent stint in rehab, so you might have imagined him as at least come to make restitution. But when she'd flipped on the porchlight last night and looked out to see who that could be, knocking so late, he'd still had the look of a man expecting a hero's welcome.

"He says he's working on six months of sobriety," she repeats now to Teresa, who sits behind her. "And anyway, this would just be for today, through dinner—they'll be gone again by sundown. He gave me his word."

For a minute there is more silence. Then: "I don't suppose he let slip at any point in the sales pitch that he and the kid aren't even on speaking terms." And in case Moira's missed the rub: "Her and us either, evidently."

"Fine, honey, yes, you told me so. But what do you want me to do, disinvite them? I already made him sleep out in the cold—"

"After letting him raid the linen closet. Probably warmer out there under a blanket with the heater on than he would have been in here."

"Did you get a good look at the state of that van?"

"Have you taken a look at the state of our boiler?" Teresa asks. "Maybe we should have budgeted for a replacement instead of for some yuppie kitchen that's not even ready yet to host a meal."

"Well, if we couldn't move, I wasn't going to leave the place as is. I wanted it to feel like a home for you—for once. And for Izz."

"You know I don't give a shit about Italian granite, Moira. What you wanted was for it to stop feeling like the place you used to share with an asshole who left you holding the bag."

"Listen, if I'm still in the doghouse for this business around the boat, that's understandable—"

"And the funeral, and Corinne, and the whole probate process," says Teresa, not one to gild the lily. *Your family's all dead or missing*, she'd said, once the will was unsealed, *so why let them hang over your life this way?* But it's precisely when you miss a chance to correct the thing that went wrong, Moira had wanted to explain, that you get a haunting. So the whole point of that fundraising email all along, of turning the transfer of the *Molly A* into a second memorial to balance out the one that Ethan had wrecked, was a kind of exorcism. Expiation. Come this time Saturday morning, they'd be free.

Knowing how this might sound out loud, of course, she turns toward the island. "I did end up inheriting the money, though. Even if it wasn't enough to cover a gut-reno. And the deed to the house."

"And for your troubles, your brother means to blow through with no warning, leave his stink on this stuff so you'll never look at it again without thinking of him. But only if you let him, Moira. Remember, I didn't even *want* to be here for Thanksgiving. We could have been in Massachusetts, at my parents'." After a moment, she adds, "It's the girl tripping you up, isn't it."

"Seems like sort of a package deal . . ."

Teresa's skied eyes are somewhere between a plea and a roll. "You know one of the advantages of not traveling for the holidays, I find? Sleeping in, in your own bed. So I'm going up to that nice, big bedroom that used to be an attic, up under the eaves, Moira, and I'm setting an alarm now for ten fifteen—that's an entire sleep cycle away—and when I come down, I want his ass gone. Not for my sake, either . . . for you, and for our son. And maybe for that niece of yours up there while you're at it." The kicker, *Or else you can find me in Somerville*, remains implied, but her ire seems credible enough; when she sets down her coffeemug on the gleaming new granite, its brittleness sends a slosh over the rim.

And now, hearing the creak at the landing, Moira finds herself yearning for the old bedroom, impossibly luxurious in hindsight, where for a year or two after moving back here, they used to spend whole weekends alone together. Then came Izzy, and Netflix—a miracle of passive absorption right up to the point where she and Teresa had started watching different shows, one on the iPad, one on the laptop—so that more and more these days when they can get their earbuds untangled they are merely alone alone. And then rising early for work, the lion's share of the week spent trying to impart the deep truths of physics amid the pungent biology of eighth-grade boy, that fug of gymsock and Axe body spray strong enough to put you off men for life if you weren't off them already. And picking up Izz on the kindergarten wing where he's the only child of color, strapping him into the Toyota with its desperate-sounding brakes; giving his chatter somewhat less than a hundred percent of whatever she's got left en route to a house she still lives in because that's what's swingable on a teacher's salary and her now-exhausted inheritance—and to a wife she knows is equally exhausted, a wife she half the time feels pressured by this closety little town to pretend is just a friend. And if they do pencil in sex every once in a while, it's as you might a routine cleaning at the dentist's; evenings are mostly just Izzy's speech exercises and meals fit for exactly no one's Pinterest board. Not that she resents any of this, she thinks (well, fine, maybe the Axe body spray), but she is far too tired to put up with the brother who at the top of the next hour lumbers in from somewhere with that shiteating grin of his, not even having bothered to knock, and takes up the mug before attempting a kiss on the head.

"Got to hand it to you, Sis, the place looks great. And you're a kind soul to make coffee. You don't have to go through the whole rigamarole of pretending to flinch, by the way, I know you're not thrilled to see me."

For all the sleep-lines on his face, he is the same old Ethan, that straining after brightness, and seems bent on keeping her the same, too, summoning a cocktail of anger and devotion strong enough to make her ill. She stays stiff, facing the window where her son still swings. After helping himself to the last of the milk and poking around fruitlessly for sugar, he tries again:

"That one's yours out there, huh?"

"He has a name. Izzy."

He evinces no curiosity if it's short for anything; just says, "I like it."

"I'm standing here, Ethan, trying to understand your thought process, coming here like a thief in the night. Really, I am. Tell me something, though: Is it that you genuinely don't see the trail of destruction you leave everywhere? Or that you just don't care?"

And perhaps there really has been a change, because he stops to consider. "Probably a little from column A, little from column B, if I'm being honest."

"I mean, after all this time, you show up unannounced—"

" 'Come for homecoming,' the email said!"

"—saying you want to me to meet your daughter. Yet somehow in the course of us packing her off to your room for sleep you forget to mention that she's decided to go mute."

"Ah. So she's been down already? And clammed up on you, too?" Not obviously displeased. "Look, if it makes you feel any better, it's nothing personal; I'm told Sarah hasn't heard a word from her in over a month."

"But it feels like there's one parent in particular who has her all knotted up inside." She's meant to punish more than to accuse, but when she turns to see the indignation flit across his face, she can't help but feel regret.

"Anyway, it's like I told you," he resumes. "I've only got her until nine tonight. You said the memorial thing starts at like two, right? With the boat? And you're obviously not looking to pump out a bird in the meantime." Gesturing at the empty range. "So we can spend the morning catching up instead, stay to give the *Molly A* a proper sendoff, try to squeeze in however much of the reception afterward—I take it there's a reception?—and by five, five fifteen, we'll be on the road again and out of your hair."

Right up to this moment, she's imagined their talking past each other as just the old familiar rhythm, but no. Somewhere in her brother's schemes and self-deceptions there's been a slippage: between the Thanksgiving feast she'd understood him last night to be inviting himself to—the one where she might have gotten to know her niece—and the memorial rites she has scheduled for this weekend. It's a confusion she could dispel right now, of course, but who's to say that, informed of the day's actual itinerary, he doesn't sweep the girl up and make a run for New York himself? Nor has the punitive mood quite left her, it seems, since she feels powerless not to scheme a little herself. "Listen to my words, though, Ethan. Unless you want this whole day to be a firefight, you need to clear out of here for a bit and let folks acclimate to the idea of you sticking around. I've already spent an hour trying to lower the temperature . . . not least with your daughter."

"Well, there's the IGA on North Main, right?" he says, after a quick phoneward glance (though still with his injured look). "I guess I could walk over there, grab some toiletries . . . but it's hardly even eight a.m. yet."

"I don't remember Ducky's Sinclair ever keeping holiday hours."

"I doubt Ducky's in the mood to mend fences, Moira."

"I'm not saying you have to climb up on the pool table and announce your presence; just go kill some time there while I do what I can to placate Jolie and Teresa, and then I'll come get you, we can sort out the rest on the way to the store."

He studies her face. "Man, you are loving this, aren't you. The black sheep and the dutiful daughter." But having satisfied himself of something, he holds up his hands. "On second thought, don't answer that. If I turn up with my throat cut, you'll know who did it."

The screen door closes behind him, that slam she wishes she'd had the contractor take a look at. Still, a little blueblack bird, iridescent as an oil swirl, continues to hop around pecking pecans from the brown back lawn. And then it hits her: Did Ethan think she'd at some point *wanted* to be thirty-six and living back in the house where they'd barely survived sixteen? She has a theory that everyone has an age where they come closest to their true selves. For him, judging by his one letter from California, it was probably those years when he first got strung out on Mom's meds and she'd thought it was just pussy, or pot; for her it came later, when she was living in Berlin. She'd believed herself to be escaping into a nineteenth-century novel or the Kathy Acker equivalent: mornings in a labcoat, afternoons on the barricades, and dancing all night . . . as if that moment of peaking on X with the dog-collared DJ looping his drum-break toward infinity could somehow be carried out of the club, and the border between waking life and dream be dissolved. She would become some fierce alloy of Madame Curie and Marius from *Les Mis* and Václav Havel. Or Harvey Milk. But that wasn't life, obviously (as she sort of knew even then, dragging herself back through Zoo Station at dawn). And the thing about conflating survival with escape is, Moira spent a lot of her teens on it, her early twenties. At a certain point, you just wear out.

In the time it takes her to think all this, she's continued to stand at the sink, having totally forgotten her purpose. What returns her to herself is just the surge of water in the pipes: Instructed to go wait next door, has Ethan instead ducked upstairs to start the shower, check on his daughter? No—odds are this is Teresa, trying to de-stress for sleep. Still, how to handle the stricken niece, buy them time to talk? She looks down and sees the heavy stockpot under the faucet, her dad's old crab pot, and recalls the five-pound bag of sweet potatoes abulge on a basement shelf, chosen because they yield a dessert with no added glucose (Izzy having arrived from foster care diabetic on top of the stutter and the allergies). To get the dish baked off and cooled in time for departure, the yams ought to be boiling already. But the peeler is nowhere to be found, and if that's indeed Teresa in the shower, filling the big pot is only going to mean further conflict; somehow the reno left no budget for the wide new pipes that might deliver hot water simultaneously upstairs and down, so it's a constant battle around here to decide who does what when. This bird pecking under the tree has given her an idea, though, and when she reaches for the phone, there it is: World's Best Sugarless Pecan Pie.

Upstairs, the study door is closed, and if there's a sound from inside save for a man's televised rasp, she can't tell over the soft slosh of the Swedish washer-dryer. For a second she feels certain that if she forces the latch, there'll be no one in there watching at all. But when she knocks, Jolie unlocks, and the TV is off, as blank as her face. It's a look Moira knows from cornering one or another of her first-formers in the hall at St. Anselm's between classes. That feeling of being sentenced to solitary with no one to tell you why. The nose ring never helps. And though her long-lost niece probably isn't gay except in the way everyone at fourteen is gay, she wants to reach out still and tell her *It gets better*—even if that's a lie. You develop an instinct for how to do this, teaching. She holds up the slightly rusty nutcracker she's just rummaged from another box, and as if they have some preexisting relationship, see each other multiple times a year, says: "I'm guessing you're still on the fence about staying for dinner, Jolie, but I'm in a rush to get my pecans roasted. Think you could give me a hand? You'll need those boots."

With a decisiveness that's almost startling, Jolie turns to grab them off the futon she's righted and tidied. And in minutes, she and Izzy will be harvesting shells from the now-bright lawn as Moira settles onto the porch steps and double-checks the phone.

"Hey, you didn't get into the sweeteners again, did you, Izz? Because this recipe calls for agave."

But her son too is quiet, as if the silence were catching. The work slows, but doesn't stop. The pecans, hulled, make a gorgeous warm brown in the bowl.

Then she hears herself begin to hold forth (as if Izzy didn't know) about type 1 diabetes and the difference between ground nuts and tree nuts, the science behind anaphylaxis, the little yellow backpack of insulin and EpiPens that has to travel with him everywhere. Is Jolie getting any of this? It's surprisingly hard to bear in mind that a person not using words can still hear them. "But since you two are cousins," Moira ventures, "I'll let you in on a little secret about your grandpa. Most people are good at only cooking or baking, one or the other, but given room to do his thing, he actually made a hell of a pie. Weekends when there wasn't a race on, he had this apron from the navy he'd let me wear to help with the crust. Of course by the time he retired and could put in more hours in the kitchen, the arthritis was all through his hands, so it was back to that frozen crap my mom used to make. Not that he ever complained."

Something in all this has coaxed the girl to within a dozen feet of the porch—her thin bent back, her pink split ends. But now Moira miscalculates: a pecan shard clings to Jolie's sweater between notches of spine turned visible by the wool, and in going to remove it, she touches the girl's body and feels her whole posture tense as if to bolt . . . as why wouldn't it? The touch is condescending. Suggests difference, possession, agenda. Which is to say: failure of vision. Yet the jacket Jolie came in is still upstairs, along with her giant backpack. And seeing as how this might be the one opportunity she gets, Moira proceeds to make the most of it. "For what it's worth, I think that was Teresa starting a load of laundry back there, not your dad in the shower. I've got him tied down at the gas station for a bit, so if you still want me to smuggle you across the bay to the bus, now would probably be the time to say something."

Jolie says nothing, though. Apart from the clank of the tongue-ring, she's a picture of dwindling receptiveness. Yet neither, Moira notices, has she made any further move to go . . .

9

WHICH MUST HAVE BEEN right around the time that Ethan, yawning nervously, scratching through his hoodie, caught the ghost of his own motion in the glass-fronted freezer case of Ducky's Sinclair. The hoodie was partly to cover his absence of shirt; he'd snuck his tee into the wash next door to get the funk off, since there'd be little chance to buy a new one before the business with the boat. Had he his druthers, of course, he wouldn't have risked a run-in with Ducky at all. But nor had he wished to add to Moira's burdens by hanging around her place to mooch breakfast, and at present he was basically subsisting on a pinch of coconut snuck from yesterday's cakebox, the better part of a Hershey bar dunked in bad ferry cocoa, and this mug of tepid coffee obviously meant for someone else—and he couldn't see himself making it as far as the IGA without some fortification.

Luckily, he wasn't choosy. These last months had left him a connoisseur of the grab-n-go, the microwave falafel, the taquitos glazed in brightness through the south-facing windows before his reflection swallowed them again. Without the beard for camouflage, he worried about being recognized here, but of course the last time he'd been in, this clerk would have been about the age of Moira's kid, so his repeated glances at the video monitors were probably just to track the intentions of a stranger. Maybe with so many junkies floating around these days (or Ducky's fearsome panopticon having weakened with age), shoplifting had become more of a thing. Certainly, there were more varieties of bottled water now than then. More colorful packaging for the diet pills. The cat on the counter was possibly a different cat. Otherwise, all seemed as before. The smell, for example: pink hand soap, mint-flavored chaw, hot dogs conceivably original to the joint.

With deliberate calm—telling himself he'd been a rounding error in Eddie's trafficking plot anyway and it had been years since he'd swiped those Whip-Its—he selected a frozen chimichanga from the case, balled the wrapper in the counter's cute trashcan (new), and popped the rest into an underpowered microwave (old, plus or minus some duct tape). To distract himself from the video poker with its mocking NO PAYOUT sign, he moved to the *Street Fighter* console demoing mindlessly in a corner. In the course of a generation, just by remaining itself, the game had gone from cutting-edge to passé and was now rounding into a senescence of nostalgic kitsch. A play was still only twenty-five cents, and the hot-drink machine on the ferry had left him with this handful of quarters he began to lay out along the bottom of the screen. Among an array of culturally insensitive avatars (how had he not noticed their offensiveness before?), his favorite had always been the lanky South Asian guy who couldn't take a punch but who, by means of his extendable limbs, had been able to scoop up a second-former's mind and carry it far from the little house not thirty yards away. Now, of course, the thing Ethan longed to get his mind off was the suggestion that it was his presence rather than his absence that was causing his daughter's suffering—that far from curing her of her malady, he may actually have brought it with him. The obvious counterargument being certain steps Jolie had taken back in April, when he'd still been three time zones away . . . and in July, after she'd frozen him out . . . and then October, when he was busy flirting with relapse. But in any case, had he really imagined they would drive off the boat at damn near ten o'clock last night and her spirits would magically lift, her tongue loosen?

Punching, lunging, hurling his golden bangles, he pushed all this to one side. And when, sometime around his eighteenth demise, a reflection troubled the screen, it was a woman's and he ignored it, lest she plug in a quarter and join as Player 2. But now she slid in alongside, her own *Street Fighter* move, and banged a hip into his.

He was startled just long enough for his Tamil insurgent to

get slaughtered by a cape-wielding Soviet. Glancing over, he saw long, dark hair and a sateen jacket with union insignia. Eye makeup, some sun damage, no wedding band . . . a six-pack dandled by its rings. "Sorry," he said, when she failed to take the hint. "Kind of in the middle of something here."

"I know it's been a while, but do you really not recognize me?"

And now he turned and looked again and felt something go tight inside him. "Natasha? Shit—it's been ages. But you're not in town for this thing this afternoon, are you?"

"You mean Thanksgiving? My folks still live here, Ethan."

"No . . . I mean this memorial deal, my old man's boat." For however pale a presence the rector of St. Anselm's had been in the mind of his son, surely he'd stood for something in the wider community. That one fall when the city had been an open wound and the country in mourning behind it, he'd brought home a national sailing championship to a town that had never won so much as a game of gin rummy.

"What boat?" she asked. "And I thought you were in New York, doing TV or something. Bummer about your dad, by the way, I should have mentioned before . . . but I guess better late than never." He took her blush as embarrassment, but maybe she was just remembering wounds they'd inflicted on each other in the dark back of time, before she'd moved on to greener pastures in the person of his ex-friend Judd. She edged closer. "You know, you could really break some hearts turning up like this, Ethan. A few Immaculate Heart girls were up on Keel last night drinking beer. There was talk of a reprise later . . ." And gestured with the cans. Her nails flashed. He was already fleeing into the sour tang of Natty Boh when the ding above the entrance saved him.

"I wish I could be there, Natasha. But as soon as the champagne's smashed on the hull or whatever, I'm on my way back north. Look, here's my sister, come to collect me. I'll see you around, okay?"

Not that Moira was going to dignify what she saw as his natural habitat by coming more than a step inside. By the time he realized he'd left his chimichanga in the microwave, they were out beyond the tarmac, facing the old house (whose blinds he would swear had been open), and since he sure as hell wasn't going to be darkening Ducky's door again, there seemed to be little point in going back to do penance . . . But speaking of shit-lists: Moira's pace as they recrossed the tracks was blistering. Had her feints at diplomacy been hiding something all along? Well, good for her, he thought. Finally owning those feelings. When she did speak, though, it was only to ask him, "Who's the hoochie?"

"You've really got a knack for blaming the victim, Moira," he said. "I mean, if anyone was the hoochie around here, it was me." Though in truth he'd been all of fifteen. And now his coffee had gone cold in its mug, with its taste of coffees past. *St. Anselm's Academy: Truth, Honor,* some third thing time had rubbed away. He wanted to ask why she held on to this crap. Instead, he inquired cautiously whether she'd managed to talk Jolie down from the ledge.

"I can't even talk Teresa down, and she's my wife."

"Wait a minute. You got hitched?"

"Three years ago this April."

"Forgot to check your hand, I guess . . . Hey, I'm really happy for you—"

"Thanks for the vote of confidence, Ethan. I was obviously on pins and needles to see if you approved."

"—but you could have at least sent me a wedding announcement."

"So you could do what . . . not respond? Don't act like that's a low blow, either," she added, after a minute. "Teresa's right; you can't disappear for fifteen years and then just swan back in expecting applause." *Swan, dwell, gallivant:* his father's words. "Which is something it's high time we talked about, probably."

"My disappearance?"

"Your expectations, rolling back into town like this."

The dinosaur tanks and the slope of Keel Hill having dwindled, he trailed her into the parking lot of the old IGA, where shadows from the roofline split the weedy traffic islands. It was here, near an abandoned shopping cart, that she finally paused. The store should have been open by now, but the windows seemed suspiciously dark behind the price-chopper ads, the only signs of life a radio playing somewhere under the cart-return and a few birds resettling up under the eaves.

"I feel like you keep forgetting, though," he said, unable to help himself: "You're the one who contacted me."

"About the memorial for Dad? It was a mass fucking email! And after the stunt you pulled last time, Ethan . . ."

"It wasn't a stunt, is the thing. Something came up at the last minute that I couldn't get out from under."

"You were supposed to give the eulogy; you were his son."

"It's not like it mattered to Dad at that point—"

"It mattered to other people, dumbass! And explain to me: what comes up, besides you calling two days later from some so-called rock bottom?"

"How I got there is a long story, I wouldn't know where to begin. But without that—and without your generous contribution, I know—I wouldn't be on the path to recovery. Not exactly a linear process, but still."

She stared at him for a minute before stalking toward the automatic doors, into which a gangly staffer was feeding a line of carts, a strangely resonant thunder. The music was the same old oldies station, yet the songs were now all from the 1980s.

"But as far as 'expectations' go," he said, pursuing, "I've learned not to expect much from anyone, anymore." The tube lights had come on; the heat he couldn't vouch for. The zipper of the hoodie sat cold against his chest. "I mean it's not like I *expected* to find myself back on the East Coast last summer. And if you'd told me six months ago that you and I would be here in the fall, roaming the baking-supplies aisle of the Cheshire IGA, I'd have said you were crazy. But then I go to pick Jolie up yesterday for our custody visit and she's . . . pretty much like you said. All twisted up. By me. So I guess the idea was, if I could give her something to focus on beyond just the two of us—you, obviously, and, ah, some sense of Mom . . . and whoever else you'd invited to Dad's ceremony, Teresa and Isaiah—"

"Izzy," she said, studying the label of a new-age sweetener. "Neither of whom you knew existed at the time—"

"Izzy, sure, then in some small way it might help. Not least by showing her how serious I am about making amends. There's this thing they say in the program, you know, about, like, connection being the opposite of addiction. Almost a mantra, come to think of it . . ."

And with all that had passed between them, she was still his sister, veteran of many of the same foxholes, so if pressed, he could have gone on to tell her about that spring, the train, Jolie's getting caught drinking, and his fear (or was it a memory?) of where all this might be headed. But now she was saying, "I'm not disputing the premise, Ethan, necessarily, but the expectations I was talking about were for the next eight hours. You keep bringing up that email from Saint Anselm's, but did you even read it?"

"What does that email have to do with my daughter's well-being?"

"You told me you were going back tonight. The rechristening of the boat's not till ten a.m. Saturday."

"It said Thanksgiving!"

"It said Thanksgiving *weekend*. What kind of moron would schedule a memorial service for the middle of people's holiday?" Into her basket went the bottle.

"And one thirty is . . ."

"Dinner. The one I thought you were agreeing last night you'd bring Jolie to."

"But I was just at your house; the burners were all cold. There's still plastic on half the shelves in your fridge."

"Ethan—Izzy and Teresa and I, we're the guests, not the hosts. Did you think I'm here for the pleasure of your company? I need agave nectar, and some shortening; I'm supposed to be bringing a pie."

"Shit," he said again. "But why didn't you say something earlier?"

"Why do you think? I knew how you'd react once you found out who'd be carving the turkey." And now, as she held his gaze, something clicked. Her evasiveness, the low-glycemic shopping list, even her adoption of a child; the amends she really wanted made—the debts she felt were owed—could only be to one person.

"And *that's* why you offered to run interference with Jolie? We're supposed to go break bread this afternoon with Eddie Sixkiller just off some guilt you feel about having left him to rot in jail?"

"Eddie Sixkiller?" she said, with a surprise that seemed genuine. "Eddie Sixkiller was in Afghanistan, last I heard. And as far as

who deserves the guilt in your whole drug-smuggling caper, that's
between the two of you—"

"And Ducky."

"So you say. The person I'm talking about is Corinne."

"Oh, fuck no, Moira. I mean, *Corinne?* Sorry . . . but unless you
want me to take Jolie and get out of here right now, you're going
to have to call this off."

"You should really try listening to yourself sometime, you
know? You say your concern is your daughter, and helping her to
reconnect, yet here you are, threatening to withhold a relationship the first time things don't go exactly your way."

They'd come back to the front of the store, where among the
less recondite brands of candies and gums, the displays still held
sealed tins of Altoids. And as he stood here counting breaths,
waiting for his heart to kick back in, he caught his mind drifting
back to a trackless place on the sand, and then to a clearing in the
woods, and those marijuana plants entrusted to his care—though
of course if they'd taken root there and flourished, Eddie might
never have started slinging the harder product that had made
convicts of them both.

"Anyway, I'm not about to let Corinne spend the holiday alone.
She just turned sixty-five, and she's part of our family. I'm telling
you this as your sister. And you're the one quote-unquote serious
about making amends."

She was right, damn her: he had said those things. Further-
more, if he could brave a few hours with Corinne, his other goals
might in fact be advanced. And not just those touching Moira . . .
That is, if Jolie could see his wicked quasi-stepmother's effect on
him at close range, she might finally start to understand, well, if
not what had made him who he was, then at least some of what
it had felt like to be that way. "I guess you have a point; we could
go."

"There's one piece I can't follow, though," Moira said. "With
Jolie not talking, how are you supposed to know if this 'connection is the key' thing has even done the trick?"

Easy, he almost said: she opens up her mouth and tells me.
But outwardly he pretended not to hear. "It sounds like you'd
better get cracking on that pie, Moira, and I'll finish up here by

my lonesome, maybe head downtown and look for something a little nicer to wear." For either he was hallucinating again, or the hoodie too had started to smell. And thinking with a twinge of the all-everything heritage bird now thawing at the back of his boss's closet, he made a mental note to grab some Febreze from the cleaning aisle—or no, given the state of his cash reserves, maybe better to try to pinch a bottle for free back at the house once his sister wasn't around to give him this look anymore, the one like there was no other person in the world it could possibly be harder for her to see . . .

10

BUT WAIT, something feels off here, Sarah Kupferberg finds herself thinking, some eighteen hours earlier. Which admittedly doesn't sound like the Sarah we've come to know (the last decade of her life having been largely an attempt to deny that feelings enter into decision-making at all). Recent events, though, have forced her to face her feelings more squarely, and to wonder at the many different moments they might secretly have been running the show. Certain mornings her last year of grad school, for example, when she would scooch back under the sheets to tuck Ethan's big arm around her only to recall that his side of the bed was still empty. Or the first time she'd had to arrange a custody visit on what she insisted be neutral ground. And what it had felt like then to see him on a park bench somewhere with no lawyers or judges around, only herself to keep from running over and saying it was a mistake, please come home. Though maybe the disquiet that's snagging her now is more the sum of ten thousand intervening moments. Coding fieldwork standing up on the bus so Jolie could canter her My Little Ponies on the seat below; looking forward to a few hours of actual writing . . . right up to the instant of dropping her off at the new preschool, when again the regrets would come flooding back in; and later, the dissertation done, teaching Methods in Ethnography to a roomful of undergraduates who could never really have understood the first thing about what any of the above had felt like, from the inside. But even after losing Ethan to California, Sarah had still clung to the idea that it was possible to know your own mind, and to stay within its bounds. So perhaps it's not too strong to say that the real watershed comes this Wednesday before Thanksgiving, when, against her long-held policy, she stops circling the blocks south of Grand Central and enters a Starbucks—her first ever—to catch up with her daughter's former teacher, Brandon Koussoglou.

Or rather when, not finding him there as planned, she doesn't immediately turn to go.

She's thought often enough these last few days about reversing herself on his invitation; it was why, not wanting to seem more resolved than she was, she'd turned down his offer to meet at her place an hour earlier instead. But here she is with her overnight bag on her shoulder . . . and anti-corporate commitments aside, the coffee chain does offer a weird sort of comfort: the comfort of being not quite anywhere at all. With its earthtones and unobtrusive jazz, it's designed to be a "third place," or even that impossibility, a non-place. If not for the homeless guys reading newspapers up front, you might have been in an airport in Omaha, or Copenhagen. And anyway, aren't its labor practices said to be decent enough, at least relative to Dunkin' Donuts? Dismissing as hopeless any attempt at objective comparison, she joins the queue . . . though when it's her turn to order she hears herself reject the menu's Orwellian verbiage and ask for a small coffee rather than a tall, "light and sweet." And before the cashier can correct her, hands him a reusable mug and snatches up a copy of the *Times* to see what fresh hell is being misreported while she waits for her order to come.

November 23, 2011, says the paper. Issue 55,598. More fires in Western Australia. Further crackdowns in Tahrir Square. But as she sinks into a club chair with a view toward Park Avenue, her sense of an alarm bell ringing somewhere is less global than local. Even the jazz is barely intelligible above the grind of the grinder, the steam from the steam thing, the repeated pounding of the espresso pistol. Inside, she is rerunning the last time she left the city, and what a mistake that had been: the wee-hours haul back from Montauk on the Fourth of July with her hungover fourteen-year-old stretched out across the backseat and her father's forty-CD audiobook of *Ulysses* spavined on the passenger's side. She'd spotted it in the footwell loading up the car and now figured it might prevent her nodding off, or at least be so punitively high-minded as to clarify to Jolie how seriously she was taking this; music would have been frivolous. Yet as the fireworks trailed off and Blazes Boylan jingled past barmaids-cum-sirens and mists from the Long Island fields crept out over the roadway to transform the steel heads of arc-lights into UFOs, the whole of reality had started to feel like a bad dream. It was then, pinching the back of her hand to stay awake, that she'd thought of the one person who'd been warning her ahead of time that she should maybe be worried about her daughter (unless you counted the ex-husband swooping in months later like some incorrigible messiah to cast everything back into disarray).

But now the rap of knuckles on glass makes her jump. In her memory, before that first phone call, Brandon Koussoglou had shot up six inches and his hands had become Ethan's. The civilian duds he wore to their lunch a week later had been familiar enough (his Interpol shirt, his desert boots), but the surprising slightness of the figure inside had made them seem the emblems of actual youth rather than of a refusal to grow up—like the catastrophe that hardens a person into adulthood hadn't yet befallen him. Though maybe she is his catastrophe, she thinks now, as he beckons her out of the Starbucks and a tiny white-haired lady frowns over from the club chair opposite. From one angle, these thrifted jeans must make her look like a cougar. From another, like damaged goods. But no, the woman's scowl is for something behind her, and when she turns, there is her little go-cup on the coffee bar's proscenium, an artifact from another, less deluded life. In this one, she has somehow missed the sound of her own name.

"You sure you don't want a venti-sized mochachino or whatever?" she prods herself to ask Brandon on the sidewalk, having given him her cheek to kiss. And nods at the clock above the terminal entrance a block away. "I'm saying, we've still got twenty minutes, we could go back and discuss this over coffee, on me."

"I grabbed tea from the teacher's lounge at sixth period," he says. "Anyway, the station'll be a zoo, with a scuffle for seats if we miss the boarding announcement. Maybe we could just talk on the way?"

And before she can answer, he is charging ahead into the

rush-hour bedlam of Park Avenue South, dragging a wheelie suitcase with the hand not reaching back for hers. One point in his favor, she reminds herself: the slightly effortful quality of his innocuousness—the sense that beneath it, certain long-range ambitions are being held in view. Of course, Brandon's vigilance about missing the train sits oddly against his avowals that no particular meaning attaches to her having said yes, that going up to Connecticut to spend the holiday with his parents needn't signify more than *So long and thanks for the memories.* As if noting the disconnect, he's now turning at the corner of Forty-Second to say how grateful he is she's decided to come. And to flash a rueful smile. "After that last time on the phone, I was worried we might have broken up already."

"That wasn't what I was trying to say, Brandon, or I wouldn't have called back later," she says. "But now I've got Jolie's homecoming to think about, too, and it's all a muddle . . . me dying to see her on one hand and at the same time dreading it. I was more just trying to help you see how messy this could get, if I then had to disclose that the person I've been dating was her teacher."

And here comes the blush he gets whenever she tries to tackle the matter head-on. "Former teacher."

"But since my mom's volunteered to keep her through Thanksgiving . . ." (*You're young, he's cute, why not see all he has to offer,* had been the line) "there's at least time here for a proper goodbye."

It's the same tack she took in that phone call, but Brandon's smile still looks a little pained. "Well, if the shoe's ever on the other foot, remind me to thank her."

"I just wouldn't want to give you false hope—"

"No, totally. Hear me out, though. If you get to the drop-off point tomorrow night and you've somehow come to feel like, hey, maybe my teenager really is overreacting to me dating again, maybe family obligations don't have to be incompatible with a person's personal life . . . well, I'm sure Jolie could be talked around."

"And if I continue to feel like this interlude we had together was really important, but that maybe it's better if we just be friends . . ."

"Then I'll look back with gratitude and affection, I swear. And in the meantime you'll have helped me get my folks over this idea that I'm still stranded in some hovel in Bushwick grading papers—helped them see their little darling has landed on his feet."

They've talked about this earlier in the fall: the only-child syndrome, the struggle against overprotectiveness, and then suburban life with its illusions of control; how after he'd stalled out on his Ph.D. three years ago, his mom had wanted him to return to Fairfield County, safe from the pitfalls they'd moved to escape when he was young. More recently, though, Sarah has almost started to wonder if his gentle sendups of his uptight two-parent household had instead been meant to reflect something to her about her own choices—the stance she was starting to fear had been wrong for her daughter from day one. So perhaps this bell will cease its ringing soon.

But first they have to get through Grand Central, which is indeed a zoo. Commuters press through side corridors, swirling down in their dozens from the street as if at some inaudible signal. Then the great main concourse, an azure-tinted mixing bowl where, at intervals, lines of travelers fan out before departure boards; they might (it occurs to her) be museumgoers standing back to admire a painting. And stopping now to scan for a track number, Brandon Koussoglou looks perfectly at home among them. How well does she even know him, after a mere forty days? she thinks. She could still turn back . . . though perhaps with added guilt for having let things get this far. Then she glances toward the steps of what is soon to be an Apple Store and sees a girl with an uncanny resemblance to Jolie slouched comma-like over a smartphone. Starts to hear again her daughter's voice through the intercom . . . through the phone from the hospital . . . and to feel anew that time is out of joint. But no, this scrolling slump is just the glum posture of everyteen everywhere, and besides, isn't Brandon right? After a decade on a high shelf, and with her daughter still under Eleanor's protection, isn't Sarah allowed just one more night of feeling desired, or desirable, or at least marginally interesting again?

These were of course the sorts of longings that must have tucked themselves away among her worries, going to meet Bran-

don for that initial lunch in July. At the last moment, she'd decided
not to tell him about the subway scare that had started Jolie drinking, feeling he was exactly the type of person from whom she'd
been sworn to keep it a secret. But she and Jolie had made no
such compact about what followed, which he'd seemed gratifyingly discomfited to hear: the resurfacing of her ex-husband and
the resulting Montauk gambit and how she'd discovered Jolie out
there with a bottle of purloined liquor. There was a larger context, too, she'd gone on, almost without meaning to: she herself had never been a drinker, but Jolie's father, her ex, was an
addict—recovering or not, it was impossible to say. And only
three years out from probation. *Right, Jolie mentioned this back
before winter break*, he said. Which was maybe another sign, she
thought, but of what? That he was trying to steer this conversation toward Ethan? Or that Jolie had felt comfortable confiding
in him about the one thing she'd never seemed to want to discuss at home? Then again, what did Sarah teach her undergrads
but that you needed only two tools to open up the most storm-
swept interviewee: a sympathetic imagination, a suspension of
judgment . . .

But now he is off again. "Train's this way, it looks like."

Through an archway into harsher fluorescence and down a
ramp onto a platform where he accelerates into a stiff-legged jog.
Armies of commuters are already threatening to overtake him,
flowing around columns and newspaper bins and into the available spaces, trying to seem as nonchalant as is humanly possible
just this side of a gallop. She reminds herself to look into those
faces—and not just because she sees it as her job. But of course
here is Sarah Kupferberg, among them too, plunging ahead as if,
for all the world, she knew where the hell they were taking her.

Anyway, she should probably just have trusted her sherpa, this
floppy-haired child of the Metro-North. The conductor idling
outside the second car from the front seems not to have noticed
them looping by into the as-yet-unoccupied first. "Eat my dust!"
Brandon says under his breath. Then, as if remembering he's
not alone: "This good?" And indeed it pays to be first, for now
they have their pick of seat, but *is* it good? Is it right? Or is this
just more personal gain won at someone else's expense? She tries

to calm herself, to see Brandon as a subject, what his choices in their own context might reveal about him: that he prefers the seat toward the back half of the window, with its unobstructed view, at the exact midpoint of the traincar (temperance, moderation, but also complacency, as if no one ever needed to beat a sudden retreat); the left or western side where, depending on what she does or doesn't do here, the Bronx River soon will or won't appear. But now along with the actual passengers trailing after them into the car glide the phantoms of others: a spectral Ethan gravitating toward the porthole in the door up front, straining to see through the darkness; herself just beside him but to the left, at what would have been the driver's-side window . . . and then, in the far back corner, slumped where neither of them seems to see, the wraithlike daughter they've unthinkingly dragged along.

Of course, if some outside context was really what she was looking for, she remembers Brandon saying at that first lunch, then it was a good thing they'd started talking this way . . . but that was the moment when, in his mild uptalky manner, he'd sprung a twist on her, saying how in his head he'd been going back over their conversations, but that Jolie had struck him as basically her mother's daughter; and how he'd started thinking that maybe a parent's feelings of concern needn't always rise to the level of fear. Like in this case, maybe Sarah had been right, and it was just typical teenage stuff? Or anyway, it was only an airplane bottle, she'd said: Crème de menthe, right? Well, right, so far as I know, she said. But then what if there was more than one, or if there's something else I've been missing? You're forgetting I've been through this before—

At which point came that peculiar blush and then a cough, as if whatever he'd swallowed had gone down the wrong pipe. But hey (he'd said, once the color subsided) . . . setting aside her past for a minute, kids were going to be kids (no?) and even at fourteen most of them could probably afford to lose control now and then, in small doses. Take himself at that age: Would she think less of him if he told her he'd done his share of keg-stands in high school, toked a little grass while at Wesleyan? Molly once or twice in grad school, at a concert? So his feelings were, underage drinking was definitely something for an educator to keep an eye on . . . but maybe also to try to see in perspective? Anyway, the most relieving thing Sarah had said was that she'd finally called in a therapist, so now Jolie would have a place to take whatever she really needed to talk about.

And still the sense of wrong persists, not least in how tentatively his hand's come to rest on hers. "Would a different seat be better? We've got our pick, Sarah, just so long as we hurry."

"No, it's fine," she says. "I guess having my mom push things back a day has just knocked me off balance. You haven't seen her this week, have you? Jolie, I mean? Around school?"

Again that uncomfortable look. "To be honest, Sarah, I've been trying to give her a wide berth ever since that night she, ah . . . buzzed up."

"But we've talked about this, haven't we? She can't possibly have known that was you in the apartment—she was downstairs the whole time."

"No, sure," he agrees quickly.

"—so she can only know what she heard on the intercom."

"I just mean . . . I'd hate for her to feel I was being put to work as some kind of a double agent, reporting back to you. She did at least know we were in touch this spring."

And now it's Sarah's turn to blush. "You're right, this whole thing puts you in an awkward position. Why I should have listened to my instincts in the first place . . ."

He doesn't seem to catch her drift, though; just takes her bag from where she's set it by the window and hefts it to the barred luggage rack overhead. And once he's settled into the space thus cleared, plops down beside her like a retriever after a good run. But then why should she expect Brandon Koussoglou (of all people) to credit these little twangs of conscience or foreboding or whatever they are? In the last forty-odd days, she has let him into her bed half a dozen times; why wouldn't he, despite assurances to the contrary, read this putative last hurrah as a sign that she instead wants it to continue? She is thankful now for having the window to look out of, even if this section of the platform seems ghostly or somehow apocalyptic with the glass's slicked-on sepia crinkling in places like bunched pantyhose and with all those rushing travelers getting sucked into invisibility behind her. She waits for the rumble of the door that will mean it's too late for them to turn back.

"You're awful quiet," he says.

"Brandon, look . . . People talk about motherhood being a job and then applaud themselves as feminists, but this is different. I can't just put up a vacation message and stop mothering for a day."

Where he might have grown annoyed again—where she might even have been trying for that, to create a pretext she could use to get up and go—he is instead saying again, as if disappointed, that he can understand.

"But anyway, you don't think there's something I might be missing even now? Maybe whatever Jolie says, or doesn't say, I should be headed down to Stuyvesant Square for that recital—"

"It'll already be over," he says, without looking at his phone.

"I thought you said it started at four!"

"Three thirty, I'm pretty sure. Or that was the update online."

"But see, there you go. I didn't think to look before telling my mom. This whole last year has me feeling like I've got these blind spots, you know?"

"If you didn't, you wouldn't be human. You have to start forgiving yourself somewhere, Sarah."

"And blind spots in my blind spots."

"Listen, you've trusted me this far. Has it done you any harm? What I guess I'm still hoping you'll take from that is, you're allowed to let your guard down for a night now and again without expecting disaster to follow. Just like you're allowed to have more than one person you care about."

And there it is again: his hand barely there on hers, the little sigh and surrender as the train jerks forward. She turns to look back along the scrolling platform, as if the girl from the Apple Store steps might at the last minute be running to catch up, and sees instead just the barest glimpse of someone frozen at the bottom of the ramp, as if seeking to bend the train to her will. But not Jolie. It is Sarah's own self at fourteen or fifteen, board under arm, so sure of who she was and where she was going. Of course, she's been trying to stay true to that self ever since, and look where it's gotten her. And of course, Brandon *is* right: Jolie is safe with her grandparents up in Riverdale, and it's not going to kill anyone, is it, one more day of missing her like this? Of this unaccountable feeling of an alarm bell ringing nearby? This ache of being in the wrong? Or so she'll remember having thought as the train slipped off into darkness that day, until even the one little glimpse of this other Sarah she might still have gone back to was gone . . .

11

AND NOW MIDDAY HAD COME, and with it, picture time: the three women assembled on the porch of the house as Ethan stood on the lawn struggling to work the camera feature on his phone. Beside him, the boy, Izzy, rocked a tiny sportcoat, and Ethan himself had managed to claim someone's unclaimed dress shirt off a rack out front of the twenty-four-hour laundrette downtown. With jeans and the corduroy jacket, it didn't look half bad, he felt—looked positively Sarah-like—and for a while, sitting in front of the Macy's parade pointing out various stars of stage and screen, he and his nephew might have been images in some postracial Currier & Ives. But through wave after wave of float, Jolie had refused to come down from the bedroom and join them, and now that she'd finally knocked off whatever she was doing up there and made her presence known, Ethan wasn't invited to be in the picture . . . or rather, had offered to serve as photographer before anyone could clarify out loud that there was no place for him there on the steps, amid the subjects.

So perhaps it was Teresa with her scowl and motorcycle boots, her long camo skirt, who would best capture his mood of mingled defiance and resignation. In the one image where no one blinked, she'd be carrying a cellophane sleeve of storebought rolls, and Moira flowers, and the kid Jolie's violin case, and Jolie nothing at all unless you counted the somehow winnowed-seeming backpack, whose straps you could barely see under the pinkened tips of her hair. After sending the image to his sister (or anyway, attempting to), Ethan suggested taking separate vehicles in case a tactical retreat became necessary, but she told him not to be ridiculous, they'd all fit in the 4Runner . . . and besides, he didn't know how to get where they were going.

"Only because you won't give me the address. I have GPS now and everything, Moira. Or sorry—is this about the van? You're embarrassed for people to see what I've had to resort to to make ends meet?"

Teresa shot her a look, but Moira remained stubborn. Maybe even protectively so. "Just go grab the pie, Ethan, all right?"

"Well, I guess if we're all coming back after, we can at least leave some of these props behind."

He knew better than to try to sunder Jolie from her backpack, but felt Izzy's grip on the violin loosen like a soft conspiracy between them. And while Moira retrieved the SUV from the tilting garage, Ethan doubled back through his childhood home, expecting to feel something more toward it now that it was empty. Apart from the sunroom, though, his sister had carefully managed the work of erasure. The violin was an excuse to go up to the bedroom where Jolie had made her blockade, but it looked more like a den at this point, its sole sign of habitation a TV cabled to a VCR. She might have just finished watching, except that it was cool to the touch. Less so the pie dish downstairs on the kitchen island. Yet beneath its foil the pie looked pale and underdone, and when he snuck a pinch of filling from where the crust had pulled away, the taste was awful, dry, like a communion wafer—surely a little jolt of flavor wouldn't hurt. The sugar he never had managed to locate, but finding a sealed maple syrup high on a pantry shelf, he fired up the broiler, adjusted the rack, waited, drizzled the top, and blasted it under for about forty-five seconds, an old restaurant trick. Then, wincing a bit from the heat, he grabbed a towel from a nearby laundry basket and carried the pie out front, trying to look like he'd just been hung up in the john.

The 4Runner was waiting at the curb, but the open door on the passenger's side made him feel less like a visiting dignitary than like a victim of extraordinary rendition. Izzy's massive carseat having failed to fit the middle of the back row, Jolie had been forced into the cramped space there, leaving Teresa perfectly poised behind Moira to aim little darts of loathing at the side of his head. Which of course he ignored, trying to focus instead on not being gelded through the towel as they rounded onto the business strip of North Main.

His earlier circuit had made clear how poorly the recession had treated his hometown. Soaped-over windows. For Sale signs a dime a dozen. And out along the bypass, where you'd think corporate parents might have stepped in to stanch the bleed, corporate hands had instead chosen to wash themselves. The Jiffy Lube had become an adult bookstore, the KFC an off-brand biscuit joint whose fragrance penetrated through the glass. And that charismatic *iglesia* with its drive-through lane and banner reading *DIOS ES EL SEÑOR*—wasn't that the old Mazatlán restaurant? At any rate, they were past it in a turn or two, and winding out on blue highways into a countryside mottled by clouds, woodsy places among the fields denoting water under a wisped pale sky. The houses and doublewides set far apart still looked to Ethan like space capsules, but in addition to the old familiar loneliness they now seemed to transmit a second layer of loss, as if abandoned on the surface of the moon.

All of which would leave him unprepared for the upmarket surge north of the river, little commercial complexes with names like "The Shops at Mewes Plaza," stands of condos with their air of well-heeled leisure. A whole other America whose hedgerows he caught himself admiring as Moira wheeled past at slower speeds. "Wait—*this* is where Dad ended up?"

"I wouldn't read too much into it," she said. "Corinne was already living out here before the wedding." She glanced toward Jolie in the rearview. "Corinne is Izzy's grandma."

"Corinne is nobody's grandma, Jolie, your grandma died when I was seventeen." (Why hadn't he thought to clear this up earlier?) "She's your grandfather's second wife."

"Well, widow, if you want to get technical about it," muttered Teresa. But too late; they were now gliding into a slot out front of a condo that matched all the others. It backed right up to the water, where already—not even two p.m.—the day was going down swinging.

To put it even more plainly: Corinne D'Alessi, the place's owner, was someone Ethan had long been content to believe was the enemy, particularly during those early days of rehab. The story had felt safe, even comforting: the scheming enchantress who'd usurped his dad, patiently casting her spell as she'd spongebathed Mom and changed her bedding. Moreover, from the huddle now forming outside her door, where crystals hung dead center of a foliage-themed wreath from Target, it seemed quite possible that Corinne actually did identify as a witch. As various muffled thumpings issued from inside ("Just a minute!") he recalled her fussiness around food and the suspicious-for-a-medical-professional length of her hair. Yet when he really tried to remember her as she'd been in the mid-'90s, coming and going from the sunroom where his mother lay dying, he could recover no designing looks toward his father, nor so much as a hint of accusation about the missing pills. In these last available seconds, it seemed almost possible that *that's* what he'd been so pissed about: that she'd been simply another person who'd found it easiest to turn away.

But now Corinne was in the door, offering only warmth. Well, that plus Nicorette smell, plus his dad's old apron, plus cheap metal bangles hanging loose and profuse as her wrists shot past Moira to enfold her in the narrow foyer. It may have been the first time since high school that he'd seen someone hug his sister. She even allowed a kiss on the side of her head, after which came similar welcomes for Teresa and Izzy (who called Corinne "Gran," with a few extra *G*'s to spare). Finally, Corinne's eyes with their Cokebottle lenses swung to the hanging plants on the porchlet, among which Ethan had been trying to hide without bumping his head.

"You remember my brother," Moira said. "He's decided at the last minute to grace us with his presence. And this is the niece I was texting you about"—gesturing back at the dry grass where Jolie gazed inscrutably at the sky.

And was there a moment here where Corinne's smile faded? Where the sun-weathered face seemed to shift or the green eyes to stand off in glassy objectivity? More likely that was some combination of guilt and wishful thinking on Ethan's part, for now the eyes resettled on him, gleaming. "Of course, Ethan, how are you?"

"Can't complain," he made himself say. Yet when he reached for her hands, she held them in midair.

"Oh, you wouldn't want to touch these, they've been handling raw meat. But Jolie, welcome—no need to reply, Moira gave me the heads-up you wouldn't be talking." And as she stepped aside to let his daughter enter first, he tried to signal that she should go right ahead, but Jolie was having none of it, from either of them.

From the macramé hangings on the walls inside—from the driftwood on the console and the brighter living room beyond and the ceiling rising to a second-floor balcony—no one would have guessed that the rector of St. Anselm's had spent the last six years of his life here. There was a TV tuned to CNN, beachy white upholstery of a kind his dad never would have countenanced on his own. The only thing legibly his was the scent of cooking drifting out from the kitchen. Well, that and the big glass door giving onto some wooden docks, a tangle of motorboats partly obscuring the woods on the creek's northern side. The concept seemed to be that you retired out here and then spent your days putzing around on the water, much as some retirees bought property along a golf course. And now Moira was up beside him to check the door's lock, seeming almost conciliatory. "Ever since I've been a mom, I can't look at this dock without wanting to reach for a lifejacket," she explained. And did a voiceover like William Shatner's on that old *Rescue 911* show: "'Little would the boy's mother suspect what was waiting for him that fateful day . . .'"

She could have no idea how close it cut for Ethan, standing here watching his daughter's mute reflection on the glass. But if he'd shrunk from telling Moira how close Jolie had come to dying back at the start of this whole clusterfuck, whose fault was that? And anyway, how did any parent do anything but worry about his or her child's safety, every moment of every day? When he turned back toward the dining area, Izzy was under a table with a laundry basket of plastic army men. You had to hand it to the kid, he really had the onomatopoeia of male aggression down, the *pching* and *tsiew*, which Ethan for some reason attributed to Teresa (though perhaps also to the CNN). He groped in his pocket, found the last of his Hershey bar from the ferry, squatted to cement their alliance, and when Izzy crawled out to accept it, smiled and placed his finger to his lips. It was so easy at that age; the boy didn't even crawl back under, but stuck around to see if there'd be more, forming thumb and pointer-finger into the okay sign when Ethan shrugged an apology. But upon rising, he noticed that the table was only set for four. Then something plunked into a hot pan and resumed its sizzle. He was about to ask was there anything he could do to help when his eye caught a glimmer from the mantel: a vaguely Celtic vessel of beaten tin for which the term of art, obviously, was *urn*. It might have come from the ruins of some castle or abbey, or alternatively from the old Salisbury mall, that store next to TCBY with the flip-top pewter steins and the polystyrene Gandalfs (which may itself have been called Gandalf's).

"Hey, these are Dad's ashes?" he heard himself call.

"What's left of them."

"For Christ's sake, Corinne. You really just put it all out there, don't you?"

She scarcely looked up from what she was searing, but added, "Sorry if that sounds harsh. With you having skipped the funeral, I realize you're not living with them right in your face all the time. What I mean is, Moira took her half out to Assateague Island—"

"—to be with Mom's," said Moira, at his side again. "And some went into the flowerbeds at home, and some into the nature preserve . . ."

"I was hoping to scatter the rest at sea before Moira traded away the *Molly A*," Corinne continued, "but keep finding there's more I have to say to him, you know?"

He did know—he had things of his own to say, it struck him, should anyone care to ask—but at present he was too flustered to try to claim what should have been his rightful legacy. His sole escape was through the back door, onto the dock.

Where almost instantly the stink of menthol became unmissable. Jolie made no effort to hide that she was its source; just took a puff and exhaled, not in his face, given the distance, but not *not* in it, either. She must have found Corinne's stash of Virginia Slims, slipped out here while he was brooding, yet what was Ethan with his history supposed to say? *You'll kill yourself with those? Bum me a drag?* No, the glass was sliding open again behind him, Izzy padding out like his familiar, and the best he could do before the kid saw how cool his cousin looked as a smoker was to snatch up the cigarette and flick it into the water. That little sizzle of extinction. He waited for Jolie to bristle, or else smirk, but got only solemnity, detachment, whatever you'd call the medium whose medium she'd lately become. And if the smoke that lingered in the air wasn't quite the same shade as the sky, Izzy made no mention of it; just pointed to a crescent of white up there, so slight it might have been imaginary.

"This moon's called Little Sp-Spirit, you guys."

It then emerged, haltingly, that they'd done Native Americans at school in honor of the holiday. And before long—as if prodded by the lack of response—Izzy was launching into a whole big thing about the action of gravity on the tides and the crocodile named Herman who lived with his family under the dock. Within a few minutes, Ethan could feel his daughter's mood soften. Only when he dug out the unopened Baby Ruth in gratitude did she flare back up, a flash of disgust that bordered on fury. And so quickly that it was like magic, she interdicted his bribe for the kid just as he'd done with her cigarette and disappeared it into the folds of her jacket. Izzy gave no sign of having noticed, much less of being deterred.

". . . And that's why he has two b-birthdays—Herman's husband Jeff, I mean . . ."

The moon would be lower, and Jolie indifferent again, when the kid reached up for her arm and turned them gently toward the condo. Covered dishes now decked the table inside. Ethan watched Teresa turn off the TV; look over to see if Corinne objected; and, when she didn't, go over to light the candles in their sticks. Then, as Moira tried to force the first of two additional chairs under the table, he realized that he should have been trying to make things easier on her, not harder. And had to remind himself he could speak. "I realize Jolie and I are the intruders here, we can just eat in the living room, if that's what you want."

She seemed puzzled by something. "Well . . . Izz doesn't need a full-sized chair. Maybe the two of them could go do a kid's-table thing on the balcony. Corinne has a whole play area set up for him up there. Anyway, mealtime's not his finest hour—ten minutes in, and he gets antsy and wants to explore."

This felt like more martyrdom on Moira's part, since it was only for the sake of proximity to Jolie, he knew, that she'd been tolerating him in the first place. And still he was touched by the gesture. "Really, Sis, it's fine."

"My fault for not owning a bigger table," Corinne said, bringing out her finished dish: not meat at all, but some dark minced green that caused Izzy's nose to wrinkle. "Your dad and I didn't often get to host dinner," she plowed on, ignoring it. "He kept his dance card full raising funds for that sinkhole of a school, and now that he's gone, the most I ever have to feed is this crew."

"I'm sure the hearth is plenty comfortable," Ethan told her, having caught just a faint flicker of grief in her voice. (Jesus, what was happening to him?) "And don't worry, this visit's not likely to lead to a repeat performance."

She would insist on loading their plates first, his and Jolie's, and as the lids were lifted from the last platters he discovered there was to be no main course, either. Perfect, he thought: a Thanksgiving with no turkey, for a homecoming with no real home. But with her passive-aggressive brand of bonhomie, Corinne was already explaining that she'd gotten the idea to do all side-dishes this year out of a magazine. "The bird always comes out dry anyway, the only thing Teresa ever touches is veggies, and my cholesterol being what it is I'd rather jazz up my kale with some grass-fed pork from Farmer Bob down the road than give my ducats to Big Poultry. Of course if I'd known we'd have extra meat-eaters . . ."

Whether this even applied to her anymore, Jolie wasn't letting on. She took a roll and potatoes and a ladleful of the larded greens and settled on the low brick fireplace with her plate on her knees and her tux jacket bundled tightly beside her; in the cardigan, she looked even thinner. And by that point the moms had taken seats flanking Corinne while Izzy lugged some coffeetable books toward a chair at the far end. To Teresa's evident annoyance, Ethan went across to help his nephew construct a sort of booster seat before sitting down next to his daughter. Then, feeling the gas logs warm his back, he got up once more to fold his own jacket, set it on top of Jolie's to mark between them a little demilitarized zone. Out of habit, he was braced for some kamikaze prayer or pagan invocation from the head of the table, but no speech came this time, just Corinne closing her eyes ("Let's all try to think what we're thankful for"). And as the next minute or two passed in quiet contemplation, the idea that his daughter with her pierced tongue might eat this food started to seem no less likely than that she'd burst into song.

Still, it was only later that he would second-guess the urge he'd then begun to feel creeping back in. Had filling the silence with his own voice been meant to remind Jolie of his charms, or to impress Izzy, or to rectify with Corinne the awkwardness of the last hour (decade) . . . or simply to distract them all from what he must already have had it in mind to do? At any rate, he now heard himself say to Corinne a little loudly, after racing through his dinner, "Seems like you've managed to stay busy out here."

She had to scoot to the right to see past Teresa, who hunched sullenly over her food, facing away. "I know one person who keeps me busy, at least. A couple afternoons each week, Izz comes out on the schoolbus to entertain me until the girls can get free from work."

"Busy hands are happy hands, right, G-G-Gran?" said the boy from atop his teetering library. Corinne laughed. She'd been the one to tell him that, she said . . . not that it was any great point of pride, when she'd made her whole career among people who struggled to survive from one minute to the next, and through no fault of their own. "Though now sometimes I wonder if I was maybe too focused on their struggles, when I could have been of some aid to the other folks struggling all around them." A look here at Ethan, right out in the open. "I don't know. But my problem's always been the opposite: not too much time but too little. I've got so much filling it now, I find myself wishing the day was thirty hours instead of twenty-four." And then, as if to round out the excuses she seemed to want to make to everyone for everyone else: "Your dad was like that, too, as I'm sure you recall. Never at a loss, even in retirement. We had good years going up and down the bay on that boat, though God knows we didn't get enough of them."

Having long ago taught himself to see Corinne's oversharing as a form of aggression, he was realizing to his dismay that it was probably just who she was. Indeed, what rankled most about Corinne was that in her habitual overstepping of boundaries, she resembled no one so much as his mother. Dad had so often chafed, been so silently irritated, at Joanna's unchecked self-expression that you might have thought he'd seek out a closed book like himself for the second go-round. Instead, he'd settled on a woman with the same compulsive openness (if without any art to channel it into)—and by all appearances had tolerated, or even encouraged it. Did this mean he'd loved Mom less, as Ethan had thought, or just that he himself had been wrong about what love really was?

"I'm glad you two were happy together," he conceded, half against his will.

"Me too, Ethan," she said. "But what about you? I'll admit I haven't kept up with your credits in recent years." And now he could have sworn he felt Jolie's attention quicken beside him.

"Oh, it's been years since my last part, as I'm sure Moira told you." He used the edge of his fork to scrape together a mélange of yam and remaindered sprout that shouldn't have been quite so delicious. Then thought of the ashes sitting over in their gaudy urn. And tried to recall how honest he'd ever been with Jolie about his life as Alan T.'s charity case. He could be honest about it now, anyway; he was feeling a desperate-ish need to walk out of here having won at least *some* distinction for himself. "Usually I tell people I'm in landscape architecture, but I suppose if you're working for a boss instead of a client, you're really more of a yard guy. Still, digging in the dirt was something my mom always liked to do."

"Don't I remember. Even before I knew her, I used to go out of my way to drive past her beds in the spring just to see the flowers bloom."

"The pay's shit, if you'll pardon my French, but I get a roof over my head for free. No small thing, given how rents in California have come roaring back."

And at last, Teresa seemed to glimpse the opening she'd been waiting for. "Funny that you'd be reaching us by way of New York, then, Ethan."

Moira froze in the doorway as if only now registering the gap in continuity, her newly delicious pie in one hand and some non-dairy travesty of ice cream in the other. He tried to sound unruffled. "A colleague said she'd cover my gig out west so I could get a little Q.T. with Jolie here."

"Ah, 'a colleague,'" said Teresa. "I see. And when will this 'colleague' be expecting you back, exactly?"

"Well, I guess that depends on the Q. of the T., doesn't it?" he said. "Maybe even as soon as this weekend, if my daughter will just open back up and let us have a conversation." It seemed a breakthrough, phrasing this explicitly as a quid pro quo—right up to the point when Jolie stood to take her plate to the kitchen. Amazing, how she could make it look like just the natural end of the meal, but it only deepened the hole that seemed to be opening up inside him. Like, was she right? Had his fumblings toward empathy been mere self-absorption all along?

He had risen from the hearth, and Teresa from her chair, but Moira and Corinne remained at the table, which, turkey or no, was impressive in its ruins, a monument to imperial excess. And now the TV had come back on—or rather, TVs, for there was a second one up there on the balcony, where Jolie must have put on a movie to try to peel her cousin away from dessert. Ethan could make out blue flickers on the ceiling, and through the banister a beanbag chair and another hamper's worth of toys, a door leading back to what seemed to be a second bathroom. A person acting under a compulsion might hypothetically be able to get some privacy up there. Behind him, after a minute of hesitation, Izzy padded toward the stairs. Oddly, there was no sound besides the smack of helmets where Teresa had moved to the sofa to await the Ravens game.

But when he turned again to the hearth, the little wall he'd fashioned there had collapsed into a puddle. He refolded his daughter's jacket to prevent wrinkles, smoothed it, slipped his increasingly unsteady self into his own, and explained to Corinne sotto voce that Jolie would have thanked her for the meal—believe it or not she normally had great manners—"but you remember what it's like at that age . . ."

"Oh, we both know I'm not the one in her crosshairs, Ethan, and anyway, she can't stay like this forever. In the meantime, at least she cleans up after herself, which is more than I can say for certain teens I've known."

"All credit goes to Sarah, I assure you. My ex," he added (as the ravening in him grew truly terrible). "But sorry, I guess I was always careful to keep the two of you apart, wasn't I? Here, let me be the one to clear." Corinne protested—he was her guest—but already he was standing with a Shiva-like arrangement of plates on his arms. "Just point me to the Ziplocs, and I'll set you up with leftovers to last till Christmas. Seeing how little Jolie ate, we may even want to take some for the road."

Any chance at palliation started with having the kitchen to himself, letting his sister and would-be stepmother murmur behind him in the same low tones they'd just been using to discuss his daughter. Maybe it was him they were discussing now, and his inability to pull himself out of a spiral . . . or no, the subject seemed to be whether Corinne could bear to sit through a second memorial for Dad, but whatever, talk was cheap. He laid the plates in the sink and began with clattery ostentation to go through the drawers to the right of the fridge. It was in the second of these that he found the baggies he was looking for. He snagged the kind meant for sandwiches and pocketed two. Then a little more rattling in the sink plus a splash of water before heading back out to the obliviousness of other people.

Up on the balcony, when he reached it, Izzy had gone uncharacteristically quiet in the shadows, while Jolie's gaze stayed fixed to the TV. He had an impulse to take a closer look at what they were watching, but downstairs the women droned on, and time was not his friend. Earlier, while still shouting questions at Corinne, he'd watched himself with whatever degree of absentmindedness put the urn of his father's ashes down on the front hall console—like they were simply the sort of thing one mislaid. The mirror there on the wall faced the other wall (he could see no one, no one could see him), so it had been nothing just now to sneak the ashes up here to the guest bathroom, where presently he went ahead and pushed the button-lock and set the faucet running . . . and where of course what he confronted, glancing up from the vanity, was another mirror.

And before I go too much further, reader, let me just pause here to say that I haven't forgotten you're in the room, too. I can even feel you wondering, like: What is happening here? (And why so many mirrors?) Or maybe by now you've put that much together, like: Yes, I get it, Jolie, your dad was an addict . . . but is the only point of this story to keep dragging us back through these same sterile spaces and locked doors? Because instead why not have one of you look up for once and decide to do something different, and spare us all the heartache of what's to come? Or if that's too great a leap and there can be no second act, then why not go ahead and end this now?

To which latter point, I say: Touché. I mean, haven't I been having such thoughts myself, on and off for most of my life? The kind of change I'd most wanted to believe in had by this point turned out to be a fairy tale. The truth was, we were all basically stuck inside ourselves. And other people? A dream, or a nightmare. They could share a stage with us, even be in the room, but nothing changed. They could haunt us but could not touch us. And yet, all these different people, locked inside themselves, mere steps from each other . . . it has to lead somewhere, doesn't it? So even if I can't see a way to make them fit together neatly, I refuse to give up on this idea of all our stories being one story. And if you're still out there asking what this one has to do with you, then I must somehow still be *"stuck in my own head"* needing to *"push harder . . ."*

So listen: Here he is, at 4:37 p.m. on Thanksgiving Day—Ethan Aspern, my father—glancing back down in time to see one hand pluck a decorative soap from its pebbled dish and begin to wash the other. He's been stalling, that much seems obvious. Or at any rate has placed the urn way over toward the edge of the formica, since with his luck he might otherwise knock it into the sink and send some of the ashes swirling down the drain. He considers this vessel almost warily. It's not that he actually believes it is his father, exactly, or that he imagines what is inside is anything beyond mere dust. But having spent the last however many years trying to live without false hope, he can no longer be one hundred percent sure, either, that nothing separates this oily and surprisingly dark soot from any other. "Sorry," he mumbles, in case anyone can hear.

Then, with the toilet lid closed (Corinne's one of those people who dyes the water blue), he plunks down on the carpeted seat, almost eye-level with the container. Fishes up a baggie and tips the urn, taps the rim so enough ash gets shaken out to plump the tinted plastic but not enough to make a telltale bulge in his jacket . . . and feels, briefly, his pulse jump a beat at the memory of the small, flaky quantity of coke that got him and Eddie Sixkiller nailed for possession with intent a decade ago.

This is what, ten times that much? Twenty? Anyway, it'll have to do. He is somewhere between squeezing out the excess air and zipping tight the color seal when it strikes him that what the second Ziploc is actually for is a failsafe: for double-bagging. The problem is, rather than fill the hole in him now longing to be given substance, this drab baggie of his dad's ashes only makes the craving worse. Well, okay, that and the weight—not in his pocket, where it hardly registers, but in the urn, which (perplexingly) seems reduced by more than he's taken. Have his hallucinations somehow gone tactile? Or alternatively, has he left a spill to be discovered tomorrow by Corinne or her cleaning lady? Through the door, he thinks he senses a shift in the condo's quiet, a thickening of alertness or concern. But being only himself, he can't stop. He grabs a scant semi-handful of the soapdish's rocks, pops them into the urn, and before he can think twice lids and agitates it, wincing at the clunk. It's not like these dumb rocks will ever be missed, he thinks. Then he douses the lights, tucks the urn behind his back, slides back onto the balcony, fiending—

And sees at once that something is off, for already Jolie is hurrying toward him with some urgent business to discuss. *Busted*, is his first thought, but then why have her cousin all flopped on her shoulder like that, the ring of chocolate gone smeary around his mouth? And why the pennant of candy wrapper aflutter in her hand, what happened to the king-sized . . . fuck, the Baby Ruth. In an instant, he has accepted the boy's gray little body as his own. His fingers are plunging past the kid's wet tongue, but he knows he'll find no obstruction blocking the airways. And is already vaulting toward the stairs, nearly tripping over a toy-basket. The urn, a thing of no consequence, clatters down on the console. "Time to go?" says his sister from the living room, but all three women are now on their feet, and the best he can do is shove Izzy into her arms.

"You tell me, Moira, the kid just snuck a whole candy bar up there—is he allergic or something?"

"What do you mean is he allergic? Listen to his breathing! And where would he even get his hands on this? Baby Ruth is fucking peanuts!"

"You put nuts in the pie, though, right?"

"Pecans, and no sugar! Where's the backpack?" she yells to Teresa, who is yelling back:

"You're saying on top of everything you forgot the backpack?"

"Jesus, his throat's a pinhole—"

Which is when Corinne takes charge: it doesn't matter who forgot the backpack, they'll have EpiPens in the ER—just go. "Now!" And so frantically do they rush to the car, so ominous does the silence grow once the doors slam shut, that Ethan will have to turn in his seat to make sure his daughter hasn't been left behind.

By the time Moira swats at him to face forward, they are burning a trail back to town a good thirty miles an hour above the speed limit, hazards faintly clicking, and through an afternoon fast to fade. Ethan closes his eyes but only feels the speed increase. Sees the needle trembling. When he dares to peek there are no sirens, though. No other cars. A few stars look out from overhead as radio towers and grade crossings whip by. "Try to keep his legs elevated," Moira blurts to Teresa, who hasn't bothered with the carseat but now holds Izzy in her lap, with the boy's moveless head on her shoulder. Ethan looks back down at hands that still aren't his own.

"You act like I've never done this before," Teresa tells his sister, so softly you'd have thought the danger lay in waking him. At which point Ethan recovers himself long enough to grasp something: that her anger up to now has been a proxy, a way of expressing Moira's; that what really signifies is this quiet, the quiet of things hanging in the balance. Yet he has no way of evaluating his own role in setting them there; only the knowledge that if he hadn't been in that bathroom, fighting off old demons, Jolie might have saved crucial seconds by going straight to Moira and not mistaking him for anybody who could help.

But then they are arriving at speed inside the ambulance bay, and Moira is leaping out to take the boy from Teresa without

even pausing to kill the engine, and between them they are racing toward the emergency room. Ethan is pulled as far as the
doors before something inside cripples him: that sense of uncar-
ing order—its wide, white feel—and a particular smell, the burning of a thing too clean.

A voice from behind nearly stills his heart. "Sir? Can't park
there. Someone's going to have to move the car."

And now he turns to spot, on a stool just past the doorway,
either a cop or a persuasive facsimile who should under no circumstances be allowed to see him drive. By this point, though, his
sister and sister-in-law have vanished into the very place where (it
hits him like a trailing punch) his dad died not so long ago—and it
isn't as if, having just come several hundred miles on a suspended
license and in direct contravention of the writ of a family court
judge, he has many lines left to cross. In the backseat, Jolie hasn't
budged. "Bear with me," he says, easing behind the wheel. But
after that moment on the landing when she seemed on the verge
of speech, she has only gone deeper into herself; on the surface
there is even more of the nothing than before.

The parking lot feels surprisingly full, but Ethan ought to
know by now that grief takes no holidays. As a streetlight flickers
on, he picks a spot right underneath that can be found just as soon
as Izzy gets discharged. He climbs out, leaves the car's keys on the
right front tire. From here, he and Jolie can reach the house and
the van by taxi, ten minutes the long way around, since they won't
want to risk crossing the woods on foot in the dark. Only just
five p.m., so he's still nearly on schedule; if the traffic stays coop-
erative, he'll have her safely back on the Upper West Side by nine
or soon after, and everything the way it was. But then from the
clash of the ER doors, his sister emerges, looking ready to tackle
him . . . And how can he think of his own safety at a moment like
this? Having sought for Moira with his own child in danger, how
can he turn his back on hers? (And if his nephew should fail to
awaken tonight—or worse—what then?)

"A moment of your time," she says. "In private."

She leads him only a few dozen steps away, around the corner
of the nearest ambulance. Through two of its windows, he sees
Jolie light up another smoke, and if this is just her way of signal-

ing open rebellion, then fine, he thinks: he's earned that much. But for a second, shielding something from the vast glare of the flame, her whole body seems to shake.

"The kid'll be okay?" he says. "You got him what he needs?"

"Just go," says his sister. "You need to go."

"Are you serious? I can't run out on you like this. Not unless you can tell me he's okay. Izzy, I mean. I know he has a name."

"And *I* know he wouldn't be comatose in the first place if you hadn't come prancing back in here like the fucking lord of misrule."

"So this is my fault now?" he says (while knowing of course that it is; and if a lapse in Jolie's vigilance had been required for that Baby Ruth to pass from his hands to Izzy's . . . still, there's no way he sells her out). "Because the kid stole candy from my pocket?"

"You realize he has diabetes, right? If I didn't know better, I'd swear you've been high since this morning." But then Moira overcomes her anger—is even admirably restrained, notwithstanding a slight ripple in her jaw. "You know what, forget it. I have responsibilities to other human beings. I realize you aren't equipped to understand that—"

"I'm *trying* to understand it," he says, feeling for a second like he's addressing something larger than just his sister. Yet even with this other audience, he retains his special genius for the fatal slip, the bridge too far. "It's just . . . sometimes I feel like every last person in my life wants me to keep fucking up, you know? To stay damaged, so I can be the bad guy."

"All I want is for you to do like I said and just go away, Ethan. And not come back. You're supposed to meet Sarah four hours from now, right?"

The show he makes of checking his phone is mostly so as not to have to meet her eyes. "Yeah, but to be honest? If we stay, it's not like she knows I'm down here."

"That's not funny, Ethan. Because I'm pretty sure the word for that would be kidnapping."

He lets it go. "And anyway, that was before you moved Dad's memorial to Saturday."

"I didn't move anything, goddammit. I've been right here this whole time. The email's been the email. You're the one who keeps changing the rules. 'I'm never coming back.' 'Whoops . . . here I am again.' Can't come talk at a funeral—can't even show up for a job at the fucking HoJo—but some do-over years later is not to be missed. Has it ever occurred to you that you're a maniac, when you're not being a total depressive?"

"Manic depression is the human condition, Moira. What do you want me to do? I'm trying to atone here. It's said to be a crucial step, you know?"

"Fuck your atonement; they're admitting my son to the ICU, I don't want you anywhere near him. I've built a family, and I mean to protect it."

From your other family, he thinks.

But now Teresa has resurfaced. Her face, apart from its pallor, is lost to the light behind her, yet the demand it makes on her wife is clearly that she choose, one of them or the other. And as the automatic doors swallow Teresa again, Moira doesn't pause for even an instant. He tries to grab hold of her shoulder through the puff of her jacket, to keep her at least long enough for goodbye, but when he moves to press his lips to her forehead as he remembers Corinne doing, she writhes away.

Which is when, perhaps, it comes: the second when, across a gulf of eighteen inches, they can really see each other. Together, apart.

Different. The same . . .

The silence would prove intolerable, though; as ever, Ethan was the one to blink first. "You're right, Moira—sorry. I don't even know what I came here for. But thanks for everything I guess. Call me when you know Izzy's okay. And maybe I'll see you in another decade or two." On the far side of the ambulance, Jolie would remain a cipher, facing the bypass. For all she knew, she'd just missed her one chance to bid her aunt goodbye for good. Or, as the case may be, to say nothing at all. But he could at least see now what had turned her away, he thought, and with Moira not around to judge him any longer, he went over to her. "Jo, listen, whatever you think you just heard, you have to know, that's not going to be me anymore—the guy who cuts and runs, okay?"

No response. Then another hole was opening inside him, and for the briefest and most searing second it was as if he could now replay the scene on the balcony not from his angle, but from her own.

"And you should know that no one's blaming you for what happened to Izzy back there, all right? In fact, you probably saved him, coming for me like you did, and he's going to want to thank you just as soon as he wakes up. Which he will any minute—I promise. So we should maybe just start looking for a place to stay until he does." He stopped, troubled by something; then remembered what it was. "But I don't suppose you've got cash for a cab, do you?" Patting his pockets. "I must have left my wallet in the van . . ."

12

NOW IT'S TRUE that were there such a thing as a do-over—a mulligan—there are certain points Brandon Koussoglou might have been a bit more forthcoming about with Sarah: not least, how he's made this trip once before. That had been 2008, Easter weekend. His traveling companion had been a grad-school compatriot who'd agreed she would marry him, yes, but only after coming out to Fairfield County to meet her future in-laws. They'd caught the same direct train out of Grand Central . . . sat in the same car, actually, right up front. And when the conductor had let them off eighty minutes later, the same pizzas had been waiting under his mom's name at Giancarlo's by the station, one clam and green pepper, one "how your father likes it" (i.e., plain). What followed was a hike up through the neighborhoods with pizza boxes to save Dad the tip on delivery—a side-benefit of Brandon's visits home. Same lukewarm slices on paper plates in the kitchen to spare Mom's china for the big holiday meal; same right-wing monologue from his father in the kitchen afterward; same rooms readied on separate floors for the unwed guests to sleep in; even the same furtive sneaking upstairs by Brandon around midnight (same settling for a handjob in his old racecar-shaped bed) before a stealthy return to the same old basement pullout and the dreamlessness of sleep. And in the morning, the puffy albums of Brandon's baby pictures set out carefully by Mom for perusal. The ham has now given way to a turkey, of course, but otherwise the correspondence between the two visits is so close as to suggest a kind of reenactment. And the thing is—Brandon can admit it to himself here at the dinner table, looking around for a little space in which to take the offensive between Dad's big soliloquy about Obamacare and Mom's getting up to fetch dessert—some part of him has probably been wanting this all along, wishing only to become their faultless son again, hungry for approval.

Maybe even more so now, given the fallout from his last breakup. This is the part he *has* told Sarah, right up front, on their second actual date: how things with her predecessor had ultimately gone up in flames, that A.B.D. spring of '08. To find a new apartment on so little notice had been an ordeal, and the degree had suddenly seemed meaningless, so he'd started looking around for full-time teaching jobs instead—a way to serve, he said. (Had he then brought up the year Wittgenstein spent teaching kindergarten? Fine: guilty as charged. And had he, even while admiring his own candor, been warning his new love covertly not to hurt him? If so, it seemed forgivable, given what Priya had put him through. Besides, a little tragedy on the CV lent a touch of gravitas, he thought—something Sarah's talk of her teen pregnancy and crazy ex-husband made him worry he lacked.)

But now here they are, in this white clapboard colonial with its breakfront and extra place-settings, its table with not one but two ornate vases of flowers, the superfluous leaf propped in a corner by the window, the half-acre of lawn framed by curtains and valences and blinds. Why deny it? Such was the soil from which Brandon Koussoglou had sprung. And if, at twenty-four, he'd been one of *those* young men in the seminars, always with a hand in the air, always racing toward the answer he just *knew* the instructor was looking for—well, he has now, at twenty-eight, started to suspect that you can't build a future on how you'd like to be seen. You have to try to be a little more transparent.

And so, having presented Connecticut to Sarah as a kind of bittersweet adieu, he's really brought her up here to begin anew. Just as soon as Dad shuts up, he'll invite her out for a walk. Under stars just beginning to glimmer, he'll guide her ever higher along the jumble of streets to a little park he could find even blindfolded, and there, on a bench, while she waits for him to lead her back through the gloaming, he'll finally say what he should have back in July. To wit: that when he'd emailed her to propose that conference last winter, he'd never expected to fall so hard or so fast (or in such flagrant breach of the faculty code of conduct). And by the time he gets around to the part about Jolie and the dance, she will of course have forgiven him. Then, on firmer ground once more, they can game out what to say to the girl when she returns, as a way of ending Jolie's peskily expansive version of the silent treatment . . . and so, all three of them, of making a fresh start.

But in the meantime: how well the introduction to his parents seems to have gone! He's always taken a little aback to discover how different his mother is from his memories of her. In his youth, she'd worked mornings as a dental hygienist, and on days when the weather wasn't some shade of New England brutal he would walk home from the bus stop to find her sitting on the swing out front, still in her important smock, awaiting her three facts about the day. Now, even as his father has ballooned outward in that way of older men, his mother reminds him of a balloon's tied-up end, trying to retreat inside. But that only leaves more room for Sarah. Who has been so impressive here, frankly—so beautiful, quick, courteous to his mother, skeptical of his father in just the right way—that maybe Brandon does decide (so sue him) to postpone his confession till after dessert. Why upset the apple-cart?

". . . Well, but you can see how that might sound to other people, Fred," he hears her saying now. "You're the C.P.A., right? Don't you think these 'job creators' you're focusing on are just going to find a way around the extra taxes?"

"But in that case, sweetheart, answer me this: Who covers the cost?" he says. "Not the folks always with a hand out saying me me me, I can tell you that much."

"Aren't we all saying me me me, though, on some level?" she says after a second. "At any rate, experience has taught me that we all end up paying a price for our selfishness, eventually."

It's the cross-hatching of pain in her voice that makes Brandon look up from his wine. The Jolie-related moodiness of yesterday has returned as a faint tightening at the corners of her eyes (a tell you might not even notice, were the two of you just meeting) and for a second, he's having that thing he's heard her describe as the addictive part of fieldwork. It's like their contexts have decoupled so that he can look across and see hers clearly from within the vantage point of his own. Specifically, he is seeing what it must be like to have sole responsibility for an actual flesh-and-blood human being now approaching the cusp of womanhood. What it must be like is: terrifying.

And in this moment before he can scramble back to the safety of fantasy, Brandon Koussoglou is recalling a third visit to this house—one he has perhaps been concealing even from himself. This was the week he'd dropped out of grad school. He'd spent the bulk of it in his climate-uncontrolled carrel in Low Library, surrounded by photographs and asylum requests, the awful-seeming heaps of other people's testimonies . . . yet blocked, as he'd been since moving out. Finally, swallowing hard, he'd begun calling around to wedding vendors to ask for his deposits back. And when that was done, had written to inform his new dissertation adviser that come September he'd be throwing in the towel. Then, in the starriness of high summer, he'd bought a train ticket home without calling first, trudged uphill from the station so consumed with his own pain that he wouldn't remember making the turns . . . And there she'd been on the swing out front, an older woman in one of those terrycloth jogging suits and glasses he'd never known her to need before. Then it was like a series of lenses were clicking into closer alignment: wasn't the same old Mom of his childhood still in there somewhere, still living? As if to prove it, he'd sat down beside her there and forced himself to confess the facts he'd been keeping from her: his jilting at the hands of Priya, the cache of explicit emails he'd found between her and their then-mutual dissertation adviser; and how he had felt, reading the specific words they'd used. "Never mind why I was in her inbox, Mom, Jesus, you're missing the point." But for a minute there in the bug-swirled light, as his loneliness lifted just long enough for Brandon Koussoglou to glimpse a way out, some other thoughts had seemed to hover right at the edge of clarity: ideas about communication and depression and secrecy and trauma, hearing and seeing and being heard, being seen . . .

These were the very same thoughts that would return to him on Second Avenue almost three years later, confronting Jolie with her empty liquor bottle. The same ones threatening to resolve on a subway platform just last month, when the girl had looked across at him like someone had put a knife in her. And how pale she'd been then. How young, and raw, and how vulnerable.

Now he reaches for Sarah's leg under the table. Feels a bit queasy, knowing it's time to stop fucking around here and share this other part, about that night when Jolie spotted him on the platform. But his mother cocks her head, as if puzzled; and unable to face the thought of disappointing her again, he instead gets up to go pee. Then, as he's nearing the sanctuary of the darkened hallway, the buzz of the phone sends Sarah digging through the bag hung from her chair. The woman in his head would never be so impolitic as to answer it, but the one now before him is headed through the living room and out to the porch, saying this is a call she has to take.

And half a minute later, barely audible through the double-paned glass and the multiple window treatments, he hears, "Goddammit!"

He turns to Mom, his channel of clairvoyance already starting to pinch like too-small shoes. "That'll be the ex I was telling you about," he says, when she doesn't react. "Call it a hunch."

"Well, I know you two were trying to make the seven fourteen," she says, continuing pointedly not to express an opinion about his having taken up with this stuck-up divorcée who is never going to give him a child of his own. "I'll just scrape the plates and get the oven heating for dessert." His dad, who three years ago had seen the iPhone as portending the end of Western civilization, is already poking around on the *Drudge Report*, so it's not even clear he notices his son excusing himself.

In the front room toward which Brandon now drifts only a single lamp burns, so swiftly has the night descended. He is listening pretty much openly now, and could probably still screw up the courage to make his admission, if Sarah would ever think to ask. To wit: that he still feels cowed by her past, as if there's something she hasn't leveled with *him* about. Through the window, though, he can hear only her side of the argument, and then only fragments. Each of which feels like another hole punched in the dream-life he's been living—not so much what's being said as the feeling with which she says it.

"What do you mean, 'one day at a time,' Ethan? Who told you you could have her in the first place?"

And:

"Well, what did you *think* my reaction was going to be? But why do you sound so upset? Is something wrong there?"

An exchange harder to make out here. Then, falling back to reason:

"I don't see how that's remotely relevant. Look, be vague about the details if you have to, just let me come get her. I can be to you in like ninety minutes on the train if you'll . . . well, then, where are you?"

Also:

"But what are you trying to say here? *Can't* tell, or *won't* tell? Listen to me, please—I know when there's something you're keeping from me; don't keep this, too."

Then:

"So help me Christ, Ethan, what you're describing is a hostage situation, you realize that? Until what, *noon tomorrow*? Now you're headed toward something even worse. And I'm done making excuses when you pull this shit, okay? If you don't have her back to me by then, there are numbers I won't hesitate to call— you understand?"

A thick description of the smartphone, by the way, ought to include the fact that there's no satisfying mechanism for ringing off in anger—that it's impossible to slam your finger down on a touchscreen. Before she can come back inside, though (not that she seems in any hurry to, hugging herself, punching up a number, facing the dark), he goes out to drop any pretense of not having heard.

"Some news, I take it?"

"Well, there's no point in rushing off to the station anymore," she says grimly, still holding the phone. "Somehow Jolie ended up spending the holiday with her father. Something he claims to have cooked up with my mom . . . who's about to get a goddamn earful just as soon as I can reach her." She holds up a finger. Listens to a recording click in; hits end. Dials again. "Because now he's refusing to bring Jolie back. He says he's on the verge of some breakthrough with her, but that he needs another day."

"Wait—he's keeping her without your permission? Can he do that? How can he even do that?"

"By not giving me an address where I can go put a stop to it, is how."

"That's fucked up, Sarah. Not to mention, aren't there laws?"

"Ethan lives by laws of his own . . . have we not talked about the person he can become when something like this sends him off the deep end?"

"Something like what, though?"

"That's what I'm trying to find out." Another recording. Down comes the phone. Then she says, as if to herself: "And there's your confirmation. Both my parents ducking my calls; he must have even gotten to my dad, somehow." Then, seeing his face: "If you have something to contribute, Brandon, let's hear it."

"No, I'm just . . . I'm just thinking of what the cops might do if you reported him." What he's thinking, actually, is that Brandon Koussoglou has lived to fight another day—has now been given more time to figure out the right thing to say if he's to hold on to Sarah, and with his rival temporarily on ice, for good mea- sure . . . Then, helplessly, he sees again Jolie's pallor on the plat- form, her gauntness. And what it might do to her to watch her dad get hauled off to jail once more. Sarah's right, he thinks, just say it—warn her about the dance, and the liquor, and that look Jolie had on the platform: *The story I've been telling's not as simple as it seems.* "I don't know, the guy already has the one felony, you said, right? Which means further trouble with the law, further absence from Jolie's life. So I guess involving the authorities at this point only causes more problems than it solves." He piv- ots, trying to sound tougher. "I mean, screw him, you're within your rights, but maybe the key is not to do anything too rash, since you'll just be getting her back tomorrow? That's what he said, right?" And when she doesn't answer: "I don't suppose your mom's intuition can have been onto something, and he really is making some headway with her?"

For of course there's this other fact Brandon knows: the harm it will cause his chances with Sarah if Jolie comes to grief in any way. Or rather, that unless he clears his conscience first, it will all in some sense be his fault.

"Such is the spin he's putting on it," Sarah says, but again with that yearning in her voice. " 'A non-linear process,' he calls it."

"So maybe it just means they're talking?" He has an urge to lead her down to have a seat on the swing, where he could more naturally slip an arm around while he works on her to open up about whatever it is she's feeling. But then that damn dog takes up barking somewhere out on Gun Hill Road, where you can't see any of the other houses, and where no one else can really see yours . . . and what to do in response to the call she's just received is obviously something for a woman of Sarah's substance to decide on her own. So at the moment when he might continue thinking in ways that lead out beyond the self, Brandon Koussoglou thinks the better of it . . . and keeps his fool mouth shut.

13

THERE WOULD BE this one hotel they passed, it was out by the highway, with barely enough letters to convey *No V ca cy* on the big board out front—a mouth with half the teeth knocked out. But behind the wheel, Dad didn't even slow to read it . . . just plowed on through the darkness until some five miles later they came to a town like the end of the world, empty towers and parking lots the only things in abundance. Or so it seemed at the four-story place they pulled into, hawking a discount rate. The van doors boomed creepily out over the tarmac where only a few other cars were gathered, all of them ill-used. One, a make of station wagon you never saw anymore, was stuffed to the gills with pillows and boxes of clothing, and as they hustled past she got a terrible feeling off it, like someone in there might be sleeping, or dead. This despite several large and prolix signs insisting the lot was for paying customers only. Like the other security measures—the medieval spikes topping the fence and the keypad on the street-side gate and the baroque system of intercoms and airlocks for accessing the lobby—these signs made Jolie feel more sick, not less. The pale brick façade as they waited to be let in was layer-caked with empty breezeways, lights clustering behind curtains two and three floors up like diners in a forsaken restaurant. She was imagining people shooting meth in there, or servicing johns, or both, when the buzzer buzzed, letting them in.

The desk area smelled almost exactly like the changing rooms at the Y: urine and the quantities of chlorine needed to cover it. And still her heart thumped. A pool? Her suit had been left back at Moira's, but if this place were truly deserted she might steal out

in her dumpy underthings, stay underwater with her eyes closed
and hold her breath until the cold numbed her worst fears about
Izzy, the feel of him still in her arms. Never before had she so
badly wanted a drink. But the clerk, a guy Dad's age only harder-
bitten, was even now advising them, with something like relish,
that the pool was closed; a guest had thrown up in it.

"Be that as it may, I need a room for me and my daughter,"
said Dad, stepping closer to flash his passport and unvelcro the
wallet. She thought she heard him hold his own breath as the guy
re-counted the twenties he'd been handed . . .

Then they were squeezing together onto a floaty-feeling elevator, on their way up to floor three. Possibly the ocean view
fetched a premium during tourist season, but now, approaching
winter, it was like the principle had been reversed: as if this hotel
were cheaper than those on the bay side precisely because of its
exposure, the wind sobbing like a trainwhistle where the breezeway ended. While Dad fumbled with a key-card, she could see the
van lit up by a security light down below, its tail stirred stupidly by
a gust. Farther out crashed a wave she couldn't see.

But aside from the keening, which persisted even within, the
room was nicer than you might have expected for $69.99 plus
tax. Or at any rate had two full beds and a shower-bath, assuming
someone hadn't thrown up in it as well. By the pasteboard desk, a
boxy old TV had been pressed into service as a stand for a knockoff flatscreen. Her brief, wild hope for a VCR (that other way out)
came to nothing. The remote had been left on the floor, and Dad
picked it up and aimed, perhaps just to drown out her silence.
Then, when the volume was high enough that the wind could
no longer be heard, he went to the bathroom carrying his plastic
sack of deodorant and toothpaste from this morning. She didn't
want to betray panic at his absence, or anything else, which was
where her phone should have factored in. Only now, just when
she needed it most, her invisibility of the last year had slipped.
From the last hour alone, here were four separate text threads and
two voicemails from Mom she knew better than to open, plus a
follow-up message from that fucker Grayson Aplanalp. She could
have unfriended him in October, had that not been its own way
of sending a message. But strange, she reflected, that he should

go completely dark on her after what he'd done and then just this week try to reach her twice. Or maybe not so strange, if it counted as the violation she'd experienced it as. No, the strange thing, actually, as the glass darkened and ghosted back her outline, was to realize how far outside all of that she'd ventured now. How, from the father returned to sprawl on the bed beside her, surfing the channels, there was no longer really anything she wanted. Which didn't mean they weren't still bound together on some deep level: associative mind, surface soft-heartedness, uncontrollable urges, and secret self-loathing. But a scant twenty-four hours in his presence had disabused her of the notion that his walking out on her three years ago had been anything but a gift.

Dad settled on a movie with the funny plump actress from that one sitcom, as if to lift Jolie's spirits—as if he knew that she too found the actress irresistible. (Which was worse, she wondered: his having forgiven her so quickly for putting his nephew in a coma, or his need to fake it?) It was to avoid giving him the satisfaction more than anything that she found herself turning back to Facebook, always good for some fresh indignation to drown out whatever you were actually feeling. But the platform, with its relentless drive for contact, had now made it harder to avoid your so-called friends; not only did their names keep surfacing, but also elided bits of text, and Grayson's, clearly meant to bait her into opening his message, was

HEY J SINCE WERE SETTLING ACCOUNTS . . .

Then, when she caved and clicked:

. . . I THINK YOU'VE STILL GOT SOMETHING THAT BELONGS TO ME.

If the desired effect was to bring home to Jolie that there was nowhere left to run—that the misery had hit a seam inside her—then he was a fucking savant. For books were indeed among the few things she'd imagined she might still need in this life, and his was right here in the bag on the floor . . . along with Mircea Eliade, a crumpled *New Yorker*, a now-pulverized Nature Valley granola bar, and the VHS tape she'd thought as late as this afternoon might have been enough to save. At least until she'd realized the second half of it was missing all its sound.

She fumbled along the side of the bed and dug in her bag till she felt the cheapie paperback. Drew it out, studied the cover: *Little Flowers of Saint Francis.* Even in the dimness, it looked the worse for wear. Some water had seeped in from somewhere so that the pages made an autumnal rustle as she turned them.

Then the acid tabs she'd tucked there fluttered out onto her chest, pinwheeling through the TV light, beautiful in the way only a dangerous thing can be beautiful.

She didn't dare move until the bright surge of an exterior shot showed Dad's face in the bed next to her. His eyes had drifted shut; maybe what he'd been feeling wasn't generosity so much as exhaustion. He was doing his moaning thing again, his breath suddenly stuck in his throat, forcing her to think about whether she wanted it to stay there. Brain cells would even now be flickering out, never to recover, but she declined to nudge him, instead waiting another minute until he started heavily and began to snore.

Then she broke for the bathroom, turning off the TV as she passed. Inside her, under a throbbing pulse, she was now hearing again the tiny music that had leaked from the earbuds on the tracks all those months ago, before she'd grasped that her phone must be okay. She reached down again to pick it up (never mind that it was still out on the bed where she'd left it), and with hands going shaky like the tunnel itself brought one of those white shell-shapes close to her ear. *Do I believe in God?* the music roared inside her. *Do I believe in me?* And closer still:

Some people wanna die so they can be free.

Outwardly she was watching her own hands, less shaky already, reach for the grimed taps of the bath. And feel the water start to flow. But it was dingy-colored rather than clear, and the bath itself so shallow, and how did you ever stop struggling to come up for air? Right: filled your pockets with rocks, which of course she didn't have. Or no, you took care of your wrists first . . . which she thought about briefly, but to try that here without the necessary preparations might be messy, she decided, and the last thing she wanted anymore was a mess. What she wanted, suddenly, again, was calm and fierce and clean and irresistible. Almost holy, if anything could still be holy. Which meant that, at least until she could find some quiet stretch of shore on which to actually carry out these steps, she remained trapped.

When she moved back into the room, she was practically blind, since the night with its blackout curtains was darker than it ever got at home. Funny thing about darkness, though, for the person longing so desperately for erasure: beyond a certain point, it made your brain work that much harder to fill in what must have been there. The phone, too, shared this structure, which now seemed to her the foundational structure of American life: the thing you turned to to forget your pain only left you with more of the pain than before. With a vehemence that surprised her, she found herself bashing out a reply to Grayson. Was maybe even trying to incorporate something of her dad, or of men more broadly—their way of reaching out to scratch an itch without worrying what got broken in the process. All caps, yes, but she did pride herself on her punctuation, even here in the otherwise blackness.

LISTEN, FREAK: I'M NOT GOING TO BE A THREAT TO YOU MUCH LONGER . . . SO PLEASE, PLEASE, PLEASE, LEAVE ME ALONE.

Then she double-checked to make sure she really had changed the privacy settings earlier this week, and could go somewhere on foot and not be found. And almost instantly, was grateful to her former self: Perhaps the biggest reason for holding your tongue? You always gave away so much more of yourself than you meant to.

Then she turned the phone back off, resolved to think no further about the plans that now promised her peace, for if she did she might never get to sleep, and the daylight never come. And when, after a minute, she risked a tiny "Dad?" in the darkness, just to make sure her voice still worked, and heard herself start to cry, the weird thing was, it didn't sound like her at all.

14

"NOT TO BE A KILLJOY, SWEETHEART," says the voice on the line, "but what exactly did you send me?"

It is 8:01 in the morning, the Friday after Thanksgiving, and Erica Morales needs no larger context; the weird thing is, it isn't even the first time she's gotten one of these calls. Still, she begs his pardon.

"I come running back from Cleveland to salvage my business," comes the reply, "only to find your pal Ethan in the wind."

She wants to interject here that Ethan Aspern is in no way shape or form her pal. In fact, the reverse: it would be difficult to imagine a sworn enemy who could more comprehensively have destabilized her own livelihood, not to mention sense of self, and all from a single indiscretion it's not totally clear he even remembers—a night back in 2008 when she was at her least rational-minded and him at his most drunk. He was more like a wrecking ball who'd come slamming into the wrong apartment and then, rather than succumb to gravity and good taste, had hit pause on Newtonian physics to gratuitously knock her books off the bookcases and fuck with the stereo. Then again, Les McGonagall had developed his own unorthodox approach to boundaries, wherein companion and colleague and fellow sufferer all blurred into one thing—the very reason she'd thought to send him a problem like Ethan in the first place. And only now does she see the flipside of such porousness: that in the mind of McGonagall, a seeker such as herself is no more entitled to sympathy than is a perfect stranger. "Slow down for a sec," she says. "Am I to understand he never went back to California?"

"I could have told you that at any point in the last four months, sweetheart, had you been around to tell."

"I've been studying my ass off to change jobs, McGonagall, you know that. Sorry, 'keister,' I should say. But I was at the working group Wednesday night, where were you?"

"I told you, Cleveland. For the holiday. When for all I know, your boy *was* headed back to California—but if so, he took my van."

A sheet of cellophane makes a sucking sound as she lifts the edge from the dish. Carries with it a ghostly orange scumble. "I'm standing here in my kitchen looking at yesterday's pumpkin pie. Is it possible he just got caught up in Thanksgiving revels somewhere and had a relapse? Got loaded and passed out? You remember he has that history of addiction."

An odd clatter on the other end. "Darlin', it's a free country, or so they say. But this is bigger than one man. I've got clients out there who are depending on me."

And now he's explaining how he'd been on the couch at his buddy's new tract-home in Richmond Heights, all full up with stuffing, a godson nestled close on either side, everyone about to bask in the glow of a warm TV—a big deal for him too, considering how his real family had iced him out years ago—when he got a message from a customer flagged as urgent. Attached was the file every dogowner was supposed to be sent upon successful completion of a walk: an image of a creature fed and cared for and blessed. "Except this one's a video, Erica, and that's not what it shows at all."

"Why do I have this sinking feeling you're going to say more?"

"Well, here's the odd part. You get a shot of the owner's medicine cabinet, then a jar of what appears to be prescription painkillers, and a hand reaching in to, uh . . . well, fondle it, almost. Unclear if anything was taken, but just the poking around is creepy enough. Especially with a soundtrack of heavy breathing. Now why would your pal record a thing like that, much less hit send?"

"Are you sure it was Ethan, though? With that phone of his, I'm not sure he can even take video."

"He can now. Though from the look of things he hasn't yet mastered how to share it."

God help us, she thinks.

"Point is, the owner's steamed—if it's not a theft, it's at least a serious breach of trust—and Ethan's suddenly got his phone turned off. I have to fly home on standby for damage control, not least to figure out who else he might have pulled this junk on before my whole client base starts to collapse, you know? Step in the apartment late last night, and before I even get the light on, I'm noticing this gamey scent from the spare room. Follow *that*, there's a corpse in a wet bathtowel at the bottom of the closet. Not a client, praise be: a frozen turkey, now room temperature. But my keys aren't on the counter where they're supposed to be. And my calls all go straight to voicemail. And my van is nowhere to be found. Poof."

"Stolen, you're alleging. By a repeat offender."

"I'm not alleging one way or the other. But it darn sure would help if I could find him."

"Anyone else have the keys?" she asks wearily, already filling out a form in her head.

"Would I be calling you personally if they did?"

"But not active-duty police, I notice."

"I've had enough experience in that arena to last a lifetime, you may remember. Still, I was wondering if it might be possible to get some kind of an intermediary . . ."

She sighs. Hears herself ask how long he can give her to reel this old case of hers back in.

"Reel him back in? I'm not sure that's what I'm asking, Erica. I mean, I could probably keep up appearances for a day or two, assuming he continues not to show. But you can't throw a lifeline to a person who's not ready yet to catch it. Have you ever thought that maybe you should instead be shortening the path between this fellow and the consequences of his actions? Cruel to be kind sort of thing?"

"I know, McGonagall. I know you stuck your neck out for me on this one. Against my better judgment. I can't explain it. Only try 'a little patience and humility'—right?"

A pause, as it sinks in that the person she's quoting here is himself. "Okay, kid. You win. I'll go down my manifest, call out sick with whoever I can't reach on foot. But think long and hard about what I said."

She rings off and instantly has a headache. Or no: instantly seems to have had a headache for some time now, just beneath her notice. But why was Ethan Aspern *her* headache, and not someone else's? She tries to recall this other thing McGonagall had once said in the working group, about the guru as that which incited and annoyed, and thus had something to teach you. She has, without thinking about it, placed her head against the doorframe next to the phone's wall-mounted cradle. It softens the ache to push against it, to equalize the pressure. But this means she misses her mother coming back until she feels a cool hand on her neck. Right. Black Friday. They're slated to go Christmas shopping in under an hour.

"*¿Está todo bien, guapa?*"

"Yeah, I'm good, Ma."

Her mother has to have known this would be her answer either way. What will tell is what she does next. But there's far too much noise coming from the fridge, bowls jostling, foil crinkling, for her mother to actually be looking for anything in there, so Erica doesn't open her eyes or move, even after a sandwich has been thrown together out of yesterday's leavings and she is once more left alone. She forces herself to wonder if it is possible she really *is* attracted to Ethan's special brand of madness . . . and if, by some slight lowering of the flag of professionalism, or possibly by not being angry enough at his return, she has unwittingly encouraged it. Which is perhaps a way of asking again whether what is exceptional about this guy is his sensitivity, or, conversely, his obliviousness. What is clear though, she feels certain, is that for months or even years before that, there had been only the one thing about him that seemed exceptional to her at all.

BUT LET'S THINK BACK. The case against him would have first appeared in her docket toward Christmastime, 2003. That means she was twenty-eight and two years on the job, just long enough to assume from the charges in his case-jacket that this white-sounding guy was in fact some other thing. Which seems racist but isn't. On DV, larcenies petty and grand, even involuntary manslaughter, crime didn't discriminate, she found, and simple possession could net you an advertising exec, a street hoodlum, a

Chinese kid needing an interpreter, a butch bartender from some farout stop on the L . . . but there were other offenses (coincidentally or not coincidentally, those most often leading to Rikers) that seemed tied to ethnicity, age, and gender, themselves tied to economic status and community-level trauma. You could get dinged for an unlicensed handgun as a middle-aged *blanquita* from Gramercy, true, but there would be some aberration in your past to account for it. Whereas if you were a twenty-one-year-old nonwhite male—Erica's meat and potatoes, her golden mean—no such accounting was needed. "Bodies," they called them. It got to where she could guess the specs on an incoming body without even checking the name on the folder. She'd come to accept, for instance, that possession with intent to sell, good old NY 220.16, correlated tightly with being young and poor and from public housing, which in turn meant black or Latino. From her statistics class at John Jay, the word "predictor" now returned with new and unsettling resonances. She had already seen the stats, of course . . . had watched her own cousin Nita's rasta husband get railroaded in the early '90s, which was in some weird way why she'd enrolled to study criminal justice in the first place: Babylon bidness, he'd called it . . . But seeing a thing and knowing it weren't the same.

And perhaps this was why she had a special soft spot for possession with intent, the 220.16s. She watched them slump in her little plastic chair and hounded them with phone calls when they failed to show; marked the excessive paperwork still filled out, circa '03, on a Tandy brand mainframe computer with a dot-matrix printer, one endless perforated sheet of human failings. Usually its subjects were even younger than she was, and it was these younger bodies in particular she was at pains to see as individuals, each with his own story. She wasn't sitting in judgment, she assured them; she was, if anything, the last thing standing between them and a judgment that had already been passed way over both their heads. What she hadn't yet realized was that Babylon didn't give a fuck or a farthing if you were working to make its business more humane. Like the IT system—like Corrections writ large, perhaps like life itself—it was the kind of ad hoc assemblage no one would ever have designed from scratch, but which might come crashing down en masse were even a single corner to be targeted for an upgrade.

And besides, in her clients' persistent refusal to be saved, she would begin to suspect a deeper homogeneity. Maybe this was what God saw when he looked down at people, too. Or maybe for him, the mysteries of identity were more like some uncanny valley. Maybe if he decided to wipe the whole thing out and start over again, a plague this time or a pillar of fire, he would fix that: nudge these images of himself in the direction of greater similarity— simpler that way, and less room for drama (though also less free will)—or of greater variety, to spare everyone the guilt and obligation you felt, facing your own mirror. And maybe like Erica Morales at twenty-eight, twenty-nine, he thought pretty seriously some days about annihilation. Maybe those stormclouds she could glimpse massing over the Colgate Clock in Jersey City from the coffee room at 100 Centre were just the inside of the mind of God, brooding.

The upshot of all of which was, aside from his name, and his punctuality, she might not have made Ethan Aspern for a white guy at all until he first shuffled into her cube in '03 with that sheepish look of his . . . except. Except that 220.16 was at the *way* upper end of what they'd let you walk for with no more jail-time than it took to clear Central Booking. He seemed conscious of his position, somehow, settling into the chair. Maybe that was the source of his embarrassment, his air of slight befuddlement at finding himself there. No actual poor person could have afforded to go around with those doodles on their canvas sneakers. Not to mention (she checked the paperwork) the private lawyer who'd argued his case, or the five-thousand-dollar bail he'd been released on almost two years ago, after pretrial motions. And she couldn't fail to see that he was easy on the eyes, too, with his broad shoulders and baby blues, teeth that had benefited from regular attention; he looked like the kind of guy who'd been told from birth he could succeed at anything he set his mind to. She walked him through the procedures for checking in by phone and documenting his search for employment—"I have some resources I'm mandated to connect you with, should you need them"—all of this pro forma, the judge would have given the outlines, probably his attorney, too, but he was doing his best to look engaged, in that way that indicated he either had had some higher education or alternatively really was a complete and utter virgin: frequent and sustained eye contact, possibly-too-vigorous nods of his sandy blond head. "You trying to hurry me along? I'm boring you?" she said finally, just to remind him who had the whip hand. She'd learned by now that what mattered was that they respected you.

"Yeah, no," he said. "Sorry, I'm new to this."

Predictably, the probation term in his plea deal came with fewer bells and whistles than most, in theory because it was his first time, not even a misdemeanor for a prior (though of course she couldn't see the juvenile record). "No drug testing regime, I see."

"Well, my buddy and I were both sober when we got picked up . . . I mean, just between us two, I'd had a nip of Popov earlier in the night for courage, but by that hour of the morning I was pretty close to clear-eyed, could walk a line, touch my toes. But can we speak candidly in here? I mean, you don't report to the D.A., right? You're not an actual cop?"

He seemed genuinely not to know, and she had to work that much harder not to be disarmed, since his judge, even for a judge, was a notorious meddler and tyrant. "Think of me as middle management, Mr. Aspern. Once that gavel comes down, your crime is your crime."

"Because the thing is, if I hadn't already been in the middle of trying to clean my act back up, there wouldn't have been any drugs left to bust us on. Nor left unsnorted in Harlem, is sort of what I'm dealing with." He looked at the floor. "And still there's that moment, you know, when you're sitting on the side of the road and the rollers are going in your rearview but the law hasn't yet come forward to flash its light in your pupils . . . that moment when you don't know if you're about to be granted another shot at life, or if this time you really are dead. That was the moment I should have remembered there was still some coke in my jacket. Eddie had gone to all those lengths to keep the car clean, not so much as a microgram for the canine squad to be tipped to, and here I am with half an eight-ball sitting in my jacket pocket from two nights earlier. If it would have just occurred to me that I'd forgotten it there, drunk, I might have had time to toss it. Instead what I couldn't stop thinking about was that I was less than a mile from a warm bed and the only person I'd ever really known how to love. I was still married at that time, you see . . ."

It was as if he'd been waiting for the smallest opportunity in which to gallop off with the interview, conscript it in the service of some larger story he needed to tell himself about himself.

"Let me just cut you off there, Mr. Aspern. Like I said, any extenuating factors are between you and your judge."

"—and in a sense it still feels like I'm back there, lights flashing," he continued. "But I guess my buddy Eddie who was driving . . . I guess you wouldn't have any update on where they sent him?" he said, craning his neck hopefully, as though she'd have left some corner of the file visible from where he sat. "No one else will give me a straight answer."

"I could ask around," she couldn't help but say. "But where he is currently depends on a lot of things, including what sentence they handed him."

It was right at the tip of his tongue. "Two to four, on account of an earlier bust. With time served for the months he was stuck out at Rikers. They had a plea deal closed by the end of February."

"But how is it you made bail and he didn't, even factoring in his prior?" she was dumb enough to ask. "I'm just curious, professionally." He looked back down at the hands between his knees.

"You have to understand, Eddie's foster family had already washed their hands of him, and so the closest thing he had to a dad was his supplier, this guy Ducky . . . the one he'd just tried to do an end run around to build his own supply line to New York. And who I'm not convinced didn't have some way of knowing all that and narc us out in the first place. A real hard-hearted son-of-a-bitch. I tried to get my own family to scrape up extra cash for a second lawyer, even found a bail bondsman who'd take our boat as collateral, but according to my sister, my dad wouldn't bend, he'd decided to pin all the blame on Eddie—as apparently Eddie had, too. I was told he filed some affidavit trying to claim sole responsibility . . . like that was some legally valid concept or something, like it could do anything but dig him a deeper hole.

And this despite the fact that we were no longer speaking, even through counsel." He paused. "Could I have leaned harder on my sister to help him? Or gone to my dad myself, found a way to reverse the estrangement that had set in between us? To tell you the truth, I don't feel great about that, but at the time I was so pissed about everything Eddie had cost me. See, there's this other family consideration I probably ought to mention . . ."

Of course. Here it came. She was expecting him to trot out something about an ailing relative needing money for transfusions, or perhaps (he seemed the type to see it this way) whose delicate health wouldn't survive the revelation that he wasn't a perfect angel—a little tender-hearted granny, say, who had to be shielded from the fact that he now had a rap sheet and his own personal P.O. But this had been the real surprise of Ethan Aspern: she would never have expected that waiting back home for him in Spanish Harlem, in that warmth he never reached, had been a daughter all of four years old.

"And now six. That's two birthdays I've had to miss, and you *know* what those mean at that age. You can't imagine how this whole thing has screwed up custody proceedings. Of course without it, maybe there wouldn't be any proceedings. Maybe I'd still be married."

It seemed so crazy that a middle- to upper-middle-class whiteboy just entering his mid-twenties could already have been the father of a six-year-old that she might have thought he was pulling her leg. But in the meantime something had flashed out from beneath his façade of doomed charm—something he didn't even seem aware of. It was fear. Or it was fear seen through the wrong end of a telescope, which was guilt: the memory of having done something by the light of your fears.

IN THE YEARS THAT FOLLOWED, the years that would carry him from twenty-five to twenty-nine and Erica on past the bourne of thirty, Ethan's whiteness would pale for her, come to seem less anomalous. Along with everything else, the drug game had liberalized. Cheap heroin was flooding the market, with prescription pills playing hype-man; she'd see college types nodding off on the subway stairwells she picked her way up in her don't-even-think-about-it clothes (her sensible shoes, her too-slack slacks), and she was catching more of them in her "IN" tray, too, on second or third possessions or on the constellation of related charges—hustles and smash 'n' grabs and scams—to which less privileged folks had been resorting for years to support the trade. Ethan's attractiveness, too, had flickered in and out of her awareness, depending on what she had on her plate and whom she was dating at the time.

No, what mostly defined him in her mind—at least in that first phase of knowing him—was that more than any particular commitment to sobriety, his daughter seemed to be the one thing keeping him tethered to the straight and narrow. Not that he wore a World's Greatest Dad tee-shirt (unless it was under that hoodie), or even (that she knew of) carried pictures of her in his broke-ass wallet. In fact, when he came in punctually each month and settled down in the plastic chair, he often didn't seem to be thinking of himself as a parent at all, much less as a criminal—more as an overgrown child, with a child's innocence, a child's inability to be blamed. But he and Erica had entered the time-marking stage of their journey together, the time-marking she'd now come to understand was, after intake, actually the bulk of her job.

And why even have them show up here, these bodies, month in and month out? she sometimes wondered. On some alternative planet, it might have been simply to observe a change, but on this one, she'd come to believe, nobody changed. Not really.

Take Erica herself: she had been in Babylon's employ now for five, six, seven years. Probation was a good union to be in, too, one whose negotiators had wrested from the city fifteen days of annual leave plus a three percent bump for cost of living. Her first February, she'd flown to the DR for a week of bona fide vacation, of the kind neither she nor the guy she was sleeping with at the time had ever gotten before. By the next February, with the next guy, it already had the same grinding feel as a workweek, but whatever—it was now what she knew how to do. What she didn't know how to do was not already be thinking of how to move on to the next next guy while she waited with this one in the piddling Santo Domingo airport for the flight back home.

No, the point of having the bodies show up monthly was to document that they weren't *not* showing up—a box you could check on the paperwork, and later in a pull-down menu in the already-obsolete new computer interface. As if in compensation for the pointlessness, she developed a kind of bedside manner, a facility for chat that gave the illusion of deep engagement just by getting them to speak on whatever she knew they cared about. And here again, variety began to assert itself. One client, re-trained to drive for UPS, heaped endless abuse on a supervisor. Another, a real tough guy—face tattoo and everything—had a whole sketchpad of fashion designs he would break out and show you if you asked. And Ethan Aspern, who had decided to give AA another chance and now filled the downtime between meetings and work and custody visits at the Union Square cineplex, seeing multiple films on one ticket . . . in another life, Ethan might have been in movies, or made them, so intelligently did he break down the units and objectives of the latest slasher flick, Pixar, Mike Leigh.

It was around this time that she began to wonder if her objectivity had somehow been compromised—a thing she had to guard against as an unmarried straight woman whose case-load was 70/30 men. Then again, with some of these, her longest-standing appointments, it was probably too late. With Ethan Aspern, it was the daughter, and the custody visits, that seemed to phosphoresce out of his otherwise indifferent account of himself, like mathematical operators imposing order on what might under other circumstances have amounted to anything at all. The daughter's name in particular had stuck in Erica's mind for some reason, and once she was done verifying that he was still working, still keeping his nose clean, still attending meetings, still out of contact with any criminal element, still domiciled in the tri-state area, she would use this name to ask after the girl, like a key cut to pass right through the various layers of self-involved bullshit and press on a latch he didn't even know he had in him. A kind of slow wonder would appear on his face, even when what was being expressed was anxiety at how fast kids grew up in the city. From their very first conversation, his ex had tried to warn him about this, he said, but it was like he hadn't understood. Now Jolie was whizzing along busy sidewalks on a green plastic scooter, getting scolded by elderly Russians. Now she was writing her name in chalk on a green bench in the park, getting the *J* backward. Getting the *J* right. Shying from that same park's sprinklers in summer, worried she was going to melt. Reading in the newspaper about the ice caps. Sitting for the gifted test he insisted on, which the mother thought a form of apartheid.

Still later, Erica would wonder at her own eagerness for those glimpses—would wonder how much of the wonder was on Ethan's face and how much of it she'd been putting there. Her own father was a memory, possibly confected from TV, of a guy who'd taken her to buy shoes one time before disappearing to South Carolina.

And there was this other thing, too, the thing no client had any way of knowing: at seventeen, she had been *this close* to having a child herself. This was when she was still at parochial school. Love had beset her the way it does in songs—with a neighborhood guy, Ricky, wiry, gorgeous, trouble, a neat little moustache he liked to run a finger over as if to check that it was still there and a fade so tight it could have been tattooed on. Veins on his forearms the junkies used to stop him on the street to admire. In the off-again cycles of his dalliances with school, he worked as a housepainter, and she loved the paint-and-sweat smell of him when he'd get off in the evening, clean but also dirty, his pockets swollen with off-the-books cash, and always (he claimed) too tired to go out. Her mother was still on the night shift at St. Luke's then, so they used to go back to the old apartment uptown and draw the blinds, order in food like rich folks, and then see how many times he could make her come before the delivery guy hit the buzzer. His spattered white pants, sound of his belt hitting the floor. Her hands' heels propped on the sill of the window (oddly like her forehead now pressed to the frame of the door). Her face inches from the blinds, catching quick little glimpses out to where no one could see in.

Notwithstanding years of Catholic school, she couldn't believe it was a sin, either; sin was supposed to leave you feeling ashamed.

The only shameful thing about sex was how much she liked it, and again: she was seventeen. If there wasn't much more to this deal with Ricky, she didn't know that yet, nor that the reason he didn't want to be seen with her on his own block was that he had a string of other girls on the side. And by the time she found out, Erica Morales was pregnant. Though she didn't know that either.

What she did know was that she awoke one day, a few mornings after the split from Ricky, with a strange low feeling in her abdomen and some spotting. Her period was a couple weeks delayed, possibly, but Erica was hard to panic, and went to class like on a normal day, made it all the way through—though the last part of Trig she would spend in the bathroom, curled against the wall with what felt like really bad cramps, as she told the nun who found her there after the last bell.

The nun would drive her personally in the parish van over to Columbia-Presbyterian Hospital on 165th, and what Erica kept saying between moans was not to tell her mother, because if she still didn't know what was in her, she'd by this point begun to suspect, or why hadn't they just gone to St. Barnabas? She was under the impression, with the same ambient provenance as her family-planning strategy, that if it was early enough you could just take some kind of pill instead of having to go in for surgery, but when they wheeled her into the theater post-ultrasound, they weren't asking about her last period; it either wasn't that early or there was no such pill, and the nun had disappeared in a rustle of plausible deniability.

What she can recall now is the sense of blood, of her own blood beating in her head like hands covering and uncovering her ears to fake an ocean. And then her own internal monologue seeking to blot out everything coming from outside. Had the panic she'd avoided earlier that afternoon simply put on a mask and slipped behind a tree to wait? Or had it been wearing a mask to begin with, flying a false flag of non-aggression to coax her out into the open, where a girl on her own made such easy prey? But this much she'd been right about: the calendar was the enemy, insofar as it was too late, probably, to go back now. These instruments at the edges of her were coldly insistent and unable to be gotten around by acts of imagination. It was like a gagging sensation you thought you could endure because you knew it would be over soon but then you kept on gagging. And she knew sex was going to be ruined for her for a while. Already, she was ruined for Ricky, who would choose among whichever of his other girlfriends could give him another little Ricky—for now, the procedure over, she was ruined for that, too. And *now* they were gentle, cleaning her up, head to one side so she couldn't see.

Later, a nurse would explain that the pregnancy had been "ectopic," meaning wrongly implanted, never to come to fruition. And had meanwhile ruptured a tube, while the surgical chaos that followed had all but ensured the unusability of the other. She could always adopt. She wanted to ask the nurse to hold her hand, but knew she couldn't. Something had been taken, an oath or something. The doctor had basically evanesced, as if embarrassed to be seen anymore, or as if she, the patient, was supposed to be the one embarrassed. And had borne away with him the clump of cells that had been, but no longer was, a part of Erica Morales. Who herself had perhaps not been fully prepared for the possibility that the New Testament God of her parochial-school girlhood, hovering on a cross just above her on her wall, would now return to stare down from much higher in silent disapproval. *See? I told you not to, and you went and did it anyway.* In the morning, the nurse gave her some pads and instructions and asked her, not unkindly, did she have a way to get where she needed to go, but the question was merely the outward form of a question, positing a connection that was even now dissolving. Of course she did, she said, not quite realizing yet that she was in no shape for the subway. She would be helped into her clothes, wheeled as far as the reception area, but there was no one there to meet her and she had no money for a cab, and the wheelchair was like a shopping cart hitting the Pathmark gate: it could take you this far, but could not take you home . . .

NOW, IT WASN'T THAT she'd be thinking about any of this in those meetings so many years later, sounding out Ethan about his fatherhood, about his daughter. (Nor that it returns to her this way even on the day in question, with her head to the kitchen doorframe: as narrative, whole and continuous and firm to the touch.) But from the tendency of the same conversation to recur, and recur, she must have felt some vicarious something or even just simple curiosity about this cosseted white guy who had nothing and everything going for him if only he could have seen it.

And so when he'd called her weeping with only a month left to go on his probation, the one collect call they allowed inmates to make from the drunk tank of Lower Township, New Jersey—when he said he'd fucked up and started using again, been picked up trying to drive while under the influence (and on a suspended license, no less)—she had, against every rule in the book, ordered him to sit tight and she'd come down there, see if there was some kind of string she could pull to get him free . . . not for herself, but for the little daughter. Then she had taken the city car she would now have to fake mileage accounts for and driven the length of the Garden State to finesse things with a local magistrate: you have to understand, the guy just lost his father, missed his one shot at reconciliation, twelve-stepping on its own didn't seem to be working, they were trying to get him into inpatient treatment somewhere . . .

And yes, it had perhaps been cruel of her to be so kind, seeing as how the girl would end up without a dad anyway—how, according to her friend who ran the detox place in L.A. he'd lasted all of forty-eight hours after discharge before slipping off to do dope—and how when Ethan next appeared, just this last summer, he'd be violating their contract again. But by this point she had found herself on the difficult road back to God, via the triple-play intercession of some Sufi poetry she'd been sent once in a desperate hour and Les McGonagall's working group of Third-Order lay Franciscans. Life, as she now felt God saw it, wasn't always about the choices you'd made, or even about what you'd wanted. A lot of it was more about what you hadn't chosen to want, or could have known at the time you were choosing.

And now here she is, three credits from her actuarial degree—Erica Morales, whose dream at this point is just to have as little as possible to do with anyone else's story—her forehead numb from being pressed to this probably lead paint, and Les McGonagall's little paradox or tautology looping like a mystery through her head, cruel to be kind to be cruel to be kind . . .

As her mother brings back her Potemkin sandwich from the next room, she asks once more is Erica okay.

"I'm okay, Mami," she says. "I'm good. Just my head, is all."

Then she reaches for the phone and, without bothering to disguise it, begins to do the thing she now knows how to do, because somehow in all this mess of other people she has come to see Ethan Aspern as her own responsibility. Her own child.

15

GOD BUT THE DAYS were getting short these days. Even the mornings seemed to roll out of bed late. Putting down the receiver, drawing back the breezeway blinds, Ethan thought of Easter weeks from his early childhood when Christ's wounds had been sponged in vinegar, the Jerusalem sky gone a midday black. He'd never done especially well in winter, but out west you got the consolations of climate, and even East 112th Street had boasted the distraction of light beyond branches, the way certain deepwater fish stage luminous displays to attract fresh meat and fight the bleakness however many thousands of feet under sea. In treeless Ocean City, by contrast, the only buffer against the early dark was this line of hotels along the breakwater—through one of whose plate-glass windows he could now observe his daughter's disappearance into the back of an antlered van far below, with intentions that, if he thought about it, might have seemed concerning.

Even the one night in the hotel had been a mistake, he could admit that now, though he didn't feel Moira had left him much choice. The light from the torchiere was awful, as light from torchieres always was, casting the crazed shadows he recalled from his mom's German-expressionist phase. Nor had much been done to conceal or otherwise prettify the emergency sprinklers issuing from the ceiling at intervals mandated by code; the shapes they threw looked uncannily barbed. But how, apart from light, to fake a little cheer, make it seem like they were still on some devil-may-care vacation rather than on pins and needles awaiting word about his nephew, Izzy, the boy who'd done nothing at all to deserve this?

Though undoubtedly Ethan was doing his thing again now, he thought. Spinning out the way he always did. Jolie had a good head on her shoulders, and would be fine. To distract himself, he turned back to the upper TV with its dim sum of cable channels. Golf was already winding down in Western Europe somewhere. A half-hour more, and it would be late enough to turn breakfast into lunch (and to hell with the fact that he'd told her mother they'd be back by noon). Then what . . . another movie—more waiting? Assuming Jolie wasn't already using the privacy of the van to dial Eleanor, or Sarah. Or the fuzz. He thought about redrawing the blackout curtains, but like most no-smoking rooms, this one had the stifled air of prodigious recent smoking. To say nothing of the moans of neighbors that had awakened him at intervals through the night so that as recently as minutes ago, when the sound of Jolie's exit roused him, he'd still been sleeping. And all this when he'd vowed not to let her out of his sight until he could establish for certain whether she was still holding herself culpable for Izzy. His mind ran briefly to whether he'd left his shaving stuff in the van yesterday, but of course he'd skipped buying a razor at the IGA. Thus the two days' growth of beard. No pills of any kind unless she was the one carrying them. He contemplated the back-pack sitting over on her bed. Specifically: contemplated searching it. But of course leaving her stuff behind was just another way of her signaling that she planned to come right back. A person could lose his mind this way. No, the next step here, clearly, was to find out the news about the boy. For if he had made it through the darkness alive and well, wouldn't the whole question of culpabil-ity be moot?

The room had a phone, obviously, since he'd just made a call, but phone books no longer existed, so he reached for the Android he'd powered off after last night's skirmish with Sarah. A hos-tage situation, she'd called it, as he'd paced the curb out front of his onetime home, lit up on worry and grief; and he knew the newspapers, if they called it anything, would have called it simple abduction—kidnapping, to use Moira's word. But not all stories are like that. Or anyway, this one wasn't. He couldn't decide now which would have been more troubling coming from his ex-wife: a flurry of follow-up messages, or what he actually found on the screen, which was none at all. What there seemed to be instead was a string of missed calls from Les McGonagall, perhaps moved by the holiday spirit to reach out from the wilds of Ohio. But never mind: a few pecks into his call-log, and the number for the hospital was his.

Yesterday, when he'd called from the darkest edge of Moira's yard, the duty nurse had refused to give him information—some HIPAA thing. Now he summoned his theatrical training and identified himself as the boy's father. No one could blame a dad, particularly one as distraught as Ethan, for forgetting his child's date of birth, could they? He was pretty sure the year had been 2005, though, he told the lady on the other end. Right, exactly: September 30.

Some keys tapped. He'd drifted to the bathroom somehow, thirsty, but the water ran faintly yellow, either manganese (harmless) or arsenic (poison). Your son's doctor will have to be fetched from the ICU, he was told, but for a second this only confused him; he didn't have a son, he had a daughter. Then the hold music. Just tell me the kid's *resting comfortably*, he thought, beautiful phrase, remarkable phrase . . . but the one he really wanted was *discharged*, which clearly Izzy hadn't been. And what if what the doctor was coming to say was that he'd died in the night? What might Jolie do *then*? And now when he sped back to the outer room and looked down, the back of the van was sealed up again, and for a second his heart stopped. But no, there she was, glancing away from the window where he stood, dropping her hand from the fedora and turning reluctantly toward the lobby. Then he hung up, because without any proof to the contrary, Izzy would still be alive. And he shouldn't—or wouldn't—let his daughter see him cry.

He crossed to the sliding door of the balcony, stepped through . . . and instantly wished he'd worn shoes. The concrete out here was cold and inexplicably damp, though maybe not actually inexplicably: some sort of condensate had dripped from the balcony above to cut glacial hills and valleys in the floor. Only a few inches from his face when he looked up were stalactites of calcification, gnarled and bonelike and disturbing to behold. But the hotel's legal team had succeeded in at least this much: what should have been balusters and railings was now a single wall of poured concrete. A second wall, higher, blocked the neighbors.

Planting elbows and leaning forward, he could see south and east to where the sun touched the clouds with implications of warmth. On the boardwalk, once so vibrant-seeming, a jumble of gulls swirled around something he couldn't quite make out, a prone rat or just a hamburger wrapper under conditions of scarcity. He leaned further. A guest could probably break his neck here if the midair contortions were managed just so. But of course once you were a parent you weren't allowed to think ever again about the coward's way out . . . one of the central terrors, maybe, of having kids: what it locked you into, knowing you'd walk through any fire to spare them loss, spare them pain. Even while knowing you couldn't. And of course Jolie was fine, probably, suffering not the torments he kept trying to project onto her, but just ordinary teenage unhappiness (as cooler heads seemed to think, Sarah's among them). Well, unhappiness plus concern for her cousin, as-yet-undischarged. If only he could stop these soft hands from mousing around in the pockets of his mind. Or see some sun here. When he turned, Jolie was behind him in the doorway.

"Jesus, honey, what have you done to your hair?"

Shaved it, is what it looked like, to a brutal half-inch where none of the dye was left. Just faint little pinkish wisps on the shoulders of her outsized tuxedo jacket. He should have remembered about McGonagall's grooming tools. But clearly she wasn't going to answer . . . unless this was her answer. The way she cupped her elbows suggested cold and/or *Shut the door, already*, but what could the hair possibly be telling him, except that she'd been trying to punish herself? In which case maybe things were worse than he thought. (No, stop that.)

"I mean, it looks cool, actually. Very Sinéad O'Connor. But your mom's going to kill me . . . which is something we should talk about, probably. Or I should."

Still holding herself as if she were a sack inclined to breakage, she stepped out to take up position near him, leaning against the unbalustered balustrade. With her boots on and his shoes off, they were so much closer in height than he was used to. Disentangling himself from his thoughts, he went on.

"So first, after you left, I called down to the desk and set us up for another night, just in case we needed it. I know you were hoping to see Izzy, and with your aunt dead-set against me, I kind of figured the hospital would be our best shot at catching him on neutral territory." (Deep breath. Honesty is a gift you give other people.) "But then when I called over just now, it turns out he's still not ready yet for visitors. Honey, listen, though. I sure would feel better if I could hear you say the words 'I know this isn't my fault.'"

And for a second something seemed to ripple in the margin of air between their arms, a kind of opening, but if so, it was unintelligible. He stood completely motionless, lest he let on that he'd sensed anything at all . . . Then the moment (if it was one) was fading, and nothing had changed yet, nothing outward anyway, nothing of her posture save the lifting of a boot to scratch the back of a leg, nothing of the gulls save for a few substitutions in the scrum, a few call-ups and demotions; nothing of the sky save perhaps for the faint expansion of a rift halfway out, a momentary brightness dull on the water.

"Hey, I don't suppose you heard that couple through the wall last night?" he heard himself blurt, maybe just to show her how extremely unconcerned he was. Or startle her into a smirk. Then, because he knew he shouldn't have said it: "I almost wanted to send flowers."

But whatever connection may have passed between them was already gone again; she might have been preparing to lean her shorn head out over the boardwalk and spit. And this terrible need he felt to dance back from the void, hadn't it been the cause of half the failures in his life to date? (*Act as if, dammit. Leap.*) He nudged her arm, and in the perfectly blank look she now turned on him, he could have read any last thing he wanted: relief, doubt, reproach, disregard, or a willingness to be dragged along behind him forever because what the fuck difference did it make? Still: they'd had that moment, hadn't they?

"Anyway, what say we go grab a bite while stuff remains open? It's not lost on me that you ate hardly anything last night, and this time of year, half these places don't serve dinner. I can show you where I used to work. And along the way, you'll get to see some of those sights I promised."

And now here came Ethan Aspern and his daughter down a boardwalk on the Eastern Shore, walking. Day-bright daylight, a diffusion of yellow-white sky; a few benched twentysomethings on the nod and some beachgoing figures in a distant mist that could have been from the jetties but seemed CGI'd in for effect . . . But when, at length, they reached what had been the HoJo, he found only chain link enclosing a slag-heap, and various signs from a successor or opportunist advertising the Acheron Diner on Twenty-Ninth Street, halfway back up the peninsula. He laced fingers through the fencing and sought shapes in the rubble. Tried to figure out what if anything he should be feeling now. Thought of something Sarah had said once about how, after man split the atom, the next race had been for some supernova that would leave the works of capital intact. And then of third-form year, before he'd seen all that addiction would cost him, raiding Mom's CDs and Moira's cassettes for a mixtape for one of his targets. Of Morrissey singing, "Come, come, come, nuclear bomb"; followed by, of all things, Simon & Garfunkel's "The Dangling Conversation." Montage effect: sometimes you didn't realize until later what it was a mixtape was really saying. And one would want to say now, as at the end of that Joyce story, that the sadness fell generally over everything, the living and the dead. But this was Ocean City in November, so the only living souls this far south and close to the water seemed to be the two Asperns themselves.

Or themselves and those gulls. Ranging north along the boardwalk, they had retreated to the guardrail pylons as if to illustrate some axiom of number theory—exactly one per pylon, no more no less—and as he came near enough each post to touch, its occupant would rear back a few feet into the sky and then hover there with great beats of its wings until the threat had passed. Even how much of themselves they could fold up inside them like that seemed miraculous the first dozen or so times. After that, it hovered between diverting and creepy.

But now came a smell of popcorn. And not just any popcorn . . . Fisher's popcorn! It seemed exactly the thing to pierce his daughter's Black Friday gloom; for a couple summers there in middle school he'd practically lived on the stuff, stopping through with Judd to replenish whatever calories he'd burned off surfing and to rehydrate with a slushee the size of his head. That quickening he'd felt glimpsing the candied colors, gold and orange and Old Bay–flavored popcorn in tubes beneath the counter . . . It seemed a kind of miracle that the Fisher's kiosk wouldn't be shuttered for the offseason, but then, neither was the haunted house farther down, a middle-aged carnie in a fleece snapping her gum out front. Only when he drew Jolie over would he discover that the multicolored tubes had been drained. Even the regular popcorn now sat unattended in a dumpy vitrine, behind a cardboard clock reading **WILL RETURN**. Still, to give up now was beyond his abilities. He leaned in and filled two empty sleeves, counted out six singles to leave on the counter, under the napkin box. Naturally, Jolie refused to take any.

"You sure?" he said. "It's Fisher's."

Still nothing.

Then the wind died and the haunted house's half-assed organ drew his eye south again, to the pier where one of the two amusement parks called the Jolly Roger stretched out to sea. The rinky-dink arcade at the entrance was for some reason still open, or uncloseable, or at any rate didn't appear to have doors, just archways gaping like neither salt nor sleet nor stormwater could touch the machines inside. None of which appeared altered since his boyhood, apart from a colossal dance game in the far corner where a willowy Asian kid with the kind of moustache Eddie would have called a pussy-tickler moved beautifully to unheard music. Closer in were the bleeps and blurps of sideshow games and the current Top 40, piped in from hidden speakers. "Check it out, Skee-Ball . . . this used to be my favorite." Three tries for three tickets cost four quarters, making six games a steal at five bucks. The tickets—now credits—came on a logoed-plastic card-looking thing. He tried to remember how much he had left in the bank after his earlier haggling with the hotel guy. But easier just to dig out his debit card and feed it into the card machine, see if it worked. "You want to play?" he asked Jolie. "I should warn you, I'm kind of a professional."

The second card, with its leering skull, got dipped in a different machine. After a sequence of synth-tones chunkier than he remembered, a queue of balls came rumbling like fallen coconuts into a slot adjoining the lane. He hesitated only slightly before reaching for one with the hand he'd been using to eat the popcorn. "My friend Eddie and I used to come in here after work sometimes." As Jolie stood beside him, giving the impression of crossing her arms without actually crossing her arms, he bullshitted some instruction involving topspin and angles. Then he bowled his first ball up the ramp, which sent it caroming among the smaller collars of the holes higher up. Justice seemed to compel his rejection, if not complete humiliation. Instead, his ball dropped into the fifty-pointer, triggering an electronic orgasm capped by a spinning red siren and a flood of further credits . . . which of course was how they hooked you.

He would play the whole next game; then another. And then another. He tried to remind himself to knock this off, offer his extra plays to Jolie, from whom even just some wordless interjection here—a groan, an eye-roll, a clank of the tongue-ring— might have eased the tension sucking him deeper, but in the end it took the growl of his own stomach to stop him. How long had he been letting himself go on like this? It was now well past lunchtime. Probably edging on toward dinner. "Are you as hungry as I am?"

She had this way of almost not even blinking.

Breaking through to her, then, was going to require something even bigger, something more, something with a feeling too large to be swallowed, further terror and awe to cut the delight. Out beyond the darkening bones of the next set of arches was the coaster called the Looping Star. Every two minutes fifty-two seconds (he'd timed it once, trying to pin down the lag between how long the ride felt and how long it actually took) it would racket past the arcade's open exit, luring you farther in. Besides, he now had all these credits to burn. Jolie could have just refused to follow, he told himself, but as he made his way toward the gathering roar he found her trailing along, Bartleby-like, only not expressing a preference.

And what they encountered fifty yards out would in his surf-rat days have been a kind of answered prayer: the coaster so empty you could jump off at the end and then rush back around to get on again, your intoxication never having to end. The problem now was that there was no carnie around to run it, just a chain across the top of the platform stairs. And this seemed a different order of recklessness from the popcorn, or the hepatitic Skee-Balls; he

wasn't so crazy (was he?) as to try to board the coaster unsuper-
vised in the automated pauses between runs. In fact, his whole
afternoon seemed suddenly ass-backward. Here he was, dragging
his teenaged daughter through the stations of his youth, trying to
save her from her feelings . . . Yet he'd been neither brave enough
nor self-effacing enough to abide the memory of what those feelings actually were, the murderous intensity that got that extra bit
worse each time the rush ran out.

For some reason they'd followed the windings of the ropeline
toward the bottom of the stairs rather than go over or under the
empty ropes. And now he turned to face her. "Listen, Jolie. I think
I'm finally understanding what you've been trying to put across
since last night. Or not *put across*, exactly . . . but you know what
I'm saying. I'm saying it hasn't been fair of me, to keep you on
for another day like this . . . Or for that matter to try to get you
to ride the Looping Star with me right now. But as to whether
to turn around and head back, I'm ready to let you be the one in
charge."

Her look was uninterpretable, yet made him question his own
motives almost immediately.

"And before you decide: *please* don't feel like you have to stay
on out of some kind of guilt you shouldn't be feeling in the
first place, okay? Because I know a little something about that."
Another breath. "See, this thing with your cousin . . ." And again,
heavier: another. "The truth is, Jolie, I'd already snuck him some
of my chocolate bar a couple hours before he got hold of yours."

Still with this belief that a secret might bind people to each other,
despite all the evidence that it only binds them to themselves.

"And as long as we're at it, I'd already drizzled Moira's pie with
a shit-ton of maple syrup, so he would have ended up eating that,
too. She didn't tell me about the diabetes, I was trying to help
that pie become its best self, I didn't know about the nut thing,
but there's no excuse. *I* was the one who tried to saddle you with
a Baby Ruth you never asked for, just like *I* was the one hauling
you down here in the first place. So the onus or whatever rests
with me. You don't owe a damn thing to anyone. We could leave
right now, if that's what you want."

Not that she could tell him.

"Or if you wanted to wait till Izzy officially got moved to recovery, I don't see how your mom could come down much harder on me than she's already threatening to. Especially if you were the one to explain to her what happened . . . maybe put it in writing or something, I don't know. And then I'd take the heat."

But had it worked after all, finally? As he watched, Jolie got out her phone, held it up for him to see. Its screen was smashed nearly past recognition, some kind of puncture wound in the center as if she'd stabbed it with a sharp object, the black glass around reflecting a million different shards of crazily angled sky. This must have been what she'd been up to with those tools in McGonagall's van, before or after shaving her hair. But did the phone still work? And either way—what would she be trying to communicate? That she was seeking to smash the way back to the child she'd been, or to shatter any path forward? That she was trying to stay here, or to go?

And now a thickset lady carnie with a money-belt and a topknot—the same one as before or her twin—came striding through the empty spaces among the rides, keys ajangle. As she unlocked the chain and an onshore gusted off the waves, Ethan would again have the feeling of some aperture trying to open between him and his daughter: that strange sense of being so close to a particular kind of suffering he knew had once been his own. The seatbelts from back then had been replaced with shoulder harnesses, but the carnie didn't offer any help, you had to pull them down into the locking position yourself. And before he could figure out which one of the two of them, father or daughter, had actually decided to board the coaster, they'd be ratcheting, balkily, toward the top, where he could now see not only the arcade roof, hotels, the water tower, but also, beyond the inland forests across the bay, the very place he'd been trying to keep his mind off all afternoon . . . because it was also the place he'd turned to once before, half a lifetime ago, after he'd found himself out of reach of every desire: not these amusements and diversions piled up mirthlessly along the shore, but, shadowing the distance a half-mile from his childhood home, the faded green bulk of Keel Hill.

16

FOR OVER A MONTH NOW, as far as anyone knows, Albert Kupferberg's days have been tennis whites and hitting around at the club, followed by the steam room and a coffee break and whatever other alibi might account for his being gone so long. Next it's on to the bathroom to wet his hair with a paper towel. A spritz of aftershave to cover any sweat left over from his exertions. And then home in the big gold Volvo he loves only the more as time darkens it, floating along these leafy culverts that coil through the secret Bronx, the radio dial in its palpable resting spot where midday culture shows yammer on in the background, and him with his own remaining secret: that not in years, not even in the city, has he felt himself more alive than he does now. Then a real shower, actual coffee, and (if there is any time left before Eleanor returns home from phone-banking for the Bronx County Democrats and Jolie from school), a little siesta before the caffeine jolts him awake in his study overlooking the creek.

After they'd moved out here in the fall of '01, he'd tried to convince himself that this was the distance he'd been needing to complete his magnum opus, the book that would trace the secret connections between the Irish and Harlem Renaissances, the hidden channels linking a people's pain to its art. Instead, when he'd written at all, it was antiwar petitions to run in the MLA bulletin and letters to the editors of *The Nation* and *Tikkun* and *The New York Review of Books*, full of whatever degree of dudgeon he could work up that day. In the great world-repair project, there always seemed to be some other, less noble claim on the attention, didn't there; the more so as one got older. Whether that pointed to a failure of his utopianism or of his pragmatism, a change in Albert or in everything else, it would be hard to say, but the lack of progress—and specifically the lack of oneself in its vanguard—was a consistent disappointment.

When one was young, of course, one took the sturm and the drang as evidence of a whole cosmos wheeling meaningfully about oneself: a hopeful sort of feeling. And obviously, things couldn't go on like they had before. Not like *this*, he remembers thinking, in the great historical lurch from Vietnam to Reagan, amid what had seemed a systematic effort to sack, suck dry, and destroy all that was best in mankind. And in womankind, for whom Albert Kupferberg had always had a fine appreciation . . . as indeed he began whisking certain nubile young colleagues and graduate students off to hotel rooms to illustrate, at hours when he was ostensibly at conferences or out practicing his groundstrokes.

Then one blinked and was older, and all the ferment and mediocrity and injustice were still right there in the very places where one had expected to find something better. That old vaudeville duo immanence and imminence again: utopia turned out to be always *at* hand, but never *in* it. Just more of the irksome myopia, the enraging quiescence, of *The New York Times*, like a lover one could no longer keep faith with but had given too much of oneself to leave. Among the parlor games to which he and his daughter had almost exclusively kept their conversations since the year Eleanor had kicked him out (before he'd consented to her terms to be let back in) was what life might have been like without *The New York Times*.

"No less hellish, probably," he'd opined, at some point early in 2002, while Sarah's marriage imploded and the war-drums grew louder. "Just without the daily columns of fine print."

"Or maybe those were the real distraction all along," she'd replied, sadly. "Maybe we'd discover they'd been blinding us to a paradise that was only ever inches away."

Which was when he knew Sarah had gone beyond him; there was obviously a reference to his own marriage here, but he was no longer capable of the hermeneutic magic that might have winkled it out. (Which in turn just goes to show that this paragon of her childhood, Albert the conqueror, Albert the exile, perhaps hadn't had enough of the truly distinguished thing. That is: of imagination.)

But now time is running short. Soon he will no longer be able to rest from his amusements, or however Eleanor construes it. On a Friday rebroadcast, a radio guest is talking about something called "neural pruning." And he's seeing the lopped branches piled in the alleys of his mind like the cleared mass of juniper and mock orange he'd stacked in a corner of the yard years ago and never gotten around to bundling for collection. Incorrigible as ever, he wonders what that pile might have turned into by now. What might yet turn out to be living there, toward the end of the day.

Retirement for such a man had been a crisis, obviously, though he'd let no one know how much of one. The departmental ins and outs were too nuanced, too game-theoretical, for phrases such as "arm-twist" or "kicking and screaming" to quite apply. Easier to say that he'd been in no greater hurry to relinquish his lectern than Ferdinand the bull to relinquish his flowers in that picture-book he used to read to Sarah in her youth . . . (Or was it that the classroom had been his arena and that, having extracted through at least some covert pawing and stamping a favorable position at Barnard for his daughter, he'd allowed himself to be eased out to pasture under whatever cork tree?) Manhattan being Manhattan, office space was at a premium, so that even the most distinguished professor emeritus could now be offered no more than a dedicated carrel in the inferno of Low Library. And for reasons of both orthopedics and pride, his carreling days were behind him . . . *Et in Riverdale ego*, as he'd put it in a letter to the new chair. He had gone on to quote *Lear* mock-seriously but had perhaps strayed into mock-mock-seriously (the new chair, in addition to being a Shakespearean, was a reader-response feminist). And how much of the joke was really left after you learned you could spend your whole first year post officio going around in a bathrobe? Sometimes he would change out of it between the time Eleanor left the house and the time she came home, but just as often not; there was no one around to care. The second year was when he'd discovered TV . . .

But then came the night of the knock on the door. What had they even been watching then? He fights for the memory mostly

as an index to how late it had been. Always hard to tell out here
beyond the ambit of the city lights, where no one but the guy
delivering your dinner knocks after five p.m. Probably one of those
police procedurals that recalled Sarah's ex-con of an ex-husband.
What it was was slightly raining. He could never remember to
put on the porchlight, a job previously arrogated to the doorman.
Did so now and brought his eye round to the peephole, expecting some badly whiskered immigrant kid already trying to fix his
face into an apology—wrong house, Mister, sorry. Found only
the top of a moistened fedora. But opened the door and there
she'd been, his granddaughter, and it was as if he'd never really
seen her before. It would be hard to say exactly wherein resided
the distress. She wasn't crying, or if she was it would have been
hard to tell, since tears weren't really the kid's style, she was like
her mother in this, like her grandmother in this (like Albert in
the year he'd returned from his sister's burial in Jerusalem and
quietly asked Eleanor what was demanded to be taken back). Nor
was Jolie significantly paler than when he'd last seen her, at that
insufferable lunch in June. If pressed, Albert would have said it
was something in the eyes—the way they kept to a region of his
chin but almost seemed to look past it, as if she couldn't afford at
least one of the following: to see, to be seen. It was a look his own
mirror had been giving him back for the better part of three years.

And before Eleanor, who knew how to do such things, could
do it, he'd pushed the storm door open, touched Jolie on her arm
as she passed.

Who told him she would need that? Would need a grandpar-
ent not to ask what was wrong or even was she okay—would need
instead the touch, the sleeve of Lorna Doones rustled up in the
kitchen and pushed across the table of the breakfast nook to the
place where she eventually settled herself (even if she couldn't
take one until after he'd stepped out into the dining room to
check the mail tray again)? "I suppose you're not going to tell us
what's going on," he said, back turned, flipping envelopes, listening to the rustling plastic. Hearing his own self-regard. Fighting
it. "But I should probably make up a bed in the guestroom. And
then call your mother to let her know you're here."

He couldn't stop himself, though, from going to touch her

again, placing a hand on the hands picking at each other somewhere in the vicinity of another cookie. And for an ever-so-slight
moment before she was recalled to herself, Jolie would forget to
flinch.

"Hey," he said then, in a voice that seemed to come from someplace else . . . from a library on the Upper West Side fifteen years
earlier, where some decisive words had once come out all wrong.
"Whatever it is, sweetie, is just life, okay? Or at any rate, you're
always welcome here."

And that was about the extent of it. In the morning, they would
again be of two minds, if not more (though at least one of them
no longer quite so alone). Jolie would have nothing further to
say about why she'd come, or indeed about anything at all. Later,
calling Sarah again, Eleanor would gather the details that only
made everyone's motives that much harder to parse. His dubious ex-son-in-law, the terrier who'd affixed himself to the pant-
leg of their life, had failed to return to L.A., and now was said to
have taken Jolie to see that superhero play on Broadway done by
what's-her-name, with the masks and the puppets and the obsessive restaging of myths . . . but the main indication from the therapist, according to Sarah (according to Eleanor), had been that it
was Sarah herself who was now somehow the problem.

It was thus arranged that Jolie would stay with her grandparents for a while. Albert had even volunteered to drive her down
to the school should she miss the bus. He'd known kids growing up who'd commuted from Flatbush all the way to Horace
Mann; how could a month of driving her in to the Village be
worse, in this big yellow car? Maybe he'd missed having a kid in
the house. Maybe he'd missed it the first time around. What was
never missed, by Jolie (though he sometimes wished it would be),
was the Bronx 7 bus.

Still, it's remarkable how the old muscle memory snaps back,
how in the space of this last month he's become his old self again,
or the self his old self had almost stopped believing in: penning
a letter of apology to the feminist chair, pleading for his carrel
back and for off-street parking for the Volvo; and then these long
sweaty hours in the campus library, poring over *Ulysses* once more,
maybe for the last time, and in the rests between chapters trawl-

ing JSTOR for the latest scholarship, tinkering with the manuscript now on the seat beside him, the one he will soon pretend
to need the girl's help editing; reorienting his commute around
public transit schedules, the twin pinnacles of Jolie's departure
and return. And then the TV at night, the simple pleasure of sitting in silence with the wife whose loyalty he's never until now felt
he deserved and their one granddaughter, half watching whatever
garbage passes for entertainment. He's even gotten used to the
odd rhythms of the dinner hour, to himself and Eleanor taking
turns supplying the talk Jolie won't or can't, where alone they
might have just traded sections of the paper. And perhaps in his
preoccupation with a person other than himself, Albert Kupferberg hasn't quite absorbed what his wife said last night about
another change in plans, about no longer needing to go into the
city to deliver Jolie's clothes—Jolie having cleaned out her dresser
already. At any rate, he is unprepared as he goes to signal his turn
into the one-car drive to find another car in his place, and his wife
on the stoop with Sarah plus a small, dark-haired man he seems
to recall from somewhere. Bright Mercury, he thinks for a second (his memory not quite having caught up with him), bearing
news that Jolie too, just out of view in this version of the telling,
has been brought home after however many twists and turns to
the Ithaca of herself, restored to all her powers and ready to share
again her voice with him at last . . .

17

"BUT HOW ABOUT I JUST drop a dime to the FBI, how's that?" Sarah hears herself say, sending her handbag hurtling toward the dining room table as though throwing it wide of an explosion. Then chases Eleanor back to the hall. "I mean, how did you possibly see this playing out, Mom? I come home to meet you and Jolie and, surprise, there's Ethan instead? So I'm holding you almost as responsible as him—which you'd know if you ever checked your messages."

And then there is (so to speak) her fucking father. "Slow down a minute, Sarah," he says. "Responsible for what? And where is Jolie, exactly?"

"Jesus Christ, Daddy, where do you think? Still with Ethan. Well? I know one of you knows something about this. He didn't just slip in here under cover of darkness and steal her away without anyone noticing. And you—" She turns to find Brandon Koussoglou still hovering on the threshold with that irksome innocence of his, as if her indulgence has turned him from a shiny new boyfriend into one of those manchildren in beer ads on TV. "Are you going to just stand there?" She's aware that her daughter's disappearance is in no wise his fault (to whatever degree it's not Ethan's and her parents', it is obviously her own), but this has been building in her through a night of tossing and turning in Brandon's too-short childhood bed, her mother continuing to dodge her calls, and then sitting for hours essentially frozen on the deadlocked Merritt Parkway in a car his dad has lent them, unable to get a cell signal out. And so, at the very moment she's all but ordering Brandon in from the stoop, she is also confirming that whatever's between them is over. And the pain of it is strik-ing: to have been handed at the age of eighteen only the one true love to last the whole of the rest of your life. "Right, guys, sorry. This is Mr. Koussoglou . . . Jolie's ex-social-studies-teacher."

For his part, Brandon remains mild in his leather jacket. Then he blurts, belatedly, "You have a lovely home," and all of a sudden she wants to kill him again. Or kill him and kiss him in a single stroke, essentially erase him, this *Homo millennius*, twiggy indie-rock man. A wave of lightheadedness overtaking her, she asks to sit down.

And is again surprised: it was supposed to be her mother leap-ing in to help. All through her growing up, Eleanor Kupferberg had been the one standing ready with helmets and kneepads and tubes of Neosporin while Albert muttered to himself in the spare room or stretched reading on the loveseat under the vibrational equivalent of a "Do Not Disturb" sign. Yet it is Albert now taking her elbow to steer her back to the dining room, his tennis outfit jiggling over his paunch, his chest lavishly thatched above the collar. Even before he sits her down at the table with its fruitless fruitbowl and the bay-window view of what might be Colorado until she adjusts to the left and sees Yonkers, it occurs to her to wonder whether her parents are getting along better these days, and what if anything that has to do with their softening toward Ethan . . . and also how it was they had stayed together in the first place, knowing about each other what they knew.

Her mother's alteration had seemed to start the morning after the one and only time Sarah and Ethan had ever slept together here, when she herself had come downstairs so bleary-eyed. Her mom, meanwhile, had been buoyant: a city girl all her life, and look at this! Pointing out little hooks in the cabinets from which decorative mugs could hang just as soon as she purchased them. And then standing at the bay window exclaiming over squirrels like there weren't squirrels in Central Park. On the other hand (as Sarah would end up arguing immeasurable years later at the close of her dissertation), everything was context, wasn't it, every-thing transformed by the ground it stood upon and the position you adopted to observe it. No, the real problem was where to draw the lines. What connected to what, versus didn't. Mom for example had wanted to see this dining table as an extension of the one from the city, filled with friends at holidays like in *Hannah and Her Sisters* (only minus the husband's philandering). Whereas Dad had always preferred Dr. Johnson—*to be tired of the city is to be tired of life*—so what was the context *he'd* been imagining for all of this? Had he thought it would now be easier to pull off his affairs, under cover of the long commute and his old tennis ruse?

About her own husband, Sarah had known from the start that he'd rather die than cheat—had seen it as the sign that she and Ethan would always be together. Yet every indication is that Mom and Dad had outlasted them, taken their Thanksgiving meal here for the umpteenth year as a party of two—another thing for Sarah to feel bad about. Then again, if this is what a marriage becomes in the end, a beautiful formal dining room where no one ever laughs or fights or fucks or cries or dreams the way they used to, then maybe it's time to let go of the larger guilt, about choosing to save herself and Jolie instead of Ethan . . . to save herself and Jolie *from* Ethan. Because it would have been no less of a hell to lose him this other way.

Her father continues to stare at her, the tiny white nubs of his whiskers rippling in the crags of his neck. It is when her mother's nervous chatter with Brandon floats in from the hall that she realizes Dad's been silent several minutes. And maybe this is where Jolie gets it: between the bursts of grandiloquence that make you feel somehow flattened, he has as many different shades of silence, her father, as there are of the color white. This isn't his abstracted silence, or the pedagogical one where he's pressuring you to come up with an insight worthy of articulation, but a listening, an almost feminine quiet. Only after it's apparent that she's still trapped inside herself does he think to go first. "All right, sweetie. Walk me through what's going on again?"

"You really don't know?"

"If I did, would I ask?"

She fights an urge to hold it back out of sheer gall. "Well, I can't say for certain until Mom stops hiding behind the teacher, but I gather she and Ethan cooked up some plan that he would come and fetch Jolie from the Wednesday recital—"

"I was there, I thought you were read in on that!" And, after a pause, "Though perhaps she let me think it . . ."

"—and then I guess he was supposed to dazzle me by being

there to drop her off at my place last night instead of the two of you—"

"In addition to the two of us," he says. "Or to your mother, at least, in the latest revisions."

"Except Ethan's revising, too: Forty-odd hours on, where are they?"

"But that's the man you married, isn't it? I'm not sure I understand why you're blowing in here so hot, Sarah, if he says he's just a day late to drop her off."

"Daddy, are you listening to me at all? It's not like I was consulted ahead of time. I didn't agree to any of this. And now that he finally has her, I have no idea when he's going to bring her home."

"But you have to know he will soon enough: that's him, too. Slip, correct, repeat," he says. And if she hadn't already sensed something was off with her dad, she would now. She's gotten so used to being the one in the middle, explaining, defending . . . while he's always treated Ethan as whatever was the goy version of a schlemiel, unfit to touch the hem of Sarah's garment. "As for your mother, it seems she may have used a little subterfuge," he continues. "But then, one of us probably had that coming . . ."

"Oh, for Pete's sake, Daddy, not now . . ."

"I only mean that your mom's done the best she could with what she was given. The current state of affairs is clearly not serving Jolie. And can it really be right to just let the kid turn aside and brood, Sarah, with no chance for the offending parent to redeem himself? Or at least, for her to get a long enough look at him to decide whether he's still capable of change?"

"It's not like I've *wanted* to keep the two of them apart, Daddy, any more than I want to get the police involved, but on the phone last night he was basically refusing to give her back."

He has turned away to check something on his own phone, and for a second she wonders again if he's paying attention. "Well, refusing or forgetting," he says finally, "Ethan seems to have blown off the custody laws already, so it's not like you've got that to hold over him." He puts the screen facedown; studies the back of his hand. "But maybe if you tried offering a little leeway . . . ?"

"Do you think I haven't done that already? I gave him until noon today. But Vikas says he's seen neither hide nor hair of Jolie, and I haven't been able to reach either of them. Ethan's got his phone turned off, and now something must have happened to hers, too. Not that she'll ever talk to me on it anyway . . ."

"So let's try them in person, air things out face-to-face. I've got the Volvo waiting right there."

"That's what's scaring me, Daddy. He's been in the city since June, but I don't even know which side of the river to start looking on, much less on which street. And what kind of a mother leaves her daughter loose to wander New York at a time like this?"

"We never knew where you were half the time, and look how well you turned out."

"And supposing he doesn't bring her back tomorrow?" she says. "Or the next day?" And rises to turn toward the sideboard with its disordered stack of mail. She hates this, hates the tears in her voice. How it feels to have to try to explain this side of Ethan, the one that he always kept facing away. "I mean, what if the reason he's acting out like this is that he's . . . you know, doing it again? What if he's back to drinking, or doing drugs? With Jolie in his care? I'm supposed to just— Wait . . . is she getting mail here now?"

The writing on the tray's padded envelope looks almost like a thing remembered: Jolie Aspern, c/o Dr. and Mrs. A. Kupferberg. And then on the back, in the same blunt scrawl,

2 Whom It May Concern...

"Oh, that arrived two days ago, she forgot to open it," Eleanor says from the doorway. "Doubtless from a classmate, the penmanship's atrocious—you can take it to her just as soon as we know her whereabouts."

But Sarah isn't listening; already she has torn the top off the mailer and removed several battered sheets of copy-paper covered in another hand, one she knows like her own, and is drinking up the words the way she used to when she was a kid, as if she can't gulp them down fast enough. There's a disorientation at first—Who is this *"they"* in the opening line; and *"despite"* . . . well, what, exactly? Who is being addressed? But at the mention of a *"Chinese place downstairs,"* a tingle sets in. She knows this rented flat, these people, this sleeping child in the next room, except that in this telling, the writer, her daughter, is somehow also her ex-husband. And as she reads on, the force of the immersion makes it hard to breathe: *"The messenger bag where he's stashed a last pill and one of his few remaining liquor bottles . . ."* They never talked about her finding his stash, the morning of his arrest. How does Jolie even know these things?

Well, okay, the drinking: Jolie had tried that last summer, plausibly even as a way to feel close to him. The problem is, Sarah can feel the pressure of something underneath, a great old sadness welling up, *"weeping . . . unvaporized . . . waking Sarah up and risking the truth . . ."* And wait—what is this bit toward the end about *"the psych ward where now I sit, writing"*? Because Jolie has been admitted to the hospital only once, long before the drinking started . . . and had been cleared to go just as soon as they'd found someone official to say she was okay. And still everywhere is this aqueousness, this *being dragged back under.* She knows that feeling, she thinks. Lord knows Ethan does. But this is her *daughter*—her daughter, having to feel it to write it.

Her daughter, sitting and writing all this in Bellevue Hospital, in April of 2011 . . . when she'd been rescued off the subway tracks only hours before.

"Oh my God," she says. Jolie had been drunk down there, not just on the Fourth of July. And louder, when Brandon pokes his head around the door: "Oh my God—are you still here?"

"Someone's station wagon's boxing me in. Why, did something happen?" And then, seeing the page that's just dropped to the floor, stoops to give it a look. And stays crouched for a while, clearing his throat, and is slow to come up again. "I guess she must have found a way to break it to you, then."

"Break to me *what*?"

"Uh, the thing I've been trying to help you see all year? That Jolie's maybe not doing so hot with the loss of her father?"

"You've been trying to help me see no such thing!"

"But I have, Sarah. Or I did, if you'd ever let yourself listen. It's like she said, though: you make it awfully hard for other people to acknowledge failure. Which is more or less a direct quote, by the way, from when I caught her with Jägermeister at the Valentine's Day dance."

"With *Jägermeister?* In fucking February? And instead you invite me in there and start talking about Clifford fucking Geertz?"

"She clearly needed to feel someone was in her corner . . . And I thought maybe I'd dropped enough hints that you'd get her some emotional support!"

"*In loco parentis,* Brandon. You were her teacher, not her peer. And she's been getting support."

"Well, exactly."

"That's what all this was supposed to be, was fucking support. But only *months* later, after what you're making me start to think was some kind of . . . some kind of cry for help."

"What?" This is Eleanor, choosing exactly the wrong time to return.

"And now thanks to you here I am with no return address on what feels like another one, and it's up to my ex-husband, her fucking *kidnapper,* to keep her safe in a city of eight million people until I can find her again."

"But are we even sure they're in the city?" her mom says quietly, and swallows. "I'm remembering that, among other things, she packed her passport."

"Oh my God," Sarah says again.

Bizarrely, it is her father who is the voice of reason. "Okay, Eleanor, calm down. I'll grant that this maybe sounds a bit worse than any of us were putting together . . ."

"I should send out one of those goddamn AMBER alerts, is what I should do. Bring the cops screaming in."

He unlocks his phone, slides it toward her until she can see his search results from earlier. The custody laws. The penalties for breaking them. And Ethan with his record. "We need to think carefully, Sarah. But if it's what you want—"

"Who cares what I want? How else am I supposed to get to her?"

She can almost see his great brain, after years in dry-dock, churning into motion. "You say you don't know where Ethan's staying, Sarah, but . . . are there friends you could call, maybe scare up some kind of lead?"

"Ethan doesn't have friends, Daddy, you should know this. He has people he fixates on, dreams can break him out of himself, and then locks back out as punishment once he sees that they can't."

He takes it in without even flinching. "I meant friends of Jolie's, honey."

And briefly her universe gets reconfigured. Since Ethan's last relapse, when Jolie was in fifth grade, the question of a social world has been eclipsed, along with all else in their little two-person life, by the matter of just getting through the day. But now that she's seeing the last year's events from a different angle, what stuns her is how barren that life appears. At some point, the procession of schoolmates and colleagues and Upper West Side neighbors had fallen away, and Jolie's whole world had seemed to reorganize itself around tribes, the swim team, the orchestra camp, the clique of girls who wanted to hang out by Grant's Tomb or the pizza place on 110th. For her bat mitzvah (the last milestone for which she'd seemed willing to accept any celebration at all) that was what she'd wanted, she'd said: no reception in the assembly room to follow, not even one of the scavenger hunts they used to organize in the park for her birthday—just the promise of paid-for slices to lure a few girls to Koronet Pizza. And Sarah's response had been, great. Easier to bring off than a real party. But she remembers now being startled to see the number of kids who'd hung around after the service. Four. Including Jolie. No, if she really asks herself who Jolie's friends have been after the change of schools—or whether, behind the blur of extracurriculars, there even *are* friends, it's like she's peering down a long dark corridor at her own adolescence . . . where against the wall a figure now appears: the girl who was supposed to sleep over the night of the dance and whose looping print this might even now be on the envelope, sending back Jolie's coded transmission. She'd spoken to the father by phone to arrange the sleepover, Nigerian last name, Londoner by accent, but hadn't thought to save his number, and now finds herself, at the precise moment it seems most critical to remember, blanking on the girl's name. Chastity, Temperance, Fidelity . . .

"Brandon?"

His head appears again around the doorframe. "No, sorry, you're right, I should go, but I'm blocked in—"

"Shut up for a second, though. What was the name of Jolie's friend, from *Into the Woods*?"

He blinks, blameless in his Perspex glasses. "You can't mean Precious Ezeobi."

"Right: Precious. Do you think you could pull up a number?"

"Um . . . why would Precious's number be in my personal phone? We'd have to go through the school office, and it's closed for the holidays." Where Ethan would already be charging head-long ahead, like catastrophe was his calling. "And besides, I'm not sure Precious is going to take you anywhere you want to go—" Then, seeing her face: "Oh, all right."

It is already dark enough that the entry preserved in his contacts glows like a candle when he sets it on the table before her ("Precious—home"), as though they were still on some curve of possibility and not in her parents' dining room with her father opposite, exploring the outer limits of his capacity for a cocked eyebrow. But Sarah hardly notices any of this. It was a month ago, that night in the apartment with Brandon tugging on his clothes, that she first admitted to herself that the person she's becoming is someone other than she ever imagined she'd be. Now she is realizing she's going to have to expose her own failings as a mom to a perfect stranger. And never has the fucking smartphone seemed so misnamed as at this moment when the planets roar in the gaps between satellites and the reason she'd even purchased it in the first place—the fear that she might otherwise lose her daughter— becomes real . . .

18

ON SECOND THOUGHT, what had come to him out there, as if breaking through the surface of the earth—what he'd glimpsed from the top of the Looping Star—was actually something of a personal Golgotha. Yet it had also, at that other hour in his life when he'd felt at such a loss for a way forward, been the one place he'd known to go. Then the coaster had begun its plunge, which Jolie had endured in silence, exiting no paler than before. Like a ghost she'd trailed him back to the van, and thence for supplies to the CVS at the northern end of Ocean City, and now, there being so little up that way to slow them, they were flying back over the long Assawoman Bridge, from whose apogee he could already see the sun sinking behind the hill, staining the waters of the bay a deep garnet. The memory was fading again; he could no longer have said why he felt such an urgency to reach it ahead of the sunset—only that taking Jolie there after all these years would obviously mean something. More, anyway, than an early-bird dinner at the diner, oyster crackers and offseason calamari.

Back on the mainland, a V of crepuscular pines was making everything seem darker, but he reminded himself not to worry, they had a while to go yet before the lightshow began in earnest. Nor did he bother to point out the hospital as they passed it . . . and Moira's too he evaded, and of course Ducky's, adopting a tortured, somewhat elliptical route off the bypass. Eventually, though, the trees fell back and the shambles of the business district hove into view. If by day North Main had looked inert—and if by night its lit-up signs might still lend a luster of vitality (big

if)—then at twilight his hometown seemed a third thing altogether. Ethan had honestly believed as late as yesterday that just
the romance of the place, his love for and hatred of it, might summon up some corresponding fire in his daughter, but the town's
true genre turned out to be zombie apocalypse: unable to die but
also, really, to live.

Still, at Keel Hill, this changelessness began to look like a gift—
for the setup here had been genuinely good to begin with . . . or
at least, you wouldn't have wanted it any other way. Along its
base, at right angles to the slope, ran a quiet residential street
lined to one side with multifamily homes. A yellow rebuke of egg
protein had hardened on someone's siding, but he couldn't have
guessed why; there'd been tenants, sure, who would occasionally
yell or threaten when the noise from on high got too raucous,
but all that ever seemed to come of it were these anodyne signs
out front of the houses. **PARK CLOSES AT DUSK. NOISE ORDINANCE.
NO LOITERING.**

On the other side of the street, however—the one they were
now crawling along—stretched a curbless berm of grass relieved
by dirt patches and the gnarled roots of aging trees. The township could have solved a lot of problems by making it illegal to
park here, but the berm, like the slope and the fenced-off area up
top with its old Martello tower and forest stretching out beyond,
belonged to the state of Maryland or to some arm of the GSA
(depending on whom you asked), leaving little room for municipal government. And from down here at the base, he recalled, it
was always easy to imagine that you'd missed the big finale until
you squinted up through the branches and spotted, way up the
hill, the shadows giving way to a line of peachy high contrast
you could almost see stealing skyward. Sometimes you'd hear the
sounds of guitars, of neohippie drums, and catch gleaming up
there, high as the eye could reach, a bonfire like a second sun . . .
as now, when the chemical smell of briquettes, burning, told him
to leave his own charcoal behind.

He decided not to show himself perturbed by unwanted company. As the wind ruffled his grocery sacks, he stooped to grope
among the trees' deadfall for two sticks of weenie-roasting proportions and waited for Jolie to emerge from the van. She wouldn't

quite go ahead of him toward the flames and voices, but no longer
would she follow, either; for a second, they might have been kids
bound by blood oath, waiting to see who'd jump first. Here again,
though, her silence revealed a silver lining: since she couldn't grill
him on exactly what it was they were doing here, or even protest
via posture or gait the long hump up the hill, he could choose to
pretend that some revelation was at hand. Another fifty yards and
he'd have brought her as far as he knew how to get from New
York, grandparents, new boyfriends (girlfriends) . . . whatever
back there besides himself had made her feel so helpless, robbed
her of her voice.

Admittedly, marching straight up the hill-face had its draw-
backs compared with sneaking through the woods as he'd more
typically done, but so long as they kept below the copperline of
dying sun, they would go unremarked by any of the smudges
seated or standing up there. What had seemed from ground level
a single group of them now resolved into several, clumped along
a hundred yards of storm fencing. The musicians were mostly
bunched at one end, a cluster of high schoolers or returned col-
legians from whom wafted an odor of pot. And where normally
these kids would have owned the whole hilltop, the group in the
prime viewing spot looked from this distance like full-blown
adults; drawing closer, Ethan could see the telltale loss of resil-
ience, the coarsening of forms.

Beside him, Jolie's breathing had grown audible. Was it possible the angle here was steeper than he remembered—or that,
with whatever of him she now carried inside her, she was chasing
a contact high? Or was it that his new exposure was already working, and she was about to open up and tell him everything? One
thing he was certain of: it wouldn't do to arrive at the top already
huffing, particularly if you weren't sure what awaited you there.
Trying to play it off as a planned thing, Ethan wedged the sticks
under his sack arm and reached for her elbow to stop her from
trudging ahead. But already she was turning, the light warm-
ing her face. He turned, too, trying to see it through her eyes.
Or if that proved impossible, then at least to look alongside her.
For here was the big moment: sunset, the reverse angle of that
early-spring morning at seventeen when he'd free-climbed the

Martello tower to learn what it might feel like to see daylight again. What it had felt like was that he was so goddamn lucky to be alive. But what was she thinking?

She was thinking, perhaps, that people wasted their time when they told each other not to look into the sun; unlike spitting into the wind or jamming a fork in the toaster, it was actively hard to do, so that only the worst sort of masochist would think to keep at it for more than a second.

And now the view was to the west-by-southwest, where beyond a thick carpet of blueblack pines the earth dropped toward the Chesapeake, bisecting a vast orange disc. The light out here felt all-consuming. A sound in the head like a blowtorch. When he touched her arm again, though: nothing. No response but to turn and continue her climb.

It was when their shadows skimmed the fire up top that the folks gathered around it seemed to twig to their presence, shading eyes against the inferno. Not to recognize any of these faces was a relief, but also a wound, in that no matter where he went these days, Ethan seemed destined to be merely tolerated. Or not even tolerated; a huge guy in flannel and a blaze-orange mesh cap was now rising to crash another log onto the fire, showering sparks upward as if to scare off the newcomers. Then, sunspots fading from his eyes, Ethan realized that the woman studying him from a dozen yards away was his ex-whatever-that-had-been. He raised the hand holding the sodas, catching a can that fell from the plastic rings before it could roll away. A beerkeg squatted nearby like a sentry, teetering slightly where the ground went flat. "Geez," he said, too loudly. "I wasn't expecting to find you up here, Natasha."

"You missed good fun last night," she said, but didn't budge from the grass where she sat. And when he came closer: "I kind of assumed you got cold feet and weren't going to show at all." In her voice was a note of reproach, like now that she was the one on home turf, and himself the visitor, she could afford to impose a penalty.

"How you got that whole keg up here I'm not even going to ask," he said. Then, quieter, so Jolie wouldn't hear about the invitation he must have been trying to forget: "Sorry, Thanksgiving itself got a little . . . complicated. I didn't think you'd still be around."

"You remember what my parents are like—if I had to spend another hour under their roof, there was going to be a murder."

Natasha's parents were among the many things he'd managed to forget about her, and parricide a topic he felt uniquely eager to avoid; yet Jolie was back at his side, and with the severe haircut, the piercings, the weight loss, it would soon become obvious, if it wasn't already, how fucked up it had been to have him as her dad. Maybe if he kept things moving, though, Natasha at least wouldn't notice the muteness. "Sorry, this is my daughter. Jolie."

There was no sign of shock that she was already a teenager; only a nod. "Nice meeting you, Jolie. My stepson's one of those goons rolling around in the grass over there. Andy, don't stain your pants, asshole!" And now he could make out here and there the little midgelike shadows of kids scampering back and forth. "And here comes Dennis, my husband. Den, Ethan and I shared a few scenes together back in junior high."

He was alarmed to see the trucker-capped guy come lumbering over to offer a Beowulfish hand. Maybe the cap was meant to be ironic, not menacing, since like Ethan he wore checked Vans? But no, even jocks wore checked Vans these days. And half the world seemed not to bother with wedding rings (or at strategic moments chose to conceal them). It was like some implosion of functions had ground every distinction that had ever struck him as meaningful or important to dust. Everyone just as good or as bad as everyone else. "Can I get you a beer, bud?" the guy said.

Jesus, could he? The sun itself might have been urging Ethan to drink. But perhaps too loudly, he said no thanks: "We're good with soda for now. And it's Ethan. Ethan Aspern, the rector's son."

As Dennis turned to greet Jolie, Ethan did his best to distract from her lack of engagement with a flourish of the drugstore sack, using the van's key to slit open the tofu dogs and skewering one on a stick. Weirdly, it seemed to work, or at least Dennis was none too swift on the uptake. And with the late rector's son and granddaughter apparently deemed not a threat by their lord and master, the company on the hill returned to its previous concerns of fire and keg and tunes—all except for Natasha, who'd fixed on him a curious look. "You really could have given a heads-up you'd be making a late appearance, Ethan, and given me some time to practice my lines."

He found he couldn't meet her gaze. "I wouldn't have known how to reach you. And anyway, like I said, I didn't think I'd still be here. You remember what a creature of impulse I am." As if to demonstrate, he opened a can of Mountain Dew, which promptly spurted foam he had to jump back from. When he turned to offer it to Jolie, he found her seated some ways off, arms around her knees, peering past the skewered dog and the globe of sherbet now melting into the tops of the trees. Far from calling her out of her suffering, proximity to his own seemed only to have driven her further away. Determined not to show his embarrassment, he set up a beef frank for himself and shoved it into the vociferating tongues of flame.

It couldn't have taken long for the first sweet char to form, yet when he pulled his stick back out, the hillside was appreciably darker, the puddled sunlight less orange than a dire, dying red. Jolie had risen and crept over to the storm fence to inspect a shadow someone had propped there. Not a weapon, as he'd worried for a moment, nonsensically; just a guitar whose lacquered face, turning in her hands, seemed to burn. Past that, the Martello tower had sprouted a cellular headdress, atop which blinked a red bulb's beacon. A ripple in the indigo behind the fence's diamonds was identifiable, with some effort, as bats. But it was Jolie who remained his fixation, Jolie he hadn't realized knew the barre chords now drifting over to him—Jolie to whom he seemed to feel closest only at these moments when she forgot he existed at all.

As the light dropped and the riff continued to develop, the laughter of the men and women seemed to get louder and to carry farther, and he had the same feeling he'd gotten up here at the start of his first Vicodin high: of fading toward invisibility. In a kind of cool swoon, he remembered, he'd stumbled off down the hill just to see if Judd or Natasha would notice and beg him to come back. Squinting, he could almost make himself out down there.

He spread out his jacket. Guzzled the foamy Dew. "You do realize there was a time when I'd have taken down half that keg," he said, unsure whether he meant to intimidate or brag. "But I gave all that up, the drinking, the dope . . . which I owe to my daughter. I couldn't keep at it the way I'd been doing and still be her dad." He paused. "Though I guess I couldn't seem to be a dad without messing up, too."

Natasha sighed and stretched and lifted herself from where she'd been sitting at the fire's far edge. Another thing about the light up here: when it went, it went fast. "Your daughter doesn't seem to be listening, though, so is the confession here for my benefit or just your own?"

He was honestly trying to remember whether that was even the relevant question when she squatted and reached for the plastic rings of his six-pack. Pulled free another can and, with the same hand that held it, plucked at the tab. If not for the aluminum rasp preceding it, the *hsst* might have come from an animal. The bats, hitherto noiseless, were either indiscernible or not there.

Tossing the rest of the soda-tackle back on the ground, she handed him the can and then bumped into it with a keg cup. And then her cool nails were digging into his wrist somehow, unless that was a memory. The fire, luffing, etched her preternatural body but left her face a nagging shadow. "But here's to cleaning up your act."

He cleared his throat and said, "Yeah, you too, Natasha," and chugged, though his airways felt no less tight, all he was getting was industrial-grade glucose and yellow number five. And for a second, he was back in the pockets of Jolie's black coat, soft hands feeling around for him in there. "Sorry, I don't know what I'm saying. It's been a long couple of days of solo-parenting."

She snorted, did a complex thing with her hair (or she had somewhere in the past). "Shit, if I'd known you'd turn out to be a family man, Ethan . . ."

"Let's not pretend you'd have gone after me in the first place."

"Speaking of people going after you, though, there's something we should probably get out in the open if you're going to keep hanging around up here."

"This is about some hangup I'm still carrying from twenty

years ago?" he said. He had a sense of Jolie's fretwork becoming a kind of cover for her listening—though probably that was only wishful thinking. And whatever Natasha might have to say to him here about the thing she'd done to or with him that day on the loading dock, he was pretty sure he didn't want to hear. "Because we were just kids then, okay? I can promise you it's all water under the bridge." He couldn't quite carry it off, though, master the shame now kicking against his insides as if it were a thing still alive. "But you know what? Hold that thought," he heard himself say. "This Dew shoots through you like a racehorse." To Jolie, he said, "I'll be right over there with an eye on you, honey, but do me a favor and stick close to Natasha here while I pee. She's good people, okay? You've got my jacket in case you get cold." And slunk off at something like a run.

By tradition, the place where you went to relieve yourself was the same place you took whatever girl you'd managed to talk into fooling around: all the way around the north corner of the fence and down a worn footpath. Another few hundred yards (and a trip back in time, he supposed), and you'd have ended up some-place else, in the woods where Ethan had later gone to drug him-self senseless. The walk now took him past the younger groups that, with the sun gone down, had begun to splinter into vari-ous factions slipping shadowlike down the hill. He nonetheless had a familiar sense of being sized up. Back then, the discomfort would have been that the people he was passing were older, and thus capable of beating his ass. Now they were all closer to Jolie's age. Yet still playing "Uncle John's Band." He seemed safely past when he heard a lone voice shout: "Narc!" Then the others exploded into laughter, leaving him almost shaking for want of that beer.

The fencing ran on beyond where he'd expected. A flaw in his memory, he figured, until he noticed how the starlight went from dull to bright where new metal joined the old. The shinier section extended to the very edge of the bluff, blocking the foot-path, and on it hung a fresh No Trespassing sign. Yet with the dumb adherence of water wearing down rock, the hill's stalwarts had merely tramped out a second path farther along. Terraced into a lower part of the slope, it punched back up through the

brush to rejoin the first path on the far side of the exterior fencing, and here, where the ground leveled off again, he stopped to
face the dark. The smell wasn't carnal, as of yore, but rather the
woodsmoke of last leaves turning, making a sound like tinkling
ice when the wind gusted up. That and the chambered earth, and
above the wind a little music, maybe Jolie's guitar-playing, maybe
somebody else's. How many millions of futures had he imagined
for himself without ever stumbling across the one that might lead
him back here?

Of course the whole quandary back then had been the way he'd
never stopped to think about the future at all. Or if he did, there
had seemed to be only the one future, drawing him onward without his desires or intentions having much to do with it: the one
where he was supposed to have died in a car crash or an overdose
or an overdosed car crash when he was seventeen. But now sounds
were coming from along the footpath behind him, whooping and
a metallic jangle like tossed keys. Rezipping, he braced for kids
coming back from doing those things any parent who wasn't will-
fully deaf as well as dumb would know their kids were doing, in
these woods in the dark. Maybe he could just fade back into the
temple of brush here around him. But no—the button-up he'd
been wearing was bright white, and he'd left his jacket back on
the grass, almost daring Jolie to find the sealed Ziploc inside. The
source of most of the noise, male, paused behind him. "Well, surprise, surprise. I was wondering when you might show, E." No
actual surprise in the voice. To the figure in the shadows, it said
go on ahead, he'd catch up with them once he'd finished with his
old pal Ethan here.

"Eddie . . . damn, man. Moira said something about you still
being overseas . . ."

"But then we couldn't have run into each other like this, could
we? Nah—I took my discharge a year ago. Came back to do some
work at the casino up in Ocean Pines. Now stop hiding, and let's
get a good look at you."

The hand on Ethan's shoulder was already pulling him into an
embrace, the slope giving an odd sense that Eddie Sixkiller had
become the larger of the two. Formerly somewhat schizoid about
physical affection—foster care tended to do that to a person—he

must have been high on something, though maybe just sex, the cumin scent of which still clung to the hands now feeling the back of Ethan's hair for length. "Man, it's good to see you."

"The casino, huh?" Ethan said quietly, once Eddie had let go.

Dirty work, Eddie admitted, parting poor folk from their money, but you got past a certain age, your ethical sense sort of reconfigured. "It was either that or sign on for Iran or who-ever the hell else they're fixing to do now, and you know . . . fuck that—"

"I just thought with your record . . ."

"I'm working security, Prep, not handling dough. And hon-estly, even the background check for croupier would have been easier than that shock shit I had to do to get myself out of the clink and into the army. Why, you down here chasing a job?"

"Listen, though." He knew an apology was owed: for not hav-ing spared Eddie those months in Rikers, for never visiting him up at Moriah, for the lawyers, or the sentencing discrepancy between the two of them, or for something less effable entirely, but Eddie waved him off.

"Like I said: everybody does what they have to do, Ethan, it's what keeps the world interesting. But when Natasha copped to seeing you over at Ducky's Sinclair, I was like, what's up with that? I thought you'd left us for good."

"I'm only here for another twelve hours. A kind of mix-up put me in charge of my daughter for a couple days—" He felt the mistake a beat late.

"No shit? You got little Jo here?"

"Well, not-so-little Jo now. She starts high school next year. And is already grown-up enough to have realized I'm her biggest problem. Probably swapping horror stories with Natasha as we speak. But there's this memorial thing for the rector in the morn-ing . . . maybe we could try to catch you there?"

They would do no such thing, of course, but Eddie said, "Aw, you weren't thinking you'd get rid of me without an introduction, were you?"

And Ethan could see no way around one, really; it had been like a full ten minutes since he'd left Jolie in the care of a near-stranger, and it might take at least ten more to shake off Eddie Sixkiller.

So he let himself be led back around the fenceline, Eddie's dogged surefootedness suggesting he'd done this plenty of times since the newer section went up. But as they neared the place where the two alloys met, an electric light snapped on in the depths and Eddie stopped, a hand formed out of the darkness. "Five-oh's out early tonight," he whispered after a second.

"Five-oh?"

"Didn't anybody think to tell you this, E.? They tightened up enforcement after 2001. It's not really our hill anymore."

Ethan stole forward to peer through the wrist-thick trunks of the volunteer trees. Down toward the street, the white eyes of flashlights were already swinging back and forth under the dark sycamores as official voices crackled and responded. The Dead-playing kids he'd passed earlier had vanished. Farther along the hilltop, where the beams had concentrated, Dennis was struggling to unfoot the keg—no sense in wasting good beer. Others were snatching up things to flee. He couldn't actually see Jolie amid the commotion, but she had to be over there somewhere. A route at the summit's far end led back through the bramble to a sidestreet, and if he could get her over there with the rest of the crew, they could circle back to the parking strip once the heat had died down. Their only alternatives were to find a place to hide or take the back way out, follow the railroad cut all the way out through the woods. As he made it around the fence, Eddie grabbed his arm. "Wait, where do you think you're going?"

"I've got to get my daughter. She's right there."

"You said she's with Natasha, though, right? Natasha knows how to handle herself. We're the ones need to steer clear of the fuzz."

"What for? We haven't done anything wrong."

"You want to try explaining that to a judge? This is federal land, Ethan, and your record's hardly better than mine. Come back to the tracks with me, circle around, and we can pretend you just—"

But Ethan was already off, making a kind of primal scramble for the spot where Jolie and Natasha had last been seen. No sign of them now, naturally. Jesus, what had he been thinking, that they'd just sit tight, awaiting his return? But then farther down, there she was at the edge of the swirling beams, the only one left, her shorn head bare, turning her upturned hat around and around, nervously: his little girl. He stooped to snatch his jacket from the ground and then hooked her arm, pulled her back behind the fire where the flashlights wouldn't reach. And perhaps something had changed in her after all, or at least loosened, because her face was transparent in its reproach—and maybe, possibly, a little scared?

"Sorry, honey, but you're not giving me a lot of choice but to grab you—it wouldn't do to get caught. Now on three, we're going to make a run for the brush there. And try not to give them a look at you in case we have to pass them again later to get the van. You ready? One . . . Two . . ."

"*Psst.*" Eddie was still where the fences met, motioning. "*Not that way.*" With no time to think, Ethan followed, looking back to find Jolie racing along behind. She was good at it, surprisingly, with that unteachable instinct for the perp-run, huddled and unlinear. Behind them faded Natasha and the others, the police with their different voices. The blinking beacon of the tower fell away to the right, and with it the old path. And suddenly they were alone in the woods—in the dark.

Since he was afraid of the scolding and pleas he might face if he turned on his phone, it would be unclear to Ethan how long they walked there, in a silence broken only by the sporadic crack of kindling underfoot and the rustle of branches he learned to catch as they snapped back. Any moonlight was now blocked by the trees, yet Eddie seemed to have a distinct sense of where he was going, and why not? He'd just come through here with that girl (or possibly boy, Ethan supposed)—the one he now seemed to have abandoned to his or her fate. But had the woods always been this overgrown? They crossed a gravelly patch that might have been the railroad cut, it was hard to say. And if it had been up to him to lead himself and his daughter out of here, he'd never have been able to, he was just thinking, when he realized he couldn't hear a thing anymore: not Eddie's footsteps, not the branches, not even Jolie's breathing. He reached back for her . . . and again, there she was. "Eddie?"

No answer.

Then a voice drifted out of the dark. "Sorry, just fucking with you. Spooky in here, right, Prep?"

And despite his exasperation, Ethan found that he could breathe again. If Eddie felt it safe to talk, they must be far enough from the cops to remain unheard, and deep enough in the night that his fears could not be seen.

"But your girl there is good," the voice continued. "She'd be like a natural born tracker."

"Look, let's not dig our hole any deeper by screwing around here, Eddie," he said. And added, so she would know it wasn't her he'd felt so ashamed of, "I already told you we're on the outs, Jolie and me."

"But that's only what you deserve, isn't it? For leaving a loved one in the lurch like that, I mean?"

"Which I richly fucking deserve, you're right," he forced himself to say. "But all that aside, I can't afford to lose sight of her out here . . . Because the truth is, she's made up her mind she's not going to be speaking to me anymore. Or maybe to anyone."

"Well, gosh, Ethan, I wonder where she got that idea?"

His voice's location, Ethan realized, still couldn't quite be pinpointed, but it was on the move again. He saw no choice but to try to keep up, pulling Jolie along by the sleeve. "What's that supposed to mean?" he said.

"What do you think, homeboy?" A stick cracked. "Who engineered the Aspern Wall of Silence to begin with? Hell, if the rector were still around, you wouldn't be talking to him, either. And I seem to remember I did warn you about that."

"Look, though. Before you go trying to drag me through the mud in front of my daughter, let's get something straight. My dad's the one who shut me out first, not the other way around."

"But what did you expect a wounded animal to do, Ethan? Put up billboards around the forest? Or write some big fucking opera about it, like, 'Oh, I'm in Pain?' No, an animal has to go away to heal, you know that. And he must have known you'd know the feeling, being his son. Think of the space it made for you and Moira when he went off on that boat."

"With her *hospice nurse*, Eddie. It was hardly even spring before he was inviting her back to the house."

"I'm not defending it, understand. Just trying to help you see the line of descent. So your old man didn't warn you he was planning to remarry . . . Hell, you couldn't warn me not to run cocaine, couldn't tell me not to imagine I could go up against Ducky—"

"Can we not, though? With the drug stuff? In front of my kid?"

"It's nothing to be ashamed of, E. You were trying to do right by your lady, provide for your little girl. But why not just come out and say you didn't want to be my wingman? Or at least come hear me afterward on how sorry I was?" And to Jolie: "It's probably time someone told you, kiddo, what a proud tradition of stubborn-ass withholding you come from. Maybe none of us is really that unique, am I right? Now watch your step."

The ground had seemed to turn gravelly again—they might already have crossed the railroad tracks another two or three times, but Ethan was now so turned around he couldn't tell. He swiped at the dark, felt the arm of Jolie's sweater. "Eddie?" But ahead, there was nothing. Or no, not nothing: some part of his mom was scattered out here in these woods, Moira had said. And now some of his father was right here in his jacket pocket. He had a crazy idea of reaching in for a handful of ashes . . .

But something had started to pale up ahead: that porchless old glider, catching lights from the bypass across the stubbled fields. His eyes drank them in like stars. Already, Eddie was over and squatting in the dirt, seeming to feel around under the glider's iron frame. Ethan braced for him to start up again, tell Jolie how her dad had left him to molder in an upstate cell. Or even worse: spent a large chunk of the '90s cowering out here in a chemical sickness instead of caring for his fading mother (much less attending to her work). But Eddie had already tucked whatever he was after into his pants and come trotting over. "Damn smart of me not to have taken my tool up the hill."

"Jesus—is that a gun?"

"I said the new angle was security, right? I can get you one if you want, by the way. Job or tool, whichever. You come and see me too, Little Jo, if you ever get old enough and feel the need for protection. But sorry, getting ahead of myself. Why don't you two go on and turn around here, start walking."

"You first, Jolie," he said, not trusting Eddie not to have planned some confrontation even harsher than the one he now saw bearing in on him. And, Jolie obeying for once, they were walking back the way they'd come until they reached those tracks he could now have found his way along in his sleep: the ones that led to Ducky's Sinclair.

But perhaps there was never going to be any payback at all. When they reached the chain gate to the gas station and he could make out faces again, Eddie's was gone, and Jolie's seemed unchanged by anything she'd just heard, unless it was possible for her to have shut down even further. No time to worry about that now, though. He explained to her once more that she should keep her hat low as they passed through the lot, in case a cop or two had come here after the raid. But there was no clientele of any description, just the empty light of a convenience store window. Not even Ducky, but just another lowly clerk. In the next lot over, his own house—Moira's house—sat dark, though it could hardly be nine p.m. He watched Jolie study it, almost heard her working out what it would mean for his sister and nephew to be stuck in the hospital even now . . . But no, there he went again, with his need for some drama in which he might redeem himself. More likely they'd been released and, worn out, had just gone to bed . . . and his chance at getting her in to see Izzy was gone.

It was when he thought to look back at the woods from half-way across the tarmac that he realized he had somehow let his fear take over again, had blown his chance to apologize to Eddie. But he could hardly go back there to look for him. Instead, in the time it took to walk around to the van, he would keep an eye on the wall of trees beside them, longing for that shadow he'd know anywhere to detach from the dark and fall in noiselessly beside them, but it never did. They reached Keel Hill to find no police cars left—no vehicles aside from the van, in fact—so maybe the cops' aim had been less to exact vengeance than just to break up the party for the night. And maybe the keg itself had been drained to douse the fire, for an acrid smell still lingered, visibly hazing the cones of streetlights. In the houses opposite, the windows were all black, reminding him of something, though he couldn't have said what. Every last other person here seemed to be on holiday, or evicted, or sleeping one off, yet as he and Jolie pulled away in the van, he'd keep scanning the hilltop and the woods for any trace of his former nemesis and benefactor. And friend. So fervently would he search, in fact, that he never noticed the headlights that had snapped on behind them at the gas station, the nondescript sedan now keeping close as they rolled south by southeast through his hometown's forsaken streets and then swung due east toward Ocean City.

19

WHAT PRECIOUS HAS LEARNED from her father? Pick up on the third ring. Any sooner and you come off as overeager; any later as hard of hearing. Which is how, when the bleep of the cordless finds her basement bedroom through the parlor's wide-planked floor, she knows this must be Dad answering, and to mute the sound on her iTunes, in case it's someone calling with news about Grace (now drifted on to Prague with some ponytailed Eastern European), or, more likely, about one or another of Precious's own exploits. For the truth is, in the fourteen months since her sister left them, there have been any number of Precious Ezeobis out there running the city—classes she's cut, bars she's snuck into, boys fooled around with, girls once or twice—and at some point she'll have to look her mom and dad in the eye and say, Yep, I've got some of that in me, too.

Though possibly by this point she is less grieving her vanished sister than furious with the remaining one (the dullard Prudence, home from Vassar and now gone with Mom to their annual tea at the Plaza like everything was the same as before). Or is just slightly addled after two days off school with her entire new set from LaGuardia away on ski vacations or visiting grandparents so that even if she had somewhere to go, there'd be no one left to go with. In any case, the call can't be both about and for Precious (can it?), so once her name comes floating down the stairs in her father's beautiful rich voice, she feels relieved, though also a tad suspicious: If someone truly wanted to reach her, why not just try her cell?

She shucks off her headphones, goes upstairs to find her father at the kitchen counter pressing his palm over the handset, watching her with the distant formality of a researcher puzzled by the results of his experiment. Perhaps he disapproves of her still not having changed out of pyjamas, even here at the dinner hour. "One moment, please . . . my daughter's in the midst of getting dressed."

And perhaps her sigh, weary as she is of being watched, is just the sound she makes preparing to be Daddy's Little Girl again and do the gestures of pretend-listening. Or perhaps she's just trying to annoy him. Perhaps two mutually exclusive feelings can be true at once. (Perhaps, Precious sometimes thinks, that's the only truth there is.)

"Hello?" The voice on the line is a woman's. "Is this Precious?"

"Um, yeah." Like: Who else would it be?

"Oh, thank God. This is Sarah Kupferberg, Jolie's mom." A fakey bright tone that nonetheless costs Precious a little twinge of regret (unless it's the name that does it). To escape direct observation, she rises with the handset and crosses the long parlor to the front window. Outside, a gingko heaves in a streetlight, its last leaves a flaming orange-gold, its rancid berries flattened by feet.

"Did she give you this number to call?" Precious says. "Because before you get the wrong idea, I should warn you that your daughter and I didn't part on what you'd call the best of terms. She sort of went rogue on me last winter."

"Oh," says the lady, disappointed. And rightly so, honestly, since Precious had clearly been some kind of high-water mark socially for Jolie (Jolie who never dared show in public the funny and caustic if frankly somewhat reckless kid she'd revealed herself to be in private). Then, recollecting herself, the lady says: "Well, she sort of went rogue on a lot of us last winter . . . as I'm guessing you already know."

Precious wonders how you might convey a yawn to someone who can't see you.

"But what I'm calling about is a matter of some urgency, and that's just whether you have any idea where she might be now."

And here Precious almost wants to laugh. It's as if the lady's confused—as if Precious had actually stayed over in Jolie's apartment that time, poking through its drawers, tippling its aperitifs, sitting in its so-called grading nook eating waffles. As if, on either side, the relationship had been any more than ships passing in the night. "Sorry, though, back up. I literally have no idea why you'd think I'm the person to ask about Jolie."

"Are you saying you know nothing about this package that came to my parents' in the mail, Precious? '2 Whom It May Concern'?"

"Not really ringing any bells."

"Shit. And the art-school joke earlier, with the crayons?"

"Um . . . yeah, no, still blanking."

Her own father clucks audibly behind her, and when she turns, motions for the phone, so that she almost misses the woman's pained silence on the other end. It is with a pantomime of long-suffering-ness that Precious instead swerves and goes to the stoop. And from there spots a lady in broken Crocs and one of those floppy sun hats you see now and again, harvesting the least-squashed berries from the slate walk a few brownstones down. Maybe it is a feeling of, like, "There but for the grace of God" that turns Precious toward pity. But maybe it is only that she knows she's scored a direct hit. "Look, Ms. Kupferberg, if you want to get all Inspector Clouseau about it, your daughter's probably just mooning around that bookstore she likes down on Allen Street. Unless she's made a date with that skeevy Facebook guy of hers who tried to friend me last month—"

"Precious, the only date she's on is with her father."

Right: Daddums. "From the all-school recital, you mean."

"Wait—you were there?"

"Obviously. I had the solo in the LaGuardia chorus! But you're talking about someone tall, kind of medium-hot, doomy-looking, asking after Jolie?"

"His name is Ethan. I don't suppose she ever told you about their past together?" *Our past together*, she seemed about to add, but didn't.

"Like I said, we were never that close. But you can always tell the girls with daddy issues a mile away . . . forever looking for the wrong things from the wrong people."

"Precious, listen, I'm sorry if this has offended you in some way, but Jolie's been getting these packages in the mail, from someone

she led me to believe was you, and if you were at the recital, that
makes you an eyewitness, so maybe there's something you can
still do to help."

"But an eyewitness to what?"

"An abduction, Precious. Or at least a missing persons case.
Possibly two of them."

And when Precious speaks again, she sounds to herself no longer quite so sure, as if she's stumbled over a doubled bit of runner
in a long, straight hall. "Oh. Fuck."

"It's going on two days since I heard from Jolie's father, and I
don't know where they went, or how stable either of them really
is right now, or even if they're still in the country . . . He didn't
seem in any way high to you, did he?"

But the woman is now sounding just like her dad lectur-
ing Grace over the phone after she'd refused to come back last
Thanksgiving—like his daughter was standing on the precipice
of some terrible dark hellhole and not a place you could get to
faster than certain parts of the U.S. just by hopping on a plane.
Precious speaks louder, hoping he might hear her now through
the tall old windows.

"Is there something you're trying to insinuate? How am *I* supposed to know if someone was high?"

And then, curiously, a second person on the phone says, "Hand
me that," and she hears a familiar voice—"Precious, let's cut the
crap, shall we?"—before the sound of another scuffle, after which
the mom comes back on the line. "Oh my God," Precious says.
"Was that *Mr. Koussoglou*?"

The next sound splits the difference between a groan and a
sigh. And suddenly she sees it: the mom had somehow gotten
entangled with that slick little otter of a teacher, who would of
course have told her Precious, Precious is the evil mastermind.
Mr. Koussoglou, who at the end of her seventh-grade year, having
caught her coming all red-eyed out of a janitor's closet one day,
had had the nerve to sit her down to say he'd had his eye on her
for weeks now, and knew she'd been smoking pot. Blinking at her
through his dorked-out glasses, like a member of Weezer gone
into the witness protection program. She might have explained
right then and there how she hadn't wanted any of the other

kids to see her crying. Instead, she'd threatened to involve her
father, the lawyer. Had even produced his number: "Go ahead,
call him." Which Mr. Koussoglou almost did before wussing
out as she'd known he would. It wasn't even the fake-concerned
slash boundary-challenged way he'd touched her leg, saying he
knew what it felt like to be misunderstood, that had pissed her
off so badly . . . it was more just the nerve of it, you know? The
presumption. Like, he would probably look at that Chinese lady
down there and just *presume* to be able to know from his own life
all sorts of things about the particular kind of pain she was in . . .
or honestly that the lady was in any pain at all, when probably that
crick in her back just happens to be her natural resting position,
you know? And maybe she reuses those old drugstore sacks out of
eco-friendliness, and maybe it's not even the same Chinese lady
who comes around on Tuesdays to pick through the recycling.
Maybe she just really likes the smell of gingko berries. And Grace
gone now for the second Thanksgiving in a row, and Mom and
that sellout Prudence having put it behind them . . . You never
really knew the first thing about what was going on inside other
people.

"Listen, though, Ms. K.—if I may. You call me up here and
tell me your daughter's hanging out with this dad you can't get
ahold of, and somebody's sent her some crayons or something,
and then you start speculating—on no evidence that I can hear—
that maybe he's taken her out of the country, or maybe they're
both head-cases, or maybe he's on drugs, and generally trying to
convince me to panic about this person I'm not even really friends
with—"

"It's Dr. Kupferberg, Precious. And it's not just speculation;
you're not seeing what I'm seeing—"

"Yeah, but I think that's sort of the one thing we're agreeing on.
And as to the rest of it, I wish I could set your mind at ease, really
I do, but the more I hear, the more I'm questioning whether she's
not the one making sense here after all. Which you can tell her for
me when you see her, you know? Or anyway, give my regards."

She hangs up but continues to hold the phone to her ear, since
her raised voice just now has made the lady with the gingko berries glance over. And for a second in the stillness afterward, she

really does try to do the ethnography thing, the leap into another person's life . . . but based on what, and to what end? To imagine herself inside the woman looking up at Precious, trying to imagine herself inside Precious, looking back? No, impossible; you get lost in the middle there somewhere, she thinks. And still, she'll sit on the stoop for an extra minute wondering what her eldest sister is doing right now six time zones away, and if she's still all right— whatever her own dad may be thinking about any of this as he watches, through this window that could probably use washing.

20

IF ETHAN DIDN'T THINK MUCH of the slam echoing across the lot behind him, or of the shadow stirring beyond the half-dead arc-lights where dumpsters still hunkered in the dark, it may have been because his mind was on Eddie Sixkiller. Had eighty minutes in the woods really been enough to discharge the debt between them, whichever way it ran? And which of these facts carried more weight with his daughter: that he'd scurried off into the night up on Keel Hill, or that he'd returned for her with the cavalry? Then again, maybe he'd just reached some kind of accommodation with the predicament in which he found himself. Best to assume of other people, even the desperate ones who seemed to populate the Elysian Shores Motel—even of Eddie Six-K—that they were no more or less real or fucked up or impossible to know than you yourself were.

The elevator now sported the same out-of-order sign as the glass door to the pool—some fresh horror—so he led Jolie out to the staircase with its stucco exoskeleton. This was the last night he could afford to stay here and still eke out a return to L.A., but it's not like there was any other move he could make to try to reach his daughter. A few hours of sleep, and then come the sunrise they would go. Through an arrowslit at each landing, you could see the parking lot (quiet again), the Looping Star (lit for no one), and beyond that the silver-gelatin blackness that meant the sea. And though the echo of Jolie's footsteps seemed unnecessarily loud, he chose to blame her heavy boots and dejected tread, never considering the possibility that this was in fact another set of footsteps entering the stairwell one flight below.

The room in their absence had only intensified its mustiness, as money shut away in a vault will magically yield interest—remarkable considering that the maids had come through and left the sliding door to the balcony half open. The scent of smoke was like a stain that refused to be gotten out. But never mind, Ethan thought; if Jolie was going to remain disengaged, then he could, too. He returned in shirtsleeves from his tooth-brushing and spread himself with a groan on the farther of the two beds, as though wearied by a hard day of accomplishment. Maybe just having made it through so many hours of her resistance was itself an accomplishment. On the TV was a crime scene, police-taped: the ten o'clock news. He was about to say something about turning in—they had a long drive ahead of them in the morning—when the knock came at the door.

You could tell at once, just from the shape of it, that what was meant here was business. Three brisk reports not loud enough to upset the neighbors (so clearly the person hadn't internalized the laissez-faire ethos of the Elysian Shores) but not quiet enough, either, for Ethan to follow his usual playbook and pretend not to have heard it, hope it would just go away. When it came again, the steel door jumped slightly in its housing. Among the many things he'd neglected to secure was the chain, and to do so now, and risk the rattle, would be as much as to admit they were inside. When he raised his head from the mattress and found Jolie's eye in the mirror, he caught a look of what may have been apprehension. Possibly even a slight nod: Well?

It was a curious feature of the fisheye peephole that it gave the illusion of enabling sight while actually doing so little to aid it. As he tried to get his bearings, something came back to him about Odysseus in the Cyclops's lair. Baked into the story's own monocular form, of course, was whose side you were supposed to be on, but only because the Cyclops was stuck in the monster role; otherwise the hero was sort of an asshole. He blinked. In the psychward fluorescence of the breezeway, he could make out a logoless cap, black-on-black, bending to check a watch or a phone, and the shoulders of a sweater-vest too light for the gathering chill. And only now did the third set of footsteps in the stairwell really register. But the figure was too short to be Sarah come to take vengeance; had she hired a private detective?

Bap bap bap—quieter this time. "Come on, get the lead out, Ethan. I know you're in there."

"Just a minute," he said, almost shouting. Whereupon, amazingly, a second banging came from the wall behind the mirror— the randy neighbors, signaling them to keep it down. And then before him in the doorway, like a wayward guest, stood Erica Morales.

"I'm going to skip the part where I ask if you mind me coming in," she said, self-evidently. "Or where I make some lame excuse about dehydration."

He heard himself answer, as if from a great distance, "No, of course." Then, stepping aside: "I can't say that the water's any great shakes down here anyway." He gestured toward the bed. "This is the daughter I was telling you about last summer. Jolie, this is Erica . . . or Officer Morales, rather."

"Pleasure, Jolie," Morales said, when no response was forthcoming, and entered.

But he lingered at the door. "I guess I know why you're here. I'll admit it, though: I'm surprised you'd be after me so soon. Another few hours and I'd have had her back to New York, and me flying west. Unless Sarah was the one to alert you . . . ?"

"McGonagall came home early," she said.

"Damn. And found the van missing."

"Not just that. He'd been getting complaints from clients . . . something about some creep filming their apartments? The wrong videos being sent to their phones?"

He thought for a second. "Well, that explains all the calls from him, I guess. But listen, is there a way we could do all this maybe not right in front of my daughter?"

"I'm sorry—did you say the kid's not supposed to be here?"

"Like, go down to the pool area or something?"

"Jesus, Ethan. And you think I'd trust you right now even to leave this room?" She moved over to the sliding glass door as if to test the lock. The ocean's black noise rushed in. "If you'd prefer privacy, we can step out here for a minute, but you're going to have to tell your daughter to stay put."

Rather than argue, he tried the bank of lightswitches on the wall near the door, but none of them worked. Still, when he stepped outside, Erica followed, sliding the stubborn glass closed. The low wall before them, now lit by the overspill of the room, showed smudged little pinnacles of stucco, snagging points for all manner of dirt. As for the pale stuff clogged at the balcony's drainage points, it was a hard call—bleached leaves, pulped toilet paper . . . gull feathers, maybe. Something nagged at him, but inside, Jolie was rising. He motioned, probably superfluously, for her to close the curtains. And just before she did, blacking them out, he could see Morales taking his inventory, as if photoshopped in from another life. Then he leaned his forearms on the wall's rough top and looked out past the boardwalk, trying to discern was there anything out there still alive tonight.

"The thing is, Ethan, I never made you for an actual crazy person."

" 'High-functioning,' is a term I've heard used. But you knew about the drug abuse, which indicates at least some kind of a loose screw."

She went on like he hadn't spoken. "I'm saying, I've dealt with some crazy motherfuckers in my time. But you're not hearing voices telling you to do this shit, are you? Instructions from newspapers, or dogs? Thunder?" He shook his head no, when the truer answer might have been *Not at present*. Or maybe *Only when I'm asleep*. "Which is not to mention the recidivists: firebugs, sex criminals . . . And the thing is, I never violated anybody without at least knowing the reason: either for want of adequate funding for mental health, or just to try to keep someone off the streets who's a danger to themselves or others. But here you are, a white guy with a good face and a high-school diploma . . . I mean, what's your excuse? The question's purely rhetorical, by the way, I'm not looking for an answer. And as to your daughter, I sure hope she's not slipping out the front door as we speak—"

"But she hasn't done anything!"

"I'm saying, I hope so for *your* sake, Ethan. You know what the second worst thing you can steal in this country is, in the eyes of the law? A motor vehicle. Do you even have a license?"

"You have to recognize I was going to bring the van back. At the outside, I'm guilty of a little grand borrowing."

"The single worst thing to steal of course being a child."

"She's my child too, goddammit!"

There was a tapping now, insistent, as of a junkie looking for a vein. He would realize she was tamping down cigarettes only when the ribbon of noiseless cellophane she'd torn from the packet went glimmering away by starlight. Perhaps disappointment had led her to be more open in her own addictions, he thought. But if so, add it to my tab.

"I'm serious. I told you in July that I was worried about her, and why, and that I'd come back to help. An opportunity arose, and I took it. Isn't that the American way?"

"An opportunity to take her across state lines for three days in a boosted Econoline?"

"Borrowed. Plus at the time I thought I was supposed to be at this memorial thing for my dad."

"Again?"

"Still."

The moon should have been making itself known out there by now, but had gotten lost somewhere toward the back of the sky. And all at once he realized that what had been nagging him about those gull feathers was where they'd come from . . . where the seagulls of Ocean City went at night. It was like his Monahan problem all over again: pigeons brooded under eaves, country sparrows had their little confusions of nests, but he could honestly say that in all his time on the Eastern Shore he'd never seen anything approaching a seagull nest, and when he rummaged among the corrupted files in his mind, the image he kept coming up with was a thousand of them huddled against the wind with their heads bowed, like in that penguin documentary.

"I asked what your problem is, Ethan; now I'm going to tell you what I think," Erica said. "Stop me if you've heard this one before. I think a bad thing happens at some point in a person's life, whether by mistake or something they can't control, and it freezes them in a particular moment like a kind of curse . . . they get stuck so they can't move forward or back. Take me, for example. I'm frozen in here at like seventeen—that's bad enough. But I'd put you somewhere between three and six or wherever the whole object-permanence thing kicks in. I think that somewhere underneath you're still the little princeling Mommy never made pick up his underwear off the floor."

The cigarettes were gone before he could reach for one, a form of prestidigitation. She'd obviously had time to stew on all this on her drive down—and perhaps even time to justify what she seemed already (ominously) to have decided to do. Which didn't mean she wasn't preaching the gospel. Another thing he realized he didn't know was what kind of powers a person's ex–probation officer retained in a state not her own, beyond the power to dial 911—not that he would have insulted her by telling her to produce the cuffs already or leave him the fuck alone. And say he did go quietly into the arms of the law: Who would sit with Jolie on their way back to the city? And who would drive the van? Where the cigarette had disappeared to, he couldn't say. Same place as the seagulls, maybe. Same place as his ability to beg for mercy.

"Cause and effect's what I'm talking about, Ethan. Three years ago, when I found you that spot in detox, I guess I was imagining the place you came from as a little more privileged or whatever than it turns out to be. Maybe I needed that to make me feel better about myself, maybe make what went down between us more your fault. You'd had too much of what spoils people, I thought. But I've been doing a lot of reading lately, a lot of painful personal growth, and now I'm thinking maybe it's a guy thing, or a generational thing: a refusal to acknowledge cause and effect. Every year, you know, when the West Indian Day Parade happens, you get these hard rocks firing their Glocks in the air as if the bullet didn't have to come down somewhere. I don't know where they think it goes. Just . . . evaporates, I guess." Her voice, quiet, had gone shaky in a way he couldn't quite understand.

"Well, they've been drinking, haven't they," he pointed out. "Getting high. Which is at least one thing I haven't done."

"And still I don't know why someone like me would be singled out to bring someone like you back into acquaintance with the law of gravity, but that's what seems to have happened. So help me out a little: tell me what you'd do if you were me right now? Because if I were me, Ethan—"

From the curtain flashed a blade of light. And suddenly something came back to him. "If I were you? I'd give me till ten a.m. tomorrow."

"You know I can't do that."

"No, but hear me out. I admit I haven't made much progress

with Jolie to date. Probably the opposite. But the whole reason we couldn't go back Thanksgiving night as planned was that my sister had this memorial service scheduled for first thing Saturday instead." Well, that plus Izzy being hospitalized, but it wouldn't help the cause to say he'd accidentally put his nephew in intensive care. "So let us stick around that long, and then I'll follow you back to New York in the van, explain myself before a whole frigging tribunal if necessary, give Jolie back to her mom. Or whatever: you can follow me, have her ride shotgun. So long as she's not left alone."

"The last time I tried to do you a kindness, if I remember, it didn't seem to change much except to guarantee you learned nothing."

"Yeah, but I managed to stay sober through all this, that has to count for something. And I never lied to you, Erica. Going all the way back to that night in your apartment. I was always giving you the truth of myself, as best I understood it. You want me to do time, I'll do the time, just as soon as we've finished this one thing, taking Jolie to pay our respects to her grandfather. Maybe I can't fix her, but I owe them both that much."

"And what were you proposing I do in the meantime?"

"You'd be surprised at how many vacancies there are in this joint. The unit next door is, ah . . . occupied, but you go back downstairs right now, I'm sure the gentleman at the front desk would be more than happy to book you a room on the far side."

"Yeah, and I bet he'd do it just as easy if I dialed up reception from your phone," she said, reaching for the sliding door.

He fanned himself, seeking to disperse the smoke from his clothes, yet into the room it came, swirling, as he followed Erica Morales. The air felt too warm, suddenly, and in the seconds before his eyes adjusted, he had an impression almost of overmuchness. The news was still on, but the sound was turned all the way down. Yet Jolie hadn't moved from her bed except to be holding a book she must have snagged earlier from the van: that *Little Flowers* thing McGonagall had been after him to read. He couldn't be certain, but he thought he'd just seen her flash a weird little smile of reassurance. If so, though, she'd already fallen back to chewing her tongue-ring. She would naturally want to know how things had gone out there, the disposition of their affairs, but he didn't feel like he could tell her, since Erica had sat down on the edge of the bed, drawn by last night's Ravens highlights or just wanting to make him squirm. "You mind?" she said, without turning to Jolie. "I lost forty bucks on this game, I'd love to know how."

Jolie did her quasi-involuntary smile thing again, but Morales was engrossed in a replay. "Ouch, you see that? He's going to be feeling that tomorrow. Or today, I guess."

She waited until the commercial break to pluck the phone off the nightstand and ask the front desk if she could have the room two doors down in her name. Amid the ensuing negotiations, Ethan would notice Jolie discreetly trying to dig something from her gumline, but didn't think much about it. It was only when the Channel 5 weatherman came on, yammering from within the whirlwind of what he called a "Doppler fly-through," that Erica seemed to decide she'd tortured him enough. "All right. I guess my keys'll be ready for pick-up now. But remember: after that, I'm only two doors away, hearing you if you try to leave. And then seeing you bright and early." She rose and smoothed the legs of her slacks and exited onto the breezeway, as though she'd just been a neighbor come to pass the time of day.

Footsteps faded down the stairs. Ethan took the remote and hunted for the button that would kill the screen. Foreplay was starting up next door, or had resumed. Behind him in the mirror, Jolie had her finger back in her mouth again, as if a popcorn husk or a rubbery bit of tofu were caught there. What he'd thought was a smile, though, was in fact a grimace. Which was weird; he hadn't seen her eat anything all day. "You okay?" he asked, but at that moment, her fingertip fished out a small lump of grayish pulp that resembled nothing so much as the detritus clogging the balcony. "Jolie?" he asked as she sealed it in her palm. "What the fuck *is* that?"

But already she was up and grabbing her bag and out to the breezeway herself, not quite at a run.

21

GRAYSON LIKES to think of himself as different—no, sorry. Scratch that. Everyone here in the States likes to think of him- or herself as different . . . at least in certain phases, certain moods. You have only to fire up a TV or a tablet to see it: that flattering address to individual taste and habit. But Grayson Aplanalp, from about the age of the endless summer day camps he'd been slow to recognize as daycare—that is, right around the time of his mother's one-way flight back to England—has been treated as if he *were* different, and so has decided to think of himself that way.

In matters of simple biology and everyday life, perhaps this has been naïve. There comes a moment in New York when you realize your signature look, the buttons all buttoned, is ten thousand other people's signature look as well. An almost bittersweet moment when you realize every other boy at the boarding school, too, has been wanking into his tube socks. There comes a moment when you realize that what you've taken as sweat stains has actually, a fair percentage of the time, been somebody else's semen (or at least when you start to doubt your ability to distinguish one from the other).

And now there comes a lonely guilty Friday about a month after the incident with Jolie when, actively seeking to be like anyone else, he rises from the couch where he's slept these last two nights and undoes the padlock on his room for the first time since his escape back to Putney and sets about expunging any trace of her ever having been here. The tumbler on the windowsill with its film of eighty-proof backwash, the hair on the pillow too long to be his own . . . these he hastily consigns to a trashbag, lest

he be forced to recognize himself as some kind of actual preda-
tor. But there are also the mussed bedsheets to consider, cov-
erlet included, each of which he sniffs carefully for any trace of
saliva or pre-come. Finding none, he wads them up with the same
jeans he's been sleeping in and carries them to the washer, which
he clears of the damp load left inside for drying. He'll have to
remember to put it back when he's done, so Consuela won't know
he was in here and get suspicious (Grayson never before having
stooped to lift a finger with laundry). And now, measuring out
the washing powder, guessing at proportions, he can't help thinking of another book he's had to read for school, where the guy is
frantically shoving a debutante's body into a basement furnace
to cover up a crime he hadn't quite meant to commit. And again
he wonders: Had it been an assault, this thing between him and
Jolie? Was he an assailant? To the extent that it's up to him to say,
he doesn't believe so, or not entirely; everything had seemed so
warmly and wetly if a little toothily consensual—at least right up
to the point where the girl's consent got abruptly withdrawn. And
even after that, he believes he'd handled himself, ah . . . nobly is
probably a stretch, but tactfully. Compassionately. The problem was, he could see where she was coming from. Where she
was coming from was he was a good three years older, and knew
her to be somewhat mentally unstable. He hadn't quite realized
until the moment the word left her mouth that she might have
been *consciously* suicidal back in April, but in hindsight, what else
could it have been? He had picked her up on a psych ward, after
all, and had gotten that queasy excited feeling later, reading the
weird little vignette she'd left there in the trash. And though she
hadn't accused him of anything worse than exploiting that insta-
bility (and at worst what had he really done, besides ply her with
blandishments (and vodka) and accept (okay, fine, insist on) a little
head under false pretenses?), it seemed possible, in the clinical
light of the laundry room, that consent behaved oddly in the presence of deceit.

On the other hand, absent a certain quantum of deceit on both
sides, it seemed doubtful that much in the way of sex would ever
have transpired at all, historically, had been Grayson's experience. People pretending to be better, smarter, older, more con-

fident and clear-minded and less pervy than they actually were was probably what the species needed to replenish itself. Which in turn perhaps pointed to a structural problem or design flaw in the reigning fetish for authenticity.

But now he upbraids himself for intellectualization and flippancy—not necessarily in that order. The simple fact is, he'd lied to her, a girl of fourteen, who, whatever she'd said about it, really had looked to be in dire straits from the very first moment he saw her. Worse, he'd transacted on the lie. Had made her feel the shittiest thing he could think of, which was betrayal. If not assault the way you saw it in movies, then it was at least a crime of some description. And wanting suddenly for some reason to be reminded of that, to have his nose rubbed in it, he remains in the laundry room for the whole length of the cycle, perched atop the machine like Rodin's *Thinker*. Then he loads the dryer and moves down onto the floor. At some point a crescendo of nails on the buffed concrete announces the coming of Wantohantoweh, who gives him a baleful look but then circles and settles himself on the floor in adjacency to Grayson's hairy bare leg. It was this dog's dogwalker, of course, the ponce with the cutoff dungarees and the van, who had left behind *The Little Flowers of Saint Francis*. And all representations to Jolie notwithstanding, Grayson has long since gone ahead and purchased his own replacement copy, which he opens on his lap but then finds himself reading the same page of over and over, its letter shapes no more decipherable than abstract art—

Not one knows how to serve me the way he should!

—when suddenly, in the polished porthole window of the washing machine, his face becomes his face again.

It is the face of a shitty person, a face crying out for some form of punishment—whose owner's future (such as it is) might already be ruined depending on what Jolie has or hasn't said to other people about what, intentions aside, he inarguably did do to her. He has scoured the New York State website for one of those embarrassingly named Romeo and Juliet exceptions to the statutory rape laws, but can find none, and is anyway about to turn eighteen. Nor can he rule out having pinged her about the book after all this time to try to smoke her out: Who has she told about him? Before he can even think about trying again, his hand has twitched to his pocket. What he is unready for—is even a little spooked by—is the message he then finds waiting for him. Not Jolie, as it turns out, but someone using her profile.

Hi. My name is Sarah Kupferberg; I'm Jolie's mother.

His heart has already stopped, yet he stumbles a little over the semicolon, wondering if he's ever seen it deployed on Facebook aside from the occasional old-school emoticon.

Obviously this isn't my account, but I trust you won't object to my reaching out this way. You show up as one of my daughter's few contacts, and it's been suggested you might have some idea as to where she's gone now that she's missing. And/or as to why.

A scuttling little crabwise doubt shoots out from the place where it must have been hiding all along and begins to insinuate things about jumpable bridges, handfuls of meds a stricken Jolie might have consumed before anyone could stop her. Then, scrolling ahead, he sees a reference to *her father, with whom she was last seen.* And tries to reassure himself that Jolie's just been caught in some kind of custodial crossfire (which: tell him about it). Yet beneath the grammatical composure, her mother seems worried. And given what little he remembers Jolie saying about the dad, this makes Grayson worry, too. So he types back that, although it would be wrong to claim any ability to know anyone else's motivations, if this is Jolie's computer the mom is using to access her account, he might be able to help.

Perhaps he's picturing a train ride in the morning to the tawdry precincts north of Fifty-Seventh Street, an apartment studded with reminders of Jolie and thus inflected with her complex mixture of sophistication and gullibility, as dogs are said to resemble their owners. (But then, who does Wantohantoweh with his withering gaze resemble, this dog who belongs only to himself?)

In such an apartment, empty of her and yet marked by her passage, he will feel guilty again, he knows. Guilty and also a little turned on.

He types out a new message, moving fast, trying to beat into the ether the reply he can see now his previous message invites. The thing is (he writes), he lives downtown, and is under the weather, not really feeling up to travel just at present—even if only to the other end of the city. And almost immediately upon his hitting send, a response appears.

That's okay. We can come to you; I presume now works?

We? he thinks. And begins to type, *It's late*, but before he can finish, another message arrives.

It's an unusual last name you have, Grayson—the only Aplanalp I can see in the white pages here. Expect us in 5 to 10 minutes. I'm writing this from a Starbucks three blocks away.

He can feel his curiosity taking over, yet the moment he sets down the phone, he's in hell again with that gymsock smell, brief as a note of music but also so loud it makes him wonder if he's missed something. Then it is gone.

And now it is 9:18 p.m. and, having checked the hi-def camera feed from the doorman's desk and spied there a tall and frightfully attractive woman in a raincoat, along with an elderly man, he hurries back down the hall, grabs from the laundry room the nebulizer he likes to use to cover the smell of bong rips—then realizes the sheets aren't dry yet, much less returned to the bed in his room. So when he meets them out at the elevator—Jolie's mom now restored to more normal dimensions and the old guy looking imperiously around but not extending a hand or introducing himself—it is to the dining area that he leads them. Situated at the juncture of two window-walls above the terrarium city, the table has room for a dozen guests, but only one place is set—the one where Grayson sits to eat takeout and watch YouTube when his dad works late.

As the mom repeats in more detail the situation with Jolie, he can feel her alternating between scouring his face and glancing around the apartment, as if wondering where all the grown-ups are hiding. Or as if looking for clues. Meanwhile, his attention keeps wandering back down the hall to his room, like a part of the mind that, through attempted repression, comes to occupy the very forefront of thought. Only bits and pieces of what she is saying filter in. That and her terrifying alertness. "I notice the two of you exchanging a lot of messages this summer, which then just stop," she says at one point. "How is it that you know my daughter again?" As if the rest were simply the anesthetic before the scalpel went in.

"Jolie and I? Well, we're . . . we're friends, isn't it?" he says, hoping the girl or the algorithm has had the good sense to delete that selfie and scrambling to remember what else was in the DMs—all of which will have been accessible to the mother. At a minimum, she will have seen the last exchange between them, about him being a freak, and her ceasing to be a threat. He decides to play for honesty. Honesty plus pity, that ought to do it. "We met last spring. At the hospital?"

The mom blanches and looks at the old man, and for a moment Grayson feels a little more confident in his position: there must be something she's concealing, too. But then he sees the way her gaze has returned to him: *How much do you know about that? And why?* "And then what, Grayson . . . you just start trading messages? Who friended whom?"

"She seemed like a cool girl," he says, by way of conveying that the friendship is of a platonic nature. One does not, he sees in hindisght, try to pressure or seduce a cool girl, or trick her into having it off with one. He almost brings up the privacy settings, but doesn't want to admit that he checked to find them adjusted. "But you said she's with her father, right . . . ? And these are Apple products she's using? I don't suppose it's occurred to you to just try the 'find my phone' feature?"

After only a slight wince, the mother reaches into the briefcase she's hung from the shoulder of a chair she's otherwise refused, withdraws a sleek silver square with yet another sticker on it: *POGUE MAHONE.* He feels that she would fasten it to her person with handcuffs if she could. But she opens it and places it on the table, says, "Show me." And when he hesitates, says, "For everyone's peace of mind, your own included, we need to know where she is, Grayson." She won't let him rest until she has her daughter back, is the implication. And maybe not even then.

"But you have her iCloud password?"

"No, but the computer's set to log in automatically."

"Okay then . . . ahem. Let's see what we can do."

22

SHE COULDN'T SAY why she'd been imagining a man behind the knock—any more than she could have put into words the other thoughts and fears that had been swirling around her head that day—but the woman in the doorway, under the black Yankees fitted, stood not much taller than Jolie herself. There was no badge to be seen, not at this distance—or anyway, not from the bed. Yet in the posture, the peremptory air, something in the face, this person unmistakably had the weight of an institution behind her. And that was before Dad made the introduction and let her slip past with her boxer's crouch and into the noirish interior.

The harsh light of the torchiere would reveal someone substantially younger than that bus-driver outfit made her seem—late thirties at the outside—and Jolie found herself thinking for some reason of Prince circa *Controversy* only minus the moustache (himself a turbanless Jafar from *Aladdin*). The interest the woman was finding in Jolie's face seemed likewise to belie the costume; could *she* have been one of Dad's old flames? But over against that was the posture, the aggression, the way that when she said, *Pleasure, Jolie*, it was like someone announcing the theme of a lecture. No, the lady was a cop, come to take him into custody for trying to keep her. But then nothing followed except those curious, almost amber eyes, sizing Jolie up. And some confusing volleys with Dad during which Jolie tried to remain very still. She even started to imagine she'd maybe succeeded in disappearing until she was told in so many words to keep doing what she was doing: *stay put*. And with that, the lady and Dad were on the balcony with the non-working lights and the door sliding shut behind them.

What erupted almost instantly out there was a dumbshow of anger, its muffled audio compensated by gesture and glare. The light from the torchiere was like the lights outside the gymtorium—like she was trying to watch a rehearsal through the mesh-reinforced window, with the difference that most performances don't lead to a life behind bars, as this one seemed destined to. Yet it was to facilitate her own leaving, rather than to honor her father's wishes, that Jolie drew the curtain and resolved not to hear, grabbed the fedora from the dresser where she'd put it. Let him go, said a voice inside her. Whatever he's done, let no one try to protect him anymore from the real world, which is the world of consequences. So why were her eyes already running along the surfaces, the baseboards, the corpselike impress his body had left on the comforter . . . looking for anything else that might have deepened the trouble he was in?

Apart from the pocket change and gum wrappers and little boluses of wadded receipt, there was nothing; they hadn't had the room long enough to really settle in. And the folding razor she'd lifted from the van was obviously legal to carry, and was about to leave the crime-scene with her, in the slit lining of her hat. She proceeded nonetheless to the bathroom, needled by something. Besides: she'd get the luxury here of another wall between herself and the drama out on the balcony, a drama with which she would have nothing more to do. The rattling vent fan, in this context, was a blessing. So too the dripping tap, the wincingly uncinematic light above the mirror making plain that the maids hadn't made it this far—another idiosyncrasy of the Elysian Shores and one frankly a little tough to explain. (Had they been called away on some other task? A fresh bout of nausea? Some supervening emergency?) But even this could be seen as a blessing, for here on the counter, laid out as in a surgical theater, was the sum total of her father's local acquisitions: the plastic IGA sack full of toiletries. And what was it she'd been afraid to find here, anyway? Stacks of currency swiped from that gas station? His ex-friend's unlicensed handgun? It was only in the interest of thoroughness that she even bothered to check the corduroy jacket left hanging on the back of the doorknob. But goddammit—here it was, obviously. The tinted baggie she scrounged from a pocket, the shadowy cargo within of what she instantly knew to be black-tar heroin. She'd heard the name, but had been unable before now to conjure an image. And it explained a lot, didn't it? Even if he wasn't back to using, which she assumed she'd know if he was— even if he'd just brought her down here to slide back into the drug game, gotten it off his friend Eddie to sell or just transport for money—it seemed like enough to get him locked away for a good long time. It was no longer possible to imagine that Jolie's life would be any the worse for that. Or that she could even still somehow live. Yet she flushed the pee that had been left in the toilet to mellow (Dad again), and didn't wait for the vortex to calm before dumping in her discovery, a mass about the size of a baby's fist that didn't scatter finely over the water, as you'd think, but proved surprisingly heterogeneous.

The second flush was weakened by the tank not having refilled, or not fully. She licked a square of toilet paper and hastily wiped from the rim a sooty residue that might still have been enough to trigger a drug-sniffing dog or a litmus strip. Oddly grayer than it had looked through the plastic. She was careful this time to wait—though it killed her—before flushing the two baggies after it. Baggies that didn't really want to go down, and may even have caused some plumbing difficulties for the room's next tenants, but at least she'd spared her dad these aggravating factors, she thought . . . which was when her focus on Ethan cleared and she remembered the other Schedule I drug that was out there, mark- ing the book she'd left in plain sight: the doubled little blotter of LSD.

She killed the light so as to kill the fear: Did she even dare go out there to retrieve it? The fan died, too. The voices that drifted from the balcony into her black box of a bathroom, her Schrödinger's cube, were no less distant than the wet slapping sounds redoubling next door, behind the particle board and the HVAC ducts. Whether it was a good or a bad sign that Dad and the officer were still out there, she didn't know, but there seemed to be nothing yet in the way of sirens, backup, radios crackling in the hall. Gently, she undid the door's lock, eased it open to find the curtains still drawn, luffed slightly by the change in pressure. And creeping to the far bed where the book was, she plucked the acid from between the pages. Her plan, to the extent she had one, was to take the tabs with her as she went, but at the exact moment she turned toward the door, the one to the balcony was sliding open, and the lady cop who'd advised her to stay put came backing through the heavy fabric, struggling there for a moment as if caught in a web. And if Jolie in that split second could have just played it cool, pocketed or palmed the tabs, everything might still have turned out differently, sweaty hands or no. But she'd long since accepted that she was her father's daughter—the second coming of Ethan Aspern, that was her. And on some pure impulse, or compulsion, she instead popped the blotter into her mouth.

What she hadn't counted on then was the spell in which the woman would just hang around. It was endless. She could feel the paper she was willing to stay solid trying instead to insinuate itself into her tongue, the tabs to uncouple, to cling to or hide behind the metal piercing, making her think out of nowhere of the illicit Eucharist she'd taken secretly in a church once, though only baptized Christians were invited to receive. Then blessedly the woman was gone, and with her heightened perceptions Jolie could hear her footsteps entering the stairwell that led down to the lobby. She ignored the question Dad looked at her when he turned—and the question he outright asked (*What the fuck is that?*) when he saw her at last fish out a tab with her finger. But it was only the first of the two, and she was up and out the door. Her mind was not on Dad or whether he followed. Rather, she kept thinking, on the breezeway, on the stairs, that she would reach up and find the tab's twin capering and hiding along her hard palate, but there were cameras everywhere, and it wasn't as dark out as she'd let herself believe. So she would still have a mouthful of poison, sacrament, whatever, when he finally caught up to her on the abandoned boardwalk and turned her roughly toward him. "Jolie?" he hissed. "We're not supposed to leave the room. Are you trying to get me taken into custody? What on earth is going on?"

Above the shuttered arcades, a solitary plane was drifting by, so high and slow she at first mistook it for a star. Somewhere up in the branchings of her head a memory swelled, but didn't drop down to where she might retrieve it.

"Jolie?"

And suddenly she was reaching up, just as slowly it seemed, and fishing from her mouth the rest of what for at least a few minutes (but how many?) had been poisoning her to save him, or vice versa, a second gray gob finding her palm under the streetlight.

"What the hell?" She smoothed it flat beside its spitting image, their winking stars blurring, one still visible, one less so. Held out her hand. "This is . . . Jesus Christ, did Eddie give you these? No, wait—how long were they in there?"

She would have this idea later that if you really, really concentrate, you can feel the moments that are going to stay with you as they're happening. Like a knot on a string that's passing through your fingers. And just before he took her hand and swept the whole damp mass from her skin and popped it into his mouth—which is to say now, sitting here in my drab apartment in the late summer years later, trying to find some way to explain what came next—she would be given just enough time to wonder if the memory that was ripening was this one.

VI

BABYLON REVISITED REVISITED

11 September, 2021
Passeig de Sant Joan 87, Primer 2a
Barcelona, Catalunya
Esp.

On a blue summer day like this one, Jolie—from the oblong window of a
plane eight miles over the Atlantic—what will strike you if you're looking
the way my mom tried to teach us to in third-form drawing (seeing not
what you hope for, but what is) is the curious fact that there's really no
such thing as a horizon. Sure, there might be a deepening blue out there
toward the vanishing point, or a haze of scudding clouds, but only under
the conditions called "severe clear" do you actually get the line people
talk about, that visible boundary where down ends and up begins. Some
trepidation at even boarding your flight can start to feel not crazy, but
downright rational. And hours in, when you sense a creeping drag, a subtle
depressurization, an altitude loss so gradual everyone including the pilot
seems to be sleeping right through it, you might perhaps be forgiven for
feeling you could use something to take the edge off. Or anyway, such
were my thoughts in the middle of 2001, somewhere east of Greenland,
returning from a belated honeymoon with your mother. I sat there trying to
remember other lessons I'd once hoped to forget: how I'd kept myself off
opiates the winter and spring I was seventeen; ways I'd infinitely delayed
the moment of opening my Altoids tin, or going over to the Sinclair to try to
score. I counted breaths, prayed, hummed songs in my head . . . held out as
long as I possibly could. Then I unbuckled, squeezed past your eyemasked
mother, and wove a slalom course through steerage to the rear galley

where one of the flight attendants sat working a crossword puzzle by the light above the jumpseat.

I should add—in all honesty—that I hadn't expected to find a soul back there. On my previous foray, I'd seen only a makeshift bar unattended on the countertop: a tower of inverted cups, some beercans footed in icemelt, plus a vaguely medicinal chardonnay . . . which last, the wine, had been the first alcohol I'd touched in the eight days since we'd flown over; it had almost started to seem again that I might be able to stop. But now, halfway through an onboard movie chosen in what would soon seem an act of hubris—I'm remembering <u>Speed 2</u>, but it may have been <u>Die Hard with a Vengeance</u>—Bernoulli's principle had begun to feel a little flimsy again. After letting the stewardess finish with the boxes she was stuck on, I heard myself ask if she had anything stronger. When she looked up, her voice had that Aer Lingus lilt.

Trouble sleeping?

Her hair would pretty much have to be red, wouldn't it? Also: she had one of those wing-shaped pins clipped over her heart, just to the right of her scarf. I wanted to say something snappy . . . like, it was broad daylight in an airborne sarcophagus, sleep was for people who weren't paying attention. Instead, I told her, truthfully, that this was only my second time on an airplane (or first, depending on how you counted a round-trip) and that anyway I'd been an apnea sufferer for a few years now, no one really wanted to hear me sleep. Then I fiddled with my wedding band as, legs still crossed, she bent forward to unlatch one of the wall's many storage cubes, a pale curve of bra flashing under her regulation blouse. In a bin were bottles of whiskey, of which two handfuls emerged. On the house, she said. Just let me know if you need more.

There was a time when I'd have rejected her charity as a point of pride, and a later one when I'd have done so to keep up appearances, but I had since managed to convince myself that I was just a regular human being. That is: a person who could sometimes be allowed to drink and also a person who could sometimes feel this overpowering need to. Not that I'd tell your mother about the surplus bottles now stowed overhead when she woke an hour later, any more than I'd show her the scrap of paper I found in my lap after the descent began in earnest and the attendants came through to gather trash. The phone number was one of those European joints starting with a plus, and would still be in my possession when the stewardess gave her finger-wave goodbye, watching me not-toss it into a colleague's trashbag . . . and that none of this got noticed by Sarah Kupferberg I took at the time as evidence of my stealth, and thus of my commitments to us both remaining intact.

We were supposed to get picked up at EWR, but she had a voicemail saying to take a car, so it would be ninety minutes and approximately four thousand dollars in cabfare later that we went up to the Kupferbergs' to fetch you.

Eleanor met us at the door with cheek kisses; you were napping, she said. Then she surprised me by asking eagerly how our trip had been. And I was just putting on my stupid faux brogue to say Grand, grand when Sarah spoke up from somewhere behind us, producing an odd echo.

Mom, what is this? You're getting rid of this stuff?

She was standing in the old Kupferberg library, but now boxes blocked the lower cabinets, flaps upward like beaks hungry to be fed. The shelves above were empty, the ladder nowhere to be seen.

Right—about that, Eleanor said. I was planning to wait until your father was here, but . . . you may as well know, we closed on a place while you were gone.

"Closed"? But what does that even mean?

A house, honey. To live in. The realtor first showed it to us in July.

What realtor?

We signed the papers on Monday.

And this is why you sent us abroad for a week? So you could slip out of the city undetected and buy a house?

Not out of the city, Sarah, just to Riverdale. It's the Bronx.

It's the 'burbs!

It's not the 'burbs, you can reach it by subway—as I pointed out to your father. Subway and then bus. No, Al, I said, just wait, she'll be happy for us both . . . and now Jolie will have some grass to run around on.

But think how much harder it'll be for you to even get to see her! And I'm standing here right now looking out at the park—

At which point, Jolie, you came padding in from the front hall in some kind of Tiger Lily buckskin, followed by a captive it took me a second to recognize as Albert Kupferberg.

Look, it's a forty-minute commute at most, he said defeatedly, and you're never home anyway. The books I've been taking up in carloads, but the big move isn't scheduled to happen for another two weeks.

And suddenly I was seeing it: everything had its price, and leaving New York had obviously been what he'd had to pay to keep Eleanor.

That your mother would splurge on another cab so quickly after having gotten out of one—your mother who'd always believed cabs to be in some way counterrevolutionary—was how I knew she'd seen it too; her dad had failed her once again, and she wanted to get away from him as fast as possible. But now, after leaning forward to tell the driver to take Amsterdam because Broadway had been a shit show, she craned back at the easterly building faces gone blue with shadow and asked how her parents could possibly be choosing to give all this up. Their whole life had been New York.

Which she would still be saying ten days later, apropos of nothing, pouring her Grape-Nuts in the morning: their whole life was New York, how could anyone possibly turn their back on this city? She seemed stuck on the same threshold I'd drifted across months earlier—am now crossing here again at forty-three, realizing you may not have been writing me from Bellevue after all this summer ("two slightly different places, two different times") but only stuck in some "humdrum apartment." In short, Jolie: none of us knew anymore what story we were in. We were all of us up in the air. Though in your mother's case, I can at least fix with some precision the date she'd lost the plot, since our return flight, ten days earlier, had been on the first of September, 2001.

But let me just back up here once more to clarify that we'd by this point lived several lifetimes. Our wedding, such as it was, had taken place almost three years earlier at City Hall, slotted into the gap between Sarah's early graduation from Columbia and the jump she'd arranged to get on her Ph.D. The previous summer, we'd shared a little two-month idyll after your birth, laundry everywhere, stacked takeout containers, all sleeping in the same bed as the mood struck us, a wondrous disarray. But ever since, she'd been working like a woman possessed, lugging her breast pump along with her briefcase onto the crosstown bus for nine a.m. classes and calling home at intervals on the cellphones we'd early-adopted so she could hear you babble and you hear her voice (also because it turned out rats had gnawed through the phone lines in our apartment). And though I hated being apart from her for so long, I assumed it was just her own inexhaustible willpower driving her back to the desk again after coming home at night, you swaddled for sleep and cupped in the crook her crossed leg made as she annotated articles and powered through tomes. I'm saying, I was more in love with her than ever, Jolie—more in awe of her too, I think. And at any rate, I had my own passion project now.

Which was you.

And I remember, oh . . . the gorgeous boredom of our morning routine after we'd put her on the bus: the walk to get coffee, egg-sandwich smell wafting from the doors of bodegas propped open for the fall; and stroller wheels made to jam on the uneven slabs of sidewalk, young dudes in airbrushed jean ensembles who'd courteously lift the front to help and then, having barely slowed, roll on; an old lady on 110th always watching from the stoop in her housedress, one rope of silver in her black, black hair, who when I loosened the buckles to show you the sun, said, You carry a baby like that? And the generations of women who called you Mami—Ay bonita, Mami, Dios te bendiga, the blessings in a different language ringing kinder in my ears. And me at nineteen, me at twenty, proudly one-arming you around Spanish Harlem like no one before in the history of the world had ever had a baby.

By nine months, I recall, you were alarmingly tan. I would have to take you out into the streets again at naptime just to get you to sleep, and then again when you cried in the middle of the night wanting to wake Sarah, so sometimes I didn't even bother to go in, bottle-feedings and changings all happening right out in the open. And I know you've painted me somewhere as sleepless at the time, which I was (maybe even problematically so), but I was also something more, because the way I got you to sleep wasn't through motion alone, but also through music; and oh, how I would sing.

Your mother had all the old lullabies from her mother, but what I had from mine, as if in compensation, was the whole lush sprawl of postwar pop, and I could feel almost close to her again as softly I sang you every last random thing I could remember the words to, "Go to the Mirror Boy" from <u>Tommy</u>, or "Johanna" from <u>Sweeney Todd</u>, or "Nothing Compares 2 U," or U2, "One Tree Hill." Even songs my mom might have looked at askance, "Friends in Low Places"; "Brandy" by Looking Glass; "Regulate" by Warren G. Because you're right about context being everything: I remember singing you that one by Talking Heads about flyover country, car parks and baseball diamonds and little toy houses . . . and I remember too the sweetness with which these details could be delivered a cappella, where their inclusion in a punk song couldn't but register contempt.

And then it was the next summer and suddenly you were older, the ten dozenth sippy cup filled, the ten thousandth grape sliced, but also these sunshowers of individuation I'd relay to your mom in phone calls I could no longer get you to sit still for, watching you repeat with slightly more mastery what she'd just missed you doing for the first time: the first sprint across the room, the first complete sentence . . . I still have a little notebook I kept of all the ways you'd reinvented language. Marching up and down on the loveseat cushions, chopping an invisible axe, saying, Vike! Vike! Vike! What were you doing? "I'm Viking!" Or when I'd ask you, Capeesh?, how you'd respond: Caposh. And how once, hearing your mother tell me, not-so-sotto-voce, that one or another of her own parents was driving her crazy, you looked her straight in the eye and said, Mommy, you're driving me happy.

     And I want you to hear this, Jolie, and to know it, whatever your own struggles may or may not be, now that you're older even than I was then: you were driving me happy. Maybe that first year, you could chalk it up to infancy, but after that, it was just the way you were.

     No, what started me using again, in earnest, was that this life I'd stumbled into—undreamt of, yet maybe the only one I was cut out for—this life, for at least two reasons, couldn't last. The first, stupidly, was money. When we'd reneged on our agreement to move in with Eleanor and Albert, I'd thought my survivor benefits would carry us further than they did, and perhaps hadn't registered the minuscule scale of the paychecks your mom would eventually be earning as a graduate teaching assistant. I was going to have to return to work, as I'd promised. And given her need to be free to teach during the day and her justifiable (I felt) aversion to going back to her parents for help, the work would have to be at night, which pretty much ruled out the TV roles for which I'd rendered myself more or less unfit anyway, via the two-year gap in my résumé. So it was to be restaurants again. Restaurants where I put in six nights a week, having already clocked days at my life's great work. Restaurants to which I was always running late when I handed you off to Sarah in the evening, before she even had time to shrug off her coat. Restaurants that meant that for months I'd hardly see her at all, and from which I'd emerge near midnight spent and lonesome and drained of resistance and knowing you'd both be long since asleep. Restaurants where, it goes without saying, I was never far from a bar.

Besides, I thought, what had all that been back there anyway, in high school, with the aerosols and the psychedelics and then the Vicodin Percocet morphine, the oblivion, the transfixing need? Couldn't it just have been a phase, like Moira the German club kid? Wasn't it presumption, or even self-aggrandizement, to think of myself as an addict? Or, failing that, wasn't it something I could grow out of? Anyway, I had too much to live for now to start using actual drugs again, I told myself—like the focus my little girl would demand playing lost boys by Harlem Meer come sunrise— whereas these bottles behind the bar just held the same mild decoctions I saw servers and cooks and managers sampling at shift's end, at worst the cause of a little bleariness the next day. I hadn't forgotten the night Jerry Garcia died, of course, the life it had nearly cost me, but I was now twenty-one, and what could it really hurt to linger behind for a drink as the waitresses were always tugging at me to do? And so on, Jolie, I think you know the rest: the telltale rationalizations I hadn't learned yet to recognize as the voice of the beast.

There was a little pub a few blocks south of work where I used to go nurse a drink or two alone before heading home. Heaven, let's call it, after that other Talking Heads song, the one where nothing ever happens: some African cab drivers, a tall couple from Legal Aid, a nattering of kibitzers, and down near the jukebox an old lady named Mary with a face like a brothel keeper's and a barstool with her name literally on it. Her sister Tony or Toni tended bar, tiny but still beautiful, bouffant dyed black . . . not that there was much to the job: each liquor came in only two different brands, and everything else was served in the bottle, save for the one tap of Guinness, which she poured like it was Coors.

And the fact that I didn't even much enjoy drinking after the first few months seemed only to prove that I must have been mistaken about myself: couldn't really be harboring some condition or disease. Likewise a mark of my virtue, I believed (rather than of a concerning slide toward secrecy, the rules blossoming and proliferating alongside their own violation), was that in this period I always returned from the bar at least sober enough to sneak into bed before your mom ever noticed my tardiness—and that, until those airplane bottles, I never, ever brought alcohol into the house. Nor do I think you probably noticed any obvious difference in the quality of our days together; in fact, I may have overcorrected for my worsening hangovers by saying yes to everything, disclosing the existence in myself of a kind of improv genius or playmate god.

No, the bottom line, Jolie, in case you ever wonder: it wasn't being your dad that made me the addict I am. Rather, at least temporarily, it helped me become something else, too, something better. And on mornings after I'd had one too many, when my head was killing me and all my powers of invention seemed to be stuck at the bottom of a well, I would still take you to the park and watch you from the safe distance of a bench, trying to make commiserating eye contact with the West Indian nannies. (Who by the way were having none of it.)

Which brings me to the other, more profound reason the life we were building together was untenable: you eventually began to outgrow it. As early as the summer of 2000, the year you turned three, it was evident that you needed more than just a dad to raise you, notwithstanding all our trips to the library, all the playdates with kids your age I was sure I could pull together if only their parents, twenty years my senior, would stop blowing off my calls. The deciding symptom may have been the "buncha books" you started asking to be left with when you took over the living room for naptime, and the hours you then spent "reading" them—the terrifying Concentrating Face you'd make while teaching yourself every last thing I couldn't. By the spring of 2001, I'd caught you trying to write your name inside the flaps. When I reported this to Sarah, she brought up preschool, but I was already feeling some distance from her, and to my shame, I couldn't bear the idea of also being distant from you for five days a week. Think of all the time you'd have to go to auditions, though, Sarah said, or to write (with some obscure note of longing here about the play she still believed me to be finishing). But I pointed to our old friend money: How could we afford preschool, when we couldn't even afford a babysitter so that we could occasionally act like married people on my nights off? Or maybe the adverb I chose was "ever." Maybe the verb was "pretend to be." In any case, I think the line may have shaken her up more than I had meant it to.

Hence: a honeymoon after all, in Ireland, coinciding with the completion of her grad-school comps. In the eyes of your grandfather, it amounted to basically a birthright trip; at any rate, he'd been offering to pay her way even before I'd met him, as if wanting her to walk in his footsteps—or as if putting an ocean between the two of us could convince her to cut me loose. But he didn't know what I'd since come to learn: that connection too can be an addiction. And now, trying to find her way back to hers, Sarah asked him to cover the cost for us both.

And of course that trip was epic, Jolie. It was as if the magus Albert Kupferberg (or perhaps, I now think, his wife) had waved a wand made of bills and granted us seven more days of the summer of '95, albeit six years later. Ireland was far to the north, far west in the time zone, so that even this deep into summer the evenings would last well into night. We tramped through cities and towns, swam in ice-cold ponds, ate sandwiches in fields where crickets sang (I was surprised to discover that Ireland had crickets) . . . even slept one night in a castle on the wild bleak coast where my mother's ancestors had committed their acts of piracy. And no matter where we were, we talked endlessly together the way we used to, only this time about the interviews she was collecting for the dissertation I hadn't realized had been giving her fits. The endless weeks spent among the streetwalkers under the El in Jackson Heights, slowly earning their trust, seemed to have destabilized something in her, or else the last several years had. Her hypothesis going in had been that these women and men were rational actors, responding to the shitty but meliorable conditions of American life; my own hypothesis, advanced in the spirit of a sparring partner, was that sometimes people were driven by forces beyond their personal ken, and that here at the end of history, life was nothing if not a mystification of choice. But it was neither one of these suppositions she saw showing up in the transcripts, she said, or it was both: this uncomfortable middle where her interview subjects seemed to feel themselves to be living, full of power yet also bereft of it, somehow.

On our last night overseas, as if to escape the problem altogether, we made a series of resolutions. We would finally accept some financial support from her parents, at least until I could find a higher-paying gig, and then would send you to the only preschool in our price range that seemed to still have a slot, this Spanish-immersion thing down by the Museo (though because I spoke only English, you'd get no practice around the house). Unbeknownst to her, I would also begin to pawn the boxes of my mom's music I'd paid the super to keep in our building's basement; maybe Albert and Eleanor wouldn't even be needed, if I could come up with some lie about where I'd found the money. Maybe I could give up my nights in the bar, too. Maybe I could support her as a real husband would. She must have sensed on some level what this was costing me, though, this idea of an end to my days taking care of you, because the final promise we made was about her and me, our marriage. We would move our futon out of the bed-sized sleeping nook of the last four years and move your new big-girl bed in, so that the larger living area would become a space for us to play husband and wife again, or at least watch a movie every so often over takeout we couldn't afford. If we could just get through this next little grind, we agreed, the completion of a half-dozen more interviews, the coding of the transcripts, the actual writing of the dissertation, we'd be home free.

What neither of us was counting on was the preschool requiring a physical from the pediatrician, and the pediatrician not being able to squeeze you in for an appointment until the third week of September. From my perspective, the delayed onset of school was something of a reprieve. Still, I now had those little bottles in my suitcase, and each night when I shuffled back from work, my tolerance slightly diminished by ten days overseas, I'd be too well-lubricated to resist a nightcap or two in our tiny lavatory. Or even a soporific dose from the regular-sized bottles I suddenly seemed to be stashing in my messenger bag, practicing coping the only way I knew with the loss of someone I loved. And what we'd actually created by moving our futon to the living room was a space where it would be safe for me to recover. In the morning, while you played with such toys as I could muster from the crannies that seemed to suck them in—you were into puzzles then, I remember, and insanely good at solving them—I would odalisque on the mattress as if observing you and . . . not sleep, exactly, that would have been irresponsible, but close my eyes and let's say feel the heaviness of the time, the emptiness of an apartment building where people fit for normal life were already off for work.

Time to play zoo, I remember hearing one morning somewhere above me, and I cracked an eye to find that the sun hadn't budged on the wall, or the gnomon of the fire-escape shadow moved relative to the waterstains on the window. The whole of time as understood by the ancients, the planetary model refurbished by Copernicus, seemed to be on the verge of breaking down again. Copernicus, who had obviously never been put in charge of childcare. You tugged on my ear, explained that I was supposed to be a lion.

Daddy's a tired lion, I said, and sank closer to the floor.

Da-deee.

Okay. Okay. My eyes still closed, I roared my terrible roars, swiped my aching claws; moved my slow thighs to punctuate the tired soliloquy of what I assure you was one extremely rough and slouching beast indeed.

And somewhere in there, I began to notice the sirens—nothing unusual at first, but then more and more. Or maybe it was the way they stood out against what seemed to be a hiccup in the air traffic to LaGuardia. Which was odd, given the conditions of severe clarity I alluded to above. You have to remember, information wasn't yet pinging around the ether in quite the same way it does now. I know at one point I broke off our game to hoist the water-stained front window high enough to check the street— unusual because that thing was a deathtrap, too big for the anti-fall bars now required by the city. And I would like to report here, as evidence of the feeling of urban togetherness that cynics would later try to write off, some special attunement in the knot of guys outside the bodega on our corner; I can at least certify that I saw cabs start to pull over and was disconcerted enough to flip on the television and hold the rabbit ears to make my whole body into an antenna. The local affiliates must have been sharing a feed, since each of the three networks seemed to carry the same low traffic-copter shot of the twin towers with gashes so high up you'd have taken it for a horrible accident, a prop plane someone hadn't known how to fly, if only there hadn't been two of them. The silence, too, I remember deepening, like a pastoral scene in a nature documentary, or the quiet of a church before the organ prelude starts, either because Sarah had left the sound down some previous night when you were sleeping and me out of transmitter range or because as the first of the silvery debris began to slide from the leftmost tower, those professional yakkers had found themselves at a loss for words. And as I moved reflexively to block the screen from your sight, I thought: Of course. Firefighters. I suppose I was thinking of those helicopters with their great buckets of water that helped fight fires in California; they must now have been cut off by the top of the screen, so that all I could see was the effect: the silvery cascade of the life-giving water. Then—in the time it took me to realize the downpour I was seeing was just glass and steel—that first tower disappeared, like an eraser had been run from top to bottom.

You'll have been too young to remember the annual New Year's party on our block, Jolie, the crowds that used to form outside bars and cafés for the countdown, but this was like that, only the opposite. A thing I've never felt before or since: the whole city holding its breath. A voiceover had at some point estimated the number of people inside each tower at twenty thousand, and for a moment I swear I could feel that number not as a number, but as the heat of twenty thousand discrete fires, snuffed out.

Then I remember the cellphone circuits all jamming, busy signals, recordings. Fighter jets began crisscrossing overhead, an unmistakable ripping in the sky. And though I saw your worried look and told you this would be okay, your mom was okay, the scale of the thing defied comprehension, such that I admit to wondering whether any of the twenty or eighty commercial airliners said to still be streaking through the blue out there (the ones, it occurred to me, the fighter jets had been meant to shoot down) might be bound for Low Library or St. John the Divine or wherever your mother was now . . . though of course if the target list was broad enough to include an unfinished cathedral for a religion no one practiced anymore, we were probably all already dead.

Still: if I knew your mom to be okay out there, to be safe, then why this unbearable tension in my body? Why, for hours, couldn't I take you out of the apartment and down onto the street with those neighbors? Why was I counting the minutes until I could put you down for the nap I knew you wouldn't sleep for, and why did I finally do it a whole hour early, knowing you'd be giving up your nap anyway once you started at the preschool? I was losing my shit, was why. I needed Sarah there with me, physically, where I could feel how alive she was. And I feared that if this moment went on much longer, I was going to die (I can say that now)—which I couldn't let you see. You had just started knocking on the sleeping-nook door to be let out when she entered, looking ashen. She'd walked all the way over from the west side, she said, the buses and subways were all fucked, but why was the door here locked—

I almost tackled her, held her close until the tears I knew were in there started to come. Then I put a finger to my lips like, don't let Jolie know we're awake; took her over to the loveseat, where we locked hands and sat. I had finally managed to get the antenna to bring in a signal without standing there to hold it. Maybe all those other times I just hadn't wanted it badly enough. And I can remember the quiet as we watched the ABC anchorman, Peter Jennings, and—I can't believe we did this, honey, but Jesus, we were so young—let you join us after you knocked again. The late Peter Jennings who, it must be said, was magnificent in a crisis—who for hours didn't seem to eat, sleep, drink, or piss, since the commercial breaks that might have allowed him to do so had been suspended. Peter Jennings who, I would later learn, wasn't even an American. Who was from Canada, and a dropout like me.

All classes canceled, your pediatrician's visit and the start of preschool further delayed, we spent the rest of the week tucking you in the umbrella stroller you'd already outgrown and pushing you for miles through the city, trading off, one-arming the handle so we wouldn't have to let go of each other's hands. Once or twice, as if on our old rambles, we kept going until we hit the cordon around Lower Manhattan where, after a few silent minutes, we would have to turn back. And when we stopped for supplies I would look at the clerk across the counter of the bodega or CVS or the bagel shop, or at the messenger idled on his bike or the teacher suddenly stripped of students or the banker waiting at a light or the trans woman taking it all in from a Siamese connection, and for a second our eyes would meet and it was like we were all really seeing other people, you know? Like, each knowing the other had to be feeling the same thing, but in this way utterly peculiar to him, or her, or them. Everybody having lost somebody, somewhere. Everybody somebody's child.

And how rare it was, I thought, to recognize a moment like this even as you were in it. Like living inside a poem. Though maybe it was just me and not your mom who knew what to do in between the lines there, where things broke down, because I'd already seen a whole world's worth of human beings blanked out once before . . .

Over the years, I've tried to tell this story in any number of meetings, Jolie, but the thing I could never bring myself to be honest about when I did was this feeling of wonder, too. Of a kind of suspension radiating outward—of a utopia inscribed inside a hell. Of life qua life, maybe . . . because "life as we knew it," the one-foot-in-front-of-another thing that had given me such trouble, stood revealed as completely absurd. I don't mean that the grief wasn't awful, or everywhere; it was on a scale to match the three thousand people whose murder we'd all just witnessed. When the little capsule biographies began to appear in the Times, Sarah would force herself to read every word, saying even one of these was worth everything the paper had ever gotten wrong. But the corollary of all those people dying was this heightened recognition that there were others still alive. And to lose sight of that again, I thought I'd learned, would be to dishonor the dead—even if you believed what you were doing was the opposite.

Of course, you can't live in a poem, not permanently. I'd just started my second year front-of-the-house at a brasserie down on Prince Street, which had reopened sooner than you might expect. It felt almost patriotic, bracing up our fellow New Yorkers with food and drink, and at the end of a shift my colleagues were no longer content to hoist a few comps at the zinc bar facing the mirror, but now wanted to go out into the East Village where, even more than usual, no one seemed to be sleeping. Through the wild free streets of the city they would want to seek out other restaurants and clubs and karaoke joints and bachata floors like the ones Sarah and I had frequented long ago. But there were also drugs everywhere, coming closer, I could almost smell them, so along with my rule about being in bed before dawn, I'd made certain pacts with myself not to enter any bar from which I didn't have an exit strategy. Nor to carry flirtation beyond flirtation, for with the wedding band on my finger and the adorable little daughter whose photos filled my wallet and my difficulty stopping anything once started, I remained catnip to two distinct kinds of women—those who wanted to ruin me and those who wanted to save me.

Yet I did find myself returning more and more to the bar called Heaven. It was there one night, for example, that a party of firemen came in from the station down the street. And I'm not sure why, but after an hour or so, when Toni or possibly Tony seemed for the first time to drop her coolness toward me and asked what line of work I was in, I put down whatever novel I was reading and glanced down the bar to where the firemen were being stood shots and answered, Construction.

Here, I wanted to believe, was a character I could inhabit if I kept the answers clipped: unskilled, no prospects, shacked up outside of Peekskill with a girlfriend and her daughter from a previous relationship . . . coming here at the end of a working day to tie one on before boarding the bus back home. It didn't occur to me that construction was still frozen all over the city while everyone waited to see if we'd be hit again—which would seem to mean, impossibly, that only a month had passed since the attacks.

And it would be later that night, in the back room, that I heard one of the firemen on line for the can ahead of me utter the fateful phrase, "greatest American rock band." In one corner, above an undersized pool table, someone had rigged a speaker to play, only at higher volume, whatever was on the front juke: in this case "Susie Q (Parts 1 and 2)," that cool descent in a black velvet box. And still, I found myself thinking . . . Really? You're going with Creedence Clearwater Revival? I glanced again at the firefighter, balding, smudgy, muscle-teed, who looked to be coming off multiple days on-duty and still had on the big clownish pants with suspenders. I know I should have left him to his epiphany, God knows he'd earned it, but sentiment and my third gin compelled me to offer that, no, if you set aside all the So-and-So and the Somethings—if the band concept had ever really meant anything at all—the greatest American rock band would still have to be the Grateful Dead. I gave him a little of Mom's riff about immanence and transcendence, and was about to go to the juke to show him when the door to the single-stall john opened, and a second firefighter turned from whatever he was doing over the junction box there. The bald one, though he was before me on line, tapped my chest. You're next, college boy.

Somehow I'd failed to realize that even these guys, everybody's heroes, were wired on the ubiquitous cocaine. And I can honestly say that in that moment the white streaks on the mirror balanced on the box looked basically harmless, like detergent left atop a dryer. What I mean is that for all my chemical promiscuity, I had never actually been much of a coke guy. Even in the days before I'd filched those first pills from my mother, I'd resisted what made you feel better, or feel more—unconsciousness being more my bag. But now this guy with his glinty little bb eyes, the one who had not long ago been rushing toward the flames rather than away as I would have been running, and who perhaps as recently as today had dug through toxic ash to recover the bodies of perfect strangers, or people he loved—that's who was calling my bluff.

I stepped into the head. It's funny what comes back to you. Or I guess never leaves. I bent to the mirror and with one nostril open did a running inhalation—"like a champ," I heard one of them say behind me, but with what level of mockery was unclear, because a new song had begun to play, heavy on the bass, "This Is How We Do It," and as I turned and found the bathroom door shut behind me, I understood that what these guys had been snorting—what was now in my body for the first time since junior year—was some kind of painkiller, obviously. My lady. (Because that's what you took when you were in pain.) On the far side of the wall or alternatively in my head, no one had bothered to fix a blown woofer, so below a certain threshold the frequencies were starting to break. Otherwise, nothing: a perfect, relieving absence. I thought of your mom, guiding Albert's Volvo through cop-infested Delaware, dropping into fourth to pass a truck.

Then a second of fear, like I'd risen too quickly. Then nothing again.

When I got myself together to emerge at last, the pool table was sort of

iced-over, the area around it deserted. Out in the bar, the party was in fact
under way, but it was as far removed from where I stood now as it had
been when I was fourteen, watching the older kids goof around on Keel
Hill where nothing they could say could hurt me now, not even if it was For
God's sake, Ethan, have another drink.

By the time I started back to chipping like this—ingesting what I'd
determined to be a safe amount of heroin at Heaven, leveling off with just
enough of the blow I'd scored from one of the busboys, booze running
behind it all—it was October, you were off to escuela, and Sarah's teaching
had resumed. The rent had to be paid and tuition procured, so I was still
working five nights a week plus Sunday brunch, but now I had no one to
get out of bed for most mornings. And I can hear your objections here, Jolie;
and it's indeed true that I could have hustled through my last customers,
batch-processed the sidework, tipped everyone out, and been home at
an hour when Sarah might still have been sitting up reading, pen dancing
over her fingers, haloed by lamplight on a cracked plaster wall . . . and
when I still could have at least watched you sleep. I could, that is, have
declined the very first drink of the night, or have left before my first trip to
the bathroom. Yet I'd convinced myself those were the hours I'd labored
through the rest of the day to earn: the hours when I could finally feel at
peace in my own skin.

   I reached peak comfort sometime around midnight, and would maintain
it until I caught a glimpse of myself in a mirror four drinks and as many
bumps later, when I could hardly stand to look—or to stand. By that point
it might be two thirty in the morning, creeping up on closing time, as if
the minutes and hours of my real life were dammed up forever ago, on
the far side of the earth. But then to keep the dam intact I'd have had
to sniff more dope, which would in turn mean more coke, and breaking
dawn, and getting caught, and maybe not being allowed to do it all again.
And instead I was in control. I would exit the subway four blocks from
our place, walk home high through the bright blighted streets at that hour
when the garbage trucks rolled through. Okay, so I might get blinded by
the stairwell lights and stumble a little, then start as if someone else were
standing there beside me to appreciate this asshole's sloppiness. It might
take whichever of us a minute to get the door open—the moment of
maximum danger; in the bathroom mirror I might already look paler, puffier,

my string played out. But it was always with the utmost care that I brushed and deodorized and slid into bed beside your mom, who never gave the appearance of being disturbed and for a long time didn't say anything at all.

Then, the morning of our third wedding anniversary, there was a ring at the buzzer, which for some reason the rats had left intact. It lasted too long for a delivery, and my first instinct was to try to smother the plastic bellbox with a pillow. You, meanwhile, were at the cramped little table where we took our meals, pouring too much milk over some pre-sweetened cereal I'd gotten your mother to soften on. Another thing about that apartment was, you couldn't buzz anyone in, you had to physically go down and see who was summoning you, so my choices were to leave you to your cereal, bring you downstairs, or ignore the buzzer and risk my head imploding. I beckoned for you with my hand. Whoever this was out front had stood back to give the steel security door a wide berth.

Still, it took me a minute to assimilate who it was: my father. For one thing, I was unused to seeing him in denim instead of chinos. The ballcap too looked new, as did the undersized truck with the Maryland plates parked behind him at the curb. The way he said my name made me feel we were standing a lot closer than we actually were. And, half a decade having passed since I'd given up on such understanding as he had to offer, you'd have thought I could have found some better opener than what came out:

Since when did you drive a pickup truck, Dad?

He let it go: And this is . . . ?

Yeah, I said. Say hi, honey. This is your other grandpa.

He'd made no move to cross the sidewalk—had perhaps even backed a step toward the pickup—and yet I had the oddest sense that he was seconds from placing a palm to the side of my head. Not the false father of the Christmas of '96, trying to decide what roles I could and couldn't play, but his real self. Selves. And of course, as I've already said somewhere, I could sympathize with that. The complexity of it.

Ethan, you look tired, he said.

Which I ignored; he should have said something when I was fifteen.

How did you find me, though? No, wait, I bet I can guess.

For now I was remembering how Moira had reached me the morning of the twelfth, and tried to call me again just last week. This despite my request to be left alone for a while.

Son, listen—

Don't.

—that morning, when it happened, we were watching on TV . . .

You and Corinne and everybody else, I said.

He balled his hands, unfolded them. I could see him wince a little.

Try to walk in my shoes for a minute, though, Ethan. How could we be sure you didn't have an appointment in those towers?

Obviously you knew better. It's not like I'm some kind of white-collar professional, and there aren't any casting agents down there—

Or that you weren't living by the Holland Tunnel, or . . . or having to abide the loss of near neighbors, people you saw every day.

I don't see you knocking doors in Tribeca. Or showing up six weeks ago, when if I'd lost someone, the wound might have been open. Speaking of which, I hear congratulations are in order.

Congratulations? he said, appearing baffled for a second.

Whatever concern you were feeling about me and my well-being, it didn't preclude you from going out and finally winning that sailing championship, did it? Moira left a voicemail.

Then, lest it become more than that (I was so hung over I could barely stand), I told him I guessed he had what he'd come for; I was now aware that I hadn't escaped his reach, and he could show up any time.

He shook his head, as if in hesitation: I don't know why I thought becoming a father would make you see things clearer, Ethan.

But what is it I'm supposed to be seeing?

Something like this happens, when you realize you might lose the person you love most, you feel like you need to find them and just . . . just be with them through it.

Yeah, but that's only if you haven't cut them loose in the first place, I said. Not that there wasn't a time when I needed you to be there with me—more than one, probably—but where were you then?

Yet when I turned to go, it was also to see whether, with all that had passed between us, he would let me walk away again. I'd almost forgotten there was a witness to any of this until you paused on the step, looked back out the door to where he was standing and said, clear as day, Hola, Abuelo. Yo soy Jolie.

That evening, partly in observance of our wedding anniversary, partly to break her boycott on their new digs, your mom and I had planned to take the subway up to Van Cortlandt Park and then a bus out to Riverdale, where we would drop you at the Kupferbergs' before going on a date—our first since Ireland. After another long day in the field, she had changed into a little black dress under my old jean jacket and looked both stunning and pretty much like the platonic ideal of herself. And you: on the seat between us, in name-brand overalls courtesy of your grandmother. Eleanor had offered to come down to our place to watch you instead, but it had been a while since I'd been in any shape for housecleaning, and I didn't want her seeing the state of our apartment and reporting back to Albert that she'd had my number all along. So we would go to dinner and maybe a movie up here in the Bronx and then come back to sleep in the Kupferberg guestroom, with you taking the pullout sofa in Albert's office. My habit in the best of times being to wear the same outfit several days running, I had packed only a tee-shirt and toothbrush, but your mom had brought along civvies for the morning, and of course I wasn't going to let you forget your pj's, so the duffel we schlepped ended up looking like those go-bags the government was now urging on everyone—and it might tell you something about the city's trajectory back to disenchantment or the sour state of my own head that I kept ours on top of my feet so it wouldn't touch the anthrax-retentive floor. As I tried to picture our fellow passengers walking across the GW Bridge, fleeing a burning city, I waited for you to say something about meeting your other grandfather, but maybe you knew more than you let on, because you never did.

The handoff, too, took place without incident, Albert not bothering to descend from his new sanctum and me declining Eleanor's invitation to come farther than the stack of boxes where I'd tucked the overnight bag behind the front door.

Walking from the bus stop to get here, we'd remarked, grudgingly, on the handsomeness of the neighborhood, but now it turned out to have gratifying flaws. The business district was somewhere between modest and effortful, and we must have roamed the length of its main drag five times— checked-tablecloth Italian, untenanted Punjabi, mock-Tudor Applebee's— not buying that there wasn't some more memorable place tucked away among them, since this was, as Eleanor said, still New York. By the time we realized we were wrong, the possibility of making a ten p.m. movie seemed purely theoretical. We settled on Italian, "Best in the City!," per the Sharpied inscription of some dead or forgotten actor's publicity still mounted to a wall. It was time to level with Sarah, I knew, about my dad and about the help I now sensed I probably needed, but it had been over a month since we'd had even five minutes to talk, and I had the feeling of fumbling over my lines.

And to be totally honest, I caught myself blaming her for that. Or rather, blaming the way I always ended up being the one in the wrong. The way I knew she'd have tried to plead his case . . . and the way she'd let me fool her with my backsliding, even as the secrets I'd needed to keep were the one thing she'd never forgive. As I tried to sound her out on her fieldwork, and to commiserate about her own parents, I made a game of counting how many of her responses included the words "no" or "not" or some contraction or implication thereof. Otherwise, I remember little, including what she ordered, until it arrived and she began to cry.

At which point my dinner, some seafood thing, lost whatever edibility it might have had. You're losing her, I thought. She's going to leave you. Again.

But out there beyond the footlights I must have seemed entirely self-sufficient, and already her own tears were receding . . . because of course (have I made this clear enough already?) the suppression of suffering wasn't just my superpower, but your mother's, too.

I reached for her hand, but she seemed absorbed in trying to get the pineapple-glass shade of the candleholder at the table's center to sit properly on its screws. And when I asked what was wrong, she said it was nothing, and not to worry.

We should walk, I realized; hadn't the best times always been when we were walking? I asked the waiter for the check. And a coconut panna cotta to go, I added. His look as he registered the half-eaten dinner and my hoarseness of voice conveyed something like, You sure dessert's what you need, buddy? But frankly I could appreciate the professionalism that kept him from saying anything aloud.

Out on the sidewalk, where Sarah already was, the Indian place had gone dark, and the other restaurants were closing up. A light summery rain seemed to materialize out of midair more than to actually fall. And I thought, well, so much for walking, except she didn't seem to notice she was getting wet. Crying again, harder now, she let me take her hand.

I had to fight panic again; did she already know? Or was any of this about me at all—was there somebody else? My instinct was to lead her to wherever it was darkest, where she would feel like there wasn't anyone to see her, or judge, but the slopes of the sidestreets carried us however wittingly back toward the river, and our daughter, and the life we'd apparently made for ourselves.

I don't know, she said finally, only a few blocks from her parents' place, when I dropped her hand and asked her once more to tell me what was wrong. I don't know what's wrong with me, Ethan. It's a feeling, is all.

She'd been burning the candle down too far, I suggested. Maybe we both had been. Working too hard.

But it's not that, she said. I like to work hard, I always have, you know that. Only now I feel like . . . like whatever work I find myself doing isn't the thing I'd choose if I really had a choice. I'll find myself, like, drafting a footnote, or standing in front of a class, and half of me can't even hear my own bullshit, you know, Ethan? Half of me is wanting to be back out there with you pushing her in the stroller to Canal Street. Or on that loveseat, holding hands. And then when I am with you guys, I somehow feel so alone all I want to do is get away, be on my own, go hide. The other day I almost found myself heading out to Beach 116th. Do you know how long it's been since I was out there?

There was no relief; only the opposite. For I knew this feeling—even knew its name. But somehow it had never occurred to me that Sarah could have felt it, too. That is: I associated depression so strongly with cowardice and inanition, with my glider and drugs and woods, that it had taken her all but beating me over the head with it to see that industry, unstinting, could be another mask for it (as in America, almost anything could). That whole time after she'd had to return to class and be away from you all day, and before that in her dormroom, hugging herself in the green chair, she must have been running from it. Even all the way back to the day when she'd reached for me in the HoJo parking lot, the day that had probably saved my life. And here I was—mad at her for not being able to do it again. At some point in there, I saw, I'd let her become a myth of herself. Worse: if my absorption back into my habit wasn't the cause of her current sadness (I think it was likely just as much September, and working motherhood), the drugs had at least blocked me from coming to her rescue as she'd always, in the end, come to mine.

We walked a little farther. The rain had stopped, but globes of humidity remained around the streetlights, now farther apart. The leaves, dark under trees that dripped when the wind kicked up, had spread to what by the cramped standards of the city felt basically like mansions. The yellow of their windows glowed. Tell her, something inside me said. Tell her what she saved you from back then.

What I said instead was: You don't have to worry about the time apart from Jolie, honey, if that's any consolation. You know I take good care of her. But maybe this should be more about your needs, trying to get you another vacation or something. With me along, too, if you want me there. Or with both of us.

The offer was sincerely meant. I was about to reveal to her the surprising amount of money I'd saved for the preschool, selling all but one box of Mom's CDs for a dollar apiece down on Bleecker Street, when I realized it had already disappeared down my throat, and up my nose. Fucking asshole, I thought.

But that's not what I'm saying, Ethan, she said, cutting me short. I'm saying, it's not even a rational feeling—like, amenable to solution. It's in my body somewhere. Which isn't even mine anymore. My hair is falling out. My ass is fat.

Are you kidding, Sarah? Your ass is amazing. And since when did you care about that stuff anyway?

And . . . and I don't even remember why I ever wanted to be a professor, apart from my dad. But now we have Jolie, and we need the money. It's like, for the first time in my life, I can't just <u>decide</u> something and walk away from the alternative. Like I'm cut up into a million pieces, and can't figure out how to get any of them talking to each other again.

I knew something about that, too, I said, cautiously. She stopped and turned to look at me. But the nearest streetlight had taken this opportunity to go out, and I couldn't quite read her face. And forgive me, Jolie, I've really been doing my best here to leave all the sex stuff aside, but in the interest of searchingness, of fearlessness: I wanted her so badly right then. I wanted her the way you want a mystery. The way you want a stranger on the subway, or a whole different life. And I wanted her to know how much I wanted her, still and always, even if I'd never seen her as clearly as I thought—and also to know what a fucking idiot I'd been to risk squandering the chance to know her better, see her deeper; that it was to my eternal shame to have ever wanted anything else. So where I should have kept going and said, yeah, honey, this is called grief, I think we're both grieving, I instead went with Iggy Pop.

All my life, I said, or sang. You're haunting me.

But what if that's not enough for me? she said. To be somebody's ghost? And I could hear her smiling . . . hear her sad.

Which is when I brushed aside her arm, stepped into her, sought her mouth in the dark, trying to remember all the parts of her she'd disparaged so that I could love them, too, show her how absolutely fucking real she was to me. It seemed important to hurry, somehow, as if the clock itself were against us, as if it were break through or die. And it seemed, too, going to our knees on someone's dark lawn in the Bronx, in these last moments when I was still capable of thought, that love should always be just that real, or else fail the attempt. The way these letters are a failed poem.

But here is another truth of the sort no one likes to hear: if you want to get free of your own troubles, try focusing on someone else's for a while. All that next week, I would wake on our marriage futon and my first thought was no longer of how far off midnight was or where I might go to score . . . or it was, but then I would remind myself of your mom, still asleep beside me, and notice what you called, way back at the start of this thing, her "rivers": how her face, unconscious, disclosed the fatigue she'd been so careful to hide in waking life. It had been hard work for Sarah Kupferberg, too, being more than one person. It had been exhausting.

I had never cared much about material attainments, never really cared where we lived, or what sorts of things we'd been able to buy. I guess none of it struck me as a fit subject for art, which I'd been taught should concern itself exclusively with identity and rebellion, with fucking and politics and salvation and death. There are no good pop songs about 401ks—and, with all due respect to "King of the Road" and Prince's "Sister," few that I can think of about the struggle to pay the rent. But then I would see those yellow windows of Riverdale burned into my memory and hear its trees in the rain, and I would think, as my mother must have thought, back in '80s DC, with her marriage going to pieces: there must be a place for us where life would be easier, "peace and quiet and open air . . ." A place in this case with a viable career path for a person like me, and a reasonably priced preschool that would deliver our daughter's instruction in a language I could understand; a place where your mother could abandon the endless striving and return to freedom—to the ocean, even—if only I could scrape together the cash to afford it. How much would it take? Six thousand to start? Eight?

With my days now wide open, I at least had time to try. I began by returning to the writing I'd once imagined might be my vocation. But I must have been farther gone than I realized, because that first week of not doing dope was even harder than I remembered, endurable only because I'd done it once before, and I couldn't even get out of bed in time for work—from which I was promptly fired.

And you might think, well, there you go, Ethan, more time to write, but in the depths of washing out, in a cold-turkey swivet, basically wanting to die, I could squeeze out only a single, four-line poem.

When I'd grown a little steadier on my feet and found a couple shifts at another waiter job, right down the street from the first, I started sending out headshots. I even attended a few auditions, but no callback ever came. And from the back row of the two or three AA meetings I made myself sit through, my main takeaway was that the work of resurrection wasn't going to be some glamorous coup de foudre, some guy on the phone saying hey, kid, we want you in the picture, but a long, slow, penitential slog.

And so one afternoon not long before Thanksgiving, I stopped off at Lincoln Center on the way down to my new restaurant. I'd disguised myself well, I thought, put on my rattiest jeans, grabbed my adolescent Vans out instead of the thicker-soled sneakers I usually wore to work. But as I watched the throngs of undergraduates bustle through the lower-level doors, I saw for the first time the subtle fashion-changes wrought by the last four years of hegemonic capitalism and felt the full Rip van Winklishness of my age. I was like a figure out of another century, or maybe an alternative present; who even knew whether my student ID was valid? Still, the hunched-over security guard raised no objections when I flashed him my wallet, and I was let through the turnstiles just like anyone else.

In the course catalog I'd continued to receive by mail (along with, inexplicably, the alumni magazine), I had noted that Hank Gregory still held his freshman drama workshop MTuWTh in the same little black box theater where I'd started, one flight down from the lobby. I couldn't very well disrupt his teaching, and couldn't seem to run down his office hours, so I dropped my decoy knapsack and settled against the wall at the top of the steps where I used to wait for class to start. As a red digital clock suspended from the ceiling meted out its uniform time—2:58, 3:01—the tempo of bodies, the volume of chatter, began to swell. Once or twice someone almost stumbled over my legs, but for all that they noticed me I might have been a street person. Finally, at 3:04 p.m., the theater's door swung outward and the first squad of jayvee thespians emerged, looking invigorated by whatever had occurred within. There came a thickening, and then a thinning, and finally Hank himself, preceded by a backward-walking whitegirl hugging to her chest a bound sheaf of scenes. Just before she could step on me, I rose to make myself conspicuous. I could almost see the moment when the penny dropped.

Now here's something you don't see every day, Hank said, in his deep purr.

My sheepishness was that of the prodigal son, or of Jacob tossing off his disguise: You've got another class?

It's a miracle they gave me this one, he said. But three hours is a long time to go without coffee. Walk with me?

When we reached the plaza outside, the snack cart was just folding its umbrella, preparatory to being hitched to the back of a Chevy Blazer and hauled off to the underworld for the night. Yet Hank was indeed served a coffee, black, whose little blue cup seemed an auspice or reminder.

My announcement that I needed him to get me back into school earned no immediate reaction—except perhaps to keep the cup at his lips too long.

I guess that means you're officially a dropout then, Ethan, he said. I thought maybe it was just my classes you'd bailed on.

I don't know, I said; isn't dropping out pretty much only semi-official by definition?

Registrar. Bursar. Provost. These are actual jobs, man, actual people. I'd imagine one of them could establish with some certainty whether you are or aren't currently matriculated.

I thought for a minute.

Well, yeah, in that case, I guess I sort of did drop out there. I was always planning on leveling with you about it, by the way. I know it probably hurt your credibility when I stopped returning people's calls, and I'm sorry about that, Hank. If you want to know what happened, I had a baby.

Damn, he said.

Well, not me, my girlfriend had it—wife—but you know what I mean. I was only a freshman when we got pregnant.

And now at least I got indignation: Damn, he said again. Didn't anybody teach you how to put on a jimmy hat? Then: You know, it was always going to be something with you, Ethan, but I kind of just assumed it would be drugs.

The shame arrived late, thunder after lightning. And rebounded as defensiveness.

It was sex ed in the '80s, Hank, I went to a religious school below the Mason-Dixon Line. What do you want me to say? Anyway, I had to get a job.

She doing okay, at least?

My daughter? She's amazing. Whip-smart—

I meant the girl you got pregnant. The mother.

Oh . . . I'm not really sure, I guess is why I'm here. We did stay together, if that makes a difference.

Well, I'm glad for that, at least. For love. But as for the rest, the re-enrolling in school, you've come to the wrong guy. I can't help you, Ethan.

Won't, you mean.

I'm an adjunct professor, I'm barely clinging to the institutional chrysalis as is, he said. What you ought to be looking for is someone with some sway on the inside . . . if that's in fact where you really want to be.

I don't know what I want, Hank. But I can't wait tables all my life. I'm a "we" now. Like in that film you used to say you liked so much. The one I made back in high school—

And if I needed any proof that something had happened to my persuasive abilities, it might have been the look he gave me then, as I watched it sink in that I'd never done any such thing; that whoever had made that movie, it wasn't me. I pressed on:

It's like you used to say, right? It's time to start thinking about other people.

Well, in that case, he told me, you'll need to go straight to the top. To the fathers.

The fathers?

The Jesuits, he said, arcing his coffee, now empty, toward the trashcan. Here, let me walk you in.

It was a peculiarity of Fordham's Lincoln Center campus that one could go long stretches within it—and apparently even longer stretches without—and not recall that it was run by priests. The architecture was International Style, not Gothic, the mascot one step up from a goat, and, apart from the freshman theology class I'd stopped attending after the first chapter of Augustine's <u>Confessions</u>, you never saw the Jesuits. Yet neither had any of my classes ever taken me above the eighth floor, and as we boarded the elevator, it struck me that there were at least four more up there, per the buttons on the control panel.

The one Hank brought me to was either the tenth or eleventh, where a subtle palette-darkening as the doors swept back marked our entry into the corridors of power. The dean of students' office was a suite of hushed and carpeted rooms down the hall. His secretary, looking exactly as you'd imagine a priest's secretary would, looked over her cat's-eye glasses and bid us sit; Father Michael was a busy man. And when the dean did emerge—a pinkish, clean-shaven man of middle age, middle height (middle everything, save for the white clerical notch on his collar)—he gave no sign of recognizing Hank as his plenipotentiary; I stood mostly so he'd know whom to address.

You're Auburn?

Aspern, the secretary said, as Hank made no move to leave. Then: You can head on in.

What wasn't middling about Father Michael was the view from his office, with the steep slate roof of a church in the foreground, kettles of birds roiling off the peak, and the corridor of an avenue rushing out to the south where the smoke from the towers had only recently disappeared. If I'd had an office like that, I thought (which I recognize is ridiculous, a thought from another life), I would almost certainly have positioned my desk so as to face the city. But though the dean had turned his back on it when we sat down, the effect was the opposite of renunciatory. Like: See all this? It's with me.

Dean—I began.

Please. Father.

At that time of day, a faint radiance off the windows of other buildings meant that I almost had to squint to see his expression. I jumped straight into my personal history on the floors below, and how it had been interrupted near the start of what should have been my sophomore year. I tried to underscore that I believed myself to have some talent, though God alone knew what it was, and that my teachers in the drama program seemed to think so, too. Since I was trying to inveigle the dean's sympathies while skirting the premarital whys and wherefores of my withdrawal, I'm sure the emphases fell in weird places. Also, I could feel my throat starting to burn. My eyes had wandered, not too obviously I hoped, to a little wheeled cart by the door and a cut-glass decanter whose stopper made a rainbow on the wall. Maybe at the end of a hard week of invigilation, the fathers liked to gather here at happy hour to cluck over transcripts like mine. Then I heard myself adding, in a voice I'd never found before, that I'd lost my mother at seventeen and had probably been in mourning for years—something I'd come to accept only recently.

I watched him unlace his hands, start to lean forward, then think better of it. There was a long pause.

It may surprise you to hear it, son, but our annual attrition rate with freshmen runs to seven or eight percent. Comparable to competitor institutions, I'd point out, so you don't think the college is getting something wrong . . . and perhaps only natural when you take several hundred eighteen- and nineteen-year-olds and plunk them down at the beating heart of Babylon. But of course every last student we admit is well past the age of reason; there's only so much hand-holding we can do without impinging on your freedom.

I thought of what Hank had said about how it had been bound to be something with me—and of legends of NYU freshmen disappearing into the East Village during orientation with a keg cup in one hand and a crack pipe in the other, never to be seen again. But what did that have to do with freedom?

I wasn't out partying, if that's what you think.

And naturally (he continued, as if I hadn't spoken), we have a readmission process for those students who've struggled to stay the course.

I heard a "but" coming.

But son . . . Ethan? You've got two knocks on you. First, it's not like you just jumped out of the plane and are frantically trying to pull the ripcord. You've long since hit the ground. You're what, twenty-three? It's four years you've been out of school and in the world—

Think of the richness of experience I could bring to the classroom, though.

Am I understanding right that you've been gainfully employed?

His tone had been hitting something stony in me for a while now. I could feel it there like a chickenbone, right at the top of my chest.

Well, I don't know about gainfully—gainful to whom? But yeah, I've been working in restaurants.

And how much might have turned out differently had the instinct, the seduction (the gift) not been lodged sideways in my throat. To keep from doing something foolish, I tried to remember my motivation—your mother in her black dress in the rain—but to no avail: doing something foolish was who I was.

Let's be real, Father. This wasn't fun and games, okay? It wasn't alcohol, or drugs. It was love. Love with a side order of sex. I got a girl pregnant.

A girl with whom I now have a four-year-old daughter. I didn't get a lot of support from my family, but on the other hand, I guess I didn't go asking for any. Did I mention my dad was the rector of my high school? Episcopalian, so I don't expect that to carry any weight with you, and really just an administrative gig at that point, but still, he had to lead our chapel services in the gym once a month, and give the blessing every day before lunch. He had this one he used to do Fridays: "Please, Lord, help us always choose the hard right over the easy wrong." And I'd be like, what the hell kind of a blessing is that? Why not just ask for the right choice to be easy? But I guess the association stuck, because I figured the right thing in these circumstances, the best thing, was to drop out of college and care for my daughter during the day so that my girlfriend—now wife—wouldn't have to. Which, for the record, I loved every minute of. Loved. So I'm not trying to blame my dad, if it seems that way; maybe I'm saying he had a point. If anything, being Jolie's dad hasn't been hard enough, you see? I mean, for me to have actually deserved her.

Ethan, he said gently after I'd been silent awhile, and tweezed the thumb of one hand between the pincers of the other. Let's say I'm willing to grant that you seem in extremis . . . the other obstacle, I fear, is that the semester's nearly over. The computer closed out the last enrollment period a month ago Tuesday.

But there's still drop/add, right?

Drop/add was in October. For those already enrolled.

Father, I said, you religious guys talk a big game about the sanctity of life. But with all due respect, how can you know what you're saying when you don't have any skin in the game? I do. I chose to. Or helped Sarah choose to. However screwed up I may have been at the time, it's the only good choice I ever really made.

And you can choose to keep waiting tables and keep body and soul together and then to come see me again in January about spring semester. And if you do, I'll do what's in my power to help.

January might be too late, Father. Assuming it's not too late now. I'm throwing myself on your mercy, and you're handing me bureaucratese.

But son . . . I'm saying this as nicely as I can; perhaps mine isn't the mercy you need.

I rose and walked out of his office so genuinely stunned by the rejection that I wouldn't notice Hank stepping back off the elevator into the '70s-looking waiting room.

I went down to my office, he said, thinking you might want this. Not that it was what got you in, by the way; that was the essay you wrote—how badly you wanted to change. But a memento, maybe.

And held out a CD-R with a peeling label I'd thought lost among the stuff I'd pawned. And as I took it, I remembered something else he'd said, not without affection, the day I'd told him I was going to be on <u>Law & Order</u>: that sooner or later, everybody goes on <u>Law & Order</u>, kid. That and six fifty ought to buy you a hamburger.

But here I am, coming close to the end of what I set out to tell and yet ever less sure of the point. Because what, ultimately, can we learn from any of this, you and I? Maybe only that a body can learn to tolerate just about anything—that it's the mind, the source of power, that is also the seat of weakness. Tell it a certain trial will last a week, or even a year, and it will promptly set to work managing that term, breaking it down into survivable units. But thrust the horizon out into the haze I described, that cloud of unknowing—the pain could take a decade, or longer, who knows—and that same mind, if it is anything like mine, will devote all its considerable resources to convincing itself of the worst: that the moment will in fact have no end.

And the worst, it had started to seem to me, in mid-to-late November of 2001, was only a synonym for how sobriety was going to feel, quite possibly to the end of my days. I would be condemned to go on indefinitely like this, not man enough to abide what is human, yet not not-man enough to embrace the beast . . . just stretched, excruciated, across the space in between.

But that only goes to show how illusory, how impoverished, are the imaginative resources of even the most grandiose heads. Because a couple days later, a hostess at work slid me a note at the end of my shift: 158, it said. I thought of Aer Lingus, that air hostess, but this was four digits shy of being even a domestic number. I was still racking my brain when I headed out into the street and glanced toward the corner and spotted Eddie Sixkiller.

It was the most purely cinematic thing I can recall from that whole period: him tilted back against a night-lit wall in his customary garb, black jeans and black tee-shirt, black shitkickers propped against the brick. If not for the way he bristled at the sight of me, he might have been standing there since 1995, waiting for the rest of the world to catch up. Or maybe, Eddie being Eddie, I'm giving myself too much credit, and he'd been watching through the glass the whole time I'd been counting tips. But now he squared himself up and spread his arms, and I got the Drakkar Noir, the air freshener, and that spurious edge of sarcasm some men feel a need to put on before a demonstration of love.

Step back and let your old pal get a look at you, he said.

Which, by the way, Jolie, is I don't think is too strong a word for what remained between us: love.

When I asked him (trying to hide my alarm) was he in the city these days, he said airily, Oh, here and there.

But what made you decide to come looking for me now?

He grinned and reached into his back pocket, pulled out a folded polygon of newsprint whose comically large typeface I recognized right away as the Cheshire Press-Times. The new regatta stinger had interviewed my dad on the occasion of the sailing team's win at nationals—and of Dad's announced retirement. An impending remarriage was mentioned in the article, to a local nurse; as was a daughter, Moira, a physicist, currently of Somerville, Massachusetts—and a son, Ethan, an alumnus of St. Anselm's and now an actor, of New York City. It must have been a month out of date.

You're telling me Moira filled in enough detail for you to find the restaurant?

I got the sense she was trying to keep me away from you, actually. But let me buy you a drink, Prep. You've put in an honest day's work, and we've got some catching up to do.

Resolving that I'd allow myself exactly one beer, I went along. There was no shortage of bars within a couple blocks of the restaurant, but we ended up in a cacophonous dive all the way over on Second Avenue where, given the right equipment, you could probably have metabolized drugs out of the air. And if I'd felt virtuous at the moment I'd made my little rule, I was already swooning under the pressure of present company, all these bodies a thousand years younger than myself, with the jukebox roaring its subliminal message to feel free. The bartender cupped his ear. Two shots of something see-through appeared on the bar, jumping a little with the bass, neon blurring the meniscus. Then I heard myself blurt that I was a father now, had made an honest woman of Sarah Kupferberg . . . as if the right mixture of candor and glibness would somehow protect me. Or maybe I wanted to see Eddie's face, always a few seconds ahead of where I was

going, show surprise at how I could change. But of course a dive bar worth
the designation is one where it's hard to see anything at all.

Then he laughed. What, did you think I ever doubted you'd do the right
thing when it came down to it? he said. Well . . . ? The kid have a name?

Jolie. Jo, we call her.

Little Jo. Shit, man. I'm really happy for you. If I'd known, I'd have brought
a gift.

Just then, the song on the jukebox switched over, and there was an
interval where the background was a babel of bar noise mounting subtly
higher. Still in his exaggerated, pool-shooter's stance, he studied the
beerbottle whose label he'd been peeling with his thumb before the music
came back in.

How is she, by the way?

Who, Sarah? Why does everyone keep asking me that? It makes me feel
like there's something about myself I can't see. And I thought you hated
each other.

Your little girl, you dope.

Oh—right.

And as I tried to summon you back before me—as I'm doing now, Jolie,
decades later—I could feel the bar receding chimerically.

Jolie's smart like you wouldn't believe, I said. And not just smart—
imaginative. Beautiful. Stubborn as hell, naturally. When she was a baby she
used to go on these crying jags of like three, four hours. The doctors say let
them cry, they're not supposed to be able to exert willpower for that long,
but she would wake up and just flat refuse to go back down. So I learned to
not fight it, you know, try to ride it out instead. And then Sarah was juggling
I can't even tell you how many classes, working toward the day when she
could support us and I could get back to acting. It was when she got old
enough to eat a French fry that Jolie calmed down. That and being able to
talk, because now she could just say what was on her mind. I think maybe
she just didn't like to depend on anyone. Like her mom in that way, I guess.

And not her dad?

Aw, you know me, I was always looking for any star I could hitch my
wagon to.

It was the sort of thing that used to come out of me when I was
drinking—that maybe was the reason I drank—but the second it passed my
lips, I could feel myself blanch and turn away.

I think you sell yourself short, man, he said. I mean, look at what you did. Showing up in TV commercials and whatnot. Getting yourself out of the home counties.

Oh, it wasn't so bad back there.

Wasn't it?

I shrugged. Anyway, that's me, I said. What about you? I know you're not here for the sparkling conversation, so what are you really doing in the city, Eddie?

Oh, same old same old. Same but different.

He looked up. I fought a small, fierce urge to seize his shoulders and shake him, a whole starveling self still coiled inside me. And for the second time in as many minutes, that happiness in his eyes flickered, faltered. But of course, I'd been expecting him to stay the same person, and instead he'd done just what was proving beyond me—had grown up. And as I blinked, mask rejoined face again. An unbroken strip of the gold-foil edge having come free, he peeled it all the way to the far end of the label, until it no longer had room to run.

But see, that's where you come in, E. Because just now it's me needing someone I can count on. And that person's pretty much always been you.

Count on for what? I said. You're going to have to be more specific.

He somehow managed to lower his voice without actually lowering it:

What if I told you I had a chance to get you ten grand for a night's work?

My response was to become instantly incapable of judgment. I was back at the bottom of a well, and here came Eddie Six-K with a ladder and a rope and ten thousand dollars. With that kind of money, I thought, I could put your mother on my back, cover a security deposit on a better place and several months' rent . . . and still have enough to cover a semester's worth of preschool while I finished my play, used it to barter my way back into college, took the pressure off Sarah's dissertation, built us a real life.

I'd say what kind of work are we talking about here?

Driving, is all. Just going for a drive.

But I don't drive, Eddie, I said, daydreams already fading. I never did get my license back after the night it got suspended.

No, I mean, I'd be the one behind the wheel. What I need is a warm body riding shotgun. For presence, let's say. You always did have that, Ethan.

But presence alone is worth ten grand to you? And driving where? And why?

Why do you think?

Jesus, I heard myself say—are you trying to get us thrown out of here?

For I'd looked down at the heat-sealed little bag that had appeared on the bar between us, what looked to be a couple grams of cocaine. I glanced around, but no one else seemed to have noticed, and sensing already that he'd make no move to claim or conceal the bag, I covered it and, when he wouldn't take the sample back, slipped it into the breast pocket of my jean jacket for safekeeping. I would remind myself to flush it the second I could get to the bathroom. Or, if that would offend him, I would do so as soon as I got home.

We take off just shy of midnight, he said, head down 95, meet a couple folks about a handoff, no traffic, and we'll be back and crossing the GW before sunrise.

And I'm to surmise Ducky knows nothing of this? Because I assume otherwise the two of you would have some kind of staffing system in place, someone else you'd call, a professional . . .

For an even split on twenty g's? I'm hurt you'd even consider it. Besides, you're the one solved the basic problem I was stuck on, Ethan.

What are you talking about?

You'd be surprised at how much fits inside a longboard once you hollow out the foam. But you can ride up and down the coast with one strapped to your roof, any hour of day or night, and no one says boo turkey.

I figured he was joking. My real usefulness to him was that I'd been away long enough that if someone in the wee hours down there spied me sitting behind the windshield of the car (or fine, helping unbungee a board), I could pass for out-of-town muscle . . . yet I wasn't out-of-town enough to ever consider ratting him out to Ducky Flaherty.

And still: ten thousand dollars.

I don't know, I said, finally, to what felt like both of our genuine surprise. How much time do I get to think about it?

Friday would be too late, he said. Thursday's when we're supposed to take off. So by Wednesday I'll need to be crossing my t's.

The feeling dropping through me was the same one I'd had the week after my mom died, when I was seventeen and junk-sick, home from school, suffering. And at the second gate of the Brooklyn Bridge on the night of your conception. And sitting out amid the chop of the Rockaways once, the whole rest of my future in the balance. Only in this case, where was the danger? I wouldn't be crossing the line for life, hardly even for a night, and I was already reimagining your mother as the kind of person who would feel relief and not fear when I did what I already knew I never would:

walked in with a duffelbag full of cash and tossed it on the bed and told her everything dragging her down had just been taken care of.

We spent another hour talking of other things—long enough to make it seem as if Eddie's proposition were parenthetical to the real business of a still-extant friendship, rather than the whole reason for us three being here in the first place. Maybe the next drink was really three drinks, I can't remember. Maybe I was thinking only of myself again. Eventually, though, we parted on the sidewalk, full of high hilarity, with nary a mention of Wednesdays or of decisions to be made. And as I walked back alone toward the subway, the tiny lights of two planes passed by overhead. The flight paths had refilled by then, cutting lines up there on the mirror of the sky like September had never happened. Which in some sense entailed me being up there too, suspended in midair over the last gasp of my youth. It was twenty years ago on the Eastern Shore, where my mother had driven out solo to catch some waves on her way to a wedding . . . and it was also twenty years on and me getting your email in Cadaqués, feeling helpless to help you through whatever conflagration you seemed to be facing. And you, reading these words now, trying to decide how much you're willing to trust me with whatever comes next, given what went down in 2011 after we ate that acid. For if I've come to believe in anything, Jolie—my own best beloved—it's that all this survives somewhere on tape, not a cold surveillance-style thing, but a mixtape you can wind with a pencil in the infinite rack of Maxell-90s that lives under the bed in the sunroom where God lies sleeping. My mother on that tape is dancing. Your mother on that tape is still trying to get you to let her back in. Back home, though, when I stumbled into the bathroom to rinse the whiskey from my breath and hung my jacket on the back of the door and pulled the chain to turn on the light, I would find Eddie's local number tattooed on my hand in black marker, where I must have written it against forgetting. After copying it onto a bookmark, I had to use half a bar of soap to get the original off—and still there would be this nagging sense of something overlooked, and a kind of lingering gray I was hoping Sarah wouldn't notice in the morning, when she woke in the bed beside me and asked how the night had been.

VII

THE MUSIC
MUST CHANGE

A | 1981–2021 | NR ☐ YES ☑ NO

The distinction between selfishness and selfless-
ness is chiefly one of range.

—MEHER BABA
Discourses

U don't need no money, u don't need no clothes;
The second coming, anything goes.

—PRINCE
"Sexuality"

23

A.1: "Deeper into Movies" (5:23)

He had never seemed more confused as to her actual age than when it came time to settle on a film. This was after she started returning to the apartment for visits, and before Netflix with its red envelopes and sixty-word synopses managed to bankrupt Mondo Kim's and Mister Video and even the Yorkville Block-buster, at any of which you could interface with an actual clerk. Yet when he did avail himself of their services, he would half the time come back with a cartoon, operating under an apparent delusion that she was still three years old. Other times, particularly when she was in fifth grade and his own dad secretly dying and himself headed toward his third and final crack-up, there would be unreturned R-rated or R-adjacent films she came to suspect he'd put in the queue with himself in mind and forgotten to mail back ahead of their scheduled visitation. For example, an early Wachowski Sisters whose S&M themes he seemed to have over-looked until about fifteen minutes in, when he cleared his throat and said, "You know what? I think this thing still gets Channel 9. Let's see if the Yankees are on."

"You hate the Yankees, Dad. Overdogs, you said."

"Well, the Mets, then."

Another was called *The Opposite of Sex*.

To be fair: if the title were accurate, it would contain no explicit sexual content. And the box prominently featured the girl who'd played Wednesday in *The Addams Family*, albeit in the midst of the self-reinvention that would strand her somewhere between indie edgy and indie twee.

But this one too got shut off early, when it became clear that a major plotline involved fallout from a teen pregnancy. Jolie hadn't at the time had more than the rough outlines of what sex entailed, nor the subtlety to grasp that the titular "opposite of sex" *was* the pregnancy, "opposite" having been garbled to mean something closer to "corollary" or "reciprocal," or perhaps just used in its old-fashioned sense—the way a sofa could sit opposite a chair. She did know, from school, that the word "sex" was verboten, and the act it referred to life's supreme end and pleasure. And she just kept thinking, from the floor where she watched: What could possibly be its opposite?

Later, as she grew, she would make a private puzzle of these opposites or abstractions. Her body was the opposite of pretty, say. What it was feeling was the opposite of drunk. But still, what could the opposite of sex actually be? For a moment, in the recovery room of the hospital in September of 2021 where I sat reading a letter from my father purporting to shed some light on all of the above, I would be tempted to conclude that the opposite of sex was having to care for a nap-striking toddler while badly hung over. But no, I'm remembering now; no . . . the opposite of sex had all along pretty clearly been tripping on acid with your own dad.

A.2: "Prelude on the Esplanade" (2:56)

The first real change is the hand. Interesting, and possibly even predictable were she to think about it harder than she's capable of just at present (for, defined by the darkness of the fedora it clutches, the hand is still just a hand, not any of the things it will yet become (a sword made of light, a fishy flicker in an indigo sea, a fist striking a blow against death itself)), but for the first time in her life, this trusty companion, Jolie's own right hand, seems no more or less distant from her than anything else. The hand, her hand, which is to say my hand, could equally be your hand or his hand or somehow its, which is to say anyone's.

Then a wave of fear moves through her, of what she might now see were she to look over at Dad. Perhaps out here on the sandy planks where the parking lot lights hardly reach, he too will have collapsed into ground.

Then again, what if she's been guilty of the very thing she was always accusing him of, othering him, refusing to see him as a person as real as herself? Then what she would be afraid to see would be precisely his specificity, his proximity. (A flicker here where she wonders if what Dr. Loesser had really meant by the term "shared subjectivity" was more like improved objectivity.) Plus of course there's the sea he now drags her toward, crashing and foaming, making the odd echoes that are maybe her first real hallucination, shaped by shells she can't see. No lifeguard on duty, obviously. And despite her injury of that spring and all the missed practices having cost her her slot on the swim team, she can still just about picture herself shaking free and running into it. Can just about imagine absorption into what she can now see only as foam swirls riding above depths she's finally ascertained to have been concealing a perfect nothing. Yet she does what she hasn't really till this moment. Looks back. Looks up.

A.3: "Hey! Orpheus" (2:28)

Look at his baby, though, there on the beach. Focus now: his little girl dropping knees-first onto sand none too clean by day but currently a soft slope of what could be nuclear ash or televisual snow. Or no: *cruzada de piernas*, as she'd corrected him her very first day home from the preschool. Point is, she's got that infernal navy surplus bag, that backpack of the damned, one-armed before her, and is scrabbling again in the hat atop it, and though there's something missing here that he hasn't quite identified yet, all the indwelling blankness of these last days has burned away to leave on her face a kind of rabbity terror he can't even say where he's getting, except as a residue drawn from the air. Try to see her: nose-ring aglimmer, tertiary piercing he hasn't noticed before in the ear, renunciatory hair of a napalmed monk; and since it can't block her eyes anymore, he can see in the bleed of arc-lights their gray, Sarah's gray—and that what she is feeling must indeed be panic. Unless of course he's not seeing her at all and she's perfectly calm and perfectly still and the little squiggles and curlicues are the acid in his own body already starting to hit. But ridiculous—notwithstanding the possibility of some sympathetic blurring between them, it's way too early for that. Besides: is it even possible to trip on secondhand blotter?

For maximum uptake, he tries to work the damp remnant under his tongue, where his mom used to place the thermometer. And remembers the test: moves a pale hand in front of his face, as if swiping at a fly ("You getting anything?"). But no, so far no trails, no *Nude Descending a Staircase*. Yet this has been Ethan's scenario since all the way back in the spring, hasn't it? To get her out of hell, you've got to re-enter hell yourself, and not sliding backward with your eyes shut, either, as he's always done before—because what makes hell hell is precisely this desolation, this panic. If he's not careful here, there's no telling what she might do to escape it. Thank God they're not up on the hotel balcony, but then again: awful lot of ocean out here, and not a lifeguard in sight.

"Sweetie, listen to me. Move your hand in front of your face. Are you seeing anything?"

She's still not going to speak, apparently, but to his surprise she does do the motion, echoing his, and he looks harder, finds fascination struggling with the terror. If he didn't know better, he would say he can almost make out the trails.

"That's the drug you'll be feeling, okay? The onset. But I'm not sure I'm going to be able to catch up to you like this. Or at any rate, it's going to take maybe twenty more minutes."

Starting to panic himself, he ransacks his brain for any other insight that might soothe her in the interim. What else does he remember from that first time up at Frank Loves Emma, when Judd McGrath had promised to drop too but then at the last second wussed out—how someone had warned Judd that acid stayed in the body forever, just at the base of the spine, awaiting traumatic reactivation? No, surely not. But how about how you could drink o.j. to take the edge off . . . fuck, wait, no, or was it that the vitamin C was supposed to make you *higher*? He settles for this:

"You're going to be fine, but you have to prepare for it to come in waves, okay? They'll feel at first like little vignettes, with some space in between for you to rest. But what we'll want to avoid as they get closer together is any panic or fright, or like shock to the system, okay? So definitely no haunted house," he says, confused for a second as a ghostly calliope starts up. "No more Looping Star, even were it still running. And then no funhouse, no mirrors—we're going to have to keep you away from mirrors."

Of course this only seems to frighten her more. What else? Comes a gentle surfer boy stumbling out of the Rosa rugosa that June all those years ago, unless the boy himself had been some kind of hallucination. That was when the fireworks had really been starting in the sky back of the pines, choirs of angels sort of kaleidoscoping around the flaming cilia of a sun he knew he wasn't supposed to look at (he wouldn't realize till morning that what the angels had been doing was leaving), and the boy must have recognized his fierce breathing, seen his knuckles white on the board, because what he told Ethan was, "You tripping? Don't fight it, man. That's like rule numero uno. Whatever is coming, you got to just go with it, try to ride it."

He repeats this now more or less verbatim, adding that, if her experience is anything like his was at her age, it's going to become difficult at some point for her to keep up the vow of silence. Though if she doesn't feel like talking right now, by all means go with *that*. "Still, honey, unless you're feeling a particular attachment to this particular stretch of beach, we should probably get a move on, because, number one, we're going to need some supplies, and number two, we're about a football field away from where my P.O. will just be putting together that we've done a runner—and I can think of few places where I'd less like to be when one or both of us are peaking five hours from now than the holding pen at One Hundred Centre Street." Funny, how the wet little nub of paper in his mouth keeps trying to dissolve on him. He sucks harder. The blood-brain barrier—that's a thing, right? Then he gives up and swallows. Takes her hat and puts it back on her head where it belongs. Holds out a hand. Little hint of a smearing thing. Persistence of vision, probably. *Have I ever let you down?* he knows better than to ask, but the answer doesn't matter—because at the moment she touches him, he can feel her enter his own head, start to move around in there.

A.4: "The Drum Thunder Suite" (7:34)

Their actual childhood home, the true one, had been an undistinguished rowhouse a few blocks from the back of the National Zoo, where on hot days in summer with the windows open, the shrieks from the monkey enclosure used to give Moira the fantods. In fact, his first inkling of sex was probably Mom perched on the lower bunk, refusing to skip over the part of the encyclopedia about assortative mating, on the principle that more transparency equals less fear. But Ethan's own personal terror was of the electrical storms that seemed to come from out of nowhere some evenings to smash apart the house and suck him away into the charred sky—what Moira took to calling the five o'clockalypse.

Which would sound like hyperbole to anyone who'd never spent a summer in DC, that collision of watch-setting punctuality and ultraviolence . . . newspaper boxes gutted along bus routes, the white flesh of cracked trees, storm drains choking on hailstones as if on their own teeth. Somewhere in memory, though, he is sitting on Mom's lap by the windowscreen of the third-floor room she used for her painting. From up there, the window could have been a de Kooning: trapezoid roofs all fishbellied silver to deflect the heat, and away over the dark swale of Rock Creek a far green furze where another unfinished cathedral drew lightning. And for however long the storm took to blow itself out, Mom would calmly talk him through her best scientific, aesthetic, and ethical understanding of what was happening: how it was powerful, and how it was beautiful, and why it would not hurt us.

Did it work? To this day, he can't tell you how a thunderstorm comes into existence, yet when he smells one gathering, it is always mixed with Joanna: homemade deodorant and oil paints, drops stippling the sill and her coffee breath in the clipped hairs near his ear and her medal swinging free of her smock's neck as she leans forward, the better to see.

A.5: "Ecclusiastics" (6:59)

Another memory, this one mine: I am walking with my father who says music. Who says water, but also music; water is good, but music will be key. Or possibly "king"? It is a little hard to hear when the ocean is trying to have sex with my ear. In any case, he is weirdly calm, my father. Calm and also the hurricane around it. And I'm realizing that it has always been this way. How his best self appears in the middle of someone else's crisis. My hand is in his hand or vice versa, but it's neither filial nor romantic, we are like two men in a medieval Islamic village out to take the air.

Are like, and then briefly are.

Have I mentioned his voice? It is not quite a tenor, yet is higher generally than you would expect for someone as tall as he is, the reason for which, I'm now realizing, is so that it has a place to descend when it wants to mean something. This octave range— more typical of a singing than of a speaking voice—is how he works his magic; how he convinces you against all experience to trust him. And is also my favorite thing about him. A question mark where you wouldn't expect it, a sudden softness, laughter of great frequency, even more than his grin, and lacking a mirror, I don't think he really knows he is doing it; for him this is just himself. He finds the voice he needs at the moment he needs it, and at the point where the words leave his lips, I think, he really does believe them. Which is how he stays so calm now, or anyway seems to, when I need that: no fixed principle, nothing he is trying to defend.

And though I know somewhere, flickeringly, that he must also feel increasingly desperate to reach wherever he's hoping to find supplies before the probation officer gets wind, he seems to be talking himself as well into this calm. He is redescribing Ocean City to me, this shit burg or berg off to our left, which I would have thought thoroughly plumbed already. We keep to the sand because it will be harder there for anyone to see us but also I suspect because the shuttered remnants on the dilapidated boardwalk are a labyrinth things can hide in, living things, and I keep remembering a rail-thin guy in Juggalo paint out at Coney Island, "Shoot the Freak," real malice to his voice, and at times the gulls tucked atop the fluid iron rail of the boardwalk seem to wish us well but other times they threaten to turn into little wrapped mummies. As at times, the red lightning going atop the hotels' cell-phone battlements feels like a warning. Everything, in short, trying to decide which way to go, what to become. And here is my father filling the world with his voice.

He remembers when that building there went up; it was the tallest one in Ocean City, just imagine, with a player piano in the lobby and ice sculptures, a shrimp buffet . . . and now that he mentions it, it does take on a gleaming aspect. He sometimes even knows when to be quiet, too. At one point we pass—I'll never forget this—one of those concrete slabs by the steps to the beach, with a showerhead at head-height and another for feet. And though obviously the water has been cut off for the winter, some leaves (but from what trees?) have blocked the drain, and maybe a pipe burst somewhere, for a puddle has formed. Just enough light from up on the boardwalk reaches it that I can see them in there, the leaves, goldbrown and rust-colored, of an oak, I guess, their fingers rippled by a current passing from nowhere to nowhere, and though they seem trapped I summon my zendo training and try what he said, just going with it, and I discover that what they're really doing is dancing. But behind me now the names are dropping off the things. And it occurs to me that I do not know where music comes from, either. Or even what it is. Still, I am trying to find a way to tell this that is like music.

A.6: "Over the Hills and Far Away" (4:50)

They rolled in by convoy, his father's design, the two of them up front in the truck in case they needed to stop somewhere for gas, the girls following behind them in the car. He would never have called them "the girls" within hearing range, of course; Mom must have been like thirty-seven by that point and would never have stood for it, Ethan thought. He was even then the worst sort of mama's boy, and as the lanes collapsed from four to two he was pretending he could read Mom's lips in the juddering sideview mirror, though if he'd been back there, he probably wouldn't even have been listening. Sometimes he used to sit on the stairs of the rowhouse, just out of sight, and let his ears go blurry while she and Dad talked, her mouth making visible shapes on the air like the smoke her friend Barnesy used to blow into soap-bubbles on the patio at parties. But with Dad he couldn't read anything, because what kind of shape does silence make? What kind of shape does watching, does judging? Maybe the discomfort was just Ethan's bladder, though, since later, after they'd finally stopped outside some rural filling station and he saw Moira in the mirror jump out as if to beat him to the john, and so (on impulse or compulsion) raced around the back of the painted cinderblock to whizz in the high grass—after all that, when he climbed back into the empty cab to wait, he could feel himself relax. He settled on his back with his feet tucked up against the door and looked out the open window that cut off the crown of a nearby oak until all he could see was the haze of a late summer sky, the dirty clouds piled there indistinctly; he was thinking for some reason of the Paramount Pictures logo, convincing himself that these were not clouds but enormously tall mountains, and that that was where they were going, up into the snowcaps, high over everything. Then Moira appeared in the window with her big fat head. "Ethan? What are you doing?"

"What do you mean, what am I doing? I'm waiting for you to finish, nerd."

"Finish what? That's the new house, next door. The truck wouldn't clear the tree. But anyway, you've arrived. We're here."

A.7: "Visions" (5:23)

Does the security state too date back to the fall of 2001, he thinks, or is that just another poetic misremembering? The bent metal metal-detector things stationed like garment racks to the left and right of the doors—likely these were in place already, as were the little beige surveillance cameras he keeps expecting to clamber down from their corners until he reminds himself to take his own advice and just go with it . . . whereupon the cameras are just cameras again. But then what of the sunglassed policeman exiting when they came in, preoccupied with a bag of Funyuns? And what of those black-glass palantirs bulging from every third or fourth acoustic square, occluding within their curves further cameras, so that conceivably the oldfangled beige ones are just decoys anyway? It seems to be not so much his refusal to believe he can actually be tripping as his sense that these lidless black eyes are judging him for it that drives the paranoia.

His daughter, meanwhile, is stuck at a tabloid rack back by the door, staring at Brangelina and/or Bey-Z, who admittedly seem to pulse right off the page. With her hair under her hat, her pallor, Jolie herself looks destitute, like a runaway in a train station, and also deeper into her own trip than before. Though of course if you're the weedy carrot-topped clerk who is the only other flesh-and-blood human left in sight you probably assume a certain level of drugginess just from the fact that someone's in this twenty-four-hour CVS on the wrong side of a late-November resort town at like eleven here at night. It is as an exercise in ceding control, steering into the skid, that Ethan goes right up to the counter. He hasn't accounted for the difficulty, though, of not getting sucked into the guy's point-of-view . . . of not reaching out to stroke his cheek and say, *Hey, buddy, shh, it's going to be okay . . . don't be so sad.* Then, seeing Jolie's eye start to wander toward a security mirror, he tightens his grip on her arm. Swallows the remaining shred of blotter he's just discovered in the process of clearing his throat, not trusting himself not to accidentally spit it onto the counter, evidence of his own depravity. "We were in here earlier . . . I don't suppose you guys carry camping equipment."

"Camping equipment?" The guy's Adam's apple jumps. Skin is terrible. He too seems to be working hard to avoid the convexities in the corners, all those reflective surfaces.

"Or maybe just beach chairs? Towels?"

"Might be a few over in Seasonal. I don't know, man, I just work here."

Christmas fever hasn't yet reached these far outposts of empire—not yet—but the Seasonal aisle, in between office supplies and adult undergarments, is choked with wheeled plastic tubs fresh off the truck, some radical advance in containerization, ready to disgorge fake fir and receive the meager lot of unsold Thanksgiving crap for whatever its life is to look like post-recycling. But now Jolie is hunching slump-shouldered over a phone that's supposed to be broken, and when he snatches it from her hand, he sees through the hypodermic jags of glass not more

celebrity gossip but "Emergency calls only" and then a message
Sarah sent an hour ago:

> Jolie, listen, I made contact with your
> "friend" Grayson. I know you're at the
> Elysian Shores Motel, 204 N. Baltimore
> Ave, in Ocean City; I just can't believe
> you'd let your father take you down
> there. And Nana says you have your
> passport, so whatever you're planning,
> or he is, it needs to stop before someone
> gets locked up—understand? Either I
> hear from you by midnight, saying you're
> on your way back home, or I'm calling in
> an AMBER Alert, understand?

He half expects to see one now, just below where the text ends:
"Ocean City MD AMBER Alert: White Ford Econoline Van, six-point
rack, tail." But what he feels, with Jolie looking panicky again,
is the surrender he's been preaching finally taking hold, or the
freedom of almost certain doom: Sarah may be bearing down on
him from one side and Morales from the other, but it doesn't matter what happens to him in some hypothetical morning that may
never come—or even that he's caused Sarah the fear she's obviously feeling, and himself such guilt . . .

What matters is what happens to Jolie right now.

He grabs the phone to power it off and pulls her toward a small
lot of brightly colored beach things huddled at aisle's end, where
he indeed finds a couple of towels, and a sweatsuit labeled **OCMD:
RIDE OR DIE** for if she gets cold. And let's see, what else . . . ?
Water for hydration, an orange Gatorade in case this vitamin C thing really does work, a boombox essentially unchanged
in twenty years, a sleeve of D batteries, and—sweet—a rack of
compact discs in dusty shrinkwrap. Let's see: CSN, *Kid A*, *Court
and Spark*, remaindered Portishead, *Skeletons from the Closet*, all
equally prehistoric now . . . and fine, some American Spirits,
because he remembers how cigarettes can make time pass, or

seem to. These are of course the things the clerk will itemize at midnight, when the policeman, alerted like every other, remembers seeing them here and comes rushing back in to take a report *(See, Officer, the guy couldn't possibly have been her father, he bought her cigarettes, it's right here on the receipt)* but by that point they'll be long gone, and the camping thing was a red herring anyhow, no way to make it out to Assateague, that local mecca of tripping, or even to the state park at Henlopen absent any ability to drive. Does the clerk seem a little twitchier than before—is his own cellphone already jumping in alarm? Of course, Ethan's would be, too . . . unless the powers-that-be have some way of hiving off the offending node from everyone else's. In any case, when he and Jolie emerge into the blighted streets, there's what seems to be a police cruiser sitting dark down there, so he wheels in the other direction and begins to march her almost at a run up the inland side of this narrow peninsula, to where no one will think to look for them—but where trees still grow and marsh grasses double as screens and the bridges to the north and south stretch over the Assawoman Bay.

A.8: "I Know Places" (3:15)

It is somewhere around this point that the trip goes narrative; naturally, the narrative is one of escape. He is Daedalus, the puzzler, maker of mazes, to her Icarus, prone to overexcitement and melting. But this must be one of those mazes that reconfigures itself behind you the farther forward you go, for at least some of the lampposts seem to have become the trunks of trees, the same ones that left the most graceful leaves aswirl in the beautifulest puddle—though weirdly the leaves have also regenerated overhead, they still flesh the canopy at the center of faintly humming lines of pale color, and about this much, he's been right: riding atop the moment offers a measure of protection from it. But now a plane is both passing behind the branches and, it seems, zippering the back of her head to the front—and wow, shit:::::though the sky up there is black, motionless, there is some kind of crazy halation effect, that infrared bomb-scope thing where you can see the person's breath coming off them like smoke but not whether they are a terrorist mastermind or a child on its way to a wedding.

Then Bong go the circles of a church, calling her back to her mother's threat to call the cops at midnight and the question of how long it's been, but maybe checking her phone, too, counts as looking in a mirror, the thing everyone seems to know not to do. And how could she be a target for someone else's drone when these leaves are breathing so greenly above and, with each street-light passed under, bristling themselves into the bearded faces of green men? It is the stubbled face of her father, her calm and confident and for a while now she's suspected strategically non-chalant father, from which she's suddenly getting the fear. But of what, when the lack of any siren must mean something's stayed her mom's hand or held off the probation lady?

They have come upon a cross-street that T's into estuary shallows, a water tower to the left, the long bridge from earlier rippling slightly to the right, as if its stanchions were playing that game Crack the Whip or doing the Wave. And before her: the Assawoman Bay. Stretching away to either side of where they stand is a circuitboard of '80s-style condos shingled in unpainted wood but also, like her grandpa's place, trailing docks out back. And she can feel her dad years from now, grandfather-aged, a monad, the power-center the maze will be constructed to protect, dipping grilled cheese into tomato soup eaten straight from the can and watching TV, so why is he out here with her right now, risking everything? Apparently it is to lead the way onto a little strip of parkland baffled by cattails along the bay . . . where he whipsaws the beachtowel as she has foreseen, exploding deep colors into the sky. And when he gets the two towels roughly squared up on grass that should be cold now but isn't and the batteries are unpacked and loaded into the boombox, he bids her sit or (if she wants to) lie down, and listen to the music; he does seem to be feeling a little funny since the drugstore, and should answer the call of nature while still in possession of all his faculties, he'll be right over there by that water tower, in actual eyeshot this time but don't move; look, here is water he bought her, here is a safe space where she can stay, he's even bought her smokes. And he must know what he's doing leaving her alone again, she thinks, for she hardly notices the weight in her hat anymore, and this water is the water of life, and Gatorade is thirst aid for that deep-down body thirst. And music is key, is king, is everything. So again: Why so much fear?

A.9: "When Doves Cry" (5:54)

But of course what had really sent him drugward was sadness, at least at first, a vibration he must have felt coming on the air, for when the words "4 p.m.—appointment" had appeared in his mom's messy handwriting on the family calendar that seventh autumn, he'd assumed it was with a divorce lawyer. Where had Dad been then? Out at St. Anselm's, running spreadsheets on his squat brown Mac, still trying to revive his failing school. Or at the marina with a bucket of boat paint and a stiff-bristled brush, as if a mania for order ever saved anyone; as if the laws of physics (at least as taught to the second form by wizened Mr. McGlaugharn) didn't require that each move toward order within the system be offset by a slightly greater increase in disorder elsewhere, in an inexorable march toward the heat death of the universe. Perhaps this was why on some level Ethan would hold his dad responsible for his mother's dying . . . but that would be later. Now? Now Ethan took it upon *himself* to be the disorder, the eater of sin, and when both Dad's car and Mom's truck with its rattletrap board-rack were gone, he would take a few nips of codeine cough syrup from the medicine chest and then go commandeer the sunroom he was no longer technically forbidden to enter—having served as her gofer and amanuensis—but not technically invited to treat as his personal party pad, either. The once-verboten record player had not only a red light that snapped on with a pleasant click, but also a second, periscopal light that sent a corridor of ridged and stable and shimmering gold across the endless revolutions of black wax. And beyond the inner rings of *Purple Rain* lay a white field pelted with flowers and a set of typefaces he could never locate on that other prodigy of the forbidden, Dad's computer. Sticky sadness. But oh, no, he wasn't *gonna let de-elevator bring! Him! Down!* He didn't hear Mom's truck rattle up, and so didn't know she was back until she was in the doorway watching him dance. He jumped a little bit, and the record skipped.

"Caught purple-handed," she said.

"You scared me," he exclaimed—like butter wouldn't melt.

"This whole room is windows, though." She reached to run a finger along the sweatline below his hair. "I'm impressed by the energy, frankly. It's still hot out."

He shrugged. "I got the lawn mowed. Half of it anyway. I'm going to go shower and change." And started to withdraw toward the stairs.

"Ethan. Come here a second, honey." He kept waiting for her to accuse him; the unmowed grass was right there for all to see. Instead she said (verbatim quote, by the way), "This is probably just easier if I go ahead and tell you, grown-up to grown-up."

B.l: "Back to Black" (4:00)

Done peeing now and shaking off in the high grasses whose kelpy writhings threaten to remind him of something, he finds himself moving closer to the water tower to squeeze in another call—one that Jolie, safely ensconced over there with the music, doesn't need to hear. It will take only a minute, but somehow feels like it needs to be done, since even if this were to end with his daughter alive and safe and restored to the overworld, there's no telling what circle of hell it might land him in, and for all time. Behind him, "Mexicali Blues" is playing, a little Fabergé egg of sound that means she's still close enough to call out to him if need be. He flattens a hand against one of the tower's great pale metal legs to soothe it, get it to stop being apocalyptic. Or maybe it's himself needs soothing. Traffic thin on the bridge in the distance, humming. The phone's light startles in his hand with something like 487 new messages from Sarah and/or McGonagall. Though still no AMBER alert, he observes. Then an electric ringing you could really trip out on, were your thoughts ever inclined that way.

"I'm eating dinner, what do you want?" says a voice. Then: "Hello? Ethan?"

"Sorry," he says, blinking. "Just returning your voicemail

from earlier in the week, Magnolia. Happy Thanksgiving, by the way."

"Is that really all you're calling about? Because Happy Black Friday'd be more like it. Or no, I guess it's already tomorrow where you are, isn't it." Out there somewhere a siren blooms, but a red one, an ambulance's, he thinks, and anyway, no one on the bridge can see him over here in the shadows.

"No, sorry again, that wasn't true. I actually just called to warn you that . . . that you're probably going to be hearing some embarrassing things about me, and maybe not hear from me again for a while—"

"You're on a bender?"

"Not exactly. But I wanted to say, sorry. I'm sorry."

"Well, I guess that finally puts us even, then. You do realize I'm not taking this call at the Casa?"

"You're in L.A.?"

"Let's just say Alan T. didn't think super-highly of my efforts to keep his garden watered. He's none too pleased with you, either."

Ethan sighs. "No, I know, I sort of started to figure the truth was going to come out eventually. But you're doing all right there, out in the world? Still sticking with the program?"

"Ethan, you're the one who sounds drunk. Are you okay?"

"What, with not having a place I can go back to? What choice do I really have?"

"I meant are things okay with your daughter, dummy."

"Oh. Yeah, she's here with me now, so . . ."

The bridge has started doing a weird echoing thing, though, it's like being in a tube. At one end, he thinks, he can see Jolie over there, but he wills himself to turn back toward Magnolia before he gets caught in the closeout. "Nope, just wanted to tell you I'm sorry . . . and also grateful. You didn't have to put my needs first, but you did. And I'd like to think I learned something from that. You're a good person, you know." He sees her in her sandals, shades: she is.

"Yeah, well, give me a ring in five years and we'll see how that's going. But is that all?"

"Just—be kind to yourself, okay, Magnolia? You deserve that."

And rings off. If not quite bathed in universal love, he can now at least feel bad in a different way. It almost gives him an impulse to keep going, right on down the Contacts list, Moira, Eleanor, Corinne, eventually Morales—all these women, he notices, but nope, there's Eddie in the mix, too, and ultimately, depending on how long this feeling lasts, even his dad. But of course what this gets you, just going on impulse, is stuck chargerless in the dark on an uncertain quantity of LSD, and he needs to conserve at least three percent battery here so he can know when word of his perfidy has officially gone out. No, best to power back down, shift his full attention to Jolie. The bay, as he turns, tosses off profligate little paisleys and arpeggios. The cattails beckon. The egg of sound cracks to admit him. There is only one problem: the towels are empty. The tube is closed out. His little girl is gone.

B.2: "Wicked Messenger" (4:05)

Now, should you ever find yourself just on the wavery edge of what threatens at any moment to become a bad trip, one thing I can't recommend you do too much thinking about is the phrase "bad trip." Though on the other hand try not thinking about it, right? BAD TRIP BAD TRIP BAD TRIP, Jolie hears in layered voices, or perhaps sees, for they carry these striations now instead of echoes, like reverberant parentheses. And the (((BAD))) part begins . . . well, it's been latent all along, but if she has to say where the trip really tips over, turns dangerous, it would be when Dad chooses to drift out beyond where she can see. There is the sheer physical sensation of the drug, of course, the quickened breath, the pulse involving itself promiscuously with various slowings and speedings she's only just noticed in the dark: fierce dilations of nostrils and eyes and probably ears, too, and other borders that now seem to have been porous all along—it's like boarding a rollercoaster already on the downhill, or perhaps streaking down the face of a wave bigger than you are (I wouldn't know, neither Mom nor Dad ever took me surfing). Were it to remain this side of panic, you might even call the feeling exhilaration.

Except both panic and exhilaration presuppose the involvement of the head, don't they, and hers remains singularly detached, in a working order of evident perfection. No, her head has never made better sense than now, or perhaps has never made sense before at all. For example: were she to seize this moment to run into the beckoning cattails or the black bay water beyond, it would be not some childish caprice or bitter lashing out at the cosmos slash God slash her father Cronos for leaving her alone—all the things she now sees had been mixed in her back on the subway tracks last spring, at the moment her world ripped in two. Nor would she be fleeing the fear and the despair she'd felt last night, when she'd realized she was going to try to do it again. No, her surrender *now* would be in obedience to a cellular longing she hadn't had the clarity to see: to acknowledge the tendency of all things to merge. And if she doesn't yet dare—acknowledge, merge—well, that bespeaks a faint still-mystified part of herself, a headroom still left to her to go.

But now in the grasses that stroke her cheek and say *shh* a door appears. She slips through it sideways, and though her boots schloop with mud, her exhilaration and good sense each go up a notch, for it is important not to disturb the musicians who are playing along here, inside. Neither in the flesh nor on a screen has she ever seen the members of the Grateful Dead, but (assuming this isn't Graham Nash doing "Marrakesh Express") they are about as hairy as you'd expect, though friendly-hairy instead of scary-hairy, like the benevolent talking animals in picture books, only ensconced in rich rough caftans, and as they strum their too-many guitars and pound their Ewok drums, color spurts from their fingers. Except hold up, wait a minute, who called the tune—what's all this she's hearing about a devil who wants to take it all away? No, shit, there he is: Spooky Electric himself, priapic, ecstatic in a long-nosed mask and striking gleeful flamenco poses and raw as a peeled clementine beneath, and if he were to look over here to the wings of the grasses and spot a morsel like her . . . shit. ((((BAD TRIP BAD TRIP BAD TRIP.)))) So despite her knowing she's supposed to roll with it, steer into the skid, she edges backward through the door. And finds that out here she has not moved, nor has time. Same length left on the cigarette she's lit. Same ambulance. Same song, whichever of them, when the ambulance moves off. But she hasn't noticed till now the red light flaring out there atop what must be the dark hill they climbed to watch the sunset forever ago. She knows this cathedral shape it clears in the night. Knows what is under there: the body of a man. Giant. Beast. All that's left is the red rose held in his folded hands, which is the red light crowning the Martello tower, flashing once, twice, and when the last petal falls he will be dead. And over here, across the bay, on that high building from earlier: an answering flash, which is the wand that casts the spell that binds him.

B.3: "Hey You" (3:54)

Up on the slope, high on Vikes for old time's sake, but with the pills in his tin fast dwindling. Mom had stopped refilling the morphine prescription in hopes that a clearer head might help her finish . . . but finish what? And if his mystique as the rector's son had ever existed, Ethan might as well have tossed it in the dirt like a flower. He hadn't been laid in over a fucking year. Had long since stopped really feeling like trying. Coming back from a piss, he began to fantasize he could hear the feral groupings of upperclassmen talking shit about him—and good, he thought, or the beast in him thought. He wanted to be an abomination to the God he no longer believed in. Wanted badly for it to hurt. So he stumbled past the spot he'd been sitting on and went to bum a smoke, mostly to confirm they hadn't been talking about him after all and were no threat. But "Who the fuck's this guy?" said someone whose face it was too dark to see. "What are you, guy, 21 Jump Street?"

"Huh?" he said.

"With the blazer?"

It was winter again, or still. He hadn't bothered to change out of it. "I go to St. Anselm's," he heard himself answer. "It's my father running the show out there. I'm Ethan Aspern."

"And that cap? Boo. The Orioles suck, man."

"You suck," he slurred, unable to help himself. "Your whole like attitude sucks."

"You know what I say? I say fuck Saint Anselm, whoever he was. And fuck your father. And mostly fuck the motherfucking

O's." And instead of striking him the guy had reached for his hat, cleared his throat, hawked a loog inside, and planted it back on Ethan's head. Considered him as you might a portrait you were trying to decide whether to add a stroke to. "Sloppy," he said.

B.4: "Death Don't Have No Mercy" -> (6:47)

(((((BAD))))), the wand seems to flash, the witch's scepter tripping sparks up the sky. It is hard to make out the real shape of it, actually, clipped as it is by the rooflines of the closer-in condos from whose windows (were there any eyes to see) Jolie might look to be either a murderer lurking in the too-tall rushes or some kind of coward. So she moves deeper out, trying to *go with it*. The roofs collapse into ruin. Conducing in turn to more fear. Her boots want to merge with the cold mud now brimming over her ankles, but again, they are no more or less a part of her than anything else, than the dancing weeds wrapping around her when she looks down, she can regard all this with curiosity, without judgment, all those modifications of consciousness thrown over her head in early sessions by Roshi Steve, who had clearly been some kind of sublunary or factotum of this dark force bleating from the rent where sky meets shore, because what else is the point of clearing her head if not to make way for—wait, holy shit: the force is not BAD, it is blind. The thing that wields the wand is BLIND, she can see it now, back between two of the . . . castles or whatever she said those were. It claws its way right out of the eyeless earth, and has to use people like Jolie for its eyes. Disguising its maw behind some administrative building where you go to take care of water bills and purchase stamps and file for benefits and such, it lures them in even now, and saps them of their vision, sends them back out into the world with every memory of who they are and where they come from erased, and all so it can keep eyes on that body on the far shore, keep it enchained, keep it amazed. It is trying to lure her over there now, she feels its venom dripping. Whispering she can just come and crouch behind a bench in a concrete plaza and watch for a second and then bear away on her ((((((TRIP)))))) the true picture of what there really is here at

the end of everything. Well, that is fine. She will just make herself small here, will just move farther out into this invisible space
between it and the body, this Assawoman Bay that drops off with
surprising sharpness and even more surprising coldness and is
now soundlessly up over her thighs.

B.5: "How to Disappear Completely" (5:56)

It was unclear what he'd thought would become of the body. Was
he anticipating something supernatural, a kind of rapturing away?
Or merely logistical: they would remain in some hospital room
while his mother in her wheeled bed was tactfully borne out, or
alternatively go out into the cold, to the car, while there in the
room she would stay? It seemed to him now that he hadn't really
thought about it at all. But a body turned out to be one of those
problems in the physical world that doesn't just vanish because you
blink or turn away or a wall interposes itself between—perhaps
the preeminent such obstacle. And now his mother's was upstairs,
but his mother, having wanted to die in her own home, wasn't.
Nor here on the little stoop by the sunroom where he sat with his
sister, called back from her freshman year to say goodbye. Afterward, for the actual dying part, they had moved Mom back up to
her room, refolded the orthopedic bed downstairs with its sheets
stripped off—so that the sole signs of habitation in the sunroom
besides the riot of her archives was the cot the two hospice nurses
would use to catch shuteye. He didn't know how they did it: he
personally wanted to throw up every time he passed the sunroom
door and saw the weird black mattress halved like a masseuse's
table, though maybe like the constipation this was all the dope
he'd been snorting on an empty stomach. The last thing in Mom's
stomach had been a bite of flan on Tuesday. The male nurse, some
kind of Latin, had noticed she could keep it down, and it was
sweet and protein-rich and so he'd brought one each afternoon
from the Mexican place out on the bypass that was the one spot in
the county where folks of different colors used to mingle. But her
insides were mostly tumors that the flan couldn't cure any more
than the morphine, and she was sleeping twenty-two hours a day

and there were certain tells, the breathing, the feet, that she was going to die soon, as his dad told him matter-of-factly the other nurse had told him so he could prepare.

But no. No. That was before.

This was after. What came between was impossible to say. Not least because he hadn't been allowed to be there to watch at the very end. It was nothing for a kid to see. Well, fuck, that just made it worse: Was dying that hard? That painful? Because living sure was. He'd gone for a walk, unable to bear stillness, hadn't even had the heart to take the last pill he carried in his tin, since what then would be left of her? Just smoked a little dope and then a menthol cigarette he'd stolen off nurse number two to cover the smell, and when he came back, his sister, who also hadn't been allowed in, was on the stoop, this stoop. And it was like, Is she . . . ? And then a nod whose precise smallness he would never forget. Chin shifted by a single degree. And already fifteen minutes later he couldn't remember if he'd cried. The sky was low and heavy and violet from the runoff lights of offseason Ocean City. And the stars already starting to come unstuck from the sky when he realized they were early snow. The flakes, trippily, went red. Then an ambulance, lights on, sirens off, exactly the combo you most hate to see, and the pool sharks coming out of Ducky's paused respectfully by the pumps, everybody somehow knowing everything already, but he would ignore them unless one was Eddie, who would understand, and would maybe have more of the weed he'd be needing now to treat the pain. The pain of not treating the pain. He lit another cigarette, his own, and silently dared Moira to say something. What she said was, "I've decided maybe he was right. That it was nothing either of us wanted to see."

"But how would he know?"

"I think at this point you can go see her, if you want to."

Was it even still her, though? And why an ambulance? Where was the emergency? Fine flakes of snow began to collect in his lashes and the fuzzy Pendleton shirt. Each was reportedly unlike any other, but how could anyone be sure? Then the EMTs came out, quietly said Sorry for your loss, shut the doors he hadn't realized had been open. Having moved to the neglected yard and looked away, he heard only the slam.

When he looked back, his dad had come out onto the porch, holding a bottle of Mom's whiskey and three Dixie cups. Dad couldn't quite pull it off, had nothing to say where she would have had some like great toast, and once they'd done their tiny shot, no bigger than what you'd use to wash your mouth with, he took the cups so they wouldn't litter the yard and said, "If you two are all right out here, I think I'll just go lie down for a minute. It's been a long night." Mark it down: nine p.m., December 15th, 1994, the first and last time they ever drank together as a family. They'd been half Irish, it occurred to Ethan as the light went out in the sunroom, but now they were down to a third.

B.6: "4'33"" (0:00)

"Jolie? Jolie!" She jolts palpably under the hand closing on her shoulder, pulling her upward and out. This part of her at least is dry, setting aside the possibility of some wicking effect from the jeans. His wake, delayed, makes the path of red light on the water splinter like cracked ice, and for a second he too is spinning, but it seems essential here to gather himself, master his high. "Honey, you can't be out here, okay? There's a dropoff to the channel. What are you even doing?"

Then the silence lifts for a second and he'd swear he can hear her thoughts. What she's thinking is, *But you told me to go with it.*

"It's just a drug, honey. It's not going to keep you from freezing to death, if you don't drown first. Now come on, let's head in."

It's not for lack of trust, he tells himself, that he keeps a grip on her upper arm as they wade toward the shore where the music still plays—for if he's starting to hear her thoughts, it's not so far-fetched after all that she can hear his, too, and mistrust in either direction is the enemy, he doesn't want to send her into another spiral. Yet the slap of cold water seems to have broken something in her, he can feel her system calming.

Even his own head seems to clear for a while. You're supposed to strip against hypothermia, but they have only the one set of sweats, and he'll probably be better off with his pants on, however wet, than naked as the Last Judgment and climbing Mount Trip-more again, so he just holds up a beachtowel while she changes.

He reminds her to take off her socks, dumps water out of boots presumably water-resistant, pretends not to register her unwrapping another pad from her bag, since she's made clear she was uncomfortable with him noticing them in the first place. It is when he wraps her in the other towel and sits her down on the dirty ashy gooseshit sand with one arm around her for warmth that he notices the lump over his heart missing. What's left of his dad's remains must have fallen out somewhere in the water. He has half a mind to go back after them, but no, if it was a proper goodbye he ever wanted, he would have had to go to this thing in the morning like he told Morales. But he can't even do that much anymore, can he? Not without guaranteeing his own arrest. Assuming it hasn't happened by then already. "One More Saturday Night" is just a totally inappropriate backdrop here, by the way. He fumbles around for the stop button on the box. For the music too was on some level just another symptom of how he'd been trying to control her experience: it wasn't even her music. Apart from John Cage, it occurs to him, he doesn't know what Jolie's music even *is*—nor, lacking words, can she tell him. And his own is at least half his mom's, the soundtrack to a movie that never got completed. His whole self is a kind of fiction built around a memory made out of a failed or imagined artwork. Capillary action, the area of greater, what, density, pressure, bleeding out into the area that is still comparatively a void. And anyway, it is only just one a.m., still so many hours left ahead of them, best to conserve batteries. Then, incredibly, a sound, a sniff: Is Jolie crying? And if so, is it the lysergic "My God, it's so beautiful" kind of crying, or the other? And how to make himself the kind of person who might ever be worthy to hear her? Capillary action, something inside him repeats: like unto like. Then: Stop hiding.

"Jo, look." He reminds himself to swallow. "I feel like I've got to ask you something now, so we're clear, and I don't want you to get mad like the last time, but if that's the cost, that's the cost. Listen . . . you weren't *trying* to get yourself killed back there, were you?"

Another sniff, and then a miracle: her shoulders lift, drop. A shrug, even in the dark he's sure of it. But go on.

"How about earlier, though, in April? The thing that brought me back, I'm talking about."

She stays still—fine, maybe he was imagining the shoulders, but no, here in the dark: a nod. "I think . . ." she starts to say, her voice catching, then rasping. And then it is just her voice again. "I think I was. I mean, I think I must have been. I think I saw my chance to just . . . be done. Go."

And her head, like something dreamed, comes to rest against him. He is the one now afraid to move. "Oh, Jesus, honey. And that's what you've been bottling up in there all this time? Because you could have told me, you know, at any point . . ."

But he can already feel the words going, her closing back down.

"I'm not criticizing. I'm trying to tell you, I wouldn't have thought any the less of you if you'd just said something. Honestly, it's probably my fault, is how some part of me knew from basically the minute I got that phone call."

For a second, she's silent again. "You're saying you *knew*? All this time?" Oh, if only she could see what it feels like here inside his head . . .

"I think I did. Or was afraid to know."

"But without Mom telling you?"

"Without her being able to see it herself, honey," he says. And then an unfreezing, a collapse, as what *he's* trying to tell *her* sinks in. "Not because she doesn't love you, Jolie . . . but because it's the kind of thing you can only really know when you've come pretty close to doing it yourself." And what it feels like to say that out loud, after all this time, is what. Amazing. Terrible. But isn't he supposed to be the one listening? "Which . . . which I guess I've never admitted to anyone else, but which I did."

"And that's why you had to go to California in the first place? And not the drugs?"

"Oh, no, honey. This was back before I even met your mother. A long, long time before you were born."

B.7: "Steady Diet" (3:42)

At first that winter, it would be lots of warm heavy casseroles, for which Ethan after the ravages of withdrawal ought to have had an appetite. By the time the donations ran out, though, it was like his thinness had crossed over into invisibility. And by then the meals that appeared under the under-cabinet fluorescence were the ones that could be put together in the morning and not require reheating when Dad got home from locking up the school: salads in the catholic sense, with mayo as a binding agent. Not that it was ever frozen pizza or the random crap from the fridge Mom used to try to sell as dinner when deep into her work ("Don't say 'leftovers,' Ethan . . . say tapas!"). In fact, Dad had expanded his kitchen duties from three nights a week to five, Saturdays being for Ethan to approximate spaghetti and Sundays for a midday meal after Dad got home, now flying solo, from St. Paul's by-the-Sea. But Ethan wanted to point out that mayo was the condiment equivalent of Wonder Bread, and no longer would the food be brought to the table; it was serve yourself in the kitchen (or maybe he was supposed to expedite for them both). Increasingly, his cold-shoulder tactics having managed to keep Corinne out of the house, he and his dad ended up taking their meals in front of the TV. It was a little less like torture to talk there; the steady flicker of external stimuli gave them more to be meaningless about.

The show they found they both liked was *Jeopardy!*, his father for the epistemological grid it imposed on the chaos of human existence, and Ethan because he was weirdly good at trivia, all these bits of disconnected info you could only pick up through not applying yourself to anything in particular. Smoking the amount of pot he now was only made him more intuitive. Also, Alex Trebek had that Canadian mildness he'd always responded to.

And because he had not fallen for the ruse of hierarchy, was a fox knowing his many little things, Ethan would become, in his junior year of high school, consistently better at *Jeopardy!* than his father, the rector of St. Anselm's (himself no slouch). Fuck sailing—if Princeton had offered a *Jeopardy!* scholarship, it would have been his. Except. Except his dad seemed pissed about something. At first it was just a kind of edge to the badinage, a tightening of the jaw, a quizzical angle at which he held his head so the light turned the lenses opaque. Ethan kept his own mouth shut; to show that he noticed would have been to admit that he cared. But then came the day, this was probably late March, early April, when he couldn't help gloating over some Daily Double ("What is 'modularity theorem'?" "Who was Shams of Tabriz?"). And Dad looked at him and said, distinctly, "You little shit."

Which, if only Ethan had known how to look, might have been the sign that Dad wasn't taking so well the triple loss, either: of his wife to cancer, of Moira to college, of his son right before his eyes. Instead, it made him decide once and for all that his dad was a fraud and he'd been found in a basket on the shores of Lake Erie while his real father, infinitely more forgiving, kept his distance somewhere north of the border.

B.8: "Shadowboxin'" (3:29)

Was it even true, though, what he went on to tell Jolie that night about wanting to kill himself? Or just more shapes his mouth made of the air—her own father, whom all this time she'd thought too in love with himself to imagine a universe without him? He said so many things back then that weren't quite true, but he generally did believe them when he said them; I can now reaffirm that much. And here is another place where the drugs introduce a distortion. On the one hand, they themselves were an attempt at self-murder, obviously, if in slow motion. I know that what he'd been chasing all that time, on that hill and in those woods, was a sort of Viking funeral: both to shove his mother's body out on the water and to climb aboard it as it burned. But shift your angle a little, and his more or less continuous intoxication from ages fourteen to seventeen either puts the whole question of ideation, choice, intention in rather a funny light, or reveals those categories to have had real problems to begin with. So right up until the moment when your great-grandmother actually died, I still can't tell you in a practical as opposed to metaphorical sense how close he came to going through with it.

I mean, there were guns, sure, he would confirm; you couldn't throw a rock on the Eastern Shore without hitting someone who'd try to shoot you for it. He knew a truant from the public school who'd had cards printed, his name and then SMALL ARMS DEALER. He knew seniors who used to squeeze in a hunt on the morning drive out to St. Anselm's; see a dove on a telephone wire and point the barrel out the window and just start blasting. But he, Ethan, had never gone so far as to acquire a pistol or rifle. The garden hose in the garage would have been another, less painful way to go. The noose from the tilting rafters. And overdose: a reward, almost. But the question of method amounted to a question of whom you'd really been angriest at, and wanted the damage directed toward—other people, or yourself—and it was this as much as anything, him saying he could never decide, that let me know how seriously he must have been weighing his options, in the period when he was held under by pills.

But then came the period after resurfacing, the decompression sickness and the pot and the *Jeopardy!* and then Corinne herself at the house, and the warm spring night when he'd caved and bought a couple Percocet someone was selling at Ducky's and fled to the beach to take them, and then decided . . . and found himself driving 110 miles an hour back from Henlopen with his lights off . . . and the question of what might have happened had he not slowed down to let that song play out and thus fallen prey to a Delaware speed trap, half a mile short of the banked curve with its big steel welcome sign at the state line. And even so, he wouldn't get into specifics now, nor even in his letters of ten years later, and I was losing my ability to see so far into his head. Maybe he didn't trust me fully even now, didn't want to give me any ideas—maybe with his highly evolved gift for not thinking about things, he would soon barely remember having told me. But yeah, he said: at one point he'd come pretty close to killing himself . . . and on the principle that authority equaled any performance of suitable conviction, what could I do but accept it?

B.9: "Possibly Maybe" [Radio Edit] (3:28)

"But the part you're still not telling me," she hears herself say at the time, or words to that effect, "is does the feeling ever stop?"

"Oh, God, yes, Jolie. Don't you know that? I'm here to tell you that it does. Or will. It might take six months—"

"It's *been* six months," she says, that catch in her voice.

"So maybe nine months, honey, or ten, or twelve, but then something will come into your life that you weren't even looking for, and change it. And change it again. I can't explain how, but I promise you—*promise* you—that it is not always going to hurt this much. The being human, I mean."

He closes his eyes to banish the things now starting to feather the spaces between the connected dots of the sky. Which only makes more of them, of course, an etching out of Doré's *Inferno* he has to fight through to get back to the question of whether, even with her silence broken or on pause, they can ever make themselves understood to each other. The words no longer come so easy anymore, though. It's like he's forgotten how to speak. And him supposed to be the fucking Virgil of the Eastern Shore.

"I mean I wish I could go back there and recover some specific strategy or trick for you, some kind of event or something. But all I can come up with is that your mom was dead center of what changed for me."

"*My* mom? Sarah Kupferberg? The queen of denial?"

"You have to remember, though, there were so many other sides to her, Jolie. I mean, that was the adventure, you know? That was the thrill, the way she couldn't help changing, shifting among all those different possibilities. It's like she'd found some way to remind me that I prefer living to dying."

"But how can someone 'remind' you of something you never got to experience in the first place?"

"Well, that's the thing, I guess, if I think about it. There was this moment for me that had to come in between . . . but which I don't even know how to describe. And that was just the moment of knowing I was done. Knowing that whatever plan I'd been carrying around would always be there, but that I just . . . *couldn't* anymore—even if the feeling I was now stuck inside was never going to end. It was the morning after that night I got caught out at the state line. I could have been pinched for a DUI many, many times before, but of course all I blew on their little machine was point zero-zero, so I got off with reckless driving. And after my dad had bailed me out and brought me home and gone back to bed like nothing important had really happened, I snuck back out and went through the woods to Keel. I don't know what I was doing. But you see that light over there? The tower? I had seen it from my window, like it was the one thing left out there still alive. I found my way to it, and started climbing it, freehand. The drugs had pretty well worn off, I was going to hurt the shit out of myself if I fell, but at that point what did I have to lose? And by the time I got to the top the sun was coming up, and I just remember feeling like my mom was really gone then. Was really and truly never going to see this again. Kind of hearing it in my head. Which was the actual hardest part, Jolie. It's so hard to know that what you're hearing in your head isn't just your same old bullshit, calling you back. But after that I just . . . I just knew that I couldn't anymore.

"So you did start to feel better."

"No. Worse. Because now there could be no trap door I was holding open. No other option, do you see? But it was a choice, even if it wasn't me making it."

And does Jolie's silence now, against his shoulder, mean that he's finally found the words she needs to hear? Or just that he's driven her back into her shell once again?

"Let me turn it back on you, though, Jolie: Isn't there anything out there that might remind you you feel alive while you're waiting, even something stupid, like a crossword puzzle—or reading poems? Because you have to know this now: whatever it was, I'd do literally anything to bring it to you. Even if that thing turned out not to be me."

"I don't know," she says, after maybe a minute. "I just know I can't go back there and face life like this."

"Back to New York? Where else are you supposing you'll go, though? You read your mom's message, you know she's not going to give up on you. Not ever."

She snorts, a sound not her own. "Yeah, just like she didn't give up on you, huh?" For another minute, she seems to struggle with something. Takes off the hat, turns it around in her hands. Rustles in her backpack. He can almost feel her willing herself to decide. So maybe he should stop talking about suicide and heartbreak with his fourteen-year-old daughter in the middle of a metempsychotic acid trip. Or how's this for a maybe: maybe he should shut the fuck up and just listen, for once. Then she says, "No, it's with my violin. That's the king. Key."

"What—you want music? Sorry, I figured it was only making things worse, here, let me put something back on . . ."

She scoots away though as if he's said the only wrong thing and then stands up and faces the water, winds up and pitches something. Hard. So he barely hears a plop. Then she repeats, No, he's been missing the point, if he wants to get her something that can carry her forward, he can get her the violin.

Which is still at the hotel. Or rather, at Moira's. Which will mean an awfully long walk, exposed along the highway, that black V of pines. Or else, assuming it hasn't been impounded, means the van.

B.10: "Sound and Vision" -> (3:03)

The soundtrack would in fact for a long time be the problem, because whatever else Joanna Aspern was, or had been, she was what you'd call a visual thinker. It was precisely this that she'd loved most in music: how it overrode thought, opening spaces where there hadn't been any before. Which was maybe all she'd been trying to do in the earliest of those videos. But something that hadn't occurred to her yet at the time when she'd put down her paints and picked up the camcorder, that first winter here on the Shore: a change of medium meant a change of rules. That is, unless she wanted the silence itself to be statement-making, every image committed to tape would require a corresponding sound.

There was always diegesis, of course: sound that came from the tape itself. As witness the following summer, the summer of '87, when she was surprised to find that the deafening cicadas of Brood X had returned. They had startled her the summer she'd moved to DC, too, 1970—how they seemed to materialize on the porch-rails of her group house like a coating of sci-fi metal. One day she'd gotten stoned with a roommate, just enough that she could still drive, and then taken her truck out Rockville Pike with the windows down, and when she felt the decibels to be at their loudest, drowning out the rattle of the surfboard, had pulled over on the shoulder and got out and walked around aiming her Nikkormat at the powerlines they fuzzed and the sky they came down out of, the deafening seventeen-year cicadas. And now here she was at thirty-eight, living where and how she'd never thought she would. The next time she saw them, it occurred to her, she'd be who knows where, and fifty-five, and married for twenty-nine years. Inshallah. After that was iffy.

In DC she could have just gone into a camera shop and ordered the parabolic mic she now saw she needed, but out here she had to call around, get something mail-ordered from B&H in New York (where she would later rack up a not insignificant amount of credit-card debt), and it was touch-and-go as to whether it would arrive first or her subjects disappear to wherever it is cicadas go to await their second coming. But the mic won. Had already won without her knowing. Ethan at nine was always opening packages no matter whom they were addressed to . . . yet how could she blame him, knowing each other as they did? She looked at him and saw only her own mirror. Once more into the breach, then, except now it was him aiming the camcorder at the sky while she tried to capture their peculiar sound, bristling. The headphones on her own ears, volume turned up to where the needle just scraped the red. Strange, wingèd things. And she had certain tricks she was teaching herself to do with the videotape, pulling it out of its plastic housing, crimping it, various corrosives you could apply and then remove to fuck the image up. Also strange, though: when she ran the sound concurrently for a last check before dubbing it onto a second tape, the images instantly became boring, indicative, a mere movie. She found she could go the opposite way, kill the cicada buzz and layer in an unlicensed song from her vast trove of music, say "Sympathy for the Devil" or the extended synth loop from *Controversy*, but the frisson produced was only that of a TV ad, or soft-core porn—which is to say, that of those music videos Moira couldn't get enough of. More interesting, because more wabi-sabi, was to take the cicada sounds or others equally incongruous and layer them in over the mundane footage she'd been taking of the Kmart parking lot or the perpetually going-out-of-business furniture barn by the railroad tracks downtown. A mood was instantly achieved; a narrative implied. But the pieces never worked, she couldn't get that uncanniness she wanted, even out of Ethan's Monkish noodlings on the piano. Couldn't tell you what made the pictures themselves so sad.

And later—and for a long time—she would have the same problem with the footage she shot for *Other People: A Requiem.* She had finally worked out an interview device that, with its double periscope of one-way mirrors dropping down between her and her subjects, would allow them to look each other in the eye (or to imagine they could). And you could have an hour with someone or a whole afternoon this way, getting out of them suddenly the most fascinating stories, intercut with B-roll of what they were describing (shot later in their homes or workplaces or haircutters', or houses of worship) . . . but when she revisited the footage, the visual component was like, why am I even watching this? Why not just stop and listen to the talking on its own, the way baseball is better on the radio? So she tried taking out the people's voices altogether. Replacing them with music. With cicadas. Kept only the faces, and the sort of still-lifes or -lives of the B-roll. It took her far too long to wonder what would happen if she went the other way, kept the voices, just never showed the people at all.

Then, all of a sudden, the other images, even ones that had nothing to do with a given story, ones looking for a home, would become not just objective illustrations, but that person's world as seen from the place you could never quite get to in waking life: the inside. As they talked, invisibly, about the world now unfolding before you, you somehow slipped your skin, became them. And also there were the suspense elements, assuming you didn't know them personally; like, who really *was* this person now talking, unseen? How long were they going to keep it up like this? And, once you got deep enough inside him or her and turned around to face outward: What was it they weren't revealing, or possibly even noticing, about what had become of all those other people who were meant to be here? A bomb? A plague? Was that the real reason the voices all seemed so lonely, underneath?

More problems, though: the no-people constraint only got her as far as the halfway mark. Why? Because this wasn't a frozen image, one of her paintings, out of time, but a whole ninety minutes she was trying to move an audience through . . . and as a scandalously underrated Who song she now had on repeat in her classroom-cum-editing suite put it, "Music must change." Also: by that point she knew from her dreams that she wasn't going to live to see the cicadas' next return. So in cutting together the second half of the film, she began to phase out the voices at intervals and let the faces back in, long, still, corporeal, only the mouths moving, silent. But she didn't want more than the ordinary silence, or didn't want the silence to be the last statement she ever made. Which left the original problem, before the film could be considered complete: What might it have sounded like if it was?

B.11: "Elysium" (5:54)

Even from a block away, the gated parking lot looms like a fortress, a fortress at the foot of a citadel, a fucking donjon—and this from Ethan, who is trying to keep his wits about him, not get sucked away along dissociative lines. How can he ever have thought it was dark? It is the planet closest to the sun, a bee planet all covered in chalky yellow pollen that comes off in your fingers when you touch it—none of which, of course, is the point. The point is for you to be able to see the iron bars, barbed wire, the signs that for some reason he can't read, but whose typography alone says *GUESTS ONLY—KEEP OUT.* This is not to mention the security cameras, which seem to have clambered down from their perches at the CVS, taken a brief wallow in black paint, and then hied themselves over here to batten onto lightposts and the corners of the hotel itself. The ocean crashes invisibly, but also misleadingly, since it can no longer help Ethan or his daughter.

What can? Well, for one, the place seems bereft of people; not even that station wagon from last night is here. Though of course empty is exactly how the authorities would *want* it to seem if some trap were being baited with the van, its ridiculous tail aflap each time the wind blows. He has another brief flash of how the two of them will look on the security monitors, only now in addition to the oleaginous desk-clerk there's a whole phalanx of SWAT guys in Kevlar and dark shades leaning to see over the guy's shoulder, plus a night-vision element to the landscape, blueshifting the sodium and leaving the ground an irradiated green. Which, forgetting his own rule number one, he tries to blink away.

And now he notices how the lot is situated on the breezeway side of the building, not the ocean side, so even assuming Morales is still up there chain-smoking her Kools, torturing herself on the rack of mercy versus obligation, she won't be able to see them down here without being seen herself.

He checks his phone for the AMBER alert, but his phone is of course off, and he's hesitant somehow to ask Jolie to turn hers back on. But he does have this keycard, which will plausibly let him swipe in at the far end of the lot and not have to enter via the lobby, though at the cost of creating another time-stamped record of their movements and perhaps, too, setting off some kind of alarm. Or the clerk is passed out on a cot in back, and Erica is still sleeping too. Or this is all a dream. Maybe coming back here a second time is like lightning striking twice, so crazyass no one would suspect it, in which case surprise is on their side, and he's just turned to pull Jolie behind a dumpster, brief her on the need for stealth, when—

"Good God, honey, what is that sound?"

B.12: ->"Always Crashing in the Same Car" (3:35)

Answer: the fucking recycling truck of all things. At—what was it now—two in the morning? And though Jolie couldn't read the signs either, she didn't need to. It was the self-driving semi from *Maximum Overdrive* or the Fury from *Christine*, or at least the light in the alley gone opaque on the windshield meant she couldn't make out who was behind the wheel. And where her previous visions had sort of built toward or effloresced out of recognizable reality—one thing disguising itself as another—this was like wholecloth hallucination: either there was something rumbling down there with its headlights on in the alley or there wasn't, was nothing. And no matter which, a something or a nothing, it had been following her around in her blind spot all day, all yesterday, maybe all year. Its great mechanical arm now swept up a dumpster, a sound that was like the shattering of every kindness that had been done to her this last however long to coax her back from the edge of a (((((((BAD TRIP))))))). An emissary from

the municipal serpent, smashing orbitals, swallowing light, guz-
zling vision, only restless now, circulating, hungry, and blocking
her way toward overseas, and freedom. Well, fine, then, let's go,
she'd be thinking as she stepped into its path, prepared this time
to smash it down with her fists, take it on alone, when her dad
showed up in the bright light beside her, and she realized he could
finally see what she was seeing, too. Which meant either that it
really was there after all, or else that all was lost. For suddenly she
and her father, Ethan Aspern, were inside the same trip.

24

A.1: "The Breaks, Pt. 1" (4:09)

But now, I'm afraid, things get seriously weird; for if I'm to convey what comes next, I'm going to have to drop the curtain or camera or what have you and fast-forward a decade, to early autumn of the year 2021, when I finally began to understand certain things that happened back there—or seem to have happened back there. There was all the Dad stuff, of course, but on some level I'd long since grasped the fundamentals: we were the same, me and him. But the reason this whole story suddenly needed to be put down on paper turned out to be different stuff, mom stuff, which even through the first two trimesters of my pregnancy remained (so to speak) *an experience whose inside I literally couldn't imagine.* And perhaps that's why in my early drafts I always got stuck right around here: the fight with the garbage truck. Only now, sitting in the comfortable wood chair I'd had to wedge my increasingly whale-like ass into for most of the composition of the memoir, in the bedroom-slash-office on Mott Street to which I'd been more or less confined for the year and a half of the pandemic (hence also in some sense the pregnancy), I was reading back over the most recent of Dad's letters, the one I thought of as his last best shot, and got to the part again about how my mom, far from being the Apollonian superwoman I'd for so long fallen short of, had been only another depression-prone human after all. And I shit you not: I'd just started going back through my material to see what else I might have missed when my jeans went wet, as if I'd sat on a water balloon. And I began to experience what would have been déjà vu, were it not . . . well, the Germans really should have had a word for this. What happened over the next few hours to time and to consciousness, I mean. For it was something I was about to discover I'd lived through before—almost as if its whole purpose was to prepare me for the day of your arrival.

A.2: "The Street Only Knew Your Name" (6:25)

"What you reading there?" Erica heard someone say, and when she looked up, there he was. She was used to guys coming up to her on the street, probably every woman was, but this one's grin, with its reddish-gray penumbra of beard, was so guileless it would take her a minute to realize he too had come out of 100 Centre Street—someone else's body—and also that his question was rhetorical, that he already knew what she was reading, or rather, battening her eyes to and trying to read. "The Guest House." *The Essential Rumi.* This was only a couple months after she'd confided to the last next guy, a colleague, about a kiss shared with a certain boundary-challenged client, and the guy had subsequently chosen to move out of her apartment, and the book, having arrived in the mail as some kind of screwy apology, had become one of the few things making her feel less lonely—or at least helping to fill the time. Certainly not like this salad from the so-called Pain Quotidien, twelve bucks and she'd barely touched it. She didn't touch it now, or make any other sign of hospitality, she didn't think, except to mark her place with a finger. But the stranger made a small and similarly performative "May I?" gesture and politely moved the salad closer to her on the bench before replacing it with a small stack of matching paperbacks and plunking down.

"Belly of the beast, huh? Must wear on a person." Then a nod back over his shoulder, obscurely victorious. "Won't be wasting my breath on that duty officer again, that's for sure. Say, I don't suppose you'd know—" and gave her the name of the fellow who used to supervise his parole, another white guy, she thought, a real prick, but then most corrections officers were, it was why she came down here to take her lunch. So were most of the bodies, too, at this point, if she was being honest. Except this one wasn't like that, she could already see. He wasn't interested in her that way—may in fact have been gay, or at least had a general sexual vibe of, like, not currently practicing—and as he volunteered that he had done a little digging into mysticism in the hoosegow (he actually used the word "hoosegow"), had read a few translations from the Persian, she reflected that she hadn't known Rumi was a Persian and not some kind of Arab or something.

"Okay, I'll bite. What were you in for?" she said, to put them back on familiar ground; she knew better by now than to fraternize.

But instead of answering, he asked her, did she really want to know?

And actually, it was this rather than the patter or the eighteen inches between them that marked the ex-con next to her as apart: how quickly he set aside whatever was his own sob story, the whole business of himself, and instead asked—gently but genuinely curious—why in the Sam Hill someone on some kind of Sufism trip would ever choose to work corrections.

She wasn't, though, she said. On any kind of trip; she had enough baggage to deal with just being a recovering Catholic.

Which may only have quickened his interest. Still, this way of seeing her as a complex human being and not just another body was the other thing that brought to mind her ex-client with the jones for poetry, whom since deciding however belatedly not to kiss back she'd generally tried not to think of at all. Except where Ethan Aspern had seemed desperate to share with someone all the parts of himself, this one was merely . . . curious. Possibly just liked people? When she commented on it, he shrugged.

"Mainly putting one foot in front of the other these days."

"Well, but also coming back down here to where it all began. Most people tend to run screaming."

"What can I say? I'm trying to put the running and screaming behind me. Doing my best just to serve and obey."

"Maybe you missed your calling, then," she said, settling back down into herself. "A rap like that, you might as well be one of them in there. 'New York's Boldest,'" she said.

For the first time, he seemed perplexed. And then the cloud passed. "What, the obedience thing? Because that's not quite the same animal as what they're asking for in there. Which, come to that, is probably why the duty officer wouldn't let me past the bullpen: subversive element, you see. Not whether to obey, but what."

His eyes glinted.

And whatever he had on his side, there was a moment when she would feel almost painfully jealous of it. Equanimity. Peace. Peace with the fact that there could be no equanimity, that the scales were permanently out of whack. But then he said, "Sorry, I'm still in visiting mode, darlin'—I shouldn't have pushed up on you like I'm on some kind of crusade."

How could she not take offense? She was nobody's "darlin'." Told him so.

But it was as if they'd seen slightly too far into each other. "You looked hungry for the company, is all. Like you could use a fellow traveler. A friend."

She could feel it trying to fill her again, a pressure to tell him that she did, in fact—Oh Jesus did she need a friend. She suspected some kind of trick. He got up to leave; then thought the better of it. Turned. Saw her looking at the book he'd left off from his stack, so that now she held two. "But listen, if you're not doing anything this Friday, some folks and I have a little lunchtime . . . working group, I guess you could call it. Reading mostly—some of it poetry—and then talking about what we read, and sometimes there might be a little singing, too. Not professionals, understand. Nobody who has to answer to anybody they don't want to. Just folks like you and me." He gave her the address—some church somewhere she already knew she'd never see the inside of—and then got up, smoothed the thighs of his pants as if they were anything other than raggedy cutoffs. This despite its being spring. "Nice to meet you, by the way. Assuming I don't see you again . . ."

"Officer Morales," she said. "Probation." Then: "Erica."

Les McGonagall, he said, like he'd been waiting for her to go first. The pleasure had been all his.

A.3: "The Sick Bed of Cuchulainn" (3:00)

Specifically he'd had—as he stood there posterized by the lights in the darkness—a vision of his daughter taking off her several earrings and handing them to some girl in some hallway while others pounded fists into palms yelling, Fight! Fight! . . . words that called what they named into being (though not so loud the teachers would hear). Had a vision of her hands skipping the formalities and going straight to the other girl's throat. You had to be willing to be a little crazy, he knew, and in that moment, in this one, Jolie was—which even more than her saying aloud, *Let's go!*, was how he knew she'd taken the fight to the real enemy, the one out there, and stopped turning the battle inside.

And then of course there was the fact that the truck just royally had it coming, the "Flaherty" in Flaherty Hauling being of course Ducky Flaherty, the first voice heard in his mother's last film. In his rare appearances around the filling station he was grizzled, shorter than he seemed, a stocky man in a Jimmy Buffett tour tee and a dingy fisherman's hat who hardly ever spoke—just toked, implacably, on a Swisher Sweet cigar. Later, Ethan would wonder how Mom had gotten Ducky to open up to her on camera: if it was some kind of fairy-tale deal where she'd then have to kiss him so he'd turn into a prince. (He used to think a lot about non-Dad people his mother might have been kissing, in those times when she started going out to shoot without him.) But the fisherman's hat somehow rendered that far-fetched, and more likely a little light extortion had been enough, since everyone but Ethan seemed to know, whether they admitted it to themselves or not, how Ducky made his bones. In addition to the Sinclair station, the bookmaking operation, the joker poker, the wholesale drug business that would give Eddie Sixkiller just enough rope to bind himself forever to the Eastern Shore—in short, what passed for organized crime down there—Ducky had an interest, as even the most two-bit kingpin will, in cleanup. Waste removal. And say that wasn't him back there shifting audibly out of neutral, laying on the horn—Ethan still for Jolie's sake would gladly have put a fist through the windshield himself. But from the moment Ducky's bugle-blast went out from the truck, deafening, four-dimensional, they'd been out of time, even for him to explain that they were out of time. The whole of Ocean City, such as it was, was immediately on high alert. He couldn't say that the truck in real life was accelerating toward them, but in any case he pulled Jolie clear and through the gate, the first time he'd ever nailed a keycard swipe in one go, and though it wasn't quite enough to fulfill his messiah fantasy, they were now on the sodium planet, lit up, fugitives legging it across a desert to the van. Gravity worked differently here, or maybe it was just advisable not to try to sprint while tripping, for Jolie stumbled, and when he looked back for her, as you never ever should, he saw that the whole lot was dotted with dead or dying seagulls, but he pulled ahead and—no time to play the gentleman—trusted her to take shotgun. Of course Morales would be taking all this from her balcony, even though it was on the building's far side. She wouldn't need to see the trap sprung anyway, she'd had the locks changed on the van, and any minute . . . no, here we go, the door was opening after all and Jolie bundling in across the front seat. The engine catching was a mercy, the only question was of the gate, which—yes!— opened automatically before them, and then they were out on empty streets again. Not even the truck was still around, though this meant that given the tail, these horns, they'd stick out like a sore, er . . . claw. Getting hauled in for another suspected DUI here would really be the cherry on top of his kidnapping plot. And still: worth the fight just to see her relief. At a red light that seemed interminable, he looked at her. "Dad?" he heard her say, quite distinctly. And in her head: *You're doing that thing again, your breathing. Are you okay?* So why all of a sudden couldn't he answer? Why couldn't he speak?

A.4: "Lament" (2:03)

From the sixth-floor library of Broad Horizons, you could see down into the courtyard hollowed into the middle of the block, and it was there by the window, watching the other kids flirt or semi-ironically hacky-sack, that she would spend much of her idle time those first few months at the new school. Or in the hallway outside the gymtorium, listening to auditions for the fall musical, the singing from behind the mesh-reinforced door where she'd sat practicing Sondheim's "Stay with Me" not an hour earlier. But at a certain point, it was judged that enough time had passed that the musicians and the cast could be joined together, and then without ceremony the orchestra was trooped in. Jolie Aspern played well, had a good ear, was maybe even talented, but the lights stayed dim over the glossy wood floors of the pit, and she would find herself drifting off the beat, longing to be one of those people up there onstage, the ones to whom life was happening, until the tapping of the conductor's baton on her music stand snapped her out of it. So she was surprised when the baker's wife hopped down one day after rehearsals, came right over to her and asked, "You want to see something grosser than gross?" They wound up in a little caesura of a space between the folded-up bleachers, the older girl showing her a piece of natural-childbirth agitprop found on the internet whose general mise-en-scène, notwithstanding the jaunty world-music score, or perhaps exacerbated by it, was like an early David Lynch movie.

That is: knowing *that* came out of *there* and seeing it with your own eyes turned out to be two different animals entirely. They must have watched it like fifteen times; at some point they were downstairs, moving out into the courtyard. And before Jolie could quite internalize that the sky above was getting dark and she should leave if she still wanted to beat Mom home, she and this girl—this beautiful girl she hardly knew—were joined in a solemn agreement that parents were the worst, and never to become them themselves. "Now promise," she would always remember Precious saying to mark the occasion, and spitting gravely into her hand. What she couldn't recall even five minutes later was which one had then been the first to make the invocation: "Or hope to die."

A.5: "Hours" (3:55)

The time is nothing or it is everything, telescoped by blackness, which in different shades, blueblack, grayblack, blackblack, delineates water and then seas of fields, strips of trees, sky, and every so often a vision of one or another sign comes newsreeling up out of the pines. And now that they are off the bridge (((BAD TRIP BAD TRIP BAD TRIP))), her dad calms down and proves himself surprisingly adept at driving while intoxicated, and to the accompaniment of that Radiohead thing on the boombox in her bag, so beautiful she wants to cry. It's like the universe in its dismay has seen fit to return them to two nights ago, when none of this had happened yet, and the black stars were still in her bag, and her aunts' and cousin's lives were still whole and inviolable, not to mention those of Dad's ex-friend Eddie, and his poor probation officer. She sees with a pang Izzy in some breathing apparatus, goes with it, and then as the image builds she hardly remembers what she's even chasing out here. For a moment, it almost seems as if Dad might solve all their problems at once, drive the van fast enough or well enough to suck all those miles back in through the grille, put the two of them on the lower deck of a reversing ferry, and then scramble tail-first up the parkway to NYC, where flights to Europe leave every twenty minutes and her violin case is under her arm again and her passport ready for stamping.

But no: a few more moves with the power steering, of man merged with machine, and they are back before that dark little house, which honestly she would be a fool to say doesn't look a little haunted, if only by previous drafts of the lives once lived there. She notices that he doesn't pull to the curb out front this time, but kills the light while swerving into the lot of the silent gas station, a trick he must have picked up somewhere. And as the dashboard lights die, too, and the music, she loses his face and the feeling of comfort it was giving her, and only wishes she could know what was going on in his head. But she has lost that power now, if she'd ever had it, even as he's gone reeling deeper into her dreams.

A.6: "Rebirth of the Flesh" (4:54)

When an ambulance starts up outside your window, it brings with it the sound of a hundred other sirens, the minute-by-minute sirens of the previous spring, and of the refrigerator trucks that had been parked outside the hospital down the street, just at the edge of visibility, their generators rumbling like construction all through the night. You have since encountered people, men, who'll talk confidently about having "done their own homework," and how the mortality rate isn't that big a deal, and have wanted to point to that auditory knowledge built up in your bones and say, "Well, but what about the fucking refrigerator trucks?" Not to speak of the wrapped things you watched disappearing into them . . . what was that term? Catastrophe actors?

But now it is nine months after the first winter and you are on your side on a futon and you remind yourself of the way you learned to calm yourself when you were fourteen, to say to your memories and visions as to a ghost: *I mean you no harm.* You are meant to be calm here, in this pause between contractions, which admittedly aren't supposed to be coming quite so close together so soon. On your side on the futon you rest for another moment and then, without conscious intent, lift your head slightly and take a sip of coconut water from a straw held at the wrong height and angle for your mouth so that it cannot possibly be your omnicompetent mother positioning it there but only dear, hapless Pete. And already you can feel your animal self taking over again, with an animal's helpless presence, which is just another word for forgetting; already the pressure around the abdomen is a memory you aren't having, it cannot hurt you for another ninety seconds you'll never even see the other side of, probably, for what is time to an animal? You regard your now-fiancé's face with the very same curiosity and non-judgment with which you regard what you remind yourself, just before consciousness goes, not to think of as pain. But it hasn't been ninety seconds yet, has it? And what is that look in his eyes? Is something wrong here he's not telling you? And where the hell is your mother?

A.7: "This Is How We Do It" (3:59)

It is so much darker here at the heart of things than at their edges, she thinks, watching his shadow slip out of view along the edges of the woods—so much darker even than the dumpy resort town seven miles to the east that what if it were to trigger some Bad Trip in *him*? He'd seemed for a minute there, crossing the sandlot, to at least be wavering. Though darker can also mean more stars—more of the lightshow she's got a firmer handle now on how to handle. *Go with it* doesn't mean *Go to it*, exactly, any more than the advice not to run from a bear in the woods means go cuddle it. It's more like *Learn to exist alongside it. Abide.* So she disregards once more his instructions to just trust him and stay put and climbs out of the van to follow. She can see the back of his corduroy jacket a ways ahead, but maybe his protective instincts weren't so dumbass after all, for Ducky's pillbox hunkers low and evil off to the right like a stone tablet where sacrifice gets made— and probably, given what she now knows about Ducky's, one bristling with cameras to boot, picking up her whereabouts, her intentions—and to the left . . . well, those woods are a void, are an ocean. How they roar.

They pass the entrance to some kind of road running into the woods—the same one, it occurs to her, they came out by last night—and then the two towers of the tanks, the front end of whose dinosaurs sort of peel and detach with flaming edges, turning to watch as first father and now daughter pass. And here is the next step she's fabricated, as opposed to actually feeling: what he plans to do when he gets there. All well and good to talk about wanting to retrieve the violin she'll need in order to leave for good, but how to do so? The house she stands below now seems to resist any one narrative. It is the gingerbread house in the fairy tale and the house the kids set out from to get there and the castle where the grail or girl awaits, and also is a tomb. Albeit with its modest dimensions, its sad little walk where shrubs made of moonlight phosphoresce and bloom. She wants to go with him now, through the beckoning plants, but perhaps that is scarier, because what she can see in his shoulders as he pauses there where no one's left the light on is how much it is costing him even now, this insane fantasy of return. His mother died in there, for God's sake. She more or less saw it with her own eyes. If only she could still be with him in his thoughts, the one place she can no longer go, she would tell him at whatever cost to her own plans to have a little faith in Moira, his sister, to just walk up the walk and knock too late at night, again, but to do it this time the right way, aboveboard—as if she might be inside, as if he might be honest about what he came for. But already behind this story of reenactment, of reconciliation, he is gone from the walk, a shape she can't pick out again until it steps from a vine onto the roof of the sunroom one flight up and, low to the tarpaper there, moves over to the window. And seems to get stuck there. She hears a brief snatch of music, as through headphones, and then an ambulance, but no, there are no lights; the streetlight that's been lighting her way, oddly cloudy for the dry weather, blinks and goes out. And of course, she thinks: there's that little safety bracket in there from yesterday morning, keeping the window from going wide enough to endanger a child even Izzy's size. And again: How does *that* fit through *there*.

A.8: "Life's a Bitch" (3:30)

It would be a mistake to call the place where you come down off the GW Bridge anything like a street, and so to invoke any sense yet of being home free. There is instead an extended liminality, the all-day all-night jockeying of traffic, appendages of exit ramp and steel-bound merges fitting one over the other with what must have been increasing precision, or at least intricacy. Eddie blinks and imagines blueprints upon blueprints. Blueprints just for the scaffolding required to build whatever needed building, since the traffic swells and then outstrips whatever you design to channel it. In another life, one consecrated to other forms of futility, he might have designed these things himself. He is good like that. But Eddie Sixkiller is about *this* life, and it's his sense that his old pal Ethan Aspern needs to be, too. If anything, his relief at coasting down to a stop behind the hospital complex on Haven Avenue where you can choose either a left or a right into Washington Heights, is the relief of having brought Ethan through the first run in one piece. For, gifted with too much of whatever it is Eddie has too little of, Ethan has a way of setting people's blueprints on fire, which is part of why Eddie still loves to see his face. Too much design, in *this* life, is just a different way of getting lost. And quite apart from the chance to get out from under the thumb of Ducky Flaherty—apart also from the chance to cut Ethan and his little girl in, to the tune of ten g's, on the clean twenty now in the trunk—he's maybe thought bringing

Ethan along would act as a kind of talisman, since the guy had that kind of luck, things always worked out for him. Or at least has believed that his sense of responsibility for Ethan might serve to keep him on his toes.

The city is talking about traffic cameras now, so he reminds himself to signal before turning right, south, toward Harlem and then sunrise. Ethan's been snoring against the window since about Exit 11 of the Turnpike, and he resists the urge to reach out like the dad neither of them has and to squeeze his knee and say, Look, see? I told you we could do it. A little drool on his jean jacket like back when Eddie used to find him passed out on his glider and stick around long enough to make sure his breathing returned to normal before slipping back off noiselessly into the woods. And even when police lights come out of nowhere to trouble the rearview, blue with just a single bloop of siren (the actual worst combo), Eddie's not sweating it. He's sure he signaled; it is only when the cops change their story to a busted taillight, which he knows to be untrue (what is he, stupid?), that he'll start to suspect a rat. But for now he almost whistles. The money, no law against that, is in the trunk, which is locked anyway, barring sufficient p.c. to get it open. And the weight was never in the car, thanks to the longboard now being sawed back in half in a chop-shop in Cheshire County. Not the least flake of snow, so bring on the canines, no? "Morning, officer," he can't resist saying a little impudently when he rolls down the window, startling Ethan from his doze. But of course it is not morning yet, and night, with its deep pockets, still has some tricks left to play.

A.9: "Who Are You?" [Single] (3:22)

She is flying blind here, climbing not so much a wisteria as a memory of wisteria, her backpack trying to drag her down and her boots even heavier with moisture. Noiseless enough to have crossed the lawn without raising alarms, they're both silent for a minute, with some effort, on the creakable roof of the sunroom, or else he is still elsewhere, up in the clouds, starting to peak, because when she touches him, he jumps. There's enough light from the streetlight coming back on to see him blinking, feel him recognize her again. *Dad*, she says in her mind. *This is going to be okay*. And unshoulders her bag of tricks and entrusts it to him. It wouldn't fit through the window with her, and something's still holding him back.

The light in there is a nightlight, uncamouflaged where the glass goes transparent, the streetlight winking out again. A nightlight plus something else: in one corner of the ceiling, a smattering of stick-on stars. How the painters managed to miss this—how she did, sleeping there Wednesday night—she doesn't know. As if it were that next morning again, or its reverse, she finds herself kneeling on the tarpaper, still careful not to creak, and turning her head sideways to where her ears will just slide through. There remains some question of her shoulders, and her torso, but she has not inherited Dad's chest any more than she has his great apse or choir of a head—and there are times when being only a junior B cup comes in handy. The weight she's lost, the winnowing of these last months, was for this, it seems. Half inside now, she can crane her neck up and look straight ahead, but she is going to have to get her arms the rest of the way in to catch herself or else risk thumping to the floor . . . and perhaps she has been trusting too much that five or however many hours are enough to put her beyond the worst excesses of the acid, because time has gone all surrealist again and the window is now trying to eat her, cleave her off right at the hipbone, the ineradicable caboose. She thinks against her will of the great machines that crunch cars, of the sentience of houses with eyes for windows and mouths for doors, she shouldn't have tried to go right in through its eye, she thinks, nor started thinking of the pain as simply pain, but now she lets go the breath that was trying to fill her and reminds herself to try not to hold it . . . and suddenly all that is outside is blackness and she is through. The little light of the nightlight is so warm-looking it nearly sets her crying again, as warm as that towel Dad wrapped her in back on the beach, and already doing her more good. The fresh white paint has its purpose, too: to be stroked this way with the light, with the stars. And there, over at the foot of the bookshelf–cum–entertainment center, as if awaiting rescue, is her violin. Except the door to the landing has come open a crack or been left that way, and when she goes to close it softly, lest she make a racket getting out of here with the case, she sees too late the other thing about this room she must not have thought to notice yesterday, back when nothing mattered: a full-length mirror mounted to the back of the door. Which—click, another trick—has just sealed her inside.

A.10: "Unreleased Backgrounds" (0:51)

~~In the beginning,~~
~~At first the glass~~
~~The window was riddled with flaws, but they did not know it then~~
~~To begin with, someone's handing you~~
~~Manic depression is the human condition.~~
~~Was the window in that apartment flawed somehow?~~
~~Her father's moods too seemed to move in waves, but none of them were aware of that then.~~
~~Exterior: a window bleared with rain.~~
~~It was a window for looking at, not out of.~~
~~They were so young then, still~~
~~All life is~~
~~But then they hand you~~
~~Just as a fire is~~
~~Our lives are~~
~~Manic depression: the human condition.~~

A.11: "Shadow of a Doubt" (3:32)

The peaks are coming too close together, says a voice in your ear as you pell-mell back down the slope and into the trough, a battered animal. He is at the end of an arm holding a hand that isn't yours, in an experience whose inside you cannot imagine: Pete who with his dear deep voice and his face you can no longer lift your face to see does not (God love him) know how to hold a hand, nor remember the protocol for if contractions are too short or not widely spaced enough. Something about a bed not being free yet at the birthing center, the letters he was supposed to pack, a backpack he can't seem to find. The pressure at the center of everything, hard enough to forge diamonds, is easing off now but too slowly for comfort, is the world's largest blood pressure cuff, and where is your mother? Why has she left you out here in the lonely open to face all this on your own?

You want your mother.

You hear "drink this drink here," forward or backward—shake your head, and when you send back down the bucket for words it comes up empty or there is no rope long enough or no such bucket. It is supposed to be three-one-one crest to crest, he is saying, but yours are more like two and a half–one–one and a half, unspeakable nonsense, you have about another twenty seconds here to recover and then the midwife's stuck in traffic on the way to the hospital, everyone back to driving again because of the delta, the variant traffic, the variant variant, and where even is here anyway? You feel yourself spread like a butter between times, you are half one place and half the other, back stuck in a window like Pooh at Rabbit's house and then here up front with this pressure rebuilding, life sloshing back and forth, so what can it mean now to need to go in to the hospital already where there will be no midwife but only so many masked others? What can it mean that that siren is starting to loop and repeat—is that for you, too? Is something wrong? And where is your mother to *shh* and tell you even this is okay, there is nothing wrong, this is just the pressure of life rebuilding and reproducing itself—something you personally have been put here on earth to go through?

A.12: "Live to Tell" (5:18)

And now just a brief little bonus cut for Magnolia, here at the end of side one: she truly was a disaster in the garden, but after blighting the kumquats, overfertilizing the limes—after restoring the Casa del Sol, in under five months, to its state of benighted entropy and barring Ethan's way back to paradise, she will finally get her face-to-face with Alan T. Will track him down at his house in Brentwood, on the mainland, and be surprised to find a guy in a golf shirt, normal-looking (if slightly on the short side), couldn't be older than forty-five, who disavows any special knowledge of what's gone on out there at the Casa—just wants to know, what's up with all these excessive-use citations from the water authority, and what ever happened to Ethan A.? Whereupon, good as her word, she will lay down her cards for him, but with the full business, the whole range of her emotional coloratura, blowing hot, then teary, then ingratiating, so that he will be suitably impressed with her range and indeed call in a favor with a casting agent. And the rest, as they say, is history. Or at least the "Personal life" section of her Wikipedia page, I'm seeing.

B.1: "Smash the Mirror" (1:34)

But the thing is, you can't not look at your reflection, right? Not a dictum, like looking at the sun, but something else altogether. Jolie has gone through a period, that year of her first depression, when in all stubbornness she has actually tried to live by rules like this. For example: that she would not take another living thing's life. Well, okay. She then spent a month having to trap mosquitoes in her hand and hastily toss them out windows, wadding toilet paper to accomplish the same with a bathtubbed silverfish, and flushing as opposed to squashing more than one spider, telling herself that down there in the world of unseen pipes somehow tying the visible world together, the spider would find its several legs and swim out to sea. But right around the time she'd left a banana in her backpack and flies had spontaneously parthenogenesized, sheer inertia or its country cousin laziness had set in. Fine: so she was back to being a killer again. But maybe she could at least give up being sarcastic? Yeah, right.

Okay, fine then, new rule: she would not cry.

That one had lasted almost three months—as it happens, the very same period she spent sinking deeper and deeper into drinking. She imagined telling some boy or girl, in the distant future where she'd finally figured out whether she was straight or gay or bi or something, that she never cried. But then came that damned Almodóvar retrospective, in the theater at Lincoln Center to which she might have invited Precious Ezeobi, had their paths not already diverged. Good thing, too, what with the bigass tears now rolling down her cheeks. Which one had that been? The one with the missing dad . . . *All About My Mother*? Or no, *Volver*, the return, where Penélope Cruz looks straight at the camera and starts singing. So anyway, yeah, one last rule: Jolie would not look in mirrors. But this was actually the shortest-lived, since the whole metropolis turned out to be made of mirrors: windows, the bumpers of cabs, elevator doors that split you in two and put you back together again. Not to speak of the literal mirrors (dressing, security, rearview). And then the figurative, back then, in the eclipse or was it horizon of other people: the way you looked at a face, real or imagined—even the face of Penélope Cruz, high as the eye could reach—and saw only yourself, looking back at you.

And with the little yellow nightlight now doubled in the black glass behind her and redoubled in the silvering before her and then given back again eightfold, still slightly atremble from the shutting of the door or the breathing of the house or from the LSD itself, all that golden light (in short) before and in back of her, the mirror she is pulled toward seems essentially an altar, which must be why she stays on her knees, crawling along the Turkish-ish rug to just shy of where her fingers might leave prints or her breath fog. Drops of light run briefly upward, as if a film were being rewound back to the original frame . . . and then stabilize, clearing a negative space around her. A mirror. And what she sees there is the worst worst thing, worse even than the field of dead birds or the snakey-snakey bridge or the wicked scepter or the devil who was trying to steal her booze, worse even than a ghost: it is the truth of herself.

She looks infinitely old . . . looks to be pushing thirty, practically, meaning at least ten more years of this burning. Her buzzcut is awful and her hair fucking ugly—who was she kidding? Not just mousy, but like straw a mouse has shitted in. Her skin is pale and untouched by the gilt of fake starlight and as thin as paper, lined and wrinkled and riven and blotted. And so, so tired. She has taken for granted all along that her outside looked as young as she felt on the inside, even as it has been breaking down, taking on river after river for anyone who knew how to look. So it is either not identical to herself or worse: is. And the hand she holds out to touch the face is only a thing made of bones, another dead bird, no longer adroit or beautiful or even interesting. Just persisting. Pointlessly there. Her body is a weird shape that still after all this time cannot find a comfortable way to kneel, and the light in her eyes is something she must have put there in her head, for they are glass looking into glass, and she is just another object, a something in the nothing, the meat suit she'll never outrun. It occurs to her that this is also how she'll look when she is dead. When even the positive space will be a negative space. No more somethings; not even the anything she was once so ready to piss away.

And still she doesn't close her eyes or yet look back. Would you call that bravery? Or mere compulsion? No, scratch that. It is not so much that she chooses to face forward as that she is helpless not to, her heart turning and returning in her chest, still dumbly hoping for change.

B.2: "West End Girls" (4:05)

Later—for he was not without culture, in his first-to-knock, first-to-enter way—he would read or see something somewhere downtown about a painting with the legend There Is No Place on This Planet More Horrible Than a Fox Farm . . . And fair enough, he had never been on a fox farm nor frankly fucking known such a thing existed, but he had to assume that what went on there involved fur, pelts, it sounded awful. Besides which, he had an inkling rightly or wrongly that the phrase was supposed to be some kind of metaphor for the virus that caused AIDS, about which he did know a little something. Two of the more beautiful chorus boys from *Starlight*, looking a tad shaky on their skates in Pittsburgh, had taken leaves of absence by the time they hit the West Coast. Still, with all due respect, whoever this artist was, banging on about the horrors of the fox farm, he had clearly never made the trip through Central Bookings.

That was what he heard the return crowd call it—plural—so he tried to call it that, too, to himself, in his head. He was too much a New Yorker ever to let on how cherry he was, all his low-hanging misdemeanors of the Bronx circa 1981, 1982 (turnstiles jumped, trainyards defiled, solicitation) having been processed through the relevant precinct houses—not that anyone asked. It dawned on him in the grim light of four a.m. that the city too had been a kind of temporary holding pen, since what trained you for one trained you for the other.

When he'd been thrust in here however many hours ago, still too high on Dex to really feel how drunk he he was also, the racial scene had unsettled him, coming as he was out of the comparative caravanserai of a drag ball uptown—but then after a brief span of immersion it became just a fact of life. Likewise the strap-hanger vibe: too many bodies, too few seats. (Though courtesy was no longer the move—there were no pregnant ladies, and you couldn't afford anyone making you for a fag.) And finally the extraordinary inversion here of public and private, inner life and outer life, less a departure from everywhere else than a kind of concentration of it. There was a little sink bolted into the wall. There was a shitter right out in the open, seatless and unlovely. And then adjacent, as if to discourage you from using either of them, a payphone. One discrepancy, though: the city was riddled with clocks whereas here, as at the casino where the touring company had been put up in Vegas, there was no clock visible, unless he'd missed it on the way in. The guys lounging along the edges had the languorous quality of great cats, their wrists resting on honest-to-God bars.

He ran his subway module: keep head down, neither initiate eye contact nor avoid it. Waited for his name to be called. After a while, he gathered through his faltering high that other bodies were being pulled out to talk to their lawyers, if they could be called anyone's lawyers, working as they apparently did for free.

And then he was jolted again by the sick thud of the body off the fender of his car—but what gave anyone the right to cross the FDR on foot like that after midnight? A microsecond of impact, was how too-fast he'd been going . . . and also just long enough for the bumper to become a sense organ, to feel the life being bumped out of the body. Then, on that minimal shoulder, arms bound behind and the lights whirling in his eyes, he didn't think to ask the arresting officer was it a man or a woman precisely because he knew it had to be a man. As in, what are you in for, faggot? Who, me? I killed a man.

He thinks it again, forces himself: That man is dead. I killed a man. It is when he has an urge to look at his own face, to see what it looks like, that he registers the other discrepancy between the highly reflective city and this specific site within it: Central Booking or Bookings does not have a mirror, either. Weird, because you'd think a key step in their degradation would be to show them themselves beefing over a corner of bench, shitting in the shitter or struggling to hold it in, lying on the floor with the shakes, stuck for all eternity in a small space with whatever it is they've chosen or failed to choose. But apparently the mind is mirror enough, and in there, where he's done pretending to be something other than what he is, he's going to have a good long lonely time to look at himself and at what he's done—assuming a difference—and can in fact not see, short of biting the bullet and punching his own ticket, how he might ever get out from under it . . .

So that he almost misses the screw calling his name. "McGon-agall. McGonagall?"

B.3: "Let Him Roll" (4:05)

"This supposed to be some like confession or something? Because I feel like you're looking for me to apologize." The voice shorn of its body. The high grasses closing again where a fat tabby, limbered, disappears. "I'm sure there are types who'd watch something like that on the PBS or whatever, shame of the work-ingman. I see them in the store, too, every summer. Come out here like they found a solution to the other ten months of their lives. When if it was a solution they'd have been out here year-round. Though you really did move your loved ones out, didn't you, so maybe you are something special. Still, the way I look at it, there's exactly as much to most folks as meets the eye." Sound of a cigarette being dragged. Little crispness of baking tobacco. "Not to tell you how to do your job, but maybe you should try explaining a little more what you're after back there. People don't like the quiet. It can feel like you're trying to push their buttons."

Off-mic: "This is me doing my best to listen."

"I don't even know why I agreed to this. Sounded interesting to be in a picture, I guess. But to your question, I'm not trying to be made out to, like, represent anything. I didn't ask to be born in this neck of the woods, I'm saying. Nor sent away to fight for it. I'm not proud of what I did over there any more than I'm ashamed of it."

"But you came back." It's the last time Joanna's own voice will be heard before the midway point of the film, where everything starts to go haywire.

"Except where else was going to take me in, in seventy-one, seventy-two? Not that I didn't love the place, either, understand. If you'll excuse me . . ." And now a series of second-long stills, like a palm full of snaps flicked through. View of the picnic tables. View of the empty pump area, looking toward the picnic tables. Same but in reverse, as seen from under the picnic tables. The tanks, with their dinosaurs, as seen from below. Close-up of a gray stripe that if you blink is a single train track. A hubcap dangling from a keyring inserted in a steel door. Too many powerlines, various oddly shaped little things to keep them from touching, dancing in a winter sky. Coin-op vacuum; diegetic flush. And now inside, the four aisles of PLUs, seen as if browsed, never just one brand of anything, alternating with the view from behind an empty register. Back for a second, forward a second: the rhythm of a surveillance camera refreshing its footage. And in the corner by the joker poker, that video game with no one around to play it, assorted algorithmic carnage already under way. A hiss, or possibly a chirr, the keening edge of inexplicable cicadas. The sound clips out briefly.

"Where were we? Right, best and worst I ever did. Probably the same thing: marriage. I was married too once, okay? It was no picnic. Now I'm married to all this. You noticed how we open late on Sundays? Well some Sundays I drive out there to the cemetery, walk out, sometimes lay some flowers . . . Do I talk to her? Of course not, we barely talked even when she was alive—and now she's dead. I don't even know if I loved her in the way you used that word, or chose her; it was more like each of us being chosen, and taking a hell of a long time to accept that for what it was. Like this place. I try to be what it requires of me, whether you think that's right or wrong. Maybe that's love." The twin tanks, seen from below, are like the legs of a parent as seen by a child. "I love it the way you can only love a thing you didn't choose."

B.4: "The Black Angel's Death Song" (3:12)

"Aspern?"

In a voice that rustles, from outside the bathroom door. Last name only, to preserve the distance his being in a place like this at this time of the night has already collapsed. Not to speak of how she's driven the like six hours round-trip on the Garden State to fetch him, as the networks waited to call the election for Obama. (Hope and Change: the Götterdämmerung of his twenties.) The future being unequally distributed, and the jailors of Lower Township not yet having hiked the cost of a call to what it's been in New York since the time of his last arrest, it is already the best quarter he's ever spent. "Just a minute!" he shouts.

But the seven years between the two cells is still a fucking blur, as with much of the car ride north, and people in AA turn out to have been right about all his reformations, his vindications: he is still and always the fucking addict he doesn't want to be anymore. When his heaves remain dry, he gets up off his knees and flushes. Sits to piss, not quite trusting himself to stand, and leans on a wall and possibly goes somewhere else for a while and then flushes again, trying for a performance of suitable conviction. And is pleased not to stumble as he crosses to the sink, but then it's only the one step. Once he's confirmed he's not going to puke there, he pulls the little stopper thing and runs water as if to wash hands but then when it is as full as he can get it without overspilling he plunges his fucking head in, since that seems to be the source of all his problems. He's seen this plunge on any number of Westerns, albeit in the horse's trough, which would still be better frankly than he deserves. But it works: underwater, he is instantly less loaded, or the swimminess inside is suddenly matched by an equal and opposite swimminess without. His father is gone. Is dead. Whatever he was so angry about is almost gone, too. He has missed his one chance to touch that face a last time with his fingertips, feel the whiskers he can even now barely recall, if whiskers can grow on corpses, the way grass sprouts from unvisited graves. He wonders is it possible to die just from holding your own head underwater. But no, that is all behind him, the dream that he might ever escape, and now, for however long he can hold on to his breath, he is simply here.

This is the moment.

This be the verse, right here.

He has not gone into the hall yet to receive from Erica Morales the ultimatum that for someone like him might as well be a mountain of raw: clean his ass up or go to jail. Has not yet leaned toward her in the confusion of their closeness and begun to kiss her—and for about eight seconds, to be kissed in return. His future is a black box, is this closed room, his closed eyes as he holds on for another second. He has a daughter now to live for, eleven years old, an ex-wife he still can't imagine his life without, and one last box of his mother's unpawned shit, the holiest of the holies, which he'd meant to carry down there to return to the collapsing garage like it was trying to hold on to it so hard that had called down the curse in the first place. But now, in this eternal present, this moment without end, he sees that he could equally well try to move it forward. Give it to Jolie.

B.5: "Pissing in a River" (4:52)

You feel helpless not to push but you're in a cab so are told you cannot. Your hand still held, your face against the glass, the siren is now blessedly silent but the lights are coming on like rabbit punches that seem almost gentle against the leaden circles of what is clearly now pain. Which at every pothole ramifies outward, too big for its borders, yet you remain bound by yours, so something must be wrong, you must be both in the pain and beyond it, here and not here, and women still die in childbirth. All. The. Time. And fucking Pete seems to be worried mostly about smoothing things over with the cabbie as, with his iPhone . . . wait, is he fucking *filming* this? And then a circle begins and for a while you go somewhere . . . else.

From which when you return you are entering a hospital, the all-hours bustle of emergency rooms everywhere—wait, are *you* the emergency? You catch a glimpse of a relieved-looking cabbie before the automatic doors crunch closed and you are being presented with a wheelchair like a door prize but go straight to all fours as a woman says Not here, Mommy. It is the horse-faced nurse from the birthing-center orientation, the one you've been hoping you didn't get. Who upstairs will tell you You're almost there but you cannot. What it is, is: this fear. You can't. This is something you can't not go through but also you can't, Oh Christ I cannot do this, Mommy—and just as the somewhere else descends to reclaim you, there she is at last, in the doorway, your mother. And not just that: behind her is *her* mother. And her mother's mother. And what they are reminding you: you have been here before. For a second, it is moms all the way down.

B.6: "Visions of Johanna" (7:31)

The one and only time she will make herself known to Jolie, it is as a light from the depths, a mass of colors like a globe of blown glass when it emerges from what is called the glory hole. It is still warm, this mass, but not dangerously so, at approximately the temperature of a body running a high fever, and is likewise about the shape of a medicine ball or a five-pound sack of flour, just barely too big for a girl of her stature to fit inside her ribcage. Where it will nonetheless seem to be: conjured not out of the night outside, but up from inside her, so that she cannot tell anymore whether her eyes are closed or open. She will know that it has a name, that the name is Joanna, but it does not come to her as a grandmother (it isn't even clear she knows who Jolie is) . . . only as somebody's mother. The colors—mostly yellows reds and blues but with a purple too that seems somehow primary—swim with patient purpose on the glowing surface they enclose, less swirling than unfolding a pattern, though through them she can see other patterns moving deeper inside, on levels where the warmth burns hotter. And she feels she could stay with it for as long as she wanted, so long as she knows that this doesn't mean forever.

When she reaches out—curiously, without conscious intent, and with what appendage is unclear—she will discover that its warmth will heal whatever it touches. But that is not what it is for. It (she, his mother) has a message, if only Jolie could find a voice to relay it so that it doesn't just sound like someone telling you their dream. Or like something as small, as embarrassing, as *Hey, I saw your mom in there; she loves you*. But in the time it takes her to hear these words in sequence—or whatever it is happens with words, inside—there is no more suffering, because Jolie has flickered out of consciousness, become an intention rather than a thing. And just on the cusp of return, there comes a second of a joy that could pass for terror. There is a heat here that could actually devour, yet that chooses not to . . . that is maybe enough. She opens her eyes, or they have been open all along, and no mother is there anymore, and in the mirror before her she is merely herself, normal-looking as anyone can be said to be—and it is only when her eyes flit past her to the futon that she realizes she is no longer alone.

B.7: "Partita No. 6 in E Minor, BWV 830: V. Sarabande" (3:41)

It turned out to be a wood-floored utility space of some kind— a gym by day, probably, or assembly room—but then everything since her discharge from Columbia-Presbyterian had been one long blur, a dissociative slide, so from here at the threshold the girl couldn't really have told anyone what precise kinds of ordinary business would have brought anyone's lives to such a crossing. Only that now, inside, the space felt at once overbright and sepulchral, such illumination as there was seeming to come from beneath the floorboards, strangely (though it went some distance toward explaining why none of the posted signs could be read).

Oh, and this: she had a curious sense of having been here before.

Maybe it was the way no one already inside had looked up to see her waiting there, squashing her printed instructions and sani-

tary pads deeper down inside her bookbag. Each, she was somehow surprised to find, was a woman, though that made sense, too.
Not that any of them could take the place of her mother; each was
too involved in carving out some of this limited space for herself
alone. The long day was fading outside, but now a whiteness could
be seen in some clerestory windows high overhead, the shadows
of the birds that roosted up there coming and going, indifferent as
ghosts. *Lent et douloureux*, she thought (odd, since the second language spoken in her home was Spanish, not French). She took a
pillowcase full of linens from a pile and chose from a folded-up row
the least busted cot and soon, in a space maximally distant from its
neighbors (much as they were maximally distant from hers), she
had set up a little area in which to lie down and try to lessen the
pain. Yet she already knew she could not close her eyes in here; it
was almost as if she were unable to stop seeing. Her own saddle
oxfords neatly paired on the floor. A spot where one panel of the
parquet had lifted slightly. Socks not quite right for the shoes. A
discolored place where she'd been leaning too much to one side
on her way down to the subway and the brush of the escalator
had rubbed.

One way people in such places claimed space was by talking
to themselves. Her attempt to tune out their voices, not to be
scared of them, only made them worse. Worse still: wondering
how many nights she'd now be doomed to live like this herself
before the telltale bleeding stopped or she too started sounding
crazy that way, muttering under her breath so as to seem hungry
or high or desperate or otherwise dangerous enough to frighten
off anyone who might try to fuck with her. Which she would then
probably by definition also be. She tried not to think of the face
of her mother, doubtless out of her mind now with worry. Her
mother who could not be told. Instead watched the birds depart
less frequently, the light go. Heard the women around her subside into sleep. But already knew that she would not sleep, not
tonight—for Erica Morales did not want to blot out the world, not
anymore. What she wanted was for someone to help her decide
whether to press on like this, keep running, whatever the cost, or
instead somehow decide to face the music, go turn herself in. Go
home.

B.8: "Changeling/Transmission I" (7:51)

Izzy, she wants to burst out, when he waves from behind the door. And *How long have you been watching?* But the seam feels fragile and might not hold. So instead she goes to him, drops down, takes his hand in hers to keep herself from squeezing his whole body; he seems like the kind of kid who might not enjoy it. But she hasn't seen him since he was carried, unconscious, into the maw of the hospital, and maybe it is the nightlight's little incandescence, or the afterglow of her visions (which may well be to say, of the drugs), but his skin, so chalky gray then, now looks warmer and darker and perfectly alive. If he has any strong feelings about this, he does not show it. Just takes his hand back. A little Band-Aid inside his wrist. What he says is, "See, I said you'd c-come back, but no one ever l-listens."

Her finger goes to her lips. His normal volume is already too loud, and in the silence of the night he's like a siren, a blare. It occurs to her to wonder if his speech thing is actually a hearing thing—like what someone had said somewhere about depression actually being a mask you put on rage (or was it the other way around?).

He is now offering from the end table a glass of water: hers, from the other morning. Her mouth is pasty, admittedly, somewhat as her complexion had looked in the mirror, but she declines it with a shake of the head. She still has half a Gatorade in her backpack outside, in the safekeeping of—it returns to her—her father. Jesus, she was so caught up chasing her own need for escape that she hasn't stopped to think about his. Though maybe it's only been a minute or two? Hard to say. She presses small hands once more, wonders if there's something she's still afraid to admit to, but then lets go, murmurs to him not to worry, she's safe, she's just here for the violin.

And as she turns her back to stoop for it he says, or blares, quite fluently—almost sharply, "B-but, is that all you came for?" She pretends not to hear his disappointment. "Then I guess we're really not going to be seeing you again, huh?"

Has he unlatched the case, she wonders—peeked inside? Seen the passport, guessed at her plans? She really should get a damn lock on the thing, but it hardly matters in this instance since Izzy seems to exist slightly outside of time anyway and probably had an inkling all along. What would he think if he really could see into her heart?

"Izzy," she says, remembering that she can talk. "I wish I could explain it to you, why I can't stay. I want to hear all about what went on in the hospital, how you got out. But a lot has happened since then. Some people are after us, and it's not really safe for me out there. I've kind of dug a hole for myself, you know?"

"No, I g-get it. You need to r-run." Arms crossed, but otherwise keeping the family poker face. "You're scared. And we're only just k-kids."

Her shrug feels feverish. "Are we? I don't know, I guess."

"But maybe you could t-take something when you go as a k-kind of suh . . . a soo-soo . . ." She thinks for a second he will change up and go with "reminder," but instead he traces that curious figure or pattern on his arm and out it comes. "Souvenir?"

And there, black on the black futon cushion, is what she hasn't noticed before: the VCR, its cords already wrapped and tucked. Jesus, this kid. Had she left fingerprints on the play button or something? But no, of course, that was her grandmother's videotape she'd been showing him at Corinne's two days ago, right around the point where the sound cut out, and maybe he knows that where she's going, VCRs aren't going to be so easy to come by. And maybe it doesn't count as stealing if it's your family giving it to you. She bends over him once more, his little body in its silk pajamas, relative in size to her as she might be to her own mother, but alive is the important thing. And whether or not he likes it, she puts her lips to his head and when she finds his scalp leaves her blessing there. Tries not to let the tears touch. Then making up for lost time she books to the window, feeds herself out face-down and feet-first, knowing she can fit this way, and as if she's dropped some additional weight makes it out with room to spare, remembering just in time to reach back in for the violin and the VCR she's left on the floor. She supposes she could've had Izzy feed them across, but through the crack in the window, the stars are gone, the nightlight in there is orders of magnitude dimmer than she remembers, and she can no longer make him out.

Only her father, standing on the tarpaper like no time has passed at all, staring wordlessly out past the canted roofline she once bumped her head on, to where their pursuers still fail to materialize. She thinks of the message she is supposed to give him before she can make her exit, and him do whatever he's decided he has to if he's to live with the consciousness of what he's done. But before she can say anything, he's returned to her the backpack and taken the VCR in his hands, looking down at it as if in thought or hallucination—as if at least one of them has just seen a ghost.

B.9: "Wait for It" (3:13)

It would be impossible to say later for how long Erica Morales had sat on the fire escape with her Rumi that week, smoking, looking out toward the other Dominicans celebrating some rite of passage in an apartment across the way with foil trays of food and Underground Kingz on repeat. "The Guest House." "Ridin' Dirty." "The Phrasing Must Change." How to get from this life over to that one, though. How does something new come into the world? It seemed a simple enough matter of crossing the courtyard through the grass nobody mowed, going up that other fire escape like some post-everything Romeo; what was the worst that could happen? Well, she could step on some metal, need a tetanus booster. Or step on a cat, and rabies. Or they could be like, Yo, you don't belong here, lady, what are you doing, there's nothing here for you, get lost. No worse than McGonagall's little band of lay Franciscans might say to her, too, if they could see all the doubts in her head. But to find out, she would first have to decide to start climbing down the stairs. And to do that, she'd first have to decide to move toward where the steps started. And to do *that*, she'd have to decide to get up from her folding chair, which she hadn't all week, save to go to the office she could neither abide a day longer nor leave. There was no moment of deciding, or if there was, you couldn't think your way into it, any more than you can think your way into your own future, or past. Or for that matter, your present.

Which might have been helpful to know during all those thousands of hours when this or that victim or perpetrator was sorely trying her compassion: we don't make our choices, so much as we are made by them. In which case what is there for the person who needs something new to come into the world but patience, or prayer, and maybe a sort of ethic of "Just go with it"? Perhaps the reflexive verb form "find oneself" is useful here: as in, on the evening of the appointed Friday, Officer Erica Morales, having sat for so long in her folding chair, was surprised to find herself in the act of leaving her own story to try something new, not the back way via fire escape, as she'd imagined, but walking right out the front door.

B.10: "Castles Made of Sand" (2:48)

The morning of November 26, 2011, has only one sunrise, and it will find the two of them up near the summit, in clothes nearly dry, sharing an afghan while trying not to touch. An hour earlier, give or take, Ethan had wrenched open—once and for all—the badly corroded chain marked **AUTHORIZED VEHICLES ONLY** and with the lights off nosed the dogwalking van a length or two down the railroad cut into the woods, then climbed out to restore the broken link (now hook) to its connection. Perhaps easier just to remove the tail and horns than to conceal the whole vehicle, but that would feel wrong, aesthetically, and anyway, he'd still have the license plate or lack thereof as an identifier. Also: he's always wanted to do this, be this flagrantly unauthorized. Live this far outside the law. And so, lit only by the strip of perhaps-just-paling sky between the two treelines, he'd contrived to edge them back along the road they'd walked out the night before, to a spot approximately even with the start of the path up the back slope of Keel, and there, where no one for the time being would think to look for it, they have long since abandoned the van.

They'll be facing west up here, of course, the wrong way for sunrise, but it turns out not to matter. Or rather, on acid (as they must still to some extent be), anything can turn out to matter. To wit: he's sitting with his nearly-grown little girl, as close as he'll probably ever get to her again, atop what in some sense is the dead dark body of his own father, still trying to figure some way to go through with what he's now realized he must do. And though the turf has now slightly re-dampened his jeans, it is everywhere else tipped in a frost he's pretty sure he's not imagining. And beyond, below, lies the outer dark of the dying little town, which, no matter how he'd cursed it, he'd never really believed he could wash off his hands. And while you do not get the whole lightshow looking west, a flaming eye or spreading curve to mirror that of the sun's going under, there is this whole interesting range of washes the sky passes through, echoed in the whiskery deadness of grass with its touch of gray. And even if you can't impute the existence of the sun from its effects, you still wouldn't want to totally write it off, either. Unclear what they're waiting for up here, but with him dumbfounded by the corner he'll now have to paint himself into and her with not much to say beyond goodbye, it is rather like watching someone try to illustrate the concept of change.

B.11: "The Next Movement" (4:10)

. . . At which point they hand you your daughter, and the real work begins.

25

A.1: "I Am Trying to Break Your Heart" (6:58)

When the climbdown, the comedown begins, it is simply as the color blue: a certain threshold in the sunrise is at some point passed and everything begins to be touched with it, as by the fingers of a paint-drunk child. First to go is the sky, not unexpectedly, the northern pinks and golds at this time of year being as frangible as leaves, and with not so much as a cloud in the sky to hold them—but still it registers as a kind of bereavement, this blue like denim almost all the color has washed out of; it will stay that way through the whole of the short day, and will flatter no one. When she finally looks over at her father, for example, to see if they are still having the same experience, it is this blue that will make the back of his hand on the grass look like a much older man's. And then the grass itself, this last however long, has stilled its pullulations and become, under the thinning frost, a calm almost-indigo. The sycamores down there with the big flaws on their trunks are a slatey blue blemished with steel, and the canopies azure where a few leaves still shimmer, letting wood the blue of veins shoot through. And the cars, so often blue to begin with; and the unegged eggshells of the aluminum-sided houses picking up the sky's blue as the blue of skim milk, of skin left too long in the pool; and then more trees and past them the scrappy signs, the blackletter of the Racanelli funeral home blued down to the outer rind of a ripe avocado, and the red-gone-purple of the Amoco station that could never beat Ducky's on price: fictions of a spectrum, mere speciations of blue. It is the death of night's heat, the world cooling back to its old orderly disorder, and there is something about the watching that pierces her, makes a little slit to let what is out there flow into her, too. It fills her flat chest, this blue, the best worst part of her first and only acid trip, until a moment or instant comes when she realizes why the blues are called the blues. But where it should be filling her eyes, it seems instead to have leapt across some border, for when she next turns toward her father, he is shaking under his section of afghan, his stubbled cheeks wet and his fingertips digging into the grass, as if that could ever stop it from growing.

A.2: "In a Black Out" (3:16)

He knew what he had to do now, but at the key moment—the decisive moment—he could not go across. And behind the plate-glass front window of an Irish-enough bar in Lower Township, New Jersey, waiting for the girl to bring around his second beer, he would wonder why he'd always insisted on taking the ferry in the first place. The view was of water, but it wasn't the *right* water here four miles north of the ferry terminal, where he'd driven in his black suit to kill the half-hour until the damn thing boarded. Cross this water here, on a line due west, and you'd have gotten only as far as Dover, Delaware, having saved yourself no time nor gained much in the way of scenery. Anyway, he couldn't go across, not yet. It was a fucking miracle, frankly, he thought, finding half a sip left at the bottom of his stupidly tall glass, but his would-be sponsor from his dues-paying years, '03, '04, had seemed glad to hear his voice—"You made yourself a little scarce for a while there, Ethan," followed by a hacking cough—and had loaned him the car no questions asked, a day and maybe a night, once he'd revealed himself to have found another meeting, to have made it to Step Nine (though of course he could never even get his head around Step Two). It was worse than being cursed, some-how. Not lying to your sponsor was like the first rule or pos-sibly defining feature of sponsorship, he thought, but then you weren't supposed to take a drink, either, where what Ethan had been doing these last months was sliding back down into what he would have then pegged as a mid-major trough, even before the drugs had come and found him. Later his erstwhile sponsor, in the more-terminal-than-anyone-realized stages of lung cancer, would die before Ethan had a chance to apologize, by which time the inpatient counselors in California, whom he was paying for the privilege (or anyway Moira's credit card company was), would have helped Ethan see that this was something of a pattern in his life: losing people before you got a chance to say what needed saying—a feeling less of being abandoned than of not having finished a project together, through some fault of his own. And all the God stuff behind it, that nodding and unjudgmental disappointment . . . and anyway.

Anyway.

Anyway. His father was dead. He was well and truly orphaned, though maybe that was misleading, self-indulgent, he was about to be thirty-one years old. *My sister and I are orphans*, he imagined himself starting with the waitress, who had definitely been giving him that look, what with the pre-distressed formalwear and the grief he was either enormously talented or not much good at all at concealing. And who now, along with a new beer, set down a bowl of peanuts, since it seemed like he might be staying awhile, and a Stygian little thimble full of poison. "You looked like you needed something stronger," she said.

Had he used it on her, his grief? Very well: he had used it, assumed a cunning doleful air, assuming he hadn't had one already. More to the point: Had he finished the requested eulogy? He had not even fucking begun it. He took out the typing paper he'd folded into eighths and shoved into the breast pocket of his rent-to-own suit. The blank page should have been less intimidating now that it, too, came as it were pre-distressed. He watched the early returns trickle in, things not looking so solid for the forces of light, and stroked his pocket for the mint-tin he would definitely not be dipping into, at least not until after the memorial, and tried to think of what you would even say about a man like that. It was no easier than thinking of what to say *to* him. He wondered if Eddie, long out of jail now, would show. Then, as he always did at times of disaster, he thought of Sarah—as if here in his mind, at the eleventh hour, she might still let go of her judgment and come save him. Or be saved. Sarah, who never used to seem in doubt, who had always known just what to do, and then chosen to do it. Sarah, whose only real mistake, ever, had been to love him. Even now, though, she could not have understood how it felt in here, or how to get from there to the right thing to do. In between lay either a decision made far inside or a change visited from without, but when he looked out the window, it seemed a storm or at least a fog was rolling in, the sky and the bay's gray water dark and getting darker, so what could it hurt to just take one more shot like a normal person, like a normal grieving person. And then maybe talk to the waitress. And then maybe go do hardly any of what he had. Perhaps it would even loosen the tongue, he would remember thinking later, stumbling through the mud to his undying sponsor's car, trying to find the hole thing the key went in, the keyhole, in the hundred percent dark.

A.3: "Is There a Ghost" (2:59)

Not for the first time this week, Sarah Kupferberg is (as the poet said) just going on her nerve, running on pure instinct as she tries to explain the irrelevance of choice to her father. "I don't know, Daddy. It's more like, if we're not ready to go out on a limb, then why did we even come here?"

He peers over her shoulder at the laptop in the motel room they've sprung for so as to recharge the fading battery and shower—Albert never could function in the mornings without a shower—and to gather themselves for a final reckoning.

"But there's nothing on this map that I can see but woods, Sarah. And you just said the location hasn't budged in hours."

"I have this sense about it, though."

"You know who you sound like when you do this."

"Who—like Mom?" For, whatever else you want to say about her, Eleanor does have a sort of gift for the insoluble problem, the solution that comes out of nowhere. But of course that's not who he's talking about, he's talking about the problem named Ethan, and she is no longer so unconscious of the piece of him that's still embedded in her. The wound now a part of her body. Nonetheless: "This announcement popped up when I looked for the address of the school and it was like I could just feel they'd be going."

"Like you could 'just feel' last night we should come tear-assing down here in the Volvo."

"Elysian Shores Motel. It said right there in the metadata."

"Which only goes to my point, Sarah. You tried the personal approach already. Occam's razor says we go home right now and admit defeat, wait for him to bring her back. The guy can barely keep his shoes tied; there's no way he keeps a kidnapping up much longer. But if instead we go and find they really did come for this thing, and then see us giving chase in public and try to run . . . well, then you have to get the law involved. All of a sudden you're talking about standing up in court and bearing witness against your little girl's dad, honey. And him facing jail for the next quarter century. Is that really what you want?"

"You think I came here chasing Ethan—like I'd give him another chance if he asked?"

"Chasing Jolie, honey, obviously. All I'm saying is, before we go making a citizen's arrest, perhaps you should ask what's been holding you back from calling 1-800-FIND-KID. And if there's some wisdom in that."

She could call it right now. Yet Sarah is discovering of late that she cannot will herself to unfeel what she feels, which is that she has to track this dot, follow this sign, be there whatever the consequences for herself and Ethan, to face them without flinching and to offer Jolie what protection she can. Though if she's wrong, and there is no sign . . .

"And this memorial service you scared up—"

The nail tapping the screen looks ugly, bitten-down. Is her own. " 'Remembrance and Rededication,' " she says. "It can't be coincidence, either . . . Like it just happens to be starting an hour from now, three point four miles from those woods?"

"And assuming it's not, and they didn't just chuck the phone after you texted her, are we planning to show up in yesterday's jeans?"

"I don't think it's that kind of event, Daddy, and anyway, this never struck me as the kind of place that stood on ceremony."

Albert opens the door to the breezeway with its fresh-smelling air, steps out to survey the parking lot and the rough landward side of Ocean City like some pompous old quartermaster on an ill-swabbed ship. Who *is* her father, really? she thinks, for the second time in as many days. And what is this new thing she's feeling toward him? Regret? Disgust? Sympathy? But no time to decide that either now. No time to decide anything. She turns. "Are we done here? I feel like we're done here. Let's go."

A.4: "Right Back Where We Started From" (3:12)

Promptly at 9:30 a.m. the first guests arrive to fill the wedding-style white folding chairs that dot the faded fescue of the old town green. These are the would-be local elders, the churchgoers, whose weekend rounds comprise just such civic ceremonies and diocesan celebrations, along with what seems to some of them a frankly unbelievable number of funerals, viewings, wakes . . . the upshot being, they are past masters at mourning: show up a half-hour early, sit near the back, tally the number of chairs for whatever akashic scorecard's being kept. This one is eight rows of four-plus-four, so that's like what, sixty-four RSVPs? Plus the projectionist's seat and standing room for the stragglers who increasingly don't even bother to reply. Last time there was this big a crowd was the car king, Gutfreund Senior, and that had to be ten years ago. And if there's a faint note of hope that not so many show up now, it is tempered by a general clemency, for the town had ultimately softened on this Aspern fellow, or at least on the distinction he'd brought to the school, now failing again without him. And if the art-teacher wife had at times seemed a little obsessive, a little fast and loose with her commitments, a little woo-woo, no one chose to remember that now; and even the spinster daughter had come home, adopted a black kid, with her roommate . . . well, it's the twenty-first century, isn't it. And of course the son who'd gone off to New York to become such a bigshot he couldn't even get away for the funeral—the father had never mentioned the son's acting career, but you had to imagine his buttons were bursting. And oh, not that it mattered, but he'd brought a trophy back here in '01. Parade and everything.

The Mexicans who'd set up the chairs—unseen, but you imagined them as Mexicans—must also have given the grass a trim, and although it was a pointless gesture in late November, the quorum now settled into the back row approves above all of pointless gestures, especially those meant to convey respect. What else is the rechristening of this boat, really, when all you need to show the IRS for the tax writeoff is a transfer of legal title and a receipt from an accredited 501(c)(3)? And maybe there is some life in it, this grass, for from the bluegray clippings scattered in damp lines comes a faint green smell riding the sweetness of the creek where the *Molly A* now sits docked and furled, ready to sail forth on her new mission—to go out and win for the St. Anselm's sailing team more trophies, and for this forgotten place a little more glory.

Time passes. The sky doesn't change. Several more seats fill. By ten minutes shy of the scheduled start of the thing (per the programs on the table at the back), a little unease has begun to circulate. One of the Mexicans (see?) has come out to pull down from its cross-brace the oversized white sail of a movie screen set up along the sidewalk where you come in, and from a projector next to the programs, or more accurately from a laptop, the obligatory PowerPoint of photos has begun. Outdoors, though, in cloudless daylight, a slide show seems ill-conceived. The Channel 5 forecast said expect some rain, but then the weather on Channel 5 does tend to be unreliable. Even after the projector gets turned around and the screen gets moved to the shade of a shade-tree right up front, behind the lectern but blocking the view of the boat, it is hard to make out the pictures of the deceased and his bride, the deceased in his uniform, the deceased handing out whatever those are, diplomas, the deceased and his kids, the deceased in the pink of his youth grinning back from the back of what looks to be a different, smaller boat. Moreover, when they turn to the lectern, the first row remains empty—not least of the widow. A man is dead, again, still, yet is this to be just a rerun of the unpleasantness from last time around, when no one had turned up to speak for him? Who will honor this man with even a modicum of punctuality?

A.5: "Finger Lickin' Good" (3:39)

It's not often you get a walker at the drive-thru of the Biscuit Shack over toward the hospital, but it does happen. The inside dining area opens at eight in the morning and closes at nine p.m., but the biscuits start coming out of the oven at six—right around the time the deep fryer gets to bubbling—and are credible enough that a market exists among the farmers and fishermen and other early risers and persists on till midnight. So in short, the clerk will say later, in a witness report taken by the Cheshire County sheriff's office, you do get some carless folks rolling through on foot at times when only the drive-thru is open. Usually said folks are on drugs, the frizz-haired manager interjects for clarity, or sanctimony. Which the black kid in the paper hat affirms, though generally wary of digressing too much to the deputy now licking bits of biscuit-glaze from his big white fingers. Late-night you mostly get the potheads, all gentle-like, so it's the mornings you have to look out for. That's your speed-freaks, your methheads, and increasingly your opioid addicts, folks underslept and edgy off the comedown and usually looking to haggle over price after you've gone ahead and punched in the order—and frankly a little scary looming up like that against the deserted parking lot. But no, this one wasn't scary, exactly. Or not yet. What had stuck out about it was that it was broad daylight, and the dining room open, so if he didn't have a car, he could have just come inside to order. Well, that and the hat. A car had actually been behind him in line, had tootled its horn, he'd seen the guy jump, but then he'd tugged the hat on tighter and come over to the window, tall enough to have to bend down, and in a voice real polite but maybe not from around here ordered two coffees and asked how many chicken biscuits he could get with the change. Which did seem to augur haggling. "I told him we don't do a chicken biscuit per se, we do chicken *and* biscuits, but for a breakfast biscuit we offer ham, sausage, blueberry, huckleberry, bacon and cheese, or if he wanted he could order plain biscuits and then some chicken and assemble his own. He looks over at that bush right there, like as if it could talk, and then says, okay, how much is the chicken. And I did what I was trained to do" (here with a look at the manager). "I said he could get a box of a half-dozen biscuits at three dollars on special, plus two breasts at two thirty-nine apiece, which comes to like seven seventy-eight before the coffees, but for nine forty-nine plus tax he could do the Big Box, which is a whole fried chicken, meaning two split breasts, two wings, two thighs, two drumsticks, ten pieces total, and which comes with a dozen free plain biscuits and then you take the coffees as your two complimentary drinks, that's a real steal for a dozen fix-'em-yourself chicken biscuits, and again the bit with the bushes and he says all right, I'll take it, and stands up and starts drumming his fingers on the pass-through right here while I wait for the order. I had to bend down some to see his face, which you could not really make out what with the shade of the concrete canopy out there not to mention the hat, but since you asked, I'd say sober, yes. The man just looked tired to me. Like he'd been through some things. And you don't really realize how big the Big Box is when two of them are being handed through the window of a Suburban filled with the whole sailing team or whatever, but it did seem kind of almost ridiculous for just this one guy by his lonesome, like food for a giant, or maybe that was . . . well, look. You can see for yourself."

On a screen back here in the manager's office, time-stamped 9:34 a.m., a tall, trim man in a corduroy jacket is seen loping off toward the bushes with a truly preposterously large yellow carton of chicken carried by its own handle and a cardboard caddy with two bigass American coffees. On his head, bowed as if to obscure his face and thwart any identification, he appears to be wearing a Pilgrim hat, black, high-crowned, with a buckle.

A.6: "Memories Can't Wait" (3:30)

His father was dying, had perhaps for some time been dying, was what Moira had wanted him to know over the phone. Round and round they'd gone, for how long he was afraid to look back at the call history and find out *(words, words, words)*, but underneath, dodge and duck as he might, he was essentially a little boy sticking fingers in his ears and repeating, "I can't hear you." And of course he could hear just fine, or better than fine. When she started with, "You should know Dad's been sick," it meant "He is dying." Ethan could hear this not only because he knew the drill, but because his father's death had been waiting out there for him for a while now, a bony figure keeping its mouth shut behind an arras—he had almost invited it in by his own actions, as he used to think his father had invited his mother's—and were he still writing a play it was the only thing that could have been left to happen here at the start of Act III, for of course "Your father is dying" meant in turn what Dad himself would never say, which was "Please come home." It would even be simple enough: go down to Ocean City; take a hard right. But why hadn't Dad at least told him about the failing kidney? Why hadn't Moira? Right. Because Ethan's own rebellions had as much as told them not to. Because he himself had made abundantly clear through his silence that the wreck of his life was their fault, and his sobriety wouldn't withstand it.

And of course today happened to be the first of his two nights off, the waiter's early-mid-week weekend. Right around the equinox, his bad moon rising, things in the balance. He had Jolie coming over tomorrow, he should really start cleaning the apartment, but the days were still long enough that the sun had not yet gone down behind its waterfall, and at some point, trying to parry Moira's thrusts, he'd left the apartment, hopefully locked and with the stove off (though doubtless still in disarray), and had begun to walk south, phone to his ear. I stayed behind through all of Mom and all the shit that came after, he wanted to tell her, while you went off to Boston. "I'm sure he'll be fine, Moira. When was he ever not fine?" From a distance, if you squinted hard enough to miss the little razor-phone in his hand, you might have thought him one of the city's ten thousand madmen, talking to himself, locked in passionate debate.

And then he rang off, and somehow he was way down by Madison Square, as if to clock in at the latest restaurant. An investment bank had failed two days earlier, there had been an odd sense of suspension in the dining room ever since, watchfulness with an edge of high hilarity, people spending money like it was a thing that wouldn't exist tomorrow, rounds of Courvoisier and Dungeness crab, and now whole structures of empire seemed to tremble in superposition about him. People straining to keep holding their breath. To know whether the cash in his pocket would be worth anything on the other side, you'd have to be able to both predict the future and know a lot more about the philosophy of money than Ethan ever cared to. Some twenty blocks farther south of here, though, he knew, was the greatest bar in the world, which would be standing even after everything else was rubble. And apparently his mind had already made itself up somewhere to remove the last block, under these extenuating circumstances; when he looked down, he saw a text he'd sent to Jolie calling off tomorrow, lest she show up and see the state he apparently was in. Surely any day now he would undo or repair this damage, find a way to go across. Meanwhile, in the bar called Heaven, he would be received as a long-lost son or else not known at all. Assuming there was even a difference.

A.7: "That's When I Reach for My Revolver" (3:53)

It is unclear to Teresa whether she even still buys this postulate about people not changing (as, in a dozen different ways, she's given Moira to believe) or if she's just too much a product of her own time and place—too much a Masshole—ever to surrender a tactical advantage. Between the week two years ago when, on a visit to her parents, they'd strayed through the city hall in Medford to formalize their decade-plus relationship, Izzy standing by with a Mason jar of confetti . . . between that week and this one, something like half the states have decided they don't give a shit who you marry, so Teresa is sure these old coots watching them walk up this particular aisle now wouldn't notice or care if she were to weave her fingers into Moira's. It's just, she isn't sure Moira would want to if she knew what Teresa has done.

Their seats are in the front row, and she's had Izzy sit beside rather than between the two of them, in case her own mind changes. But on a white screen stupidly placed under a tree more or less blocking the stupid, stupid boat, pictures of the family now flit past. And though you might think this would make the boat itself less of a beam in her eye, and though the images are still barely visible due to the sun, the striking thing about these Asperns, all of them, is how stubbornly they resist change. It's like they'd moved out here to try to draw a circle around the family, seal it against whatever forces the mother had set loose by the scale of her longings, safe in this little town that time forgot. Having managed to run as far as MIT—as Berlin—Moira had proved ultimately as privy to the delusion as anyone else, and had ended up back here, a placeholder for the brother . . . and all the while,

Teresa's realized, waiting on his return. Even now, she can feel Moira counting on her brother to come release her from these burdens she's had to carry all by herself. And Teresa has realized something else, too, sitting here in front of the murmur she's trying to hear as impatient rather than just disapproving (and feeling punched in the face every time the guy appears on the screen, his mother's spitting image): that what she'd told the probation officer this morning was true, that she really does expect him at the last possible minute to show.

See, there's a paradox, she thinks, though possibly also a solution. She's long known that you can't let the past contain all information about the future—there is an actual law of physics— even as she's been arguing to Moira that at bottom most folks are incapable of change. But what if an inability to change is not predestined but is one of those things a person like Teresa, through sheer New England mulishness, can believe into being? Then, conversely, to change would require the belief that you are capable of it, either your own or someone else's. About her own capacity to change the woman she loves through her scheming— whatever may become of the brother—Teresa would still take the short side of the bet. But at least it means that, pretty soon here, one or the other of them is going to turn out to have been right.

A.8: "Nothin' but Time" (10:55)

You have not lived as a citizen of your time, not really, if you haven't spent a Saturday in summer at New York City's lone IKEA, way down by the salt domes and abandoned granaries of Van Dyke Street, on the far wrong side of the BQE. Ethan had pitched it to Jolie mostly for the excuse to ride the water-taxi from Thirty-Fourth Street—"the Swedish Children's Museum," he'd promised—though how and whether this comported with the unwritten amendments to the custody agreement was anybody's guess. At any rate, he'd been picturing it as a quick in-and-out affair, to get her a proper kid's bed, but inside found a logic not dissimilar to a casino's, with the exits and the action placed maximally distant from each other; and now that they had boarded the escalator to the Showroom Floor, they were too far from the door to turn back. He held Jolie's hand tighter in his, unable to imagine finding her again should they be separated. But here at the top was a labyrinth of cute roomlets along the lines of what he'd been imagining for the sleeping nook at home—he could actually feel her pulse speed up. Though of course the new bed would have to work for him, too, the other eleven out of every fourteen nights, since he never could get to sleep in the living room anymore, feeling obscurely troubled by the window's flaws—and all this provided he could talk Sarah into the next logical step, which was allowing overnights on weekdays and alternating weekends.

The kids' bedrooms were right up front, unavoidable, like a gift shop you had to exit through, only in reverse. "What do you think?" he asked Jolie, striking a mattress. "Too firm?" But it soon became clear that, transfixed as she was by the bedframes, rugs, and lamps, and by his presence, she would have said yes to anything. It was a lady in an Eagles jersey, grandmother of five, who would help them pick out the right one.

And only now, their decision made, did the IKEA reveal itself as labyrinthine in the Greek sense, a prison. Shortcuts dotted on the "You Are Here" maps had been bricked over in real life. Every jewelbox room, every sleek storage unit and kitsch painting on this involuted circuitboard would receive its due. And though Jolie was too much Sarah's daughter to say anything, she was his as well, and so of course she wanted everything. Even when Ethan had managed to discover some fire stairs, they found themselves fed onto what various signs denominated the Marketplace Floor. Which was crazy—had they not just been in the Marketplace for over an hour? But no, the Marketplace Floor turned out to be a kind of shadow-self of the Showroom Floor; same massed shoppers, same anfractuous path, except here you could actually place in your giant cart the items whose ideal forms you'd only been able to yearn for above (to the degree you'd made it through Plato in college).

He felt on the verge of epiphany about a cultural order that could yoke together such seemingly unlike things: the assembly line that made the furniture, the cattle chute that bore you past it, the ships on the harbor and the landfill beyond—people working at IKEA who could afford only IKEA. It was like a nineteenth-century utopia where all superfluity, all deviation and excess, had been sheared away. His response, this time around, was to let Jolie fill the cart with the sundry fripperies about which he'd been so disciplined above. Her room, the sleeping nook, would become her room again. He himself was no longer even landing auditions, it was as if somehow the terrible self-consciousness of AA had sapped him of his powers (as if now when he said yes to everything, it was for the wrong reasons), and was back exclusively to restaurant work. He didn't want to think about whether the sum of cash in his pocket was sufficient to cover these lampshades and sheets and fuzzy throw pillows, but perhaps it was like riding a wave, you just didn't look back, didn't look down . . .

It was only in the too-long line that he had time to slow himself and reflect on the other problem: this was just way too much stuff to haul back on the water-taxi or in the yellow cab it would also leave no money to pay for. At some point, he was going to have to tell her what he'd realized—that something was going to have to be sacrificed for something else, or all would be lost. But just look at her, his little girl full of hope: he couldn't, not now. So he held off, and held off, and inched forward in the line, and for as long as he could, and did, he was the greatest fucking dad in the world.

A.9: "Bigmouth Strikes Again" (3:13)

At 10:05, with the slide show on its fourth or fifth pass and the older folks now audibly restive—when Corinne in tasteful tie-dye has settled into the second row and it has become clear that there will be no brother or niece to fill the two remaining spots up front, leaving herself and Izzy the sole Asperns present to discharge family duties—Moira tries to get Teresa to look at her and then, having failed at last, rises to go do what Ethan can't, or possibly won't. She motions for someone to kill the projector in back. The gesture feels spurious, the authority unearned, and as she stares out from this tree-shade into the lightening, looking for further faces, she is startled to see instead toward the back her ex-sister-in-law Sarah Kupferberg, fifteen years older but still as killingly beautiful as on that day at the HoJo, squeezing past to a line of free seats. She is trailing an older man, plausibly her father, whom it occurs to Moira she's never met. Perhaps she has underestimated Ethan after all, she thinks. Perhaps he's orchestrated a massing of everyone he can get hold of to bid goodbye to the *Molly A* and whatever she stood for; perhaps if she looks hard enough even Squatch will have overcome his bruised feelings at her never sleeping with him and have turned out, too, swelling the thinned ranks of the bereaved to make this seem something more than a tax deduction. Something more like a proper goodbye.

But Jesus, what is wrong with her. She has only to look at Sarah's face more than a decade after Ethan left to see her own vexations mirrored. Some people might change; her brother never does. And is this how Teresa will feel about her, too, should they fail to pull through? She digs out her rolled sheet of paper and is surprised to find herself shaking. She tries to focus on the projector's lens back there, its cold black eye. Then she switches to Izzy's bright face and feels her spirits recover; takes it and multiplies it a million times over, uses it to populate the seats. Her son is alive. And she is a professional: she does this all the time. And thus can even confidently go off-book and just say what's in her heart, battered though it may be.

"Okay, everybody. It's my pleasure—honor, actually—to welcome you here for this rededication, or memorial, or what have you. I know it's been some time since my dad died. And longer since he last set sail. A lot of you will remember from the year we won nationals that he was really most himself out on the water. What fewer people know is that it was my mom who actually picked out this boat for him, and was the one pushing for the move out here in the first place. So to the degree that the championship was a credit to the town, they both had a part to play. And I just want to say on all our behalf, it was a way of giving something back to a place that for too short a time gave two such different people the space to coexist. But now, as is only fitting, my son and wife and I would like to give something back, as well . . ."

A.10: "Sweet Little Jesus Boy" (2:51)

Izzy, of course, knows how important the object world is, for he is its secret master. Not only the swingset chains he can creak just so or where all his army men are buried in the graveyard of the turtle-shaped sandbox out behind the garage, but the whereabouts of his yellow backpack (usually), and the wedding ring one of his moms keeps removing in anger and putting back on, and the clothes he keeps crisply folded in his floral-papered drawers, and the candy bar—the forbidden, the delicious—disappearing into a tux-jacket pocket. The objects of this world are his friends. It's related somehow to his being an only child and half-magic and a sissy and changed at birth and various other things he's aware already set him apart but are also all he knows. And the objects are good friends, not false ones. They do not Indian burn or titty-twist, do not make fun of his stutter, do not say Spit it out when he talks to them. And they will tell you things, if you listen. Like with his Cousin Jolie's violin: he went right up last night after coming home and spotted its case in the room where she'd slept, and when the violin asked him, he spent some time explaining to it with great fluency what he remembered of all that had happened to him back in the hospital, or what he imagined, since he'd mostly been asleep. The mask on his face. The ivy in his arm. The needle as big as this. The violin listened attentively, wanted to know was he scared. He was a little scared, he admitted, dialing the cool dial on the bow with its wonderful flaxen hair, fiddling the little velvet latches, flipping open the secret-feeling compartment with its big scarred gemstone and its water bottle and its passport all ready for running away. The violin was what had told him Jolie would come back here, and the passport how he knows that when she goes it will be for good. If he were an object, Jolie wouldn't have to be scared of him, and then he could just tell her We're all scared; you can't always be running away, but consonant blends were hard, and someone had to be free to run for staying to mean anything, and people, unlike objects, rarely listened to each other anyway. On the other hand, objects rarely surprised you. But then sometimes they did. All of which is to say that he wasn't much listening to his other mom's speech, he was more interested in the sound his own voice made in his head, when he turned back to see who that was arriving now to make her hitch and noticed what no one else had, yet: a new something placed beside the laptop on the table at the back. And there, in the wire trashcan where people could recycle their programs later after the boat belonged to the school, was a yellow cardboard suitcase for the chicken Izzy wasn't allowed to eat on account of the molasses they put in the batter or the crushed-up nuts or something, though honestly it didn't seem to fit at all.

B.I: "Many Rivers to Cross" (3:02)

The thing no one talked about was the pressure. It cut against the self-image of an open meeting, the all-are-welcome, call-me-by-my-name and so forth, yet for Ethan, it was always there, in the prayers before and after, but especially when people got up to tell their stories. This was the meat in any meeting and clearly a key part of the propulsive mechanism of an organization with no leader and no form of linear control. You'd have someone visiting from another meeting, working off their debt or gratitude or whatever by standing in front of some basement room to share his or her story, but you'd already heard it all a hundred times before. Nor was it any amount of grit or specificity that held the attention: the details of this or that self-inflicted loss, autoamputation with dull knife, disastrous sacrifice to Booze or Pills or Blow or whatever was your lady. Rather, bizarrely, it was something in the posture toward the room. You knew when something was being protected—when the story about a moment of maximum vulnerability was being contrived to protect exactly that vulnerability. You knew, that is, when the person wanted something from you. And you knew, conversely, when all someone wanted (standing up there in fellowship, bearing witness to his or her own life) was just to Give It Up. And somewhere in there was the source of the pressure. These people were too naked, too far from any reflecting surface to really know, but as they stood up there speaking from within the white light, powerlessly a part of something larger, you, who remained out here in the shade of the room, wanting things, suddenly burned to be part of it, too. He would think sometimes of Hank Gregory. And of a Wednesday-night gospel concert Mom had taken him to at the A.M.E. Zion church over in Millersville where they'd been the only white people. (How she would have loved AA, with its pluralism of the hajj.) How, when they'd snuck in an altar call between sets, he'd thought, at nine, at ten, Yes, I, Ethan Aspern, am ready to lay down the terrible burden of my sin, and she'd had to put a hand on his jeans to stop his going forward to be saved. Research purposes only, she said. And he thought of the five-hundred-pound column of air people were said to carry around on their shoulders and heads. (It was this, he would decide later, that everyone not in the white light seemed to be carrying around at all times, and that had almost cost him his daughter. The burden he was ready to lay down, could not imagine carrying for another twenty-five or fifty years: the weight of air.) But every time he gave in to the pressure, got up to Give Back, gripped a lectern or if there was no lectern laced hands in front of him (the hardest question of acting, Hank had said: what to do with the hands), what came out no matter how hard he was on himself amounted to what he could never forget Sarah once accusing him of, which was the narcissism of mere explanation. Here's why I did what I did. Look at all this shit, and poor me braving it to stand before you. Admire me please. Vindicate me. Slightly envy me. Love me, please. A performance, but to all the wrong ends. He could feel the long-timers' lips pursing in the dark. To them, it didn't matter, what mattered was that he had done it. Got in his reps. The idea was you couldn't keep hiding forever. Just work the steps, and sooner or later something would change. But they didn't know the real him, the essential him, not least because he had not let himself be known—knowing as he did that the problem was not what he did, but who he was . . . the kind of person who could not let himself be known. And the more he tried to thrash his way out of these loops and bonds of thought, he thought, the further away from actual Service he got.

B.2: "Call the Police" [Radio Edit] (4:11)

As for Erica Morales, her choice is getting harder and harder to avoid. If it was ever possible to save anybody, it may well be too late now. She is too late to grab a seat, certainly, but then, she's not sure she'd be a welcome presence here anyway, given the occasion and the job she now knows she has to do. All his protests to the contrary, Ethan had indeed lied to her last night, assured her he'd stand and face the music. And sometimes justice, the real kind, is the only kindness there is. Scanning these largely pale faces, she finds no trace of him here. But with a cool assessing eye now trained for the aftermath of floods, fires, frauds—for the human propensity to inflate all claims—she does note the chicken box wedged unceremoniously atop the trashcan, and then the VHS recorder, a real antique . . . the little, human details that tempt her to relent.

She'd slept surprisingly well last night at the Elysian Shores, once the orgy in the room next door had subsided, and the sound like human sacrifice in the parking lot, but had awakened not an hour ago to find no answer at Ethan's door, and when she looked down from the breezeway, McGonagall's broke-ass van was gone. Yet it's the girl who needs saving, she reminds herself, not really listening to what the woman is now saying through the speakers. Maybe he means well but, as her mother had told her when she'd come home after her one night in the shelter and confessed (and as her experience with Ethan would seem to confirm), you can protect your child only so much before you start to do damage. Beyond that you have to set them free.

She takes out her phone and stands for another minute amassing the details she will have to hand off if she does decide to go through with it, punch in the number for the local constabulary, and behind that the FBI with its interstate jurisdiction, and ultimately the U.S. Attorney who's going to have to make a felony case off the testimony of the sole witnesses against him, not including herself: the ex-wife—and, if she can be tracked down and persuaded to flip on him, the girl. *And how exactly did you get yourself mixed up in it, Officer?*

Of course it would just be *ma'am* now, she reminds herself.

In any case, she'd already had the name of the sister, recovered from old notes she'd never bothered to return to Probation, and though she'd written it like Laura with an M, it hadn't taken more than a few swipes of the thumb to scare up the home address she'd staked out last night, only to watch Ethan and his daughter in no time come slinking out of the woods. Of course, when she'd showed up at that house again just an hour ago and in daylight knocked on the door, what she got was an Asian woman saying Moira was already gone to set up chairs for the event. But no sooner had Erica mentioned her quarry than the woman's eyes narrowed in calculation. After a minute's rummaging in the house, she had handed her one of these same programs she now sees paperweighted by a VCR to the table before her, fluttering in the breeze. Moira was still holding out hope that Ethan would come make a speech, the woman said. Some comment he'd made two nights ago . . . and then some fraudulent phone call placed the next morning, one day into the kidnapping.

The sister standing before her sure as hell doesn't seem like an accessory, and is now returning to her seat, leaving behind on the lectern an as-yet-unbroken champagne bottle. What had she said to elicit this limp applause, other than "I'll shut up now"? Right: that they would try to run the PowerPoint once more ahead of the unveiling of the boat's new name, see if the clouds now coming in made for easier viewing, there have been some complaints—and this time, fine, yes, with the music synced up. And when a little black boy, a changeling in a corduroy suit, leaps up and bowls along the aisle, Erica half expects him to leap into her arms, before realizing he's headed to help with the projector. Which is when, beyond the edge of the tree's shadow, a second woman appears, as if disgorged from the earth. As if out of nowhere. Not standing, but stooping over something (a backpack?) as if to administer first aid or make sure the thing is dead. Or maybe just a girl, actually. And when she rises again with her thin white hand held aloft like a rapier, interrupting the order of service, Erica recognizes her face even before she starts speaking.

B.3: "A Poem on the Underground Wall" (1:52)

Star light, star bright,
First star I see tonight,
We need to net at least 25k this year
Post-taxes

B.4: "Essence" (5:51)

There was a specific age, maybe at times a specific month or even day within that age (at least if you were wired like Jolie Aspern), when the distinction between substance and essence, quite possibly semantic, or even imaginary, became a missile precision-guided to penetrate and then blow the mind. It was Albert who explained it at the time, and who mostly had it, she'd later realize, from Aristotle via Joyce. The context was the bat mitzvah, about whose guest list she'd been dithering. What if she invited Sam Wohlgemuth and Melissa Gutierrez from fifth grade like she wanted to? But then what if the regrets ran to like ninety percent, and the remaining ten percent showed up only to bear witness that she had no real friends? The question she asked out loud was why they were bothering at all, since neither Mom nor Albert nor Nana believed in God. Well, but it was a rite of individuation, he said, and they could believe in those, couldn't they? Individuation and then the one he'd always had more difficulty with, incorporation (as in corpus, the body)—these were demonstrably marked with some kind of ceremony in cultures throughout the world.

But could he not at least agree that the age of thirteen was arbitrary? Like, what happened to the body at thirteen that hadn't already happened at twelve?

Another of his long pauses, this one to gather his thoughts. Well, from the standpoint of tradition, your question's nonsensical, sweetie. It's the ceremony that creates the thing ceremonialized, if you follow me. The idea being that even as you remain substantially the same, your essence is altered by the presence of others—in this case, you are seen to go from girl to woman.

Essence?

Take away all the tangible, molecular, identifiable stuff . . . then whatever's left that makes you you, that's the essence.

You mean take away all the stuff we Kupferbergs actually believe exists.

All the stuff, let's say, we don't have good reason to be suspicious of, he said, looking over at Mom. Then: Always one step ahead, your daughter.

"Izzy," she says now, into the mic, breathing hard. "I think someone's already cabled that thing in, if you wouldn't mind doing the honors."

B.5: "Just Like Tom Thumb's Blues" (4:50)

In the coffered ceiling of the yawning auditorium, there burned a kind of brightness, or that was his impression, yet it didn't seem to filter down to the hundreds of empty seats below. There, the only light that he could see came from the goosenecked lamp of the sound supervisor's mixing board, halfway back. It was here that the bald man running the audition was to take back the microphone after a shadowy conclave with the rest of the panel, offering, by way of dismissal, only *Okay, thank you.* But even then, save perhaps for the faint embossing of the arc of a waxed skull as he turned away, none of that light a hundred feet overhead reached him. It remained trapped up there, as if bound in a net, its source invisible, and its main effect, in conjunction with the strong footlights of the stage, was to lend the whole auditorium a dreamlike intensity. And instead of the singsong "Okay, thank you," he heard, after reading from the script they'd handed him, a woman's voice asking if that was it, or whether he had anything else. He had nothing. A few lines from his mom's old *Masnavi,* a Shakespeare soliloquy he could remember little of right now. But he'd hammered out so many revisions on that play for Hank four years ago that the lines of the opening were still recoverable, if he tried. Or monologue, really, in the end, for he never could get any of the other people in it to speak as convincingly as himself. It was like his trouble moving from poetry on the page to poetry in his soul: a question of how to get life, which was change, to happen. Still, he'd get points for audacity, or if they didn't like the performance, he could always blame the material, lie and say someone else had written it. But now, the boards of the stage feeling both springy and overhard beneath him, he realized he should have listened to the terrible difficulties even this monologue had given him in the composition, such that he hadn't ultimately been able to tell whether its authenticity was hard-won or spurious.

Whether the white light he'd wanted so hard to make happen was there. Whether the pain . . . He squinted, shielding a hand against the glare, but could see nothing. The microphone's little crackle of activation.

"I'm sorry, which one are you again?"

"Aspern. Ethan."

"Whenever you're ready, Mr. Aspern."

And so, without really thinking about it, he began.

B.6: "Do Nothing Till You Hear from Me" (5:00)

"Ladies and gentlemen," Jolie begins, as a title card appears on the screen behind her. And stops to catch her breath. "And also, I guess I should add, aunts, cousins, grandparents, Oh God, Mom, why are you here, too, please don't—"

And though she knows now the list was a stalling tactic, Eleanor Kupferberg feels a flush of vindication that borders on pain every time she refreshes the video on her phone. See? She was right all along to do what she did. Now stand aside, Sarah, don't frighten her off. Then there is mostly just relief again that this sweet, quick, exasperating girl, almost certainly the only grand-daughter she'll ever have, is whole and intact and herself again, whatever that means. A voice that was the same as six months ago, and also somehow different: more layered. Though perhaps it's just the doubling of mics, or all that saliva, the tongue-ring clank-ing against teeth.

"And okay, so long as you'll stay seated and give me the floor, I might as well go ahead and throw in step-grandparents, friends of grandparents, ghosts of grandparents. Probation officers; yes, I see you out there, or I guess I wouldn't have come jumping up here like this, would I? For those of you who aren't read in, I'm Ethan's daughter, down from New York. James and Joanna's granddaughter . . ."

A pan here to the title card frozen above her, which Eleanor can never read given the glare but has decided must bear the dates of the grandfather's birth and death. Then that watchful look and an odd worry you could almost miss the first time if you weren't her grandmother, an unnatural hand flourish to bring attention back to the uncanniness of herself, there at the quivering edge of the shadow.

"Now I have to admit, I don't really get all this fuss over a boat . . . but then, I'm not from around here, am I? I think I was like ten before I realized the city I'd grown up in was surrounded by water; I'm what you'd call a lubber. And of course, I used to not get the thing where people go to temple on High Holidays and do all the old superstitious mumbo-jumbo they don't believe in, either." There is a Latin word for this long-windedness Eleanor used to mark as *pl.* when she was the one editing Al's articles, a sense of redundancy, a kind of filibuster. "So maybe the point is just to bring a bunch of different people together to say good-bye to something. All of which I guess is by way of an apology for interrupting whatever is supposed to be happening here . . . though I'm also begging your indulgence for just a few more minutes before we pop or smash this bottle and send this beauty off with her new name . . ." She looks down. "The T.S., er . . . *Sea's the Day?*"

A look back up, for something curious has by now begun to happen on the screen, not the projected slideshow at all, but some sort of low-budget movie—startling even now to see the picture begin to jolt forward after all that stasis. Beginning in medias res, it offers no razzle-dazzle to hold the eyes, just what you'd see if you were there and turned around in your seat to scan this town Eleanor has never had occasion to visit. This actual town, but virtual, seen as if everyone were sleeping, or dead. Eleanor wants to call out to the person holding the camera to turn it back on Jolie. Which, as if hearing her, he does.

"Now it's been a long time, more than a month, believe it or not, since I've had much of anything to say, so you'll forgive me for being a little rusty. And then this isn't the plan I had in mind. Which honestly, if I wasn't going to try to kill myself again, required me getting the fuck out of here. No, no reactions yet, *please*. Just listen. Like, maybe the move all along was to steal one of these boats, you know? And like sail it to someplace I could grab the eleven fifty-five bus to the nearest available airport? And if I made that bus and could get reception, then I might look down at my phone and find a ticket already waiting in my email, bought and paid for with other people's money. And by nightfall I could be declining drinks from the drinks cart. And by morning be as far away as I could possibly get from the long arm of American law, trading on my natural gift for improv plus whatever funds I could unvelcro from my wallet."

Eleanor has since learned what's happening here behind the screen, of course, behind the speech; the question that keeps her coming back is how much Jolie already had this prepared when she stepped to the lectern from under the tree, and how much of it had just come together in the moment, in the collision of people and circumstances and whatever else exists.

"But what a cockamamie scheme, right?" she presses on. "No one ever taught me to sail. And then, how could I just run away from the life I'd been given, knowing all the sacrifices my parents and even my grandparents had made so that I could be a little more empowered-feeling, a little more free? It's like my Cousin Izzy was trying to tell me, I think—what my dad of all people kept trying to tell me: you can't really go forward if you're not willing to go back. So for me, running away would have only led deeper into the hole I've been living in for the last year or so. Yet standing up here after the night I've had, I can imagine, somewhere very nearby, the person for whom running might also be the opposite. The big sacrifice. The last last chance. Context is everything, see? And for better or for worse, the context—to commandeer a phrase from my maternal grandmother—is always somehow other people. Sorry, starting to flag a bit. Could you possibly fast-forward to the part where we actually get to see them? Thanks, Izz."

A mercurial cloud, thinking the better of things and moving back off again, makes a strange effect for a minute on the gathered faces. The camera tilts clumsily toward the screen, where the mute and dreamlike tracking shots of high-school hallways, parking lots, rusty gliders in woods have given way to faces, their mouths moving without sound, in a close-up defeated by the distance of the phone . . . only one of whom Eleanor recognizes.

"That was the title she gave this, by the way. *Other People*. Like: Have you done your best by them? Have you tried to hear what they're saying? And where you've fallen short of perfection, can you still try to forgive them? And be forgiven?" Something is happening to her voice, the auditory equivalent of a bulb threatening to burn through the frame. Then it is just her own voice again. "Can you just stop fucking hiding away for once and maybe let yourself be forgiven?"

The faces on the screen are two now, speaking to each other in silent alternation . . . but also, one senses, behind each other, maybe past each other, or possibly it's a Rorschach thing, and that's just the construction Eleanor is putting on it. In any case, between this moment and the end, Albert will not move the camera again, or if he does it is likely an involuntary tremor, not meant to communicate anything in particular.

"Oh, right, so there they are up there, my Grandpa Aspern, my Grandma Aspern, right there in the flesh. You might be asking yourself what this little speech of mine has to do with the rector and his boat, but if we can just drop the whole not-speaking-ill-of-the-dead thing I'd like to flag for a second that my grandfather was not a perfect man. Maybe even sometimes not a good one. I mean, he clearly left a lot of people around him feeling lonelier than when they started. As did my grandmother, it would seem. But then again, are we any less stuck inside ourselves than they were? And they were probably only doing what they felt they had to do. See, look at them there, trapped in their own perspectives . . ."

She is watching. Thinking. But you can't see her anymore. Just hear her voice over her grandmother's face (on her grandfather's phone (on her other grandmother's)) echoing inward and outward to infinity.

"She could never finish this, you know: Joanna. Couldn't figure out what the people should sound like, if they were really going to be heard at the level of what she would even at that late date probably still have called the soul. I've thought about it a lot these last couple days since finding the tape: what I'd say if that were me wielding the camera and I knew it was going to be a permanent goodbye." More watching. A lull, a spell it's unclear even now whether she's casting or falling under. A siren starts up somewhere. "Shit," she says. "I can't believe it. Maybe there was never enough to get this done. Time or whatever else." Then this: "But no, wait, hold on, I think I'm getting it now, how it was supposed to go all along. Because the whole point was . . . fuck, sorry—if

you could just bear with me here for one teensy little more minute and just keep all your attention pointed this way . . ."

B.7: "I See a Darkness" (3:42)

It had warmed the day of the funeral, so what should have been
snow was instead rain, and once the requisite spadefuls of earth
had been flung under a hastily pitched white tent and the plein-
air service Joanna had insisted on was over, a reception always
meant to be outdoors was instead reconvened at a backup location: the tragic multipurpose room above the rector's office out at
St. Anselm's. Save for the attic-like elevation, Ethan would later
think, it would have been perfect for a recovery meeting. But
none of that had happened yet. At present, what he registered
was just blue industrial carpeting and awful tube-light, the utter
absence of beauty. His dad was chatting with various board members. Ethan, stone-cold sober and three days sick, stood by the
window looking out at the long crescent drive, the dead brown
playing fields and woods, trying to send through his shoulders and
stiffened neck a signal not to approach or try to comfort, he didn't
want comforting. And thus it was that he finally spotted Eddie
Sixkiller out by the flagpole, straddling his foster sister's bike and
looking up at a window through which he doubtless couldn't see.

His customary black clothes were now an ill-fitting funeral suit,
as if he had only slightly upgraded a mourning he'd been in all
along. So maybe he'd been at the service, too, undetected? There
had at least been a surprising number of people, and Ethan, feverish with withdrawal or despair, could be forgiven for not having seen him there and feeling the actual worst thing, which was
alone. Without excusing himself, he went downstairs, his pulse
quickening from its sluggishness for the first time all day.

In fact, the whole reason he'd had no pot to treat his symp-
toms was that Eddie had been keeping his distance ever since the
death, in a manner that struck Ethan as canine. Not slinking the
way a cat does, but like a dog hewing to the edges of somewhere
it knows it shouldn't be but still unable to master its concern.
A half-dog, half-wolf whose eyes and waiting Ethan could feel
vectoring across the schoolyard now collapsing between them.

The rain would have to have stopped, wouldn't it. At some point, Eddie had sat down on the skate-chipped base of the flagpole, so that it was in the midst of rising that he said Hey man, I'm really sorry.

Ethan lied and said no worries, and after checking that no one had come to the window to watch, lit a cigarette. Eddie knew better than to give him that guilt shit now. They stood shivering in companionable near-silence until Eddie said, as if following up a thought, "I figured your dad wouldn't want me coming by the house."

"Why's that?" He was already feeling an ache at the root of his tongue, the light shrinking. He wanted something for it, the pain. Oh, how he wanted . . .

"Bad influence."

"Fuck that, though," Ethan managed, from the bottom of his well. "Fuck my dad."

But Eddie said not to say that about your own flesh and blood; you never could know who you'd end up needing, and for what. Then, as if it were a message he'd been sent to deliver, he rubbed his hands together in that way he had and claimed he had to get back to business, time waited for no man. Handed across a dime-bag; there'd be more where that came from should he need it, on the house. And climbed onto the bike and set off down the drive, beads clacking, his black pants going blacker in a stripe where the water kicked up from the back wheel, his hand-me-down coat flapping like a scarecrow's. Like the boy inside had all this time been nothing but sticks and wind.

B.8: "Raised on Robbery" (3:06)

Later, in the driver's seat of the dog-smelling Econoline, caravanning the long way back to New York, a shaken Albert Kupferberg will reflect on the upheaval behind him and wonder if he got what he wanted. When there isn't a car or two intervening on the highway, he can see clear through the Volvo's rear window to its backseat and Jolie's shorn head held high above, but only the back of it. And from Sarah, driving, not even that: no body language to read or interpret, nor has she given him much to go on after the ceremony ended, either, when they would wind up practically next to each other—not that there was any real chance, given the raised voices and how close she seemed to need to be to Jolie and then all of a sudden the commotion when someone thought to check behind the screen. The little tugboat of the officer's or whoever's car in the rearview is now nudging them along to where some of the pieces can be picked up and glued back together. But not every piece; there are laws.

He had said, if only to himself, that chasing his granddaughter here wasn't about him and what he needed, about attempting to make up for fifteen years of having let Sarah down, the damage he might have caused by his own crimes. But maybe he'd been hoping she would notice at some point how well he'd done, would turn to look directly at him like those faces on the screen. (Though that's just the montage effect, isn't it? In one sense they'd be seeing only the lens, in another, only the audience, but at no point actually each other.) And then he would say, "Hey, look, honey, I'm sorry, for everything. Forgive." And she would say: "No, it's okay." Or "Water under the bridge." *Und so weiter.* And then they could walk on into the rest of their lives unfettered by guilt, and by doubt. Outside of literature, though, things don't work that way, is the theme he's now left to embroider upon. And the only material left to support it is a video of Jolie on his phone talking about forgiveness, a message somewhere in there to be decoded by the right hearer—but how could that possibly be him? Had he been forgiven? And either way, what came next?

As if reading his mind, or one of them, or as if his mind or minds is or are not quite inside his head, Jolie had at some point amid stonewalling the police as to the current location of the boat reached into her bag and handed across to him the battery-operated boombox for the ride back . . . which by rights should now be playing the Ithaca disc from *Ulysses* but isn't. Some frisky lady of the canyon instead. Still, she's right. Music—music is what his condition requires. Expansion joints bump underneath. The wheel beneath his hand quivers, but not as badly as it will in a few years, when he has to surrender his keys. They will be coming up now on the Walt Whitman Service Area. Hot dogs. Carvel. Cin-

nabon. Pretzels. The grass. And then at some point soon after it
will all be gone.

B.9: "I Think Ur a Contra" (4:29)

He would be traipsing through a pine forest, searching, always—
searching—when he'd find himself in a soft straw clearing with
a structure at the very center, an old barn or possibly church. It
looked abandoned at first, but around back would be this crude
rackish thing made of wood, like a frame for stretching canvas, and
beside it a woman who both was and was not his mother, glancing up from the biggish spliff she'd just gotten lit, an expression
as blank as paper. Which is when the moaning would begin; he
was always the one who was startled. Plus, by the dream's fourth
or fifth recurrence, a little pissed to boot. Like: Where was *his*
spliff? Wasn't *he* supposed to be the one with the secrets? Eventually he'd recover enough to say something along the lines of, How
long were you planning to just keep hiding back here? There'd
be a moment of pity when her face would seem to burn. Oh, she
said then. Did you think this was hiding? Because if you're ready
to look I can show you what really is— Whereupon the daylight
would come crashing back in, trailing the rest of his life behind
it like a note tied to a rock. He'd be however many thousands of
miles from the home where the gas station next door used to stain
the curtain white. Tug this one aside, you might get not a glowing dinosaur, but a green solidity of mountain, a blue sky dawning
behind a thorny crown of clouds. And spring in its Queen Mab
phase, fucking with the proximity of moon and earth, with the
tides and the winds and, evidently, with the head of the late-rising
rooster in a courtyard a block farther up the hill, who has only
just begun to sing.

B.10: "If Music Could Talk" (4:36)

And then, outside, the wind died, and inside also. I can't report to
you with any conviction how long I might have stayed standing

there, waiting for something to stir. At some point, though, from across the water, it came to me, an arpeggio, a chord sequenced into component notes I could fakebook with my bow: the broken little synth riff from the start of *Who's Next*. On record—on CD, on tape—it was pitched somewhere between the human and the nonhuman, its discontinuities mathematically produced, and though normally I tend even now when playing to rush and slow, rising and descending, my heart, I found, was suddenly a fucking metronome. I could pause for a day between notes, and the beat would wait for me, to be picked up right on time. So I could focus simply on getting the feeling in, the feeling I wanted to send across to my father—your grandfather—who if there was a God would have taken the time I'd bought him with all my sentimental claptrap to sneak onto the boat behind the screen and then do whatever one did with a boat, loosen the lines, untie the moorings. It was precisely the size of this feeling, I knew, that would keep their attention over here, on me, the now-descanting power chords seeming to sync briefly with the faces onscreen. But at the moment the boat obediently detached from behind, was birthed as it were from the forehead of my risen grandmother, I could feel my audience wanting to look over there too soon, for humans want drama, and music must change. So I listened harder to myself or whatever was now trying to sing through me, and was surprised to find my fingers working in a bit of melody from "When You Were Mine," by my lost love of earlier that year, Prince. It was basically the same chords, after all, in basically the same sequence, albeit with one more in the mix. And with the relative minor entering, coming and going, and that Who arpeggio the thread running through, it turns out you've got enough notes and chords to play any of about a million songs. So as my dad's father on the screen tried to move his mouth in reply, I found myself interpolating a bit of "Crimson and Clover," and then, because my own dad hadn't gone yet, the outro to "Sweet Jane." I played a verse of Patti Smith's "People Have the Power" and another of Sinéad's "The Emperor's New Clothes." I remember I played a decent-sized chunk of "I'm Goin' Down." And then suddenly I was moving freely back and forth among them, as if the borders had grown very porous, taking what I needed and leaving the rest, and finally, when things started to get a little ragged, rising back into "Teen-age Wasteland" (sorry: "Baba O'Riley") and then to the best of my memory the actual violin solo that comes after . . . which I'd subsequently discover is pretty much also note-for-note the gui-tar coda to that one Smashing Pumpkins song about a season where the singer finds himself blocked, unable to speak. (Go lis-ten to it, daughter; tell me I'm wrong.) And all the while, behind the music, beyond sight of the audience, the boat with its unheard motor was nearing the bend in the creek where, I had noticed after spotting the probation officer but before pushing Dad aside and dashing to the lectern, it could possibly just with a little help slip out of sight behind the trees. On the screen, my grandparents were still singing to each other soundlessly across a human gulf, and maybe this is me imagining things, but I'll believe till the day I die that their faces had changed even from the midpoint of the film, had gentled and aged. I know, too, that I wanted the boat to disappear already, and at the same time I wanted it to stick around long enough to know that he could hear all I still couldn't put into words. Which I recognize is more like what a parent is supposed to feel toward a child—the thing I'm feeling toward you now, years later, looking over from my desk to where you're sleeping in your bassinet—but whatever. I was on drugs. I guess what I'm try-ing and failing to capture here, even now, is my entirely subjective sense of how it feels to be so naked up there, playing your whole heart out for another minute for one specific other person. Then two. And then to stand up there before them staring fiercely out at your own mother, grandmother, cheeks hot, trembling hard, like a kid who's been dragged from a fistfight.

B.II: "Love Will Tear Us Apart" [Permanent Mix] (3:37)

Jesus Christ it is all she can do, though. All she can do not to just get up and bowl through the bodies between them and honestly just tackle Jolie before she can get out that very first word, for there is a violence here mixed in with the love. And maybe this has been part of the problem grown up between them, that she couldn't admit to either of them how angry she was at how her life had turned out, and how hurt sometimes, and how scared; to do so would have been to raise the question of whether Sarah Kupferberg for all her formidable will was a person for whom a whole fuck of a lot of human experience was sometimes in fact just baffling. For without that kind of honesty, or alternatively a lot of trust, the essence of love could not be there. There was some strange entanglement between the two of them, Jolie and Ethan—a lot of him in her, or (double the helix, reverse time's arrow) a lot of her in him. It is a lot of what Sarah herself has been running away from this last year, has refused to see in her daughter, lest she get depressed again at being unable to escape it or keep hating herself for her inability to stay or to weaken and reopen the door . . . but it was also, it seems, what had brought Ethan back to see their daughter through. The cure derived from the disease. The speech she has barely even heard, for at the sound of that voice itself there is just a joy that passes understanding, that lives in the body: to see her standing up there intact, adult, and to know that they will again have their years together, with whatever degree of recrimination. That Jolie will not try to leave again, and will come home. Returned her to her whole self, is what he's somehow accomplished in the space of three days. Does it even count as a crime? You're damn well right it does, she reminds herself. Legally: yes. Also morally. It is, impressively, the most fucked up thing he's ever done. But in the end, it is also the opposite; and he must still be here somewhere, since there's no way he'd leave Jolie standing solo in the end without saying goodbye. Maybe instead of going along with whatever legal trap the probation officer has just triggered she can slip off alone, find him out in his hiding place and look once more upon the face she loves and say to him, as if she were his own too-trusting mother, just go, I'm not going to press charges or report anything if you don't stick around, so just take this last last *last* chance I am offering you and please go. And will she be breaking as she says it? Grief-stricken at the loss of that face she loved even before she knew it? Will there be some twist of vindictiveness, of punishment, revenge? Well, fine, then—those belong to her, too. The essential Sarah Kupferberg. But for now, she knows, her calling is just to not leap up from her seat and fuck it all up as Jolie picks up her instrument and begins to play.

B.12: "With or Without You" (4:56)

But wait, he thought—he knew this song. It had come to him across the margin of water between them, found him on the boat Jolie had talked him onto through the P.A. as if guiding him through a dream . . . and for a moment nearly caused him to forget himself and the impossible thing she was now asking him to do, not only because he'd never till now heard her play the violin, but because the song had come to him like this once before, at the moment he most needed to hear it. And a third time before that, sitting cross-legged on the sunroom floor while his mother was off somewhere chasing a doomed love or a wave or some things with wings and he could touch what his fingers had so badly wanted to back in the third-floor room in DC: the forbidden stereo. The little pop-up periscope of the turntable. Its light on the black ridges of the record like the path moonlight makes on water. And the black square on his lap, young men ranged there three and one in sober black and white. By that point the album was already four years out of date, they were on to sunglasses and banks of video monitors and special effects on MTV; they would never again be this young.

Yet the song these four chords made, for anyone with ears to hear it, was side A, track 3. Back then, with the record player, his hands had known just what to do, what switches to flip as his mother had patiently taught him. And he was surprised to find now in the knotted lines he continued to unravel that something of his father remained with him a little longer, so Jolie had given him that back, too. He couldn't see the screen he was hidden by—only hear the song flitting out of this particular melody and into something else again. As he might never again hear her voice, see her face if he kept on going this way, into the freedom she was obviously trying to grant him.

But how could he just leave her like this? How could he live another decade, maybe a lifetime, without her? He couldn't. And yet there is no alternative; it's not like he can just go off some-where to die. Not anymore. And suddenly, like a violence, comes peace: at least this once, he'd got to hear her play.

So maybe he gets caught on a bus somewhere between the dock in Ocean City and the airport . . . well, he was already a criminal, wasn't he? And the anxiety, the worry that the engine would blow his cover, or that he wouldn't remember how to work the throttle, or would hit one of the other boats scuttling back and forth in the channel up around the bend, all dropped out of him as he became for a moment pure hearing, pure seeing. The markers were all right there. The music was only getting stronger. The worst that could happen was after all only just what he deserved.

And yes, with the legal predicament whose knot he had not yet cut, it was perhaps a caprice, perhaps a risk, certainly not a necessity that had him going up to the foredeck like this, just at the point where his home and past were to slip from him entirely, and loosening the lower of the two sails, but then he felt he owed it to her to leave her with some legacy of her own, give her what he'd so far been unable to through the whole of his befogged return. The trees ashore were still and black, and maybe he'd got-ten something wrong with the rigging; as he rounded the marker at the headland, the canvas just sat there, calm. There is such a thing as wanting something too badly. But time runs on, and music is change, and as he rounded the turn at last, about to slip from all their sights, the wind kicked back up again to fill the sail just so, as it never had for him before, and though he could no longer find her face anywhere, or even hear whatever song she would now be playing, he had to trust that she'd seen it, this white flag, this angling brightness, and that it would stay with her and help her should the dark ever choose to return. He couldn't protect her anymore, if he ever could—couldn't save her, couldn't even stop her suffering—nor would he, could he, since it was part of what made her who she was. All he could do here in the end, really, flawed as he was but her father now and forever, her father to his bones, was to haunt her no longer. To love her, his daugh-ter, and to let her go.

CODA

THE MEAT SUIT (SLIGHT RETURN)

2022

"You will grow up, you know," he said . . . "I mean, when you grow up you will be free." She shook her head. She knew better than that now, at fourteen. There was no freedom except to cease to love.

—MAVIS GALLANT
"The Remission"

SHE WOULD BE SOMEWHERE over an ocean when it occurred to her that it was not too late—that she could still change her mind. Or a sea, she supposed, but in the night, from tens of thousands of feet up, there could be little solace in the distinction. On the online maps she'd kept checking these last months for reassurance—feeling like nothing so much as herself at fourteen checking and rechecking the international flights out of New York, Philly, Baltimore/Washington—it had seemed that the last part of the flight would be over land, the country's mountainous interior, yet here they were tracking coastline for the interminable minutes of what may already have become descent: a studding of small lights a wintry bluewhite, intensified by their own reflections on the water. Which just went to show that anything was still possible. Sometimes the only thing worse for acrophobia than looking out the window was to pull the shade so you couldn't see.

And she wasn't even that bad a flyer! But now she was flying for two. Children under twenty-four months traveled free, supposedly, but the American Academy of Pediatrics recommended a three-point restraint for these same nominal "lap babies" during takeoff and landing, so you ended up buying a ticket for the carseat. Her daughter had like most of the rest of the cabin been asleep now for several hours, and the man in the next seat over, nervous and hirsute and looking uncannily like her junior-year French teacher in college, seemed to have relaxed somewhat, even lowering his face mask long enough to eat a few peanuts he fat-fingered out of a bag. Under twenty-four months was of course also the age that was too young for a face mask—the uncartilaginous ears—suggesting perhaps his stiffness had just been fear of infant germs. From within her own mask she now resisted the urge to reach out and float an index finger below the tiny nostrils, not to make sure her daughter was breathing (or not primarily), but just to feel the puff of air, that smallest possible unit of breath already getting bigger.

She had thought of this often in recent days: how there were things people could tell you over and over again, but that you still had to live through to understand. Certain kinds of truth you could know only through your body. The way you were always losing people, for example, every second of every day, and the crazy things it could incline you to do. Or how in times of impossibility or danger or change what you wanted was to be physically close to the ones you most loved, even the ones who, for you, might be just as dangerous, just as impossible. Maybe her hormones were still out of whack from nursing or from the birth five months earlier. She could feel herself sliding into a chasm of cognitive dissonance as her former French teacher who was simultaneously just a middle-aged Alsatian business traveler began to ask in an accent about her travel plans and to recommend some sights in this city where they'd be landing before she knew it, he said—for all the world as if there had been no mutual mistrust, no six hours of silence. Or perhaps there was simply an intimacy in now having nearly crossed the night together, the only two people still awake in this tin-pot kingdom of the dead. As he complimented the baby's beauty and behavior both (you should see her at three a.m. at home, she wanted to say) and began to talk about his own granddaughter, static electricity activated his arm hair and made it seem to dance. Of course, being a man, he wouldn't notice. For a moment, as he informed her that no, this really was the start of descent, she even imagined he was her father: a normal person, as Dad kept claiming in those too-long letters he'd wanted nothing more than to be.

But then forty minutes later, down on the concourse, this man made no offer to help her carry the carseat, which was perfectly normal of him but not at all like her actual father, the lunatic—back then and possibly still. Who would also have insisted on taking every last bag, leaving her embarrassingly unencumbered, almost uncomfortably free. The carseat, at 450 pounds, was precision-engineered to bang into her leg just above the knee as she lugged it, and again each time she shuffled forward in the wee-hours customs line. And still the baby slept. Would perhaps have slept straight onto another plane, this one headed promptly back home.

What was the purpose of her visit? the douanier asked, or whatever was the Catalan. It was complicated to explain, so she said Business, in English, which seemed only slightly less inaccurate than Pleasure. Her business? Filmmaker. It was only the tiniest bit of a fib. And then they were out in these vast, emptied spaces built for an Olympics: an airport so beautiful, so sleek, so seashell-colored, so European (at least compared to JFK's dowdy Terminal 8) that, if you could somehow have gotten rid of the masked infantrymen standing watch with enormous machine guns, you might almost have wanted to live in it.

The cabs outside had the same sleek quality as the airport, and the light was just beginning to pinken. Palm trees and groomed poplars lined the road. Everything a perfection of itself, clean, smooth, not at all what you heard about Southern Europe, but then this really wasn't Southern Europe, the man on the plane had said . . . these Catalans were their own thing—the same tone people who didn't realize what you were would sometimes use to cast aspersions on New York Jews. In America you'd have to strap the carseat in backward to face the car's actual seat, but here she turned it sideways and trusted her grip on the handle to keep it reasonably safe. You couldn't shield them from everything, as her mother used to say; and should some hidden imperfection jostle her daughter awake, she wanted her to be able to see. They were rolling now through industrial districts, but even the factories had those elegant slatted shutters, the pastel walls. Trees thickening dark-greenly along the hill to her left, like what L.A. might become if it ever managed to grow up. She did not know what the temperature was; she'd rushed distractedly into the cab at the airport and no longer smoked and had kept the window rolled, as if it were still seventeen Fahrenheit degrees out, still New York. The language on the radio fell somewhere between the two she'd studied in school, and still, on no sleep, at what would have been only like one in the morning her time, she could not puzzle it out. She recognized something on a sign, though: a bullfighting arena. She wanted to point it out to Pete, who would have been torn between his ethical vegetarianism and his insatiable curiosity, but Pete had a work thing he claimed not to be able to get out of, and wasn't scheduled to be arriving at the airport till Sunday. "Leaving me to cross the ocean with a five-month-old," she'd said, suspicious of his motives. Yeah, he'd said, but maybe she would want a day or two to reconnect with her father after all this time, without himself in the way? Not to mention the jetlag, she said, ignoring it. Before the pandemic, Pete had often traveled to London for shoots; she knew his method coming off a redeye was to stay up all day, then a glass of red wine, a bath, and sleep forever, but neither she nor her father drank anymore, if his account of himself was to be believed. And though in some sense this had been his great gift to her, and he really had always been amazing with babies, the thought of leaving one in his care while she slept for ten hours was yet another reason to turn around.

And then with the virus numbers back up everywhere, another wave, it would be just the three of them in his apartment until Sunday. Or possibly the four of them: somewhere in between the lines of his responses to her manuscript, his agon about the stepmother, she'd had an intuition there was a lady friend he was hoping she wouldn't hate. Though on the other hand, wasn't every single thing in his letters exactly what he would have said if he were trying to manipulate her, or whatever you'd call the thing he used to do when he was in the middle of an episode? Wasn't that why she'd ultimately thrown up her hands and realized she had to just include the letters wholesale? It was really less that he'd proven anything to her in writing—or even could—than that she was still trusting or gullible enough to want to take him on faith, she thought, as the cab entered a traffic circle among beautiful, almost Parisian apartment buildings.

And the crazy thing about modern life is that the more inevitable things feel, the more they are actually up in the air. Nothing was stopping her even then from wising up, telling her driver to go all the way around the circle and head back to the airport. She was lucky, sound-editing documentaries was work you could do from home, plus she had the inheritance from when Albert died, and by tonight, which after all would only be late morning, she could be in her own bed and the baby Pete's problem. Moreover, however naïve she remained halfway through her twenties, she was also tough enough to carry through with almost anything. She'd learned that about herself now.

But then abruptly they weren't moving, and the driver killed the radio and said something she couldn't understand except for the word "euro." There were mopeds whizzing past, mostly as the roar they made, even when stopped at the confusingly designed stoplights. Yellow over here seemed to mean a weird kind of go. The sound caromed off walls angled to form a wide diamond around the intersection. She looked past the carseat. It seemed too early to see families out pushing their own kids in strollers, but there they were, them and the garbage collectors and the homeless. And then a peculiar sculpture of an owl atop a building across the densely wooded traffic island, just shy of where a park started . . . Ropes of steam from the tops of buildings. She realized that the cab had pulled right up onto the extravagantly wide and cobbled sidewalk, and when she looked back out her own side's window, she was facing one of those apartment buildings. The ground floor had double wooden doors high enough you could have ridden a horse through. A smaller porter's door had been cut into one—a medieval effect overall. But up on the second floor was a small metal balcony, probably not original, a couple of folding chairs and two new-looking surfboards leaned against the stucco, one taller one shorter, and a table with some kind of struggling potted tree.

And suddenly there came a silence, inside and out—one she knew was going to stay with her for a long time afterward. It was as if the sound had dropped out somehow, or not yet been selected and synced. The sun had just cleared the top of the building opposite and in an access of thinnish February light she'd picked out a man in his bathrobe up there, ten years older, even taller than she remembered, but still shockingly small against the city, shockingly young in his early-mid-forties. Sensitive enough to be waiting for her this early in the morning, yet oblivious enough not to realize she had come. It was a face she had been sure for so long she would never see again, stupid beard or no. The face of either a prodigy or a fool; either everything had changed for him since the last time around or nothing had. And the thing in her chest just then hurt so much that she found herself too timid to move.

There is even a story, reader—there are perhaps many such stories—in which she is sitting there still, a pillar of salt, frozen on the event horizon of the rest of her life, unable to stay or to go.

But this is not that kind of story, and in it two things would happen so simultaneously that it would be hard to say later what led to what. One was the cabbie turning the radio back on. Another was her daughter's eyes, Hannah's curious still-colorless eyes, coming open. You were supposed to be able to see hardly anything at that age, but that was bullshit, she knew. You saw everything at that age—it was afterward that practically the whole of existence became a loss. She would remember later tilting the carseat slightly, as if to give her daughter a single look through the glass.

And of course, human as she was, she thought about fleeing. Really she did, as a light somewhere went yellow. All this time, she'd been waiting for a decisive moment, and here one seemed to be.

But in truth it wasn't a choice, what she did then—more like a step on a path she could no longer quite imagine walking alone. The path was shaped by her steps, of course, but also, being a path, helped shape them. She could feel it shaping her now, as she reached for the carseat's handle, and then the button that would unlock the passenger's side. For how could she not open the door and take off the goddamned mask and at least find out how the air here might feel? And having gone that far, how could she not give voice to the thing that was even now stirring inside her, beneath the pain, calling Dad's own name up to him? How could she just leave him there, in midair over his own life, in his bathrobe, with his highly conjectural girlfriend and his sad little lemon tree? How could she, since it wasn't just her or him deciding anymore, but had to somehow be both of them, together?

I mean, where the hell else are we supposed to look for ourselves, if not in each other? All life is suffering, obviously—Jolie knew that now. But then again, honey: she was your mother now, too. And our lives are not our own.

ACKNOWLEDGMENTS

It is a good and a joyful thing to give thanks:

—to the peerless Diana Tejerina Miller, who gets a line of her own;

—to Chris Parris-Lamb, who dug deep, and to Rebecca Gardner, Will Roberts, Sylvie Rabineau, Aru Menon, and all at The Gernert Company and WME (particularly Sarah Bolling for her early insights);

—to the house of Knopf: Reagan Arthur, Jordan Pavlin, Maggie Hinders, Zuleima Ugalde, Erinn Hartman, Jordan Rodman, Oliver Munday, John Gall, Zachary Lutz, Anne Achenbaum, Emily Murphy, Nicholas Latimer, Kristen Bearse, the tireless Rita Madrigal and Amy Ryan, and the legends Kathy Hourigan and Andy Hughes;

—to Paul Bogaards and Stephanie Kloss for having my back;

—to Sigrid Rausing and all at Granta (including Pru Rowlandson, Bella Lacey, Josie Mitchell, Luke Nema, and now Jason Arthur) for support early and late, and to Caspian Dennis in perpetuity;

—to Walker Lambert, Antoine Brown, Chris Eichler, Daron Carreiro, Sergio de la Pava, and Thad Ziolkowski for all manner of help, and to Nuria Ferrer for keeping me going;

—to Naomi Lebowitz for continued inspiration (and for *Lucky Per*);

—to Paige Ackerson-Kiely at Sarah Lawrence and especially to Brian Morton for his unfailing generosity;

—to the fine people at Watchung Booksellers;

—to the Allen Room of the New York Public Library, and then on

—to the seekers of Woodley Road and environs, who once saved my life and will find bits and pieces of their own lives mixed herein;

—to Matt, Will, and Kurt, wherever they may be, and to whoever left that fortune-cookie fortune under my windshield wiper in 1996;

—to my mother and to my sister (I love you);

—to Cynthia Oakes, for being so kind to my kids;

—to Sonny Mehta, to Frankie Kata, to Julie Hallberg, to my dad;

—and to Elise, my love, my forever and ever, Amen.

ILLUSTRATION CREDITS

A NOTE ON THE TYPE

This book was set in Janson, a typeface long thought to have been made by the Dutchman Anton Janson, who was a practicing typefounder in Leipzig during the years 1668–1687. However, it has been conclusively demonstrated that these types are actually the work of Nicholas Kis (1650–1702), a Hungarian, who most probably learned his trade from the master Dutch typefounder Dirk Voskens. The type is an excellent example of the influential and sturdy Dutch types that prevailed in England up to the time William Caslon (1692–1766) developed his own incomparable designs from them.

Composed by North Market Street Graphics, Lancaster, Pennsylvania

Printed and bound by Berryville Graphics, Berryville, Virginia

Designed by Maggie Hinders